CW00501606

The Hermit

Book I of
Kahverengi's Dilemma

Zephyr Axiom

"Every way of a man is right in his own eyes,
But the Lord weighs the hearts."

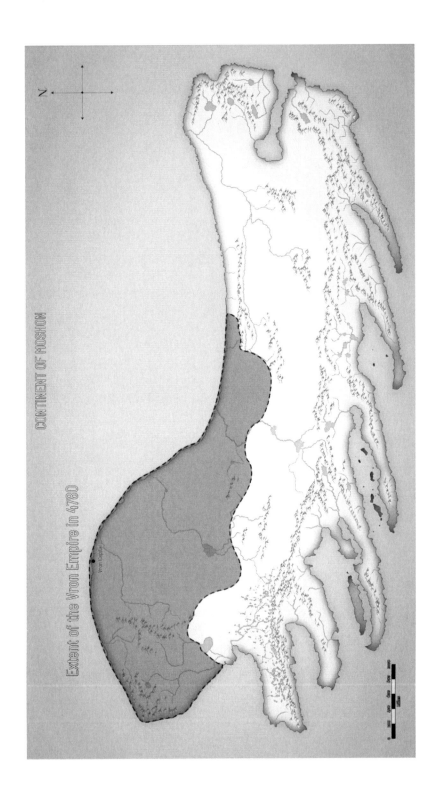

CONTINENT OF MOSHON

Extent of the Vron Empire in 4780

Leverie as depicted c. 4770 on a mural in the Highcity Council Dome.

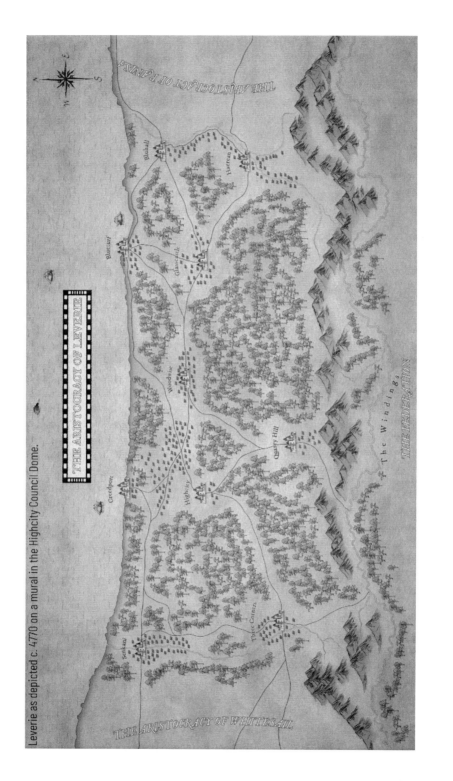

Part I:
The Pebble

Chapter 1

*"If, by some chance, travel back through time should prove
possible, I provide a single firm piece of advice:
Do not try it."*

—Kahverengi the Thinker,
On the Feasibility of Time Travel.

Retyar hated quiet days. Problem was, those were the
only kind of days he ever had any more. He'd quickly gotten
used to the routine of his new job. Get up at six. Have a quick
breakfast. Put on the uniform, the ballistic armor, his pistol,
and his rifle. Then stand around in a guard tower doing
nothing for nine hours straight.

Today's weather in the Kingdom of Govunari's central
region was nice and clear, the sun bright as it hung halfway
between noon and dusk. A full moon poked out low over the
Brittle Mountains' needle-like peaks to the east, its blue disk
hard to see against the afternoon sky. The crisp air bit at his
cheeks. Looking northwest from his tower, Retyar could
make out the skyscrapers of downtown Crystal Ebb
shimmering above the forest trees. On typical days, fog or
smog tended to obscure Govunari's fifth largest city in a thick
haze. He raised his binoculars to study the rare sight, hoping
to distract himself from his own thoughts.

And from memories that still stung.

His vision shook as something pounded against the wood

floorboards. Retyar lowered his binocs and turned in annoyance. "Khyle, get those things out of your ears and actually do your job."

The other security guard sat with his eyes closed, bobbing his head in unison with the tapping of his foot. Oblivious, he started humming and snapping his fingers to the beat blasting through his earpieces.

Retyar sighed and grabbed the wires dangling down over Khyle's chest. "Work for your pay, raze it," he said as he yanked the little speakers from his ears.

Khyle opened his eyes and tsked. "Don't you ever lighten up?"

"You're a guard, not a DJ," Retyar said. "Do not make me put you on report."

The other man rolled his dark green eyes. "We're in the middle of the kingdom. Who's there for us to even guard against?"

Retyar glanced past Khyle at the sprawling compound of single-story concrete bunkers and white antennas that made up Obsidian Aerotech. Far as he'd seen, nothing interesting ever happened within its premises, but that was beside the point. He turned again to the forest and the twenty-yard open space separating the woods from the electrified chain link fence.

"There's always Ytanian terror groups."

"Even the lime eyes don't go this far south," Khyle grumbled. "And what interest would they have in a defunct R&D facility?" He nonetheless scooted his chair closer to the low wall of the guard platform and stared out at the dirt clearing. "Ah, hey, you want me to tell that squirrel there's no trespassing?"

"Can you stay serious for at least the five minutes until our shift's over?"

"Sometimes, I wonder—why out of everybody do I get lumped with the Uni graduate? You academic types are all so stuck-up and by-the-book."

Retyar hated being reminded of the University, but if he ever told Khyle he'd come here to run away, he'd never stop pestering him to open up about it. He drew in a deep breath. *Someday, you'll look back at what happened and laugh*, he told himself. *And laugh at how stupid it was to walk up to the corporate recruiter and take the first job offered.* He absently scratched at the black Obsidian patch on his uniform. Of all the things he could have done after getting his degree . . . .

Someone knocked against the support beams down below. "Shift change."

Retyar looked at his watch. "A few minutes early."

Khyle was already at the ladder. "Finally! I'm starving."

He went on down. Retyar waited for the relief to come up and formally switch off before following. He felt stiff descending the wood rungs. With how badly the ladder bobbed, he wondered if one of these days he'd finally slip and break his neck. He shook out the tension in his arms when his boots touched gravel.

Despite his eagerness to get away from the tower, Khyle was still there waiting. "Hey, I was just kidding with you, man—it's not that bad hanging with the scholar. Want to head over to Pine's for dinner?"

Retyar shrugged. "Sure." Even if the food there wasn't the best, most evenings provided enough noise to drown out his thoughts.

"You going to regale us with more tales of Idari the Mighty?"

"I keep telling you, just because I majored in history doesn't make me a bard."

"Yeah, but you're sure good at it after we get a couple drinks in you."

Retyar sighed and smiled despite himself. "Fine. What would you rather go for? I could talk about the Cobalt Spires before they were toppled by the Awandars, or Evena the Beautiful, namesake of a continent."

"Sounds too sappy."

"Okay, then, the Yellow Fields of Frost's Night and the invasion of the Sheyi, or the story of Jale the Soarer. With five thousand, four hundred and fourteen years to weed through, we've got plenty of material."

"Well, what's your favorite part of—"

Something flashed over toward the south end of the compound. The ground shuddered under his feet and a loud boom pounded through him. Retyar and Khyle both snapped around to see an orange ball of dirty flame roil up into the sky.

"What in the six continents . . ." Khyle said.

Sirens blared throughout the compound. Retyar snatched up his radio as it came alive with chatter.

"Bomb detonated at the south entrance! Guards down! I repeat, guards down!"

"Intruder spotted driving a company four-door! Last seen heading up the main path toward C Block!"

"We need medics at the gate, now*!"*

Retyar and Khyle shared a look. Khyle turned his eyes back to the column of black smoke. "My shift's over, man."

Retyar slipped his rifle into his hands and swept the charging handle, chambering a round with a metallic click. "So's mine." He ran into the compound.

There weren't many people typically milling about the facility even on the busiest days, and today was no exception. He saw only one white-coat fleeing to a security door, and behind him two blue-uniformed guards running around like decapitated chickens.

"Where are we headed?" one of the men asked.

Another explosion rocked the facility to the east, followed by the crack of gunfire. "That way seems right," Retyar said. He fished a couple foam plugs from his pocket as he moved and shoved them in his ears. Never mind the bombs; his .309 would leave a man deaf in short order. And he foresaw he could be doing a lot of shooting.

Voices on the radio reached him, distant and muffled. *"The intruder is heading north on Avenue Five! Requesting —"*

"He's heading for Building D-9. All security, make for Building D-9 immediately."

A personnel truck rounded a corner and screeched to a halt in front of Retyar and the others. "Get on!"

Four guards were already in the back. One of them held Retyar tight, the truck speeding off before he could even drop into a seat.

"The intruder has been identified as Doctor Grigon Ashkyn. He is attempting unauthorized access of a weapon in Building D-9. He is not to be allowed into proximity. All

personnel are ordered to shoot on sight."

"Raze it, one guy's doing all this?" the guard next to him asked.

"Grigon?" someone else asked. "I remember him. He's one of the section chiefs for Block D."

"Then why's he breaking in?"

"I heard he got fired last week after going off on the other chiefs."

"Mad scientist with a vendetta. Great."

Retyar gripped the side rail as the driver banked hard around a turn and careened down the road to Block D. Old, cracked cement walls and ranks of spindly weeds whipped past in a blur. Hard to believe anything special would be kept in a place like this.

They went right past the site of the second explosion. A personnel transport like the one he rode lay on its side, its cabin a mangled, smoldering wreck. Men in blue uniforms were strewn about in a bloody mess. Retyar gritted his teeth. He had no way of telling if they were people he knew, but these murders got his blood boiling. *This doctor's a dead man.*

More gunshots echoed between the concrete bunkers, followed by another explosion. This time, it was close—just two structures away.

"Let's take this guy down!" one of the guards shouted.

The truck was there in seconds. The driver swerved through choking black smoke and braked hard, lurching them to a stop. "Move! Move!"

Retyar jumped down, rifle ready. It took him a moment to orient himself in all the smoke. He held his breath and blinked against the tears in his eyes, moving forward until he found a wall with large figures stenciled over the gray cement. D-9.

"Entrance is this way!" someone shouted.

He followed the voice to a blast door. Or rather, what remained of one. Its twisted form apparently hadn't been rated for the ordinance class used on it. Retyar picked his way through scraps of metal, stepping over a body in blue. The downed guard had been shot in the face.

The guards stacked up, Retyar at point. He held out his

hand and counted down to zero with his fingers, his heart pounding. They stormed through the hole, weapons forward. The area by the entrance sat dark. Shattered glass from broken florescent tubes crunched underfoot. Water sprayed on the floor from a broken sprinkler main. A red strobe light flashed in silent alarm about ten paces in. There was no one—

"Trap!"

A hand shoved Retyar forward an instant before the area behind him exploded. He landed on his rifle, breathless, the wind knocked out of him. He rolled over, his ears ringing even with the foam plugs. The guard just behind him lay dead, the back of his vest torn to shreds. The entryway was caved in. He was on his own.

"Raze it," he hissed.

A gunshot cracked and echoed from deeper inside the building. Retyar lifted himself up on shaky limbs and forged on. The passageway turned bright further in, where the force of the blasts hadn't broken the lights. Pristine white walls served as a sharp contrast to the carnage he'd just been through. He could hear men and women sobbing behind locked doors.

He smelled burned circuits before finding the shorted electromagnetic lock on one of the doors. He stepped through the gaping passageway, rifle first, into another hallway. A red strobe light spun round and round. He passed several sealed rooms until he spotted a dead engineer around a corner. Blood soaked the chest of his coat red. Further on, he saw a set of double doors with another shorted lock. And voices.

"You can't do this, Grigon!" someone shouted in a shrill tone.

"I can. I will." The second voice was low, gravelly. Angry.

"You'll kill millions! Billions! You will erase countless lives from existence!"

Retyar crept along toward the yawning entryway, his finger on the trigger.

"We have the power to change history, Ayrn. How are we to live with ourselves if we let this technology go to waste? We can stop the outbreak of the Intercontinental War. We can save the kingdoms of Corene, of Sandspring, of Wayprice, of countless others. We can prevent the collapse of Fractora's

Peace. You fear losing billions of lives? We can *save* billions."

The far side of the double doors was dimmer than the hallway, but partially lit by an undulating, golden glow. Retyar was close enough now to make out control boards crammed with knobs and switches.

"Nothing is free, Grigon. Gain one thing, you always lose another."

"Some things aren't worth keeping."

"Like the peace our world has finally found?"

"Coordinates are set. Goodbye, old friend."

Retyar hadn't been able to make heads or tails of the conversation so far, but the last two sentences didn't sound good. He rushed the remaining four paces to the doorway and jumped into the room.

And stopped short at the sight that greeted him.

In the center of the darkened chamber stood what he could only describe as a tear in existence. A thin black line of deepest black stretched from ceiling to floor. Light bent around it, warped by tendrils of golden light that looked like flame, but which moved like seaweed in an ocean current. Lining the walls and ceiling and floor on the rift's side of the room were scores upon scores of needle-like antennas. Retyar thought he could feel them vibrating, but they and the crack in space were utterly silent.

In front of the tear loomed a man in heavy ballistic armor. His outfit sported rips and gouges from his assault on the facility. A helmet lay discarded at his feet, its shape deformed from bullets and shrapnel. Blood matted the hair at the back of his head, and dripped from his fingers. In his right hand, he had a pistol aimed at a cowering white-coat with a bloodied leg. Retyar clenched his jaw. *I'm stopping you here.*

The lock panel outside sparked and triggered the sprinkler above it just as Retyar aimed his rifle. Doctor Grigon Ashkyn turned and saw him. Retyar fired the same instant the madman twisted and pointed his pistol at Retyar's chest. He felt the kick of his rifle against his shoulder and the punch of a bullet to his gut. Retyar fell gasping to the floor, pain squeezing his vision black. He struggled to snatch his senses back from the shock and agony.

"Get up!" someone screeched. "Stop him!" It was the cowering white-coat.

Retyar grunted and forced himself to his knees.

"Don't let him get to the Rift!"

Grigon was already getting to his feet. Retyar had scored a hit only on the man's arm. He tried to lift his rifle for another shot, but doubled over from a stab of pain. *So, this is what it's like to take a bullet.*

"Stop him!"

"Yeah, you could try doing that yourself." Retyar could do no more than wheeze out the words. He channeled his anger and forced himself to stand. He took one step, and then another.

Grigon wasn't even paying him or the scientist any attention. Slowed by his wounds, he stumbled toward the dark crevice in a daze. Retyar shoved through the pain and staggered over to grab him by his armor, his fingers latching onto the rigid edge of an embedded steel plate. Grigon jerked and elbowed him in the side of the face, nearly knocking him loose.

"It's down to me to fix this world," Grigon said, grating out the words.

Retyar had been so focused on getting to the doctor that he hadn't realized how close both of them were to the Rift. The fissure stood only four feet away. The golden tendrils waved lazily, inches from Grigon's face. The eerie sight gave Retyar goosebumps. He held on to Grigon's armor and tried to drag him back.

The doctor's will proved stronger. He pulled Retyar with him closer to the Rift. "The lot of you can all burn."

"Stop him!"

One of the tendrils of light caressed Grigon's arm. Retyar flinched. His grip slipped off the doctor's armor. He snatched at the satchel hanging from his shoulder, but the bag fell loose and Grigon lurched into the Rift. His body warped and compressed to the width of the fissure. The last bit of him to go in was his good hand. It held something in its grasp—a detonator. His thumb hit the switch.

The last thing Retyar felt was the blast at his back as the lab erupted into a flash of fire.

Chapter 2

"Considering this, a man's mere presence
in the world will invariably change everything."

Retyar awoke face first in a clump of grass. He pressed his eyelids tight and groaned, trying to pinpoint his body's aches and throbs. Why did—

The facility. Grigon. Superweapon.

He snapped his eyes open and dug his fingers into damp leaves, pushing himself to his knees.

What?

Silver-barked trees surrounded him in every direction. The facility was nowhere in sight.

He felt his stomach where he'd been shot. His fingers found Grigon's bullet, lodged within the weave of his ballistic vest. He plucked it out and chucked it away in disgust. Next, he felt his back. He found a bit of singed cloth, but no gashes, no broken skin. No bones seemed broken.

He pulled out his ear foam and tried looking around for any sign of the person or people who must have dragged him out here. Nothing. Not just that. Having grown up in the country and been on a good number of hunts with his father, Retyar had a decent eye for tracking. Yet he didn't see any signs of footprints.

"Hello?"

Silence.

His heart pounded in his chest. He thought about the Rift

and what Grigon and the white-coat had been arguing over. *No.* Retyar couldn't have gone through the fissure. The explosion couldn't have pushed him through.

He tried to force down his rising panic. "Calm down. Take proper stock of your situation. What are your resources?"

He had his vest, obviously. His pistol and knife were still on his belt—he cursed himself for not even thinking to use them on Grigon—as was his radio. He had his watch and binoculars, plus two spare magazines of ammunition for each of his guns. He spotted his rifle nearby, as well as the satchel he'd pulled off the mad doctor.

He took his radio in hand, still on and tuned to the Obsidian security's main channel. He didn't hear any chatter. He pressed the talk button. "This is Retyar Venon, badge number one zero five. Anyone respond."

Nothing.

He swallowed, fighting to stay in control. *Keep a level head in a crisis or you die. You've been stranded in the woods before, Retyar. This is just like when you fell off the trail in Fluen.*

Except these weren't any woods he recognized. The trees were some kind of oak he couldn't identify, and definitely different from anything in Govunari. Even the birds sounded strange. He looked up at the rays of sunlight poking through the canopy. It was just after noon, but his watch showed it should already be getting dark.

What in the six continents is going on?

It was getting harder to pretend his situation had nothing to do with the Rift.

Grigon's satchel. Maybe it held some clue. He reached over and pulled it close. The brown canvas bag was heavy for its size. "If there're bombs in here, they better not be armed," he muttered. He let out a relieved breath when he found a canteen and several tins of food. "Hope you starve to death wherever you are."

Wherever was probably south Originate. Retyar unfolded a map of the First Continent, its lower end marked all over in red ink. The numbered circles and lines must have outlined some plan, but he couldn't decipher much of it. And he noted a disturbing detail. The nation borders and kingdom names were way out of date. It was a map of the continent from right before the outbreak of the Intercontinental War in 5343. Seventy-one years ago.

Great.

He rummaged further into the satchel, increasingly desperate. He found more maps detailing specific areas of Originate, all from the same time period. Underneath those, a tablet computer, a flashlight, a solar charger, and a little book with a well-worn paper cover. Any fan of science fiction would recognize its title. *On the Feasibility of Time Travel*, written by the classical philosopher Kahverengi of Hurmaben.

"Raze it!"

Retyar threw the book back into the bag and lowered his head against his palm. He wanted to shout that the idea he'd been sent back in time was ridiculous, but he couldn't. Not after seeing that tear in reality.

No, there's still a chance. There are less impossible ways of explaining my situation. He clung to that hope and snatched up his rifle and the supplies from Grigon's satchel. He looked around one more time at the pristine forest floor, at the carpet of leaves disturbed only by his own isolated movements. Taking a deep breath to try and slow his racing heart, he took his first steps forward.

With each minute that passed, Retyar became better convinced he'd simply jumped to conclusions. If he'd really been thrown back in time, the white-coats at Obsidian would be desperate to find him and bring him back. In the novels he'd read, the scientists and philosophers always obsessed over the dangers of contaminating the timeline. They wouldn't let some castaway bumble his way through history. And if they were really capable of time travel, they'd be able to pick him up the very instant he arrived. The fact they'd done no such thing proved this was something else.

And proves I've read way too many of those novels.

Yet despite his growing conviction, he still tread lightly

through the forest, keeping his footfalls quiet and his tracks faint. The plants and wildlife he encountered were all strange species to him. Squirrels were all brown, missing the red stripes he was used to. Lizards were two sizes too big. A deer he spotted had a snow-white tail. He was definitely not in Govunari. Probably not even on the continent of Falcone.

About two hours into his trek, he found a stream. *Finally! Now it's just a matter of time before finding people.*

The water was crystal clear, and small fish darted through the current. He refilled the canteen from Grigon's satchel before following the flow downriver.

But what if he *had* been thrown back in time? This could be five thousand years in the past, before the First Explorers set out from Originate. Could he be the only human here? He went on another half-hour trying not to let that question get the better of him. Telling himself he was crazy for even having such ideas.

At last, he thought he heard voices over the gurgling of the stream. He focused until he was sure it wasn't his ears playing tricks on him, then burst into a sprint.

The forest thinned and gave way to a small settlement of wood-framed houses and dirt roads. The buildings seemed handcrafted, but that wasn't too strange even in Govunari out in the country. *But power lines. There are no power lines.*

The voices drew him into the town. They had been loud enough for him to hear all the way in the woods, but he'd been too excited to notice the angry tones. And now it sounded like a crowd.

He spotted his first person within the window of one of the houses. She was a middle-aged woman, wearing a simple light green dress. A lock of dark hair fell off her shoulder as she leaned out to look toward the commotion.

Retyar raised his hand. "Ma'am, excuse me—"

The woman snapped around with wide eyes and pulled the shutters closed with a bang.

"All right." At least the encounter gave him something. The woman's eyes had been deep blue. *Does that mean I'm in Moshon?*

He closed in on the voices and started listening to what they were saying. There were a lot of people speaking all at once, but he caught snippets from some of the loudest.

"This is Senkani land, you conniving shyles!"

"Get out of our town!"

"Out with the Leverie dogs!"

Retyar came to a market square lined with open-air stalls and stuffed with people in bright clothing. At least fifty were crowded together, many with fists raised, some holding produce ready to use as ammunition. Someone on the far end of the market shouted above all the others.

"It is the right of House Leverie to do business anywhere in the aristocracy! If you expel us, you will answer to the Council's judgment!"

"We've no want of your rags! Out!"

Retyar tried to look over the heads of the crowd, but could only catch glimpses of the small group they were arguing with. He glanced around and spotted a stool next to an abandoned market stall. He climbed up to get a decent view.

What he saw put his heart in his stomach. Simple cotton or silk tunics with buttons and strings rather than zippers were still customary in many parts of the world. He could shrug away the absence of polyester shoes, plastic jugs, or watches. Even bicycles were a luxury in some places. But no one—*no one*—in the fifty-fifth century wore chainmail armor like the four men guarding a trio of merchants in green silk vests.

Raze it!

"We will not budge from this spot until the customary hour of market closing!" one of the men in green shouted at the crowd. "We have a charter straight from Crenden Thrake himself! If you—"

The crowd downed out his voice with a united chant. "Gricall! Gricall! Gricall!"

Retyar wondered what the word meant until he saw a man striding in from one end of the marketplace. People shuffled and pushed to give him a path up to the merchants in green. He wasn't dressed anything special, and seemed a bit on the short side. The only feature that might distinguish him as anything other than average was the rare purplish tint to his dark hair.

"Don't you think it's about time Creedport gives up on this?" the man asked.

The merchant who'd spoken earlier sneered at him. "I have nothing to say to you, Gricall."

"No, the correct words are that you have nothing to sell here in the province of Senkani."

"Nothing to sell!" the merchant scoffed. "We have better quality fabrics than anything on offer by the rest of this sorry little community, and at a quarter price less than what normally counts as premium. What in the six is wrong with all your heads?"

"You're not fooling anyone," Gricall said. "Thrake plans to choke our textile weavers out of business and make us dependent on him. Senkani has and always will sustain itself."

"You are part of the Aristocracy of Leverie," the merchant said. "We are one nation, and a proper nation does not place embargoes on its own markets."

Retyar told himself he should be stepping down from his vantage. He'd achieved his primary goal of confirming his fears. He was definitely not in the right year.

Yet he couldn't. The historian in him was captivated by the scene playing out right before his eyes. *What does it say about me that I'm engrossed in a blasted trade dispute?*

"We may be part of the nation of Leverie," Gricall said, "but this is an aristocracy, not a kingdom. The provinces have their sovereignty, and unless you possess a letter of writ showing you have Crenden Arzan's leave to sell in his domain, you *will* be gone from here."

The merchant thrust his finger out at Gricall. "You've no title of authority to be making demands."

"Title?" Gricall spread his arms. "Who needs a title when backed by the people?"

The crowd took this as their cue to raise their voices and shout.

"Out! Out!"

"No more tyrants!"

Okay, now was probably a good time to get some distance. Retyar slowly lowered himself down from the stool.

And came face-to-face with a scrawny teenager staring at his outfit. The boy raised his gaze and frowned. "Green eyes. You're Falconian. You're one of their mercenaries!"

Not good. "No, I'm just a, uh, I'm traveling through on my way to Breakpeak." Was Breakpeak in Moshon? He was pretty sure it was in Moshon. *Raze it, but what year is this?*

The boy's frown deepened. "Breakpeak's a long way from here."

"I—"

The merchant's voice rose again above the protests, "This is violence! Hands off or I'll—"

"No!" Gricall called. "Don't resort to—"

Someone screamed. Retyar jumped back onto the stool to find a fight breaking out between the crowd and the merchants' guards. Townspeople were trying to grapple the men in armor, while the guards responded with fists and feet. Someone threw an apple that bounced off a guard's head. He drew a sword and roared. "Who was that?"

Gricall tried to shove his way between the two sides. "That's enough!"

The words were barely out of his mouth before someone toppled him off balance. He fell into the guard with the sword. The two hit the ground together, and Retyar saw the tip of the blade rise up through Gricall's back.

The entire marketplace went silent.

Someone shrieked and everything collapsed into mayhem. The green-clad merchants and two of the guards turned and scrambled away. The one guard who remained standing drew his sword just as a now enraged mob surged forward.

They're going to think I'm one of them.

Retyar leaped to the ground and ran, not waiting to see what became of the guards or the merchants.

He didn't stop until the village was far, far behind him.

Chapter 3

"There are essentially two basic forms of time travel logically possible."

There were no more villages in the path of his flight. After running from his encounter, he'd crossed footpaths and roads, all unpaved. Retyar didn't follow any of them, but cut straight across. He had no idea what he was looking for, only what he was running from. Eventually, he reached a point where it was impossible to continue.

The coast consisted of a sheer fifty-foot wall of granite plunging down to a base of dark boulders. Only a little ways from where he came across the cliff, past ancient looking trees with roots dangling here and there out into the abyss, he found a small cave that seemed as good as any to use as shelter. Though fairly tiny, it had a decent vantage with two openings. One of those allowed access to a little clearing in the woods. The other was right along the cliff, providing a wide view of the ocean. The two openings were offset from each other, meaning he could be at ease he wouldn't silhouette.

Further investigation turned up a gorge forty feet from the cave. At thirty-some feet across, it cut off his access going eastwards, but also served as protection against anyone wandering in from that direction. More importantly, it sported a nice little stream at the bottom that he could access via an old rockslide along the western wall. He'd been able to use it to drink, as well as catch a few fish after Grigon's tins ran out. Now, three days after getting stranded, his basic needs were secure enough that he had nothing else except to focus on his bigger predicament.

Retyar listened to the crashing waves and stared out at the endless expanse of sea. He was recovered somewhat from a bout of travel sickness that had laid him waste right after reaching the coast. That had been another proof of him being far from home—a day of fever and chills as his body adjusted to a foreign environment. Flying from one end of the Kingdom of Govunari to the other could give him a moderate ache and sore throat. Getting totally wasted confirmed this was a different continent. But *where* he was wasn't nearly as bad as *when* he was.

What in the six do I do?

He tapped his finger against the case of the tablet computer from Grigon's satchel. It had turned out to contain a very sizable encyclopedia covering the entire span of world history. Cross referencing the bits of information he'd gleaned in the village, he concluded he was in the years somewhere between 4503 and 4784. Leverie was a relatively small aristocracy along the north coast of the southern continent of Moshon. It had originally been part of the Aristocracy of Whitesail-Leverie until it broke peaceably in two at the start of the forty-sixth century. That was less than twenty years after Whitesail-Leverie had itself formed from the fragments left over from the civil war of the Aristocracy of Tarkandan in 4487. At the other end of Leverie's timeline was its conquest at the hands of the Vron Empire in 4784, interrupting a civil war between two of the aristocratic Houses that started in 4780.

He sure hoped he wouldn't be getting caught up in that whole mess, even if he'd always wondered what real life sword and shield warfare looked like. If his studies at the University were anything to go by, it would have been nothing like how movies always portrayed things.

As for the country itself, Retyar knew fairly little about the aristocracy form of government. Most of the world conformed to either the kingdom or warlord models of governance, with a few kingdoms taking on elements of democratic representation. Moshon was an outlier continent. The nations here had deposed their kings early on in world history and replaced them with ruling councils composed of elected crendens from the noble class. Each of those crendens would be something like a provincial lord, with authority over their city and the surrounding rural territory. That held mostly true except for a handful of exceptions, like the Vron Empire, which had a senate and powerful generals with broad autonomy on campaign. *I wonder what differences that makes on the street level of society.*

Retyar shook his head. He couldn't let himself get drawn in by questions like that. He'd finished rereading Kahverengi's book on time travel. He knew the dangers of altering the timeline. Worst case scenario, he could cause reality itself to break down by creating a causal paradox. Best case, he'd completely erase from existence all he'd ever known. His family, his friends, his country—if he changed anything, none of it would come to pass. *A fate worse than death: never even being alive in the first place.*

He stood, fighting a wave of nausea, and walked out of the cave. "This is stupid. This is totally, utterly stupid."

Seagull cries filled the air around him as the birds circled and rode the wind. Waves battered endlessly at the rocks below, the sound of each one like a hammer against his mind. He paced the small clearing outside the cave.

What were his options? It came down to two possibilities. Affect the timeline or don't.

The only moral choice was the latter. The problem: that wasn't possible. The most famous aspect of Kahverengi's writings was the Pebble Effect. The slightest of changes can influence everything that comes after. Retyar simply living here in this forest would mean fishing or hunting rabbits, which would impact the local wildlife, which would alter the minute day-to-day lives of hunters and fishers, who would in turn have slightly different routines when heading into town, which would alter the city's economy, and on and on up the chain of cause and effect.

He stomped on a rock and turned on his heel as he continued pacing. What should he do then? Kill himself? Even that would leave ripples. The very presence of his body would still impact the ecosystem. And with him dead, how would he safeguard the things he'd brought with him? The tablet, his guns, his armor vest—even the cut of his pants or the material of his boots could potentially revolutionize local technology. If he chucked it all in the ocean, it could wash up somewhere. If he buried it, someone could dig it up. If he burned it, there would still be components or materials that survived.

He wanted to yell and scream, but he couldn't. He didn't dare multiply the impact of his presence. Snatching up his radio, he put the receiver close to his mouth. "Someone, anyone, just pick up and tell me you're here!"

Nothing back. Always nothing.

Even if he did find some way to erase his presence, he'd already interacted with people. They'd seen him in the village. Spoken to him. He'd stuck out like a sore thumb. Did that mean the timeline was already altered? Maybe the reason no one had come to rescue him was that his world was already wiped from existence. Yet, wouldn't that mean he shouldn't exist either?

Raze it!

Time paradoxes were fun enough to puzzle through so long as you weren't actually stuck in one.

So then, what do I do?

He had at least his immediate answer. He'd do everything possible to keep himself out of history's way. It was all he *could* do to keep his world safe.

But even in the midst of all his fears, Retyar still felt something else that he couldn't quite suppress. He went up again to the edge of the cliff and looked out at the expanse of ocean. He breathed in the sea air, listened to the cry of seagulls, absorbed the sounds of water crashing against rocks and wind rustling the forest leaves. This was the past come to life. It was a world that people knew only from dusty tomes and faded paintings.

The historian in him couldn't stand letting this opportunity go to waste. He had the chance to be an eyewitness to events that scholars from his time could only imagine and theorize about.

"I don't have to touch things," he muttered. "I don't have

to be seen."

He'd already left his footprints in the timeline, and yet he was still here. He hadn't erased himself from being and he hadn't ended the world. The universe's existence clearly wasn't so fragile as to be ruined by his actions so far.

How much could he dare to test the bounds? If he just poked around a little, checked out a town here and there—that might be all right, wouldn't it?

Several sets of double fins broke the water about a hundred yards out. Shyles on the hunt. Retyar closed his eyes. No way to tell until he messed something up. It would be like swimming out to sea, testing how far he could go from shore until one of those predators tore into his flesh.

Don't entertain these thoughts, Retyar. With deliberate effort, he broke his gaze away from the ocean's surface. He went back into the cave and switched on the tablet.

Chapter 1

"There is the predestined category
and there is the open system."

Arzan Redleaf, crenden of Senkani, burst through the door to Thrake Leverie's study, his blood pumping furiously through his veins. "You have gone too far!"

Thrake didn't bother to contain the scowl on his bearded face as he sat hunched over the pile of sales reports stacked on his desk. "This is my palace, Redleaf. Kindly see yourself back to your own blazing city."

"I will," Arzan said, marching forward and slamming his fists upon the fine hardwood slab, "as soon as you keep your stooges to yourself and stop *murdering my people!*"

The other man dropped his pen into its inkwell and scraped his seat back across the finely polished floorboards. He stood, his eyes of deep sea blue coming level to Arzan's. There was hatred there. Hatred of the kind that only arose from years of enmity. "That little incident in the village was an accident. One brought about by senseless acts of instigation on the part of the people of Senkani. Where are my reparations for the merchant and two guards killed by your insane mob?"

Arzan leaned in. "This case will be brought before the Council, Thrake. Until their ruling on this matter, not one of your merchants is to set foot on Senkani land."

"Oh, this will be heard by the Council all right," Thrake said. "I will be sure to put in every detail of how unrestrained your savages are, and how the young head of House Redleaf barged into *my* city, into *my* study with a sword at his waist and ckols in my hall."

"What else do you expect after you send hired thugs into my province?"

Thrake laughed mockingly. "You'd have my people go into that backwater of yours unarmed? Everyone knows the Senkani to be unruly brutes—much the same as their ruler. Smoke and ashes, every third man in your province struts around with a sword on his belt!"

"You act all high and mighty, as if Senkani isn't the first line of defense for the western border. Tell me, whose blood was spilled in the Tarkandan Split? Certainly not that of House Leverie."

"Ancient history," Thrake said with a toss of his hand. "But, of course, you always bring that up. House Redleaf's antiquated heroics are its only claim to importance."

Arzan's vision clouded with rage, though he forcibly took hold of his emotions. He raised his finger. "Not one merchant." He whirled around, his red cape twisting through the air at the motion, and stormed to the door.

"Your House has always been a blight upon the Aristocracy," Thrake said after him. "A shame the ship didn't have you aboard as well as your father and mother when it sank into the bay. How better it would have—"

His voice cut as Arzan slammed the door after exiting into the hall.

His ckols and Thrake's stood tensely in the crowded corridor, their hands close to the hilts of their weapons, each side eyeing the other. Arzan fiddled with the clasp of his cape. "Come."

Chainmail scrunched as his men fell in around him. Arzan drew in measured breaths on his way towards the exit, noting as he did Thrake's clerks and maids ducking into rooms to stay out of his path. *The Council will see Thrake has finally crossed the line. They will rein him in.*

Plenty of good that would do Gricall.

He descended the stairs to the ground floor and let the servants open the main door. Filgneir awaited him outside. His trusted adviser sighed and passed a hand over his bald head at Arzan's arrival. "You have completed your objective, my liege?"

Arzan nodded to the carriages. "Let's return home."

"I do think we should have had the Council deal with this first rather than coming in person," Filgneir said quietly. "It only ever riles both of you up when you meet face-to-face."

"Some things are only properly done in person. And how I wish I could punch that man. Because of him, one of the most honorable individuals in Leverie has lost his life."

"At the end of the day, it truly was an accident."

Arzan grabbed the handhold on his carriage. "Which is the only reason I didn't draw my sword in there."

"I do hope you never have to stoop to such a level, your grace." Arzan stopped and turned to see an old man in simple clothes standing beside the escort wagon. The man stroked his wispy white beard with fingers smudged by green dyes or inks before bowing his head. "I apologize on behalf of the city of Creedport, since my crenden is unlikely to do so himself. What happened in your province is a terrible tragedy."

"Are you one of Thrake's advisers?" Arzan asked.

"Were that it were so," the old man said wistfully. "I might have been able to talk some sense into that stubborn head of his before we reached this point."

Filgneir leaned to Arzan's ear. "This is Honorable Maltan. He's a tinkerer patronized by Crenden Thrake's late father."

"I've heard of him." Arzan looked over at the round, hundred-foot tower not far away, rising up above the tile rooftops of the rest of the city. "You're the one who operates the tower, correct?"

"'Operates' is a word that gives me too much credit," Maltan said, smiling. "I live there, and the stipend the former crenden and crendess left me in their will allows a little bit of continued dabbling in the sciences."

"Well, I'm afraid I cannot accept your apology, Honorable Maltan," Arzan said. "I'm not in the habit of holding to account those not responsible for a wrong."

Maltan grimaced. "Then it's likely you'll never have one. Thrake is a stubborn man, never willing to admit a mistake—especially to his enemies. For those who oppose him . . . It's a testament to his unforgiving nature that he sent his daughter all the way to Falcone simply for questioning him."

Arzan had heard rumors about that. He crossed his arms. "The story's true, then? She's exiled until she's an adult?"

"Thrake's rant wasn't altogether coherent as he marched her off to the docks," Maltan said. "But that was likely his intent."

"Her grace Charva would be sixteen this year, I believe?" Filgneir said.

"Already a year in the land of the kings." Arzan shook his head. "It boggles my mind that a father would subject his child to such a place."

Maltan sighed. "Knowing her, she's taking it as an adventure."

Arzan had only met her two or three times, and then only briefly. The girl had certainly matched her spirited reputation. He didn't doubt the old man was right. "May she be experiencing a better life than I have." He nodded his farewell. "An unexpected pleasure to speak with you, Maltan. Let our paths cross in future."

Maltan raised his hand. "If circumstances allow. Good health to you, your grace."

Arzan and Filgneir finally boarded the carriage and set off through the city. He stared out the window as the vehicle rolled across the cobblestones, amazed as always at how disorganized Creedport's streets were. They were on one of the two main avenues cutting straight across the city, but every path that branched off melded into a twisting labyrinth of chasms lined by close wooden walls and choked merchant stalls. Both main avenue and narrow alleys alike were congested with merchants and commoners. The carriage matched pace with a Leverie-marked wagon filled to the brim with rolls of vibrantly colored cloth. All such a far cry from the more honest and, in his mind, simple beauty of Senkani. *Of course, this city does have one thing going for it.* He breathed the fresh sea air blowing in from the bay on the north end. It wasn't a smell one always got back home.

"As harsh as it may sound," Filgneir said, "I doubt Gricall's death will have much impact on anything."

Arzan fiddled with his cape's clasp. "I'm thinking he may

have more influence in death than he did in life. We can finally get the Council to stop Thrake from meddling with our markets."

"We're still part of the Aristocracy of Leverie, my liege. We can't simply cut off all our relations with the other provinces."

"Even when one of those provinces is trying to strangle us to the point of servitude?" Arzan angrily rapped his knuckles against the side-boards. "How did Father deal with that man?"

"I recall Thrake being easier to work with when his wife was still alive," Filgneir said. "She did wonders to even out his temper and ambitions." He grinned slyly. "Perhaps it would be of benefit for you to find such a balancing influence for yourself?"

Arzan laughed. "Do I seem all that troublesome on normal days when I don't have House Leverie causing me problems?"

"No. In fact, you normally seem the most controlled person in the room."

"I'm in no rush to get married," Arzan said, waving his hand. "I'm only twenty-six—plenty of time left to sort that out. It's not like we're in the monarchies, where they're always under pressure to have an heir or five."

"The rest of House Redleaf would certainly be happy if you did have a successor in line."

Arzan chuckled. "Moshon is probably the only place in the world where most of the nobility actively *avoid* trying to take part in politics."

"Well, that's the only natural outcome when there's no money to be made in taxes," Filgneir said.

"Too bad it doesn't solve all our problems."

The carriage rolled through the south gate, trading old wooden buildings for a patchwork of fields filled with vegetables and livestock. *Out here, one province looks much the same as another. I wonder how well the common people would get along if it weren't for the feuds of us nobles.*

A question in futility, he decided. As long as society existed, so would authority and politics.

Chapter 5

"In the pure form, the predestined variety
is perhaps the easier to understand. In this model,
there is only a single timeline, and the time traveler
was always a part the causal chain."

Reckless and stupid. Retyar knew that was what he was being, only weeks after resolving to stay put. He should be at the cave, hiding from the world, not exploring it. But exploring he was.

And right now, it was worth it.

The city that lay in front of him was exactly what he had dreamed of seeing in person during his time at University. The forty foot-walls were the most immediately striking thing. The very concept of setting physical boundaries around a city was strange to Retyar's world, but here they existed to create a stark divide between urban and rural. From atop his wooded hill, he could see all too clearly the contrast of densely packed tile roofs inside against the patchwork of acre-sized farm plots without. *That's something they never put in the movies for some reason. Farms.* That was an oversight he'd often wondered about. Why did filmmakers not seem to realize that food needed to come from somewhere?

And this city definitely needed plenty of food. He wasn't an expert, but he estimated it was big enough for at least twenty thousand people. Tiny by fifty-fifth century standards, yet impressive looking nonetheless. He wanted to walk its streets, to slip in among the line of carts ambling along through the gates. He yearned to do more than just watch the hundreds of wisps of smoke from so many kitchens. After day upon day of rabbits, fish, clams, and foraged greens, he craved bread, beans, spices—anything civilized.

He wanted to talk to somebody.

But he had to draw the line here. Observe only. No interaction.

He took the tablet out from his satchel. After searching and cross-referencing the encyclopedia for over an hour, he was fairly certain that this was the city of Creedport. Considering that the village dispute he'd stumbled into was apparently in the province of Senkani, that was the closest coastal city to the east. And this place definitely had a port. He could see three cargo sail ships moored in the bay. If he were to get closer, he might be able to confirm for sure by getting a good look at the crest on the green standards hanging at the gates and from the circular wall towers. He would also take note of the round tower in the middle of the city. That might be a landmark of enough significance to be in the encyclopedia. Something else that caught his eye when peering through his binoculars were the carvings that adorned the battlements. He wasn't a hundred percent positive, but they looked like lizards. *They had to have taken a lot of work —and money. But what sort of ruler puts up hundreds of carvings of lizards?*

So fixated was he on the city that a sudden crunching of leaves made Retyar's heart jump into his throat. He ducked down between a tree and some bushes, stowing the tablet back in the bag. The footsteps drew closer, the gait clearly human.

Within moments, he heard voices.

"Uncle, why are we coming all the way out here?"

"To get a good view of the city. I want you to have some perspective if you want to be part of the guard."

I should have realized this place is too good a spot to view the city from. Retyar pressed himself deeper behind cover as a man and an older boy came trudging into sight. They were both blond, the man wearing a green surcoat over chainmail, a helmet nestled in his arm.

The two of them walked within five paces of Retyar before stopping to survey the settlement. "The city guard's main purpose is to keep the peace, but we also have the responsibility to protect our home in the event of war," the man said. "That means being able to envision the mindset of an enemy."

"Uncle, I don't want to be part of the guard. I want to be a ckol."

"All the more reason for you to learn all this. A ckol is the crenden's bodyguard, but he must also be able to take on all the martial tasks his liege assigns him. He is a protector, a shieldsman, an investigator, an executioner, a strategist, and more besides. It's not just swordsmanship and prestige."

Six continents, I wish I had a video camera! Retyar thought.

"I understand," the boy said.

The man smiled and patted the boy's shoulder. "Good. So, here's an exercise. Pretend you are an invader trying to take the city. What is it that you see?"

The boy looked out. Retyar did the same, interested himself in the question. "Well, of course, there's the walls. Those are the main defense."

"Obviously. And assuming they were to assault instead of lay siege, how would the enemy overcome them?"

"Any number of ways," the boy said. "Ladders, battering ram to the gate, going around into the harbor . . . ."

"Which do you think the city is strongest against?"

The boy shrugged. "None of them would be easy. They'd lose a lot of men trying to attack the wall directly, but the harbor is probably the hardest if they don't have ships."

"But easiest if they do. They wouldn't necessarily lose many men attacking the walls, either. The city guard is well manned for keeping order, but there aren't enough of us to protect every part of the wall at once. We'd supplement the defenses through enlistment, of course, but they won't be as skilled and well equipped as we are. And the enemy would very likely be able to capture these hills and see exactly where the battlements are weakest. They would lock shields against our arrows and march their ladders where they are sure to win. Maybe they'd even have incendiaries to light the rooftops of the towers on fire, slowing the redeployment of our forces."

"That sounds like we should change the tower roofs to tile."

The man grunted. "I've tried bringing that up with Crenden Thrake. He likes the look of the wood roofs and doesn't think there's enough threat to warrant replacing them. To be honest, he definitely has a point." He crossed his arms. "Regardless, I'll leave it as an assignment for you to come up with a good defense against the scenario I gave you."

The boy grinned. "Are we moving to fighting lessons?"

Retyar shifted quietly, trying to get a good view of the two. *This is just too cool.*

The uncle removed a bundle of cloth he had strapped across his back, as well as the sword and scabbard tied to his belt, and dropped them to the ground. "Yesterday, we practiced your swordsmanship. Today, I'll teach you to fight hand to hand."

The boy's face dropped.

"Don't look at me like that! The poets all love to sing about the blade, but in the real world, it's an unlucky guardsman or ckol who ever has to kill. Tell me, when was the last time anyone seriously tried to harm a crenden of Leverie?"

"Um, was that the Mad Fisher?"

"Right—thirty years ago," the man said. "Of course, in the city guard, you'll sometimes have to deal with the odd murderer on the run, but by and large the worst you usually have to face is a drunken brawl."

"Or a mob."

The uncle's face soured. "What those mercenaries did in Senkani was stupid. If they'd escorted their charges out of that mess instead of trying to stand and fight, no one would have died over a few reams of blazing silk."

Retyar rubbed his chin. They were talking about what happened at the village the first day he'd arrived. *Good to know violence like that is a big deal here. Then again, what are the odds of me stumbling into that kind of rare disaster?*

"We'll talk strategy and ethics later," the uncle said.

"Come at me!"

The boy shouted and jumped forward, fists raised. He jabbed at his uncle's jaw. Faster than Retyar could follow, the man caught the boy's arm and flipped him around and into the dirt. The boy groaned.

"That's something I learned from your grandfather after he came back from Fractora." The uncle grabbed hold of the boy's elbow and twisted it behind his back until he cried out and slapped the ground with his free hand in submission. "Most of the city guard rely on muscle and numbers. It's techniques like this that helped get me promoted to captain. Use your opponent's momentum against him, take advantage of his own reflexes." He let off of his nephew and helped him back up.

"Felt like you were going to pull my shoulder out," the boy said, rolling his arm and wincing.

"Effective, isn't it? Here, I'll show you how it's done."

The lesson continued. Interesting as the whole thing was, Retyar was getting hungry and didn't want to sit through an hour of repetitive practice throws. He looked around and spotted a gap in the brush that would let him sneak off without much noise.

Carefully . . . .

He timed his movements to coincide with one or the other of them hitting the ground, inching his way toward the slope. They didn't notice him at all as he slipped away through the forest.

Chapter 6

"Here, a time traveler was always going to be a time traveler, his actions were always going to happen, and his effect on the timeline was always part of original events."

The clap of Arzan's palm against the marble tabletop echoed throughout the Council chamber, amplified by the sweeping dome high above. "This is unacceptable!"

Ylnavar Leverie, Crenden of Highcity and Speaker of the Council, rapped his wooden block in answer to the outburst. Thin and gnarled by age, the old man's voice still boomed with authority, "Arzan, such displays are unseemly in this chamber. Remain civil, or else the ruling will default to Thrake's favor."

Isn't that what's already happening? Arzan thought bitterly. He nonetheless controlled his voice as he responded, pointing to Thrake at the far end of the round table. "I repeat that I find it unreasonable for Thrake to be allowed continued access to Senkani's markets. He and his merchants have already shown through this incident that they are little more than thugs."

"By your own admission, it was the people of Senkani who initiated the aggression," Mansar said. The Crenden of Blueturf brushed his hand through his square beard, the jeweled rings on his fingers bobbing in and out of the brown whiskers as he frowned at Arzan from his distant seat. "I fail to see why it should be Creedport that is punished."

"Thrake's party killed a man," Arzan ground out.

"And the man whose sword he fell on is already dead," Crenden Roth said. The ruler of Glasscastle was just a tad older than Arzan, but with the sort of angular features that made him dashingly popular with far too many women. His face and oiled hair were set perfectly aglow from a shaft of sunlight through the high windows, and that only served to heighten Arzan's annoyance with him. "By both the Council's and your own mob's standards, it would seem justice has already been served."

"And then some," Athar wheezed. "The Senkani mob killed three to their losses of one." The Crenden of Haerean was a man Arzan liked to describe as a person of excess girth and deficient spine. As the man adjusted the cushions in his seat to better accommodate his opulent weight, Arzan tried not to despair at being attacked by someone who only ever took the side already certain to win.

"Compensation should be made to the families of each of the men killed," Ylnavar said. "That is more than generous for both this Gricall and the first of the guards to draw his sword. I believe that shall be the end of the matter."

Across the table, Thrake kept his face mostly neutral, but Arzan saw a faint, smug quirk to his lips. Arzan clenched his fists in his lap.

"I have something to add about this matter," Crenden Pundur of Three Corners spoke up. Even sitting beside Athar's copious form, the man looked huge, but in muscle rather than fat. He was his neighbor's opposite in other areas as well, most significantly in his tendency to voice unpopular positions. "I do not disagree with Ylnavar's decision on compensation, but there is an underlying issue here threatening to bring about a repeat of this tragedy. Namely, the people of Senkani themselves do not want Leverie merchants dealing cloth in their province."

"Your point being?" Roth asked.

Pundur crossed his massive arms. "It doesn't matter what free trade agreements the Council guarantees if the people aren't going to buy Creedport's wares anyway, and if Thrake keeps trying to push the matter, we're just going to end up with another mob."

Thrake straightened. "Not if the Council decrees strict protections for my merchants."

Arzan rolled his eyes. "Thrake, when will you stop trying to rule my province? You don't even need my markets—you already have more trade dealings with Falcone and Fractora than you can keep up with!"

"This isn't about money!" Thrake said. "It's a matter of a unified country. Senkani and House Redleaf have always viewed themselves as set apart from the rest of the Aristocracy. The strength of our nation depends upon a sense of unity and common purpose. Ranisa and Whitesail are giving us increasing competition as they put more and more of their resources into the textile trade. At the rate things are going, they will both be outproducing us in no more than a decade. Senkani needs to be drawn out of its subsistence mindset and join in the common good."

Arzan shook his head. "Overspecialization invites disaster. Leverie has become so focused on growing cotton and silk that half the provinces don't even supply enough food to feed themselves. Can we call our country secure if we're dependent on the Federation selling us grain?"

Ylnavar rapped his block against the table. "This discussion is growing beyond the scope of the topic at hand. The Council will take a vote of agreement on the matter of compensation to the victims' families. Discussion on trade rights and production shall be placed on the agenda for the next meeting." He slid his gaze across at Pundur. "Until then, I think it is reasonable that Creedport's merchants have a moratorium on dealings within Senkani, for the sake of the safety of all involved."

Arzan smiled as Thrake growled something under his breath.

"All votes in favor of compensation to all parties, paid by the opposing House?"

All ten crendens raised their hands.

"Unanimous agreement. Votes in favor of moratorium on trade?"

Arzan put his hand up, as did Pundur, Ylnavar, Athar, and three others who had thus far been quiet. "Seven in favor, three against. Motion successful. Now, on to the issue of gold reserves in Quarry Hill . . . ."

Arzan exited the Council building with the sun already dipping below Highcity's western walls. He felt stiff from sitting in place for hours on end, and he did not look forward to the hours more it would take to ride back home. He turned around and looked up at the majestic Council dome, still lit by the late afternoon's orange light.

"I'd call that a victory in there."

Arzan lowered his gaze back down to see Pundur descending the Council steps, his silk vest tight against his chest. "Thank you for your help. At least I have one neighbor who's on my side."

Pundur shook his head. "Thrake's a blustering fool. He gives the rest of House Leverie a bad name."

"Mansar and Roth stuck by him."

"A little popularity doesn't make a fool any less a fool."

Arzan laughed. "That's a statement I can get behind."

The tapping of a cane against stone announced someone's arrival atop the steps. Arzan glanced over as Crenden Hashan came out of the building. The older Leverie had been one of the crendens to remain silent through the whole debate, but Arzan was still grateful he had come through on the vote. He was about to step aside, but Hashan caught sight of him and came on straight with a grandfatherly smile.

"Crenden Arzan, I'm glad you're still here. I wanted to say I intend to give you my support in the next Council."

"Thank you, Hashan. It's a relief to have Woodwise as a friend."

Hashan rubbed the whiskers of his white, close trimmed beard. "I think Thrake has a point about the importance of a unified country, but he's going about it in the wrong way. The answer is in friendship, not force." He rested his hand on the ivory handle of his cane. "Besides, we all know Senkani does its part for the Aristocracy. House Redleaf has the best vineyards this side of the continent, and your province can be trusted to guard the northwest border."

"Too bad Thrake doesn't see the value in either of those," Arzan said.

Hashan chuckled. "Oh, he certainly appreciates your wines, though he wouldn't admit it to your face."

Pundur grunted. "Well, that's something. What makes him such a staunch enemy of—"

"He's a prude!" Hashan said. "For all his talk of economic unity, what he really wants is for Leverie to be ruled by one House. Even if we have a supermajority on the Council, he can't stand the two provinces that are run by their own Houses."

"I hardly ever see him giving Warth trouble," Pundur said.

Hashan lifted his cane in the air. "Even he knows he needs to be careful attacking the House that holds the gold mines. House Redleaf is the easier target." He shrugged. "He probably figures he'll wait on fighting that battle until it's nine on one."

"He's pretty clear on his target," Arzan said. "When we argue, it's always House Redleaf he attacks—not just me and my father."

"Then he's far sillier than I thought," Pundur said. "It was the Leverie who originally appointed the Redleafs into the nobility. Since then, your House has more than proven its loyalty, and not just through its part in the Tarkandan Split."

"Well . . . " Hashan rubbed the handle of his cane and straightened his dark silk vest. "Arzan, I confess, the reason I chose to speak with you is that I have a proposal to put to your consideration."

Arzan raised his brows. "Are you planning to spite Thrake and set up trade with Senkani yourself?"

"Perhaps, but that's not what I currently want to discuss. The details are something I would want to leave until you can make time to visit me in Woodwise. Would that be possible?"

Hashan's reluctance to speak here what he had in mind had Arzan immediately intrigued. "The grape harvest is just starting, so I'll have my hands full for the next few weeks. Perhaps in a month?"

"A month . . . " The wheels turned behind Hashan's eyes. He smiled. "Yes, I will expect you in a month's time. Be sure to take that adviser of yours with you—the bald one."

"Filgneir hates people identifying him by his lack of hair."

"Then he should take to wearing a hat!" Hashan looked past Arzan to the broad driveway. "Ah, seems that my horses are getting restless. I shall see you next in Woodwise, Crenden Arzan. Good day."

Pundur watched the older man stride over to his carriage before slapping Arzan on the back. "I suppose the two of us should get going as well. No point hanging about and risking a run-in with the more absurd elements of House Leverie."

Arzan frowned and rubbed the spot where he'd been hit. "That's sound advice. Thank you again, Pundur."

"I'm just a neighbor with common sense!"

The two parted and made for their own carriages. Arzan found Captain Vighkon, head of his bodyguard, waiting alone with the driver.

"Filgneir's not back yet?" Arzan asked.

Vighkon shook his head. "He finished his tasks in town about an hour ago, but left again saying he had an idea of something else he wanted to do."

"That's unusual."

The captain grunted and scratched at the old scar running along his face from forehead down parallel to his nose. "He already sent the wagons on to Senkani, so I don't think he'd be getting anything—"

"Ah, you're here," Filgneir called as he walked up from the Council building's servant wing.

Arzan fiddled with his cape clasp. "If you had time to spare, you might have accompanied me into the meeting. I needed whatever support I could get."

"I knew you would manage well on your own," Filgneir said.

"You didn't even ask if the Council ruled in our favor."

Filgneir had a glint in his eye. "Because I know you managed well on your own."

Arzan shook his head and boarded the carriage. He gave Filgneir the details of the Council rulings as the driver took them out into the city streets.

"Gricall didn't have much family to speak of," Filgneir said. "The man was an orphan. His wife passed away in childbirth, and she was from a lower family in Whitesail. I've tried tracking them down, but so far no luck."

"So still no relatives to care for the girl?" Arzan asked.

Filgneir held out empty hands.

Arzan looked out at the streets of the city, now growing dark as the sun took its leave. Highcity was the richest urban center in the country, traditionally doted upon by the other provinces in honor of it being the Council seat. The roads were paved with smooth flagstones and statues marked every street corner. Firekeepers in pristine gray outfits raised sticks with burning wicks to ornate oil streetlamps.

"There's that old retreat in the woods from my grandfather's time," Arzan said. "We'll put the reparations towards fixing it up and raising her there."

Filgneir rubbed his chin. "That will ruffle some feathers. Your family has been arguing about that plot for years."

"You think they'll complain I'm repairing it? The property will only be tied up until the girl comes of age."

"Meaning for the next fourteen years. She's only four."

"They've waited this long," Arzan said. "They can wait a little longer."

Filgneir tapped the window frame. "I doubt the reparations will cover the entire cost."

"I will pay the shortfall, and for whatever servants we hire." Arzan glanced at him. "You're not going to talk about how unreasonable I'm being putting so much into a commoner child?"

"Unreasonable?" Filgneir said. "Gricall was a symbol to the people. I couldn't imagine the outrage if we *didn't* do something for his daughter."

Arzan rubbed the edge of the window frame. "I don't want to make a big deal of it. It wouldn't be fair to the girl to turn her into a political tool."

The driver stopped their carriage at the gates to allow a firekeeper to light the lamps hanging on the front and side. It was going to be a long trip through the night, but Arzan couldn't be absent at the beginning of the harvest. Things were going to be busy these next few weeks. Perhaps it would be enough to take his mind off all the craziness for a bit.

Chapter 7

"Notwithstanding depressing consideration as to the nature of free will, this is the safest variety of time travel, and in my opinion the most ideal."

A little later than he'd promised, Arzan finally found his way to Woodwise.

The city was in many ways the opposite of what a city should be. Originally founded as a plantation surrounded by woodlands, it had since expanded over the centuries into a sprawling population center. The original forest was long gone, cut down and replaced by miles of cotton fields. The locals always kept their fondness for trees, however, and turned the city itself into a cultivated woodland. From outside the walls, the city looked more like a patch of forest surrounded by endless fields of farmland. Inside, it was absolutely stunning. Every one of its broad avenues was lined on either side with wizened elms, and most houses had enough space around them for at least one row of woods. A handful of squirrels didn't even feel the least bit out of place as they darted between horses and people.

It was one of Arzan's favorite places in the whole country.

His carriage rolled along the main avenue beneath a green canopy, the horses clomping over cobblestones clothed with fallen leaves. He was about a week late to his appointment with Hashan—the harvest had encountered a few problems, requiring extra time to sort out. He was here now, however, and dying to hear what this proposal was.

"You know, I really think we should plant some trees in Senkani," Arzan said.

Filgneir didn't look up from the reports he was reading through. "Mhm. You say that every time we come here, my liege. Senkani's streets are too narrow to realistically allow it. Besides, do you know how much work it takes to maintain the roads when there are tree roots tearing everything up?"

"I'm sure there are some places where it would be appropriate."

"Then pick out the spots. And not that area on the south end of the square this time. That would have thrown the flow of traffic completely out of order."

Arzan smirked. "Who's the crenden here?"

"You are, of course. And it's my job to remind you to act like one, and make sure you plant vines if you really want some extra green."

The carriage reached the Woodwise palace grounds. Servants pulled open the iron gate, granting them access to the gravel driveway and the other wonder of this city. While some palaces strove to impress with elaborate architecture, this one put its stock in the four acres of exquisite gardens on the perimeter of the estate. Impeccably tended fruit trees and flowers formed rows to either side of the carriage, boasting every conceivable color. Only a few of the plants were native to Leverie. Most had been procured over the course of decades from all over the six, and only thrived because of tender care.

The driver brought them to a wooden building two stories tall. It was of fairly simple craftsmanship with few embellishments, though its finish gleamed a rich golden brown. It had a homey feel, and Arzan found himself smiling as he stepped down, his boots crunching on the gravel driveway.

"Crenden Hashan is currently in the gardens, your grace," a servant said from the base of the palace steps. He pointed to a pathway. "He informs you that you are free to meet him by the hibiscus beds."

Captain Vghkon slid down from beside the driver and took a deep breath before coughing. "So it is possible to have air so sweet you choke," he muttered.

Arzan patted his ckol on the shoulder. "You exaggerate."

The path into the gardens was set with smooth stepping stones spaced by patches of dark grass. Various types of apples hung ripe from bowed branches, the fruit skins a collection of yellows, oranges, and reds. Beyond the miniature orchard, Arzan found vines set on arched trellises. Long bean pods hung from above, their green tips dangling just shy of his head. Past the living tunnel, they found hibiscus flowers planted in violet rings around a set of covered benches.

"See, this is so much more eye-catching than the drab stones around our palace," Arzan said.

The benches were empty. Arzan and Filgneir took two of the seats, while Vighkon strolled slowly about.

"Hmm, should have brought my reports along if we're going to be waiting," Filgneir said.

No sooner had he spoken than Arzan heard the approaching taps of a walking cane on stone. He turned and saw Hashan coming up the path, the handle of his cane in one hand, a plate in the other. "I thank you for making the time, Arzan! Please forgive me for not greeting you at the door. I was feeling antsy and decided to take a stroll through the garden."

"No problem at all, Hashan," Arzan said. "Meeting out here is far preferable to a dark little room."

"Very much so!" The older crenden held out the plate. "Some fruit? Freshly picked."

Arzan picked up one of the yellow slices and raised it in thanks before popping it in his mouth. Soft, sweet, and cool, it was just the sort of thing he needed coming from the road.

"Now then," Arzan said. "What is this proposal that needs to be made in such secrecy?"

Hashan set the fruit plate down on the next bench over. He stood his cane upright in front of him and rubbed the ivory handle. "We spoke of this issue last month in Highcity, but I'll ask again: what's the biggest obstacle to you being respected by the rest of the Council?"

Arzan narrowed his eyes and fiddled with his cape clasp. "I'm not of House Leverie."

The older crenden stroked his close cut beard and smiled

nervously. "Here's my offer."

Ellaniel pierced needle into cloth, drawing her yellow thread through the sleeve of the turquoise dress spread in her lap. Her hand moved smoothly, her motions methodical and precise. She was hardly conscious of the individual strokes, focused only on the image in her mind and how it manifested on her silk canvas. Her humming voice kept rhythm with her strokes.

"You pick the drabbest places to work, Goldeye."

She halted her needle just shy of pricking her finger. "I didn't know you were visiting today, Odavan."

Her cousin strolled along the garden path, hand to his chin as he regarded the tall grasses surrounding the two of them. This time of season, most were a ripe brown, their tops weighted with many different varieties of grain. Ellaniel often found this spot inspiring. At least, when she wasn't being pestered by dandy aristocrats with frilled collars and haughty smiles.

"Really now," Odavan said, rubbing dirt between his fingers after brushing his hand across the top of a brick retaining wall, "our current crenden has such odd tastes. Wheat and rice as garden plants? Bah!"

Ellaniel pointed down the path. "There are plenty of thorned flowers off that way if it's more your preference."

Odavan dusted his hands and laughed. "Oh, there's one here already. And this one's thorns are made of silver."

"What do you want, Odavan?" she demanded, pinching her needle between her nails.

Leather scraped on stone as he shifted his feet, twisting to look back towards the palace, visible above the fruit trees a little ways over. "I heard Uncle Hashan was meeting with that savage Redleaf. I simply wanted to ensure he wasn't making any silly deals. There are already enough things I'll have to clean up when I eventually become crenden."

Ellaniel tightened her grip on the cloth she was working on and glared up at him. "My father is far wiser than you."

Odavan snorted. "Wise enough to marry some barbarian princess from the Old Continent? We saw how that turned out, what with her leaving the moment she realized there were greater riches to be had elsewhere. Didn't even have the decency to bring her golden-eyed runt with her."

She slapped him before she was even conscious of having stood. Odavan held his face and rolled his jaw. "And once again, she shows she has the blood of Originate in her. This is why the House will choose me to succeed Hashan as crenden of Woodwise."

"I don't care to be crendess," Ellaniel seethed. "But don't you dare insult my mother."

Odavan bared his teeth in a humorless smile. "Till next time, cousin."

Fists shaking, she watched to make sure he disappeared around a bend in the path before crouching down to pick up her project. "To the shyles with you," she muttered, but she immediately chastised herself. Her getting riled up was just what he wanted. She turned the cloth until she found the spot she had left off at, but noticed her right hand was empty. *Wonderful. Lost the needle.* There were three more of the same size in her box, but the needle really was silver, and she hated the waste.

"Down by your left foot."

Ellaniel jumped at the voice and twisted to see a man not five paces away on the path. "Six continents, why are so many people sneaking up on me today?"

"Forgive me," the man said, tilting his head in apology. "I just wanted to make sure I was close enough to intervene if things turned into a slapping match."

"You saw and heard all of that, then?" Ellaniel eyed the sword at the man's hip, at his tough build. The features felt to her at odds with his refined clothing. He also wore a red cape, which made his appearance all the more strange. Still, his blue eyes harbored what seemed like genuine concern.

Probably that Crenden Redleaf's ckol, wandering around while his master is busy with Father.

"I admit, things sounded rather interesting," he said.

Ellaniel found the needle on the edge of a stepping stone, right where he'd indicated. She plucked it up and set about rethreading it. "Well, the interesting is now over. Thank you for pointing out my needle."

The man regarded her in silence a moment, apparently oblivious of her dismissal. She looked both ways down the path, uncomfortable at his continued presence. "Excuse me, are you aware of who I am?"

"Ellaniel Leverie, daughter of Crenden Hashan," the man said. "Do you know who I am?"

The amusement in his voice told her she'd just made a grave mistake. "Are . . . you a noble?"

The man smiled and bowed his head. "Crenden Arzan Redleaf. A pleasure to make your acquaintance, your grace."

Ellaniel felt her cheeks burn at her gaffe. "My apologies. I don't attend House functions very often, and with your sword . . . . Crendens don't normally bear swords."

Crenden Arzan placed his hand on the pommel without taking his eyes off her. "Senkani has traditionally seen itself as the guardian of the Aristocracy. The Crenden Redleaf wears this as a symbolic reminder of his duty." He removed his hand and quirked his lips somewhat sheepishly. "Though, I do hope its existence doesn't frighten you."

"Frighten? No." She remembered when she was a child, watching her mother practice in these very gardens, her father occasionally looking on in disapproval. *What do you need these skill for, Extereal? What place do they have here in Leverie?"* She returned to her embroidery. "So, out of curiosity, what is it you were here to discuss with my father?"

"A possible alliance between Woodwise and Senkani," Arzan said. He fiddled with the clasp of his cape. "You know, your needlework is very impressive. Are those patterns on your dress yours as well?"

Ellaniel nodded as she pulled needle and thread. "People say I've an eye for detail."

"And I'm sure other things about your eyes, besides."

Her brow twitched. "Yes. In fact—"

"They're beautiful."

The words she was about to speak caught in her throat unfinished. She blinked. "What?"

"I've never seen golden irises like that before," Arzan said. "And it goes well with the brown shade of your hair."

He turned away and blushed. "I'm sorry. I'm not normally one to throw women cheap compliments. Forgive me if I'm being untoward."

"You're not!" Ellaniel blurted. She bunched up the cloth in her hand. Why was her heart beating so fast? "I, um. Thank you." *My parents and my grandmother are the only ones who've ever said anything good about my eye color.*

Arzan loosened his shoulders.

Ellaniel put her project aside. It didn't seem she'd be able to focus much on it. "So, I confess I don't know much about the border provinces. Are they all about swords and such?"

He leaned against a retainer wall. "Definitely not. Senkani is probably the province most focused on the martial skills, but remember that we haven't faced a war in generations. We're farmers and tradesmen, just like everyone else."

"I see." She put a finger to her chin. "I don't recall ever seeing Senkani fabric or thread in the markets."

"Our specialty is in wines. Other than that, we largely keep to ourselves."

"Oh."

"I would go so far as to say we have some good playwrights, though," Arzan said.

"And if it's not too insensitive to ask, what would Woodwise get out of an alliance with such a quiet people?"

Arzan smiled. "For one, a stable country. Did you hear about the incident between Senkani and Creedport two months ago?"

If she recalled correctly, there had been something about a mob and a Creedport merchant killed.

"The second gain is . . . something a bit more personal to your father," Arzan said.

Ellaniel knit her brow and tried to think what kind of involvement her father could have with the western border province.

Arzan tilted his head to stare at the sky. "He asked if I would be willing to marry you."

It was a good thing she had put down her embroidery or she would have dropped it now. He turned back to her and locked his gaze with hers. In her shock, she couldn't look away. Couldn't even decide what thoughts were going through her own head.

Well, he's handsome.

She mentally shouted at herself, *Out of everything, that's what you go for?*

"For what it's worth, I postponed my answer," Arzan said, breaking away his eyes. He rubbed the clasp of his cape. "I wanted to ensure you were open to the idea. I would not in a hundred years wish to force you into something like this against your will."

"And I'm sure you also wanted to make sure I was someone worth your consideration," she said flatly.

He chuckled. "Honestly, yes."

She bit her lip. With how the rest of the House viewed her, she'd figured there was a big chance she would end up a lonely old maid, or else married to a lower merchant seeking into the nobility. To be a crenden's wife . . . .

Her eyes went to the sword at his side. She opened her mouth to ask a certain question, but stopped herself. Instead, she looked him in the face. "So, what do you think of me?"

"I think you are the first woman I have ever felt the desire to be with."

Ellaniel flushed hotter than she ever thought she could. She cleared her throat and stood. "That's a quick judgment."

Arzan splayed his hands. "But I have a suspicion it's a feeling that's not going to change. You're an interesting woman."

"You've not even spent a quarter hour with me. What at all have I shown that's interesting?" *Ellaniel, what are you doing trying to push him away? You'll not get anyone better than this.*

"Truthfully, I'm not quite sure," he said. "Maybe I'm just entranced by what I see in your eyes. Maybe it's because it seems we're in a similar state. We're both part of a privileged society that doesn't want us. But I do hope it's something deeper, and I'm willing to find out."

Ellaniel glanced around at the garden, wondering what life would hold for her if she said yes. She fixed him with her gaze. "All right, let's find out."

Chapter 8

*"The next category of time travel, by contrast,
is entirely chaotic, and could turn
the world into a living nightmare."*

Grice shifted his too heavy pack from one uncomfortable position to another. Looking around over his shoulder, it seemed like the walls of Highcity were still right behind him, the rising sun setting the curves in the crafted stone aglow. He grumbled to himself as he thought about the long trek ahead. If he didn't stop at any of the cotton plantations along the way, he'd be able to make it to Creedport soon after nightfall. Of course, if the master's horse and cart had not been making a delivery to Bluhall, he'd have been able to make the return trip and be sleeping in his own bed tonight. He did not look forward to ending the day by searching out an inn and spending a quarter of what he'd just earned in getting there. Were that not enough, he could count on the customer being angry at the delivery being half a day late.

A bend appeared in the wooded road up ahead and Grice sighed. Here was another thing about the trip to Creedport. Why did the road have to twist around on its way down the hill and then veer off towards the Jagged Fields before deciding to go straight towards the coast? Sure, Grice knew most of the traffic around here was between the Jagged Fields and Highcity, but anyone going to Creedport had to waste an hour going the wrong way. Well, not today! Grice knew where the road *ought* to be, and by going straight from the get go he'd be able to save that hour on his trip. As he came upon the bend, he went up to the fence separating the road from the hill's steep incline and hopped over as best he could with his full pack. He smirked to himself until his foot landed in a loose drift of leaves and hit the ground beneath at a sharp angle. The heavy pack made it impossible to save his balance, and Grice crashed and rolled down the hill in a flurry of leaves and twigs.

He came to a rest on his stomach and spit out some bits of soil as he waited for the dizziness to go away. Gradually, he took stock of the feeling coming in from his limbs and figured he was still in one piece, more or less. His pack felt like it was weighing down extra, though. Had he really been setting out on a day's trek with this much of a load?

A groan came from above him and Grice yelped in shock. He strained to twist his neck around and found a man sprawled on top of him. It took him a couple of false starts before he found his voice, "Oi, you all right up there?"

The stranger stirred and then rolled to the side, clearly disoriented. Grice got himself to his knees and set his pack on the ground. "A lot of ground for me to trip on, and outta this whole forest I smack into you. Sorry about that, friend."

Now that he looked more attentively, the fellow appeared to be a beggar. He was wrapped completely in an old, dingy blanket, and what was visible of his face under his makeshift hood was half-covered in a scraggly beard. He couldn't quite see the man's eyes. He had some rod or something wrapped up in cloth that was strapped to his back, but in stark contrast with the rest of his appearance, the strap seemed to be very finely made. A remnant of another life, perhaps.

"Yes, of all the forest," the beggar said in a hoarse voice as he slowly lifted himself up and pulled his hood even further down over his face.

Grice stood and offered a hand to aid the fellow up. "I really'm sorry 'bout that. Was hoping to cut through the forest to save some time, you see. Hadn't planned on misjudgin' my footing and inconveniencing another traveler."

The other man, already half to his feet, did not take the offered help, instead merely staring at Grice's hand for an uncomfortable length of time. Grice frowned. "Look, friend, I did not crash into you on purpose. I know it's rude to barrel into someone out of nowhere, but it's also rude to be suspicious when someone apologizes, which is what I'm doing. Were you heading into the city? I'll see you through the gates." That would cost him some daylight, but Grice was feeling bad about the whole incident, and his uncle had taught him to always be a friend to fellow travelers on the road.

The beggar was silent for a bit longer before shaking his head. "I was just leaving town," his voice was still hoarse. "I thought to take a shortcut as well."

"Heading to Creedport, then?"

"Just the coast."

"Well, then, we're both heading in the same direction, and we'll both need to be coming across the main road. If we travel together, I'll be able to take us along the shortest route."

The stranger gazed northward towards the coast. "I prefer to travel alone."

Grice shifted his feet uncomfortably. "Please, friend. It'd be a burden on me if I couldn't compensate you in some way."

"It wasn't that big a deal. All you did was push me down a hill."

"Not a big deal! I coulda broken your neck!"

"It really—"

Grice sighed and reached for his coin purse. "Fine then. At least lemme give ya a chip silver. It would bother me to no end if I could not make up for your trouble."

The stranger held out his hand to refuse, but looked up to the sky as if contemplating the inevitable. "Wait, fine, I'll travel with you. Don't pay me, raze it."

"Finally," Grice said, returning the coin and clapping the stranger on the back. He retrieved his pack and strapped it on, then held out his hand once more. "Name's Grice."

The stranger just nodded. "Let's be on our way, then."

Maybe you really should have just let the grouch be, he thought to himself. In any case, it was still a long walk ahead of them. Best to go and get started. Grice led the way through the low underbrush, glancing over his shoulder every once in awhile to use the visible bits of the city wall as a directional guide, and then checking the sun once the city was out of sight. The land after leaving the area right around Highcity was pleasantly flat, though the beggar's silence began to wear on him after about an hour or two. *Wait, is he a beggar, though? What kinda beggar refuses a silver coin?* The other man clearly didn't want to talk and reveal his story, though, and Grice wasn't going to pry.

But hang him if the quiet wasn't giving him an itch.

"Not my usual thing to be cutting through the forest like this," Grice said eventually as he navigated his way across some large roots. "This delivery to Creedport'd normally be sent by cart, but the master's horse is off somewhere else today. This load's for some important customer over there. Lives in a tower and has the sponsorship of the House and access to the palace. I've only seen the first floor—of the tower, that is—but by the looks of it he's a tinkerer. I tell you, the place's just filled with gears an' glass an' rope, but I ain't got a clue what half of it's supposed to be for. I'm just happy the stuff he ordered from us this time's pretty solid and well padded, so I don't think anything broke on the way down."

Grice kicked a loose stone and watched it bounce off a tree trunk. His travel companion still didn't say anything. *Probably just boring him with my rambling.* But he didn't complain either, so he figured he'd continue on for the sake of his own sanity. "Whatever he makes probably isn't very good, though, since his crenden's always threatening to kick 'im out. It's only 'cause the prior crenden issued a decree on the matter that things're still going well for the guy. Me, I don't think he can't be all bad. Word is, old man Maltan gave the crenden a talking to about that mess in Senkani. That's the kinda fellow I like. Doesn't take any tomfoolery from the aristocrats."

Grice scratched his neck. "Anyway, trade's doing pretty well, all 'n all. Woodwise's been increasing their production, so we've been sending them a lot of loom material. I hear the Council's negotiated some new trade routes in the east, and a new type of dye's come in from the south. They say it's a new yellow that the sun can't fade. That's most like exaggerating. Last time they said something like that, the color stayed a few years, sure, but then eventually went brown. The real way to preserve color is to just wear your fancy stuff indoors. Now, when it comes to dyes . . . ." he trailed off. Somehow, things just felt more awkward than when they were both silent.

Surprisingly, the beggar spoke up, "That's all quite interesting. What kinds of things do they make dye from?"

Grice frowned. "Plants, flowers, and a few minerals mostly. Everyone knows that, right?"

"I . . . don't get out much. To be honest, I don't even know what the year is."

Grice couldn't help but laugh as he stopped and turned around. "That's something, losing track even of the number of seasons! Course, that's easy enough how mild this part of the world is. You're some sort of hermit, I suppose? That makes sense of yer garb!"

A slight smile appeared on the stranger's bearded lips. "A hermit. Yes I am, I suppose."

"All right, I won't ask what drove you to such a life," Grice said. "I know a lot of your type do it for real personal reasons. Don't hold it against you for not knowing what year it is. What use does a fellow have for dates out in the woods, anyway? We're in 4774." The two continued walking. "Wanna hear any of the day's news?"

"That thing between Senkani and Creedport—how have things been going after that?"

Grice shifted his pack. "Eh, you know how it is between those two crendens. It was always plenty o' tension there, even with their fathers, but now it's gotten especially bad. Fortunately, the Council stepped in and made sure all the families got paid and the like, and Thrake's not allowed to trade in Senkani for a bit. That doesn't mean Senkani's all hunkering down again, though. Rumor is, Crenden Redleaf's making a deal with Woodwise, and Senkani'll be selling him foodstuff that's normally shipped in from the Federation and Vitran and the like. Me, I think that's a pretty good idea. The Leverie always want to put everything on cotton and mulberry and all the dye plants, but what does that leave us to eat when the ships have trouble? Don't get me wrong—my master's able to pay me because of all the loom business, but we're putting all our eggs in one basket here. I get to see a lotta stuff, and I know the danger of not diversifying. More than one prominent merchant has bit the dust because the market turned against his one product, and him having nothing else to fall back on."

Grice stopped himself short with a glance at his travel companion. "Ah, here I am going off on tangents. This stuff is out of my hands and some'd say over my head. You'll find many who think like me, even so. Those've us who aren't part of a House, but have the means to learn and to think end up wondering if this is really the best path for the country. The Leverie've done well for us so far, making us all wealthy as a whole, but can things stay as they are? —Oi, I think I see the road!"

The break in the trees became more distinct as they drew nearer, and its width confirmed it to be the main road to Creedport. "We'll make far better time walking on a clear path," Grice said. "I wonder if we might even try hitching a ride on someone's cart. That'd be a laugh. What's the point of hiring a deliveryman when he doesn't even use his own means to deliver?" Still, he was tempted.

"I think this is where we will have to part ways," the hermit said.

Grice turned again. "What? Right when we get to the road?"

The man nodded. "I wish to avoid people, if I can."

"If you must," Grice said with a sigh. "I won't be so disrespectful as to argue again. It'll take you much longer getting to the coast if you don't take the road, though."

Grice could see that slight smile again. Was there a tinge of sadness in it? "Time is something I find I have too much of."

"Well," Grice held out his hand. "It was pleasant enough being able to travel with you."

The hermit hesitated, but then accepted the handshake. "And I thank you for the news." He glanced one last time at the road and then started deeper into the forest. As he did, Grice caught a glimpse of his boots, which matched with his ragged clothing and beard just as poorly as that fine strap.

They were heavily dusted, but clearly the work of a master cobbler and in good condition. The thick soles in particular were made of an odd-looking material he'd never seen before. He looked down at his own boots, which were tearing at the seams and nearly worn through the bottom. He opened his mouth to ask where the hermit got his footwear, but the fellow was already gone. *Ah, well, can't be that hard to find the shoemaker who makes such quality.* He started up the dirt road and set his path for Creedport, wondering if the inn would have any breaded tuna tonight.

Chapter 9

"What else can we call a universe which practically rewrites itself at a whim?"

Retyar paced the cliff's edge, his mind replaying over and over his run-in with the Highcity deliveryman. It had been stupid of him to risk another expedition. Stupid, stupid, stupid. With that much interaction, could there be any hope of an intact timeline? No. A pebble was shifted. There were now ripples in history. The past was changed, and it was entirely his fault.

Stupid.

A heavy wave pounded the stones below as if to punctuate the thought. Retyar looked down, eyeing the hard granite and clenching his fists tight at his sides. The brisk sea wind pressed at him, a safeguard against his falling, yet the surf seemed to draw him in, seemed to wrestle to possess him. It promised an end to him, a guarantee against further contamination.

Stupid.

Retyar drew himself away from the edge and stalked to the mouth of his cave. He snatched up his rifle from where it lay propped up against the stone and pulled off the cloth wrapping. It would need to go.

The crashing waves drummed out a constant beat as he stripped the weapon down to its basic parts and threw them all onto the cloth. When he was done, he stared at these pieces strewn haphazardly at his feet. Separate, they were still dangerous, but not so much as the whole. He picked up the barrel and rushed to the cliff's edge, his arm drawn back.

But as his foot braced against the stone, his arm refused to swing. The barrel remained in his hand, its weight promising excellent distance if he could just throw, yet he couldn't summon the will.

"It needs to go," he whispered to himself, the words drowned out by the pounding water.

"It needs to go!" he shouted.

His arm still refused to move.

You're a coward, Retyar Venon.

He backed away from the edge and dropped the barrel atop the rest of the pieces. He pressed his back against the stone wall and slid down. In his mind, he pictured his father and mother, his brothers Dev and Kar. He thought of the people he'd grown up with, the friends he'd made at the University. For certain, he'd failed them.

Abruptly, he stood up and went to the satchel lying nearby. He rummaged violently through its sparse contents until finding Kahverengi's book on time travel. If only his theories hadn't existed! At least then Retyar could blunder his way through history oblivious of the damage he caused to a world he'd never again see. He screamed and threw the book over the cliff.

"It's not fair!" he snarled. "History is here, all around me! I should be able to watch it, explore it, experience it! Why do I have to be afraid that every step I take is wrong?" He slapped his hand against the stones. "It's not fair," he whispered.

But there's nothing you can do about it.

He grit his teeth and went to the little rockslide that let him climb down the chasm. He followed the stream at the bottom out to the sea. Careful of the shells clinging to the rocks, he searched the water until he found Kahverengi's book bobbing in a little eddy. He snatched up the soggy bundle of paper and made his way back up to the cave.

Chapter 10

"But first, to understand these dangers,
we must establish an appreciation for
the exponential effects every action
invariably has on the world."

Hundreds of confused shadows splayed against the tower's inner walls as Maltan set the flame to one of his mirrored oil lamps. The space was a veritable maze of pulleys and glass even during the day, but in the night, with only a single light at the room's center, it would be a challenge for anyone to make out even the exit from the stairs. Maltan loved the play of light and shadow, but managed to tear away his eyes and focus on the book sitting open before him. He'd been trying to acquire it for months, discovering only a few moments ago that he already had a copy shoved in the back of his library. Funny how often things turned out like that—what you searched for the hardest tended to be right beside you the whole time. The text was several hundred years old, written by an inventor of some small renown from the continent of Evena. The entry Maltan pored over detailed experiments on how variously shaped objects affected wind flow. The knowledge had been put to good use in designing extremely efficient windmills.

Maltan finished the entry and nodded to himself in satisfaction. He took the lamp and twisted his way through the maze of ropes to the stairs and climbed to the tower's second floor. Here he had the hooked end of a rope hanging from a pulley. Below it was a hole that allowed the rope to descend all the way to the ground floor. Maltan selected a lead weight from a shelf nearby and set it on the rope's end, then climbed back down.

On the first floor he had a circular fan, somewhat like a windmill, but with reverse intention. It was attached to the weighted rope, which would spin the fan once he flipped the release. Maltan wrestled his way through a mass of ropes to reach a box heaped with scrapped wood pieces left over from other projects. He selected a small segment of softwood, thin cut with a curved top and flat bottom, and took it back to the fan, where he placed it gently on a stand.

He plopped the lamp down well out of the fan's way and cracked his knuckles. "Let's see if this works, then!" With a pull of the release, the fan turned into a whizzing blur, and created wind strong enough to blow the piece of wood off the stand and bound across the table. The spinning blades came to a halt in moments, but the current test was done, leaving Maltan rubbing his stained hands together. *Excellent so far. Now to build a holding mechanism with a vertical slider.* If the observations in the book were correct, a horizontal wind flow could be transferred into upwards lift using a correctly shaped fin. This should be fun.

A shout came from just outside the tower's entrance, disrupting his thoughts. Maltan took up his lamp just before the door swung open. Crenden Thrake Leverie stood outside for the barest moment, his face grotesquely lit by his own lantern, before storming into the room. His guards uttered a few faint pleas, but they were all but ignored as the crenden stumbled through Maltan's contraptions. Maltan remained silent at his approach, a single question going through his mind and a single answer responding. Thrake finally reached the table where Maltan had been conducting his test and slammed his lantern down against the smooth wood. The smell of wine carried strongly to Maltan's nose, not a good sign as the crenden's blue eyes bore into him with barely contained fire. Maltan looked sadly about at his tower. *So, this is to be the night I am finally thrown out of here.*

Thrake remained silent for a long while, either busy

contemplating how to start his tirade, or else somehow content merely with glaring at the old tinkerer. As the heartbeats dragged on, Maltan began wondering whether or not the crenden had really come to denounce him or if something else was at issue. At long last, Thrake grabbed a nearby stool and unceremoniously crashed his rear into its seat. "There's news from Woodwise," he said, his voice only slightly slurred. "It's official. Hashan's marrying his daughter off to the Redleaf."

Maltan blinked, surprised as much by the news as by Thrake's decision to confide in him. He grabbed a stool himself. "Pardon my asking, but why are you speaking about this with me?"

Thrake slammed his fist into the table. "Because you're going to hear about this sooner or later, and I'd rather not be surprised down the road when you find some way to rub it in my face in front of all my advisers!"

Maltan straightened his thinning sleeves as he thought. "I admit, I would not have expected this of Crenden Hashan, but what is it about the marriage that is a problem, exactly?"

"What's the problem?!" Thrake roared. "Smoke and ashes! That snake Redleaf is trying to weasel his way into House Leverie! He's trying to undermine our House from the inside."

"And how do you come to that conclusion?" Maltan asked.

"What else do you expect from him? The Redleafs have always opposed the Leverie ruling structure. They don't want to take part in the textile trade—the backbone of the nation— and thus drag down the rest of the country with them. Why do you think the Aristocracy of Whitesail outdoes us? It is because we still cannot harness our full potential. The Redleafs are too stubborn to let us unite under a single vision!"

Maltan folded his arms. "Why outdo Whitesail? Leverie already prospers."

"For now," Thrake said. "Perhaps we do not need to overtake them, but we do need to rival them. We need to distinguish ourselves from all the other Aristocracies around us. Why should buyers come to us if we are not as good as

Whitesail or Ranisa, not even distinguishable from the rest of the mediocre producers here in the north? We are ahead of the pack now, but other nations are specializing. They are focusing on making better and better cloth. If we stagnate, we will be overtaken."

"It seems to me that Redleaf's actions would help us survive such an eventuality," Maltan said. "From what I hear, he wants to make the nation self-sufficient."

Thrake glared at him. "He prepares for our fall. I seek for us to excel! So long as we can sell our wares, we can buy as much food from abroad as we need, for the same price it would cost us to grow ourselves. A plot of cotton returns more than double the value of a plot of vegetables or grain, and so we gain money even when buying food from elsewhere. Every field growing kale or celery is a field wasted."

"Have you tried discussing this with Arzan?" Maltan asked.

"I discussed it with his father, not long before he died in that capsizing. Could hardly stand the man. Arzan was there. He knows what I said. The lad is so hardheaded it defies belief. Even sitting at the same table at the Highcity Council makes my blood boil!"

Maltan opened his mouth to say something, but Thrake continued unabated, "And now for him to try marrying into the House! The girl's got foreign blood from her grandmother, so she's not a full Leverie, not truly. Not even truly Moshon. The others, though—most don't care she's mixed. Woodwise is trouble, just as Senkani. There should have been more of an uproar in my father's time, when that fool Clarnd deigned to corrupt the Leverie line with that Originate woman. There should have been more to stand by me when I spoke out against Hashan marrying their daughter. Now look! Hashan's branch should be cut from the House!"

Maltan folded his arms and shook his head. "Do you think perhaps it might not be the Redleafs who are hardheaded?"

Thrake jumped from his chair and loomed over the old tinkerer. "Do not play me the fool, Maltan. I shall not be mocked."

"I do not mock you, crenden," Maltan said calmly. "I

make an observation."

Thrake tightened his jaw and raised his hand to strike, but managed to keep from following through. "If Father and Mother had not expressly forbidden me . . . ." He turned around abruptly and stormed towards the door. Unfortunately for him, any dignity in his retreat was foiled as he tripped over the innumerable ropes strung about. When he finally found the exit, he sharply ripped a pulley out of place and threw it to the floor. "Worthless plaguing contraptions!" He slammed the door with what seemed enough force to shake the tower itself.

Maltan let out a long sigh after the echoes died down. "This cannot be good for my heart."

A tentative knock came at the door and Maltan looked up just in time for it to open ahead of a deliveryman carrying a large pack. "Ah, Honorable Maltan. I've come with your order."

Maltan remembered he had some special wood planks he was waiting for. "Oh, those. You can just set them down where you are. You're a whole day late, you know. I find you're making a habit of it."

The deliveryman bowed his head as he slipped off his pack. "My master sends his apologies. Lost two horses and a cart to a landslide, so we're feelin' the strain 'til we can get another team fitted."

Maltan rubbed his chin. "I suppose I can't blame you. I hope your master gets things back in order shortly."

The man nodded. "Makes two of us."

"Did you walk all the way here, then?" Maltan asked.

"Nothin' else for it."

Maltan had the man wait as he went up to retrieve his coin pouch. Once he returned, the new planks were all piled neatly by the wall. Maltan handed the deliveryman a few coins above the required fee. "To compensate you for your extra trouble. Just make sure you are timely when things return to normal."

The deliveryman accepted the coins gratefully. "Will at that!" He bowed his head and turned to leave, but hesitated at the threshold. "If I might ask, who d'ya say are the best cobblers in the province?"

"The best?" Maltan pointed down to his own plain, well-worn sandals. "I do not make use of their skills, as you can see, but I hear that the masters in Creedport are Urvan and Ronsh."

"What of other cities?"

"Well, I recall someone speaking highly of one Valhar in Woodwise," Maltan said. "Really, though, you should ask someone with greater familiarity with footwear."

The deliveryman grimaced. "Done that already, I have! These past few months I've already visited every master cobbler I could find in all the cities I've made runs to. None of them've turned out to be who I'm looking for. I thought maybe you'd have a different idea of skill and give me new names, but s'pose not."

"What is it you are looking for?" Maltan asked, genuinely curious.

The deliveryman leaned against the stone wall. "Well, you see, on one of my prior errands bringin' you supplies, I happened across this hermit fellow who said he lives along the coast. He had some real well-crafted boots the likes of which'd make a House folk green with envy, and I've been lookin' everywhere tryin' to find the craftsman who made 'em."

Maltan rubbed his chin. "Do you think he might have made the boots himself? Some hermits use their time alone to develop themselves into masters of one art or another. I'm a little bit of that, I suppose."

"'Tis possible," the deliveryman said, "but I hope that ain't the case. My life bein' the way it is, I doubt I'd ever be able to find the time to scour the coast for him."

"They must have been very good boots for you to be so intent on finding their crafter," Maltan said.

The deliveryman slapped his hand against his thigh. "That they were! I know you aren't a cobbler, but I'm sure one such as yourself would've recognized the skill in 'em."

"If you find the man, let me know his name, then."

"That I will. Good night." The deliveryman walked out into the city.

Maltan sat and passed his fingers through his beard for a few moments. Finally, he turned back to the table with the fan and went about contemplating the next step in his experiments. Before long, he was humming a happy tune and had completely forgotten about the evening's distractions.

Chapter 11

"Imagine, for a moment, that we have a pebble.
A pebble with no inherently special traits."

Nevygar, general of the Vron western campaign, rode his horse down the soot-covered road and glowered at the thin trails of smoke rising towards the noontime sun. *Idiots*, he thought, shaking his head at the wasted ashen fields to either side of him. *Bleeding idiots.*

Ash floated around him as his escort kicked it up with their march. Not far from the road, soldiers in silver surcoats lifted a wounded comrade onto a stretcher. The injured man was first to see Nevygar's passing and saluted sharply with no sign of the pain he had to be feeling from the arrowhead lodged in his leg. The general nodded to him. "The empire is proud of your service, private."

The battle hadn't been that hard. Fewer than twenty had fallen in the approach, despite the enemy creating a prime killing field leading up to the city walls. Part of it was how pathetically short those walls were at only twenty feet, giving the archers sub-optimal range advantage. The better part of it was the Vron legion's expert use of proper shield formations. The Vron ladders still stood against the walls, the Alamask banners hanging from the towers rustling mournfully in defeat.

Nevygar's horse carried him through the broken city gates. Inside, the real carnage presented itself. Silver uniformed soldiers dragged dead men to the sides of the main avenue, blood trickling between cobblestones. Other legionaries stood guard in front of buildings, ready to deal with anyone stepping out of their homes. The army's Aiv Chahai marched on patrol, ensuring adherence to the codes.

The street ran straight to the palace in the city center. At five stories, it was the tallest structure to be seen, and it stood out even further with the intricately painted geometric patterns adorning its doors and window frames. Imperial soldiers held the entrance for him as he dismounted and climbed the short steps. Removing his helmet, he halted briefly in the foyer—just long enough for his eyes to adjust to the point that he could make out the walls. He noticed framed artworks pinned up around the room, but there was no reason to dally long enough to see details. Ahead was a grand staircase ascending all the way to the top floor. He climbed, stepping on runners wet in spots with blood. The stairs brought him to the top level and beyond, depositing him on the roof, where a circular table sat beneath a canopy of trellises grown over with vines and white flowers. Out along the balconies, the city spread open before him, as did the ruined fields beyond.

Marred beauty, Nevygar thought to himself. He traced his finger down the length of the scar running vertically in front of his ear. His eyes turned to the table, and the six men and women fidgeting in their seats around it—the crendens and crendesses of Alamask. Their faces were all ashen white. As they should be.

A gentle breeze played with Nevygar's silver cape and brushed the feathers decorating the helmet held under his arm. "Rulers of the Aristocracy of Alamask," he said, "the Vron Empire has conquered your country. We are not here to destroy, however. We do not wish to pillage or sack. Our empire does not tear down, but rather builds up. We strive to bring greatness to the whole continent of Moshon."

"The people of Alamask will not bow to you tyrants," one of the crendens said.

Nevygar walked up to the table and set his feathered

helmet down beside one of the five empty seats belonging to the crendens he had already captured in battle. "Bow? They need only obey, and their reward will be greater than anything Alamask would ever have provided on its own. And the empire's decrees have the opportunity to reach the people through your own mouths." He paused long enough for the implication to sink in. "Like I said, I am here to uplift, not destroy. The empire respects wise rule, and has no problem with competent crendens and crendesses continuing as vassals."

The sense of hopelessness around the table melted away. Blue and steel gray eyes locked onto him and the vision of opportunity.

"To that end, I pose to you a question. Explain to me whose decision it was to raze the fields and why it was done."

One of the men sprang to his feet. Though balding and rounded at every edge, he was spry with eagerness. "That was my idea, your grace. Alamask hasn't fought a war in nearly a hundred years, but I read the histories. I know that in siege, you need to burn anything the enemy can use to their advantage. You can't leave food to sustain the attacking army while they starve you out."

Three of the others rose and slammed their palms on the table. "Don't take all the credit, you weasel. It was a vote of four on two."

Nevygar pointed to those standing and snapped his fingers. Soldiers moved in and dragged them to one of the balconies, where they forced them to their knees.

"What—what's going on?"

Steel whispered on leather as Nevygar slipped his blade free and stalked towards the four. "A wise leader would have understood the Vron method of warfare. We do not waste time laying siege against such underwhelming opponents. Our goal is not to ruin the prize." His voice grew angrier with every sentence until he loomed over the now cowering city rulers. "What benefit did burning your fields bring to anyone? What do you expect your own people to eat?"

The captives struggled against the soldiers holding them down. "No, that's not—"

Nevygar hacked his sword through the neck of the man

pleading. The rest screamed as his head hit the floor and the soldiers let go of the body to let it follow. The general moved methodically from one to the next, executing them all without mercy. He tore a scarf from the body of the last one and used it to wipe the blood from his blade. Shoving his weapon back in its sheath, he turned to the crenden and crendess who remained at the table, their stares fixated on him in wide-eyed horror.

"Your provinces?" Nevygar demanded.

The man opened his mouth several times before anything came out. "Claissad."

"B-Bujr," the woman stuttered.

Nevygar scooped up his helmet. "You are the vassal rulers of the new imperial provinces of North and South Alamask. Prove yourselves good stewards of these lands." He turned and strode back to the stairway, his silver cape rippling behind him.

A messenger awaited him at the palace steps. "Dispatch from the Senate, general."

He received the letter with a nod and tore the seal on the spot. His eyes went over the words set into the paper.

> *"General Nevygar, Commander of the Vron Western Legions,*
>
> *Upon complete conquest of the Aristocracy of Alamask, you are ordered to take command of the eastern campaign. You may take any one legion of your choosing on your march.*
>
> > *For the glory of empire,*
> > *The Senate of the People of Vron"*

Nevygar folded the letter and tucked it away. He mounted his horse, his mind accessing the many maps of the continent he'd memorized. Last he'd heard, Elofe, Evasne, and Ashathan were ready to fall, but the empire was expecting strong resistance in the Aristocracy of Heartsong. The general smiled. Perhaps there he would find a challenge. If not, the aristocracies beyond would fall like a child's straw fort.

Trenlon, Roell, the Ogdon Partnership—the inland countries weren't known for their military prowess. Along the coast, Whitesail, Leverie, and Ranisa were even more ripe for the picking.

Time to gather his legion. The nobles in the east were about to see the glory of empire.

Chapter 12

*"In this experiment, take this pebble from
its natural, quiet home and place
it in the center of a busy square."*

"Crendess," Ellaniel said, the word feeling strange on her tongue. "Crendess Ellaniel. Ellaniel Redleaf. Crendess Redleaf."

The city stood out beyond the windows of her studio room in the Senkani palace, low roofs of wood, thatch, or occasional tile. Beyond the walls, brown fields angled up towards a forest clothed in red and yellow leaves. Ellaniel had to admit that there was charm to the place, but it wasn't quite enough to overshadow her melancholy as she slouched in her chair and leaned against the window sill. Three days had passed since her marriage to Crenden Arzan. The entire city turned out for the event, but was nothing like the grand Leverie weddings she'd witnessed back home. Festival banners had lined the streets, flapping in the breeze, and a feast set out in the square, yet the crowds had been lukewarm. Ellaniel wasn't the most socially adept person, but even she could sense that the city didn't trust her.

Fine. She could work through that with her new husband. Except that Arzan had abandoned her right at the ceremony's end. She learned only after the fact that he'd set out for Three

Corners on one of the stable's fastest horses. Not even any word on why. *So this is how much he actually values me.* During their courtship, he'd been charmingly romantic. Were these his true colors? Did he really only marry her for political expedience?

Ellaniel sighed and stood. Sitting around pouting wouldn't accomplish anything. She glanced at a half-done project she had lying on a nearby table, spools of thread ready and waiting. She wasn't in the mood. Perhaps try the library? Would there be anything there besides economic treatises and trade reports?

A knock came from the doorway.

"Come in."

A curly haired maid entered, pushing a wooden case that looked absolutely massive compared to her small frame. "The last of your affects just arrived from Woodwise, your grace."

Ellaniel had the woman settle the case in the corner. Most likely just some extra dresses she hardly ever used. She'd look through it later.

"Anything else you'd have of me?" the maid asked.

"Can I—" As soon as she was about to ask if she might go horse riding, she already decided no. The maid (what was her name again?) waited expectantly. "Perhaps I can take a tour through the city?" Might as well start getting to know her new home.

The short woman's face lit up. "Certainly! As you are or common clothing?"

The question caught Ellaniel off guard. "Common clothing?"

The maid's smile froze and her eyes widened. "The Leverie don't do that, I take it." She snapped into a bow. "Sorry, your grace. I didn't mean offense."

"No, I'm just confused. The Leverie and common . . . What?"

The maid looked back up, playing her fingers against each other. "Well, you see, Arzan and some others of the House often like to visit the city pretending to be common folk."

"Why in the six continents would they do that?" Ellaniel had difficulty even imagining the man with a penchant for red capes wandering around in rough clothes.

"For one, some Redleafs don't like the attention that comes with being aristocratic. Your husband, he says he likes being able to see what his people really think about things, what they say when only in the presence of their own class."

"That . . . " The concept was new to her. Trying to blend in with commoners? She could think of more than one of her relatives whose hearts would stop at the mere suggestion of such a thing. Odavan would probably choke right to death.

That image alone made the prospect alluring.

"Let me try."

The maid's face glowed and she skipped into the hallway. "I'll bring you a cloak."

Kalla. Ellaniel finally remembered her name. It was so annoying how popular the double L was in her generation. Why couldn't there be more variety to make things easier?

The small woman returned with a dark green outfit that was enough to conceal Ellaniel's dress all the way down to the bottom fringe. The maid helped her slip it on and they were off to the back entrance of the palace. Ellaniel's heart beat with excitement. The prospect of a forbidden adventure already had her feeling like a girl.

"Earlier, you spoke of Arzan by name," Ellaniel said.

"Hmm? Oh. I'm a Redleaf, after all, so I don't strictly need to go calling him my liege and all that. I'm Arzan's grandfather's sister's son's daughter."

Ellaniel stopped dead on the palace threshold. "You're of the House? But you're a maid!"

Kalla shrugged. "My parents and brothers already have the vineyard well managed. I didn't want to do field work, so serving in the palace seemed a good idea."

"But you're an aristocrat!"

The woman gave her a quizzical look before stepping outside. "So?"

The response left Ellaniel flabbergasted. What in the six . . . . What kind of House had she married into? *They're not going to expect something like that of me, are they?* No, ridiculous. She was crendess.

A plain-dressed man waited for them by the gate, a longsword hanging at his waist. The way he carried it showed him to be more than a simple servant.

"I am Ckol Magar, your grace," the man said. "Would you be more comfortable that I escort you at your side or at some distance?"

Ellaniel eyed the sword. "Won't that make you stand out?"

Magar tapped the scabbard. "It's not so unusual carrying arms in Senkani, your grace. The people take pride in their role as the border province."

Kalla stretched up to pull Ellaniel's hood into place. "Keep a little ways back anyway, Magar," she said. "Everyone knows you're a ckol." She opened the iron foot gate, and beckoned them both out, smiling all the while.

The little Redleaf maid led them down the cobblestone streets all the way to the market area. With the sun approaching noon, the city bustled with people doing business. Men and women carried bags or packages or baskets through the street. Storefronts displayed their fresh produce, fabrics, or ceramics. Craftsmen plied their trades by the doors of their shops—carpenters shaving down lengths of wood, basket makers weaving reeds, seamstresses patching clothing. Ellaniel stepped past the entrance of a blacksmith's workshop and got a blast of hot air from within, her nostrils filling with the scent of smoke as hammers clinked away in the darkness.

"Everything's so close here," she said. "People have so much more space in Woodwise."

Right on point, Kalla led her through a throng of washerwomen so tightly packed Ellaniel's cloak almost caught as she squeezed through trying to keep up. When she stopped with Kalla at the next corner, she gave her guide a solid glare.

"We would not have to deal with this if we just took a carriage," Ellaniel said.

Kalla smiled. "But isn't this different? Don't tell me you're not having some fun."

The way the woman spoke so informally with her while wearing a servant's dress continued to throw Ellaniel off balance. "House Redleaf is so strange," she muttered. She was starting to feel all the things the Leverie said about them not being real aristocrats wasn't so far fetched. At the same time . . . .

It is *a little fun.*

They continued on along the street, Ellaniel feeling amused by the novel experience of walking amongst commoners as if their equal. Kalla kept close beside her, pointing out different shops and explaining in whispers the services they provided and the intricacies of their work. Some of it was such basic knowledge that she almost felt insulted at the lessons. Other details were entirely new to her. She kept her mouth shut, her father's words coming to mind. *Better to look stupid at first and reveal yourself later to be competent than to insist you know everything and actually be an arrogant fool.*

An hour after leaving the palace, they took a break on the central bridge. Below them, the river that ran through the city's middle sparkled and cast playful webs of reflected light dancing against the floodwalls. Ellaniel leaned against the stones and stared down. "A pity the water's so murky."

"Well, can't be helped," Kalla said. She pointed at the cultivated slopes outside the city. "Farmers cart water to the top of the hill and let it run through the fields. They do that all along the banks upriver too. That flushes a lot of mud and such."

"'And such'?" Ellaniel eased her weight off of the wall as she thought she caught a whiff of something less than pleasant.

Kalla shrugged. "Oh, are you hungry? There's a stall nearby that has the best beef wraps in the province." She hopped away as Ellaniel's mind was still trying to comprehend that last sentence. Did she say stall? As in *street food*?

"I hope Kalla's not too much," Ckol Magar said. The man had been a quiet tail through the whole excursion and now propped himself casually against the side of the bridge. "She can be a handful, but right now she's more just excited to be serving you."

"But why? She's a noble."

Magar looked around, and Ellaniel wondered what he was searching for until she remembered she was in disguise. Best keep better watch over her words.

"I'd thought the Redleafs despised being subservient to the Leverie," she said quietly.

"I mean no disrespect correcting you," Magar leaned closer while keeping his eyes on the flow of traffic, "but you are Redleaf, your grace."

Kalla returned with something bundled in her hands. *And everyone's really trying to make me regret it.*

"You'll love these," Kalla said, holding out some sort of flatbread roll. "They fill it with beef, lentils, and rice, and it's absolutely delicious."

"I was willing to go on a little excursion outside, but this is crossing the line," Ellaniel said. "I am not eating something from a street stand."

Kalla's face scrunched up, but not with any sign of proper chastisement. "Well, if you really don't want to I'll get something from the palace kitchen, but these are really good. Arzan and all my other cousins eat here all the time."

"All the Redleafs eat this . . . this *finger food?*"

Kalla smiled and kept it held out for her. "Try it?"

Ellaniel stared down at the bread wrap and sighed. "If this is all some elaborate prank, someone's going to spend tonight tied to a pole hanging over a cove of shyles."

"You hear that, Kalla?" Magar said as the maid handed him his share. "You better drop the act and admit you're a Falconian silver eye come to steal her grace's bed sheets."

Kalla snorted and slapped the ckol's shoulder. "Shh!"

Magar tried to hide a smile by taking a bite of his wrap.

Ellaniel cringed at his terrible etiquette. She drew in a breath and willed away imaginings of her tutors screeching in horror (the ones she liked, anyway). She had come this far.

Her eyes widened in surprise when she took her first bite. "This is good!"

Kalla giggled. "Isn't it? I daresay it's better than they serve the Highcity Council." She quickly covered her mouth. "Not to suggest I've been eating the Council's food, mind you."

Ellaniel cocked an eyebrow at her.

"Like I said, Kalla can be a handful," Magar muttered straight-faced.

"Crenden Roth wasn't even there to eat it!"

"Not until five minutes after you licked the last sauce off the plate."

Kalla's light skin went beet red as she buried some more food into her mouth.

Ellaniel was about to make some comment, but the next bite made her forget all about it. She finished the rest of her meal in bliss, no more care for the impropriety of eating beside a maid and a ckol as the two joked back and forth. This wasn't as bad as she'd been starting to fear.

"So, what is it that Leverie women usually do all day?" Kalla asked.

"Depends on who you're talking about," Ellaniel said, taking a handkerchief from her pocket to wipe some oil from her fingers. "I spent most of my time working on fabric. Some of my cousins in Woodwise manage the estates. A few of them . . . I don't actually know much about what they do."

"Well, what did they say they did?"

"I . . . didn't speak with them all that much." Ellaniel spotted a crowd gathering at one end of the bridge. "What's that?"

Kalla peered over. "The theater. A play must be starting."

"You mean they're going to tell a story?" Ellaniel asked. She had heard talk of plays before, but no one performed in Woodwise. She brushed her fingers off over the water. "I want to see."

Kalla nodded excitedly. "Then we need to hurry before they run out of seats."

The trio joined the line flowing through the wooden gate. Kalla paid the two coppers for each of their tickets and they proceeded into an open air theater square with a raised stage and enough benches to seat about two hundred people. They took a place along the inner aisle. Ellanial sat with Kalla on her left, separating her from an elderly woman and young boy, and Magar on her right. She worried again about his sword, but true to the ckol's assurances, several other men in the audience wore their own weapons and he didn't stick out in the least.

A man with a small drum walked across the stage and tapped a few beats, hushing the crowd. "Men and women, old and young! From the roots of the world to the heart of

Moshon! History or fiction, insight or fun, all tales, all wonders, all intrigues and songs!" He bowed and splayed his hands to the side. "Today, we present to you a story you've heard time and again, but only in words passed between fellow men. It concerns one of our province and his grandest of deeds. Hero to many, villain to a few, his memory deserves to be told, and this we will do." The man retreated from the stage.

The introduction done, the audience waited in quiet anticipation. A few bird cries fell from seagulls gliding up above, but the walls around the theater square did well to block out the noises of the city.

"This is the last time, you ungrateful dog!" the shout came from behind the stage, right before a well-dressed man dragged a whimpering fieldworker up onto the wood platform. "Did you think that my mercy had no limits? That I would tolerate your dishonesty without end?"

A small noise escaped from Kalla, not unlike a strangled chipmunk, and Ellaniel glanced to the side to see the maid's brow come together in a frown. "What is it?" she whispered.

"Perhaps this isn't the best play for us to be attending," Kalla replied hesitantly.

"Master, please," the fieldworker cried. "I meant no disloyalty. I'll repay it all."

"What, does this have rude jokes or something?" Ellaniel asked. "Don't worry about me."

"What is this, might I ask?" Another man in field clothing appeared on the side of the stage, looking like someone just passing by.

Kalla fidgeted. "Th—"

She was drowned out by the field master, "I am disciplining my worker. He shall be lucky if he only loses his job—"

"Please no!" the worker interjected.

"—But who are you? This is none of your business!"

"I am Gricall," the newcomer said. "I own some land near to here."

Gricall. Ellaniel thought she had heard that name somewhere before. Kalla was now balling her skirt in her fists and biting her lip.

"We can leave now, if you wish," Magar whispered.

"Is there something I should know about this play?" Ellaniel asked, irritated that she was starting to miss lines.

Magar glanced around. "Well, if you're not familiar with him, I suppose this is a fair enough way to learn."

Ellaniel frowned at them, but the two shared a glance and didn't volunteer any more information, so she turned back to keep watching.

"This is the fourth time I've caught the man stealing from my field," the master said, pointing an accusing finger at the worker.

"How much was stolen?" Gricall asked.

"Only three strawberries," the fieldworker said. He was on his knees and holding his palms out for mercy. "Please, it was only three. The master can take it from my wages, but I didn't have the strength to continue. I've had nothing to eat since yesterday."

"The thief only offers to repay me after I catch him in the act!" the master said, raising his hand to strike.

"Hold!" Gricall said, arms crossed. "You've no right to strike a free man. This isn't Originate or Fractora that you can treat a fellow like property."

"It's only justice for stealing from me!"

"The laws of the province do not call this justice."

"The crenden's palace is far from here, Gricall," the master said with a scowl. "The laws of the House are nothing to me."

"So it matters little if I send word to Crenden Redleaf?" Gricall asked.

The master glared at Gricall for a moment, and then slammed his heel into the stage and held his tongue. Gricall turned to the fieldworker. "Now, why haven't you had a proper meal today?"

"I . . . I haven't much coin, friend Gricall," the worker said. "I have a family to support, and my wages are all for them."

Gricall nodded. "How much do you sell your strawberries for?" he asked of the master.

"Two coppers for a pound," the master said with a grimace. "He owes me three coppers all told by now, I recon."

"Three coppers?" Gricall walked to the edge of the stage and looked out, as if surveying a large field. "Field master, do you ever go out and shift the soil?"

The master snorted. "That's what I pay him and his lot for."

Gricall rubbed his chin. "Then I suppose you do not sow the seeds either. Nor pull the weeds. I would venture to guess you do not haul the water, nor fertilize the fields."

The field master adjusted his collar and started looking decidedly uncomfortable. "No, but I own the land and its produce."

"You hold the deed," Gricall said, "but you rely on others to make the land productive. Without this man, your field would grow naught but weeds, and yet you refuse him a handful of strawberries when he is too weak to do your job!"

The field master thrust his finger once more at the worker. "I pay him for his service! He gets fair compensation."

Gricall stepped up closer. "Well then, you try working in his place with an empty stomach, earning his wages. When you have done a day of that, let us see if you think it fair."

The audience clapped and cheered. The field master looked around, shocked, as if just noticing a hostile crowd.

"Now, if you see the error of your ways," Gricall said, "I suggest you treat your work hands a little better. If not, you can be sure I will have the crenden's men here to weigh in on the right of it."

"This . . . This . . . " the field master stamped his foot and then lowered his head and fled the stage.

Ellaniel pursed her lips. This was how commoners viewed field masters? She was a noble, not a common landholder, but this portrayal still disturbed her. *And Arzan lets this get shown?* Maybe he didn't know about it. But Kalla did. That would mean . . . . She looked at the actor playing the part of the fieldworker. *Does this kind of thing really happen?*

The play continued for at least a good hour. Gricall got involved in other worker disputes, each one involving a more powerful landholder than the last. Every time, he defended the downtrodden against a callous master, and each time he won. At one point, an actor appeared wearing a flowing red cape after Gricall had put yet another tyrant in his place. Ellaniel shifted forward in her seat, interested in seeing how they portrayed Arzan. He gave a nod of encouragement, and left the stage without a word. *Disappointing.*

It was then that she noticed an older woman seated diagonally two rows up. She had her head canted, and turned quickly when Ellaniel focused on her. Perturbed, Ellaniel pulled her hood closer to her eyes.

She did her best to return her attention to the play, but there was something more in the air. She became aware of angry whispers and mumbling undercutting the performance. Here and there she even saw a few people crying. She turned her eyes to the stage, but nothing all too serious was happening.

She touched Kalla's sleeve. "What's with everyone?" she asked quietly.

"Mm, well . . . ."

Ckol Magar put his hand over Ellaniel's wrist. "I think perhaps we should take our leave."

Just then, a man at the other end of the audience shot to his feet. "To ashes with the Leverie!"

Ellaniel's mouth gaped, the outburst taking her aback.

"Flog any of the wretches who sets foot in Senkani!" someone else shouted.

Magar pulled Ellaniel firmly to her feet. "Time to go." She saw he had his free hand on the pommel of his sword.

Her hood ripped away from her head. What—

The old woman from before had circled around to the row behind her and now jabbed a finger an inch from her nose. "It's her! It's the Leverie that seduced our crenden!"

The theater went dead quiet as all heads turned. A sea of blue and violet eyes stared at her, first in frowns of befuddlement, then in rage.

"Get her! Get the Leverie hag!"

Magar pulled her into the aisle and drew his sword, the steel giving a flat hiss as it dragged on the leather of his scabbard. "By authority of the crenden, I command you to—"

A ripe fruit splattered Ellaniel in the face. The next she knew, Magar was trying to haul her through a clawing mob. It was no use. The crowd pulled them apart.

Ellaniel didn't know the first thing about how to defend herself. She didn't even see the strike that caught her in the side of the head, dazing her. Her feet dragged uselessly as the shouting mob took her out of the theater grounds. Even the terror flowing through her wasn't enough to urge her sluggish limbs to fight. *Six continents, what's going on? Why are they angry?*

She heard the voices of rage form into a chant as the mob carried her over the bridge. "Drown the Leverie! Drown the Leverie!"

Ellaniel regained enough strength to grab at one of her assailants and try to twist loose. It accomplished nothing. One of the men she struggled with was built like a bull. It felt like he had enough power to snap her bones as he gripped down on her other arm. She struggled anyway, screaming at the top as her lungs as she put all her might into breaking free.

"Drown the Leverie!"

The mob pushed her against the bridge wall. She looked down at the murky brown water, her hands latching tight to her attackers now instead of trying to push them away. "Help!"

"Drown the—"

A roar of incoherent rage boomed above the voices of the masses. The mob's single-minded energy sputtered into confusion. Someone cried out in pain. A fight broke out, men punching and wrestling as they forced a path to her. In the center of that path was Arzan Redleaf, his cape rippling behind him as he advanced with sword drawn, his face masked in fury. "Unhand your crendess!"

Most of the mob broke and scattered, leaving only a half dozen crowded around Ellaniel. The large man pulled her away from the side of the bridge and threw her to the paving stones. She scrambled away on hands and knees to the protective reach of Ckol Vighkon, who placed himself between her and what little was left of the mob.

"Senkani will not stand for this, my crenden," the large man said. "There can be no alliances with the Leverie snakes."

Arzan stalked right up to him. Ellaniel put her arm out, wanting to call him back, but her cry of fear died in her throat. Even half a foot shorter and a third thinner, Arzan's sheer presence felt overwhelming against his adversary as he stared the man in the eye. "Are you a man of Senkani?"

Her assailant puffed his chest. "In life and death I shall always be of Senkani!"

"By birth or by action and spirit?"

"Everything I do is for our people, Redleaf." He thrust his finger at Ellaniel. "I will not let the House of Leverie undermine us!"

"So you acknowledge that birth alone is insufficient in defining your identity?"

"What does this have to do with your betrayal of our city?" the man demanded.

Arzan shoved him in the chest, pushing him back. "Everything! The woman you have attacked was born to their House, but her family has shunned her. Now she seeks to become one of us not through blood but through action, and you attack her?"

"My lie—"

Arzan raised his sword, point forward. "What is the punishment for attempted murder?"

The man planted his feet. "I am not—"

In one heavy motion, Arzan drew back his weapon and swung it around to hack it through the man's neck. Ellaniel heard the disturbing sound of the blade passing through flesh, saw his head and body fall separately to the ground. She turned and vomited out over the water.

The ckols and city guard rounded up the rest of the mob who hadn't fled, but now likely realized they should have. Arzan came up beside Ellaniel. He placed his sword atop the low wall and put his arm around her. "I am very, very sorry."

The stress and shock of everything had her weak in the knees and she leaned against the stones with shaking arms. "Better late than never, I suppose." She had tried restraining her anger, but the venom still came through in her voice, so she added, "Why the blazes would you leave me before our wedding night?"

"I'm sorry. I should have explained things."

"You're saying there's something that could possibly be more important than our wedding? Than leaving me on my own in this . . . this wretched city of yours?"

Arzan held her tight. She turned and saw him looking at the buildings around them. At his home. He focused on her, and she saw trouble in his eyes. "There's word that the Feathered General has been assigned to the eastern campaign. I decided I couldn't put off speaking with Pundur about the possibility of an imperial invasion."

A near hysterical laugh escaped her lips. "What?"

He was serious. She looked at the decapitated body. Her wedding woes suddenly felt very small. She'd heard of the Vron silver legions, how they crushed whole countries, put the nobility to the sword.

Two figures limped together through the perimeter of guards. Ellaniel let out a sigh of relief to see that Kalla and Magar had survived, albeit with scrapes and bruises. Magar looked to have had the worse of it, and Kalla lent him her support until they both reached Arzan and Ellaniel and each dropped to their knees.

"I failed, my liege," Magar said. "I was unable to protect her grace. If you demand it, I shall relinquish my title of ckol this instant."

"It's my fault!" Kalla said. "I should have been more insistent that we leave the play earlier."

Arzan pointed to the body. "Or you shouldn't have taken her out in the first place, knowing people like them have been stirring up trouble!"

"But, I—" Kalla cut herself off. "Yes, you're right. I . . . I will go back to the family holding, if you wish."

Ellaniel balled her fists and stood beside the two. It hadn't been long, but the pair had already grown on her. Besides, they had tried. "The fault rests most with me. In the end, it was my decision to go into the city and to attend this play."

Arzan fiddled with the clasp of his cape. He sighed. "No one's going anywhere. If we want to throw around blame, I'm the one who abandoned my wife in the first place. Let us all learn from this, myself especially," he glanced at the dead man, "and not let it happen again."

Ellaniel balled her fists and sucked in her lips. *To that end* . . . "I want to learn how to use a sword."

Everyone looked to her in surprise.

"My mother was a swordswoman," she said. "I want to have the means to defend myself."

Captain Vighkon laughed before quickly snuffing himself out. "Wants to be a Redleaf indeed."

Arzan regarded her. He produced a handkerchief before picking up his sword and wiping the blood still coating the blade. "All right. Only fair."

Chapter 13

*"Most would not give this pebble a second
thought. Who of us cares about such a
trivial thing in our busy lives?"*

The Council chamber sat in uneasy silence as Arzan finished his request. The nine other crendens cast their attention furtively around the room, or else stared intently at their documents and notes. The elderly Ylnavar rubbed his wood block softly against the marble table, the polished surfaces squeaking quietly together.

"This is too much power to put in the hands of House Redleaf," Thrake said.

Arzan ground his teeth. *Of course* he'd *object.* "I didn't say Senkani would be the only province training men for the shield wall. We should all start putting an effort into readying ourselves for the Vron threat."

"There's nothing else for it," Pundur said. "The only chance we have of repulsing the imperial legions is if we have a properly trained and outfitted army."

"The two of you are assuming they'll even come as far as Leverie," Roth spoke up, his fingers absently smoothing a corner of his oiled hair. "I think the idea is positively silly. Do you realize how much land stands between us and the Silver Tide?"

Crenden Mansar straightened his papers, tapping them noisily against the table. "Do you have any idea how much this would cost? To outfit thousands of men, like you suggested, with not only weapons and shields, but also armor —it would bankrupt the House! Not to mention the hours of labor lost if we took people away from the fields for this training! It's preposterous!"

Arzan balled his fists. "We would go a year or two in the red, yes, but if that's what we need to do in order to survive, then so be it!"

"Easy for you to spout those words," Thrake said. "You don't even contribute to this country's productivity. You want us to worry about some theoretical possibility in the distant future when we're struggling in the markets here and now."

Arzan resisted an urge to let out an exasperated sigh. "We're discussing the possibility of your head rolling on the cobbles."

"There's also a possibility that the Federation might hand us twenty trunks filled with gold bars and a note thanking us for being such pleasant neighbors."

"I can't help but wonder," Roth cut in, "if this isn't actually a ruse to distract from that debacle of yours two weeks ago."

Arzan frowned. "Excuse me?"

"Yes, what about that little incident?" Thrake said, pouncing on the opportunity to attack. "Wasn't it not long ago that you were blaming my merchants for riling up your provincials? Now we see who it is that's truly out of control."

"That—"

"Nothing short of despicable how your people behaved," Roth said. "Attacking not only their own crendess, but a woman of House Leverie! And you want to teach them how to fight? I think it's sheer madness!"

"The people responsible for the attack have been dealt with," Arzan said. "I assure you, I've sent a very clear message that such actions will not be tolerated." He grit his teeth and remembered the men hanging from the gallows in the main square, their bodies swaying until long after their lives had already expired. Executions were a rare thing, but he didn't at all feel sorry at ordering the traps pulled. "They were part of an extreme minority. The average folk are loyal to the Aristocracy and accept Ellaniel as their new crendess."

Mansar twisted the jeweled rings adorning his fingers.

"Hashan, surely you have something to say about all this. It's your daughter who was nearly murdered."

Arzan tried not to fiddle with his cape clasp as Hashan closed his eyes and leaned forward, putting his chin against his knuckles. "I was highly distraught with what happened, but I believe that Arzan has dealt with the matter satisfactorily. As far as raising a trained army is concerned, I understand all of your reservations, but the Vron present a real danger. I do think it prudent to at least make some effort to prepare ourselves."

A little bit of Arzan's tension left him, but he still felt an acute guilt at having failed to shield Ellaniel from violence. He and Hashan had already discussed the incident, and despite professions of forgiveness, Arzan knew this would always be a mark against him.

"Whatever you all may think about my leadership leading up to and following the attack on my wife, the Vron legions are the matter at hand," Arzan said. "I am trying to ensure the security of the whole of our Aristocracy."

"And I'm not convinced that your proposal is the best means towards that end," Thrake said. "What Leverie needs is money, plain and simple. We need to focus on building our profits and strengthening our hold on the market. If, in fact, the Vron actually make it here, we should have the option of hiring mercenaries from Falcone or Fractora."

Mansar nodded. "Thrake's right. I'd wager it would cost a similar amount—and if the imperials never reach us, we never spend the money."

"And we don't turn our country into some hardened monstrosity yearning for blood," Thrake said with a scowl.

Pundur shook his head and pressed his palms together. "No, you'll just invite foreign hounds into our country whose only loyalty is to coin. Do the two of you really think that's preferable?"

"Overseas mercenary companies would certainly be more effective," Crenden Warth said. "Even if we trained an army, we haven't fought a war since the Tarkandan Split. All our techniques would come from dusty manuals and whatever bits the ckols have passed down."

"Do you imagine none of the western aristocracies hired

mercenaries?" Arzan asked. "How many of them managed to fend off the Silver Tide?"

"And again, a Leverie trained army would be even more pointless," Roth said.

"They were all nearer to the imperial homeland," Mansar pointed out. "The further east they spread, the more strained their supply lines and avenues of reinforcement. We have better chances of victory—especially if we use professionals possessing actual experience."

Arzan leaned back and set his hands on his armrests. "Let's say we hire mercenaries and win. What then? The empire will still be at our border. If we have an army of our own, we would be able to ally with Whitesail and Heartsong and send the fight to the Vron before they reach us."

Thrake lifted his arms in a show of strained patience. "Does your bloodlust know no bounds? You'd send our people into a war when it's not even our country at stake?"

"It's because it's our country at stake!"

Warth motioned for peace. "Arzan, even in that scenario, we still don't have to use our own men. Fractorans can be sent in aid for our neighbors."

Ylnavar shifted forward on his bony elbows. "Pundur, do you have anything to add here?"

The large Three Corners crenden crossed his arms. "I believe everyone has brought up valid points. I personally favor raising our own army, if only for the fact that it would be more loyal and more willing to sacrifice for the sake of Leverie. Fractoran or Falconian soldiers would possess experience, true, but their bravery would be limited by their level of greed. They won't have their families at their backs, their homes on the line. Ideally, I'd want the best of both worlds, but I know the cost makes that unfeasible."

"Does Pundur's statement change any minds?" Ylnavar asked.

None of the crendens spoke up.

"It will now be put to vote. Those in favor of training an army?"

Arzan pressed his lips together as only Pundur and Hashan raised their hands with him.

"The vote is three to seven. The Council shall take no

action."

Chapter 14

"But there are those it would influence. There are those it could make stumble. Carriages it could make bump. Children it could entertain."

Retyar watched through his binoculars as the sail ship glided gracefully through the water, its rigging spread full before a brisk wind. *Topmost flag is a dark green mulberry leaf against a teal background. Leverie ship. Heading northwest, likely bound for Volcana.* The thoughts passed through his mind without him really thinking. He kept his eyes on the vessel more out of habit than anything.

An electronic beep sounded, just barely audible against the crashing waves below Retyar's dangling feet. He let his binoculars fall and hang from his neck before climbing off the cliff edge. He checked the tablet's battery meter, confirming it was finished charging, then disconnected it from the solar panel and turned it on. The familiar startup animation played, proudly showcasing the manufacturer's logo. *Still the same. All still the same.* The words were a mantra, repeated every time he activated the tablet and accessed its contents. He repeated them again when he opened the encyclopedia and went through the articles in his routine, checking every sentence for some historical detail that might differ from his memory. He used a broad selection, including pieces about the fifty-fifth century, the year 4774 when he'd arrived, and numerous periods in between. *All still the same.*

His sweep out of the way, he tapped the search bar. What to read about today? He brushed his fingers through his beard. It was months since he'd cut it, and the whiskers were touching his chest again. Better take the knife to it today. Before that, he'd have to sharpen it.

"Later," he mumbled. He thought of a topic—a bit of history he'd meant to look into connected to some of his research last week. He tapped in the search words and brought up the relevant article. As with all things in an electronic encyclopedia, the material led him down a never-ending hole of connected stories and concepts. He let himself get drawn into it all, let himself forget about the reality he was trapped in. It was already several hours past noon when he looked up and realized he was hungry. He grabbed some strips of dried fish he had stowed away in the cave. *Supplies running low. Better catch some more.* But he'd need the knife sharp for that. He looked up at the bright sky. Still time.

He went back to reading for another hour or so until the sun really started threatening to set and keep him from getting anything done. Grudgingly, he set the tablet down. He took out his knife and whetstone. A close inspection of the blade revealed curling all along its edge. He went to work, forcing himself to focus on the methodical sound of scraping steel. His meditative trance held through the whole process, keeping his mind from wandering to places it shouldn't. Questions. Despair. He tested the blade on a leaf, shearing clean through without effort, and placed it back in its sheath.

The ravine had already long since darkened in shadow by the time he climbed down and planted his feet in the chill stream. He waited, watching fish dart around his legs. He'd long ago learned to suppress his worries about influencing the ecosystem. So long as he did what he could to minimize his impact, that was the extent of his control. He struck his hand out as soon as he saw a suitable target—an older-looking fish not bloated with eggs. He threw the creature clear of the water, landing it on the rocky bank a few feet away. It flopped there as he sent it a couple more companions for company. Once he had a sufficient catch, he dispatched them all with his knife and carried them to camp. The rest of the remaining daylight he spent on dressing his scaly harvest and hanging the strips just inside the cave's north porthole, where the constant breeze would start drying it through the night.

That done, Retyar gathered up the tablet and a sheet of thick canvas that he'd found washed up on the shore some months ago. He covered himself up, preventing any light from the tablet carrying from his cave, and went back to reading. It was near midnight when the corner icon warned him his battery charge was in the single digits. He powered off and set the tablet aside. Only as he was settled down to sleep did he remember he'd planned on trimming his beard. Whatever. He'd do it tomorrow. He had nothing but time.

Chapter 15

"Any one of these things may seem insignificant, but every action, every alteration in behavior will have a cascading effect."

Beads of sweat broke free from Ellaniel's nose and chin as she blocked another strike from Arzan's wooden training sword.

"Parry!" Arzan barked. "Deflect it, don't catch it!"

Her whole body throbbing, she angled her practice blade to knock his next attack to the side. She didn't have time to feel a sense of victory. He struck again, forcing her to twist her sword into a low guard. The weapons connected with a thunk, the shock traveling up her aching arms. She didn't even see the next swing—only the edge of his blade hovering next to her face as her chest heaved for air.

"I suppose that's it for today," Arzan said. He was barely sweating and didn't even look tired. Ellaniel scowled, or at least tried to. It was hard doing a proper scowl as she labored for every breath.

Kalla was at her side almost instantly with a water skin and towel. "You held out longer today," she said, holding the skin to Ellaniel's mouth.

Ellaniel drank greedily before shuffling through the carpet of forest leaves to an old tree stump and plopping down.

"Why," she asked between wheezes, "do men . . . have so much . . . blazing muscle and stamina?"

Arzan smiled as he took the towel from Kalla and gently wiped her face and neck. "It's good to know your limits and what happens when you grow tired. Your defense started getting sloppy, and you were absorbing the force of each blow instead of turning it aside, making you even more exhausted." He flopped the towel over his shoulder. "You are getting stronger, though. I feel your strikes hitting harder than when we first started your training."

She put the point of her practice sword into the ground, using the weapon as a support to keep herself sitting upright. If she didn't, she was sure to drop her face into Arzan's chest with how tired she was. It wasn't just the training bout. They'd spent a long ride on horseback out from the city, which left an entirely different set of muscles sore.

"You still haven't explained what we're doing here," she said, pointing her chin at the bare forest around them.

"When you're ready to stand, I'll show you," he told her.

She groaned, but she was starting to recover enough to move. "All right. How far?"

"Just a hundred paces up the road."

She closed her eyes and drew in a long breath before forcing herself to her feet. Arzan helped her back to the road a little ways away. Vighkon and Magar were standing guard, and handed the two of them their real weapons. Ellaniel secured her shortsword to her belt. After months of wearing it, she was getting comfortable enough with the weight that she felt wrong with it absent.

Their horses were tied nearby, but Ellaniel was too tired to climb in the saddle. Kalla and the ckols took charge of the reins and they all set out on foot.

"The place we're going is an older Redleaf estate," Arzan said. "I've asked your father and Pundur to meet me here."

"Ah. Is it about the empire?"

Arzan nodded grimly. "What we're going to talk about could get us in trouble with the Council. We couldn't afford to meet in the city."

The sweat soaking Ellaniel's clothing began to chill. She planned to change out of her riding outfit the instant they reached the property.

"You know," Arzan said, "when I first spoke to your father about your training, I expected him to be appalled. Instead, he seemed oddly resigned." He sighed. "I guess even he buys into House Redleaf's reputation as a bunch of muscle heads."

"I don't think that's the issue." Ellaniel wrapped her arm around his and focused him with her gold eyes. "I'm a quarter Originate. My mother and grandmother were both trained in the sword. He hated it, but Mother forced him to tolerate that little eccentricity."

Arzan looked thoughtful. "You mentioned that about your mother, didn't you? After something like what happened at the theater, most normal people would expect you to demand more guards, not learn the sword."

"Well, honestly . . . ." She brushed the pommel of her sword with her fingers. "A part of me wanted to do this to get an idea why she left us."

"What do you mean?"

The leather wrapping around the hilt fit into the contours of her palm as she closed her grip. "My grandmother came to Leverie after fleeing a rebellion against her father in Originate. I remember her always being so bitter, but my mother never seemed to care about having royal blood. When the reports came that the rebels were finally being ousted and the loyalists demanding a return of the former princess to put down the usurpers, everyone anticipated grandmother would set sail."

"But your mother went with her."

She nodded. "I've tried thinking it over again and again. She was born here. She loved Leverie. She loved us. The idea I keep coming back to is that maybe she felt the urge to use her skill with the sword, something Leverie would never give her the chance to."

"A desire to test herself," Arzan murmured. She felt him tense up. "You're not planning to follow in her footsteps all the way, are you?"

Ellaniel smiled at him. "I just want to understand. I want to see if I can temper my disappointment in her."

Arzan stroked the clasp of his cape. "Have you gotten

anywhere with that?"

"Not in the slightest," Ellaniel said, feeling every sore muscle from her training.

"Whatever her reasons, she left behind something more precious than she knew," he said.

"Ah, there's that silver tongue that made me marry you."

Arzan smirked and pointed ahead. "We're here."

A little further up the road, Ellaniel saw a small mansion nestled in the woods behind a brick wall. A pair of guards pulled open the iron gates at their approach, and a stable boy came to take charge of the horses. Ellaniel stared at the ivy clinging to the building's panels and the moss decorating the shingles and wondered who normally lived here. One of his relatives of House Redleaf, no doubt.

"This estate actually fell out of use some time ago," Arzan said, practically reading her mind as they removed their boots inside the entryway. "I decided to have it fixed up for the sake of Gricall's surviving family."

Ellaniel raised an eyebrow. *Gricall's* family? "You're letting commoners use . . . . Never mind. I shouldn't be surprised at that by now."

He turned towards the stairs with a wave and a smile.

She followed his gaze and saw a girl crouched on the steps behind the banister. Around five or six, she was a skinny and frail-looking thing, but with dark hair tinted a shimmery purple that would set half the woman in the country green with envy. The girl came down the steps and curtsied. Her violet eyes evaluated Ellaniel up and down appraisingly. "Are you the crendess?"

Ellaniel smiled and returned the greeting, even if a curtsy looked extra silly when done in a split-skirt riding dress. "Ellaniel Leverie Redleaf. And your name is?"

"Fellone," the girl said. "The other kids call me Fell."

"Do you have brothers or sisters?" Ellaniel asked. "Is your mother here?"

She felt Arzan's hand on her shoulder. "It's just her," he said quietly.

"Really?" She looked around at the spacious manor. All this, prepared for a single girl?

Fellone stepped close and peered up into her face.

"You've got yellow eyes."

Ellaniel kneeled down to come level with her. "I get them from my grandmother. She was a princess from Originate."

The girl's mouth became an O. "You're from the First Continent?" She leaned close and whispered, "Do they really eat people there? Do they kidnap folks off the street and make them slaves and force them to stack big blocks all day?"

"Fellone! Stop bothering the crendess and go play with Yalla and Ith!" A plump woman in head servant's clothing swept in with a bundle of firewood in her arms. "Your grace, I'm so sorry! You look absolutely exhausted. I'll have a hot bath drawn up for you immediately."

"Those two are so dull, Magratha," Fellone said, locking her arms at her sides. "They don't even know we call our bees asmsweets."

Ellaniel didn't know that either, or what it had to do with anything. She smiled charitably. "If you want, you can tell me about bees later this evening. Magratha's right—I do need a bath and a bit of a rest."

The girl's eyes lit up. "You'll really listen? Can we talk about Razmiah's Anthologies?"

"After my bath," Ellaniel said, impressed that the girl could so easily pronounce a word like 'anthologies'.

"I'll help bring the wood and buckets!" Fellone said as she ran off.

"Very sorry, your grace," Magratha said, bowing her head before scampering after her.

Ellaniel blinked as a realization hit her. "Did she say *Razmiah's* Anthologies?"

Arzan held out his hands. "From what I've heard, her favorite pastime is reading things that others tell her are out of her age group."

"Razmiah isn't just out of her age group. My oldest tutor told me he couldn't get through the opening chapter without his eyelids drooping!"

He laughed. "Be sure to tell him he's been outdone by a six-year-old."

Ellaniel shook her head and kissed her husband. "I'll see you later. Make sure Father doesn't leave before I can say hello."

The estate's head butler showed Hashan and Pundur into the parlor the moment they arrived, and to Arzan's pleasure they got straight to business.

"I know what you're planning," Hashan said, taking a chair and tapping his cane on the floorboards between his feet. "I'm telling you, it's risky."

"Not as risky as not preparing at all," Pundur said, crossing his arms and putting his back against the wall. "Leverie needs an army, no matter what the rest of the Council has decided."

Arzan leaned forward in his seat, mounting his chin on his fist. "We'll begin training soldiers in secret. Get far enough that by the time the Council discovers us, it will be too much to stop. By then, if the others are nervous about the ridiculous notion of me trying to seize power, they'll have to put together a fighting force of their own."

"All well and good, but how?" Hashan asked.

"I've been considering that very question." Arzan stood and clasped his hands behind him as he walked up to the window, his cape rustling. "We start small. Take volunteers in batches of one or two hundred and hold their drills in the woods, rotating in new groups once the old reach proficiency. We make only as many weapons at first as will be training at any one time."

"I foresee the problem of spreading a request for volunteers without the wrong ears catching wind," Pundur said.

Hashan nodded. "Right. I don't know about Senkani, but Pundur and I get a lot of merchants and craftsmen from other provinces mingling with our own. The secret will be out within days of us starting."

Arzan began to pace. "How are we going to do this?" he muttered.

"Senkani can start first," Pundur said, rubbing his chin. "You could probably do it in secret for a while, and one province is better than none. As for Three Corners, I have an idea. I'll focus on building our horse stock."

"How does that accomplish anything?" Hashan asked.

"Cavalry," Arzan said. "Pundur might not be able to train the soldiers right away, but at least we'll have the horses they can ride."

"It's ideal for Three Corners," Pundur said. "Cavalry can take full advantage of our grasslands."

Arzan raised his finger. "Woodwise can help with the armor, without really making armor. Start stockpiling linen— have it ready to be sewn into gambeson when the time comes."

Hashan twisted his cane, thinking. "If we do that, why not go further? We can have even more supplies readied. Spear shafts. Bowstrings. There must be plenty of materials that wouldn't draw attention, so long as we don't put them all together."

Yes, this can work. Arzan smiled with strengthened hope. The three crendens continued picking out things they could start in secret, finding new ideas even as the servants brought out supper and the sun began to set. The Council might be filled with fools, but Leverie would not succumb to invasion without a fight.

Chapter 16

*"Some of these changes would be
more profound than others."*

Charva's boots thudded against wood as she strode down
the gangplank and stepped onto the Creedport docks. A grin
spread on her salt-sprayed lips, her black hair flowing free in
the coastal breeze. *And so I'm back*, she thought to herself,
her eyes on the iconic gray tower in the center of the city. It
looked just as she remembered it, welcoming her in the warm,
late morning sun. After four years abroad, it was a truly
welcome sight.

Dock hands stepped wide as Charva cut between them.
Likely few recognized her—she'd grown a lot, after all—but
her dress made her stick out. All red, cut in the Falconian
style, with long, hanging sleeves and a more decorative than
functional split-skirt over her loose pants, it certainly made
her stand apart from the typical Leverie woman. That and the
rapier. She'd bet a purse of gold that not three souls in
Creedport would recognize the style of her blade, but not
three souls would mistake it for anything but a sword. That
she could walk into town with it and call it her own was itself
worth her exile. She stopped at the last dock plank and gazed
at the stone buildings, savoring the moment of her return
home.

Her maid Nynilla brushed past with a long, relieved sigh.
"Creedport!" She glanced back at her charge with a look of
victory. "No more chasing you through woodlands and back
alleys. No more spice and gravy. No more seasickness. No

more barbaric customs and suits of armor around every corner. Never am I setting foot under the same roof as you ever again!"

Charva widened her grin at her. "Love you too, Nynilla."

With a huff, the maid tore away, the luggage boys trailing behind her towards the palace.

Unperturbed, Charva walked alone up the main avenue. Merchants and laborers alike stole glances at her appearance, more than a few sets of eyes darting away as they came to the sword. She stopped at a food stall and slapped two coppers on the counter. "A bowl of lamb and rice."

The vendor raised his brow. "That's foreign coin. You need to change it for aristocracy currency."

Charva put two more coppers down and set her elbows against the stall as she leaned in with her biggest smile. The vendor cleared his throat. "Well, I s'pose I could change it myself."

She hummed as she continued down the street, wax paper bowl in hand. The first bite was a little bland, but nothing a sprinkling of spices from her pouch didn't remedy. She scooped the last grains into her mouth right as she reached the base of Matlan's tower. She didn't bother knocking, but shoved the door open and stepped inside.

The tower was more or less how she remembered it—a complete mess. There were a lot more ropes strung about than before, but it was all familiar handiwork. Charva set her empty bowl upon a knee-high crate, where it had to share space with a row of mangled iron rods and a pile of nails, and clasped her hands behind her. "Malty! Where is Old Malty?"

There was a thud and scraping of something against stone, then the slapping of sandals as Maltan rushed down the spiral stairs. "My dear Charva! Is that really you?"

Charva's heart warmed at seeing the old man once again. She spun around, her sleeves and mock skirt twirling around her. "You are observant for a tinkerer, truly."

Maltan reached the base of the stairs and sidled through a mass of ropes before wrapping his arms around her in a tender hug. "Your father finally called you back?"

Charva laughed. "I'm sure he's conveniently forgotten I even exist."

"You have returned of your own accord, then." Maltan stepped back, his face serious.

Charva waved her hand. "Oh, please. I'm of age now. Father's authority isn't absolute anymore." She let an edge sneak into her habitual smile. "Something I'll be very sure to make him remember."

Maltan opened his mouth to speak, but Charva jumped into the tangle of ropes suspended over the floor and danced from space to space, touching nothing. "You should have been there, Malty. Sailing the oceans wide, schools of dolphins all around our ship, fleets of flying fish gliding beside the hull, and waves that glowed in the night. And Falcone itself. Towers and castles, and cities that stretch for miles and miles. And mountains. We don't have true mountains here in Moshon." She hopped deftly onto a workbench. "I climbed the highest peak in the Feathers, where the snow made the whole mountain white and I could see the world."

She jumped back down and tapped her scabbard. "They let girls and women train with the men. They know true war there and they encourage everyone to know how to fight. Have you ever seen, Malty, a parade of knights in full armor, their boots thundering through the streets?"

Maltan seated himself on a low stool. "I hope I never do. But you seem to have enjoyed yourself immensely."

Charva brushed her fingers along a vertical rope. "There's one thing Falcone will never be able to give me. I—" She spotted a shadow by the entryway and grinned. "Throrne, I know you're there!"

A boy entered hesitantly into the tower. He was taller now than when Charva had last seen him, reaching up almost to her own current height of five-foot-six, but for all his rich shirt and vest tried to hide it, he was still spindly and awkward. His jet black hair was slicked back in emulation of their father, and Charva thought it just made him look pretentious. His blue eyes, the same dark shade as hers, darted between her and the tower walls.

Charva skipped across the room and gave in to the urge to tussle his hair. "And here's my favorite little brother."

"I heard the guards whisperin' they saw you in the

streets," Throrne mumbled.

"Yes, it's only a matter of time before Father catches wind." Charva put an arm around her brother's shoulder and felt him tense. She responded by using him as a lean-to post. "Heh, I missed this."

Throrne suffered her weight, but the irritation came through in his voice. "Are you still aiming for crendess of Creedport?"

"Do you still not want to be crenden?"

"Father will never nominate you."

"I don't need to be nominated by him. I just need to be voted in by the House."

"And why should they vote for you when Father nominates me?"

Charva put her forehead against his cheek. "Because they'll know you lack the aptitude and desire to rule."

Maltan cleared his throat. "If you are done disparaging your brother, perhaps you will want to know how things have changed in your absence."

Charva hopped away from Throrne. "Ah, yes. Did the House flog Father for sending a fourteen-year-old off on her own to a barbaric land of warmongers? Did the cotton workers finally lynch our plantation managers? Throrne, head on back to the palace. We don't want your sensitive ears contaminated by seditious speech."

She meant it as a joke, but Throrne walked out. She felt suddenly bad for teasing him, but she shook her head and put him out of her mind.

"All right, what's happened really?"

Maltan filled her in on the recent state of affairs with House Redleaf. By the end of it, Charva was gleefully back to dancing between the ropes.

"I love it! I'm glad the new Redleafs can still rile him up. I want to meet them."

"Thrake is not the only one Arzan has been rubbing the wrong way," Maltan said. "Approach them and others on the Council will be watching. That risks your bid for crendess, does it not?"

Charva balanced atop a sawhorse. "That makes it fun." She stepped onto a neighboring workbench, carefully avoiding the tools strewn over its surface. "Have you written your book yet?"

Maltan sighed. "No matter how much you bug me about that, my dear, the answer will always be no."

She lowered herself to the floor with a shake of her head. "Why not, Malty? You so truly admire those books of inventions. You're as brilliant as any of their authors, even if this city's silly crenden is too great a fool to recognize it."

"The child should not call the parent a fool."

"Only you may speak the obvious?"

"It's too cruel for a man to find enemies even in his own offspring."

Charva kept her smile plastered to her face as she remembered the day she was ushered onto a ship and sent off for an alien land, likely in hopes that a sword would somehow find its way into her chest. "He started it."

Maltan sighed heavily. "What is to be done with you?"

"You just wait here and watch," Charva said. "When I'm crendess, you and I will make Creedport the jewel of the aristocracies."

"That is not—" Maltan started, but Charva leaped to the threshold and twirled through the doorway, catching herself on the handle to stop her spin.

"See you, Malty. I love you, truly." She shut the door without letting him respond.

"Willful child," she heard Maltan mutter, followed by the slapping of sandals. Charva reopened the door just a crack to get one last look at his workshop and to hear him start humming a tune.

"There is something that exists only here," she whispered. She tucked a lock of hair behind her ear and pushed herself off the door.

Chapter 17

*"One of the key changes
would be that of timing."*

The carriage rolled smoothly across the Highcity paving stones, the ride much more enjoyable now than the bumpy, jostling journey along the country highway. Ellaniel rested her arm against the wood siding and gazed out at the statues adorning each street corner. In the corner of her eye, she saw Arzan fiddling with the clasp of his cape.

"Don't be nervous," she said. "This is just a normal Council meeting. They don't know anything."

He snatched his fingers away from the clasp with visible effort. "You're right. We've barely even started. There's nothing for them to be suspicious of."

"Unless you can't keep your hands still." She smiled. "Perhaps it would help if I had Filgneir hide all your capes."

Arzan raised an eyebrow. "Oh? After I finally won you over to my fashion sense?"

Ellaniel brushed her fingers down the red, two foot capelet hanging from the shoulders of her pale blue dress. "Yes, it would be a shame, so stop your bad habit already."

The horses slowed and stopped, parking the carriage in front of the high-domed Council building. Filgneir hopped down from the driver's bench and opened the door. "My liege."

Arzan nodded. He kissed her and stepped out. She hoped silently that the meeting really would be nothing special.

Kalla came from the following carriage and up to the open door. "Anywhere you'd like to go, your grace?"

"In fact, I was hoping to stop by Natsha's shop," Ellaniel said.

The maid's face lit up and she passed word to the driver before jumping in and sitting beside her charge. "I've only been once or twice. Her designs are gorgeous! Almost as good as yours."

"You mean to say mine are almost as good as Natsha's," Ellaniel said. "She and her women are the best embroiderers in the country."

"But yours are wonderful, Ella," Kalla said, reaching out and pinching Ellaniel's sleeve, which was decorated in a complex pattern of intertwining birds and flowers. "And you're so fast too!"

She shook her head. "All right, enough flattery! You're supposed to be a maid, not a sycophant."

Kalla giggled. "But you're so lacking in sycophants."

"If there's one thing I like about House Redleaf's lowborn sensibilities, it's their lack of butt kissing," Ellaniel said, rolling her eyes.

"Here we are, your grace," the driver called.

The two women stepped down from the carriage to stand before an elegantly carved doorway nestled in between two plain fabric shops. The vertical signpost spelled out "Natsha Leverie" in flowing letters.

"Holler if you need me," Magar said, taking his station beside the entrance. He'd been riding unobtrusively on the carriage's back bench, making it easy to forget he was even there.

"I already know that we do," Kalla said, taking his elbow. "You have to help me pick out a new scarf and handkerchief."

He looked mortified. "What, me?"

"You made fun of my dress yesterday. You're showing me what you think is proper taste."

"That was a joke! It wasn't—"

"Hush," Kalla said, dragging him into the store.

Ellaniel grinned and stepped in after them.

The interior was larger than it seemed from without, stretching back like a cavern. The whole length was well lit by a series of windows set right into the ceiling, which illuminated the decorated cloths and clothing that lined the racks all along the walls. Intricate designs of every conceivable pattern and color vied for attention, and Ellaniel was sure at first sight that she could spend days looking everything over. Standing a few yards away, checking over a collection of lizard embroidered handkerchiefs, was a middle-aged woman in a dress adorned top to bottom in expertly stitched roses. Beyond her, at the back of the room, four other women sat busy threading needles through cloth.

The rose woman looked up at the visitors. Her dark blue eyes fell first on the guard, then Ellaniel's dress, the short sword at her waist, and finally her eyes. "Ellaniel Redleaf, if I'm not mistaken?"

Ellaniel curtsied. "Natsha, I presume?"

The woman stepped closer, her finger on her lower lip as she leaned in to study Ellaniel's dress. "I'd heard Hashan's daughter was good. Indeed, excellent sense of balance and spacing. You make great use of the contours of the dress, molding the patterns to complement the form. The direction of the motifs and how you fit them together are quite creative. Crendess or no, should you make this your trade, you could do quite well for yourself."

Ellaniel's cheeks burned at the compliment. She cleared her throat. "Thank you. My father always has praise for my patterns, but receiving it from a master . . . . Thank you."

"Well then, what brings you here?" Natsha asked.

"I was hoping simply to see your work, your grace," Ellaniel said. "I've studied only a few of your pieces that made it to the Woodwise market, but they were all incredible!"

Natsha nodded, her face an unreadable mask. "My shop and studio are always open to those who harbor an appreciation for our art."

Ellaniel bowed her head gratefully. "Thank you. I—"

"Just do leave that barbaric tool outside, will you? As well as that shiny buffoon."

The rudely stated demands made Ellaniel choke. She glanced at Magar and Kalla, who had both stopped in the middle of perusing one of the racks. "I'll put my sword in the carriage if you insist," Ellaniel said, placing her hand on her scabbard, "but surely my ckol isn't a problem."

"Instruments of violence have no welcome in my shop," Natsha said, her tone of voice barring any dissent. "A crenden's hound cultivated in the art of murder is no exception."

Ellaniel balled her fists. "Excuse me, but that is not how you speak of one of my servants."

Natsha loomed over her with cool hostility. "I will speak however I wish of whomever I wish."

"Your grace, I will step outside," Magar said.

"No." Surprising even herself with her boldness, she clenched her jaw and glared at the woman before her. "You will leave when you are asked politely to do so."

"I'm sorry," Natsha said. "I mistook you for a civilized woman of the House, not a pretentious bully who forces her will in someone else's home. But I suppose I should have known better. It seems one can't expect much from a gold eyed mongrel married to a Redleaf."

Ellaniel grit her teeth hard, but caught herself before lashing out any further. She was right. This was Natsha's domain. And as much as she wanted to fight, she knew there was no point. "Fine. We will leave. Magar, Kalla, come."

As she was reaching the door, she heard Natsha mutter, "A shame that such talent should be wasted on her blood."

No longer thinking, Ellaniel scooped up a basket of silks and dumped the contents on the floor before stepping out.

"You didn't have to go that far," Kalla said in a mortified whisper once they were in the street. "She's going to boycott Senkani for sure now!"

"Well, so be it," Ellaniel said. "No one speaks of my friends like that."

A new voice joined the conversation, "I knew I'd like you."

Ellaniel looked around and saw a woman leaning against her carriage, to the very visible annoyance of the driver. She had typical Leverie features with inky black hair and dark blue eyes, but wore an exotic red dress with a split skirt. Stranger still, she had a sword fastened to her belt. *Six continents, don't tell me I've started a fashion.*

"Do I know you?" Ellaniel asked.

The woman pushed off the carriage and spun a full circle, fluttering her skirt, sleeves, and hair before taking a bow. "By both name and reputation, most likely. Oh, and I think I remember seeing you at Ythyl's wedding way back when."

Ellaniel tried to think back. "That doesn't help at all. Half the House was there for that."

"I was the one who got in trouble collecting eggs from the top of the lamp post."

The memory fell into place. She narrowed her eyes. "You're Thrake's daughter."

The woman smiled. "Charva Leverie. Pleased to make your acquaintance. Flame and embers, don't look at me like that! I know my father's got a spat going with Arzan, but I'm a different beast entirely."

"What is it you want, then?"

Charva clasped her hands behind her. "Plenty of things. Adventure, friends, fame, Creedport. One thing at a time, though."

"So, which of those are you seeking right now?" Ellaniel asked.

Charva's grin had a distinctly mischievous quality to it. "How about a duel?"

"What?"

"Wood blades, of course, but . . ." she pointed to Ellaniel's sword. "They say you've been learning to use that. It's been months since I've had a sparring partner. None of my father's ckols or any of the city guard will fight me. Just as well. They claim they wouldn't strike a woman, much less the crenden's daughter, but I suspect none of them is good enough to even land a blow."

Ellaniel raised an eyebrow. "That's a tall claim."

Charva leaned in. "How good are you?"

"A noble doesn't fight for entertainment," Ellaniel said.

"Not Moshon nobles, maybe. But fine, let's make it more than a game. If you win, you get a boon from me. A favor owed from the daughter of your husband's prime enemy.

How's that?"

"This is ridiculous!"

"I warn you, I'm going to pester you until you accept," Charva said. She paced with light steps. "Let's see. I guess I'll have to try splashing water in your face, saying disparaging things about your parentage, insult your wife— oh, wait, you are the wife." She tapped her forehead. "What are the proper ways of enraging a noblewoman?"

Ellaniel sighed. "What do you want from me if you win?"

Charva stopped and spun once more to face her. "If I win, you have to be my friend."

The condition was so unexpected she laughed. *The friend of her father's enemy and a social outcast*, Ellaniel thought. *She's a few eggs short of a dozen*. She seemed sincere. But if that was really the condition, what did Ellaniel have to lose? "All right."

"Splendid!" Charva pointed to Magar. "You, go fetch us some training equipment from the city guard and meet us at the north gate. Finally, I can have some fun!"

Half an hour later and they were in the woods just outside the walls. Unlike most other cities, the Leverie capitol didn't have much agriculture in its immediate vicinity, thanks in large part to the steep slopes all around. Conveniently for their purposes, there were still a few level clearings here and there, and they found one large enough for a duel. And an audience.

Ellaniel secured the last buckle of her padded jacket as she reflected on how much of a mistake she'd made. Word had spread of a fight between two noblewomen. Dozens had followed them to the impromptu dueling grounds. She could see equal parts disbelief, horror, and amusement in the faces of the commoners and city guardsmen surrounding them.

"We should call this off, your grace," Magar said. "This is going to be a scandal talked about for years."

"It's already too late for that," she said with a sigh. "Even if we walk away now, the rumors and gossip will say we fought anyway. Might as well get something out of it."

"Give that Leverie girl a good thrashing, Ella!" Kalla said, holding out a wooden shortsword.

"You're into this," Ellaniel observed.

Kalla pumped her fist in the air. "Team Redleaf!"

Several paces away, Charva was already geared up and making practice thrusts with her weapon. She had discarded the short training blade Magar offered her and instead picked up a pole the length of a longsword.

"Are you sure you don't want a shield?" Magar asked Ellaniel. "Your opponent has the reach advantage."

She bounced on her toes and jumped side to side to warm up. In addition to donning padded armor, she'd also changed into her riding skirts for maneuverability. "I want to test how good I am with sword only. Arzan's trained me with the shield, but that's not something I'll normally have on me."

"Ready?" Charva called.

Ellaniel twirled her weapon and stepped towards her opponent. The gathered crowd buzzed.

"Those two are really going at it?"

"What in the six is happening? Aren't they House women?"

Charva grinned and drew an arc through the leaves on the ground with her rod. "Lesson one of dueling: Don't let the crowd distract you."

"What are the rules we're going by?" Ellaniel asked. "There are rules, right?"

"We'll make it simple," Charva said. "Round ends with any contact. No strikes to the face or neck and no thrusts. We'll do best of three."

Ellaniel pushed their audience out of her mind and settled into her basic offensive stance, sword and right foot forward, knees bent and ready to spring. Charva mirrored her, wielding her weapon with one hand despite its length. "Those golden eyes—you look like a lioness. I love it."

"That's not how you hold a longsword," Ellaniel said.

"Because it isn't one," Charva said. "So, how do you want to signal the—"

Ellaniel lunged and swung at the woman's arm. Charva dodged backwards with a laugh. "All right, then!"

Ellaniel continued pressing the attack, slashing at her arms and shoulders, coming up short each time as Charva danced nimbly out of the way. "You're leaving yourself terribly exposed, you know," Charva said, letting Ellaniel's sword pass an inch away from her.

"And you're getting incredibly cocky," Ellaniel said. She anticipated Charva's dodge to the side and pushed in closer, swinging at her torso.

Charva finally twisted her own sword and blocked the attack with a solid *thwack*. "Now it's on."

Ellaniel barely moved to parry in time as the other woman whipped her rod at her left leg. Charva's weapon slid off Ellaniel's guard only to come around and snap at her right shoulder. Ellaniel fended off the attack, and the next. Every time, Charva was instantly at her again, leaving no opening for a riposte. Ellaniel retreated under the onslaught, her boots kicking up leaves around her riding skirts.

"You're good," Charva said excitedly. "How about this?" She launched another high strike. Ellaniel guarded, but it was a feint, changing at the last moment and slashing at her torso. She felt the blow hit her just below the ribs, stinging even through the padding.

Charva flourished her weapon. "One point for me!"

Ellaniel tapped the flat of her blade against her thigh. "How in the six to do you move so fast?"

Her opponent smiled and saluted with her rod. "Practice."

"Get her back!" Kalla shouted.

Ellaniel wiped sweat off her forehead, Kalla's voice reminding her of the existence of the crowd. The Highcity folk were speechless at the spectacle, and even the guards were visibly impressed, muttering to each other with awed faces. She turned away from them and raised her sword once more. "Come."

Charva took her stance. "Guard!" She leaped forward, opening with a shallow slash.

Ellaniel stepped into the attack, slapping her blade into Charva's weapon and sliding it down the rod. Charva's eyes widened in surprise and she dropped her weapon before Ellaniel could catch her fingers. She dodged Ellaniel's slash at her chest and ducked the follow-up before dancing out of reach.

"You're as slippery as a fish," Ellaniel growled.

"Thank you," Charva said cheerfully. She clasped her hands behind her and began circling casually, her eyes on the fallen weapon Ellaniel guarded at her feet. "This is an interesting conundrum."

"Forfeit?" Ellaniel asked.

"Embers no! I'm getting my sword back."

Ellaniel put her foot on the fallen blade. "All right, then. Just try it."

Charva shrugged and continued circling. "You know, maybe—" She rushed in.

Ellaniel slashed. Charva clapped her hands together as if trying to catch the blade, but for once her speed wasn't enough. The edge smacked her in the chest.

"Flame and embers! I thought that would work!"

Ellaniel gaped at her. "Did you really just try that?"

"My training master did it to me once," Charva said. "I thought I'd practiced enough to finally do it myself." She rubbed the spot she'd been hit. "You really put your all into that one. Ouch."

Ellaniel glanced around at the spectators, noting some of the men blushing and averting their eyes. She cleared her throat. "That's not exactly the most appropriate place to be touching right now."

Charva rolled her eyes and pushed her arms out in a stretch. She scooped her toe under her weapon before kicking it into the air and catching it in her palm. "Ready for round three?"

"Ready to lose your stick again?"

"That was a fluke."

"No, that was your overconfidence."

"And now you're the one getting cocky."

Ellaniel smiled and shrugged. "Magar, shield."

Magar had a medium-sized roundshield for her in a heartbeat. She took hold of the center handle and twisted it to test the balance.

"I see you're getting serious," Charva said.

"Don't start complaining."

"Who, me?" The woman bent down and picked up a foot

long stick. "I'll just go ahead and use my real style too."

"What in the six is that supposed to be?" Ellaniel asked.

Charva looked down at her mock weapons. "Sword and dagger, obviously."

"Hmm, I don't see how that's any good."

"Wish to try me?"

Ellaniel obliged. She kept her shield angled against Charva's longsword and struck at her opponent's left. Charva smoothly swatted the attack aside with her "dagger". Ellaniel was mildly impressed she'd managed to parry at all with something so small, even if it left her with too little reach to follow through. *She's got great control and reflexes, I'll give her that.*

Sweat rolled down her face as she tried several more slashes, each one deflected by Charva's excellent dagger work. A bead went into her eye, making her blink. She saw Charva's sword strike almost too late. She twisted her arm just in time to avoid a hit to the wrist, but the rod still clashed against the pommel of Ellaniel's weapon. The wooden blade ripped free of her hand, flipping end over end and forcing a pair of commoners to jump out of the way as it planted itself where they'd been standing.

"Ha!" Charva shouted. "Now you're disarmed!" She pressed her advantage, striking with her longsword. Ellaniel grit her teeth and braced her shield against the attacks. Charva went at her in earnest, mixing up her angles to try and get around Ellaniel's guard. She clearly thought the match was as good as won.

Her mistake.

Ellaniel saw the sloppy lower strike she was waiting for. She let it past her shield and raised her foot, allowing the rod to hit dirt. She brought her heel down, pinning the tip to the ground, and struck her shield into the middle. She meant to tear the stick from Charva's grasp, but instead it snapped in half with a pathetic crack. *Just as good.* Charva didn't have a chance to get over her surprise before Ellaniel shield-rammed her in the chest. She heard the wind whoosh from her lungs and the woman flew onto her back in a splash of leaves. Ellaniel stepped over her dazed opponent and gently dropped the edge of her shield over Charva's clavicle.

"A shield's a weapon too," Ellaniel said wish a satisfied smirk.

Charva let out a deep throated groan and dropped her weapons to either side. "Ow."

Kalla ran up and raised Ellaniel's arm into the air. "Ha! Ella wins!"

Whistles and claps came from the audience, which somehow had grown much, much larger than before. Ellaniel glanced around, seeing far more excited faces than she expected for what was almost a blood sport. She found the rush of the fight lingering on as the energy from the crowd pumped through her. *This . . . . I kind of like this.*

Charva laughed, still lying on her back. "That was the most excitement I've had in a while!" She sat up, her pale face flushed, strands of hair plastered by sweat to her skin. "Want to go at it again sometime?"

Ellaniel offered her an arm up. "So long as you remember the boon you owe me."

Charva took her hand with a palm rough with callouses. She grunted, rising back to her feet. "Oh, you'll get it, but you might want to keep it safe for a bit. You're looking at the future crendess of Creedport."

"You weren't fighting me seriously," Ellaniel said.

Charva raised her eyebrows in false surprise. "Oh?"

Ellaniel pointed to the broken rod. "The sword you carry. It's too thin to be meant for slashes. It's a thrusting weapon, which you expressly forbade in the rules."

The woman smiled and patted her cloth armor. "Even if it's just a wooden stick, a thrust can kill through this. That's the problem sparring with rapiers."

"I want to see your real style."

"Then I'll have to see you in plate."

Ellaniel hadn't ever contemplated wearing steel armor before, but now she decided she absolutely needed a set. *It will probably be the strangest commission any of our blacksmiths have ever had.* But then, it would also provide an excuse for them to learn armor forging. Her mind turned over the possibilities of helping Arzan with his army. Yes, she could make it a competition between the blacksmiths to craft her their best suit. She couldn't wait to tell Arzan her idea. *To think it would be the daughter of Crenden Thrake who would give us this opportunity.*

"I've never enjoyed sparring as much as today," Ellaniel said, starting at unfastening her gambeson. "I *will* challenge you again, Charva."

Charva took her hand in a firm hold. "And next time, I'm going to beat you."

"Oh, that's wishful thinking."

"I had a handicap and you barely won today," Charva said. She accepted her sword back from Magar and raised it in the air. "But it doesn't matter that I lost. We're friends, right?"

Ellaniel felt a smirk cross her face. "You little cheat."

Charva slid her blade through her belt and gave a bow. "Truly."

A messenger came sprinting through the crowd. "There you are! Your grace, Crenden Arzan sends word that the Council session is adjourned."

"Well, then." Ellaniel slipped out of the sleeves of her armor and fastened her sword to her side. "He's in for an odd story."

Chapter 18

*"Again and again through history, battles
and social upheavals have been decided by the
right man at the right place at exactly the right time."*

It was week's end and Arzan wandered the streets of
Senkani to take a break from reports and figures and politics.
As was his custom, he wore a simple disguise of commoner's
clothing, tussled hair, and dark oil to tint his skin. It was late
in the day, and clouds made the sky even darker as he found
an empty stool at a promising-looking food stall. He ordered
a bowl of the barley soup bubbling in the cook's cauldron and
listened in on the conversation between the two other patrons
on the seats next to him.

"Whole fields burned right down to the ground. Not a
grain o' wheat left."

"How many dead?"

"Near half the capitol as I hear it."

"Poor sods."

"Most from hunger. The Vron burned the crops and left
'em all to starve."

"Plundered down to floorboards, I'd bet."

Arzan blew on his soup and wished the topic would shift.
He wanted to hear about Senkani's harvests, or the price of
Ranisa leather, or their thoughts on the latest play. For talk of
the empire, he could have just stayed at the palace and
continued hashing out plans with Filgneir.

"Not the story I was told," the cook said. "Way I hear, it

was the aristocrats were the ones to set the fires. The Feathered General slew them right by the Council table for doing it."

The first patron scoffed. "A pretty lie the imperials put out. Makes 'em look like heroes instead o' usurpers. Watch. When they come here, they'll kill our crenden and put a new man in charge worse'n any Leverie."

The other patron pulled out his knife and rammed it point first into the counter. "I'll die before I let that happen to Arzan Redleaf!"

The cook's mouth dropped open and he yanked the blade from the wood. "Oi! What you think you're doing to my stall?"

The man hunched his shoulders and looked half his former size. "Ah, sorry."

"This is the third time, Bavants. I'm keeping this knife."

Bravan't face paled, and Arzan noted that it looked like a really good knife. "I'll bring you a new counter tomorrow," he said timidly.

The cook tossed the blade into the remainder of the man's soup. "Good."

The first patron chuckled. "He has the truth o' it, though. We're not going to roll over if the empire comes to our borders. Even if they promise us carpets of gold, we're not handing our crenden to 'em."

Arzan stirred his soup, feeling both humility and pride. Whatever the Leverie said about his ways, he wouldn't trade this kind of loyalty for anything. He took a spoonful of his soup and savored the taste that other aristocrats were too foolish to enjoy. With a smile, he decided he had something of his own to contribute to the table. "Did you hear what the crendess did in Highcity?" he asked, imitating the tone of a gruff field hand.

The cook stirred his pot. "Didn't she have some fight with one of the Leverie embroiderers up there?"

"Oh, so you didn't hear about what happened *outside* the walls." Arzan's grin widened.

Arzan hummed merrily as he slipped through the back palace entrance, shrugging off his street cloak and letting Vikghon shut the door on the darkening city behind them. Filgneir came to meet him even before he finished putting on his proper crenden attire.

"You're in a good mood," Filgneir said.

"The city's eating up the story of Ella's duel," Arzan said gleefully. "It's already spreading through every quarter like wildfire. Our whole '52 vintage stock if the playwrights don't have the performance ready by this time next week."

Filgneir's jaw dropped and he slowly thumped his bald head against the door frame. "Arzan, that's the sort of thing you're supposed to keep hush on. Do you realize how much trouble I went through trying to quiet the rumors?"

Arzan slapped his aid on the back. "Sometimes, it's better to just say to ashes with etiquette."

Filgneir let out a heavy breath before lifting his head and shoving a stack of documents into Arzan's chest. "The manifest the clerks finished while you were gallivanting around town." He stormed off, hands clawing at the air. "Diplomacy, not provocation!"

He'll get over it. Arzan finished securing his cape and went upstairs while flipping through the manifest. The southwest vineyards were doing slendidly this year. Their food crops were also faring very well. *We're in a good position here. At the very least, there's no reason to worry about getting weakened by famines or such before the empire arrives.* More and more, he was becoming sure it would be a matter of when, not if. Five years, ten—the Vron were not going to stop, and it was his responsibility to be ready for them. For the sake of the city and its people his father had left in his care.

He entered his study to find the desk lantern already lit and Ellaniel in his seat reading. She glanced up, her finger keeping her passage. "There you are. What's a flujuin?"

Arzan dumped the manifest on the corner of the desk and peeked at the book she was reading. It was an essay of current economics. "A type of ship they've started using out east. It's got more space than the usual tri-decks. Three masts, rather fat-looking, and they use a lot of block and tackle. Not the best for open sea, though, since it's got a shallow draft."

Ellaniel folded the book closed. "That explanation is already more interesting than anything in these pages. This, though," she slipped a sheet of paper from under the book. "Charva has much interesting to say about her plans if she becomes crendess."

"Oh, her letter's not a challenge request?"

Ellaniel laughed before going sober. "I think she's serious about usurping her father. She's no interest in waiting thirty years for him to step down."

Arzan put his knuckles to his chin. "As much as this turn of events appeals to me, I feel we need to be cautious here. It's one thing to disagree with a troublesome crenden and another entirely to work towards getting him replaced."

She shrugged. "Probably wise to be hesitant. I hope it's still all right for Charva and me to be friends, though?"

"That much I think we shall risk." He smirked. "How's the armor competition coming?"

"Ah!" His wife pulled a bundle of folded papers from her pocket and flattened them on the desk excitedly. "These are the concepts they've sent me. What do you think?"

Arzan came around to view them with her. "There's a lot of variety here. I can see this one's been influenced by Originate suits. Hmm. This other one's rather . . . basic."

"Honestly, that design's the ugliest thing I've ever seen."

"Doesn't even look that strong." He checked the signature. "Master Lert. Makes sense. That man's nails have so many warts they make toads jealous."

Ellaniel put the page gingerly to the side. "We'll have him stick to arrowheads."

Arzan studied the next design. "This is ambitious. Full suit, Falconian style."

"I can only imagine how hot these get."

"Excellent protection, though. The problem is, they take so much steel and work we couldn't possibly afford them for a whole army. Even just for our ckols feels extravagant."

"We're training men for the shield wall, anyway," Ellaniel said. "Our people won't need all this."

Arzan tapped the desk with his finger. "Helmets,

armguards, and greaves. Maybe chest pieces if it looks like we have the resources, but it might be better to just go with chain shirts."

Ellaniel made a face. "But that won't do for my duel."

Her mother's spirit really is waking up in her after all. A sliver of fear stabbed through him. Maybe she actually might follow in her footsteps. No, if Ella did get the itch to test her skill, she had friends here to be her opponents. Charva was one. Arzan was always up for a bout. Even some of the ckols were showing interest in trying her.

And before long, we may not have to travel far to find a war.

He shook his head. If the Vron reached them, there was no way in the six he would let her near the battle line.

"What is it?" Ellaniel asked, picking up on his expression.

"Nothing." He pointed to one of the designs. "How about this one? I think it has a nice balance of protection and aesthetic."

"Yes, that's one of my favorites."

Arzan eyed her and tried imagining her in plate and chain. Even if he didn't want her fighting, he couldn't help but think the look would suit her. She was beautiful in her dresses, tailored perfectly to the curves of her body, the fabric a canvas for her masterful needlework (today red dragonflies spiraling up blue silk). Even so, he wanted to see her in a set of steel molded to her form, her brown hair just a tad lighter than a rich tardish wood stain draped atop her shoulder guards. *I am a strange man.*

He wasn't sure when he'd started staring into her gold colored eyes, or when she'd started staring back. The corners of her lips turned up in a smile. "You know, we don't spend as much time alone together as we should," she said.

"We need to find more opportunities to discuss armor and duels, then."

"This is fun and all, but . . ." Ellaniel stood and nestled up to him. "Sometimes, we should do other things than just talk."

"Well, perhaps I should latch the—"

He forgot the second part of his suggestion as she pulled him down into a kiss.

Chapter 19

*"What then happens when this
man is delayed a moment to pull
that pebble from his shoe?"*

*"Shoals with clear waters, bright amber meadows, skies
sunny and gentle and sweet. This land full of beauty, the
plenty around me, Evena, I name this for you."*

Charva sang to herself as she sat atop the wall's parapet,
her legs dangling out over the fields below, her split skirt
rippling in the gentle sea breeze. A few workers looked up in
perplexity or concern every now and again as they plowed the
fields. Or maybe it was annoyance at her off-key notes. She
chose to assume the former and smiled and waved whenever
she felt their gaze.

She liked the view from the walls. The forested hills
stretched out before her, their branches swaying in the wind,
birds flitting around them. Off to her right, the ocean was a
majestic blue mirroring the brighter color of the sky. To her
left, the farms made a patchwork of greens and golds and
browns. She smoothed her hand over one of the parapet's
sun-warmed lizard sculptures beside her and thought about
how small people were in this vast world. So much forest
unsettled. So much sea. Civilizations built great walls and
towers, climbed the highest peaks, and called themselves
grand. Yet when Charva sat atop such things, she couldn't
help but see how tiny humans were. How tiny she was.

It made her want to create something greater than anyone
ever had before.

The soles of someone's shoes scuffed against the stones behind her. "You asked for me, your grace?"

Charva lifted her feet and swiveled around to plant them on the ramparts. "Eventide, biggest landowner in Creedport outside the House. Just the man I wanted to see."

A tad over forty, Eventide suffered from pattern baldness and a terribly plain face. That didn't prevent him from being one of the most influential people in the province. The fifth son of a lowly fisherman, he'd climbed his way up through shrewd land acquisitions and excellent management skills. "Word is, you're seeking to oust your father and take his place. I heard Ulmar and Guilish saying they're ready to throw their lot in with you."

"Right to the point. I like you already!"

"I've no interest in giving you my vote," Eventide said.

Charva raised her eyebrows and put her hands on her hips. "Why not?"

The man smiled and scratched his stubbly chin. "Well, you're no less blunt than I am." He shook his head. "Why would I want our crenden replaced? Thrake's been running the province just fine. Business is up almost twofold since last year, thanks to his trade deals with the Falconian kingdoms. There's no reason to kick him out—especially not for some some girl without any market experience. No offense, your grace, but I just don't see what you bring to the table."

"The cotton gin, for starters," she said. "Surely you remember Maltan's machine, before Father had it banned and forbade him from crafting any more of his contraptions."

"So that's your angle." Eventide crossed his arms. "I remember that thing. Absolutely remarkable, but weighed against Thrake's merits . . . . To be frank, it's a better bet pressuring him to bring Maltan back as official city tinkerer than to replace your father altogether."

"And what about his spat with the Redleafs?" Charva asked. "Surely that's a serious problem?"

"You're grasping at straws, your grace. He's been abiding by the Council's peace."

"He wields the Council against Senkani. Arzan has valid concerns about the safety of Leverie. Whether it's the issue of the army or the dangers of overspecialization, Crenden Thrake opposes him for no other reason than his petty grudge."

"You speak of things with which you have no real experience," Eventide said, shaking his head. "You're still a girl, trying to be an adult in matters you don't fully understand."

Charva clasped her hands behind her and kept her back straight, refusing to let the insult faze her. "That seems an opinion you came here already decided on. I wonder why you even bother accepting my invitation."

Eventide rubbed the stubble on his chin. "You may not be crendess material now, but in ten years or so, perhaps you'll stand as a proper contender against your brother. I wanted to get a sense for who you are."

"If this were a monarchy, you'd be hanging from your toes right now for your impertinence," Charva said with a wistful grin. "That's why I love Moshon."

The man regarded her with a critical eye. "That sarcasm, your grace?"

"No. Even if I don't like what you've told me, at least I know your honest thoughts of where my failings lie. Now I can either address your doubts, or prove them wrong, and then you'll be an ally."

Eventide let out a quick chuckle. "Yes, there's hope for you." He turned. "Another time, your grace."

Charva sighed and leaned her elbows against the parapet as the merchant left. *That could have gone better.* Her quest to gather backing was definitely not going as smoothly as she'd hoped. The city standards snapped in the wind overhead as she wondered if she was taking things too fast after all. Most in their right minds would think it madness to appoint someone her age.

She turned around and looked at Maltan's tower rising up above the city center. *I don't have a choice.* Maltan had the genius necessary to revolutionize the country, but he was getting old. He'd die long before her father stepped down. If Charva wanted to make something of Creedport, it was now or never.

She heard heavy footfalls before seeing Throme and his

pair of ckols ascend from the nearby tower. Her brother was huffing and sweaty. "Here's where you were. Father wants to see you."

"Well, it's been a while since I've heard those words," Charva said. She pushed away from the battlements. "I wonder what in the six he could possibly want to speak to me about."

"Does everything out of your mouth have to be sarcasm?" Throrne asked with a sour face.

Charva ruffled his hair. "Of course not. I can do straight insults too." She smiled in response to his glare. "What happened to your sense of humor, dear brother? Thank you for delivering the message." She strode to the tower and descended the steps, tipping her sword scabbard so it wouldn't tap the stones.

Nary seeing me except at dinner, and not saying a word to me even then, but he has to speak now, she thought. She hadn't gotten as far as she'd like raising support for her cause, but being summoned by her father meant she was getting *somewhere.*

She made quick time through the familiar twisting labyrinth of Creedport's streets, coming around to the main avenue right in front of the palace gate. She strode purposefully up the steps into the foyer.

"The crenden is awaiting you in the guest lounge, your grace," the head butler informed her.

She narrowed her eyes. "The guest lounge? Is someone with him?"

"Crenden Roth arrived a little over an hour ago."

"Did he now." A notorious womanizer, Roth was one of her least favorite men in the aristocracy. What's worse, his sheer handsomeness could make her nearly forget his serial infidelity the moment she set her gaze on him. She bit her cheek as she ascended the main stairs and knocked on the doorway of the guest lounge.

"Come," her father's voice called.

She opened the door. The curtains of the far window were tied open, allowing the sun to try its might at cheering a room dominated by drearily dark furniture and crimson red carpets.

"Ah, the elusive beauty is here," Crenden Roth said,

turning away from the paintings on the walls and flashing a roguish smile.

She thought she'd steeled herself, but Charva still got lost staring into his wonderful face like a total idiot. *Flame and embers, to blazes with your good looks.* "Your grace," she said, "what cause brings you to Creedport?"

"Alliances," her father said, stepping from the window and slamming his goblet of wine down atop a table stand, sloshing liquid out onto his sleeve. "What took you so long to get back to the palace?"

She laughed. "I see coming straight home the moment I receive word simply isn't fast enough."

"I sent Throrne out nearly an hour ago!"

"Then it's his incompetence in finding me that you should be upset about."

"Don't speak ill of your brother!"

"Oh, I truly wouldn't dream of doing such. He's your treasured pup, after all."

"Please," Roth said, raising his hands, "this is unbecoming of our stature. We nobles are meant to be the ideal to which the commoners aspire, and you besmirch our image with such trivial quibbles."

Thrake whipped a handkerchief from his vest pocket and scowled as he pressed it to the stain on his sleeve. "You mean well, Roth, but my daughter needs to understand the value of punctuality."

Roth stepped up behind a sofa and placed his elbows on its back as he leaned in. "She's here now. That's all that matters."

Charva clasped her hands behind her. "So I am. Which I must say is very unusual. I can't think of any time I've been invited to any of your meetings, Father."

"And why would I have? Smoke and ashes, you'd only make a flaming mess of everything."

She felt her cheek twitch. "So why is it you call me now?"

"You are here because I happened upon an idea that might please everyone here," Roth said. He rounded the couch to stand between her and her father. "Thrake tells me you've been trying to get a vote of no confidence going against him.

That seems a bit extreme."

"Well, Father's a bit of an extreme person."

Roth smiled and rounded the sofa. "You want to become crendess. Your father wants an end to the unrest you've been stirring up in Creedport. I—" he slipped his hand under hers and raised it to his lips, "—am looking for a wife."

Charva forgot for a moment how to breathe. She stared into Roth's violet eyes, framed in a face poets would swoon over. Her blood pounded in her ears. She leaned in almost nose to nose.

"No," she said.

Her father slammed the table stand. "This matter is not open to negot—"

"You're absolutely right it isn't!" Charva said, tossing away Roth's hand as he blinked in surprise. "How stupid do you think I am? What use is it to be the crenden's second? I shall be ruling crendess—and Creedport shall be my city."

Roth recovered his charming smile. "My dear, I believe you are too quick to make a decision. I'm willing to share rule of Glasscastle."

"I find even that suspect. I'm sure you've whispered all manner of empty promises to your lovers. What number of those are you at now? Thirty?"

Her father gulped down the rest of his wine and threw the goblet aside. "This engagement is final, Charva."

Roth cupped his hand gently around the side of her neck. "Look, we—"

She grabbed him by the collar and shoved him into the sofa. With her other hand, she slipped one of her hidden daggers from her sleeve and held the finely honed edge to his cheek.

"W-What?"

"I shall make this very clear," she said. "The next time you touch me, this blade is severing your throat." She cocked an eyebrow. "Or perhaps your manhood would be more entertaining."

She was satisfied to see him go pale as she pressed the tip of a second dagger into his crotch.

Thrake stepped forward. "How dare—"

"Don't provoke her!" Roth squealed.

Charva looked between the two of them. "You don't control me." She pushed herself to her feet and slipped her daggers back in their wrist sheaths. "You will not be rid of me. I will unseat you, Father, and Creedport will be mine." The two men remained still as statues as she went out the door and shut it behind her.

"She's flaming insane!" Roth said.

Charva lingered and put her ear near the door to listen

"Just calm down and—"

"Your daughter's not worth any price, Thrake. I sympathize with you, but you're going to have to deal with her on your own."

Charva smiled to herself. *If this is the best Father can throw in my way, I have a chance after all.* She strode down the halls of the palace, confident in her course.

Chapter 20

*"A seemingly smallest of alterations
has the outcome of entirely changing
the original state of the world."*

"I wish his eyes were gold," Fellone said as she tottered with her hands on the armrest of Ellaniel's chair. "Gold's a more fun color."

"Blue is as beautiful as any," Ellaniel told her, stroking the tiny bald head of her baby as she held him in her lap. *And no one can use the color of his eyes to say he's not Leverie.*

Fellone blew a lock of her purple-tinted hair away from her face. "Well, at least Avlan is a good name."

Ellaniel flicked the girl's forehead.

"Ow! What?"

"Of course it is."

Fellone rubbed her injury and pursed her lips while Avlan waved his hands and laughed. Ellaniel smiled, holding out her fingers for her son to play with. "I wonder what the First thought when Dawn was born."

"*Umukur's History* mentions a lot of singing and dancing," Fellone said.

"He wrote that two thousand years after the fact. I doubt it was anything more than a guess."

"You think they were like us, just staring with gaping

mouths like the pond fish out back?"

Ellaniel shrugged. "What would be going through the mind of someone who's never seen a child before? Would they even have imagined that tiny person would grow up to be like one of them?"

"But they would have seen animals, right? A lot of animals grow kids faster than people do, so they would have known about the whole children thing."

"That does make sense. You really are a smart girl, Fellone."

Fellone put her elbows on the armrest. "I wonder where the First came from, though. Why did they just appear in Originate?"

"That's a question scholars have spent millennia puzzling over," Ellaniel said. "Chances are, we'll never get the answer."

Fellone pouted. "That's just not fair!"

Avlan wriggled and started crying.

Ellaniel sighed internally. *And here's the other side of motherhood.*

Fellone was already at the door, hands over her ears. "Hey, you little traitor!" Ellaniel called.

"Your baby!" the girl said before escaping into the hall.

Ellaniel rocked Avlan back and forth. "All right, I hope you're just hungry . . . ."

The sound of dozens of shields locking in place was even more intimidating than ringing steel or the cocking of a crossbow. Arzan welcomed the sense of primal fear it instilled in him. If he felt it, so would the enemy.

"Hold fast!" he ordered. Vighkon and the rest of his ckols joined him at his side in the forest clearing as he charged the formation, sword in hand. With a roar, he struck a shield with his blade. The solid wooden board gave only the slightest bit under his assault, and a moment later a blunted training spear jabbed him in his chest plate.

"Attackers, retreat!"

He backed off with his men and sheathed his blade. "How's that?"

"They look solid enough," Pundur said from the sidelines. The man's emerald green sleeves strained at the seams as he crossed his arms. "How are they doing on maneuvers and assault?"

Arzan pointed to the other companies marching in step elsewhere in the forest clearing. "Second unit, arrow defense!"

The company immediately stopped and all ranks behind the first raised shields above their heads.

"Third unit, quick advance!"

The next group jogged in near perfect unison, shields and spears held up and ready.

"Fourth unit, intercept!"

The last company dropped out of their slow marching drill, changing course and charging the third company. The third company came to a halt and locked shields. The sounds of battle cries and crashing wood crowded the air as the two groups clashed.

Pundur turned to the side. "What do you think, Hashan?"

Hashan rubbed the ivory handle of his cane as he watched the mock battle. He shook his head. "I don't like it."

Arzan looked at his trainees, trying to find any fault with their techniques. "Is there a particular area—"

"I don't like how proficient we are becoming at the art of war," Hashan said. "Your volunteers are good, Arzan, and that frightens and saddens me." He sighed. "But the country needs men like them. Needs men like us."

Arzan watched the soldiers in silence. He agreed that this need was a tragedy. He'd asked the volunteers what it was that drove each of them to sign up. There were those who simply wanted the excitement and bragging rights, but the greater part had more sober motivations. They knew how serious a threat the empire was and wanted to defend their families. Arzan felt a kinship with them that was stronger now than ever. He yearned to be with Ellaniel and Avlan, to be holding his son in his arms. Yet more than that, he wanted them to be safe. To ensure that, this was where he had to be.

"I had Filgneir go through the archives," Arzan said,

waving him forward. "He managed to uncover schematics for the ballistae used in the Split."

"They had those?" Pundur asked as Filgneir unfolded the silk sheets and spread them for the crendens to see.

"There were a number of different types of catapults used in the war," Arzan said. "These are the only diagrams we've uncovered so far, but I think that's fine. A ballista is the most versatile style of anti-infantry artillery."

Pundur rubbed his chin. "It's like a giant crossbow."

"That's pretty much what it is, yes. It launches bolts big enough to plow straight through a shield wall. These were even designed to fit on both wagons and wall turrets."

"We need these for sure," Pundur said. "What are the materials?"

"Most of it's wood, with only a few bits of iron here and there. The most expensive part will be the sinew for the tension cord."

"Another acquisition to keep hidden," Hashan said. "What sort of cover can we possibly use this time?"

Pundur patted the man on the back. "We'll come up with something! Maybe say those leather girdles are coming back into fashion."

Filgneir folded up the artillery schematics and put a palm to his face. "Oh, not those. They were a pure travesty."

"Whatever we go with, it's going to be expensive," Hashan said. "Again."

"We can afford it better than total defeat against the empire," Arzan said.

The trainees' mock battle was nearing a conclusion, with one side pushing the other right up to the forest's edge. Hashan sighed and forced a smile. "Well, if we're done deciding all that, how about we take another look at my new grandson?"

Arzan laughed. "I can agree to that suggestion!"

Chapter 21

"How, in this type of reality, could any man predictably control the outcome of his touching any part of history?"

"For the last time, I am not going to help you usurp your father," Maltan said, not even looking up from his task of twisting two silver wires together.

Charva pressed her palms against his workbench. "Malty, you have the most cause to want him replaced! Why do you always resist this?"

Behind her, one of the three allies she'd invited with her shuffled his feet and cleared his throat. "Honorable Maltan, her grace has brought up many significant grievances against Crenden Thrake. It isn't as her detractors have said—this isn't just a personal vendetta aimed at her father. Leverie would benefit greatly from the policies she would put in place, many of which specifically involve your skills."

"And I wish it weren't the case that she would sell my services without my consent, Master Carlehn. Surely you wouldn't like it if a member of the House were to promise twenty of your wagons for public service, but without ever consulting you on the matter!"

"You served the city when Grandfather was crenden," Charva said. "The only reason you seclude yourself now is because Father forbids you from releasing your inventions."

Maltan finished twisting his wires and dipped them in a pan of water. "It's not just because of Crenden Thrake."

"Then what is it?" Carlehn asked. "I remember the days

when you were a font of knowledge. Not just the gin. You had ways of speeding up weaving, improving the crop harvests, making it easier to load the ships. Creedport could use a return of the sage."

"Hear, hear!" Master Danar said, raising his hand. "My fieldworkers still use the techniques you gave us all those years ago. They have done us wonders! But Creedport is always growing, and that means we're always in need of more."

"There was a fire on the south side earlier this week," Craftsman Remmesh spoke up. "Three buildings burned down, but a mill in the center of the disaster was left untouched. It was built with a coat of your flame retardant, and the man you gave the formula to died near a decade ago. If you would but train some of my apprentices, it could be a matter of saving lives!"

Maltan sighed and set his experiment down. "If you gentlemen would kindly leave, I wish to have a word with Charva alone."

Charva turned around and saw the hopeful looks on her supporters' faces. She nodded and they filed out of the tower.

"You do not see the bigger picture," Maltan said. "You don't understand what inventions do to society."

"I'm getting real tired of people going on about this big picture business," Charva said. "If you wouldn't mind enlightening me on what I'm missing?"

Maltan pressed his thin lips together. He arranged the pieces of his project neatly in the center of his worktable before striding over to his tangle of pulleys, his fingers pinching at his beard. "Do you know what happens when you pull this?" he asked as he placed a hand on one of the ropes.

"I assume it lifts something somewhere."

He tugged, causing a weight at the opposite end of the tower to bob and sway. He touched another rope. "And this one?"

Charva shrugged. "I'd think it would do something similar?"

He pulled. Another weight dropped from a perch, but this time it served to snap the shutters closed all around the tower. "Well then. Do you think your guess was right?"

"I'd give myself a half score."

"Meaning you were half wrong. You failed to predict the full outcome of my actions."

"The point, Malty?"

"The lesson," he said, walking over to the second weight and putting a stop to its pendulum swing, "is that even with comparatively simple systems, it is often difficult to know what will come of your actions."

Charva put her hands on her hips. "I'd hardly call this mess of pulleys a 'simple system'."

"Compared to both the natural world and human society, these pulleys are utterly laughable. Practitioners of science make it a habit to strip complexity from their work. We do everything in our power to refine and isolate so that we have the greatest opportunity to reproduce our results." He brushed his frayed sleeves. "And once we've mastered our knowledge of one little area, manifest it in physical form, and then unleash it into the world as some clever device or system, invariably it results in something we do not expect."

"That's not something you were afraid of before," Charva said. "These people who were just here—they remember when you blessed this city with your ingenuity. Even if the exact outcome of your inventions is unpredictable, it was certainly all positive!"

"Ah, but there you are mistaken. Tell me, what do you expect would have happened if my cotton gin had taken hold?"

"We'd have the highest cotton output of the whole continent."

"It would quite likely contribute to such," Maltan said. "One of my machines was capable of doing the work of twenty men. But what of those twenty men? What would become of them?"

Charva blinked. "I hadn't really thought about that."

"If the cotton gin were to gain hold, we would have thousands of laborers instantly out of work. Not only that, but with increased supply, the price of cotton would plummet. And inventions such as these do not stay put. The rest of Moshon would find a way to replicate my machine. We would eventually end up right back where we started, struggling to keep up with everyone else in a world where cotton is now so plentiful it's practically worthless."

"It's not like nothing of the sort has ever happened before," Charva said. "Look at the looms. Our weavers can make tapestries or rugs more than twice as fast as they could before the Desihm frames were introduced, and the market didn't become undone. In fact, we might have more weavers now than ever, with better quality and far more affordable prices."

"In the end, perhaps. In the process, how many livelihoods were disrupted? How many of the old weavers never regained stability, their mastery of the art now obsolete?"

Charva shrugged and leaned her shoulder against a shelf. "The world never sees everyone happy. Does that mean it's better not to have discovered fire? Or not to have developed steel? Should horses never have been tamed and trees never have been carved into ships?"

"And the things we have done with all of these," Maltan muttered. "What was war before fire, before swords, before cavalry and fleets?"

"That is a big change of subject."

"Is it?"

She narrowed her eyes. "What's this really about, Malty?"

He turned his back to her. Charva pushed off the shelf and went beside him. When she peeked at his face, she saw tears glistening in his eyes.

"I killed a child," he said quietly.

"What?"

"There was more than just the cotton gin. I'd also built a harvester meant to roll along the fields and gather the fibers straight off the plants. Thrake didn't want you to know what really happened, and so he never told you about the second machine. During one of the demonstrations, a seven-year-old boy got caught in the device. He was playing and got too close to the . . . . I will never forget the sound of the cogs jamming as his bones snapped, or the screams of his parents as they pulled out his broken body."

Charva remained speechless. She hadn't . . . . Why had her father kept this from her?

"Leave me be," Maltan said as he busied his hands gathering up tools. "My work doesn't deserve to travel beyond these walls."

She balled her fists. "That doesn't follow. Surely what happened was an accident."

He dropped his tools in a box with a clatter. "My machines are not safe!"

"Neither is a wagon. Would we burn all of those whenever an axle breaks and crushes someone?" She slammed her palms on a workbench. "People will always die somehow. That doesn't mean we can't try to make a better world."

"Out, Charva."

"You can't let yourself be blinded by—"

"Out!"

She drew herself back. Maltan had never shown her the fury that now molded his face.

"I never imagined you were this silly, Malty," she said before stepping out and slamming the door.

She instantly regretted that. Her merchant supporters shook their heads at her clear defeat.

"I had thought you already had him on board," Danar said.

"I will turn him around," Charva assured them calmly. "He . . . revealed to me his issue, but there should be a way to work through it. Just give me a little time."

"Fortunately, we can still get by under Thrake's policies," Carlehn said. "It's more a matter of things being better if Honorable Maltan returned to his old self."

Charva nodded. "Thank you for your understanding. I promise I will find a way to convince him."

"I certainly hope that you do," Remmesh said. "We can really use that man." He took his leave, followed by the others.

Charva let out a long breath and went over the story she had just learned. She put herself in Maltan's place, imagining what it would be like to witness a child die from something she had built. What she had told him was absolutely true. At the same time, she now understood that he was dealing with some deep scars. She didn't at all blame him for the accident, but there could be no way he wouldn't blame himself. How could he be healed?

She rubbed the hilt of her sword. She could really use a duel. *Maybe Ella needs a break from nursing.* She glanced back at the tower. *Maltan, you are going to help me—one way or another. And somehow, I'm going to help you.*

Chapter 22

"Between these two forms is a third
—a middle ground between fate and chaos."

The palace study was silent for a long while as Arzan leaned back in his chair and regarded his two visitors. Kalla and Ckol Magar stood across from his desk, he at rapt military attention, she a barely contained fidgety mess. Off to the side by the window, Ellaniel sat with a huge grin, Avlan on her knee and the fabric she had been working on discarded on the floor by her feet. Arzan fingered the clasp of his cape with deliberate exaggeration as his eyes passed from Kalla to Magar and back again.

"This—"

Kalla jumped at his first word.

"—is a serious request."

"W-well, yes, cousin-ah, my liege, um, Arzan."

Arzan struggled to keep an even countenance. "Are you ready to face the possible repercussions?"

"I-I am. O-or at least, I think I am. Um . . . what are the repercussions?"

He sighed and tapped his finger on the desk. "The House may disown you."

His cousin went pale. She balled her fists tight and pressed her arms to her sides. "Then so be it."

Arzan turned to Magar. "And you?"

"Being disavowed by the House is not something I wish of her, my liege," Magar said solemnly. "However, even if that happens, I vow on my honor that I will cherish her and dedicate everything I have to making her happy."

"I've heard other men make such vows," Arzan said. "And I've seen them broken."

Magar puffed his chest. "If I should fail in my promise, then may I be stripped of my title of ckol and banished from Senkani. Even that punishment would not match the torture inflicted on my soul by my own heart, for I love this woman and would sooner throw myself from the northern cliffs than bring her sorrow."

Arzan steepled his fingers in front of his face and pretended to debate with himself a difficult decision. He intended to leave them hanging a few moments, but Avlan's riveted infant stare threatened to break him. He slammed his palm atop the desk and grinned. "Welcome to the House, Magar!"

Ellaniel took Avlan in one arm and leaped from her chair to hug her friend tight. Kalla swayed, her eyes wide with shock. "I'm not being cast out?" A storm of emotions raced across her reddening face until finally she lunged out and slapped Arzan hard on the shoulder. "You were playing with me!"

Arzan doubled over laughing at her expression until his sides hurt. When he could finally breathe again, he found Ellaniel and Kalla already planning out the wedding. The mood was so contagious even Avlan started giggling.

"Next Wednesday. Magar's family won't be able to make it to the city any sooner."

"We'll send word to the rest of the House by nightfall. Do you want to hold it here or at your family estate?"

Magar stepped up to the side of Arzan's desk and put a hand up over his chest. "My sincerest thanks, my liege."

"In a little over a week's time, you won't need to use that title anymore," Arzan said. "Magar Redleaf. Has a nice ring to it, I think. Did you ever imagine when you signed up as a ckol that you would end up part of the House?"

Magar shook his head. "Not in a thousand years. In fact, I hadn't even put any thought into it when I first realized I was in love with Kalla. Know that I do not take my new station lightly. I will do everything in my power not to embarrass the

House with my common farmer heritage."

Arzan stood and put an arm around the man. "We're Redleafs, not Leverie. Besides, Kalla's a younger child of a lesser branch. It shouldn't upset even the more stuck up nobles too badly."

"The Leverie will still have something more to complain about."

"More than Kalla serving as a maid?"

Magar smiled and took his leave to rejoin his fiancée. Some time later, the two left with Filgneir to get matters moving. Ellaniel got back to her project, a hopeless smile stretched across her face from ear to ear—a look Arzan was sure he mirrored.

"I was starting to wonder if those two would ever go for it," Ellaniel said.

"A year overdue," Arzan agreed. He rubbed the spot where Kalla had hit him. "A lot of energy for someone that size."

"Did you really have to tease her like that?"

Arzan snickered remembering it all and even Avlan laughed. Ellaniel threaded her needle through the cloth. "And I'm outnumbered."

After a deep breath to steady himself, Arzan went back to the document he'd been reading before Kalla and Magar's little interruption.

Wallonta's Forge: One hundred fifty long spears, twenty-three shortswords. Secravan's Forge: Twelve long spears, thirty-five short spears, twenty gauntlet sets. Dargav's Forge: Five cuirasses, ninety-five helms. Carpenter Adlun: Forty tall shields, three thousand arrow shafts. Carpenter Rakr: Sixty longbows, four thousand fletched arrows. Craftsman Hadkein: One wheeled ballista. Tailor Devnalla: Two hundred gambesons.

Arzan ran a mental tally of their armory before adding the fresh arms. He knew he was going far above and beyond the pace agreed on with Hashan and Pundur, but it was only a matter of keeping things secret. The arms, and also the extra men he'd taken for training.

If I can keep it up, Senkani's army will be ready by this time next year. He stood and went to the map hanging on the wall. Ashathan had already capitulated, placing the empire right up against Heartsong's borders. Should Heartsong fall, Whitesail would be next, and then Leverie.

"That's the eighth time you've taken to staring at that map today," Ellaniel said.

Arzan forced himself around and back into his chair. "I wish we could be doing more."

"You grow more obsessive with every passing week. Slow down a bit, Arzan. At this rate, the empire will kill you with worry before there are even any blades drawn."

He fiddled with his cape clasp. "Perhaps you're right. But I simply can't rest easy knowing the Silver Tide is marching closer."

Ellaniel raised an eyebrow at him.

"I'll try, I'll try." He took a deep breath. "Your father's coming tomorrow, isn't he?"

"Yes, and we will keep it a simple lunch date. None of your—Avlan, don't tug at that." She gently pulled her spool of thread away from the boy's grasp.

"If you insist." Arzan got to parsing through the stack of petitions on his desk. "I wonder if he'll have another Xuo puzzle box."

"I keep telling him, Avlan's nowhere near old enough for those. He still isn't making sentences yet."

"That doesn't mean much," Arzan said with a grin. "He may only be a year-and-a-half and not talking much, but it's the quiet ones that hold the most surprises."

She held their son up in front of her. "You hear the expectations your father has for you? You'd better start reading soon so you can catch up to Fellone."

Avlan stared with wide, solemn eyes.

"How can you look at that face and see anything other than a contemplative spirit?" Arzan demanded with a laugh.

A knock came at the door, followed by the polished top of Filgneir's head. "Some letters for the two of you. Your grace, this one has the look of another duel request."

"Charva's certainly getting more and more antsy," Ellaniel said as she accepted the mail. She tore the seal and passed her eyes over the letter before glancing at Arzan with a half smile. "Perhaps it is about time I accepted another bout."

"You think you're back in shape for it?" Arzan asked.

Filgneir sighed. "So uncivilized. Swords are meant for smacking the enemy, not each other." He shook his head, closing the door as he went back into the hall.

Ellaniel rolled her eyes at him, stretching out her arm and clenching her fist. "I'm ready."

"Any news on her bid for crendess?"

She perused the letter one more time. "Hasn't written any more about it, so I'm guessing she's hit some snags."

"I never figured it was going to be easy," he said. "In any case—"

Another knock. Arzan didn't even have time to answer before Filgneir swung the door wide. "My liege, a messenger from Highcity. You're summoned to the Council immediately."

Arzan pressed his palms to his desk, jaw clenched. *Bloody shyles.*

Chapter 23

*"Helpful in the understanding of this
form of time travel is the concept of gates."*

All eyes in the Council chamber rested on Arzan as the echo of Ylnavar's block faded away. He kept his features neutral under the Speaker's scrutiny.

"Do you know why you're here?" Ylnavar asked, his voice ever professional, but now touched by a twinge of anger.

"I wait for you to tell me," Arzan said.

Ylnavar glared before putting his bony hand atop a sheet of paper and sliding it close. "I have here no fewer than forty signatures from witnesses testifying that they have seen Senkani men equipped for war and training in the martial arts. There are others attesting to seeing evidence of large numbers of weapons being produced by your blacksmiths, and even a *siege engine* sitting in one of your workshops." The Speaker crumpled the paper and threw it behind him with a sharp flick of his wrist. "The Council expressly forbade you from raising an army, Crenden Arzan!"

Arzan held tight to his armrests. "I recall you did."

"Did you have the slightest intention of following our decision?"

"No."

Roth rolled his eyes and exhaled loudly. "Well, at least he's not skirting around it like *some* people would."

Ylnavar rapped his block. "Silence! The Council hereby

demands that Senkani desist its militarization immediately and destroy its weapon stockpiles."

"You haven't put it up for vote," Arzan said.

"Smoke and ashes!" Thrake said. "You think a vote would change anything for you?"

"This was already voted on when you were forbidden from this nonsense in the first place," Mansar said.

"Haven't circumstances changed?" Arzan asked. "The empire is already on Heartsong's border. They're no longer some distant threat."

"This is no excuse for defying the Council," Ylnavar said.

Arzan brought his fist down on the stone table. "The Vron are going to crush us if we do nothing!"

"That is irrelevant to your violation of the rule of law," Ylnavar said. "You will disband your forces."

"No." The word left Arzan's mouth without hesitation.

Ylnavar stared at him as if Arzan had gone mad. "Take this any further and I will put a vote before the Council to have your House title removed from your name."

"Then you'll have to cast me out of the House as well," Pundur said, standing, "for Three Corners will not disband its army either!"

Athar wheezed. "What? Three Corners was raising one too?"

Hashan tapped his cane. "And Woodwise," he said calmly. "Are you ready to remove me also?"

Ylnavar ground his block into the table. "Arzan was little surprise, but you two? This is a gross insult to the authority of the Council! I call an immediate vote to remove all titles from Arzan, Pundur, and Hashan!" He raised his hand.

Thrake put his arm up. The others shifted uncomfortably.

"Removing three crendens is a bit much," old Loftham of Bluhall said. "How far along are their armies?"

"If the Council's concern is about lost profits, the money's already been spent," Pundur said. "Would you waste it all out of spite?"

"We shall not call enforcement of the law spite," Ylnavar said.

Thrake flicked his fingers. "Can't you see what this really is? House Redleaf is trying to get power to strong-arm the

Council!"

"We can't really say that if Hashan and Pundur have armies also," Athar said before shriveling into the opulent folds of his coat and vest at Thrake's glare.

"The rule of law is important," Hashan said. "However, we must also consider what laws are for—the security of the people they govern. My fellow crendens, we cannot allow for blind obedience to the law to overcome the actual needs of the country. While we squabble, the Vron Empire continues its approach. Do you expect Heartsong to hold off the Silver Tide? And once they fall, will Whitesail be able to withstand without our help?"

Crenden Warth rolled a pen between his palms, his eyes focused on the center of the table. "I hate to say it, but things are getting worrisome. I'm starting to think Arzan and Hashan are right."

Thrake jumped to his feet. "Smoke and ashes! This military nonsense is going to destroy us. We need to focus on the weaving race with Ranisa!"

"You're the fool here, Thrake!" Pundur growled. "So what if we fall behind in the markets? That's better than being dead."

"Mercenaries," Loftham said. "Perhaps it's time we look to hire some Fractorans."

"Flaming expensive," Mansar grumbled.

"Didn't we agree that would be our course of action?"

"The Vron are still as far as Heartsong."

"And how long will it take to contract an army and ship them over here?"

"Flaming expensive."

"All our choices are flaming expensive, Mansar!"

"What if we surrender?"

All argument paused as everyone stared at Warth. The man wrung his hands slowly. "I, um. I've heard that Nevygar's not as ruthless as all the stories. He's fine leaving the old crendens as vassal rulers so long as the empire gets its taxes. It's the resisting that gets them killed."

Arzan had been glad to no longer be the center of attention, but he couldn't let that go. "If you truly believe that to be an option, Warth, I suggest you step down right now."

Warth raised his eyes to him and bit his lip.

"I-Isn't it a possibility, though?" Athar said hoarsely.

Hashan struck his cane against the floor. "It is our duty to the people to keep them free from tyranny."

"In all Moshon's history since the overthrow of the monarchy, the aristocracies have recognized the commoner's right to his own labor," Arzan said. "We do not have the right to demand through taxation that which is not ours, and we certainly do not have the authority to give that right to a foreign invader!"

"It's not as if we recognize more rights of the commoners than the Vron do," Warth said. "They have a democratic republic allowing every citizen a vote in their government."

"To what end, mob rule?" Arzan countered. "Popular vote isn't an instrument of freedom—it's a shallow justification for lording over any minority."

"As opposed to the minority lording over the majority," Warth murmured.

Ylnavar rapped the table. "This is all far besides the point. We shall conclude our vote on whether to remove House titles from Arzan, Pundur, and Hashan."

No one joined Ylnavar and Thrake's votes.

Ylnavar stood, his block held tight in his bony fingers. "The Council has spoken. You three fools are allowed to do whatever you wish, to the shyles with law." He turned about and stalked out of the chamber.

Arzan fingered the clasp of his cape and regarded the remaining crendens. "So you know, I don't feel victory in this. Unless all of you prepare for war, we're still on the path to defeat." He rose from his chair, his sword plain at his side. "Even if you don't join us, Senkani at least will fight to the last breath. Freedom is worth that much."

Chapter 29

"While there are many things our pebble can influence, that influence can still be limited by certain factors of causal dependence."

The boots landed on Maltan's workbench with a thud as the deliveryman Grice dumped them from his bag. "Whaddya think? Good, eh?"

Maltan cut through shafts of sunlight pouring through his tower windows as he bent over the specimens, noting the respectable leather work and exceptionally thick heels. "You finally tracked down the cobbler you were looking for!"

"Six continents, no. Fellow's like that gnat always flyin' in the dark corner of the room—never sein' any of it except little buggy shadows in the corner of your vision." Grice patted the boots. "Made these m'self! Got 'prenticed to Master Harleaf in Highcity. Well, half 'prenticed. He shows me a thing or two whenever I'm in town."

"These do look like quality work," Maltan said. "I suppose this is the last I'll see of my favorite deliveryman."

"Favorite—Ha! As if I'm not late on half yer orders!"

"Speaking of . . . "

"Ah!" Grice lowered his pack and produced a padded bundle. "Boss says it was flamin' hard getting a hold of this."

"Which is why I paid such a handsome fee, so tell him his complaints will get him nowhere." He undid the cloth, unveiling a bronze measuring rod set with three little glass vials of oil. "Yes, this will make it so much easier leveling my sliders upstairs."

"I've no idea what you mean by that or how that contraption will help you, but glad it's working out. S'ppose I'll be off, then."

"Don't forget your boots!" Maltan called as the deliveryman turned for the exit.

Grice smiled back at him. "They're yours. I've a good eye for foot sizes, so it's sure they'll fit. You can finally get rid of those beat up old sandals of yours." He hummed a tune as he stepped out and thumped the door closed behind him.

"Such a nice fellow," Maltan said. He looked again at the boots and tried to remember the last time he'd even worn shoes. *I'll need to stop by the market and get some socks.*

The door swung open as he was setting the footwear aside. Crenden Thrake marched on in, stopping short of the maze of pulleys that never failed to trip him up when he proceeded any further. His face was stormy. "Maltan," he pointed his finger upwards, "with me."

The crenden started up the curved stairway before Maltan could even ask a question. Maltan sidled through his contraptions to get to the stairs and follow him. Thrake didn't stop at the second floor, but continued on all the way to the observation deck. When Maltan caught up, the crenden was leaning into the base of one of the arched windows and staring at the city below.

"Do you see what that is?" Thrake demanded.

Maltan followed his gaze to a large cluster of people crowding the main avenue. "That's new to me."

"It's Charva, riling up the mob."

Knowing what to look for, Maltan found the speck of bright red in among the mass.

"I ordered Ulman to put a stop to her nonsense," Thrake growled. "Even the captain is on her side, saying Council law affords her the freedom to undermine me!"

"He's right, as far as I'm aware," Maltan said. "So long as she's not advocating violence, it is perfectly legal to declare grievances, perceived or real."

"She's not even content turning the merchant class," Thrake said, ignoring him. "Now she's trying to paint me a villain to the commons. Do you know what she's saying?"

"I've a feeling you're going to tell me."

"She's feeding them all the lines the Redleaf gave the Council. She's fear mongering, promising the Silver Tide will crush all of Leverie unless she's named crendess. She wants to train up an army and march it together with Senkani to fight the empire in Heartsong. And what else? When they go, they'll have war engines designed by the great tinkerer Maltan."

Maltan sighed and shook his head. "She's saying that?"

"Are you working with her?"

"I'm abiding by your decree," Maltan said. "I produce nothing for use outside this tower."

The crenden glared at him. "And yet in every speech she gives, she boasts about how you will help her bring about some new era. She's so very confident your inventions will deliver us into a golden age."

"Much to my chagrin. I assure you that she is making these promises on her own."

Thrake pushed away from the ledge and stepped close to him. "You'd better be telling the truth. Leverie can't afford an upset in the established order. If we can just unite the aristocracy in focusing our all on the silk trade, we can become the biggest producer on the continent. We're winning, and we don't need you changing the game."

"I understand your ambitions, but isn't someone else already reordering the board?" Maltan asked. "Don't you think your daughter has a point about the Vron?"

Thrake laughed. "The empire is helping us, you old fool. It's their war that's upended our western competitors."

"And it's our turn soon on the chopping block, or do you really think the Silver Tide will just stop at our border?"

"Smoke and ashes!" Thrake said, waving his hand. "I'm sick of everyone using them as some boogieman to try and get power. The empire's stretched so thin we need nothing more than to smack them once or twice with a hired army. They're not worth taking our people from the fields." He narrowed his eyes on Maltan and scowled. "And I suppose if they came so far as Creedport, you probably would have some war engine up your sleeve that could turn the battle all on its own."

"My machines are not for killing," Maltan said softly.

Thrake snorted. "When his back's against the wall, any man will bend his principles." He abruptly turned away and stomped towards the stairs. "This is a waste of my time," he muttered. As he reached the first step, he paused. "If I do find you conspiring with my daughter, there will be repercussions. Do *not* defy me."

The crenden descended into the shadows, leaving Maltan standing alone by the arched windows. He let out a long breath and gazed down at the crowd Charva had gathered around her. "I think it's safe to say we're heading for tumultuous times."

Chapter 25

*"Regardless of most daily variation, a man
still wakes at dawn. A town's women still
draw water from the same well.
A harvest is still brought in during Fall."*

It was high noon by the time the carriage rattled its way out of the woods and into the Senkani training grounds. Eager to stretch her legs, Charva swung the door out and hopped free before the driver even had a chance to rein the horses to a stop. Her boots hit the bare ground without the slightest puff of dust, the soil still damp from last week's rains. A dozen yards away, within a wide circle of wood huts, the current batch of trainees practiced their shield maneuvers. The commanding officer's shouts alternated with the crashing of hundreds of wooden boards knocking into each other, creating an atmosphere not so different from the drill squares she had seen in Falcone. Horses drew to a stop behind her and two pairs of feet thumped to the ground, belonging to the two guards Captain Ulman had recommended to her. She smiled, feeling good about her growing influence. *I suppose I look official now with an escort.*

She spotted Arzan's familiar red cape underneath a wide blue tarp, surrounded by a small entourage of ckols and servants. Captain Vighkon saw her as she approached and gave a friendly wave.

Charva came under the tarp, thumbs hooked casually in her sword belt. "Things are lively around here."

"Good afternoon, your grace," Arzan said. He was

studying a campaign map on the table in front of him. Carved soldier figures marked spots all throughout Heartsong and Whitesail. Three little soldiers stood within Leverie.

"Ah, this game," Charva said.

Arzan nodded. "This game."

They both silently regarded the map for some moments before Arzan spoke again. "What brings you out, Charva?"

She smiled and rocked on her heels. "Boredom. Want of air. A desire to see a couple hundred dashing young men labor and sweat for the sake of honor and valor. I'm disappointed on the latter point. You need to find more handsome farm boys for your province."

Arzan snorted and tapped one of the carved soldiers, deep in thought. "If you want to see Ella, she's in the sparring circle past the hut over there."

Charva nodded. Instead of moving on, she waved to her guards. "Say, why don't you fellows go take a look at the shield training. Seems like the sort of thing boys are interested in." Her tone made it clear it wasn't a suggestion.

The Creedport guards left and Arzan looked up at her, brow raised.

"I'm calling the no-confidence vote," Charva said. "You may believe your voice is not respected in House Leverie, but if you speak at the proceedings I assure you it will give weight to my cause."

Arzan stared motionlessly at her for some moments. Out in the field, the commander shouted out his orders. "Shield wall!" *THUD*. "Arrow wall!" *THUD*. "Shield charge!"

"I have no love for Thrake," Arzan said at length. "Even so, he has not troubled me for some time now. I'm willing to leave things in the past and have peace."

"Hasn't troubled you?" She laughed. "What about the last Council meeting? He puts his vote into trying to get you untitled every chance he gets."

"Which is fully legal and within his right. I'm talking about nonsense like the Gricall fiasco."

Charva picked up a spare carved figure sitting along the map's edge and tacked it down over Creedport. "I will add to the army."

Arzan leaned over the map, once more deep in thought.

"I've already been gathering support with the people," she pressed. "Creedport sees the threat. They're ready to join the cause. My father is the only thing standing in their way."

He tapped the table with his fingers, then called that bald aide of his. "I'm going to need to discuss this with Filgneir. Your grace, would you afford me a few minutes?"

I have him, Charva thought. With a solemn nod but inward smile, she strode away from the tarp in the general direction of the training circle. The ground here was packed hard from months of foot traffic, and even the rains looked to have done nothing to soften it. The commander shouted more orders. A dust cloud preceded the mass of a four-layered shield charge three yards away from her. Charva watched and listened to their thundering boots. She could feel the vibration of their coordinated charge passing through the ground beneath her. It was impressive, if tempered by the motley look of the trainees. The men varied widely in age, from teenaged to perhaps middling forties. Aside from the rectangular red wall shields and wooden training swords, the only consistency of appearance was that there was none, everybody wearing whatever mix of clothes and colors they felt like. She wondered how much of an effect that had on their mindset. There was a reason professional soldiers had uniforms, wasn't there? At least, she remembered someone saying something about it being more than just telling allies apart on the battlefield.

The nearest men caught sight of her and Charva couldn't help feeling flattered as a few started tripping over their feet and messing up the formation. Feeling mischievous, she flashed a playful smile before going on her way, the commander shouting insults at the trainees.

The sparring circle lay on the other side of two huts and consisted of a thirty-foot arena ringed by a waist high picket fence. Half a dozen ckols stood watch around the perimeter, while inside a training master was set about bashing a stick relentlessly against Ellaniel's wooden sword. The speed with which the crendess defended impressed her, and she was made all the more striking by her outfit. Wearing a hardened leather cuirass atop a gray dress with split skirt over a set of dark brown chaps, she looked fully the part of a rogue adventurer ready to challenge the perils of some untamed wilds. She'd even taken a page from her husband's wardrobe sense with a red capelet that trailed her movements together with her loose brown hair.

One of the ckols bowed to Charva in greeting. She recognized him as Magar, the head of Ellaniel's guard. She put her palms atop the fence next to him and tipped forward to balance on her arms. "This brings back memories. Of course, you don't block so much with a rapier, so my training involved a lot more running away screaming."

"Not something I can imagine, your grace," Magar said.

"Your mind needs exercise, fellow." That brought a smile to the man's face. "Look, see, I knew some sense of humor existed beneath ckolish stoicism!"

The trainer called a halt and Ellaniel backed out towards the fence, her face and clothes drenched in sweat. Charva dropped her feet back to the ground and waved excitedly. "Still practicing with just a sword, I see."

Ellaniel paused her step, surprised at her visitor. "Charva? You came looking all the way out here?"

"One can't call a place out of the way if there's a crenden or crendess there," Charva said.

Ellaniel glanced around. "I don't know. This looks a lot like nowhere."

Something pressed up against Charva's leg and she turned her head down to see a small child using her to steady himself as he gazed between fence posts. Ellaniel's curly-haired maid was right there to heft him up and put a cloth in his hands. "You want to give your mommy a towel, Avlan?"

The boy held the cloth out over the fence. "Momma!"

Ellaniel pressed it to her face before putting her forehead against his and smiling. "Thank you, Avlan."

"Already two years old!" Charva said. "Hey, Avlan, can you say 'Auntie Charva'?"

The boy focused on her with wide, blue eyes. "Charcoal."

Ellaniel snickered into her towel as Charva ran a lock of her inky black hair through her fingers. "Huh. Well, close enough."

"So we have permission to call you Charcoal?" the maid asked.

Charva squinted at her. "Oh, that's right, you're the mouthy one."

Kalla stuck out her tongue.

"Careful, you don't want that snark rubbing off on your crenden-to-be," Charva said.

"Then you'll need to excuse yourself as well, your grace," Kalla said.

Charva leaned her hip against the fence. "If I could just get a maid like you, the Creedport palace wouldn't be half so boring. First thing when I'm crendess, I'm taking a lower-born Leverie girl and setting her to scrubbing the halls."

"Make sure she's short and prone to stealing bites from the kitchen," Magar said.

Kalla hopped around Charva and kicked Magar in the shin. Ellaniel wiped some more sweat from her neck. "So, what business brings you here, Charcoal?"

Charva gripped the fence and hung back. "Well, I thought I might challenge you to another duel, but it truly wouldn't be fair to fight you when you're already exhausted from training. Disappointing, that is."

"Don't tell me you want to bet again so you can cancel out the favor you owe me," Ellaniel said.

"I just want a fight!" Charva said. "No one in Creedport ever plays along."

Ellaniel glanced at Magar.

Magar cleared his throat. "I wouldn't be comfortable fighting a woman. What about the training master?"

The man in question happened to be drinking a water skin within earshot. "I train Redleafs and their ckols only. If I draw my blade on anyone else, it's to the death."

"Morbid fellow, isn't he?" Charva murmured.

Ellaniel nodded. "Very. Look, Magar, I could order you."

Charva sighed. "He'll just go easy on me. No fun in that." A thought crossed her mind and she snapped straight. "What about this: we'll appoint champions! That should be fun."

"Appoint what?"

"Champions," Charva repeated. "Out in the kingdoms they'll have tourneys where the nobles have a knight or someone represent them in the arena. Duel by proxy."

"I thought *you* wanted to duel," Ellaniel said.

"I can't do that, so next best thing. Here, I'll get one of my guards." Without waiting to hear any opposition, Charva jogged off to the main training area. She found only one of her escorts doing as she'd ordered. The young man stood watching the formations with utmost attention, and even looked as if he wanted to join in with the exercises.

"Where's the other one?" Charva asked.

The guard didn't remove his eyes from the trainees. "Off to find if there's any cook fire going, or so he told me, your grace."

"Come with me. I'll see if you've any sword skill."

Back at the circle, she found Magar already doing practice swings with a wooden sword. Kalla looked Charva's guardsman over. "Is he even a ckol?"

Charva shrugged. "Not as far as I know."

"It's been my dream since I was a kid," the guardsman said, "but Crenden Thrake took a dislike to me on account of my uncle."

That piqued Charva's curiosity. "Your uncle?"

"Captain Ulman."

Her interest rose immensely and she actually looked at him. Blond hair, violet eyes, square jaw with shaved chin, fairly well muscled. "What's your name?"

"Ersch, your grace."

"How about this, Ersch. Put up a good showing in your duel with Magar and I'll name you ckol."

It took a moment for her offer to sink in, but when it did she could see the excitement blossom in his eyes.

Ellaniel put her hands on the fence. "Wait. Only the crenden or crendess can appoint ckols."

"It won't be long until I fulfill that requirement," Charva said. "When the time comes, he can call on all of us here as witnesses to my deal."

Ellaniel raised her eyebrows. "Well, not my city." She hopped the fence and took Avlan from Kalla's arms. "Magar, if you win, you and Kalla get the whole week off for the harvest festival."

The prize caught Kalla's attention. She jumped up and shook the posts. "Magar, take his head!"

Ersch vaulted into the circle and caught a wooden

shortsword the training master tossed to him. He nodded his thanks without a word then proceeded to the center of the ring and saluted his opponent.

"Three rounds," Charva said. "Only hits to the body count. I suppose the training master can serve as scorekeep."

"Start at three paces," the trainer said, taking up position between the duelists. "Swords up."

Both men set into basic one-hand stance. Charva was able to identify tiny differences in each side, but both were typical Moshon style, with grounded footing and offhand at the ready to grab the hilt should reach need to be sacrificed for power. Only one big thing distinguished the two: Magar was left-handed.

Hmm, how well is Ersch going to deal with that?

"Fight!"

Ckol Magar went on the offense immediately, swinging straight in. Ersch's parry would have been magnificent were the blade not on the reverse side from normal. Magar's weapon slipped right past Ersch's defense to land with a *thwak* on his hardened leather chest piece right below the heart.

"One for Ckol Magar," the training master announced.

Ersch put a hand where he'd been struck, grimacing as he put pressure. He took a deep breath before tipping his head in respect. Magar returned to his starting place. Before the trainer shouted the beginning of the next round, Ersch glanced over at Charva with eyes that seemed to beg her forgiveness. She kept her face neutral and waited.

"Second round. Fight!"

This time it was Ersch who made the first move, dashing in and swinging hard from the left. The sweep connected with Magar's blade, throwing it out to the side, but Ersch's blade went with it. A follow-through slash would give Magar enough time to regain his guard. Instead, he reached out and grabbed the ckol's collar with his offhand, then twisted around and flipped him over his back and to the ground. The next Charva saw as the dust dissipated was Ersch's blade pressed to Magar's stomach.

"One for Guardsman Ersch."

Ersch reached out his arm to help up his opponent. Magar

accepted the gesture and sprung to his feet. "Good one, guardsman."

"Don't compliment him, beat him!" Kalla shouted. "You're captain of the crendess' guard."

Magar retook his starting position. "Sorry that I'll be beating you this round. Can't let the wife down."

"Oh, that's how it is," Ersch said settling back into stance. "Sadly, I can't yield. My family honor is on the line."

"Third round. Fight!"

The two men launched forward at once. Magar struck first. This time Ersch caught it on the correct side and parried it away. Their blades clashed several more times in a flurry of attacks, neither man getting close to a solid score. Ersch hopped back.

Kalla shook her fists. "You can do better than that, Magar!"

"He's not as—" Magar started.

Ersch rushed in, feinted with a slash, then hooked his foot behind Magar's ankle. Off balance, the ckol took a wild swing at his opponent, whacking the side of Ersch's head with a loud *thunk*. Kalla gasped as the guardsman dropped to the ground. Charva jumped the fence and ran up as Magar and the training master knelt over him.

"Six continents, I didn't mean to do that!" Magar said.

The trainer felt at the scalp. Charva saw a trickle of blood under his light hair. "Doesn't feel bad. He'll have a headache, but no permanent damage."

A groan escaped from Ersch's throat and the man opened his eyes.

Kalla crept up beside Magar. "D-did we win?"

"That was a foul," Charva said, not hiding the displeasure in her voice. "Seeing as how the points were tied and the fight won't be continuing, I think it fair to grant Ersch the win."

Ersch grinned and tried pushing himself up on his arms. "I think I missed something, but I'll take it."

"Don't just stand there, Kalla," Ellaniel said, coming up with Avlan in her arms. "Get the man a wetted cloth."

The maid pressed her lips and ran off towards the water barrel.

"I'm not the greatest expert in Falconian dueling rules,"

the training master said. "Does that foul count as a forfeit?"

Actually, in a proper duel their equipment alone was already breaking all manner of regulations, but Charva didn't bring that up. "Never mind that. Truly, even if Ersch here had lost in terms of points, I told him to put in a good showing. And so, Guardsman Ersch," she held her hand out to him with a smile, "I think you're due for a promotion."

Ersch gently grasped her hand and tipped his head. His voice verged on cracking, "You have my lifelong loyalty, my liege."

Hearing the title sent goosebumps up Charva's arms. Even if she wasn't the proper liege of Creedport just yet, she didn't correct him.

Kalla came back with the cloth and they got Ersch back to his feet and cleaned off. Charva turned to Ellaniel, grinning. "So, think you've rested up enough for a fight?"

An hour of sweat and bruises later, Charva and Ellaniel made their way back under Arzan's tarp. Crenden Redleaf was waiting.

"When do you want me to speak?" Arzan asked.

Ellaniel looked at both of them, the unspoken question in her face.

"Two days after the end of the harvest festival," Charva said.

Arzan nodded. "I'll see you then."

Chapter 26

*"Picture a traveler who has had many
chance encounters through his journey,
but when he comes to his destination, there
is still only one possible entrance into the city."*

"No."

Charva faced Maltan with her hands on her hips, glaring down at his worktable. "Yes."

"We're not going to start playing a child's game, my dear," Maltan said with a heavy sigh, not looking up from his springs and gears.

"If there's anything childish here, it's your refusal to help this city. Hundreds—thousands of lives are at stake."

"And wouldn't thousands of lives be lost if I did help you?"

"Vron lives."

She saw his eyebrow lift. "Really? Only Vron?"

"What is that supposed to mean?"

"It's weapons you want from me, is it not?" he asked. "That's what you've been promising the people, as I hear it."

Charva held one of Maltan's pulley ropes. "Yes, I want weapons. What is wrong with seeking tools to tip the balance in our favor?"

"Have you considered that one of the key strengths of the Vron is their readiness to adopt the things they encounter? You want an advantage today, but if you get it, do you expect the Silver Tide will sit idly by and let us keep it? They will learn. They will make it their own. And then they will use it against any who stand in their way."

She shook her head. "So what, then? You're saying we should face one of the strongest armies in the world with nothing they don't already have? We. Will. Lose."

Maltan stopped his work, setting down his tools and pressing his palms to the edges of the table.

"What's worse?" Charva asked. "That they get ideas for some new toys or that they conquer our country?"

"There are times when the greater good must be considered at the expense of a single nation."

Charva pressed her lips together and narrowed her eyes. "I don't want to be harsh, Malty, but you're not one to talk of the greater good when you don't even want to help the people outside your door."

"Charva—"

"The world is always moving on. The only difference is whether you're a leader or a follower, or if you're left behind entirely." She walked out.

It always ends the same. She bit down on her frustrations, wishing Maltan would just see reason. *I've enough support to succeed with the no-confidence vote, but Malty's backing would push it to a certainty.*

Preparations for the harvest festival were already well underway. Reaching the main avenue, she found the sides of the street lined with stalls half set. She ducked under strings tied with silk streamers as people readied to raise them into an overhead canopy of color. A few children darted around her to play in the low-hanging net, adults shouting at them not to damage the decorations.

What would it take for Maltan to move forward? He could change the world if only he cared. That was why Charva had wanted to become crendess in the first place. If her only accomplishment in life was to be his patron, she could die content.

Well, maybe I wouldn't settle for that being my only *accomplishment . . . .*

A girl ran giggling and screaming right into Charva's path as she played a game of tag with her friend. Charva blocked the child with her palm before she could ram head first into her stomach. The boy chasing her stopped and looked up.

"Charva! It's Charva!"

The folks nearby paused in their work and glanced over. A few men raised their fists in respect. The women tightened their lips. One went so far as to slap her man's arm down. "I can't believe you support her! She's going to send you off to war if she has her way."

"*Someone* needs to fight for the country!" he shot back.

Charva continued along the street, consciously holding her head high. *Two days. Two days will decide if I'm right.*

She went a ways before turning off the main street and finding Master Carlehn's estate. There wasn't really anything she needed to discuss with him before the no-confidence vote, but after her argument with Maltan she wanted an ally to talk to. She stepped up to the entrance of the two-story home and raised her hand to knock. She paused, noticing the door was slightly ajar. With a frown, she toed it open the whole way and peered into the foyer. "Carlehn?"

No one answered. She didn't even hear the slightest bit of activity from any of the servants.

She stepped into the house, her fingers loosening one of her daggers in its wrist sheath. "Carlehn?"

There was no one in the lounge or in the downstairs study. She poked her head in the kitchen and saw a pot steaming on the stove. The door to the firebox hung open, a log on the floor as if dropped on its way to the flames.

She drew her dagger as she went up the stairs. *Flame and embers!* The second floor was more of a mess. An end table sat on its side in the center of the hall, vase shards splayed across the floorboards. Paintings were scattered all about, their frames cracked. The door to the master bedroom hung on one hinge, the frame in pieces from being forced open. Charva advanced with soft steps to check each room. Most bore signs of a scuffle, but there were no bodies.

As soon as she confirmed the building was empty, she rushed back outside. "City guard! Where's the city guard?"

"Won't do you any good, yer grace."

She turned to see a wizened old woman sitting on the front steps of the house next door. "Did you witness what happened to Master Carlehn?"

"Crenden's men came and rounded them up."

"Ckols took him?"

"A couple. Most looked like hired thugs with badges." The woman spat.

"Where did they go?"

The old woman shrugged. "I don't know. I've been sitting here this whole time."

"Father's stepped over the line," Charva said tightly. She set her course for the town guard headquarters. "Forget the no-confidence vote. I'll have him arrested for abuse of authority." The turn of events almost made her laugh at how easy it made things, but she worried for Carlehn's safety.

She arrived at the guard office at a quick jog, her split skirts fluttering. A pair of guardsmen came out the front just as she ascended the short steps.

"You," she said. "Where is Captain Ulman?"

The two glanced at each other before waving her urgently to the side. "Your grace, you can't be here! The crenden removed Ulman from his post an hour ago and put Sergeant Rand in charge. There's a ckol inside with orders to apprehend you on sight!"

Charva gaped. "What?! He . . . he can't do that!"

"The guard's loyalty is already evenly split between you and your father, but the crenden's hired mercenaries to tip it in his favor. If we fight, there'll be a lot of blood, your grace."

"Embers! But where have these mercenaries come from?"

The sound of jingling armor pulled the guardsmen's attention back inside. "That's some of them right there!" They moved to cover her just as a set of five men in hardened leather and chain hurried out the door.

"That's the southeast section of the city. They say this one's a hothead, so we might have to rough him up a little. Careful of the . . . ." The mercenary's voice faded off as the group rushed down the street.

Charva put her back to the guard office wall. "Southeast. They must be going for Master Babar." The art commissioner was one of her latest supporters.

"It's a complete purge," the guardsman said.

The other shook his head in disgust. "A party even set off for Honorable Maltan's tower a few moments ago. The crenden isn't leaving anyone out of—"

Charva was already running. *The flaming shyle wouldn't dare!*

The festival preparations were just a blur in the side of her vision as she raced down the main avenue. Men and women shouted as she shoved past them, their curses breaking off when they recognized her. Charva barely even heard.

She reached the tower with her heart pounding in her chest. She didn't pause even to catch her breath, but shoved open the door and bulled her way inside. "Malty!" she wheezed.

A form moved at the far end of the tower, too deep in shadow for her to identify without letting her eyes adjust from the bright daylight outside. Even without seeing the details, she could tell from the man's gait that it was not Maltan.

"I wondered how long it would take for you to finally come whimpering back here," Crenden Thrake said.

Charva swallowed, forcing control of her rage and fear. "Where is Maltan?"

Her father strode deliberately through the tower until coming up against the tangle of pulleys that crisscrossed the center floor. He grabbed a rope and held firm. "This ridiculous game of yours is come to an end."

She put all the menace she could into her voice, "Where is —"

The clicking of armor stole her attention to the edges of the tower. Ckols and mercenaries in chain and plate stood ready on all sides, their hands on their hilts, prepared to draw. One particularly ugly one with scars crisscrossing his face even already had a dagger drawn and was testing the point with his finger.

Thrake rubbed the rope in his hand. "I always hated these flaming things." He produced a knife and sawed until the rope snapped, dropping two counterweights at opposite ends of the room.

"This is criminal!" Charva said. "I'll have this brought before the Council!"

Her father cut through a second rope, crashing another weight to the floor. "I am taking the necessary actions to maintain order in Creedport. You and those who support you, dear daughter, are guilty of treason."

"Every step I've taken is legal! You can't—"

"I can and I have! The businesses of your supporters have been seized and are pending new ownership. Everyone intending to vote against me has been imprisoned or expelled from the province. And Maltan—that lingering blight on this city is finally rid of!"

Charva struggled to keep her voice from breaking. "What did you do with him?"

"You and the Redleaf are always going on about how I don't do my part preparing us against the Vron. Well, I've tasked him with traveling to Heartsong and reporting to us on the status of the war. Funny how Arzan's insistence turns out to be useful, isn't it?"

She lunged forward, right into the hands of his ckols. "You've done what?!"

"He should be aboard the next ship west as we speak," he said. "They're set to sail, oh, right now."

She tore free from the ckols' grasp, ripping her sleeve, and dashed into the street. She made for the docks as fast as her legs would carry her. Tears turned the city into a blurry smear of color. Her lungs burned, but desperation drove her on. *Flaming shyle—that flaming shyle!*

She reached the water's edge to find the bay empty. A single ship was already at sea under full sail.

Her legs gave out beneath her, bringing her knees thudding against the wooden planks. She wiped her good sleeve over her face with a shaking arm to remove the sweat, and also her tears. She struggled to breathe and not to sob. Only faintly did she hear voices around her.

"Is she all right?"

"Get a guardsman, hurry!"

"Your grace, how may I help you?"

She tuned everything out. Everything but the lapping of the water against the docks. She listened to that sound until her father's voice came to her from behind.

"I've said it before, Charva. No one defies me. No one."

Chapter 27

"Despite the variation in events that the
traveler may have experienced leading up to
this moment, the city gate serves as a bottleneck
through which the ramifications may manifest."

The harvest festival was always Arzan's favorite time of
year. The city of Senkani became a riot of color—silk banners
flapping in the wind, painted stalls lining the streets, and
people from all over the province wearing their brightest reds
and yellows, greens and blues. Countless food stalls engorged
the air with the smells of a hundred different dishes. At every
corner could be found a juggler, a flute player, or a chorus
singing traditional songs a thousand years old. The theater
was always packed from dawn to dusk. Even now, with the
sun already creeping close to the western treetops, there were
hours of festivities still to go. Well, so long as the dark rain
clouds lumbering in the north were kind enough not to cut
things short.

"Perhaps one of these days we'll actually use our House
privilege and get a seat for one of the harvest plays," Ellaniel
said, glancing at the long theater line from under a headscarf
worn close over her golden eyes.

Arzan smiled and put his arm behind her as they strolled
on past. His other arm kept Avlan propped against his
shoulder, fast asleep after all the day's excitements. As
always, he had chosen a disguise for them—this year as a
merchant family of modest means. "You know I couldn't

stand being pampered all day. Besides, the festival's designed for commoners. Aristocrats always miss half the fun."

Ellaniel grinned. "By fun you mean getting crushed by crowds and smacking balls with a bat?"

"What else would I be referring to?"

She laughed and shook her head. "So undignified."

"It's worth it being undignified every once in a while."

"You have me there," she said, resting her head against him. "It's not so bad pretending to be a normal family."

They walked across the Middle Bridge. Arzan remembered the day years ago when he'd rescued Ellaniel here from the mob. He eyed her discretely, but saw no sign of her mood darkening.

At the other end of the bridge, they found a familiar woman dragging her bemused husband around by the sleeve. "Magar, hurry up. The sweet bean cakes always sell out before sunset."

"We've already had enough sweets to hold over a normal six-year-old for a year," Magar said. "How many—Oh, good afternoon my—" he interrupted himself with a cough. "Having fun, brother?"

Arzan smiled at the near slip. "Always."

Ellaniel took Avlan and walked over. "Kaa-ll-aa," she sang ominously.

Resignation set into the maid's face. "All right."

"You can still visit the cake stall, but bring him home straight after," Ellaniel said, handing the boy over.

"Come on, Magar, we're getting a whole basket." Kalla didn't wait for the guardsman's response before rushing on down the street. Magar nodded to the crenden and crendess and then followed.

Ellaniel locked her arm with Arzan's and they continued on. They passed a performer doing a disappearing act with a large hamster and dodged a group of teenagers splashing dyes on the street lanterns. Not much further, they saw a man with a wooden blade and makeshift shield playing soldier with some youngsters. The scene reminded Arzan of the days his father had spent giving him sword lessons.

"What do you want for dinner?" Ellaniel asked.

Arzan looked around at the stalls. The competing smells

in the air were all delicious. "We could just pick any of these at random, I'd wager. Everyone's secret family recipes come out during the festival."

"Does House Redleaf have one?"

"Of course it does. It's for wine, though."

"Naturally."

They settled on a professional-looking place in the main square that had tables set out for patrons. They ordered their food just as the sun began to dip below the tree line. Each dish was cooked on request, so Arzan and Ellaniel found a place to sit and wait out by the edge of the tables. They watched the light keeper set the street lanterns burning. The nearest had a splotch of dye thrown across its glass pane, making it cast a blue shadow over Arzan's half of the table.

"Ah, matching colors," Ellaniel said. "You've got blue, I've got yellow."

Their dishes arrived after some minutes, Arzan's a roasted duck with potatoes and spinach, Ellaniel's a set of fried pork slices, rice, and mushrooms. Without a word, they split them both between them and set about devouring their dinner. It was only halfway through that Ellaniel finally asked a question. "You're still serious about testifying in Creedport?"

"I said I would, didn't I?" The seats just around them were unoccupied save for the one being used by a disguised Captain Vighkon. It was safe for them to speak so long as they kept their voices low.

"The rumors of Charva losing her power base yesterday . . . ."

"Rumors," Arzan said, slicing a piece of breast off the duck. "Unless we get word from her or there's clear evidence of her fall, I am holding to my end of the deal."

Ellaniel poked her fork at her rice. "Good. Thrake needs to be held accountable for the wrongs he's done us."

"I can't say I disagree. However, a ruler can't let grudges guide his decisions. The real issue is that Leverie needs a strong army. That's all I'm fighting for."

"You can use that for your reason. I'll be sitting in the audience with a smile and a glass of wine as you roast him at the hearing."

Arzan chewed and swallowed a piece of meat. "I feel

sorry for Charva, living with that kind of father. That temper and arrogance . . . . What's it like having that for family?"

"You could read some of her letters if you really want to know."

He had to admit he was curious what kind of writer the young woman was. Did she show the same boisterous personality, or did pen and paper cultivate another side of her?

Someone started up a stringed melody nearby. They let the conversation drop in order to listen to the music. Arzan's eyes wandered around the square, happy to see his people having a good time. The food stalls were getting busier now, not just with the usual laborers finishing their day, but with families and couples. Even if he doubted there was such a thing as a perfect society, at the moment this felt close enough. His gaze fell on Ellaniel's face, or what he could see of it under her headscarf. She noticed his attention as she reached for her water cup and smiled.

A clamor of excited voices rose all around as someone with a torch approached a large stack of wood and straw in the center of the square. The sun was now sufficiently set for the flaming stick to be the most brilliant light around. Arzan dropped his fork onto his plate and stood, hand outreached to his wife. "Ready to dance?"

Ellaniel took his hand with a childlike grin and let Arzan pull her to her feet. Bright light washed over them as the bonfire was lit and the square cheered.

Someone pressed against his shoulder. He frowned right before hearing a whispered voice in his ear, "Crenden Thrake sends his regards."

Alarmed, Arzan kicked back his chair and twisted away, shoving Ellaniel out of the man's reach. He saw a flash of reflected firelight and felt a blade slash through the flesh of his forearm. Without thought to the pain, he grabbed at his longsword and swept it from its scabbard. "Ckols, to me!"

Another flash and Arzan caught a second strike with his blade. He saw his attacker now—a man with scars crisscrossing his hardened face. He wore a black cloak, clearly mercenary. It had to be such. No ckol would serve as an assassin, no matter what his crenden's orders. He pressed into his sword and shoved his assailant back.

Steel rang from a few yards away as Vighkon parried a blow from another assassin. Behind, he heard Ellaniel slip her shortsword from where she'd hidden it in her skirts. "Arzan . . . ."

He snapped his gaze around and saw that they were surrounded by at least half a dozen more cloaked men. Someone screamed from the next occupied table over. Arzan held his blade ready to meet whoever came at him first.

Three of them rushed in at once. With only a sword and no shield, he knew it was over for him. He lunged at the center assailant—the man with the scars. If he could take one down and buy even a little time, his ckols might at least be able to rescue Ellaniel.

Before he could close the gap, a ceramic bowl exploded against one of the assassin's heads, splaying food and shards all around and throwing the attackers off. Arzan's sword hit scarface, but slid off a metal plate hidden under his cloak. The assassin dodged Ellaniel's slash at his neck. Rather than follow through, the attackers backed off and formed a defensive circle.

The rest of his ckol guard contingent arrived. Four of his best fighters. Alone, they might have a difficult time, considering they only had hard leather under their commoner disguises. What really saved them was the growing mob of commoners. Commoners with swords and months of basic combat training.

The change of fortune brought a satisfied smirk to Arzan's face. "You picked the wrong place to carry out a murder."

The scarred assassin spit on the ground. "Flee!"

As one, the men charged the thinnest section of the mob. They cut down two Senkani in an instant, and the gap only widened as the villains wedged themselves through the opening, expertly parrying the few assaults that came at them.

"After them!" Arzan barked. He took the first step to lead the charge, but was stopped by Ellaniel's hand on his shoulder.

"Arzan, the palace!"

He turned his head and saw smoke billowing into the air across the river. His breath caught at remembering they'd sent

Kalla and Magar home with Avlan. By now they would surely
—

Ellaniel was already pushing her way through the crowd. Arzan sheathed his sword and shoved his way after her. Once out of the throng, they ran nonstop through streets where people grew increasingly alarmed at the smoke gushing out over the rooftops, too massive and messy to be from a festival fire. As Arzan gazed at it, a drop of water struck his face. The start of a storm. When they reached the main gate, Filgneir already had servants and commoners in a bucket brigade in front of the main doors. Black clouds poured out of most of the north wing's windows. Ellaniel was first inside, her headscarf long abandoned and her hair streaming as she dashed up the stairs. "Where's Avlan?"

Arzan noted the absence of guards and the blood staining some of the rugs. "Ella, sword ready!" He drew his own, Vighkon and the other ckols catching up to him as he ascended the steps. Ellaniel either didn't hear him or didn't care, ducking under smoke and running through to the north wing without pause.

He hurried after her, comforted only in the knowledge that at least the stone building wouldn't come crashing down on them and that the flames would burn themselves out fairly quickly—furniture and cloth the only fuel to feed them.

A ckol lay dead against a wall. Arzan's boots squished in carpet soaked with blood as he went past. Avlan's room was just ahead, Ellaniel already there, banging on the door while servants rushed past her down the hall with buckets and wet cloth. The smoke thickened as Arzan pushed her aside and rammed the door. It barely budged.

"Who's there?" a familiar voice called from inside.

"Magar! It's us! Where's Avlan?"

There was a crash inside the room and the door swung open. Magar stood hunched in the entryway, his arm clutching at a blood soaked gash in his tunic and leather armor. Kalla was at the other end of the darkened room, huddled protectively over the toddler. "I held them off, my liege," Magar said. "I managed to . . . ," he winced, "barricade the door."

Arzan dropped his sword and went to Avlan. He found his

son unharmed, though the child was staring out with wide, confused eyes at the chaos around him. Ellaniel swooped by and took him up in her arms. A moment later, Kalla cried out. The maid sobbed and clutched at Magar, now crumpled to the floor. "Magar! Magar, no!"

Arzan shot his gaze between Avlan and Magar before dropping to his knees beside the ckol and checking for a pulse. "I don't feel a beat."

Kalla bent her head over her husband's face. "No!"

Ellaniel came over, still holding Avlan tight. She knelt down and hugged Kalla with her free arm, careful to keep the dead body from the boy's eyes. Tears glistened on her cheeks. "I'm sorry. Thank you. I'm sorry."

"He always . . . regretted," Kalla said, her body and voice shaking, "He was sorry he . . . could not protect . . . you at the . . . theater." No more words followed as she broke down and wept.

Rage clouded Arzan's vision more than the smoke that surrounded him. One word burned in his mind hotter than any physical flame could. He let it growl from his lips, wishing its utterance could bring it into being in front of him so that he might have a target for his blade.

"Thrake."

Chapter 28

"Of course, there's also the possibility that the traveler's encounters and decisions could make him change his destination entirely."

The rain hammered down in cold, heavy sheets, forcing Retyar to pull his blanket tighter against himself as he bemoaned his carelessness at getting caught out in this blasted weather. Even if his usual foraging spots were getting thin, it was stupid to come out so far with the storm approaching. Now here he was, covering on a rocky ledge beneath a creaky wooden bridge upstream of his cave hideout, having to decide whether to soak himself making it back or brave through the night where he was. Already, the stream was turning into a raging flood underneath his perch, making the latter option less and less appealing. The only thing keeping him from moving this instant was the dread of navigating the slippery rocks in the pitch darkness. That and the group of travelers choosing now of all times to come down the road. *It's only going to get worse here as the night goes on. Better climb down and get to the cave as soon as the travelers are past.*

The travelers reached the bridge, their splashing and pounding boots against wood amplified by the chasm walls. They had a horse with them too, pulling a cart or carriage. Rather than carry on down the road, though, they went halfway across, then stopped.

Retyar frowned. Who in their right mind would want to stand out here in this weather? As if to punctuate the point, the rain doubled its downpour. A sudden thought seized him. Were these men planning to do maintenance on the bridge? His fingers tightened on his makeshift cloak. *No, that's stupid. Unless the bridge were in complete shambles, no one would do that on a night like this.*

Would they?

Minutes passed. The chasm's acoustics turned the thuds of the restless horse's hooves into heavy drumbeats.

"Much . . . you reckon?" The man's voice carried incredibly well despite the rain and the rushing torrent.

" . . . tience."

A different kind of unease settled over him. There was something ominous about this group. Retyar waited with shallow breaths, hoping that the sound amplification didn't work the other way as well. A long, tense hour went by until he heard the splashes of another group approaching.

An orange glow seeped over the edges of the bridge and gave hints of shape to the top the chasm. Another horse with cart or carriage rumbled overhead and came to a stop. Hinges creaked and boots clambered over wood. A lull in the storm made it easy for Retyar to hear their words.

"How'd it go?"

"There were some complications. The crenden and crendess were better defended than we anticipated. We did manage to do some damage to the palace. Killed some ckols before setting it ablaze."

Retyar held his breath at the realization of what kind of people these were. He felt at the wrappings on his rifle.

"And the other target?"

The rain picked up again, drowning out the response.

There was a loud *thwak* of something getting hit. "Blood and dirt! That was the simplest job!"

" . . . shouldn't have . . . too soft . . . . Cracked after second child."

"What . . . her?"

" . . . second cart."

"And . . . couldn't finish . . . . No loose strings."

Someone walked down the bridge and into the mud.

Retyar tried not to let his emotions get caught up in what was going on. There was nothing he could do. It was just history. Matters done with and sealed under hundreds of years of dust. Try as he might to think that way, it still made him queasy to hear the creaking of wood as someone climbed onto a cart. He couldn't help but imagine the man drawing a blade on some kid.

"Don't like . . . wetting . . . blade with children's . . . ."

" . . . questioning orders."

The chasm flashed with stark white light that for an instant revealed the sweeping waters mere feet from Retyar's perch. He covered his ears right before the thunder boomed all around, rattling him to the core. The storm came down harder than ever, pelting every surface with heavy droplets. Knowing this wouldn't be the end of the thunder, he wrapped part of his blanket over his ears and tied it firm. Like this, he wouldn't have to listen to the atrocity being committed above, either.

Another flash came right as something tumbled over the side of the bridge and splashed into the water. Retyar started. *They just threw the kid into the river.* In moments, the men left the bridge.

Horrified with what had just transpired, Retyar fidgeting in place until the killers were likely some hundred yards gone, then scrambled up to the surface. He moved as quickly as he could manage over the dark, rain slicked stones, careful not to step into the mud and leave footsteps. Lightning flashed at least every half minute, giving him some idea of the footing before him. His soaked clothing weighed him down, adding another burden over that of his heavy heart.

He used the lightning to check the waters as well as his path, but saw no sign of the child. He pressed on until finally reaching the end of the ravine. Feeling for the edge, he leaned out and waited until a bolt flashed him the sight of a white dress and pale arms pressed against a boulder at the very mouth of the river. The rock was the only thing between her and the open expanse of dark, chaotic sea.

Retyar remained frozen in place. What should he do? *Nothing*, he reasoned. *She's probably already dead. Even if she's not, this is history. It's out of my hands.*

The next crack of lightning revealed a new terror. Twin fins cutting through the ocean waves. A shyle, probably attracted by blood.

Retyar bit his lip and sprang into action. He slid down into the ravine, landing on a ledge with what he guessed would be about five feet of water separating him from the boulder. He wanted to use his flashlight to make sure, but the glow might travel for miles even in this storm. Another flash of lightning gave him the exact distance to the rock. He jumped out as the ravine faded into darkness, the cloth over his ears muffling the rolling rumble of thunder. His feet landed at an angle, making him slip sideways and bang his knee before he could get a serviceable grip. He gritted his teeth against the pain and hurried to his task. The icy cold numbed out his fingers, making it hard for him to hold on and feel out for the girl. On impulse, he glanced out to sea. Right at that moment, lightning illuminated the waters and the double fins that were now dangerously close.

Retyar's heart thudded in his ears as he fumbled for his rifle. He stripped off the cloth covering, charged a round, and pointed it out at the darkness with his finger over the trigger. The rain hammered against his back, the wet seeping through even his armor vest. The roar of the storm came through the cloth over his ears in a smothered breath. His foot shifted on the slick stone. His eyes strained to see. He held his breath.

The sky flashed, showing him two rows of serrated teeth leaping straight at him over the water. He squeezed the trigger, the air in his lungs escaping in a pathetic gasp. The recoil rammed his shoulder hard right before the shyle crashed into him full force, throwing him into the raging torrent. His arms instinctively thrashed about and found purchase on a crack in the chasm wall. He pulled himself up and sputtered for air, then lifted completely out of the intense current. No longer caring for the possible consequences, he ripped out his flashlight and swept the area. The monster was nowhere in sight. Was it dead or had it retreated? He'd take either one.

Figuring he'd let himself freak out over the encounter later, Retyar jumped back onto the boulder. The girl was still there. He couldn't tell if she still lived. Up close and with a steady light source, he saw that she was a mess of bruises and cuts. Who knew how many bones were broken. Even if he wanted to save her, he was no doctor. He grit his teeth. It might be better for her at this point to just die.

He pulled her from the water.

Part II:
Ripple

Chapter 29

Mud squelched underfoot as the procession trod through the grassy field. To either side, stone pillars poked up through the green, each marking a spot where a prominent man or woman of Woodwise lay buried. The line of mourners in black flowed slowly between these on their way to a fresh hole in the ground, beside which sat a coffin painted in the Leverie colors. Off in the distance, a deer eyed the scene, then escaped into the forest.

Arzan glanced up at the late morning sun, then down at his wife, who clung tightly to his arm, her eyes fixated on the field. The messenger had come early in the morning following the Senkani attack, bearing news that the Woodwise palace had been struck as well. Crenden Hashan and three of his guards had not been as well prepared as the Redleafs. The assassins had killed Arzan's father-in-law and slipped away without any of the servants even hearing a thing. His blood boiled remembering Ellaniel dropping to her knees and sobbing at the news. And only moments after, a ckol arrived from Fellone's mansion. There it had been a slaughter, the whole staff killed and the estate burned to the ground. The bodies were charred beyond recognition, but Fellone was surely dead.

The other crendens attended Hashan's funeral—all except for one. Ylnavar claimed Thrake's absence could mean anything, but there was no doubt in Arzan's mind that the attacks were all his handiwork. His anger overflowed at the thought he had been ready to forgive the vile snake. Yes, he'd been planning to testify at Charva's no-confidence vote, but not out of spite. All he wanted was the country's security.

And this was how Thrake responded.

Athar was the last to arrive at the grave site, his bulbous face streaming sweat from the short excursion. Ellaniel's cousin Odavan nodded and began his eulogy. Arzan hardly listened, and Ellaniel stared blankly at the coffin. She was without doubt the hardest hit in all this. She had lost her father and a girl she treated as something between a sister and a daughter. Her closest friend had lost her husband. Her life and that of her son's had been threatened. All in one night.

Odavan finished his speech and six ckols lowered the body of their former crenden into the pit. Pundur leaned over. "I can see it in your eyes." he said quietly. "You mean vengeance."

"Shouldn't I?" Arzan asked. "Why would I let him get away with this?"

"We don't know it was Thrake."

"One of the assassins as much as admitted to it," Arzan said.

"The Council will decide," Pundur said. "A lone crenden cannot directly convict or punish another crenden."

Arzan glanced around at the rulers gathered. "And can I count on them?"

Pundur placed a hand on Arzan's shoulder. "This is a serious crime. Have some faith in the Council."

Arzan clenched his fists. "A Council composed of Leverie."

"And so was Hashan. Your vision is clouded. The House will not let the culprits go unpunished."

Dirt thudded on wood as the ckols began filling the hole. Ellaniel held Arzan even tighter. They shoveled more and more, each scoop getting quieter as the coffin got covered. Arzan took a deep breath to steady his rage. "We shall see."

The Council gathered in Hashan's upstairs meeting room. Though it was nothing like the capitol in Highcity, the large table served well enough for the eight of them. There was also adequate space along the walls for the aids and ckols, even if they did block the wide windows. Stormy faces contrasted sharply with the bright gardens outside. Pundur was right. The Council was not going to let this crime slide.

Ylnavar rapped his block. It did not have the same quality as when hit against the stone Council table, but it served. "We shall now discuss our response to the murder of Hashan Leverie of Woodwise and the assault against House Redleaf of Senkani."

Crenden Lofthan raised his hand. "First, who are the possible culprits?"

"The victims were Thrakes enemies," Arzan said, not bothering to conceal the anger in his voice. "My attacker identified Thrake as his employer. You'll also note Thrake's not here."

"Thought he already learned his lessen last time his mercenaries flew off the handle and killed Gricall," Warth muttered.

Roth raised his hand. "Before any further accusations fly about, I must mention I received a letter from Creedport moments before setting out for Woodwise. Thrake declares his innocence in this."

Arzan struck the table. "He wants to play at that, then? He knows full well he has no case or he would have come in person."

Roth produced a folded paper from his vest pocket and set it on the table. "He wrote he was afraid emotion would take the place of reason and evidence."

Arzan rose from his chair. "Certainly he would rather have the chance to weasel out with word games when the family of a murdered man stands before him!"

The rap of Ylnavar's block cut through the air. "Arzan, sit down. Roth, why is it you were the one he sent his letter to?"

Roth shrugged as Arzan grudgingly lowered himself back into his seat. "From the wording, I suspect he sent others out to everyone else and I was simply the one to receive it in time."

"My aide will sift my letters as soon as I return," Ylnavar said. "In the meantime, his claim of innocence is noted."

"Are there . . . any . . . other suspects?" Athar asked, his wheezing more pronounced than usual. He kept his eyes on the table as he fiddled his thick fingers, the whole ordeal clearly overwhelming him.

"Thrake is the culprit!" Arzan said. "Try him and hang him!"

"The laws of the Council will be obeyed," Ylnavar said. "There will be a fair trial, with the defendant having a chance to present his side in person."

"In person? And how long will that take? There's enough evidence here now for a conviction."

"Oh? I'm not so sure of that." Mansar weaved his fingers through his beard as Arzan turned an incredulous gaze on him. "All we have really is speculation and a single supposed confession heard in the middle of a fight. With only one witness to that, no less."

"Just me? No. Ellaniel, my ckols, the commoners—there was an entire crowd there." Even as he said it, it dawned on Arzan that the assassin had spoken in a whisper. Maybe he really was the only one to have heard it. What other evidence was there? The use of mercenaries? Anyone could hire them, and there were no captives to corroborate what Arzan heard.

Pundur raised his hand. "We should conduct a thorough questioning of the Creedport palace staff. If Thrake is guilty, there should be evidence in their testimony."

Arzan remembered the rumors of Thrake carrying out a purge. The new staff would be those trained to derail the investigation. By common sense, clearing the palace of those disloyal was obvious evidence of guilt. By the letter of the law, it completely protected him.

Without waiting to hear more, Arzan pushed back his chair and rose. "Deal with this as you will, then."

"Arzan, don't be hasty!" Pundur called. "We're just trying to get a handle on what happened."

"I'll be back when the Council shows it understands the meaning of justice," Arzan said, throwing the door open and storming out.

He found Ellaniel alone in her father's study, Hashan's cane in her hands. Her eyes, red from crying, stared down at the ivory and wood. Her hands and the cane stood out sharply against the sea of plain black fabric that made up her dress. Wordlessly, he went to give her a comforting embrace.

"Have they decided what they will do with Thrake?" Ellaniel asked. Her voice was flat and hoarse.

Arzan closed his eyes. "The Council needs to have him present in order to hold the trial."

He felt her tense and let go just as she struck the cane into the hardwood floor. She leaned into the handle, her hands trembling, her hair hiding her downturned face. Arzan rubbed her back and looked around at the study. The shelves were filled with volumes on the textile trade, but also on the growing of exotic plants. Paintings of far off landscapes hung on the walls. On the corner of his desk, he saw a Xuo puzzle box of the kind he had given Avlan. His own throat caught at thinking of the joy his father-in-law must have felt when he traded for it off a cargo ship from Originate.

"They killed him in this room," she said quietly. "His body was there by the window. A single stab through the heart. I can only imagine how frightened he must have been, alone against a man in armor and cloak holding a sword wet with his ckols' blood. And what did Fellone have to . . . ." she choked on the words. "And . . . all the servants . . . ."

Arzan held her shoulders and put his head to hers. "He won't go unpunished, Ella."

Voices seeped in from the hall, low, yet words discernible.

"Irritating timing this was." He recognized Roth's flippant tone. "I was just getting in the best mood with this lovely girl from my north plantations."

"That's every other day for you, isn't it?" Mansar's voice.

"Ah, that gives me too much credit."

Arzan wished the two would find some other corner of the mansion to prattle in. He contemplated going out there and kicking them down the stairs to the first floor.

"There's a silver lining to it all, though," Mansar said. "At least we no longer have to put up with Hashan's idiocy."

Ellaniel's shoulders tensed. Arzan could hardly believe his

ears either.

"Cousin," Roth said, "that's a bit harsh to say on the same day as the funeral."

"And it would be more tasteful tomorrow? Whether now or then, I'll tell you it's better having Odavan in charge of Woodwise. This army nonsense was draining the city dry. Whatever the tool he used, Thrake did good for the House."

Ellaniel shrugged away Arzan's hands and stood to full height. She gripped the cane tightly in her hands, a fire blazing behind her golden eyes. Arzan stopped her from stepping towards the door. He knew how she felt. He also knew that clubbing the man to death wasn't going to solve anything, no matter how much he himself wanted to do just that.

"We can't really condone murder, Mansar . . . ."

"I'm not condoning it. I'm just saying we're better off for it. The others must all be thinking the same thing, even if they don't spell it out."

"It's still bloodshed. Not the sort of thing a Leverie should be dirtying himself with. Six continents, this is the aristocracies!"

"Certainly. The House is above such things. For sure, there's no evidence Thrake was involved in any way."

Roth sighed loudly. "Sly, dirty politics. Almost as complicated as a woman's heart."

Floorboards creaked as the men moved on down the hall. With their receding footsteps went any reservations Arzan had over what he must do. He drew Ellaniel close to him and let the resolve solidify in his mind.

"Ella, we're returning to Senkani."

Chapter 30

"The crenden is not to be disturbed."

"Flame and embers, I don't care!" Charva growled. "Let me in!"

The ckol guarding her father's study rolled his eyes. "You're lucky as it is you're only under house arrest, your grace. Don't make me take you to the dungeon."

"Ah, so you wish to add unlawful imprisonment to the list of Thrake's crimes? Go ahead!"

The guard sighed. "Your grace . . . ."

A servant rounded the corner with a covered tray. Charva glanced at the angle of light streaming through the window at the hall's end. Lunch time. Perhaps this could be her chance to—

"No, you don't, your grace." Another ckol, her appointed prison warden, stepped in with hands up to shoo her off.

Charva grounded her stance. "I am not lea—"

The cuff to the head caught her completely by surprise. She staggered back, reeling in equal parts from the blow and the fact that a ckol had just *hit* her.

"I'm to maintain the security of the crenden's study," the door guard said. "By any means necessary."

Furious, Charva's hand went right to her sword hilt, but she stopped cold as she saw the ckol's hand move to his. She swallowed a dry lump in her throat and balled up her empty fist at her side.

"When I'm crendess, I'll see you in the street eating the fish stall's leftovers." The words felt weak to her even as they left her mouth. She turned on her heel and stormed down the hall, trying not to show she was absolutely terrified. Her personal warden shadowed a few paces behind, matching her every step until she stopped in front of the library. She caught sight of Throrne inside. Her brother was seated right and proper at the table, face studiously buried in a book. Charva made to enter the room and was barred by the ckol's arm. "What, you think I'll take him hostage or some such?"

The ckol remained as he was. "Flame and embers," Charva muttered. She undid her sword belt with a flourish and threw it at his feet, weapon and all. The man lifted his arm and Charva went in and slammed the door behind her.

Throrne kept his nose in his studies, making a conspicuous point of ignoring her. He hadn't really changed that much over the past few years. Now taller than her by a few inches, he was still thin and awkward-looking even in tailored vest and trousers. He wasn't any warmer to her, either. Charva went to one of the shelves, her eyes sweeping over the books without real interest. Still paid no heed, she pinched his book off the table. "*On Practical City Logistics*," she read. She dropped it back down, the cover folding closed on impact. "Father isn't seeing me."

Throrne leaned back with crossed arms, grudgingly focusing on her. "I could hear as much. No surprise."

"The Council will not stand for this. At the very least, Ellaniel and Arzan will do their best to help me once they hear what's happened."

With a deep breath, her brother reached out for the book. "I guess you haven't heard."

She narrowed her eyes. "Heard what?"

"Assassins attacked the Redleafs and set fire to the palace in Senkani. Woodwise too. Crenden Hashan is dead."

Charva raised a hand to her mouth. "Hashan? What . . . what of Ellaniel and Arzan? Avlan?"

"I don't know. If people aren't sure, they're probably alive."

She gripped the back of a chair. "This is why he's hiding away in his study, then? He knows he's stepped over the line!" Without a further thought, she strode to the window and shoved the pane open.

"Sis?"

"Don't call the guard," Charva said and, steeling her resolve, swung her feet out onto the narrow ledge outside. If her father wasn't letting her through the door, she'd just have to find another way in. Servants yelped and shouted below as she shimmied her way along, yet she calculated she had enough time before they could rush upstairs. Her Falconian split skirt and pants made it exquisitely easy to navigate without getting caught on the window trimmings, and in moments she was outside the study. Trying the window, she found it locked. She slipped one of her daggers into her palm and rammed the hilt into the glass, shattering the pane closest to the latch. In moments, she was twisting inside and landed her feet on plush rug.

And came face to face with a wild man rushing towards her with a sword.

A broken squeak escaped from Charva's throat as she brought her dagger up and caught the blade. The sword slipped to the side, edge scraping along her weapon with a spark, the tip gouging a line down the front panel of the cabinet beside her. She fumbled backwards from the force, her foot catching on the curtain and bringing her crashing into the corner wall. The man loomed over her, his sword held out to her chest. It was Thrake, but nothing like the man she knew. A steel breastplate was strapped tightly over his usual finery, his hair was disheveled, and the look in his dark blue eyes was that of complete terror.

"Of course!" he shouted, spittle catching on his dark beard. "Of course it was to be you! You're the one to slit my throat, get the better of me in my own palace!"

A fist banged against the door. "My liege!"

Charva shot her eyes from her father's rabid face to the quivering blade in his hand, then to the dagger in hers. "What, no! That's not—"

The ckols kicked the door in and rushed inside with weapons drawn. Their arrival shocked Thrake more than it did her, leaving her an opening to scramble to her feet. That was as far as she got before her father grabbed her by the throat and slammed her against the cabinet hard enough that her vision reeled. Next she knew, a ckol was twisting the dagger from her hand while Thrake held his sword up to her face, his grip on her throat tightening like a vice. She gagged, trying to draw in breath.

"Family means nothing to you!" Thrake screamed. "You side with upstart vagabonds against your own father in your childish quest for power! Ashes and smoke, smoke and ashes!"

Charva tried to gasp for air. All that came of it was a strangled croak as she clawed at his fingers with the hand she still had free.

"You. The Redleafs. The Council. Maltan. My own aides. Everyone conspires against me! Throrne—he's the only one I can rely on!"

The edges of her vision started to darken. The sword tip blurred. She felt her left hand pulled away and restrained.

Thrake abruptly lowered his sword, drew her forward, and bashed her into the cabinet once more before releasing his grip. Charva fell over, her breaths coming in broken gasps and coughs.

"The dungeon with her," the crenden commanded.

The ckols were quick to obey, dragging her out of the study before she even had the strength to lift her legs. She never would have thought she'd be so happy to get such a sentence. Still struggling to fill her lungs, she seized one last glimpse of her father as they carried her from the room. The man fell down into his chair and rested his blade on his knee. She couldn't be sure through the tears still in her eyes, but she didn't see smugness or anger in that posture—only fear.

The door frame veiled him from sight, and Charva's concerns shifted to frantic worries about the future.

Both hers and the country's.

Chapter 31

Arzan fastened the clasp of his crimson cape with a sharp tug. Out through the bedroom windows, white clouds blanketed the sky in every direction as if trying to smother the world. Pale gray light cut drearily past the listless curtains, the shafts ending on the inscrutable black of his coat and pants.

He turned towards the door. Ellaniel, already prepared, was staring at her reflection in her bared shortsword. Her crimson and black dress matched his, her pants and high collar giving her a military bearing even with the slit skirt she accompanied them with. Arzan placed a hand on her shoulder and she snapped the blade back into its sheath. The two walked out the door to where Filgneir and a host of guards and officials stood waiting in the hall. Arzan nodded and the group proceeded out of the palace and through the outer gate. He glanced back at the north wing and the black soot stains left around the upper windows. A figure shifted in the shadows. No doubt Kalla, seeing them go even if she still wasn't ready to come down herself to face the world of the living.

The city was quiet. No one else walked the streets. No faces peeked from windows. Instead, Arzan heard the sound of a large crowd in the distance ahead. The low hum grew louder as they approached the market square, where he had called the people to gather.

Before long, their group reached the square and came into view of the massive crowd. A wall of city guards and the current batch of two hundred soldier trainees cleared a path for the crenden's entourage through the sea of bodies. People quieted as they saw the Redleafs, and by the time they climbed onto the commandeered festival platform, there were only murmurs. Arzan squeezed Ellaniel's hand as he looked out at the thousands pressed into the square and the streets beyond. She squeezed his hand in turn, but kept her gaze cold. He saw her lips move to words too low for him to hear, and could only guess they were an encouragement.

Arzan unfastened his scabbard from his belt and thumped the tip into the stage in front of him. "People of Senkani!"

Even the murmurs died. Men and women, farmers and craftsmen, food stall owners and merchants all turned their eyes to him and listened.

"House Redleaf," Arzan said, his voice solitary and loud enough that he could hear its faint echo off the buildings around the square, "has ever had one role in this city, this province. We are here to serve the people. Since the day in which our House was founded, when we rose from our roots of mere wine merchants to be called not master, but liege and grace, our lot has been to protect and nurture Senkani. You look to us for authority, and we represent all of you to the Council and the world at large. We ensure your contracts and keep the peace through the enforcement of common law. My forebears did their best to earn your faith and your trust. I have done my best to continue in their footsteps and maintain the honor of my House."

He paused. "In recent years, I have deemed it necessary to take up another responsibility as steward of my people—a responsibility long abandoned because we had come to live in easy times. I took up the task of preparing us for war. I set out to train you and to arm you, and to make our province independent and ready to stand against the threat of the Silver Tide. And in these past months and years, Senkani has become strong. I say this all not to boast. It is you who put in the greatest effort. Just as you are the ones who plow the fields and bring in the harvest, the ones who put in the labor of building our roads and crafting our goods, you were the ones who spent hours and days in training. It is your strength that is the strength of Senkani.

"And so when Crenden Thrake belittled and threatened my House, I took offense not on my own behalf, but for you. It is of you that House Leverie has always been jealous and fearful. Senkani's solidarity fills them with terror, for they know you cannot be pressed beneath their thumb. Thrake's mercenaries tried once before to ruin your resolve when they killed your champion Gricall. They tried again this week, aiming to slay me, my wife, and my kin. It is only because of you that they failed!"

"My brother was cut down by those villains!" someone shouted.

"We need justice!"

People shuffled in the crowd, and he could taste the fury in the air. He could see in the men's eyes the thirst for vengeance.

"Justice!" Arzan repeated. "The Council knows that Thrake is guilty. In a lawful and right society, it is up to the Council to dispense justice. In a lawful and right society, I would be content to leave it to them. But do you know what Ylnavar and the rest of House Leverie have decided to do?" He clenched his jaw as he let the question hang. "They do *nothing*!"

A rumble went through the gathered masses. Arzan saw in their faces bitterness and anger, but no surprise.

"You know them well. The Council speaks for the interests of House Leverie above all else. Their profits and their power—that is their only care. For that, they will turn a blind eye even to flagrant murder!"

He thumped the stage with his scabbard. "But then what are they? What is a Council that does not enforce the common law? What is a Council that ignores its duties to its people? There is an understanding between ruler and ruled—a crenden holds power because he serves the people. It is no different from a contract. And when the terms of a contract are broken, its provisions no longer apply. The Leverie Council, having abandoned its duty, has likewise abandoned its authority!"

"Aristocracy of Senkani!" someone shouted.

"Aristocracy of Redleaf!"

"Independence!"

Arzan banged on the stage again. "Should you agree with the creation of our own sovereign nation, the Aristocracy of Senkani shall be our namesake, for you are what make this nation. But our name is not the important task at hand. No, I return to our prior topic. Justice.

"Justice is a principle which exists in its own right. It is a principle of correcting wrongs and punishing evils. When the judges show themselves corrupt, that does not mean justice is dead. It means only that it is up to the people to see it through." He looked out over the crowd, saw their agreement, but was it enough for them to go through with what he was about to ask of them? He resisted an urge to fiddle with his cape clasp.

"The conclusion to this line of thought may sound extreme. It is to march on Creedport and take Crenden Thrake by force. I will not butter it up. This will be an act of war, and be seen by the Council of Leverie as an armed rebellion. Quite likely, they will respond with martial force. If this is more than you are willing, I will not hold against any of you the choice not to answer my call. I will not hold it against you, but your own consciences will condemn you enough. You will know that you let walk the villains who murdered your brothers, your cousins, your champion. You will set free the men who killed not only those of my House and my wife's House, but also Gricall and his daughter Fellone."

A wave of surprise went through the crowd, seen in frowns, heard in gasps.

"Ah, I forgot news has not yet spread. No, it wasn't just the market and the palaces of Senkani and Woodwise. These despicable fiends burned one of my House estates to the ground, putting all within to the sword. It was an estate I had set aside to care for Gricall's only offspring. Not one man, woman, or child there survived."

Murmurs and mutterings roiled through the people, quickly transforming into an angry roar of competing voices.

"The cowards!"

"We can't let Thrake get away with this!"

"Get the head of that disgusting filth!"

"To arms! To arms!"

"Let the Council try and stop us!"

Arzan let out a tight breath as the crowd's fury continued. *They will go with me*. With the victory came the pressure of the next burden. But he would see it through. He drew his sword from its scabbard and raised the blade to the sky. "I ask the people, do we go to war?"

The square reverberated with thousands of voices raised as one, "War!"

Chapter 32

"You have two weeks to decide, Mr. Venon."

The door closed behind Retyar with a gentle click, leaving him alone in the white-walled corridor. He glared sourly at the paper form in his hand. Grades good enough to get into the University on scholarship, but they'd kick him out if he couldn't pick a major by the end of the semester. What kind of ridiculous timetable was that? What was the point of taking one year of General Studies if he couldn't use it to figure out his interests? He almost wanted to turn around and storm back into the planning office to tell them how stupid it was.

Swallowing down his frustration, he walked down the hallway, still staring down at the paper. *Aviation Technology, Biology, Computer Technology, Education, Electrical Engineering* . . . . His attention drifted from the list as he cut through the beams of gold sunlight streaming in through the windows. Somewhere out on campus, the old bell tower chimed out the fifth hour. He contemplated getting an early dinner and then heading to the dorms, but he hadn't any appetite with this threat of expulsion hanging over him. Instead, he went off in the direction of the library.

The outside air was chilly with the approach of winter, making Retyar glad for his new felt coat. He'd have to remember to thank his parents for the sendoff gift next time he called home. He pitied a few of the other students he saw shivering as they rushed around in short sleeves. Obviously freshmen from down south, not used to days getting cold so fast. Even travel sickness couldn't fix that.

I wonder how obvious it is I'm a freshman too. He tried not to show it, but the campus left him in a sense of awe even four months into his studies. The whole place, even the more modern Lower University he currently walked through, exuded a sense of age and majesty. Tall buildings of cement and glass were interspersed with stone steeples and brick arches. While the main roads were paved with asphalt, narrower cobblestone footpaths could always be seen shooting off into side alleys. Most impressive of all was the granite castle crowning the hilltop in the center of the compound. University ads always boasted about the fortress, which had been donated by the king hundreds of years ago, when gunpowder artillery made the structure militarily useless. It was there that the highest level students conducted their studies, surrounded by their Govunari heritage. It looked like such an awesome place to take classes in. If for nothing else, he had to choose a major so he could get that far.

The three-story library sat somewhere between old and new on the University scale of things. The red brick walls, fluted sandstone columns, and gently sloped roof of tan clay tile spoke to an era a century gone. Ironically, it was clear to see its design was intended as an architectural defiance against the even older records hall across the square, with its traditional gray stone blocks and black, vaulted roofs. Retyar pushed through the library's doors. Despite being heavy hardwood, they hinged open with the ease of turning a page. The cozy warmth within felt a part of the building itself, just like the yellow glow of incandescent lights set behind glass shades twisted to look like cloth or flower petals. He walked across the hardwood floors of the antechamber, glancing at painted wall hangings depicting the coronations of Govunari kings and queens.

"That's right, run, filthy lime eye!"

Retyar stopped in his tracks at the end of the antechamber, barely avoiding a collision with a girl rushing out of the library. She looked young, middle teens perhaps. He saw a flash of Ytanian light green eyes behind a set of thin rimmed glasses before the girl bowed a quick apology and hurried past him.

What was that about? Retyar knew things still weren't great between Ytanians and normal Govunari, but that sort of outburst seemed kind of excessive in an academic setting. Education promoted reasoned dialog, not bigoted outbursts. He entered the main chamber and looked around at rows of tables, but whoever had shouted was already back in the books like everyone else. With a shrug, he made for the stairs.

The library was certainly one of his favorite spots on campus. There was something inherently inviting not only in the warmth and the books lining every wall, but also in the architecture itself. He liked the way the second and third floors formed a ring around the open center, creating a kind of balance between intimacy and community for the tables pressed up against the upstairs banisters. The wooden floors and railings also created a degree of homeyness, even if every surface shone with a lacquered polish. It gave Retyar some comfort as he sat down at an empty table on the second floor and stared at the major form.

"Well, I don't want to go into engineering," he said with a sigh.

"What's wrong with engineering?"

Retyar jumped at the sudden voice right beside him. He turned to find a woman with dark green eyes and roundish features leaning in and staring at the form.

"Sorry," she said. "Just couldn't help being curious why you looked so glum." The stack of books in her arms started to slip and she hastily dumped them on the table with a heavy thump. The long sleeve of her traditional Govunari dress caught under the pile, checking her arm and making her fail to catch the top book as it toppled to the floor. "Not the most graceful of me," she muttered, yanking the fabric free so she could offer him her hand. "Thesha Dinria."

Retyar accepted the handshake cautiously. "Retyar Venon." He scooped up the fallen book and set it back atop the pile, then rested his chin on his knuckles and waited for the woman to get on her way. What he didn't expect was for her to take the seat next to him and flip open one of her books. "Um . . . " he eyed the empty tables nearby.

Thesha slid the book in front of him. It was open to a set of illustrations showing the development of passenger airplanes over the years. "Look at that and tell me engineering isn't interesting!"

Retyar pressed his lips tight for a moment, trying to make sense of her.

She saw the look on his face and laughed. It was a clear and pure sort of laugh, and it more than anything set him at ease with her. "All right, so you're supposed to go into engineering, but you don't want to. Want to talk about it?"

He wanted to say no, but something about that face of hers, framed by wavy locks of dark brown hair, broke down his defenses. "It's not engineering specifically. It's just . . . I don't know. I don't want to be restricted to one path before I even know what I like. Besides, my brother's already an engineer."

"Ah, so it's just general majoring blues. It hits freshmen every semester, but the university's supposedly got this super brilliant reason for keeping the deadline. Biologist then?"

Retyar shook his head. "I mean, it's interesting, but so's all this other stuff."

Thesha ran her finger down the list. "So, it's not so much that you don't like all these subjects, but that you might like them all."

Retyar shrugged and folded the airplane book closed.

"How about history?" she asked.

"Seems just as interesting as anything else, but it's less likely to get anyone a job."

She smiled. "You could aim for the National Museum. History is an unappreciated field, and they say the Museum is in desperate need." She leaned in conspiratorially. "It's what I'm going for."

"You're a history major." With her so close, Retyar suddenly felt his coat was far too warm for the room.

"It's the best subject in the world, and it's perfect for you," she said. At this proximity, he could see individual streaks of gray running through the green of her irises.

Retyar tore his gaze away from her and focused on the major form. "How's that?"

She backed off and spread her arms. "History is everything, all subjects, all knowledge. It encompasses everything on that list."

Retyar sat back and frowned, rerunning those sentences in his head.

"Everything has a history," Thesha continued, "and that history defines what it is. An engineer might know how something works. A historian also knows *why* it works and what else's been tried. He knows the context of its origin, the refinement of the process." She bent over and plucked the form with her thumb and finger. "So, what do you think?"

Retyar stared at the paper, then smiled. "Why not?"

Chapter 33

Retyar heard the whimpering as he returned from gathering herbs. A small sound, barely audible between the crash of each wave, possibly just his imagination. He wouldn't be surprised if his mind was playing tricks on him by this point. In the couple of days the girl had lay unconscious, he'd oscillated nonstop between hope and dread. On the one hand, he couldn't stand the thought of a child dying in front of him, victim to such brutality. On the other, her existence now threatened the timeline, could destroy everything Retyar had ever known, the family and friends he still so longed to see.

When he entered the cave, he found the sound hadn't been in his head. The girl was awake, propped against the stone, tattered blanket hanging from her shoulder over her white sleeping dress and hands clutching weakly at her splinted leg. Her purple-tinted hair lay matted across part of her face, hiding slightly her tears and the dark bruise on her left temple.

"Good morning," Retyar rasped. His voice sounded strange to him after years of disuse.

The girl tried weakly to shuffle away, but had nowhere to go in the confines of the small cave, unless she were to take the dive through the cliff-side porthole. Seeing the fear in her wide, violet eyes chased away any wish Retyar had that she might take that route. He placed down the herbs and picked up a tin he'd filled earlier with fish broth. "Here. You haven't eaten for a bit."

The offer only earned a suspicious stare. Retyar lifted the tin to his mouth and took a sip. "Here, it's safe. Might not taste the greatest from going cold, but I'm sure you're hungry."

The girl hesitantly opened her palm and Retyar gave her the soup. She grimaced with the first mouthful, though drank it all down.

"Who are you?" the girl asked.

"A hermit. I live alone out here. Happened to be under that bridge when those folks threw you in the river."

"Your eyes are green. You're Falconian."

Retyar reached out and retrieved the now empty tin. "Try not to move too much. Your leg's broken, possibly a rib or two as well. I'll go make some more broth."

He left the cave, but found himself pacing instead of starting the fire. The girl lived. The girl *would* live. Now what? From the words of the murderers, the people of her household would be dead. Still, there would be someone alive who knew her, and she would want to return to them.

No, there was a chance all those who would care for her were dead. He could play into that possibility. Tell her she had nowhere to return to.

If that worked?

The girl would have to live with him. That was the only answer.

Retyar started the fire and put some dried fish in the tin with some water. He didn't leave the cook spot until the broth was ready, then let it cool before going back inside.

The girl was still in the same spot, hunched over sniffling and crying silently. Retyar set the broth beside her, going through in his head how he was going to keep her here, while at the same time feeling guilty at what he was trying to do. No matter how much of a wretch it made him, though, it had to be done. He opened his mouth.

"Take me to the city," the girl said.

Retyar held the tip of his tongue between his teeth, calculating furiously how to respond. He cleared his throat. "I overheard the men talking who tried to kill you. They said everyone was dead."

The girl didn't look up. "I know. I saw it. Take me to the city."

"Who will look after you there? You have family?"

"I'm ward of Crenden Arzan and friend of Crendess Ellaniel."

Six continents, Retyar thought. *She's involved with the regional bigshots.* "That seems a bit far-fetched."

The girl lifted her head, revealing under her bruises and hair a face filled with a mess of emotions Retyar couldn't begin to decipher. "I am Fellone, daughter of Gricall. Take me to the city and you will know."

Retyar could only hope he did a decent job at keeping his internal crisis out of his expression. "All right, maybe you're speaking truthfully. Matter still stands that you've got a broken leg. Won't be easy getting you through the woods."

"You can carry me."

"You need to stay in place and rest and heal up."

Fellone's jaw shook as the she struggled to keep back tears. "I want to see Ella."

Retyar turned away from her and rested his hand on the cave wall as he gazed at the woods outside. "It's a long way to the city. Lots of wilderness. We need your leg to recover."

There was a long pause. He didn't dare turn around. Already, he wanted very badly to give in and help her out.

"You can go," Fellone said weakly. "Tell them I'm here."

"Just lie down there and rest," Retyar said. "When your leg's healed up, we'll take things from there."

"That'll take months!"

There was another stretch of silence before the girl spoke up again. "You're a criminal."

The accusation caught him off guard. "What makes you think that?"

Fellone's tone was sure and hostile, "Alone in the woods, you don't want to be around people, your green eyes—you're, you're a pirate aren't you? Marooned or shipwrecked."

The girl certainly had an imagination. Still, she wasn't nearly creative enough for the actual craziness she'd fallen into. But it was the perfect cover story. Best of all, she already believed it. "Maybe I am," Retyar said, putting a subtle edge into his voice. He turned to her, and even if he had a self-congratulatory smile on his face, he knew it could be taken for something suitably sinister. "If so, what do you think will happen to the little girl who tries to go out and put a man's life at risk?"

Fellone's fight all drained out of her and she shrunk in on herself. She swallowed and waited until after the next crash of wave before speaking in a barely audible squeak. "I, I won't tell anyone about you. Just let me go out on my own?"

"You think I can trust you? Kids don't know how to keep secrets. Not when they have adults pressing them for details."

"Then . . . why did you bother saving me?"

Retyar brushed his beard at hearing out loud the question he'd been asking himself over and over. "I don't like seeing a little girl die."

"But you won't let me go."

Retyar crouched down. "Maybe you should be happy I'm not the type to leave you for dead or kill you myself."

"I don't even know where this is."

"It's the coast. A manhunt just has to go in a straight line."

"You could relocate."

"I like my spot."

"I can ask the crenden to pardon you."

This girl's way too fast a thinker, Retyar thought. "No is no," he said with finality. He set the tin of broth beside her. "Drink your soup."

The glare she gave him had in it an assurance that the days ahead were not going to be easy.

Chapter 39

The horse's hooves clomped along the cobblestones as the animal approached the eastern gate. The sun only barely shone over the treetops up ahead, but where its light fell inside the wall, it set banners aglow and glinted off of helmets, chest plates, chain mail, and spearheads. Metal clinked against metal and against stone. Ellaniel sat erect on her mount, her eyes focused straight ahead as she exited the gate. She led the last group of volunteers coming in from the western side of the river to where they would join with the rest of the army now preparing to depart. The total force amounted to nearly two thousand, all of them with basic training from Arzan's rotation program. Far more than enough to overcome anything Thrake could muster in his defense.

Ellaniel trotted her horse through the ranks, feeling almost like she was in the mists of a dream. The sloped farmlands outside the walls were transformed into something surreal. The thousands of men with weapons and armor, the wagons and carriages loaded with supplies, the artillery being hitched to draft animals. Everything was so strange, so different. Including her. Steel cuirass over chain and light gambeson, arms and legs covered across the front in plate, she was just as ready for war as any of those around her. Even if she masked the hard edge just a little with sleeves and riding skirt of black lace with red leaf patterns, she was not at all the woman of a week ago. As she checked the knot of her crimson capelet, she shifted her thoughts away from memories of sheltered gardens and needlework, of days ignorant of politics and the cares of state. Days when the words "war" and "murder" belonged in stories of other countries, other continents. She focused instead on the burning, clawing desire to see someone's blood.

With the briefest of commands, she directed the troops behind her to the rear of the formation, then rode for where Arzan sat on his horse in counsel with Filgneir. Like Ellaniel, Arzan was fully armored, and though he lacked the decorative lace, he still had his ever present red cape to identify him by. Somehow, it looked more fitting now than ever before. Filgneir had forgone plate, being content with mere chain and gambeson.

"It probably won't even come to fighting," Filgneir said, passing his hand over the smooth dome of his hairless head. "When they see our numbers, the guard captains ought have enough sense to just let us in."

"We can't count on that," Arzan said. "Remember, Thrake strengthened his administration with those most loyal to him. If they open the gates, fine, but I will have no dallying about with the ladders."

Ellaniel reined in her horse beside them. "Those who defend him are complicit in his crimes. If anyone gets in our way, I want no hesitation in cutting them down."

Arzan opened his mouth briefly, a conflicted look in his eyes. She knew he wished she would stay here in Senkani. But he wouldn't dare oppose her decision to go. Likely his only comfort, and Ellaniel's regret, was that she was unlikely to take part in any of the fighting if things went even vaguely according to plan.

"There is no question in that," Arzan said. "Thankfully, even if Thrake's ckols and guards are loyal, he has no army. Whatever happens, he should be in our hands within the second hour of us seeing the walls. I just hope those assassins of his are still on the payroll so we might take their heads along the way."

A ckol came riding up to the trio. "My liege, you have—"

"Arzan!"

Crenden Pundur came stomping down the road after his shout. Ellaniel saw his carriage up the road, dust still settling in its wake, the driver wiping the sweat off the horses. "Arzan, what is this madness? Secession? An army ready to march on Creedport?"

"Go back to Three Corners, Pundur," Arzan said.

"I will go back when you disperse these men and return to civility and reason! The law—"

"This is the law," Arzan broke him off. "The penalty for murder is death."

Pundur threw his thick arms out to his sides. "After a trial!"

"The Council refuses the trial. They require he be there in person, but don't have the care to bring him in. Their rule is a fraud."

"The Council needs time. There are procedures, Arzan, a way these things are done."

"You may have faith in procedures," Ellaniel said, "but I've heard speak the people who would carry it through. They don't care about justice."

Pundur started at hearing her voice and now looked her over. "Six continents, I didn't even recognize you, Ella. Have you seen yourself in a mirror? You're not a woman, but a beast ready to slaughter."

"Good. That is what I mean to be."

The Three Corners crenden shook his head. "Do you think that is what Hashan would have wanted?"

Drawing in a deep breath, Ellaniel dropped off her horse and went up to him, her armor clicking with every movement. Large as Pundur was, the man retreated a step with her approach. "Thrake destroyed what my father wanted."

Pundur held her eyes but a moment before lowering them to the ground. "There is no dissuading you, then." He looked at Arzan. "We built up our armies to protect this country, not destroy it."

"That's what I'm doing," Arzan said. "Protecting my country."

Pundur grimaced and turned on his heel. He made it several paces before pausing. "The world doesn't end from a single wrong. That happens from the thousand wrongs that follow it."

"We're cutting the chain, Pundur," Arzan said. "The wrongs end here."

"No. No, they're not. And if you have any respect, you will give me back the warhorses I've sent you." Pundur returned to the carriage, ducked inside, and slammed the door shut.

Arzan signaled one of their ckol officers. "Get the front of the column moving. We march!"

Ellaniel climbed back onto her horse, ignoring Pundur's carriage as it turned around and rattled away. She put his comments out of her mind. It wasn't difficult.

Chapter 35

Charva sat with crossed legs atop her coarse straw mattress and stared at the flickering oil lamp across from her cell. She'd spent hours shouting threats, offering bribes, and finally being an all-around annoyance, but to no avail. Four days after being locked up, she had nothing left but seething anger and a growing sense of despair. *At least I'm used to cramped quarters.* One of the unexpected perks of her experience crossing the sea to Falcone. Still, she was *really* starting to want for a fresh set of clothes. Having the chamber pot almost within arm's reach at all times was also something of a novel experience. Aside from that, she didn't want to guess what the greenish-brown coating on all the stones was. At least, she thought it was greenish-brown. The hue of the lamplight made it hard to tell.

Growling out a sigh, she rolled her back onto the mattress and lifted her legs in the air, letting the bottom cuffs of her pants slip away from her boots and down to her knees. How long was her father going to keep her down here? He hadn't even given her a chance to plead her case or explain herself.

But then, she'd probably have taken the opportunity to sock him in the face, so he could be justified there.

"Nice that you've stopped screaming at the guards," came a raspy voice that bounced off the wall across her cell, "but now it feels too quiet."

Charva turned her head. "I'm not going to start singing for you, if that's what you want."

The laugh that echoed through the dungeon had a hollow quality to it. "That would be something! The crenden's daughter giving the condemned of the world a song to pass the time." There was a stretch of silence. "So, what goes on in the realm of the living that a woman such as yourself should end up here, hidden and forgotten, under lock and key?"

Charva lowered her feet and pushed herself up. "Who are you?"

"Freuce, son of Erkshan. A merchant, or at least that's what I used to call myself. Crenden Thrake found I was mixing fool's gold into the ornaments I sold the aristocracy. Suppose I was a fool myself for doing it. Anyway, he's probably forgotten he has me down here. That's the impression most of us get, eh, Veltar?"

A guttural grunt came from somewhere else in the dungeon.

"How long have you been here?" Charva asked.

"Hmm, not too sure," Freuce said. "Can't keep track too easily. I ask the guard sometimes, but you've already seen he's the prickly sort. Oh, but you know what year it is. 'Twas 4768 last I saw the sun."

"Eleven years, then," Charva said. "Can't imagine. I think I'll go mad if I have to stay here even one."

"So, why *is* the crenden's daughter gracing us with her presence?"

Charva stretched her arms and leaned against the bars. "My father's angry I called him a murderer. Oh, and he thinks I tried to kill him."

"Ah, yes, that would get one a trip to the dungeon," Freuce said. "Things must have changed quite a bit outside. I confess I didn't recognize you when you were brought in. Eleven years, you say? Yes, you've grown in that time. Normally, I wouldn't bring up that weird dress, or the unbecoming purple around your neck, but I'm already here. Not much more anyone can do to me, is there?"

Charva rubbed her neck. It still hurt to press the skin, but at least the swelling was long gone.

"Is it true?" Veltar asked. His voice was so deep that she could imagine the sound rumbling off the walls was the dungeon itself speaking to her. "Were you trying to kill the crenden?"

"No," Charva said. "He's a villain and a coward for trying

to kill the Redleafs, and he's done everything he can to ensure Throrne inherits the city over me, but I would not do such a thing. The fool that he is, he's still my father."

"What do you know?" Veltar muttered. "Aristocrats really are people on the inside after all."

Freuce's voice echoed, "There aren't many ruling crendesses in Leverie. The firstborn daughters who aren't married off usually pass up candidacy. Why do you want Creedport?"

Charva grabbed the bars and leaned back as she watched the flicker of the lamp. "Didn't I say? He may be my father, but he's still a fool."

Freuce chuckled. "No minced words. You still leave the question of what he's doing wrong."

"I wouldn't expect you to ask that, seeing how he has you locked up here."

"Sure, I've a bone to pick with him, but most folk were pretty happy with Crenden Thrake back when I was still a surface walker."

She reached through the bars, stretching her hand absently towards the lamp. "To explain it to the lowest of scum who deserves to rot down here like that one horrifically shaped and justly neglected tomato I saw in the corner of someone's stall last week, Creedport has an opportunity to become the pride of the continent. Or rather, it had. Thrake sent that opportunity off abroad to get crushed under some imperial's boot." It still set a knot in her gut remembering Maltan's ship sailing out of the harbor. "Then there's this stupid feud he has with the Redleafs. If it's true he sent assassins against them . . . ."

A heavy clang carried through the dungeon. Charva didn't think it was time for gruel. Someone coming to see her then? Hope quickened her heart as she tightened her fingers around the bars. Finally, she could explain to someone other than the ever cynical curmudgeon of a guard that she hadn't been trying to kill anyone.

"Look here—" she started as her visitor came into view, but she stopped the moment she saw who it was. "Ersch!"

Her ckol-to-be grinned at her and raised an iron key. "My liege, I talked the warden into letting you out."

Charva grabbed the key straight from his hand and forced it in the lock. "Don't just stand there with it!" The bars clanged against the next cell over as she thrust them open and hopped free. "What took you so long?" She asked the question, but was surprised the man had come to her rescue at all. For all she'd promised him, he was still a lowly city guard.

"Crenden Thrake had me posted off on the wall ever since the purge," Ersch said. "It's only now with all the confusion that I was able to get away from there and onto the palace grounds."

"What confusion?"

Ersch's face turned cloudy. "Senkani's declared war. People come in off the road say the Redleafs are marching an army. The whole city's in chaos. Thrake is putting the entire guard on the walls and every hunter with a bow besides."

Charva thought of the Senkani trainees she had seen only days before. "They aren't going to be enough."

Ersch raised his hand over his heart. "I'm your ckol, my liege. Whatever you wish me to do, I shall do it."

Charva nodded. She glanced into the next occupied cell as she strode for the exit. She matched Fruece's voice to an old man in dark, ragged clothes sitting on a mattress even rattier than hers.

"Thanks for the chat. I'll be sure to review your sentence when I'm crendess."

"My liege," Ersch said behind her, "are you going to—"

"I'm going to speak with the crenden. Where will I find him?"

"On the south wall. That's part of why I was able to slip away."

Passing through the guardhouse, she found the warden hadn't been "convinced" so much as knocked out drunk with a bottle of hard liquor. Ersch dropped the key on the man's desk with a cough as they passed.

Once they found daylight, Charva turned from the dungeon and barracks block and went straight across the small square to the palace. She'd been afraid of running into ckols, but there was no need to worry. Glancing to the side, she saw even the gate sentries were gone, replaced by a set of servants with fire pokers.

Inside, the palace was a flurry of servants and clerks who must have been about some sort of important business, but to her eye were more a flock of headless chickens. No one bothered to stop her on her way through the halls. She sent Ersch off to get a basin of hot water and some towels brought to her room. She *really* wanted a bath, but a quick wipe down would have to do. He had her water and cloth in record time, and she was quickly back out of her room in a fresh blue dress, a scarf to cover up the bruising around her neck, and a new compliment of hidden daggers up her sleeves.

"Here, I spotted this in one of the rooms," Ersch said, holding out her rapier and sword belt.

"Praise the day your mother gave birth to you," Charva said, taking the weapon and strapping it to her waist. Geared and ready, she went back downstairs.

Upon reaching the main entrance, she found Throrne waiting for her in front of the dark double doors.

"Where are you going, sis?"

"To see Father. Out of my way."

Her brother glanced at her sword, pressed his lips together, and raised his eyes to hers. In the strongest display of resolve she had ever seen from him, he stood firm and held the knobs shut behind him.

Charva stared at him. "I need to speak with Father," she said quietly. "Move."

"You've done enough to unsettle the province," Throrne told her, a discernible quiver in his voice despite how much he may have tried to hide it. "You split the city against Father, forced him to use a heavy hand."

"You're not defending him! Throrne, you don't even want to be heir."

"But I have to be! Creedport needs stability. You're planning to throw everything into chaos."

Charva held her hand to her chest. "I'm planning to make a better Creedport. One that surpasses what you read about in dull and dusty political treatises. And one free from the rule of a murderous madman."

"And how will you accomplish that if you become a murderer yourself?"

Charva ground her teeth. "I never said I was planning on killing him. Why does everyone assume that?"

"Then why the sword? If you are so innocent, so reasonable, then why do you go everywhere with edged steel?"

She didn't have a ready answer for that, didn't even know how to start approaching the question. "Throrne, one last time, out of my way."

Her brother swallowed hard. He didn't move.

Ersch started forward, but Charva put out her arm to stop him. She stepped up to her brother and grabbed his silk vest in both fists. He tried to stand his ground, but even if he was a young man and she a woman, his life as a bookworm couldn't face up to her training and athleticism. She ripped him aside and threw him at the wall with enough force to pop a nearby painting off its hook. She let him go and shoved open the palace doors.

The main street was as desolate as if it were midnight. Houses and stores were shut and barred, stalls empty of all merchandise. The guardsmen were all presumably at the walls. There did seem to be some bustle down in the direction of the docks. Charva guessed any Leverie or administrators who could escape Thrake's attention were getting out of town the surest way they could.

Reaching the south gate, she was disappointed to see there were enough commoners loyal to her father to form a decent-sized crowd. Charva estimated about four hundred or so men, armed with knives, hammers, spades, iron bars, or pans. Ckols ordered them about, outlining points of defense and flanking strategies for when the Senkani breached the wall. Ersch made a path for her through the bodies. It didn't take long for a ckol to spot her. He shouted and rushed up the gate tower. Charva glanced up at the wall and the guardsmen and ragtag archers lining the top. She spotted her father amongst them.

Ersch got her through the last of the crowd to the base of the gate tower, where they were stopped by a pair of guards. "Didn't they say she was in the dungeon?" one of them asked the other.

Captain Ulman came exiting out the stairwell. "Her grace

is allowed up." He waved for Charva and Ersch to come and they followed.

"I don't know what you're planning, your grace," Ulman said as they climbed, "but whatever it is, I hope it can get us out of this mess. Ersch, I won't say anything about you leaving your post and releasing a prisoner without permission. In future, remember your loyalties."

"I do, Uncle."

The captain glanced back at them. "Even if I want you to fix things, remember I am the crenden's man. Even if I was willing to back you in the no-confidence vote, by law my obligations still demand I defend him so long as the vote hasn't taken place. I don't want us facing each other across our blades."

"I only plan to talk," Charva said. She hoped she was being honest with that statement, that she wasn't going to prove Throrne's accusations against her right. In truth, she didn't quite know what she was going to do.

At the top of the stairs, Ulman blocked the path and looked her in the eye. "I don't know what to think about what happened in the palace study. I'm gambling everything on the hope that was all some misunderstanding. You have a good heart. Know that so does your father, somewhere in there." He stepped out of her way.

I somehow have a hard time believing that, Charva thought.

She went out onto the wall. Thrake still had his steel breastplate, as well as a sword fastened to his side. She had expected to be swarmed by guards the moment she arrived, but instead found everyone sent off some yards down the ramparts. With an extra touch of surprise, Charva noted that Thrake was using one of Maltan's telescopes to observe the southern tree line.

"Here arrives my first enemy of the day," Thrake said, putting the implement down upon the crenel, but not turning to face her. "Escorted by what should be my own men."

Any sign of the frenzied madness from before was now gone. Charva had little experience seeing nervous breakdowns or panic attacks. Was four days enough time for that sort of thing to pass?

"With all that approaches, you should be down there at the docks," she said.

"This is my city. I have fought for it. I will not flee from it."

Charva laughed sharply at him. "Fought for it? By hiring murderers to keep you in power? If you won't run, have the decency to give yourself up. If you truly care about this city, don't use the lives of its people to protect you from your just end."

Thrake finally turned to her, fixating his deep blue eyes on hers. "If I give myself up, will there be a trial? Will I have opportunity to give my defense? Or will Arzan Redleaf hack me down right on the spot?"

"Does it matter? What defense could you possibly give to justify what you've done?"

"I didn't do it."

Charva laughed again. "I might have had a chance believing that before you all but admitted your guilt in your study."

"As you were clearly trying to kill me?"

"I wasn't there to kill you," Charva said. "As much as it might have looked—"

"I know," Thrake cut her off. "That's what I'm saying. Thinking back on it with a calmer mind, I know you are not the kind to do such a thing. Or at least, not with the information you had at the time. And so, we are more alike than you'd care to realize. I need a trial. With the evidence in plain sight, we can figure out who is trying to pin this on me."

Charva shook her head and scoffed. "What?"

"I didn't send the mercenaries to Senkani or Woodwise," Thrake said. "Someone bought them out from under me."

"You're just spinning some story to—"

"Of course, you don't believe me." He turned back to the south. "You've never believed in me."

The bitterness in his voice came with such sincerity that Charva found herself doubting. Could he . . . possibly be telling the truth? "Who would want to frame you?" she asked cautiously. "Why?"

He turned his eyes to her, and she saw something in them. Hope. "That's what we need to uncover." He reached out a hand and placed it on her shoulder. "Charva, I need your help."

She flinched, remembering the last time he'd touched her. It occurred to her that maybe the madness hadn't actually left him, but just taken some other form. Perhaps Thrake was simply so unhinged now that he no longer remembered sending the assassins. No, that had to be the case. There was no way in the six continents that her father would ever ask her aid in anything.

"I will see if I can get you to trial," Charva said. *If he's really guilty, it hardly hurts to indulge that request.* "You better have evidence of your innocence."

Thrake opened his mouth, but was cut off by a shout further along the wall.

"I see them!"

Charva turned together with everyone else. Thrake snatched up Maltan's telescope and trained it on the road. Even without lenses, though, Charva could see that something was off.

"Ah," Thrake said, "well, this changes things."

Chapter 36

Arzan rode his horse out of the woods hoping the scouts had been wrong. Looking out across the level farmlands towards the city, he was quickly disappointed. Just in front of Creedport's walls was a mass of men bearing the standards of Highcity and the Leverie Council. Ylnavar had come with an army in Thrake's defense.

One of the scouts came riding hard up the main road. "What are their numbers and equipment?" Arzan demanded.

"Near three thousand, my liege. But they've got just farm tools and normal tunics."

Arzan's horse shook its head and shifted its footing as if the beast knew what was going through his mind. Senkani could easily take the Highcity force, even outnumbered. Yet Arzan wasn't sure he wanted to fight the Council and the Highcity commoners.

Columns of his men marched along the road beside him. Ellaniel reined in her horse next to his, her eyes on Ylnavar's force. "Everyone who gets in our way, Arzan," she said quietly.

Arzan listened to the drum of soldiers' footsteps. Pundur's warning whispered in his ears. *The world doesn't end from a single wrong. That happens from the thousand wrongs that follow it.*

Ellaniel pushed her horse in front of him so she could look him in the face. "You're wavering. Arzan, we're past that point." She thrust her finger out at the city. "Thrake is there. We can't back off now."

"Messenger approaching!"

Charva watched as the Senkani army flowed from the forest. Down below at the wall's base, the Highcity commoners tightened their line. She could sense their unease from the tone of murmurs that wafted up to her, even if she couldn't make out words. She understood how they felt. Even atop the battlements, armed with a sword and surrounded by ckols, she found herself swallowing hard as she thought of Senkani steel bearing closer.

Ylnavar reached the top of the wall and stepped from the gate tower. The thin old man held onto one of his ckol's arms, his breaths ragged after the arduous climb. "You've gotten us into a right mess, Thrake," he said between two wheezes.

"I'm innocent," Thrake said. "I submit myself to trial before the Council."

The Highcity crenden glared, pausing long enough to regain a little breath. "Then you should have been there in Woodwise when I called an emergency meeting."

"I was . . . " Thrake tightened his jaw and glanced towards the palace. Charva could see his temper boiling. "I was indisposed at the time. I will stand trial now."

"This isn't about you anymore," Ylnavar said, his mouth drawn into a scowl. "The country is falling apart. Before all else, the Council's authority must be reestablished."

"So, you are taking him to Highcity," Charva said.

Rather than answer, Ylanvar turned to the south and rested his bony hands on the battlements where two carved lizards stared glumly out with him at the armies massed in the fields.

The Highcity messenger stopped his horse a fair distance away, his eyes focused straight ahead as he tried to pretend the two thousand armed men fanning out to either side did not exist.

"Speaker of the Council, Crenden Ylnavar of Highcity, issues a message to Crenden Arzan of Senkani. H-He is aware that you have declared rebellion against the aristocracy and march an army on a fellow city of Leverie. You are hereby commanded to s-s-surrender and submit yourself to the Council's authority."

Arzan's momentary hesitation crumbled at this reminder of Leverie double standards. "Thrake attacks Senkani and the Council sits around hemming and hawing about rules. I hit back and Ylnavar's here in an instant. Go back to your liege, messenger, and tell him I am coming. And if he values his life, it will be he who surrenders."

Without watching the messenger's return, Arzan turned his horse for the front of the army. "Formation!"

The messenger only just started riding back to Creedport, yet Charva already knew the outcome. She balled her fists, her nails biting into her palms. The Senkani army, now fully emptied from the woods, began lining up and readying for attack. She turned on Ylnavar.

"Speaker, what are you doing?! My father's surrendered to you!"

Ylnavar folded his hands behind his back and regarded the southern fields. "Law and procedure must be upheld. Crenden Thrake will be tried by the Council, but first will be Crenden Arzan. He is committing high treason!"

Charva couldn't believe what was happening. "People are going to die! Don't fight the Redleafs!"

The old man ignored her plea. Thrake leaned into the crenel, face inscrutable.

"Fools." Charva ran past Ylnavar's ckols to the gate tower and down the steps, barely even noting Ersch follow her. As soon as she hit the street, she went for one of the crowd of horses the Highcity ckols had tethered nearby. "Let me through the gate!"

She got on the horse and rode it through the massed defenders, but the gate remained closed. "Flame and embers. I'm the last thing standing between you all and slaughter!"

Two guards glanced at each other and hurried to engage the mechanism. They opened the passageway just wide enough for a single rider, and in a heartbeat Charva was galloping along the road past Ylnavar's hodgepodge army outside the city, then leaving it all behind. It was a strange feeling having desolate farmlands on either side while thousands of men massed in front and back. She forced the eeriness of it from her mind and focused on the figure in the red cape at the head of the Senkani force. No soldiers or ckols came out to screen her before she reached him. She pulled up her horse so fast she nearly fell straight off.

"Arzan, my father surrenders to the Council. You don't need to fight."

The Crenden Redleaf stopped his horse, but the Senkani army continued its advance around them. "That's not good enough. The Council will just find him innocent."

"It's possible he *is* innocent," Charva said. "I admit I didn't get much news down in the dungeon, but what's your evidence?"

"This discussion already took place in Woodwise." It was Ellaniel's voice. Charva had mistaken her for a fancily armored ckol until she spoke. Any other time, she would have thought her armor indescribably dashing, but right now it filled her with stomach-turning dread.

"And what does that mean?" Charva demanded.

"That means we're done talking," Ellaniel said. "The Council won't hold an honest trial. Ylnavar's presence here all but proves it."

"Whatever. This will be a slaughter. Don't attack."

Ellaniel fixed her with her gaze. Not for the first time, Charva fancied she saw the soul of a lioness hidden within her golden eyes. "If you had a son whose life was threatened and a friend who died protecting him, you wouldn't be trying to stop me."

"Ella—"

"You owe me a favor, Charva," the crendess broke her off. "Anything I might ask, remember? I call it in now."

Charva's heart sank. "No, don't—"

"Bring me my father's killer. Bring me Thrake."

Charva opened her mouth, but found she hadn't any words. An hour ago, she would have readily said yes, but now . . . .

Ellaniel saw that she had no answer. "Then Charva Leverie of Creedport is not a woman of her word," she said, voice ice-cold.

The Redleafs spurred their horses on. Soon, Charva was left alone in their dust, surrounded by empty fields of trampled crops. She tightened her grip on the reins until it felt the leather would break her skin. Her mouth moved with half-formed words as she still grasped for something to say. But it was too late. She had failed. People were going to die. When she heard the shout of, "Archers, notch!" she bowed her head into her horse's mane and cried.

Chapter 37

Before leaving Senkani, Arzan had divided the army into six main parts. The first three consisted of the shieldsmen companies, eighteen hundred total, which formed the brunt of their force. They were lined up side by side, looking like a single mass of soldiers for now, but ready to break into separate wings at his command. The center and leftmost wing had the ladders. The next part were the two hundred archers, following immediately behind the shieldsmen. Behind them were Arzan, Ellaniel, and their ckols, forty strong, who made up the cavalry. Finally, there were the artillery teams, which had raced ahead to set up on the western hills and were already cranking the six ballistae and loading the bolts. *Let this show of force be enough to cow Ylnavar into standing down.*

He slapped his leg plate in frustration when he saw the arrows streaking through the mid-morning sky.

"Shields high!"

He needn't have bothered issuing the command. The defenders were using weak hunting bows and were untrained in war archery. The air filled with the sound of wood boards locking into each other over the shieldsmen's heads, but not a single arrowhead found its mark, every one striking the dirt at least a hundred feet short.

Arzan shook his head, disgusted. *If they want to play the game, we will show them how it's done.*

"All halt!" he shouted. "Archers, notch!"

Hundreds of men slipped shafts from their quivers and set

them to the strings of their war bows. The shieldsmen knelt low to give the archers line of sight to gauge the distance.

"Draw!"

The archers bent and aimed high.

"Arrows loose!"

"For Senkani!" a man bellowed, and two hundred arrows whooshed into the sky as one. Arzan watched their flight as they shot upwards, reached their zenith, seemed to hang lazily in the air for the briefest of moments, then rained down on the unarmored glob of men in front of Creedport's walls. He heard horrified screams from their ranks, saw men fall to the ground.

This time, Arzan witnessed the archers on the walls sending back a volley. Even with the height advantage, the arrows still landed harmlessly in the dirt far ahead of them. The Creedport bows were simply too weak.

Arzan's jaw was clenched tight. He forced the muscles to relax enough to speak. "Archers, second volley!"

Again, the Senkani arrows hit their target, and more screams carried across the fields to Arzan's ears. He imagined being one of those Highcity commoners, feeling sharpened steel digging into his flesh. He felt sick.

"Break," he whispered. "Run. This isn't your fight."

They held firm.

He wanted to stop, heed all the urgings to turn around and go home. But he remembered the night of the attack. The fire tearing through the palace. The blood-soaked carpets. Magar's lifeless body and Avlan's terrified face. He hardened his heart, drew his blade, and raised it high above his head, signaling the artillery teams on the hills.

The ballistae shot their bolts, each machine issuing a loud snap and bucking forward from the force. Two of the bolts went too high, smashing into the stone walls. The other four threw up puffs of pinkish mist as they connected with people's bodies.

This time, Arzan did not dwell on whatever suffering he had just unleashed. He ordered another archer volley. And another. He didn't let up until the second round of artillery bolts tore through the Highcity ranks and the line finally collapsed. It was only a few at the eastern edge at first, a handful of men fleeing for the woods. Within moments, it turned into a complete rout, everyone capable of moving on his own legs stampeding away from the city.

The Senkani lines whooped in victory. "Leverie cowards!"

Don't taunt them, Arzan thought. *The fewer men who fight us, the better.*

Ellaniel pulled her horse up beside his, her eyes asking for his next move.

"Left company come with me to the western wall," Arzan ordered. "Filgneir has the center and will lead the diversionary to the south. The rest are under the crendess' command. Your job is to keep Crenden Thrake from escaping and the Highcity army from rejoining the city."

Ellaniel nodded and raised her blade, riding off to the right flank.

Arzan went with his ckols to the front of his six hundred. He dismounted and grabbed a shield Vighkon had ready for him. "Men of Senkani, we take the walls!"

An enthusiastic chorus of shouts answered him. His soldiers drummed their shields with their swords. Vighkon stepped in on Arzan's right and set his shield in place. He saw the disapproval on his captain's face, but Arzan had already made himself clear. A leader was only worthy if he was ready to lead into danger, especially when it was at his request that these men were here to fight. The rest of his ckols formed up in the front line around him. Some fifty feet away, Filgneir nodded from the head of his unit.

"Forward march!"

The formation moved in perfect unison. Despite the kale and carrot plants littering the ground, any time he looked around him he saw that everyone kept the square straight and solid. His training program was paying off.

They reached the first patch of ground the Creedport archers had hit. Arrow shafts stuck up from the soil like scores of bizarre planting markers.

"Incoming!"

"Shields high!" Arzan ordered.

The formation raised shields while only slowing the barest amount. Many arrows still fell short, digging into dirt and crop. Dozens more thudded hard into wood. No one screamed.

They advanced steadily on the city, multiple volleys coming at them, not one arrow reaching flesh. Kale field gave way to lettuce, then squash. They came within two hundred feet by the time the wall archers abandoned volleys and began unleashing a steady barrage, forcing the Senkani to keep shields up permanently. It slowed progress and impeded vision, but they still lost not a man.

Arzan saw they were now fifty feet from the city. He slowed his company's pace, allowing Filgneir to gain the lead. Almost immediately, near all the archers' attention shifted to the other company. That left Arzan and his men with only the dead and injured of Highcity as the last obstacle to the wall. He did his best not to step on the bodies or brush the arrow shafts sticking out of those still alive and moaning. They might not be spared the boots of those blind soldiers behind him, but he'd at least do what he could to show them mercy.

Filgneir's ladder teams reached the wall and got to work. Up above, men shouted warnings and orders, their attention redoubling on his company. Just as planned. Arzan's company came up to the wall. Instead of raising their ladders, they followed Arzan's lead along the base and around the southwest corner. They moved as quietly as possible given their armor and equipment. The clamor of battle near the gate aided their stealth. Once a fair distance along, Arzan quickened their pace, hoping to get a good head start on his goal before the defenders wised up to his gambit.

The coast loomed ahead, and beyond them the calm blue waters of the bay. The city walls stretched on about seventy feet past the land's end, enough to deter anyone with armor and weapons from going around. Arzan wasn't going to try swimming, but he ordered the ladder teams to set up as close to the shore as possible. The wood beams thumped onto the stone battlements and Arzan was first to take the rungs. The ladder wobbled back and forth with every step he climbed, the top scraping a little against the wall in tandem. However rickety it felt, it got him to the battlements without a hitch. He slipped past the city's famous lizard carvings to set his feet on the ramparts. Glancing either way, he saw his ckols reach the tops of the neighboring ladders.

He also found a wave of Creedport guardsmen charging along the wall not twenty feet away. *Bloody shyles!*

"Arms!" Arzan shouted, brandishing his sword.

The ckols to his right instantly locked their shields to intercept the attack. Arzan and Vighkon rushed in to lend support as they were pushed back by the Creedport surge. They put their weight against the frontliners' backs, and Arzan quickly felt more of his men press in behind him.

The Creedport guardsmen had numbers on their side, at least until more of Arzan's company could scale the wall. What they didn't have were shields. The first few fell easily to Arzan's ckols. Seeing the problem, the next in line raised their swords in high guard as they tried to tackle the shield wall, kicking, shoving, hoping to break the solid Senkani defense. The front shieldsmen became bogged down simply trying to keep solid. Fortunately, Arzan and those with him in the second rank were free to counterattack over the shoulders of the first. He thrust through every opening he spotted in the Creedport men's guards, striking clean blows at hands, faces, and necks. The press of both sides against each other left no room for the dead and injured to fall, unless it was out left, plummeting down to the alleyways below. The bodies that escaped that fate remained pinned upright, bloodied mouths agape, heads and eyes rolled up towards the sky.

More Senkani scaled the wall and added their strength to the push. Arzan felt their side gradually stop giving, then turn around and begin taking ground. The layer of dead was now too thick for any meaningful fighting to take place. Everything went into the press and it felt like Arzan would be crushed to pieces. The Creedport guard struggled hard, but it wasn't enough. The Senkani moved forward by inches and feet, forcing the defenders back towards the nearest tower. As they were shoved along, a row of guardsmen lost their footing and slipped screaming over the side. All resistance collapsed —Arzan and those at the front nearly fell on their faces as the defenders broke and fled the other way down the rampart.

The Senkani cheered and raised their swords and shields in celebration. Arzan let them have their moment as he wiped the sweat from his brow. Blood dripped from the tip of his blade, prompting him to wipe the steel on the outfit of one of those he had killed. He took a moment to study the dead man's uniform. A guard captain. Like Arzan, he had taken to the front of his men. "You were better than that snake deserved," he muttered.

Arzan strode to the tower, his cape tugging at his neck as the coastal breeze tried to snatch it for its own. They met no more resistance on the way down into the city, where they found empty streets and alleys. He knew Creedport was a maze except for the main road which ran from the docks straight to the south gate, and so the plan was to start at the docks and from there march on to the palace. Assuming Thrake had not already fled before Senkani arrived at the city, this would cut off his last avenue of escape. The walls of this city would be his cage, and he would be stuck in it with wolves.

Chapter 38

Ellaniel saw Filgneir's company retreat from the wall and hoped their distraction had worked well enough for Arzan to get in through the north. Honestly, it looked like they could have taken the south gate on their own, but Arzan wanted to minimize casualties. Just take the palace from behind. Ellaniel knew in her mind that his plan was the more sensible one. In her heart, she wished she could personally cut down every rat who even entertained the thought of protecting Thrake.

With the break from action near the city, Ellaniel could now spare a glance at where, some distance away, Charva and her guardsman sat alone atop their horses. The young woman still had her face lowered against the neck of her horse. Ersch, unmoving and silent, kept his eyes on the Senkani soldiers. Ellaniel didn't feel sorry for making the request of her, nor for her harsh words. If Charva were to become a ruler of any worth, she would need to put honor and justice above all else. It was sad she had somehow fallen into trusting Thrake and the Council. After such a lapse in Charva's judgment, Ellaniel doubted the two of them could ever return to being friends.

Filgneir's company got out of bow range of the wall. They didn't appear too badly harmed from the assault. She started her horse forward to get Filgneir's report, but the man removed his helmet and started running out to her, arm pointed southward. She turned around. People were emerging from the forest's edge. A lot of people. And they bore the banners of Woodwise and the Council.

Ellaniel sat still, confused. What was her father's army doing here? Why . . . . *You need to take charge, Ellaniel!* "Turn the formation around," she commanded. "Send out a rider to reorder the ballistae."

More and more men flowed out into the fields. Hundreds. A thousand. Two thousand. The same strength Senkani had marching against Creedport. But with the Senkani force now split, Ellaniel was outnumbered.

"Ckols, with me." She rode through the fields towards the newcome army. The Woodwise commander noted her approach and rode to meet her with his ckols on empty ground. She recognized Odavan from his arrogant posture even before she saw his face. They stopped within yards of each other.

"Quite the place to meet you, Cousin," Odavan said, his curved breastplate making him look even more puffed-chested than ever.

"What meaning do you have here, Odavan?"

He pointed his arm out at the Senkani army. "I ought ask you the same question, Goldeye. I was outright shocked when Ylnavar sent a message requesting help against a Senkani rebellion. Yet here you are! Dressed all up for war, lots of angry commoners lined up behind you with pointy objects!"

"What is your meaning here?" Ellaniel repeated.

Odavan sighed heavily. "Your husband is to be arrested and brought before the Council. Where is he?"

"Apprehending your uncle's killer," Ellaniel said. "I would think any respectable man would be sympathetic to that cause. But here *you* are, coming to the defense of one who killed your own blood."

"I am saddened by the loss of Uncle Hashan," Odavan said, though he certainly didn't look it. "The fact of the matter is, there's no evidence pointing to who committed the crime."

"You're just happy you're finally in charge of Woodwise," Ellaniel put all the sugared venom into her voice she could muster.

Odavan's face darkened. "Careful, Goldeye. You can only

stray so far from your old demure self ere I treat you as one responsible for her words."

"You want to take me to account? Certainly. How about a duel?"

Odavan shifted his jaw as if gnawing on the thought. "My army outnumbers yours. Why bother exposing myself to your trained blade?"

Ellaniel shook with rage. "You would send Hashan's men against his daughter?"

"Leverie men," Odavan corrected her. "And you're just a Redleaf barbarian."

She kicked her horse into a charge, her sword in hand without any memory of drawing it. Odavan recoiled, nearly dropping from his saddle, but her thrust didn't even get close, her blade deflected by a swift parry from Odavan's nearest ckol. Ellaniel's ckols charged in around her, turning the ground into a forty-man melee, steel ringing off steel and curses flying like arrows. Odavan recovered his seat and turned his horse around to gallop full speed for the Woodwise lines. His ckols remained only long enough to make pursuit impossible, then broke after him.

Ellaniel spit at the ground in their wake. "Coward!" For a moment, she imagined she could still chase him down, tear her way through, slip her sword's edge across his throat. Instead, she turned back for the Senkani army.

"That could have gone a lot better," Filgneir said on her return.

"Archers, ready your bows," Ellaniel ordered. "Tell the artillery to attack when they deem Woodwise is in range. Shieldsmen?" she looked Filgneir's company over. They were still in good shape from what she could tell. A few were a bit roughed up, outfits slightly ruffled or torn, some light gashes in their gambeson. Regardless, they still had fire in their eyes. Only, she noticed some glanced between her and the Woodwise army. They remembered where she came from. "Woodwise is on the side of House Leverie," she said. "They are on the side of Thrake. They trample on my father's memory, and thus I shall trample on them. Friends of Redleaf, we fight!"

The army cheered and raised their weapons. Ellaniel

shifted her horse around to face her enemy. Odavan was already on the move, the wide Woodwise battle line marching across the same fields Senkani had advanced through earlier in the day. She took the kite shield she had lacked the chance to draw earlier and secured it to her arm. She still wanted to charge right in herself and hack these traitors down, but she let reason have its due and rode with Filgneir and her ckols back behind the archers.

The Woodwise army drew into artillery range. Tight snaps cut the air as the ballistae launched their assault. Only two bolts found their target. Shards of splintered shields blasted skyward along the west flank. The sections around the impacts slowed their advance, but only for a moment.

"Command the archers," Ellaniel told Filgneir.

Filgneir nodded. "Archers, notch!"

The volley did far less damage to Woodwise than to Highcity. As soon as the arrows were in flight, the enemy lifted their shields, and the *thunks* of arrowheads hitting wood were the only sound to carry across the fields.

Woodwise's response was quick in coming. Hundreds of arrows launched up from behind the shield wall, arching through the air and then raining down on the Senkani. The shieldsmen took the brunt of the attack without issue, but a few arrows peppered the archers, and one streaked down right in front of her to land in a head of cabbage at her horse's hooves. Her beast jolted back in surprise, nearly throwing her off. Not far away, one of the archers screamed in anguish. She regained control of her mount and saw a man dragged out of the formation by a pair of his fellows, a feathered shaft sprouting from his chest.

"Answer them in kind!" Ellaniel shouted. "Aim past their shield wall!"

The Woodwise army drew nearer as the two sides traded more volleys. After Senkani's first counterattack, the enemy wised up and focused on their archers as well. Ellaniel kept her shield raised to fend off arrows, worried for her exposed horse. Two of her ckols found themselves dismounted, one breaking his arm in his fall. She let a companion of his get down to help him to the safest part of the formation, the man's injured and dying horse thrashing in horror all the while. More archers went down, many of them screaming.

The ballistae got off one more round of bolts. With a closer target, five managed to hit. More splinters sprayed upward, and spurts of blood caught the sun's light. Ellaniel thought she even saw a dismembered arm tumble over a few soldiers' heads and felt vomit rise up in her throat. She swallowed it down and grit her teeth, angry that she felt even the slightest bit of disgust at what she was doing.

The Woodwise arrows stopped. Their archers likely still had ammunition, but now the shieldsmen were too near the Senkani line. Ellaniel's side needn't consider such inhibitions and kept up the attack to the last arrow, which happened to get spent right when the Woodwise shieldsmen were close enough to start the charge.

And they were ready to charge. The Woodwise soldiers paused to beat their swords on their shields and roar a war cry that sent a shiver through Ellaniel's body despite her best efforts at composure. The Woodwise commander bellowed his command and they surged forward like an ocean wave. A wave that carried at its fore a wall of shields and sharpened steel that glimmered in the sunlight.

Even as the sight elicited Ellaniel's instincts to run, she analyzed the field. Woodwise had enough men that the wings threatened to envelope the Senkani, but she saw their formation was becoming disorderly with the charge. *We can win with discipline.*

No sooner did she think such than her sheildsmen spontaneously shouted a war cry of their own and countercharged. Ellaniel shot out her arm as if after an invisible rein. "No! Hold the line!"

The two forces crashed together in an uneven mess. Some sections maintained shield formation, while others went to straight-up melee, each man fighting for himself in a sea of shouts and steel. Ellaniel didn't have time to worry about parts of the line getting cut up and isolated, however. The flanks of Woodwise's larger army were already bending around and enveloping Senkani's edges.

"Filgneir, lead the archers to aid the right flank!" Ellaniel ordered. "Ckols, with me!"

"Your grace!"

But she didn't grant anyone the chance to hold her back as she raced her horse to the left flank. The Senkani there were already hard-pressed, surrounded two to one against hundreds of Woodwise soldiers, men fighting back to back to fend off assaults from all directions. She slipped her blade from its scabbard and raised it behind her, ready to swing. The Woodwise soldiers' attention was fully on the Senkani footmen. They didn't see her coming until she galloped past them, her sword shearing through the exposed back of someone's neck. She felt the instant the sword hacked through meat, nearly lost her grip from the force of impact against bone. Her swing and the horse's momentum brought the steel clean out the other end.

She looked at the blood on her sword. *Bloody shyles, I just killed someone!* Her heart pounded faster than her horse's hooves against the ground. She'd really . . . .

No time to dwell on it! Fight! Screaming, she swung again at another soldier as she rode parallel to the back line. This time, her aim was off. The sword glanced off her target's helmet with a metallic *clang* and vibrated in her hand.

The next soldiers saw her approach. Ellaniel veered away from the battle, checking back as she did so and seeing her ckols shaving away at Woodwise's outer ranks in her wake. Slowing her horse once she was a decent distance from the enemy, she saw her assault had the desired outcome. Most of the Woodwise flankers were pulling back and forming a defensive wall against her small unit of cavalry, providing the Senkani shieldsmen a little more room to breath. Still, it wouldn't be enough. The main body yet outnumbered them.

"Follow my lead!" Ellaniel said to her ckols. She kicked her horse back in motion, circling around until she was truly behind the enemy formation. Some of the Woodwise soldiers saw her unit and turned their shields, but she galloped in where they were unprepared. Like before, she rode parallel to their rear lines and swung at the first exposed neck she saw. This time, she killed one, two, three soldiers and just kept going. Attacking from the back like this, every victim of hers taking a sword through the vertebra without even realizing she was there, she had to pull away from exhaustion rather than any waiting challenge. She trotted her horse out behind the very center of the Woodwise army, her arm heavy from all the hacking.

Taking the opportunity to survey the battle, Ellaniel saw that Filgneir's archers were successfully harassing the western flank. Their combined disruptions were working. The Senkani line was holding.

But was it her imagination that the Senkani ranks looked a little thinner?

"Your grace," one of her ckols said, "we need to be careful of the—"

"Get ready for another go." Ellaniel flicked her sword to throw off the blood. Her arm was still tired, but the enemy wasn't going to wait for her. She lifted her shield above her head. "Char—"

She cut off as her horse suddenly jolted and reared, throwing her clear from the saddle. Her back hit the dirt hard, knocking the air right out of her. Shock and pain kept her down for a moment, at least until she grew conscious of the panicked horses and riders around her. She rolled and pushed herself to her knees to see a mess of writhing animals and dismounted ckols. Not ten feet away, one of her men hollered in anguish as two companions tried to free his leg from underneath his dying horse. Ellaniel saw now the arrow sticking out of the creature's neck. The Woodwise archers. She'd forgotten about the archers. *You idiot!*

"Watch out!"

Ellaniel jumped to her feet only to feel something dig into the back of her thigh. She cried out and felt the strength go out of her leg, making her stagger and catch herself on her horse's carcass. On instinct, she reached back and touched the shaft, but even the slightest brush unleashed a deep, biting pain. A short, high-pitched whimper escaped from her throat as she snapped her hand away from the injury.

"Her grace is hurt!"

A number of her ckols solidified around her, shields up to defend against further volleys.

"A surgeon! Get a surgeon!"

Ellaniel bit hard on her lip and tried reminding herself that childbirth had been a lot more intense than this. Remembering that day did help. A little.

"Your grace, I'll break the shaft."

Pain flashed her vision white as the ckol took hold of the arrow. "No," she gasped, "just leave it!"

When a third volley failed to land, Ellaniel looked back to see what had become of the Woodwise archers. She didn't get that great a view—they were covered by the sight of Odavan's mounted ckols bearing down on them, fast.

"Move her to safety!" one of her men shouted.

She felt hands around her arms and inhaled sharply as they lifted her up, shifting her leg in the process. Through grit teeth, she just managed a question, "What of the army?"

"They're holding for now, but that leaves us stuck between—"

"Brace!" As they dragged her, she heard shields bang together. She looked over her shoulder just as a horse and rider crashed through her ckols' shield wall. One of her men landed a clean cut across the animal's flank, dropping it and its master. Another Woodwise rider came up right behind, his beast leaping over the fallen mess to let him take a swing at one of Ellaniel's escorts. She heard metal clash against metal. The next thing she knew, she was down on her good knee, chaos all around her, Senkani and Woodwise ckols intermixed, blades swinging everywhere. One of her ckols dropped to the ground in front of her, hand clutching at his gut just below the breastplate. She stared at him, shocked that things could have turned into such a disaster.

A Woodwise ckol shadowed her, stepping in front of the midmorning sun. Ellaniel desperately lifted her shield in time to catch the man's sword. The impact and her poor footing landed her on her side. She tried to scramble away, but the arrow shaft in her leg caught on dirt, digging the point deeper into the wound. The pain slammed her to a halt and wrested another agonized cry from her lips. The last thing she saw was the ckol's sword as it swung into her head.

Chapter 39

Charva watched the Senkani and Woodwise lines crash into one solid mass on the fields of Creedport. Tears blurred her sight, but she watched.

"Why? We're all Leverie. Why!?"

Soon enough, despair and grief gave way to anger and disdain. She laughed bitterly, flinging her arm out at the battle and turning to Ersch. "Why are we all so stupid?"

Ersch looked as though searching for words, but gave up and merely turned his eyes to the fighting.

Just as well. Charva didn't need any pretty sophistry from anyone. She could supply enough of that herself. She'd been the one enamored by Falconians, with their martial traditions, their shining mail, their knightly honor. She'd been the one playing with swords and talking of adventure and heroism, all the while trying to usurp her father's rule. Throrne had been right about that. It had been creeping up on her all day, an understanding that now solidified in her mind.

This was what happened when you put stock in swords.

Wanting to look away, but knowing she shouldn't, Charva played the role of silent witness as her country tore itself apart. It was the least she could do, it being her fault it had come to this. *I should have been able to talk Arzan and Ella down!*

Ellaniel, easy to recognize in her distinctive lace sleeves and leggings and red capelet, rode around the eastern flank, her ckols close behind. A shiver went down Charva's back and a stone settled in her stomach when she saw her swing her sword through the necks of the unwitting Woodwise ranks. Nearer at hand, the Senkani archers, quivers spent, charged into the west flank, desperate to save their fellows from encirclement. As proud as she'd been up to now of her Falconian sword training, Charva had no idea who was winning this battle. But when Ellaniel swooped away from the battle and slowed to a stop, she instantly saw the mistake. In the distance, the Woodwise archers, having hung back from the close quarters brawl, saw their chance and put arrows to string.

"No!" Charva breathed. Unthinking, she kicked her horse forward, but Ersch was faster in putting himself in her way.

"My liege, race in there and you die."

"Let me past, Ersch. They'll kill her!"

"There's nothing you can do. You haven't even a scrap of armor. Their fight is their—"

The arrows loosed. Charva traced their path with wide, horrified eyes. Her breath caught in her throat as she saw them hit. Horses reared or fell, throwing their riders to the ground. Though a few remained unharmed, she was sure Ellaniel wasn't one of the lucky ones.

Charva bolted her horse around the back of Ersch's. The guardsman twisted around and tried unsuccessfully to grab hold of her reins, then galloped after her.

Hoping beyond hope that Ellaniel was still all right, she didn't even see the second volley until it was already raining down on the Senkani unit. Charva spotted the crendess just as she fell against the dead body of a horse, an arrow buried in her leg.

Though she hadn't a clue how she could have helped before, now it was clear. She was getting Ellaniel off this battlefield.

Ersch's called out behind her, "The gates open!"

Charva glanced north and saw Ylnavar's ckols racing out of the city. With that, Senkani had now certainly lost. Outnumbered, outflanked, their own cavalry crushed and a fresh mounted enemy force coming in from the rear, there was no way of turning the tide.

She was horrified when she turned to look back ahead, saw the Woodwise cavalry crash through the Senkani ckols' hasty defense. Ellaniel was on the ground, a Woodwise ckol advancing on her. Charva could just barely get there in time. She struggled to pull out her sword, cursing herself for not thinking to do so earlier even if rapiers were worthless on horseback. The ckol swung his sword, catching Ella in the side of her helmet. Charva screamed and jumped out of the saddle, forgetting about her weapon and slamming into the ckol with her body alone. Pain flashed all through her left shoulder as she connected with steel plate, but she succeeded in smashing the man off his feet. She landed on top of him and rolled, her training taking over and sending her springing back to her feet a yard or two away. Her shoulder burned, and she'd no idea if she'd broken bone. Her horse escaped across the field, leaving her alone in all the mayhem, Ellaniel unmoving at her side.

The ckol sputtered something and pushed himself up. Charva drew her sword, easier now that she wasn't on horseback, but still a challenge with how badly her hand shook. In that moment, she remembered something her swordmaster had said. Someone could train his or her whole life in how to wield a weapon. When it came to actually using it against another human being in a moment of crisis, many forgot it all. The only way to find out if you were that kind of person was to see the crisis arrive.

The ckol flicked his eyes from her blade to her face, his expression first surprised, then hard, and Charva knew this was when she discovered what she was made of.

"I'll give you one chance to run, woman," the ckol said.

"I extend the same offer," Charva said. "Leave the crendess alone." She tried to sound her usual nonchalant self, but heard the quaver in her voice.

The ckol scowled and stepped in to thrust.

Charva's shakes melted away. Her opponent's attack was in perfect form, and that only brought her back to her sparring and training. Her body knew how to respond. Her foot moved a half step to dodge, her hand raised her sword to guard. The steel connected. She deflected his blade to the side, leaving him open. Almost of its own accord, her sword darted in. It carried past the point where in training she'd always stopped short. And for the first time in her life, it found flesh.

For a moment, time seemed to hang still as Charva

comprehended what she'd done. Or perhaps the both of them just froze, neither believing what had happened. Whichever the case, the stillness broke when the ckol tried to breathe, only to have his throat suck inwards on the length of embedded steel. She pulled the sword free and stared. Belatedly, she realized the man still had his own blade in hand. She backed off and guarded, but the ckol merely grabbed at his neck and doubled over, choking on blood.

Someone shoved her aside and she heard the clash of steel. She swung around, stepping out of the way as Ersch dueled with another Woodwise ckol.

"If you're going to grab the crendess, then grab the crendess!" Ersch shouted.

Charva remembered why she was there and ducked down beside Ellaniel. Her friend's helmet was deeply dented, and she feared the padding underneath hadn't been enough to save her from the impact. She fumbled for a pulse, but couldn't calm enough to do it right. She wasn't sure if she was touching the right spot, and even then she hadn't any hope of separating the pounding in her ears from the sense in her fingers. The shouting and screaming all around certainly didn't help her focus.

Not that Charva could even help if Ella was alive. Fool idiot! Ersch had been right. What was she going to do? Drag Ella out of here? Where to? It was just soldiers and bare farmland everywhere.

But still she had to do something. Even if it was merely getting her away from the immediate fight.

Charva spied the arrow sticking out of Ellaniel's thigh and snapped off the shaft, then pulled the crendess' arms up around her shoulders, gasping as she put pressure on her own injury. She tried straining forward, but Ella had always been the heavier one and her armor on top of that made it impossible to move anywhere faster than a crawl.

The fighting dwindled. Even weakened by the arrow barrage, the Senkani ckols had managed a good number on the enemy, leaving only ten in Woodwise colors still standing. But there were only seven Senkani left, none near enough to help.

Leaving three extra Woodwise free to face off against

Ersch. As soon as she saw it, Charva nearly set Ella down to lend aid, but the guardsman held his own, somehow blocking every attack and throwing his opponents to the ground with the same style of move he'd used on Ckol Magar. Charva suddenly had a hope that maybe they could do this.

But then came the rumble of ground beneath them and the approach of fresh cavalry. In moments, the Highcity ckols surrounded what was left of the skirmish, having finished whatever task they'd been set to in the main battle. Casting her gaze northward, Charva felt her heart sink. It was all over. The Senkani were defeated. The Woodwise soldiers were breaking up, and between their ranks were scores of Senkani kneeling in surrender.

"Stand down, your grace," the lead Highcity ckol said. "We've enough nobles being charged with treason today."

Charva gritted her teeth. She didn't care how outnumbered she got, or if it looked she had no way out. She wasn't going to—

Someone pulled Ellaniel away from her, having come up behind without her noticing. The next instant, she was face down in the dirt, wrists locked in a ckol's strong grip. She tried to kick her way free. "I won't let you kill her! Let her go, you—" Her shin struck metal plate, and she broke herself off with a whimper of, "Flame and embers." She squeezed her eyes shut to the pain. Not to the burning in her leg or the fire in her shoulder, but to the pain of seeing her world collapse once more around her.

Chapter 10

Thrake was nowhere in the palace. Arzan's soldiers swept the building room by room, turning it upside down. A few went overboard, smashing furniture and windows. Arzan didn't stop them. This wasn't like in the streets. Everything here belonged to their enemy. He would have personally set fire to the place—the only thing stopping him was the concern that some of the servants wouldn't flee. A handful of them put up a meager fight, armed with sticks and kitchen knives. Those were promptly captured and dragged outside. The rest fled or cowered in corners. Among them was Throrne, who Arzan had bound and hauled out for interrogation.

"Where's the crenden?" Arzan demanded.

"I-I'm not telling you, c-criminal," the young man stuttered.

Arzan grabbed him by the collar and threw him to the ground. He gave him enough time to recover his senses, then put a blood-smeared boot on his chest. "Where?"

One of the servants dropped to his knees nearby. "He's at the south gate! Please, don't hurt the young master!"

Arzan eased off. The south gate, nearest to danger? The last place he would have expected. He should have made Filgneir's assault the main attack rather than the decoy after all. He nodded to Vigkhon and pointed to Throrne. "He's coming with us."

The street was just as desolate and silent on the way to the gate as on the way from the docks. No one challenged them, windows and doors shuttered and barred closed. Only at their destination did they meet opposition—a mass of commoners waiting with tools and knives as their weapons. Arzan pitied them. Doubtless fellows threatened into this role of human shield.

And the culprit—he saw who could only be Thrake, standing with Ylnavar atop the wall beside the gate tower. Arzan would be able to identify the thin Highcity crenden's condescending stance from a mile away. Thrake . . . the man gave Arzan pause. It was too distant to make out his expression or the subtleties in his bearing, but something about him looked broken, defeated, and remorseful. Arzan smiled grimly. He'd expected Thrake to be his arrogant, haughty self up until the end. Perhaps he might actually acknowledge his wrongs before Arzan took his head.

The Senkani halted in front of the pitiable defenders before slamming their shields into the ground in a single intimidating *crack* that rattled the street. Arzan stepped through the shield wall with his ckols and looked between the commoners before him and the Leverie crendens on the wall above. He settled his attention on the people.

"Men of Creedport, I have no quarrel with you, only with the murderer who rules your city. Let us pass and I have no cause to harm you."

"Don't go playing the noble champion of the people!" someone shouted. It was an older man at the forefront wielding an iron hook and footstool. "I'm sick of Senkani self-righteousness every time we get traders from your province. Always pushing your weight around. And now you want our crenden! You ain't having him, I says!"

The response left Arzan speechless, and he had to work his tongue to retrieve his voice. "Crenden Thrake is a criminal. A murderer!"

"So you say, Redleaf, but who's the one marching through a peaceful Leverie city with swords and armor?"

A chorus of supporting voices backed the man up. "Warmongers!" "Brutes!" Along with the stream of insults came a rain of ceramics and produce that battered against the Senkani shields.

Arzan felt his blood boil, but it was his men who shouted

back. "Mindless lackeys!" "Peasants!" "Spineless cowards!"

"Enough!" Arzan said. He pointed to the Creedport commoners. "I gave you a chance out of the goodness of my heart and the demands of fairness. If you won't stand aside now, we will make you."

To their credit or condemnation, the commoners braced. They would not be moving.

Very well.

Arzan raised his sword.

A sharp clap split the air, interrupting before he could drop the point. A second and third followed, carrying enough authority to quiet both sides. Arzan looked up to the ramparts, where Ylnavar stood with wooden stick touching stone.

"Crenden Redleaf," the Highcity ruler called, "lay down your arms. Your army is defeated."

Arzan laughed mockingly. "By what stretch of the imagination?"

"No stretch. Odavan is outside the walls with the full strength of Woodwise province. Your men outside have surrendered."

The words hit Arzan like a hammer to the chest. If that was true, then Ella—no. It had to be a bluff. Even if reinforcements from Woodwise had arrived, there couldn't have been enough time for them to—

The city gate pulled open, the doors creaking on their iron hinges. Ylnavar's ckols came riding back in through the arch, looking not the least bit like they were running from an enemy. One of them shouted a command and the Creedport commoners made way, allowing Arzan to see that two of the lead riders carried a limp body by the arms between their horses, legs dragging listlessly along the ground. His strength fled from him as he recognized the bald head and chain armor. He nearly dropped to his knees when they threw the body to the street.

"Filgneir!"

"The crendess is in our hands," Ylnavar called. "If you wish her to see another day, submit yourself to the Council's judgment."

The words were but distant sounds. Arzan's soul felt hollowed as he gazed at his lifelong friend lying dead on the ground. The emptiness fast gave way to fear when he thought of seeing Ellaniel in the same still pose, her beautiful golden eyes empty and cold. Fear, and then rage.

How *dare* they!

Body shaking with anger, Arzan snapped around and shoved his way through his men. He found Throrne, wrists still tied behind his back and shoulders hunched as he tried to be forgotten. Arzan grabbed the lad by the hair and forced his face up.

"I have Throrne Leverie. Give me my wife and my men, or he dies!"

"F-Father!"

Shocked mutterings went through Creedports and Senkani alike.

"So the proud House of Redleaf would lower itself to such a level," Ylnavar said.

"What's good for Leverie is good for me. Let us through, Ylnavar."

Thrake doubled over, putting his hands on the rampart's edge and leaning dangerously out over the street. "Arzan, let my son go!"

"There is no negotiation to be had with traitors of the aristocracy," Ylnavar said. "Kill him if you will. It will only add to your punishment."

"No!" Thrake launched himself up at the Highcity crenden. Ylnavar's ckols were at the ready to intercept, but Thrake's were even faster, and atop the wall more numerous. Thrake reached the Speaker and held him by the edge, sword at his throat where all could see. "He will have safe passage! Hold to your word, Arzan, that he will not be harmed!"

The mounted Highcity ckols jumped off their horses and tried rushing the gate tower, but the Creedport guardsmen had it securely defended. After a moment's confusion, the commoners sided with Thrake and held a lane open, barring the Highcity ckols from interfering. One ckol did manage to ride back out the gate. Fearing what message he might bear to those outside, Arzan didn't waste time. Pausing only long enough to have Filgneir's body retrieved, he took his men through the arch under the watchful gaze of the man he had come here to kill.

Any frustration he felt at failing his goal was overshadowed by the horror that awaited him outside the wall. Woodwise was indeed here, its soldiers massed along the open fields. Corpses in Woodwise and Senkani colors lay strewn in a long line where the fighting had taken place, and those that remained of Ellaniel's army were on their knees in the dirt. Arzan's eyes searched frantically for any sign of his wife. He found Odavan first. Hashan's nephew rode through the carnage, pushing his horse up to within speaking range, but no closer. He looked pristine in his shining breastplate, though the half dozen ckols who accompanied him were a mess of smeared blood and dirt.

"This is the spectacle." Odavan glanced up at the walls and then rested his eyes on the captive Throrne. "I see old Ylnavar didn't have all his contingencies covered."

"Enough, Odavan," Arzan said. He moved his blade up to Throrne's neck. The young man inhaled sharply and tried fruitlessly to shift away. "Where's Ella?"

Odavan shook his head. "This is going to come back to bite us." He turned and pointed. "You'll find Goldeye with your surgeons." Before Arzan had a chance to think of a next question, Odavan urged his horse away. "Hurry up and release the prisoners! You want Crenden Ylnavar's blood on your hands?"

Arzan gripped Throrne's arm tight as death as he hurried to where the Senkani surgeons were busy treating the injured. Men moaned and whimpered and screamed around him as the physicians dug out arrows and sewed up flesh. A few quieted as they saw their crenden in their midst, gritting their teeth and putting on a brave face for their liege. Arzan's chest tightened at the state of his people. This was a disaster. For his part, Throrne seemed ready to vomit.

Arzan spotted Ellaniel's armor strewn on the ground before he saw her. His wife was flat on her back, leg bare as a surgeon bandaged her thigh. Another busied himself gently probing her scalp with his fingers. Arzan shoved Throrne off on Vigkhon and rushed to her side.

I shouldn't have let her come. I shouldn't have left her in charge outside the wall.

"Ella." He choked on her name.

"Minor concussion," the physician checking over her head reported. "The helmet padding absorbed enough of the blow. Don't feel any noticeable fractures."

The other surgeon finished tying the bandage around her leg. "Minor injuries, my liege."

Almost as if herself waiting for the report, Ellaniel stirred, knitting her brow and letting a low groan escape her lips. Arzan breathed a sigh of relief and gently cupped her cheek. Ellaniel's eyes cracked open and she pressed a hand to her temple. "Arzan? What—" She snapped alert and shot up on her elbows. "The battle—" She broke herself off to turn and vomit over a carrot plant.

Arzan rubbed her shoulders and eased her back down. "Keep calm and rest. The fight's ended."

Ellaniel gripped his armguard. "Did we get Thrake?"

Arzan forced himself not to glare back at the city wall. He swallowed hard, loath to admit the truth. "No. We're retreating."

Charva pushed her own way out of her captor's grips the moment word got out that the prisoners were to be freed, then ran towards the surgeons' field. When they had taken Ellaniel, they hadn't killed her on the spot. There was still a chance she was alive.

A set of freshly released Senkani soldiers blocked her path as they lined up around the injured. Though absent their swords and shields, the men pressed tightly enough together to make passage impossible.

"No one who's not Senkani gets past. The crendess fought for us, and we'll die before we let anyone of you close!"

As if I didn't fight for her! Charva wanted to say, but she spotted Ellaniel on the other side before the words could leave her mouth. Arzan was already with her, and it looked like she was sitting up and moving. She breathed a sigh of relief. Tension flooded away, leaving her ready to topple over.

A strong arm steadied her. "I'll get you through these fools if you wish."

Charva looked to see Ersch standing next to her, eyes fixed on the Senkani guards.

"They . . . ." she trailed off as she remembered the disdain in Ellaniel's voice last time they'd spoken, before the battle. "It's enough to know she's all right."

Truthfully, she was dead tired and her shoulder and shin were killing her. If the battle was over, she wouldn't mind getting back to her room and dropping in bed. Yet she still had to find out if her father was alive and whether he was still going to trial. She had to do her part cleaning up this whole ridiculous mess. The city was turned upside down, the fields were ruined, corpses and injured lay everywhere.

. . . And was that Throrne with his wrists tied and surrounded by Senkani ckols?

Charva navigated her way around clusters of injured getting rushed to the surgeons. Throrne's sour face lit up just a tad when he saw her past the wall of guards, then went back to being even more dour than before.

"Keep your distance, your grace," Captain Vigkhon said. He stood behind Throrne, bared sword in hand. Now it made sense how Arzan had been able to get the prisoners released.

"These are the kinds of friends you have, Charva," Throrne said, scowling. She could see him shaking. Did he actually believe Arzan would have him killed? Her brother didn't know the Redleafs like Charva did. Throrne hadn't anything to do with what happened in Senkani, and Arzan wouldn't murder someone he knew was innocent.

She paused and looked at the carnage around her, bodies strewn about, clothing and armor darkened with blood. Would he? Did she really know the man if he was capable of ordering this?

"I'll stick with you, Throrne," she said. "Things will be fine."

"Oh, because you and your guardsman can save me from ten ckols," Throrne said.

Charva held her tongue against the reminder of her own helplessness.

"The carts are here," a Woodwise soldier announced. "Load whoever you want and begone while you have the chance, Senkani scum."

A Senkani soldier shouted, "Hey, there are men still need treatment!"

"You're lucky you already had this much time, rebels."

"There's more wounded than will fit on the carts, even after dumping the supplies."

"Then pick who you're leaving behind!"

Charva anxiously eyed the groups of Woodwise and Senkani soldiers, hoping things weren't about to escalate.

Arzan pushed his way into the open. "Get as many onto the carts as you can."

"My liege, my brother can't be moved!"

"Then he stays with the Leverie surgeons. We return to Senkani!" Arzan's gaze swept over Throrne, paused a moment when he caught sight of Charva. He ignored her and went on to oversee the withdrawal.

"It'll be fine," Charva repeated. "It's almost over."

She knew a lot of things could still go wrong. She wished she'd been handed back her sword. No doubt plenty of Senkani soldiers felt the same. At least the Highcity ckols had been in too much of a rush to find her daggers. She also had Ersch, and after his display in the battle, that did give her a lot of comfort.

Even rushing, preparations to move out still took half an hour. When the first of the Senkani supply-turned-medical wagons started rolling towards the woods, the sun already approached its zenith. It tore at Arzan's heart that there weren't enough to carry everyone who needed to be moved, and Odavan wasn't giving them any more time to make stretchers. Several dozen were going to have to stay behind, reliant on whatever aid the Leverie chose to give them. He consoled himself with the fact that many of them were injured badly enough that they stood a better chance here than if they were to suffer the return journey.

"Is the last one loaded?" Arzan demanded.

"As best we can manage," the head surgeon said. He kept his eyes off the men still lying in the dirt beside the road.

A soldier kneeling over one of them rose and approached the final cart. "Please, just one more! We can't leave my friend with the Leverie!"

Arzan glanced over his silently suffering comrade. Both his legs were mangled. He doubted the fellow would ever walk again, even if he survived the broad wounds to his chest. Imagining the pain he must be going through tied Arzan's stomach in a knot.

"I can still make room for one more." Ellaniel said weakly as she tried to sit up against the front board.

The surgeon was quick to ease her firmly down onto her back. "No, you can't, your grace."

"If she's offering—" the soldier started.

His wounded friend stopped him with a voice more firm than Arzan would expect possible with those injuries, "Don't trouble the crendess. My crenden, take the last cart and go before the Leverie try anything."

Arzan knelt down and took the man's hand in his, heedless of the dirt and drying blood on his skin. "Senkani will not forget you."

"Just lead our people to victory, my liege," he said loud and strong, though tears ran down the corners of his eyes.

The cart started forward. Arzan motioned for Throrne to be kept close. He'd have him released once the last of the troops reached the woods. Odavan might or might not pursue at that point, but his numerical advantage would be lost on the narrow road. Arzan's soldiers who had come with him into the city were still fresh and fully equipped. Nothing would get past them.

He noticed Charva again, following as close to her brother as the ckols would allow. He trusted her not to do anything stupid. Despite his threat, Arzan wouldn't seriously kill Throrne, and Charva knew it. Let the younger man have some comfort, though.

A few soldiers chose to stay behind with the abandoned casualties. Arzan and the rest raised their swords in salute and farewell. It felt like it took an age for them all to arrive at the woods' edge, and all the while Arzan expected to see arrows take flight at their backs. He let out a long breath when they entered the forest without incident. Behind cover of trees, he finally untied Throrne's wrists and let Charva and the guardsman Ersch approach him.

"You can be his escorts back to the city."

"Arzan, there is a chance Thrake didn't do it," Charva said. For the first time, he noticed her torn sleeve and the dirt stains on her dress and wondered if she'd somehow gotten involved in the battle. What side had she been on? *The one defending Thrake, obviously.*

"I trusted and supported you," Arzan said bitterly. "I would have hoped for you to return the favor. Take your brother and leave."

Charva's eyes flared and she looked about to argue, but one of the rear watch rode up shouting, "They're killing the prisoners!"

"No!" Arzan ran back out of the woods. "No!"

Far as the battlefield was, it was hard to see, but he could make out glinting steel and clusters of men in Senkani colors trying to fend off the horde of Woodwise blue. Arzan drew his blade. "Bloody villains!"

Vigkhon grabbed him tight. "My liege, we can't do anything!"

A dozen or so of his men rushed past him, weapons drawn and screaming in rage. They barely made it twenty paces before they were met by a storm of arrows. Three of the soldiers stumbled and dropped. The rest stopped and raised their shields. "*Cowards!*"

Arzan shoved Vigkhon away, but it was too late. The prisoners were already overwhelmed. He balled his fist, his arms shaking and his vision blurring. "Odavan, Ylnavar, you are going to pay."

"Leverie swine!"

Charva held Throrne's hand tight. *This is bad. This is very, very bad.*

"Why is Woodwise doing such a thing?" her brother asked. "This is against the war codes. How can—"

"My liege, I think we should be getting out of here,"

Ersch said, putting himself between her and the nearest Senkani troops.

Several soldiers scooped up stones and threw them towards the distant Woodwise soldiers. "Death to all their filth!"

Charva stepped off the road, pulling Throrne with her. "Come on!" she urged quietly.

Throrne turned wide eyes on her. "Sis, this doesn't—"

Movement to her left. Charva slipped out a dagger and braced herself, but felt her brother torn from her grip.

"Here's Thrake's bloody spawn!"

Charva reached out. "Stop!"

She heard steel slice through flesh. Throrne stared at her, shock and confusion in his face. The two of them looked down at the sword tip jutting out of his chest.

Ersch grabbed the Senkani soldier by the wrist and twisted him around, audibly popping the man's arm from its socket, and slammed him face-first into the packed dirt. Charva caught Throrne as he fell free, easing him to the ground. Her brother gripped her arm, fingers digging hard into her skin. His mouth move wordlessly. She saw terror take hold in his blue eyes.

"Throrne, you'll be fine. We . . . we'll get this . . . " The sword was still buried in his chest, straight through the heart. His hand dropped away and she felt the strength seep out of his body. His eyes went dull.

Ersch fought off another soldier who came at them. Charva knew she should fight to protect herself as well, but her mind and soul were numb. She didn't resist when someone grabbed her by the shoulder. Hardly noticed the flash of red cape when Arzan threw her attacker away. She watched the scuffle through a haze. At some point, Arzan regained control of the situation and had the offending soldier kneel in front of her. The crenden opened his mouth, but she didn't hear the words that he spoke. Ersch took up a sword he was offered and lopped off the soldier's head.

Moments later, she and Ersch were alone along the roadside with the last two bodies left in the wake of the beginning of war.

Chapter 41

Retyar raised his binoculars, bringing the army column into view as he lay flat on the large rock nestled a good distance within the woods. *So, today was the First Battle of Creedport.* He nodded to himself. History was still on its proper course.

Its violent, bloody course.

The soldiers he saw were in sorry shape—torn outfits, missing equipment, many of them bandaged. He could only imagine what they'd been through. Back home, there was no shortage of movies with epic sword battles, but as a historian he knew that those were mostly all bogus. Entertainment directors had little idea or respect for proper formation and tactics. Most of the time, they couldn't even get the weapons and armor right. But the truth was genuinely hard to come by. So much of this world was lost to his time. Historians made do with fragmented documents, memories put to paper years after the events. Archaeologists dug up rusted leftovers of battles and peeked at naked bones in mass graves. Museums preserved swords and suits of plate. It was all so piecemeal, little more than echoes of a living world.

Raze it, I wish I had a camera!

The nagging urge he thought he'd gotten rid of came back to him. He wanted to crawl closer, get right in there and see these people in person. He wanted to talk to them, get their stories out of their own mouths. History's truths were right there. All he had to do was walk up and ask.

And destroy the timeline.

He sighed and stayed where he was. *I'm better than this. I'm disciplined, and the best person to have ended up in this situation. Don't mess it up.*

Like by taking a ten-year-old girl under his care?

He tightened his lips and fiddled with his rifle strap, waiting for the end of the column. It took some time, but the last of the soldiers eventually slogged past and out of sight.

Retyar got up and dusted himself off before heading back for the coast.

The cave was quiet when he returned. He took a discreet peek inside, saw the girl sitting by the far hole, staring glumly out to sea. The sun caught in her tangled hair, making the strands glow vibrant purple. He pulled back and set himself on the project he'd been working on earlier that morning. The comb was coming along nicely. The piece of driftwood he'd scavenged had turned out perfect, and from this point it was just a matter of carving out all the fingers without breaking any. Fixing her hair would give her something to do, at least.

Retyar emptied his thoughts and lost himself in the work. The seagulls circled above, cawing down at him. Waves crashed endlessly on the rocks below. He'd finished freeing the center fingers when he heard the *tink* of something getting thrown against the cave wall. With a sigh, he put the wood and knife away and went inside.

One of the food tins lay on the uneven ground, its edge sporting a prominent dent. Retyar picked it up and set it aside, then turned to the girl.

"I've only got three of these tins, you know," Retyar said. "Unless you know how to hold soup with your bare hands, you might want to take care of them."

"I'm bored," the girl said, her eyes still on the open waters. At this angle, it was easier to see the dark bruise along the side of her face.

"Not much I can do to help you on that count."

Fellone turned to give him one of her glares she'd been refining over the last few days. "Well, you must be the world's dullest pirate. Can't you at least tell me some stories?"

That was precisely what he didn't want to do. The more

he spoke to her, the greater threat she was to the timeline.

Greater threat than her even being alive? Retyar shook his head.

He felt awful for her, but he clicked his tongue in pretend annoyance as he sat back against the wall opposite her. *That's what a pirate would do, right?* "Well then, girl. What kind of stories you want to hear?"

Fellone looked surprised for a moment, but only a moment as eagerness quickly lit up her face. "How did you get marooned?"

Retyar unstrapped his rifle and set it, still covered, on his lap. "I was chasing after a traitor who stole something from us. Fellow drowned during the chase, but my boat hit the rocks and my crew couldn't come after me." Near enough the truth to be easy to remember.

Fellone waited eagerly for more. None came. "That's all you're saying about it?"

"Hey, I'm not a bard."

The girl narrowed her eyes and twisted her lip. "What was it he stole?"

Retyar caught himself fingering the satchel hanging from his shoulder. "Maps. Provisions."

"That was important enough for you to go after him?"

"Well, the captain thought he might have taken some of the gold. Didn't know at the time he hadn't."

"So, you were able to find out he only had maps and provisions," Fellone said. "I thought the traitor died before you could catch him."

"He died, sure, but I found his loot."

"Is that where those metal bowls came from?"

Retyar nodded.

"Can I see the maps? I love maps."

"Destroyed in the water," Retyar said with a shrug.

Fellone crossed her arms. "They're treasure maps, aren't they, and you're keeping them for yourself."

No, just maps of a place that won't exist until hundreds of years from now, Retyar thought. "Look, if they were really something so valuable, my captain wouldn't have just left me here, would he?"

"Or maybe he didn't leave you. Maybe the crew are the

ones you're really hiding from. Maybe *you're* the thief."

"You've too much of an imagination, little girl. If I had any treasure map, why would I be hiding instead of going out looking for the goods?"

Fellone had a look that said she wasn't quite convinced, but she changed the subject. "What kingdom are you from?"

Out of the pan, into the fire. Retyar hoped the sweat gathering on his brow wasn't too obvious. "Govunari." The girl would have no way of checking whether the country existed or not. "The kingdom holds the Falcon's Heart in the center of the continent."

"I thought Malruon held the Falcon's Heart."

Retyar silently cursed himself. "Not anymore. The Malruon dynasty lost the throne years ago." Six hundred years ago from his perspective. Several decades in the future from hers.

"What's it like there?"

"Big cities." Millions of people each. "Lots of towers." Over a hundred stories high. "The biggest university on the continent." A city unto itself.

"Ella said Charva—that's her friend from Creedport— said she went to Falcone and visited the Feathers. That's where she learned swordplay. They have knights with so much armor they're like crabs."

He nodded, remembering the suits of full plate that lined the halls of the University castle. "They use those all over Falcone, but Govunari has the best armor smiths in the whole world." Which helped in part to pave the way for the era of industry. Intimate knowledge of iron and steel made it easy to craft the parts needed for the machines of the 5200s.

Stop wanting to tell her all this, you nerd, he chastised himself.

"What else are Falconians good at?" Fellone asked.

"Other than metalworking? Like I said, we've got great builders. Massive towers and grand castles. The roads are paved even out in the country. We have bridges that have stood for thousands of years." He would have gone on about the canals, but he wasn't sure if they were built yet in this time.

"Why did you leave?"

Retyar didn't have a ready answer. He'd already used up the chasing a traitor story, and he was sure anything he constructed on the spot wouldn't hold up to the girl's questioning. He stood and hung his rifle back over his shoulder. "That's it for today."

Fellone started to protest, but Retyar was already outside, where the crashing waves drowned out anything she said. He sat down with the knife and comb. As he carved the blade into the wood, he tried planning out the next part of his story, but his mind wandered to his parents and brothers. For the first time in a long while, he thought of home not in the abstract, but in the faces of the people he'd known. He thought of the house in the country he'd grown up in and the University where he'd spent half a decade of his life. He remembered a place where he wished he could be, but was ever more certain he could never return.

Chapter 42

Retyar left the classroom with a light step and a binder stuffed with notes. If the rest of his classes were anything remotely like Professor Parvyn's, he wouldn't regret majoring in history anytime soon.

"I see you came to the light." Thesha popped up next to him in the hall with a broad smile. "One more recruit for the wondrous National History Society!"

Her traditional long-sleeved and split skirt dress coupled with the bits on old time etiquette at the end of the lecture prompted Retyar to give her a bow. "Greatest of pleasures to see you again, my lady."

Thesha responded with a gracious curtsy that Retyar was sure did justice to their ancestors. "And a delight to be graced with your presence. May the sun light your steps and the stars guide your path."

"Um, okay, I admit I don't know the response to that one."

Thesha adjusted her satchel. "You have much to learn, honorable sir. So, where you heading?"

"Going into town. I wanted to get supplies for dinner."

"Then our destinations are aligned." She started down the hall. "Well, Mr. Venon?"

Retyar joined her company, noticing his quickened heart and finding it surprisingly difficult to gauge the measure of his steps. Walking through town with a beautiful girl hadn't exactly been on his agenda when first coming to the

University, but he certainly wasn't going to complain at this turn of events.

"Are you always wearing that style?" Retyar asked after a pair of girls in hooded jackets and denim pants giggled on their way by.

Thesha waved her arm, long green sleeve trailing her motions through the air. "Why not?"

"History isn't just a subject for you."

"I guess I'm a sucker for the old ways. We have so much now. Planes, cars, computers, the Ledgerweave, all that. Humanity's stronger now than it's ever been, but I just can't help but feel like we've lost something. There's a sort of romance, a beauty, an elegance that disappeared when machines took over. I don't know. Maybe it's just me."

Retyar looked at the University buildings all around them. "Well, they don't make too much stuff like this any more."

They walked the campus streets to the nearest bus terminal just in time to meet the lumbering, blue-painted whale of a vehicle that served as regular transit for students. Retyar took the aisle seat, but the windows were large enough that everyone had a perfect view outside. As the bus passed out of the old fashioned campus and into the normal part of Parnyven, the transformation was dramatic. Concrete walls, backlit florescent signs, intersections congested with rivers of cars, advertising boards and electrical lines cutting up the sky . . . . It all made Thesha's point without her having to say another word.

The bus dropped them off about a block from the grocery. Retyar wrinkled his nose at the smell of poorly burnt gas. "I don't like how bad those buses rattle, but at least they've got air filters."

"Wow, sensitive nose," Thesha said. "Not a city kid?"

"Wheat Strips area."

"Didn't figure you for a farmer."

"I'm not. My parents work in the civil service. We just happen to live out that way." He hesitated a moment. "What about you?"

"The capital. Dad's a weatherman. Mom works in the shipping offices."

Retyar felt a stab of anxiety as he considered the

possibility Thesha had aristocratic blood. Then he felt stupid for jumping to conclusions. The capital was a big place. Even if a lot of the noble families lived there, that didn't mean most of its residents were aristocratic. Besides, those weren't the sorts of jobs aristocrats had. No reason to think Thesha's blood was too good for him.

"That saying about the sun and stars," he said, but cringed as his voice cracked. He cleared his throat. "What's the proper response to that?"

"'Strong legs, sharp eyes.' It was used in the days of the First Cartographers of Falcone."

"Oh, them. I remember the standard texts had about a paragraph on the Cartographers. The book was in a rush to get to Govunari."

They reached the grocery and gathered up the basics. The store had some great-looking crayfish crawling around in the tanks, which would have sorely tempted Retyar to splurge if only he had a pot large enough for one in his dorm. While waiting in checkout, he noticed the television up in the corner was streaming news on the Bumanali war. The volume was off, but infographics and video of Govunari tanks rolling through rubble got the point across that the kingdom was making strong advances.

"Feels like the war just goes on forever," Thesha said. "You'd expect the Bumanali would have surrendered months ago."

"You think we should just back off now? Their military's already wasted. They won't be able to pull off another incursion for years."

Thesha shrugged. "Maybe. Maybe not. If they haven't raised the white, they've still got fight in them."

They came to the counter and paid. The cashiers still used the old mechanical cash boxes that Retyar found endearingly quaint. It was one reason he liked shopping here. He'd used one while working part-time one summer, and it was indescribably satisfying feeling and hearing the click of each key stroke. Most stores now used computers with membrane key pads.

Outside, strips of clouds were starting to cast shadows across the castle overlooking the city. "The 'bastion of learning'," Thesha said. "I wonder what the creator of the phrase would have thought seeing it literally come true."

Retyar regarded the fortress as they crossed the street to the opposing bus stop. "Imagine how difficult it would have been for commoners like us to see the inside of that place back in the day. You could probably live your whole life in this town and never step inside the walls."

"It's still a little like that. How many people here do you think have anything to do with the University? Anyway, what classes are you taking this semester? We might be sharing one."

"Aren't you—"

The sound of breaking glass interrupted him mid-sentence. He and Thesha looked ahead to the bus stop, where a group of students stood ganging around a central figure. At their feet was a shattered bottle.

"You lime eyes ain't wanted in Scholar's City," the man said. "Pack up and go home."

Retyar and Thesha exchanged looks and circled around to see who he was talking to. It was a girl with short, light brown hair and thin-rimmed glasses. She looked a few years younger than Retyar and Thesha, which was interesting considering they were still freshmen themselves. He recognized her as the same one who'd almost rammed into him that one time at the library.

"Whatever Admissions was thinking letting you in, don't get the idea the rest of us'll stand for it," another of the group said.

The girl kept her gaze straight ahead.

A female member of the group, a senior by Retyar's guess, reached out and pulled the girl's satchel straight off her shoulder. The girl turned and glared at her, her lips a pale thin line. Retyar took a step forward, but felt Thesha's hand on his arm.

"She's Ytanian," Thesha said. "Just ignore it."

The bag thief opened the satchel and spilled the contents out over the trash bin. "Well, rat? Getting the message now?"

Retyar pulled away from Thesha's grasp. "Hey, quit it!"

Several sets of eyes turned on him, most deep green or gray, one lime green. All of them were incredulous.

"Seriously," one of the guys said. "Sticking up for her?"

"Did she do something to you?" Retyar asked.

"She's Ytanian. They're traitors who sold us out in the Great War."

"And did *she* do something to *you*?"

The man gave him the dirtiest look he'd ever seen. Retyar subtly shifted his footing, wondering if this was going to come to blows. He was outnumbered here, badly, but if his father had taught him anything, it was that some things were worth standing up for. After one very long moment, the guy spit at his feet. "Sympathizer. Come on, we're done for now."

Retyar watched the group until they were a good number of paces down the way, then yanked the plastic waste bag from the bin so he could pick out the girl's supplies.

"I'll do that part," the girl said.

Retyar grabbed the heavy engineering textbooks and let her rummage for tools.

"What's your name?" Retyar asked.

"Laski. They'll be targeting you from now on, you know."

"Are you saying I should have let them keep bullying you?"

"I'm saying . . . ." Laski drew in a breath and wiped a layer of oily crumbs off her pencil case before stuffing it in her satchel. "I could have handled that myself," she muttered quietly.

"Well, you're welcome anyway. Thesha and I are heading back to the dorms. I think it'd be a good idea if we all went together."

The girl bowed as she gathered the last of her things. She seemed about to disagree, but flicked her eyes to him. "I'm grateful."

Retyar glanced over at Thesha, who stood leaning silently against the sign post as she watched traffic flow by. Seeing how she kept quiet, he decided not to say anything to her either.

The bus, when it arrived, was about half full with students returning to campus. Laski made for the back straight away, her head turned so as to keep her eyes from most others' sight.

"You could try wearing shades," Retyar said. He'd ended

up with the middle seat, staring straight down the aisle, while Laski stowed herself away in the corner. Much to his disappointment, Thesha chose a spot a couple rows up. So much for a girlfriend.

"I'm not ashamed of my heritage." Laski's words would have been more convinced if she weren't slouched down to hide behind the seat in front of her.

Retyar let the silence hang before speaking again. "So, what drew you to engineering?"

She shoved her hands in her pockets. "I'm sick of people seeing Ytanians as second class. I want to show that we have worth."

"And Admissions let you in? Times really are changing."

"They didn't have much choice. I had the highest academic record in my province."

"Uhuh." He had another question he really wanted to ask, even if it was sure to be stepping on a landmine. *Blazes, I'll just do it.* "So, um. You're also pretty young, aren't you?"

She glared. "Fourteen. You got a problem with that?"

Retyar whistled. "Now I really see why the other students are bullying you. You're right that a lot of people see the Ytanians as lower than dirt. What do you think that does to the self-respect of someone who's your elder and scores lower than you?"

Laski pouted her lips. "Then to save their self respect, they'll just have to accept that Ytanians are people too."

He chuckled.

The bus dropped them off by the dorms and Laski bowed to him once more. "I just remembered I need to turn in some paperwork to Administration. Thank you for helping me . . . you didn't give me your name."

"Retyar. And if you want a place you can study without being harassed, you can pop by my table in the library."

The girl smiled and went on her way. Retyar glanced side to side to make sure no one else was paying her any undue attention, then turned for the dorms.

Plastic rustled as Thesha shifted her grocery bag from one hand to the other. She stared off in the opposite direction from Laski. "I can't fault you for having a big heart, but you really shouldn't be so friendly with an Ytanian."

"She needs friends."

Thesha sighed. "You really are country-bred." She looked him in the eye. "There's a reason the Govunari treat the people of Ytania the way we do." Before Retyar could provide any response, she turned down the path to the female quarters. "See you around later."

Retyar stood there trying to decide if he'd messed up. Did he still have a chance with Thesha after this? He certainly hoped so. But he wasn't about to admit that standing up to the bullies was wrong. It wasn't ignorance that made him sympathetic toward Laski. His father always said that every person deserved a chance, regardless of heritage. Thesha obviously had a somewhat different upbringing, and even if he didn't agree with it he wanted to know more about it. If she was still willing to talk to him. With a sigh, he started down the path to his dorm, wishing again that he had a pot big enough for crayfish.

Chapter 43

As the wagon bounced along beneath him, Maltan figured he genuinely was an idiot. He could have discarded Thrake's orders and fled in any direction he might choose after coming to port in Heartsong. There was no one here to escort him, and he knew his mission of reporting on the empire's advance was just a flimsy excuse to send him into exile. He could have made the best of it and found some other life for himself someplace peaceful.

Instead, he'd spent every bit of his coin hiring a wagon driver to take him where nobody else wanted to be. Maltan and the driver were far from the only ones on the road, but they were the only ones heading west. A steady stream of refugees passed them by on their left, burdened down with whatever possessions they could carry on whatever form of transportation they could manage. He saw in their faces the look of the desperate, the fearful, the determined, and the lost. More than a few, he was sure, thought him and his driver mad to be going the other way. Perhaps he was. For once, however, the letter of Thrake's command was more important than the intent. The war with the empire was important, and Maltan agreed that someone needed to be Leverie's eyes.

The coppiced woods gave way to rolling grasslands and farms shortly before noon. Though still distant, their destination stood clearly within sight as they crested a hill. The towering slope of rock the city of Breakpeak was built upon was impossible to miss for anyone within twenty miles.

Poets called it the sinking city. Maltan could easily see why. The rock looked just like the bow of a ship lifting up into the air as the rest of the vessel got swallowed into a sea of green and brown hills. A wreck frozen in time.

The river of refugees turned to a trickle by the time they came near the city gates. Looking north provided the reason. Soldiers holding the flags of the Aristocracy of Whitesail were lined up by the thousands in battle formation. Over their heads, Maltan could see the silver banners of the enemy they faced.

The driver pushed his horses to the limit, racing the wagon the last stretch to the gates. The city guards were already poised to close the doors as they rumbled through and came to a stop just inside the entry square.

"Not yet! Not yet!" the driver shouted, jumping to the ground and frantically unfastening one of the beasts.

"They've been open too long already," the gate captain said. "Close it up!"

"The enemy's still a quarter mile away. Just let me out."

A man and woman pushed their way out of a nearby building, two children in tow. The man grabbed the driver's hand and forced a coin pouch into his palm. "Please, your other horse."

The driver shoved the payment into his coat without even looking at it or the family. "Whatever, yes, it's yours. Hold the gate!"

Maltan got down and helped the family untie the second horse. The beast was scarcely freed before the parents sent their two children out through the gates on its back. The driver and his other horse were already long gone. The guards closed the gate with a heavy thud.

Well then. My fate is quite literally sealed.

A group of men came from nowhere to jostle him aside and tear through the wagon's contents. He just barely managed to snatch his travel bag to his chest as they pilfered whatever wasn't nailed in place.

"Wood rods: get them fitted with spearheads! Get the cloth sent to the surgeons and leather and rope to the—"

"Numbweed. Is there any numbweed?"

Maltan had no reason to remain with the cart. He stepped

back into the ominously empty square. Besides the group mobbing the wagon, the gate guards, and a handful of men atop the wall, he saw no one around. Surely the entire city hadn't been abandoned? But no, he saw them further up, where the elevation rose high enough to see over the walls. Crowds of people clogging the streets and rooftops.

Maltan set about climbing his way up through the city. Breakpeak was a picturesque place, with low, orange-tan houses and shops layered up like a giant's stairway into the sky. He navigated the steep roads and footpaths cut irregularly upwards, catching glimpses of the palace high at the city's peak. He noted the people here didn't paint their dwellings, but vines made up the difference in color, adding streaks and splashes of green to near every wall and rooftop.

Years of climbing up and down his tower steps allowed him to get a good ways up the road without so much as feeling out of breath. Men, women, and children alike ignored his presence, standing about in an eerie silence as they kept their eyes on the armies. A few uneasy whispers passed between the watchers here and there, but most lips were pressed tight. Not particularly wanting to draw attention to himself, he forewent asking questions and settled down on a low wall outside a small residence.

Despite being already in position as far as Maltan could tell, the two armies had still yet to engage. Off to the left, the Vron were arrayed in precise square formations, making them easy to count. Around ten thousand, he calculated. Standard numbers for an imperial army. Off to the right, Whitesail looked to have half again as many, but set in a ragged, disorderly line in mismatched colors. It was a stalwart wall of silver shields and shining helmets against a sea of men he was sure still thought themselves farmers.

Maltan's curiosity finally got the better of him and he leaned over to a thin young man propped against the wall nearby. "Why only Whitesail banners? Where's Heartsong's army?"

"You been hiding under the flagstones, old man? Crendess Galdava was defeated out in the Crooks. The Whitesails're the only thing left standing between the imperials and Breakpeak."

"Why is no one readying to defend the walls?"

"City elders decided it yesterday," the young man said. "If the Vron win the battle, Breakpeak surrenders. We don't have the resources for a siege."

Maltan looked about at all the fighting age males in the crowd. "You have the manpower. The harvest was just taken in . . . ."

"The harvest all went to the crendess' army and the Council, and it could take weeks for another army to come to our aid. Meanwhile, the Vron give good terms to cities that don't resist."

Maltan held his tongue rather than getting into patriotism and loyalty. He went back to watching the fields. The armies stood in place for a good while longer. Sometimes, when the wind was right, he heard distant shouts and chants as the soldiers taunted each other. The spectators around him occasionally wandered away, heading indoors for a bit of bread or water, but they always came back.

Maltan's legs were starting to fall asleep when he heard the trumpets. The notes were clear and sharp, coming in a quick tempo of highs and lows that went on for a span of moments. The silver lines of the Vron army shimmered and started to move.

"What's with them?" someone asked. "They're not keeping a straight battle line."

"Inverted wedge," Maltan said. "They mean to disrupt Whitesail's formation, cutting it into pieces."

The Whitesail army began responding, but if they had any fancy orders like the imperials, Maltan couldn't tell. Parts of the formation started to inch forward, while others hung back in no discernible pattern, bracing with their shields and spears.

Unit cohesion is nonexistent. This will be a slaughter. Maltan gripped the wall beneath him with tight fingers as the prongs of the imperial formation closed in.

"Whitesail has them outnumbered!" a man down the street said at a near shout. "They can't lose this." From the quaver in his tone, he clearly spoke the words to reassure himself more than anyone around him.

"Tear those silvers apart!" someone else said.

The prongs touched the uneven Whitesail line and sliced through as if their soldiers weren't even there. A few people cried in dismay at the one-sided fight. In rapid order, the Whitesails were broken up into three parts, with the center group swallowed up in the Vron's inverted V. The other two parts still had the outer flanks, but they made no headway against the imperial shield wall. The Vron started closing the wings encircling the center. The Whitesails broke, running out the small gap quickly closing in behind them. The flanks saw the rout and started dropping their own weapons and fleeing.

The Vron sounded their trumpets. The silver soldiers disengaged, reformed in a solid line, and watched their enemy scatter. A handful of men on horseback, presumably Whitesail ckols or officers, galloped about trying to restore order, but the effort was futile. Not even a half hour after the first trumpet signal, the battle was lost.

Most of the city folk started disappearing indoors, barring the entrances of their homes and shops behind them. An older woman around Maltan's age bowed her head against a wall nearby and wept quietly. Another woman leaned in with a hand on her shoulder. "Don't worry, Mama. The Vron will be good if we don't fight back."

"The war's not over," someone else said. "The imperials gain nothing from capturing the city. We've no stores to share with them. They'll be forced to move on, and we'll be independent again."

The Vron waited long enough to be entirely sure the Whitesails didn't catch a second wind, then another trumpet call set them marching towards the city. The few Whitesail soldiers who had tried escaping to the walls, only to find the gates shut, now ran eastwards like the rest of their companions. They looked to Maltan like mites fleeing a rising tide.

Pathetic as those soldiers appeared, as the gates swung open for the victorious Vron, he wondered if he was on the right side of these walls.

But then, what better place to observe the enemy than from within?

Chapter 99

Charva sat alone in the palace library. For the first time in a long while, the fancy frills of a Leverie aristocrat dress hung in layers at her shoulders and waist. She didn't have any Falconian dresses in black.

An evening breeze brushed through the open window, ruffling the pages of the book in front of her, carrying with it the scent of smoke and a scattering of ashes lingering after the funeral ceremony outside. *On Practical City Logistics* was the last thing Charva had seen her brother reading. His studiousness had always annoyed her. Theory had its place, but it had to be informed by an understanding of people. Book smarts alone weren't enough for ruling a city. It occurred to her that she'd never actually pointed that out to him.

"But what do I know about people?" she whispered, lowering her forehead to the table and folding her hands over the back of her neck.

There must have been some way to save him. If she had been more persuasive with the Redleafs, or with Ylnavar, or had been here at the palace to keep Throrne from getting captured. She had failed on every point, been less than worthless.

She heard the door swing open and someone walk up and take the seat across from her.

"Go away," she mumbled.

There was a gulping noise before something thudded against the table. Charva shot her head up. "I said—" she stopped short.

Thrake stared emotionless at her, his rich clothing heavily ruffled and a half-empty bottle of wine clutched in his hand. Age had always seemed to elude him, but now wrinkles were finally starting to find their foothold. The low angle sunlight from the window did him no favors.

The two of them sat quietly for some moments. The whole time, Charva wondered why her father would choose to be here with her. Her first instinct was that he needed a target for his anger, but his face showed nothing of that and the silence stretched on without the slightest inkling of an outburst.

At long last, Thrake took another swig from the bottle and slammed it down on the table with a scowl. "Imported Vasnum. Nowhere near as good as Redleaf wine and three times as expensive."

"What do you want, Father?"

Thrake didn't so much look at her as look through her to stare at the wall. "I want my son back, but we don't all get what we want."

The sheer sadness and resignation in his voice stole whatever retort Charva may have had. She couldn't reconcile such emotions with the man she thought she'd known all her life. Indifference, hostility, and anger had always seemed the essence of his being. This different him . . . . He seemed more a person, and she didn't like it.

"Do you still have ambition, Charva?" her father asked.

She didn't answer. This wasn't the time to ask the question. Everything was in such a shamble she didn't know what was up or down.

"Throrne is gone," Thrake said. "I staked everything on him being my successor. Without him, the next crenden may as well be any Creedport Leverie, but none of them would have even considered the role before yesterday. Charva, do you still want to be crendess?"

"I . . . " she wasn't sure what to make of his tone.

Thrake drew in a long breath. "I will back you as my successor."

Charva felt her mouth hang open as she stared incredulously at him. She sprang to her feet. "No! You are *not* turning around and giving me your backing! Not after all you've done, after all you've done to hurt me!"

Thrake sat stone still, hands clenched tight, eyes on the table. "This is about more than just you and me, Charva. This is about the country, and about justice for Throrne." He lifted his gaze, and she saw a face full of determination. "You won't even consider a deal with me?"

Charva eyed him for a long while. "I'm not carrying out vengeance against the Redleafs. The man who killed Throrne is already dead—Arzan handed him over himself."

"Of course I'm not asking that of you. Arzan and I, we've been toyed with like puppets on strings. Someone took advantage of our history to destroy us. Find out who it was and I will ensure you become crendess of Creedport. I'll step down immediately after I bring him down."

"You're serious." Charva retook her seat. "You really didn't order the assassination."

"No. But it no longer matters. After putting a sword to Ylnavar's neck and forcing him and his ckols from the city, I'm a dead man regardless. He'll keep his promise to deal with me after Senkani is taken care of."

"Who . . . ." Charva was still trying to gather her thoughts in this unfamiliar reality. "Who would want to frame you?"

A hint of Thrake's old self showed through with the flicker of anger in his eyes. "A man who will be very much dead once I get my hands on him, but I have no idea beyond that."

"You've made a lot of enemies, Father. Just how many servants and merchants might you have ruined by giving into that temper of yours?"

Thrake shook his head. "It's not someone in the city. Only sheer chance saw Creedport through the battle with the fewest casualties. Our streets could easily have descended into a bloodbath. Too much risk to a conspirator's life, his assets, his family."

"If it's not someone from Creedport," Charva said slowly, "then it would have to be one of the other crendens. They're the only ones who could have enough stake to push the country into war."

The look in Thrake's eyes showed that was exactly what he was thinking.

"But how do we . . . ." Another thought occurred to Charva. "The assassins. Were they even—"

"I'm sure they were the mercenaries I hired for the purge," Thrake said. "The dogs disappeared on the same day as the attacks without even taking their pay."

"They abandoned their fee?"

Thrake nodded. "It was no small amount."

Charva tapped her forehead. "They were committed to this plot and their other employer. If I were a simple freelance mercenary, I'd have taken the money as backup in case I had to cut the other job and run."

"The counterpay had to be great for them not to take both."

"And that much money you don't pay in advance. There's a chance we could track down their movements after the assassinations to find out who hired them."

"Which would have been the obvious first step if everyone hadn't already been convinced of my guilt," Thrake said.

Charva leaned into her hands. "No doubt it isn't as easy as all this. But whether it is or not, we have two paths of investigation: the assassins and the crendens." She fixed her eyes on her father. "All right, I'm doing this, so long as I'm granted one more condition."

Thrake waited and braced himself for whatever it was she was going to demand.

"I want authority to appoint my own ckol."

"No one aside from a current crenden or crendess has that power," Thrake said. "Name who you want and I will appoint him and assign him to you."

"It has to be me. I promised I would be the one to do it when I became crendess. I understand this is bending the rules, but I need a loyal man for this."

Thrake shifted his jaw as he mulled over the request. "No one's following the rules anymore in any case. Do what you wish."

Charva pushed her chair back. "I'll start at once."

"Daughter," Thrake stopped her. His mouth twisted around several near words, then he simply put a gentle hand on her shoulder. For a moment, Charva wondered how things would have been had she been the favored child. What if he had been someone better at controlling his temper and knew better how to show love? Charva lingered, caught in a half-formed image of Thrake and her brother together with her in the same room, none of them scheming, all merely happy with each other's company.

The sun set below the tree line, dipping the room in shadow. The imaginary scene faded from her mind's eye. Charva slipped through the door, steeling her heart for what she knew was going to be a journey into very dark places.

Chapter 45

"Ylnavar, Odavan, Loftham, Warth, Mansar, and Athar. No banners for Pundur or Roth."

Arzan fingered his cape clasp as he listened to the scout's report on the approaching forces. "I would have wished Pundur to join us, but at least there are three crendens we don't have to fight." *Interesting that Roth is staying out of it.* "Keep me briefed on the Council's movements."

The sound of hammers carried up from street level as Arzan walked Senkani's eastern ramparts. Archers practiced along the wall to his left, stringing arrows from basket quivers kept stocked by a stream of children running relay. The bare slopes outside the city, stripped of cover by the harvest, were now a lawn of feathered shafts, with dense lines focused around colored distance markers. Elsewhere atop the wall, engineers were busy with the ballistae emplacements, their wooden mallets raising a ruckus with each adjustment.

Arzan descended to ground level to oversee the rest of the preparations. Vighkon remained his constant shadow, but Arzan still felt a hollowness at his side as he weaved around the wood barricades being nailed into place along the main street. He kept feeling like he'd see Filgneir when he glanced beside him, the familiar bald dome of his shining in the sunlight like a polished knob, his tongue ever ready for a dash of dry humor.

The loss wasn't only personal. Senkani needed as many level-headed men as it could get.

One of his unit commanders jogged past a barricade. "The

report you requested, my liege."

Arzan accepted the set of papers: an account of the battle performances of the surviving commanders. It was depressingly thin. "Only two of them made it," he muttered, shaking his head bitterly.

"How many commanders do we need?" Vighkon asked. "We're only defending the city, and then only even one wall."

"If Ylnavar has half a brain, he'll understand how much of an advantage the river gives us," Arzan said. He swatted his palm with the report sheets. "We've destroyed the bridges, but that only slows them down. Someone's going to need to lead parties along the bank to oppose attempted crossings."

Vighkon scratched his grizzly beard. "If they're smart, they'll cross far enough upriver that we won't even know it. Maybe that's why we don't see Roth's or Mansar's banners."

"Bloody shyles, I don't like this. I'll send one of our scouting parties up to the boundary with Three Corners."

The captain nodded.

Arzan eyed him. "Maybe I should put you in charge of something."

"Ckols are swordsmen, my liege, not strategists. In any case, there's no way in the six I'm leaving your side. Can't exactly be your bodyguard if we're a mile apart."

"I can lead a portion of the troops."

Arzan bit his lip. He turned around to find Ellaniel standing with a crutch nestled under one arm.

"You're in no condition to command," he said. "You can't even walk properly."

His wife drew her sword and let her crutch drop to the ground with a clack. She took a limping step towards him, her face tight. "Put me on the wall. I won't need to move much to —"

"You're staying in the palace, Ella," he said firmly.

"Arzan, I'm fit enough—"

"Your job is to protect Avlan."

"The only way to protect him is to keep this city!"

"You lost most of our army. You're not competent for the task." It was a ridiculous excuse. By all accounts, her response to Odavan's attack had been excellent prior to her fall to the archers. Yes, she'd lost the battle, but against a force of equal quality and superior numbers, anyone would have.

Seeing her injured, remembering her unconscious and bleeding in the fields in Creedport, her skills didn't matter to him.

Ellaniel shook as she stared down at the cobblestones. She turned her golden eyes back up to him. "I know I wasn't able to save as many as I should have. I messed up with the archers, but I won't make that sort of mistake again."

"Ella—"

"This is *my* war, Arzan! *My* father they killed!" She pointed her sword at the eastern slopes. "*My* city that's turned on me!"

Arzan looked into the eyes of a lioness and understood what it must have been like when Hashan had stood before Ellaniel's mother as she declared she would be returning to Originate. He was conscious of the people around them, paused in their work on the barricades. *You know where we are, Ella. If nothing else, I can't keep giving in to my wife on military matters.*

He opened his mouth.

"My liege," one of his soldiers came forward. "I know I'm stepping out of line, but the crendess is wrong about not doing enough at Creedport. We'd have been crushed by the opening maneuver if it weren't for her."

Someone else came up beside him. "I trust her with my life, my liege. Goldeye is the best person you can have as your sub-commander."

Arzan saw his wife's jaw clench. The soldier quickly bowed his head. "I'm sorry, it's what the men are calling you, your grace. Redleaf Goldeye."

Ellaniel snapped her sword back in its sheath. "Shyles!"

Arzan curled his fingers around his cape clasp, grasping it tight. He cast his gaze around him and saw nothing but hope in the faces watching all about. *Six continents, I haven't a choice, have I?*

He turned to her. "I know how much you hate that name," he said, "but it looks like Odavan's lost his grip on it." She was stiff as he put his arms around her, holding her close and digging his hand through her hair. "I lead by the grace of the people, and it appears the people have spoken."

Ellaniel relaxed and looked up at him. "Arzan?"

A shout rose from the east, "They're here! The Leverie are on the rise!"

Arzan breathed in and fought the clenching in his chest. He let go of his wife and turned to the east. "Put on your armor. See me on the wall."

Chapter 46

Another empty supply cart went by them on its return from the Council war camp, but Charva was too deep in thought to give much heed to the driver's odd stare. Everyone she and Ersch had passed on their way west had given strange glances at the armed woman in the black foreign dress, but the ckol's crest on Ersch's shoulder always scared them off from asking questions. *Wonder how many people actually recognize me.* It didn't matter. There were bigger things to focus on right now.

Which crenden stood most to gain from either Arzan's or Thrake's downfall? She really didn't have enough information yet to answer the question, but she hoped to glean something soon. Most of Leverie's crendens were gathering in one place, and that was where she was going. In the meantime, ideas based on too much speculation and too few facts spun circles around in her head.

Ckol Ersch dropped his horse in step beside hers and held out a linen-wrap. "Something to eat, my liege?"

She caught a whiff of smoked pork and remembered she hadn't eaten yet today, having been so busy with her preparations to leave Creedport. She grabbed the bundle as her stomach caught up and grumbled. Even riding a horse, she managed to wolf down half the wheat wrapped pork and rice before she realized it. She wiped her mouth with the back of her hand and slowed to a more dignified pace as she glanced at Ersch. His grim, brooding attitude wasn't at all tempered by his sudden promotion to ckol.

"Aren't you going to eat too?" Charva asked.

Ersch raised his head and glanced her way before reaching into his saddle bag and pulling out food for himself.

"Something bothering you, Ersch?"

"Nothing you need trouble yourself over, my liege."

Charva stiffened. "A ckol's responsibilities do not flow only one way. I'll decide if what's on your mind is my business or not. Or you can quit your new station if you think that unreasonable."

Ersch immediately put a hand over his heart. "Not at all! I just saw no reason to bother you."

"Well, I have now been bothered. What's the issue?"

"I was simply wishing my promotion could have been under happier circumstances."

Charva took a solemn bite. "This isn't the way anyone wanted things to go," she said in between chews. "Well, anyone other than those assassins and their mastermind."

"And certainly not my uncle." Ersch undid the cloth around his food, but didn't immediately eat. "He was my inspiration. Of anyone, he was the one I most wanted to have at the ceremony."

"Captain Ulman?" She dropped the remainder of her food in shock. "I . . . . I'm sorry. I should have paid more attention to the casualty report. I'm sorry, Ersch."

"You've been busy with your own loss. No fault of yours to miss his death in all the chaos." He drew in a deep breath. "He led the defenders on the western wall."

The wall that Arzan breached. She didn't want to think about the implications. "Do you have any other family?"

"My parents live on the silk plantations with my brothers and sister. It was only me and my uncle in the city."

"I suppose he taught you how to fight?"

Ersch nodded. "He learned his grappling style from a Fractoran friend of his. I don't think he had quite the same knack for it that I do, and it wouldn't have helped him up on the wall. It's not something suited to the formation. Worked well against common street thugs, though."

"Do you think it's something you could teach me?"

"Well, I could, but . . . the style involves a lot of . . . contact, my liege."

Charva frowned, trying to figure out what he meant. *Oh.*

She turned her face away before Ersch could catch her blush. "Yes, um, right."

Oh, it wouldn't be that bad, Charva. He's reliable, he's got looks. It might not be all that terrible to—

No, not going there. He's a commoner. Besides, you've got your hands full trying to stop a war.

A cloud of dust from a slow-moving supply cart up ahead provided a convenient distraction from the topic. As they passed it by, Charva saw it was loaded with tower shields in Highcity colors.

"Seems Ylnavar actually cares to equip his people this time," she commented.

"With how I hear the last battle went, I doubt it would even be worth the trouble marshaling Highcity for battle otherwise," Ersch said.

Charva's grip went tight on her reins. "Ylnavar knew he was killing his people when he put them in front of the wall. There's no way anyone could think they stood a chance against the Senkani."

"Why do you think he did it?"

"Because he cared more about justifying himself than he did about his people's lives." The more she thought about it, the more Charva wanted Ylnavar to be the assassins' master. He had some degree of motive. As a man who valued order and authority above all else, Arzan and Thrake were the bane of his existence.

She smiled bitterly. She hoped things could be so easy.

The forest outside the city of Senkani was completely transformed since last Charva had seen it. Where once there had been thick brush and low branches, tents and cooking pits now occupied every space. Instead of bird song, there was raucous shouting and laughter, orders barked this way and that, and the scraping of whetstones on steel. Rather than pristine woodland air, there was smoke and the smell of horses and human waste. This all before even coming within view of the cultivated slopes outside the city.

Curious and leering gazes tracked Charva's movements as she weaved her way through the war camp towards the Council tents. Even if she wasn't quite the only woman there, she was still the odd sight. Her sword and Falconian dress (which the tailors had managed to fashion from black silk just before she left Creedport) made her even more eye-catching. Together with Ersch's escort, there was no question she was special, and no one blocked her way.

"What's your plan?" Ersch asked quietly.

"Walk in and ask questions?"

He gave her a skeptical look.

"Fortune favors the bold."

They found the command tent deep inside the camp, marked by Council and Highcity banners. Ckols from six different provinces guarded the perimeter, suggesting the crendens were currently in meeting. Charva made her way to the guards by the entrance flap.

"I'm here for an audience with the Speaker."

The Highcity ckol stared at her. "You're the one who stole my horse."

Charva narrowed her eyes back at him. "To be fair, you tried to steal my city."

"You're in over your head here, your grace." The ckol motioned for one of the other guards to go in and deliver her message. "Bit of advice. Don't let any of the Woodwise men catch wind of you."

Ersch sighed and nodded towards a guard at the tent's far corner. "Too late for that."

Charva could practically feel the hostility leeching out of the ckol in Woodwise colors. *Flame and embers.* She put on a brave front even if her back went cold with sweat. "If he wants to come at me, he can try. He and his fellows will be known as Leverie killers."

"Your problem, your grace," the Highcity ckol said.

The messenger came back out of the tent. "Crenden Ylnavar demands to know why he should hold an audience with you rather than place your head on a pole, your grace."

"Because he believes in due process," Charva answered. She congratulated herself on how steady her voice was.

Flaming six, my nerves haven't been this bad since the first time I tried standing up to Father. "I should also think he would be interested in keeping relations civil with the next candidate for crendess of Creedport."

The guard delivered the message and returned. "You are to wait until Crenden Ylnavar is better disposed to speak with you. Step anywhere west of the war camp and you will be deemed an ally of House Redleaf and an enemy of the Council."

Charva wasn't stupid enough to do such a thing, but the spoken limitation still irked her. "I understand. When Ylnavar is ready, then." She turned away from the tent and headed off in the direction opposite the Woodwise ckol.

"What are you going to discuss with Crenden Ylnavar?" Ersch asked.

"I haven't the slightest idea," Charva said. "For now, the plan is to be here, to watch and listen and be visible. There's a chance we can pick something up, or that the culprit will get nervous."

"Nervous? And then what?"

"And then I'll be counting on you to keep your eyes sharp and your sword ready."

"You think he'll be so foolish?"

"Only if I start to push." And if she could figure out where she could push, that was just what she would do.

Ylnavar wouldn't allow her to head into Senkani, but there were no restrictions on her seeing it from the camp. She weaved her way through trees, soldiers, tent pegs, and supply carts until she reached the edge of the woods. The city lay open before her—far more open than she would have liked. The slopes gave the attackers a distinct height advantage, allowing them to see into many of the city streets without even needing to climb a tree. The Leverie archers would be able to loose from outside of the defenders' range, and at an angle that would make the crenels atop the wall near useless.

But what quickly drew Charva's eyes from the city was the catapult being hammered together at the edge of the Leverie camp. The huge stone thrower was several times her height, with a basket big enough for a three-foot boulder. From the looks of it, the weapon had some ways to go before it was finished, but she guessed it could be ready sometime tomorrow. Up and down the Leverie line, workers were busy on another dozen identical siege engines.

"I don't like this," Charva said.

"Perhaps you won't have time to find the culprit," Ersch said. "Senkani may fall before the week's out."

She considered sabotage before quickly rejecting the idea. Her own mission took priority. She would have to trust that Arzan and Ellaniel could hold the Council off long enough on their own. Arzan was perhaps the most qualified military strategist in the country, and that had to count for something.

Just don't die, you two.

"Six continents, she really is here."

She turned around to find a trio of Woodwise ckols stepping between the perimeter tents. She smiled sweetly at them. "Ah, you fellows. Can we let bygones be bygones?"

The rank and file soldiers saw the approaching storm and gave a wide berth. Even the catapult workers stopped their hammering and leaned into the frames to watch.

"You killed Ckol Jrak," one of the Woodwise men said. "Don't come in here pretending you aren't on the enemy's side."

Charva let her smile turn harsh. "You're one to talk of loyalty. Your crenden is murdered and only a few days later you try to run his daughter through."

"Our loyalty is to our living crenden. What honor is there in siding with a rebellious woman who left and then turned on the House?"

"If you have to ask the question, you don't know what honor is."

"Neither respect," Ersch said. "Is this how you address a daughter of the aristocracy, snakes?"

"Traitors have no claim to House." The three Woodwise ckols spread out around them, hands on their pommels.

Charva rested her mainhand on her own hilt, and with the other discretely loosened a dagger in its sheath. "Are you seriously planning to attack me? As far as I'm aware, the House hasn't declared me thrown out. So much as bare your blades and there are enough witnesses here to see you die the moment an officer shows."

She spoke of the crowd all around, but they may as well have been alone for the sound that came from them.

"You expect us to throw away our friend's vengeance?" the ckol demanded.

Charva smirked. "What was that a moment ago about you owing no loyalty to the dead?"

The ckol scowled at her.

"So, which is it?" Charva asked. "Are you the traitor for turning on your crenden's daughter, or are we ready to admit a battle's a battle and not hold grudges?"

The man glowered for a very long moment. Long enough for a bead of sweat to trickle its way down Charva's back as she braced herself for a three-on-two fight.

The ckol slapped his thigh before turning and storming away. "Bile and grime!"

The other two glanced between Charva and their companion and grudgingly retreated after him.

Charva let out a relieved sigh as she and Ersch both eased their hands away from their weapons.

"Funny how a month ago I would have been jumping at the bit for an excuse to pull out my sword," she muttered.

Ersch let the aside go without comment.

The sound of a clearing throat demanded her attention. Charva shifted around to see Crenden Loftham standing with a pair of ckols. The elderly ruler was second only to Ylnavar in age and had been in power twice as long as Charva had been alive. He had a reputation for being the most long-winded member of the Council, which she figured must compensate for his lacking sense of presence. Short and frail, Charva couldn't help fearing the slightest gust would tip him over.

"I like how you ended that, my dear," Loftham said in a voice far stronger than she would have expected from the look of him.

"Do you think we might end the rest of the war that way, your grace?" Charva asked.

Loftham shrugged his bony shoulders. "One could hope, but I think what we have on our hands are feelings that go beyond what words can express. And when you're at a loss for words, how can you use them to mend the problem?" He exhaled deeply and gazed out at the city.

"You sound sympathetic towards the Redleafs."

"Sympathetic? Yes, I suppose I am sympathetic. No one can deny the Redleafs have cause to be angry."

"Is that why you aren't with the rest of the Council? It looked to me Ylnavar was holding a meeting."

Loftham waved his hand. "Not at all! I may feel for the Redleafs, but that doesn't make Ylnavar and the Council wrong. Rebellion is still unacceptable. I simply have no use in a military setting. Trade is my forte. I am here to provide men, not strategy." He knit his snowy white eyebrows together, his dark blue eyes scrutinizing her. "The question is, why are *you* here?"

"I . . . ." Charva really wished she had been able to come up with a plausible explanation by now. She'd just have to see how much she could stall. "I was friends with the Redleafs, it's true. I don't think it's fair what's happening here. That's not to say I want to go against the Council's decision, but if there's at least some way to minimize the violence, then—"

An idea occurred to her. She looked around at the men in the camp as a little tidbit she'd learned from her time in Falcone came back to her.

"Crenden Loftham," she leaned closer to him and spoke in a more confidential tone, "has the Council remembered to reinstate the Order of Aiv Chahai?"

"The what, my dear?"

"The Soldiers' Witness. Leverie hasn't waged war in so long that most have likely forgotten, but by the codes every army should have some of them present."

Loftham looked dubious for a moment. "Soldiers' . . . . Ah, I recall them now. When I was a boy, I heard tell of their part in the Tarkandan split. Kept the fight clean, they said. You're here to make sure they're brought back? As noble a cause as any can find in these sad days. In fact, now that you bring them up, it seems stupid we forgot about them. Great fortune you remembered!"

Charva nodded and began to pace. "Sadly, I'm not in the best standing with Crenden Ylnavar. I wouldn't be surprised if he intends to keep me waiting until the war's over before he even so much as speaks to me."

"I see you hope I will intercede on your behalf."

She stopped and faced him gratefully. "Will you?"

The old crenden put up his hand. "I will mention your objective, but you know how Ylnavar gets. Once he's set it in his head that his way's right, you have to stick a mountain in his path to change his course."

"That is enough. Even if he doesn't want to hear from me directly, at least he'll get a reminder that the Aiv Chahai should be reinstated."

"One can hope," Loftham said. He nodded to his guards, "If you aren't thrown out, I expect we shall see each other again, my dear. Do stay away from the Woodwise portion of camp in the meantime."

"I'll try my best, your grace."

Ersch waited until the crenden was gone. "That was an interesting turn of events."

"Do you think I've misstepped?" Charva asked.

"The move was brilliant! My liege, if you become head of the Aiv Chahai—do you realize how much influence you'll have?"

"That's the very problem," Charva said. "The Order at full strength can wreck an entire campaign. Do you suppose Ylnavar's going to see fit to let me anywhere near it? No, at most, this will just be our excuse to stay here in camp until he hears me out and says no."

Ersch grinned and shook his head. "You don't give enough credit to this card you've played. The Order can only be run by women, you're the only woman of standing here, and by the codes of war the Order must always be present."

Charva waved her hand. "You already see how little most of the Council remembers of the codes, or cares about them. But in the meantime, let's see about finding some more information around here."

Chapter 47

The catapults struck before sundown on the second day.

"Take cover!"

Ellaniel hunched down low behind the battlements and grit her teeth. A shadow flicked in front of her feet as a three-foot stone tore overhead and crashed into a nearby rooftop, splaying shards of wood in every direction. Screams carried up from the street, but she couldn't tell if it was from injury or plain terror. The soldiers to her sides remained silent except for scattered curses. Blood pounded in her ears, but she forced herself to appear calm. *A commander is as immovable as a mountain*, she told herself.

She stood back up, mindful of her injured leg. Up atop the slopes, just in front of the tree line, the Leverie wound the artillery for a second barrage. Thirteen in total, the machines had enough stones piled up beside them to keep up the attack for hours. She glared at their crews and at the soldiers formed up and ready to charge the gate should the city try a counterassault. *To blazes with you snakes.*

Another stone lobbed skyward to the north, aimed at Arzan's section of the defenses. She tightened her hand around the pommel of her sword, afraid for his safety. The rock hit with a thud somewhere out of sight and she bit her lip.

A soldier tapped the wall with the knuckles of his

gauntlet. "Here comes another one."

Three Leverie men lifted a stone into the catapult nearest her. The instant they were clear, an engineer hammered the lock, snapping the arm forward. The boulder hurtled skyward, the meaty crack of its launch reaching late to her ears as the stone itself raced to its peak. She watched it tumble through the air, trying to stay calm and judge its trajectory.

The soldier next to her pressed himself to the rampart. "Six continents, it's coming straight here!"

"Bloody shyles!" She broke and covered. A moment later, she heard a solid thump outside the city. She peeked over the crenellations to see the stone lodged in the dirt far to the left and some twenty paces short of the wall. She cursed her reaction. Only a few minutes of this and the tension was already going to bleed her dry. She straightened to her full height and began walking the ramparts, hiding as best she could the pain in her leg.

"Their artillery's not accurate," she said. "Stand brave! Do not be intimidated! They stand off and hurl stones because they're afraid of our walls—afraid of us! We only need to persevere until nightfall!"

The catapult crew launched a third boulder. This one cracked against the base of the wall at a steep angle, sending a jolt up her legs.

"Look—their stones do nothing! Even if they hurled every rock they can grab from the granite coasts, the wall will stand! All they're doing is wasting their time, and time is on our side so long as the eastern bank remains ours!"

There was another crack, this one distant and more wooden. A cheer rose up around her. She turned, smiling when she spotted one of the catapults in pieces, shattered under the stress of its own tension cords. Soldiers carried several bloodied engineers away from the wreck.

"Ha! Looks like they can't even build their weapons right!" one of the men said.

Hope we'll be so lucky that more of their artillery will follow suit.

Even if there weren't any more failures, Senkani only had to hold until after sundown. Ylnavar was going to see he'd made a mistake bringing the fight here.

Dusk's shadows swallowed up the last towers along the city's eastern edge and crept up the slopes below the Leverie camp. Charva set her foot atop an old stump and watched the sun sink into the far western tree line. The catapult nearest her snapped its arm forward, tossing a stone back up into the waning sunlight, where it gleamed orange until hurtling back down to the ground. She didn't follow its last leg, not wanting to see yet another person's home or shop destroyed in this senseless barrage. She cringed when she heard the distant crash.

"Keep this up 'til we've smashed the towers and scared the defenders senseless and the city will be easy pickings," one of the engineers said.

"Think we can crumble part of the wall?" the man beside him asked.

"Reckon it's worth a shot."

A soldier came and hung a lit lantern on a branch nearby. Out in the city, windows were starting to come alive with the glow of oil lamps or candles, but only on the west side of the river. In the growing darkness, the eastern half looked cold and dead.

Charva stepped a few paces out into a fairly empty patch between tents and drew her sword. She measured her breathing, tried to drown out the continued racket of the artillery, and settled into her basic fencing stance. A few soldiers lingered about, watching while she practiced her footwork. Leaves and twigs broke beneath her boots as she weaved side to side, forward and back. She flicked the blade in a parry, dodged an imaginary follow up strike, parried again, then thrust—

She remembered her sword in the Woodwise ckol's throat and nearly dropped her weapon.

She grabbed the hilt with both hands. "Flame and embers," she muttered. This wasn't what she'd wanted when she'd taken up swordsmanship.

Leaves crunched next to her. "A messenger from the

Council, my liege."

Charva nodded to Ersch and sheathed her blade. She wondered if anyone had noticed her slip. Maybe it was dark enough that they hadn't. She met the messenger by the flickering lantern.

"You are expected at the Council tent, your grace."

"Lead the way."

They took a twisting path between tents and cook fires. Outside of the spheres of scattered lamplight, the forms of soldiers lounging about or running errands shone a faint blue under the half moon. More than once she wondered if their guide had gotten lost in this makeshift city of cloth, but they eventually found the Highcity banners marking the Council tent. The ckols guarding the entrance nodded as she stepped into view, then pulled up the flap for her and Ersch to enter.

Little expense had been spared on the tent's interior. No patch of bare ground could be spied between the thick wool rugs, and silk tapestries lined every bit of wall and ceiling. Several mirrored lanterns hung on stands all around, illuminating the polished table in the tent's center, on top of which rested a detailed map of Leverie and the neighboring aristocracies. Cushioned chairs sat along the perimeter, but only one, occupied by Crenden Ylnavar, was stationed by the table. Two of his ckols stood at his flanks, hands on their pommels. With nowhere left for her to sit, Charva remained standing across the table from the Speaker.

Ylnavar regarded her with unmasked disdain. "Loftham tells me you want to bring back the Order of Aiv Chahai."

She clasped her hands behind her. "The war codes require it, your grace. Truly, you should have reinstated it the moment you determined to mobilize the army."

"And why should I care one wit about the opinion of a murderer's daughter and a traitor?"

"I—"

"You killed a ckol of Woodwise. This is your trial, Charva."

She swallowed. *Embers, I'm stupid.* She was in shyle waters now. Nothing else but to go all in. "I was enforcing the codes, your grace. That ckol was about to kill a daughter of the aristocracy who was already defeated and unconscious. It is the duty of the Watchers to stop such breaches of conduct."

The old Speaker's eyebrows knitted together in a heavy frown. "You are not a Watcher, child. The Council never appointed you to such a position."

"The Council failed to appoint *anyone* to this position," Charva countered. "Under such circumstances, it is the people's duty to elect Aiv Chahai for the war."

"You do not have the authority to—"

"The Aiv Chahai are outside the Council's jurisdiction, Speaker! The order was founded upon the principle that men cannot be trusted to respect their vows in times of war. Being subject to the whims of crendens or kings or generals undermines the very purpose of the Watchers."

Ylnavar curled his fingers around his wood block. "You expect me to bow to any woman who decides she wants to pick up a title?"

"I expect you to follow the law!" She placed her palms on the table and tried not to show fear at the Highcity ckols tightening their grips on their hilts. "That's your spiel, isn't it? That's the whole reason you're at war with one of our own crendens! But I see you're just a hypocrite."

The old man shot to his feet. "Do not presume to judge the Speaker of the Council! You will—"

A soldier burst through the tent flap. "My liege, the camp is under attack!"

Ylnavar clapped his block against the table. "The fools have left the walls?"

"No! Arrows are coming at us from the rear!"

Charva heard shouting in the camp and clattering armor.

"They must have had skirmishers hiding in the woods since the army arrived," Ersch said. "They probably intend to whittle away at you every night you're camped here."

Ylnavar stormed around the table and towards the tent entrance. "The cowardly swine will not have an easy time of it. Sweep the forest. Leave nowhere for them to escape."

The messenger ran off. Charva exited ahead of Ylnavar. They were far from danger this deep in the war camp, but things were in chaos. Men ran about as if lost, while others fidgeted around asking for commands.

"Speaker," Charva said, "this seems like a chance for—"

Ylnavar thrust his finger at her. "You are going nowhere near the front. Guards, keep an eye on her."

Charva shook her head and looked up at the blue half-circle shining in the sky.

"There's a commotion in the camp. Our skirmishers have started the attack."

Arzan nodded, though it was unlikely the scout could see it in the dark. He turned to the ckols who stood with their horses in the street behind him. "Get ready." He mounted up and pulled his cloak close over his armor to make sure the moonlight found no metal to reflect off.

They gave the Leverie some time to focus their soldiers to the east, then Arzan ordered the gate opened. The moment the massive doors swung in on their well-oiled hinges, he urged his horse forward, his and Ellaniel's ckols in tow. His wife stood above the gate, watching them leave.

The catapult crews had ceased their bombardment on hearing news of the attack. Hopefully, that was a sign there were fewer eyes watching the city. Regardless, Arzan needed to make this fast. His raiding party fanned out as they galloped up the slope.

Arzan and the two ckols in his unit were the first to reach a catapult. The crew shouted in surprise as he burst into their circle of lantern light with sword drawn. Most ran in horror, leaving only three men to huddle together and guard the machine. The ckols shot their crossbows, taking out two, and Arzan sliced through the neck of the last.

"Oil, now!" Arzan grabbed the bags tied to his saddle and splashed the contents over the catapult's frame. As his men emptied their own oilskins, he cantered over to the nearest lantern and lifted it up with the tip of his sword.

"Cavalry! Cavalry are attacking the catapults!"

The ckols finished their task just as Leverie soldiers started storming out with spears. Arzan threw the lantern at the catapult. He smirked with satisfaction as the glass shattered across the wood and the flame caught, engulfing the entire machine in fire and smoke. With plenty of distance still between him and the spearmen, he turned his horse around and retreated back towards the city. With a glance over either shoulder, he saw bonfires erupting all along the Leverie line.

"Tooth and claw, Ylnavar."

Chapter 48

The stretch of ground in front of him was the ugliest place Retyar had ever been. Trash littered the open expanse in the form of old plastic bags and battered styrofoam boxes and cups, brought there by wind or by rainwash, some of it probably years ago. Standing tall in the midst of the refuse were dozens of hanging steel sheets cut out in the shapes of people, lined up at various ranges, their faces pitted and worn.

"Everyone find a firing station." The instructor's voice came loud and clear through the earpiece embedded inside his muffs. Not like the muffled scraping of spent shell casings Retyar was practically wading through underfoot. He hefted his rifle and glanced behind at Thesha, who smiled back at him. Even during militia training, she still wore her traditional garb, determined to bring some color to this dreary place. Past her, about twenty other students slogged through the range, most of them looking like they had better things to do. Which probably was the case—midterms were next week, after all.

Retyar picked out a firing station at random and set his rifle down beside the piled boxes of ammunition. Thesha took the spot next to his, while others of their University mates spread out along the rest of the line.

"About turn!" the instructor called. The trainees swiveled around to face the man. Despite his heavy voice, he was a short fellow, and certainly had plenty more fat than muscle on his bones. "All right, you lot—" Retyar grimaced and switched off his earpieces. The man was speaking loud enough that he could hear him well enough through the muffs anyway. "Every month I get kids complaining about the militia. I tend to find you University folks get even more mushy about it than most. It all really baffles me—all you're doing is learning how to use a gun. Six continents, you don't even have to do laps! Let me tell you, anybody who complains will get failing marks and have to repeat. Am I clear on that?"

Retyar nodded with everyone else, though he secretly had the urge to complain for the sake of the "punishment". This was a lot of expensive ammunition sitting behind him and he really couldn't wait to start using it.

"Now, you're all supposedly the intellectual types, so I do hope you'll understand the importance of the militia. A lot of folks think of the military as Govunari's first line of defense. The army, the navy, the air force. When the bullets and bombs fly, they're the first ones to fight. But they're not the first defense. The kingdom's first defensive line is composed of fear and respect. No one has invaded our soil since the Intercontinental War because they all remember what happened last time anyone tried. The Kreks didn't make it ten feet before finding out that behind every window was a gun and a person who knew how to use it. No invading army can ever outnumber the civilians of the place they try to conquer. Whether you understand that or not, that's why we have the militia, and that's why no one leaves here until they can put at least half a mag on target at a hundred paces."

The instructor had them turn back around, and Retyar grinned at finally being able to load up. As he pushed rounds into his first magazine, Thesha leaned over to him. "I'm guessing you shoot a lot out in the country?" she said, loud enough to get through his ear protection.

Retyar nodded. "Did hunting with my dad and brothers. I'm a decent enough shot."

Thesha smiled and started loading a magazine. It was an interesting sight with her old-fashioned dress.

A few of the nearby trainees needed help from the instructor getting the rounds loaded, then in priming their rifles. Retyar's finger was itching above the trigger long before the last person caught up and he heard the clear to fire.

He raised his weapon and lined up the iron sights to the fifty-pace target. Letting out his breath, he steadied his aim and pulled the trigger. The steel target jumped, the sound of metal pinging coming back at him an instant after the bang of his shot.

Having gotten a feel for the recoil, he made the target dance to a flurry of lead, unleashing his remaining fourteen rounds in seconds. He smiled to himself as he ejected the magazine. Only two misses, and that because the jittery target. "Way easier than deer ammo," he muttered. As he glanced to the side, he saw Thesha was already slapping in her second magazine. Her dark green eyes flitted over him, then focused downrange. She blew through her fifteen rounds in five seconds flat, missing three shots on her hundred-pace target. She dropped the second mag on the table and shrugged. "A bit out of practice, I guess."

Retyar rammed his next magazine home. "The hundred fifty-pace targets. Ten seconds." He sighted on the metal sheet and let loose on the trigger. The rifle spat out a rain of bullets and shell casings, making the target sing out nine clear notes. As he set the gun to rest position, Thesha immediately answered his challenge with a frenzy of shots, setting the steel ringing ten times.

"I can't just let that go," Retyar said, loading his third magazine. He sighted the target, only then noticing that the rest of the range was silent. All the other trainees had put their own practice on hold to watch the competition.

Well, if I'm going to show off, might as well go all the way.

He put all his concentration into his aim, into controlling his breathing, and properly maintaining his stance. He pulled the trigger. *Bang.* The now familiar recoil jolted his shoulder and an instant later he heard the ring from the target two hundred paces out. He emptied the rest of the magazine, getting fourteen more solid hits. With the last one, the trainees gave him a round of applause.

"Three hundred paces," Thesha called, slapping in fifteen fresh rounds.

"Six continents, she going to do that without a scope?"

someone said.

She smirked and fired. The three hundred-pace plate jumped, the sound of the impact hitting them half a second later. The students gave an excited cheer. "This girl's awesome!"

Their voices cut short as Retyar shot off a round and hit his three hundred target. "First to miss loses," he said with a grin.

Thesha lined up her sights. "You're on."

They traded shots, their audience getting louder with every hit. By the tenth round, Retyar started feeling the pressure. *Pretty sure that one only nicked the edge.* He wiped a bead of sweat off his brow, but kept his aim up—Thesha's hits kept with his without any hesitation. On the fourteenth shot, he forced himself to slow down and breathe.

"Getting tired?" she taunted.

He pulled the trigger and was sure he hit the steel dead center. She followed up immediately.

"Blasted—" she bit her lip. She'd missed the target.

The other students cheered his victory. Retyar ejected his last bullet and raised his rifle over his head. "Woo!"

He felt a hand slap him on the back and turned to see the instructor staring flatly at him.

"All right, you're done with the course, hotshot. You too, lady. Let's see if you can keep that aim up when it's an actual person you've got your sights on."

Retyar and Thesha shared a glance and grudgingly set their rifles down. The rest of the trainees resumed their practice as the two of them chuckled behind the line on their way to the transit station.

"You didn't tell me you were a rifle ace," Retyar said between bursts of gunfire.

Thesha shrugged. "You never asked."

"Figured you were only interested in the days of swords and arrows."

"And I suppose you think I write my reports with a feather pen?"

"Well, you know, I wouldn't put it past you."

She pushed a lock of hair out of her face and laughed.

A trainee they passed missed the nearest target five times

in a row. Retyar looked over and halted as he recognized Laski simmering behind her rifle.

"Don't. Stop. Here." The girl practically growled out the words.

"Wait, I thought Ytanians were exempt from the militia," Retyar said. "What are you doing here?"

"Proving her people can do anything a normal Govunari can do, obviously," Thesha said with a smirk. "And doing a great job of it too."

Laski thumped her rifle down on the table. "Raze it, Thesha!"

Retyar sighed. "Can't you two ever be nice?"

"Hey, you're the one who's got her always hanging around our spot at the library," Thesha said. "You're lucky I even still show up at all."

Laski stuck her tongue at her.

"Enough, enough," Retyar said. "Laski, you want me to give you any tips?"

Thesha rolled her eyes. "Yeah, sure, coddle the Ytanian like you always do. I'll be over there waiting for the ride back."

"Thesha . . . ." He held his hands out to his sides, at a loss with how fast her mood always flipped when Laski was around.

Laski watched her leave, then took off her glasses to wipe them on her shirt. "You're a nice guy, Ret. What do you see in a girl like that?"

He could read a long list. "She's only nasty like that around you. Maybe she had family hurt by the Lime Sabotage during the war? I still haven't directly asked her about it."

"If you say so. Anyway, you said you'd tell me the secret to getting this blazing thing to shoot straight."

"I'm pretty sure the rifle's shooting straight and it's your aim that needs work. Show me how you line up the sights . . . . Okay, that looks good. Now pull the trigger and —"

She fired and went completely off the mark.

"All right, there's the problem. You're twitching as you fire, probably because you're anticipating the kick. Don't be scared of the gunshot."

He saw her mutter something, but couldn't hear it under the muffs. She raised the gun again, but it took another magazine before she was able to force her aim steady enough to hit the target once. Retyar opened a new box of ammo and helped her load up again.

"This is going to take me forever."

"You've only been here half an hour," Retyar said. "It's not that hard once you start getting a feel for it. And you could be worse. Some people underestimate the recoil and get thrown on their butts even with this low caliber."

He was going to mention a few more rookie mistakes, but he noticed her take a hand off the gun to brush dirt off her pants.

"Anyway, practice and you'll be fine. It's not like I was born knowing how to shoot, and I'm sure Thesha wasn't either."

"Are you two actually a couple?"

The question took him off guard, and even Laski looked like she only realized what she'd asked after speaking. Having started, though, she plowed on ahead.

"I mean, well, you're always together studying or in town. It's pretty obvious you like her. I think you're totally stupid on that count, but hey. But, uhm, what about her?"

"I know what you're getting at," Retyar said. "I should get it clear."

"Just so we're straight, I hate her guts, but you've been a good friend to me, Ret. I want you to be happy."

Retyar found he'd lost his voice, and it wasn't just because he'd been nearly shouting through ear protection and gunfire. He cleared his throat. "Thanks, Laski."

She smiled and adjusted her glasses. "All right, so stop hanging out here and have a talk with her. All I need is practice."

Retyar patted her shoulder and left to take her advice. It had been a while since he and Thesha had met, and he thought he had built up enough courage by now to say things plainly to her. He contemplated how he would open up the conversation. Was there anything clever he could say about their common interests? Any good quotes he could remember? Or was that all too sappy? Only once a range attendant put out a hand to collect his earmuffs did he realize he'd reached the bus bay. As he gave back the gear, he searched about the covered benches until he spotted Thesha's wavy hair and old-fashioned dress.

He balled his fists. No, he'd just come out and say it.

Thesha saw him coming and waved him towards another student who was sitting on the bench next to hers.

Retyar tsked in annoyance.

"Ret, this is Waylar Unavin. He's another history major training for the NHM. I told him about your—"

"Your undergrad thesis," Waylar's obvious excitement made the interruption a tad less rude. His steel gray eyes glistened as he extended his hand for a strong shake. "It's fascinating. 'Nothing becomes obsolete; personal and social conditions determine the acceptability of cost-value tradeoffs.'"

Retyar scratched his neck. "The wording can use some work. Hey, Thesha, you mind—"

"The idea comes through. The concept's really interesting."

"It's a Uni paper anyway," Thesha said. "Not like you need to compete with anyone to sell it—the professor's a captive audience."

"I think you could get it published for real, though," Waylar said.

Thesha twisted a lock of hair between her fingers. "Most people who hear about it usually laugh it off and automatically bring up battery life."

Waylar rubbed his square chin. "Oh, yeah. Do you have a response to that?"

Retyar put a lid on his growing annoyance and decided his talk with Thesha would just have to wait for later. "I can go in different directions," he said, shrugging. "Reword the thesis to be less all encompassing—"

"Don't!"

"—or point out the hidden costs of better batteries. It's not as simple as, 'Wow, modern batteries work better.' Better technology requires more resources and more sophisticated manufacturing techniques. The tradeoff is whether you're willing to put that much effort into a better product, rather than invest those resources elsewhere."

"Right! And the same logic can be applied to all sorts of things."

Thesha put a hand on Waylar's shoulder, "By the way, I want to mention I offered for him to join our library study group. He's eager to help you out with any research you need."

Retyar stared a second too long at her hand. *Come on, no reason to be getting jealous about that.* "I don't have a problem. Waylar, welcome aboard. What's your thesis, anyway?"

"It's on the dynamics of economy in trade between societies of different developmental levels," he said. "A lot of people don't realize how significant the influx of certain types of goods is to countries like ours. For instance, did you know that when we opened up trade with the Madavaran Tribes a hundred years ago, the gold that came in ended up causing the market crash of—"

The screeching of bus brakes interrupted him.

"Plenty of time to talk about it on the way back to the castle."

And plenty of time to have the discussion with Thesha, Retyar thought. *Plenty of time.*

Chapter 99

"I want to go outside."

Retyar sighed inwardly at the girl's persistence. She'd been bugging him nonstop for over a day now, and any urgings from him to wait until her leg was a little better were long past useless.

"I want to—"

"All right, fine! But you're not going anywhere out of my sight."

Fellone's face lit up in triumph, and she instantly pushed herself up onto her good leg. Her smile quickly turned to a wince and a hiss.

"Look, see—"

"I can do it!"

Retyar tightened his lips and clamped a hand on her shoulder, forcing her back down. "Just wait one more minute. I'll find you something you can use as a crutch." He went to the cave entrance, glancing uneasily at her before heading out. "I mean it, don't move. I'll be right back."

The girl nodded reluctantly. With another inward sigh, he went outside.

You weren't going to keep her cooped in there forever. Still, this was a lot sooner than he would have liked. He could hardly blame her for being antsy, trapped in that cave as she was for days on end. He still had no good plan for how he was going to deal with her going forward.

Where's that branch? He remembered seeing one earlier

that could be used for a walking stick. He found it poking out of a layer of leaves, most of its bark hanging in loose rings around the wood. A lizard scurried along its length as he bent to pick it up, and he flicked the stick to toss the creature aside.

Losing all caution now, aren't you. Retyar shook his head. He was past the point of stopping the small ripples. His impact on the area simply by living here for six years was just too great. He'd have to focus his energies on keeping his distance from people.

If only Fellone wasn't there to complicate things.

He brought the stick back to the cave and held it out, expecting her to snatch it from his grip. Instead, the girl took it in tender hands, her lips pressed tight and her violet eyes on the verge of tears. "Thank you," she said quietly.

Retyar bit his own lip and turned around. *Why do I have to be the bad guy here?*

"All right, you've been pestering me for hours. What are you waiting for?"

He heard her draw a deep breath and grunt as she pushed herself up. In a moment, she went past him, limping out into the sun with the kind of enthusiasm he'd been waiting for. The brighter lighting made it all the more obvious that the girl's tattered nightgown needed a wash. Pretty soon, no one would even be able to tell it had originally been white. At least her hair was in better shape. He smiled a little as he remembered the moment he'd given her the comb and how happy she'd looked. Maybe it was that act of kindness that gave her the courage to press for some freedom.

"Careful by the ravine," Retyar called. "That's a long drop."

Fellone nodded but leaned out over the edge anyway, her arms shaking a little as she braced herself on the walking stick. "This is where you said you rescued me?"

"Don't make me do it a second time."

She straightened out and looked around at the woods. After a brief pause, she limped over to Retyar's usual cooking spot and sat down. Relieved at her lack of further exploratory impulse, he picked a rock to settle on as well.

"I do have an idea you might like," he said. "It's

dangerous climbing down to the banks, but I could bring some sand up here for you to draw in."

Fellone looked at him, but her focus seemed elsewhere. It took some moments before she actually seemed to process his suggestion. "Well . . . I guess so."

"I'll do it right now." Retyar grabbed one of the tins from inside and used it to haul several scoops of sand into a shallow pit by the cave entrance. Fellone watched him quietly.

"Come on," he prompted once he figured he had enough for a decent writing slate.

She rolled her eyes and hobbled over. "I want books," she murmured.

"Can't give you that, but I'm not leaving you alone until I find a way cheer you up."

He did make some progress as the day went on. By the time the sun was lowering and he had to prepare dinner, Fellone was quietly drawing intricate patterns in the sand with a much less morose aura about her. They ate outside, accompanied by a particularly audacious squirrel that made her giggle as it tugged at her purple-tinted hair. For that moment, at least, all the problems she posed him became insignificant.

Twilight set over the forest as they finished their fish soup. Retyar made a quick trip to the creek to rinse out the tins, coming back to see Fellone staring into the darkened woods.

"If you want, we can wander a bit farther tomorrow," Retyar said. "For now, let's get some sleep."

Fellone hobbled into the cave with only a pained grunt. Retyar sighed and followed her. He stowed the tins and readied their bedrolls in silence, wondering what kind of thoughts were going through the girl's head. Whatever they were, there was little chance of him finding out. He watched in the fading light as she rubbed her hands over the walking stick before setting it against the wall.

"Good night," he said, turning on his side and pulling over his blanket.

He heard her draw in a deep breath. "Good night."

Retyar's dreams had him back in the University library, roaming between the shelves trying to find a book he'd recognize when he saw it. He felt he was on the verge of discovery when his bladder brought him awake. He quietly slipped outside to relieve himself over the seaside cliff face. The blue moonlight made the woods and ocean waves more distinct than the minutes right after sunset. Out of habit, he searched the water for any signs of sharks or shyles, but he saw no telltale fins break the surface before he turned back for the cave.

He settled back into his blankets, sparing a glance at Fellone's end of the cave, then frowned. He couldn't see much in the blackness, but something seemed a bit off. Probably nothing, yet . . . . He looked at where she'd left the walking stick.

It was gone.

Retyar jumped to his feet and snatched at Fellone's empty blankets. "Raze it! Blasted raze it!"

A chill took hold as it occurred to him she might not have run off, but just fallen over the edge. He swept the beach and the creek with the flashlight, but to his relief and frustration found nothing.

"Stupid! I should have seen this coming!"

He paced around outside the cave to gather his wits. For the sake of the timeline, his only option was to find her. He grabbed his rifle and his satchel and moved southwest. It seemed impossible that he'd chance upon her in the dark, but he had to at least try. He turned off the flashlight, using the moonlight to determine his steps. Speed was of the essence and he didn't bother being careful with his footprints.

Retyar traveled for a good half hour, his eyes searching for her somewhat still bright dress, his ears keen for any sound of her limping walk.

He stumbled and nearly tripped on his face when he noticed a yellow-orange glow in the trees ahead of him. A campfire? If she came this way, she'd surely be drawn to it. Cautiously, but still quickly, he set towards the flame.

He slowed only as he started to hear voices. He ducked low, trying to get as close as possible and hear what they were talking about. If he could—

There she was. He saw Fellone leaning against a tree, barely enough white left in her dress to set her apart from the surrounding shadows. She was but one step away from revealing herself to the group of five men who drew Retyar's eyes next. Soldiers. He had no idea of their exact allegiance, but their swords and armor made no question that he didn't want to deal with them. If he could just sneak up on the girl before she decided to step into sight . . . .

He hissed as Fellone stumbled into the firelight. "H-hello?"

The soldiers started, several of them reaching for their weapons before seeing it was only a child.

"Six continents, what are you doing out here, girl?"

"My name's Fellone. My home . . . . Everyone was murdered. I need help getting to the city."

Every fiber in Retyar's being was stretched taut as he crouched in the bushes, mind whirling. How did he get her out of there? No, things had gone over and beyond disaster with her telling her name.

The soldiers glanced at each other.

"Likely enough story," one of them said.

"Don't just buy into it like that," another said. Retyar guessed he was the commander of the group, judging by him wearing plate armor while the others had only chain or gambeson. "Remember the attack last night. This could be some kind of ruse."

"She's just a girl, Grasnakar."

"She's Senkani. They're all fanatics for their crenden. She'll probably lead us into some trap."

Fellone fidgeted. "Um, who are you? You're not Senkani?"

One of the soldiers stepped behind her and grabbed her by the neck. Fellone squealed in fright. "Let me go!"

"Dravs, Meckle, search the woods," Grasnakar ordered. "There could be Senkani waiting to ambush us."

The other men shifted uneasily. "If they're out there waiting to attack, shouldn't we stay t'gether?"

The commander spit at his feet and addressed the woods, "You out there, Senkani rats? Show yourselves if you value this little mouse's life."

Retyar heard Fellone's whimper. "Please, I'm telling the truth. I'm alone."

His hand was on his rifle stock before he even realized it. He reined himself in from drawing. The rational part of him argued that this could be the timeline's way of fixing itself. The girl was supposed to die.

"You have till the count of four," Grasnakar said, putting the tip of his sword towards Fellone's chest.

"Hey, what if there's really no one there?" Dravs or Meckle asked. "Look at 'er leg. I don't think she's pretend'n with that."

"What if?" the soldier holding her said. "She's a Senkani mouse. They like taking cheap shots at us, we'll pay 'em in kind."

"One," Grasnakar called.

Fellone struggled weakly against the soldier's grasp. "I'm telling the truth! Let me go!"

"Two . . ."

Retyar forced himself to stay put.

"Three . . ."

This had never been his business. History was set.

"Four."

What's done was done.

Fellone's scream threw all rationalizations out of his head. He sprung forward, tearing the cloth cover from his rifle. The soldiers were half drawn by his sudden appearance, and half by the metallic snap of him locking the chamber.

"What were you saying, little mouse?" Grasnakar asked.

"Let her go," Retyar ordered.

The soldier holding Fellone shoved her to the ground and pinned her under his boot. "Where'r the rest of you, rat?"

Retyar aimed his rifle at Grasnakar. "I said let her go."

The commander laughed. "That's not how you hold a

spear, friend."

"That a spear or a club?" one of the soldiers asked. With only the moon and the campfire for light, it would be hard to make out the length and shape.

"He's holding it like a crossbow," another one muttered.

"There's no bow."

"Could be some weird Senkani contraption."

"He's just bluffing," Grasnakar said. He twirled his sword as he approached Retyar. "Isn't that right, rat?" He jumped forward with a confident shout.

Without another thought, Retyar pulled the trigger.

The *bang* and *thunk* sounded in the same instant, his bullet splitting the air and punching straight through the commander's chest plate. The man's pounce turned to a falter. He had just enough time to let loose a surprised gasp before falling on his face in a clatter of armor.

All the men around the campfire shared a moment of shocked stupefaction. Even Retyar could hardly believe what he'd just done. The fire crackled, a log shifting and throwing out a gush of sparks. The rest of the soldiers went into action.

Three of the soldiers charged him at once, swords raised to strike. Retyar's reflexes took over. Three gunshots hammered out, dropping each of the attackers in quick succession.

The fifth and last soldier managed to notch an arrow and let fly at half draw before Retyar could get a bead on him. He felt the arrowhead smack him hard in the abdomen, but the arrow bounced off his ballistic armor, landing on the dark forest floor. The soldier's eyes were wide when Retyar trained his rifle on him and sent a bullet through his head.

A thin stream of smoke twisted away from the barrel as he slowly lowered his aim. Six continents, what had he just done? He found it hard to breathe as reality hit him. History. The timeline. He'd just . . . .

He'd just killed five people.

A strangled squeal brought his attention back to Fellone. The girl was still on the ground, one hand over her head, the other across her mouth to stifle her own voice. The firelight reflected off eyes wide in horror or terror. She flinched as he shifted, then approached. He squatted in front of her, the hot barrel of his gun resting on his legs. He looked hard into her face.

"I gave you rules, Fellone. Follow them."

Chapter 50

Maltan had always imagined the conquest of a city to involve a fair bit of death and pillaging. In his long life, he'd never actually seen a violent transition of power, but the stories of the Tarkandan split painted a picture of blood, chaos, and resentment. Here in Breakpeak, the Vron takeover seemed outright benign. There were no burning buildings, no mass executions, not even a curfew. The market still opened in the morning, carpenters still chiseled away in front of their workshops, and washerwomen still gossiped about mundane affairs. If it weren't for the imperial flags flapping above the walls and the Breakpeak palace, as well as the soldiers in silver uniforms patrolling in place of the regular guard, he'd have wondered if the battle outside had been a figment of his imagination.

Well, that and the fact that one of those soldiers had him shoved against a wall, sword bared. There was one group that didn't have it as easy as everyone else.

"I said hands where I can see them, old man."

"And I told you I'm not an aristocrat," Maltan said with every ounce of calm he could muster. He desperately hoped for someone to come to his aid, but every commoner up and down the sloped street did his best to ignore the scene.

The soldier waved the point of his sword at Maltan's feet. "Likely story, if it weren't for those handsome boots of yours." The man's armor clicked as he leaned in, his teeth gleaming in a threatening grin. "So, where does a normal old fellow like you get fancy footwear like that?"

"A gift from a cobbler friend," Maltan said.

"Right, well, there's a sure way of seeing one way or the other. Let's have your coin pouch."

He felt the urge to channel some of Charva's perpetual bravado, but knew it would only make matters worse. He couldn't think of anything clever at the moment, anyway. Nonthreatening, and holding back a sigh, he untied his pouch and handed it over.

The soldier hefted it with a disappointed grimace. He shoved the pouch into a pocket and lifted the point of his sword. "This isn't all of it. Off with the tunic."

A mailed fist smacked the imperial in the side of his helmet. "What's this, soldier?"

Maltan's accoster shifted furiously and started to raise his sword, but stopped immediately. It was an Aiv Chahai. Maltan had seen them about town, roaming major streets and alleys in their distinctive silver split-skirt riding dresses, patches with their stylized eye emblem sewn to the shoulders of their uniforms.

"Suspected aristocrat, Watcher," the soldier said. "General's orders are to arrest them all and bring them to the palace."

"What part of that involves lining your own pockets with their coin?" the woman demanded. She reached into his surcoat and pulled out Maltan's looted pouch by the string.

The soldier grunted, but held his tongue. The Aiv Chahai tossed the pouch to Maltan. "Take him to the palace. If he is a noble, requisitions will decide what happens with his belongings." She eyed Maltan. "Try anything, though, and I'm not stopping him from cutting you down."

Maltan accepted the warning in silence, and in silence followed the soldier's gruff directions up the main street. Chances were this case of mistaken identity would be cleared up when no one already in the Vron's hands recognized him. A part of him looked forward to the soldier getting reprimanded for roughing up a commoner without cause. The greater part of his mind, however, had already retreated into the realm of detached analysis. What were the imperials doing with the nobles they rounded up? Scant little information about that trickled down to the limited circles he'd managed to get into.

Even Maltan's endurance started to wear upon nearing the top of the main avenue. He puffed with each step, sweat trickling down his brow. The soldier breathed harder too, though he tried to hide it. Both of them were grateful when finally they left the last of the regular residences behind and reached the iron gate marking their destination.

The palace was nothing special compared to those of other cities in the aristocracies. Built of the same tan bricks as the rest of the Breakpeak, its most notable features were that it sat on several tiers cut into the rock face, with the roof of the topmost level reaching past the peak. The view from there must undoubtedly be astonishing.

Silver uniformed guards let them through the gate. The soldier led Maltan into a wide patio overlooking the city. As they passed through, an officer emerged from a palace door on his way to town.

"Still some aristocrats left scurrying about?" the officer said. "And here I thought I was done processing."

"Quite likely you are," Maltan said. "I'm not nobility."

"No reason to be in hiding. We've already identified and dealt with the staunch House loyalists. Pledge yourself to the empire and you will be granted preliminary citizenship."

Another officer walked through the main gate, this one more splendidly arrayed than the first and flanked by two men in heavy armor.

"We'll see if our guy recognizes him," the first officer said. "Tell us your name. If we find you're lying, you won't like the repercussions, mind you."

"Maltan."

The officer nodded and pointed to one of the outlying buildings. "Take him to the registrar."

The commander who had come through the gate went a few paces further, silver cape flowing gently behind him, but then stopped and turned. "Maltan?"

The first officer started, not realizing the commander was at his back. "Sir! You . . . you know this man, sir?"

The commander stood in front of Maltan and looked him in the eye. At the close proximity, Maltan could see the details of the pale scar running up the side of his face. Even without the insignia on his shoulder, he knew precisely who this commander was.

"I've heard of a Maltan," General Nevygar said. "But he's not a man of Heartsong. What are you doing so far from your home of Creedport?"

An unsettling chill went through Maltan's body. "How did I come to be known by the great general of the Vron?"

"Men of learning naturally attract to one another, tinkerer," Nevygar said, a shrewd look in his dark blue eyes. "You are the preeminent scholar of north-central Moshon. Any real seeker of knowledge on this continent knows of you."

The curse of fame, Maltan thought.

Nevygar waved the soldier and officer off. "You two are dismissed."

The men left, the soldier who'd arrested him noticeably stiff. Maltan had the slight satisfaction of seeing him catch his foot on his own ankle.

The general waved again and someone carried a glass table and two chairs onto the patio. "Sit, Honorable Maltan."

He obliged, and in a moment a bottle of wine and glasses were set out before them.

"I hope my soldiers were not too harsh with you. Power too often goes to one's head, making men you thought were reasonable into the dregs of society in short order."

Maltan shifted his jaw, wondering if he was meant to answer. Speaking with the feared General Nevygar himself had hardly been on his itinerary when he got up this morning. It was also an impossibly good opportunity. He drew in a breath. "It almost went a lot worse," he said, rubbing the spot where his back had hit the wall. "An Aiv Chahai was there to keep him in line."

Nevygar rested an elbow on his knee and gazed out at the city. "I'm always grateful to have the Order along. It would be a headache trying to keep discipline in the ranks without their oversight."

"From what little I've heard, I had the impression commanders hated being subject to the Aiv Chahai's authority."

Nevygar poured himself some wine. "What is is. A true commander takes what is dealt him and turns it to his benefit."

"That philosophy seems like one which would preclude war," Maltan said.

The general's eyes seemed to smile at him as he touched the glass to his lips. "An interesting conclusion," he said after a sip. "Care to elaborate?"

Maltan felt some of his nerve drain out of him. Years of bashing his head against Crenden Thrake had made him speak too freely. What was he doing, challenging the most powerful military man of the continent? No ducking out of it now.

"Someone who accepts the card he's dealt and makes the best of it is peaceful by nature," Maltan said. "To act in aggression, to take someone else's card as it were, that is war. So it feels like a contradiction to me that you could have such a, I would say, noble mentality while at the same time being a fearsome general. Taking—" he gestured at the city below them "—this card through such violent means."

A fresh bead of sweat rolled down the side of Maltan's face. Hopefully, it could just be taken as a product of the early afternoon sun and the exertion of the climb. He poured himself some wine.

Nevygar didn't look at all offended. "A fair view to take. It fails if you complete the analogy. I do not argue with the dealer, but the whole point of accepting a hand is so you can pit it against your opponents."

Maltan sipped his wine, taking his time before speaking again. "Why does your opponent have to be the aristocracies? What has a place like Heartsong ever done to you? Can you not instead challenge poverty or hunger? Why focus your aspirations on killing your fellow man?"

"And who are you to say such things as poverty and hunger are not my real enemy? Honorable Maltan, I suspect you fail to see the meaning of empire."

"The purpose of empire is greed," Maltan said.

"Indeed. And is that bad?"

"Now you contradict yourself in your question. How else does poverty and hunger come about if not through greed, through men taking from others to fulfill their own selfish desires?"

"Let me turn that around on you." The general leaned back comfortably in his chair. "What is it that brings a man out of poverty if not greed?"

"That's twisting—"

"I'm not twisting anything. Want is the nature of mankind. You reveal that in your very use of the word 'poverty' as a horrendous state of existence. You understand that it is terrible to live on only the basics of bodily needs, that a man must to be allowed to seek more so he can be fulfilled."

"And so you crush nations, so that you can satisfy your own desires."

"Quite the opposite," Nevygar said, a faint smile curling the corners of his lips. He drank the remainder of his glass and filled it up again. "It is nations that fulfill their own desires at the expense of others. They are the ones that look out for themselves above all else. Empire, the kind of order I bring, erases the 'us' and 'them'. The Vron seek the elevation of all."

Except the ones who die in the process, of course, Maltan thought, but he held his tongue on that. He'd been far too forward already. He was lucky enough the general had humored him this far. His eyes fell to the ground to where their shadows faced each other across the circle of focused light from the glass table. Plain black and white, except for the wine in Nevygar's glass. It looked as if the man's shadow held a grand ruby, or perhaps a ball of crimson flame.

"What wine is this?" Maltan asked. "I hadn't been paying attention earlier, but it tastes familiar."

Nevygar turned the bottle so the label faced him, revealing a red leaf Maltan instantly recognized.

"Best wine this part of the continent," Nevygar said. "There are certainly things for your aristocracy to be proud of."

Maltan was disturbed to hear the general praise Leverie. After a moment, he figured out why. When imperials like something, they take it, and Leverie was only two borders down. "General Nevygar, you've spoken of the empire's aspirations. What about you? Why do you yourself fight?"

Instead of answering, the general smiled and stood. "I have tasks to attend to. We will speak again, Honorable Maltan."

Chapter 51

Charva fidgeted where she sat on a stump behind the camp's front row of tents. On the other side of thin sheets of fabric, thousands of men were finally getting ready to charge Senkani's walls.

"Something . . . . There has to be something I can do."

"You already decided you were going to focus on your own mission," Ersch said. He was standing nearby, between her and the soldiers, his hand on his hilt.

Charva shot to her feet. "There has to be some way for me to talk them out of it."

"If there was ever a chance of that, it was lost hours ago."

As if by more than coincidence, Crenden Odavan's voice suddenly came from behind the row of tents opposite the soldiers. "Enough blithering. We are attacking. The Council is decided. You even cast your vote."

Athar's constant wheezing was unmistakable. "That . . . was only because the rest of you . . . wouldn't stop persisting! . . . If there were . . . . Odavan, stop walking . . . . Can't breathe . . . ."

"Six continents, Athar, stop eating like a whale and get some exercise. I wouldn't be surprised if it takes two provinces to feed you."

Seeing an opportunity to add her voice against the attack, Charva started to step forward, but felt a hand clamp down on her arm. She turned on her ckol. "Ersch—"

He put a finger to her lips. "My liege, Odavan is one with a motive. This is our chance to listen."

Charva glared at him, but bit her tongue.

"Do you have any alternatives, Athar?" Odavan was asking. "Some sort of incredible treasure you're sitting on that can pay for the siege? Some way to cross the river so we can encircle the city?"

"We . . . " Athar trailed off into an extended fit of wheezing. Charva started wondering if the man was really dying until he continued, "We can leave . . . . Ylnavar's devotion to this . . . this rigid, unyielding law is madness . . . . Let the Redleafs go."

"You can't seriously be saying this."

"This . . . war will destroy us."

"*Us*! Destroy *us*! We have an army ten thousand strong. My men alone sent them packing from Creedport with their tails between their legs. It's ridiculous that Ylnavar insisted we even bother trying to soften them with the catapults."

"Impatient to . . . finish off Ellaniel?"

Charva's heart pounded in her ears, filling the stretch of silence that followed the words. When Odavan again spoke, it was so low she could barely hear, but it was with frightening menace. "My patience with you is what wears thin. To the shyles with you being a fellow crenden. Say something like that again and my fist will be the next thing talking."

Forget Ylnavar. Charva would be more than happy if this piece of filth were her man.

A horseman galloped past the soldiers. "Ready! Ready!"

Charva ducked around a tent corner as Odavan marched off to where everyone was marshaled, sinking back even further when his ckols followed behind him. "Where's the Woodwise line? Spit and dirt, can't you people at least manage a straight formation?" He continued berating the troops, his voice fading as he moved away.

"Still upset at me?" Ersch asked.

She stared in the direction of Odavan's retreat, though the tents cut off her field of view within twenty feet. "You think he's the one?"

"Hashan's death made him crenden. He then sends his assassins after Ellaniel, who had the next closest support as successor after Odavan. Stick the whole thing on your father and he goes free with no one suspecting a thing."

"It makes sense. But what about Fellone's mansion? What

does she have to do with any of it?"

Ersch shrugged. "Maybe something extra to throw everyone off the trail?"

"Maybe." Charva tapped her forehead. "Embers, I want it to be this simple, but we need some kind of proof."

The next moment, the army roared its battle cry and her thoughts of conspiracy were cast aside for more immediate disaster.

Arzan stormed along the battlements and shouted at the top of his lungs.

"Archers, ready!"

The hundreds of men with him on the wall hardly needed the order. Bows were already strung and arrows in hand. No one could miss the thousands of Council soldiers who had lined up at the top of the eastern slope. It had apparently taken two days of deliberation after the loss of their catapults, but the Leverie were finally going for the assault.

"Ballistae crews at your stations! Shieldsmen—"

The sword and shield units were already filing out onto the wall. His captains knew well enough what they were doing.

In moments, Arzan was walking between two flanks of men—the archers against the battlements, and on the inner side spear and swordsmen standing ready to switch once the ladders arrived.

And the Leverie did have ladders. Scores of them.

"I used to play all the time in those woods as a boy," he heard one of the soldiers mutter to his companion. "Now they hack down our trees to take our walls."

Arzan glanced over at the young man, saw the simmering anger in his eyes and the eyes of his fellows. The sight fueled the same kind of personal anger he felt burning within himself. Everything the Leverie did seemed designed to make him hate them.

"Ready," Arzan said. "Ready to kill them all."

The Leverie issued their war cry. The ten thousand voices

raised in unison were like an ocean wave raging against the shore. The Senkani responded, and to Arzan it felt the stronger, erupting spontaneously and rattling the stones almost as violently as the earlier catapult boulders. Or perhaps that was just his own bones resonating with the sound.

The Leverie started the charge.

Arzan saw little fear in the enemy as they raced down the slope over bare farmland. Perhaps they were just emboldened by their numbers, but to dash straight at a wall topped by hundreds of archers was still something to be acknowledged.

"With that many of them, nothing will miss," the archer nearest him said. The man notched an arrow and readied to draw. "They near the first distance markers, my liege."

"They do." Arzan's hand went to his pommel. "Archers, notch!"

Even as he said the words, a line of men dropped out of the Leverie charge and stopped. The enemy archers.

"Loose!" Arzan shouted.

Countless *twangs* sounded as one as his men sent out the first volley. The arrows flew true, striking the Leverie hard. Men stumbled and fell everywhere along the ragged line, disappearing into the sea of men to be trampled underfoot. The exception were the soldiers in Woodwise blue, who intercepted the volley with shields and armor.

Arzan spent only a handful of heartbeats surveying the damage. The Leverie archers were drawing. "Shields, forward!"

Hundreds of Leverie arrows sprang skyward. Wood and armor clattered as the soldiers atop the wall rushed forward and raised their shields over themselves and the archers in front. Arrows thudded into shields and cracked against stone.

"Shields, back! Archers, draw!"

The second volley was as effective as the first, bringing down at least a hundred Leverie. Only a drop in the bucket of thousands.

The ballistae loosed their bolts, their distinctive *snap-cracks* carrying over everything else. The artillery opened bloody furrows in the Woodwise shield formations and around the ladder teams.

More arrows thudded into Senkani shields, then Arzan ordered a third volley. As they notched, more troops dropped out of the charge. More archers, but wielding short hunting bows—the best anyone not from Woodwise would be able to manage. "Ignore them. Focus on the main army."

Ballistae bolts destroyed a ladder team and another Woodwise shield wall, and made a shower of splinters out of a covered battering ram the enemy tried rolling down the main road.

Shortbow arrows pelted the wall in a steady barrage, too inaccurate and too weak to do any real damage.

The defending archers got another volley off, and then the first of the Leverie hoard were at the wall. Arzan wiped sweat from his face as he looked either way down the battle line. The enemy army seemed the same size as when it started.

"Archers, back! Shields, forward, swords at the ready!" He pulled his own blade free with the order. At the same time, he spared a glance to his right along the wall in the off chance he might spot Ellaniel commanding the southern portion.

A ladder *thunked* into the crenels three feet from Arzan. The defenders had a few scant moments to toss stones over the side, and then the enemy was there. Gambeson-clad Leverie reached the top, swords and shields up in front of them. Too bad for them, the Senkani had room for two men per ladder. The first Leverie to appear before Arzan's eyes got a quick jab in the face. The man toppled backwards and screamed horrifically all the way to the ground. The next fared no better, swinging his sword wide into the crenel like a rank amateur before a blade found his throat. A Senkani soldier came in with a pole to push the ladder away. The enemy cursed as they fell. Arzan took the chance to rotate his swordsmen before the Leverie put the ladder back up at a shallower angle.

The assault lasted a quarter hour, with bodies piling rapidly at the wall's base. Arzan rotated the men three more times before the enemy stopped climbing. The two swordsmen who had just stepped forward leaned over the side and jeered. An arrow plinked off one of the men's helmets, sending him back with a grunt. Arzan checked him over and slapped him on the shoulder when he saw he was fine.

The defenders tossed more rocks and shot arrows at near point blank. The screaming down below was incredible, sounds of pain drowning out shouts of challenge.

The Leverie army broke. First in ones and twos, then in waves, the soldiers started retreating up the slope.

This is it. Arzan stepped back with a relieved sigh. *We held them off. Our city is saved.*

"Archers, keep shooting! Don't let them regain their courage!"

It was quickly a full rout. His men cheered in victory, and Arzan joined in, shouting at the top of his voice.

A wooden thud drew Arzan's attention to the gate. He frowned. The gate was open. His confusion lasted only briefly before his blood went cold.

The ache in Ellaniel's thigh intensified as she strode out of the city and into the ruined fields. She ignored the pain and tightened her grip on her sword. Soldiers followed behind her, but she didn't bother looking back to see how many. Instead, she scanned the slope, taking in the army now retreating into the safety of their camp and the bodies littering the ground. It didn't take long for her to find what she was looking for.

She climbed the slope to a man in Woodwise blue. He was on his side, weakly attempting to crawl up towards the camp. An arrow jutted out of his lower abdomen, just below the bottom of his chest plate.

Ellaniel pointed with her sword. "Bring him to his feet."

The injured man cried out in pain as two Senkani soldiers lifted him up by the arms. Ellaniel stepped between him and the Leverie camp and looked into his face. He was about her age, she judged, but it was hard to tell with the helmet and the dirt smeared over him.

"I'm . . . I'm bleeding," the man croaked.

Ellaniel removed her helmet. A lock of dark hair fell over her brow, sweat gluing it in place. She swept it aside as she turned toward the camp. Some of the Leverie were starting to take notice, pointing to her from the safety of the camp.

Good.

She took one last look at the injured soldier, then slit his throat. The man gagged and gurgled on his own blood, his eyes filled with panicked horror. He thrashed about with sluggish limbs after the Senkani soldiers dumped him back in the dirt.

"Kill all from Woodwise," Ellaniel commanded. "Spare any other colors."

The soldiers shouted their agreement and set about their hunt. Ellaniel started her search for her next victim, but found her arm snatched in a tight grip.

"Ella! What's this madness?" Arzan demanded.

She turned on him. "Madness? I'm only returning the same treatment they gave us."

"It's still a crime! Killing a captured enemy is against the codes."

Vigkhon was at Arzan's side, his eyes on the top of the slope. "My liege, the enemy are preparing another assault."

Ellaniel tried to pull away, but Arzan held firm. "What good are the codes when only one side follows them? This is justice!"

"They're just commoners," Arzan said. "Average men following orders."

"They're traitors!" Ellaniel screamed. "These were my father's people!"

"My liege, they're coming."

"Vigkhon, help me."

"Keep off!" She tried once more to jerk her arm free, but Vigkhon had her other side in an instant. She struggled only a little longer before letting herself get dragged back towards the city. Even she saw that the Leverie were on their way. The soldiers who had accompanied her were already falling back to the wall. "I'll see that they pay, Arzan," she said, then kept her silence.

Chapter 52

Retyar and Fellone sat at opposite ends of the cave, the crashing of waves and seagull cries outside the only sounds either of them had heard for a long time. He knew the girl was terrified of him. More so than when she'd thought him just some fugitive criminal. He also knew her well enough to expect her curiosity to get the better of her.

The question came. "Who are you?"

He had already decided he'd tell her. To blazes with the secrets and stupid cover stories. He wasn't a good liar, and besides, he was sick of having no one to talk to.

"I'm from Govunari, a kingdom in Falcone. But I'm from a version that won't exist for another six hundred and forty years."

It took a moment or two for the girl to process the sentence. When she did, her blank stare turned into a scowl of insulted intelligence, then an uncertain frown when her eyes went to the covered rifle at his back.

Uncertain was good. That was better than outright disbelief.

And so Retyar told his story, all the way from the beginning.

Fellone asked a lot of questions as he told his account,

some easier to answer than others. Many of them were pretty basic, but that didn't necessarily make for a simple explanation.

"What's a security guard?" "Aerotech?" "What do you mean 'timeline'?" "What's a radio?" "Why do these 'scientist' wear white coats?" "You're a scholar?" "What's a bomb?"

There was fairly little for him to say about his six years in hiding, but with all the interruptions, it took the better part of the day to even get there. Even with all of his detailed telling, it was the tablet computer that finally won her over. The girl's eyes became full circles as he turned it on and scrolled through an encyclopedia entry.

"What is it?" her voice was filled with awe.

"A computer. It uses complex microscopic electrical logic gates to execute programs that let you do calculations or simply input and output data. This particular one lets you interact with the processor using a touch interface that detects the minute electrical charge in the skin of your fingertips. Below the sensor layer is a back lit display containing a film of liquid that crystallizes in the shapes of words and images."

Retyar was intentionally technical. He made careful note that Fellone's eyes didn't glaze over *too* badly with all the jargon. There was no way she could understand what he had just said, but she was listening, and he had no doubt she was going to do her best to figure it out.

"You said you like books. This computer holds more pages than all the books you've ever seen put together. Fellone. . . . " This was perhaps the riskiest thing of all he was doing. "I can give this to you, but it will come with a condition."

Her eyes were glued to the tablet. She deliberately closed them, and when they opened again they were focused on him. In their violet depths, he saw she knew this condition was going to be serious.

"You can't ever go home," Retyar said.

Fellone was silent for a long while. She looked between him and the tablet several times, glanced at the rifle at his back, then focused her gaze on the glittering ocean.

"Why?" she asked quietly.

Retyar set the tablet down on his blanket and laced his fingers. "You remember the thing I said about the timeline? How I was afraid of changing anything because that would mean the place I come from will never exist?"

Fellone nodded, though he could see her dubiousness returning.

"Just as I'm not supposed to exist here, the knowledge you have, the knowledge you will gain by reading what's in this computer is not supposed to exist in this world. You have the power to change everything. To destroy everything."

"But you won't let me go home even if I don't look at that computer."

Retyar drew in a deep breath. He knew how she was feeling. He'd been coping with it for six years. "Fellone, just as the things you know don't belong here, you don't either. You're supposed to be dead. The way history plays out, you died the night those men threw you in the river."

"But that doesn't make sense. I didn't die. I don't remember ever dying."

"That's not how it works. You don't remember things that —"

"*I didn't die!*"

He slapped his hand on the cave wall. "That's the problem!"

The words finally broke something in her. The girl chewed on a quavering lip and blinked back tears. Retyar wished he didn't have to say these sorts of things to her, but it had become unavoidable from the moment he'd saved her life. He knew that now. He put a hand on her shoulder.

"You're dead to history, have to stay dead to the world, but your heart's still beating. I know it doesn't seem like a fair trade, but I can at least give you the opportunity to read and learn about things that no one else can possibly know. You can share it with nobody and do nothing with it." He left unspoken that there were people who were more than content with that. Obsessive researchers—seekers of knowledge for knowledge's sake. It was a personal choice, or perhaps an inclination that certain individuals were born with. It wasn't something someone should be pushed into. Not that Fellone had any alternatives. Still, he didn't want to push.

Fellone wiped some tears on her sleeve before raising her eyes. Retyar didn't expect the defiance he saw in them. "Your world isn't mine."

The words hung in the air between them, punctuated by the crashing waves. Retyar fought down the anger they brought him. "My world is what yours will become. What it's supposed to become. It's the natural progression of things."

"So what?" Fellone demanded. "Why do you decide what's the right way of things?"

"We're talking about billions of lives." Memories of his family rose in his mind, joined by thoughts of his one-time friends at University. "Change the timeline and their fate will be worse than death, because they'll never have existed in the first place." Even as he spoke, another image came unbidden: five soldiers lying face down on the dark forest floor.

"Those lives don't exist," Fellone said stubbornly. "This isn't your world."

Retyar stood to tower over her. "I saved your life!"

"And now things are different."

It was what Retyar knew to be true, but not what he was willing to accept. For the wisdom to be from the mouth of a ten-year-old child made it easier for him to ignore.

"You are not leaving here," he said. "There will be no negotiation. Try and escape and I will find you. I did it once in the dead of night, and I can do it again. Don't make me choose between your life and the whole of my world."

She glared back at him. "But didn't you already?"

His fingers curled into a fist at the words, his nails digging hard into his palm. His teeth clenched so hard together he couldn't force out another word. He gathered up the tablet and stormed outside. Why did the girl always have to be so difficult? Why did he have to always come out being the bad guy?

He'd made a mistake saving her. Worst of all, he couldn't correct it. Despite his threat, he wouldn't be able to kill her— and she knew it.

And if he couldn't kill her, the only way to deal with the situation was to win her over. He ran his fingers through his hair and glared back at the cave. "And what a great start at that I've made," he muttered.

Nonetheless, he returned inside.

Fellone already had an expression saying she was planning something drastic. Retyar spoke before anything could come of it.

"Think about what happens if my world doesn't arrive. I won't exist. If I don't exist, there's no one here to pull you out of the river."

The girl opened her mouth, but closed it again, her angry frown turning into more of an angrily considering frown.

"That's stupid," she said. "You're already here."

"'Already' doesn't mean anything with time travel. Everything here is my 'already'. You dying is my 'already'."

"But you're here."

"And the last time it was the year 4780, chances are I wasn't."

Fellone opened and closed her mouth again. She crossed her arms.

"There are philosophers who have spent years thinking through all the possible implications of time travel," Retyar said. "One of the more famous ones was a man named Kahverengi. He argued there were several possible kinds of timeline. The first is the type where everything is set. With all things that have happened and all things that will happen, it will always play out the same no matter what. Someone who travels back in time was always meant to travel back in time, and anything he does was already a part of the original timeline."

"Then—"

"That's not the case with us. In my history, you don't make it out of that river."

"Or nobody knows that I do because you keep me here."

Retyar scratched his beard. "So it's decided either way."

Fellone pushed herself up to stand on her good leg. "Unless I leave right now."

He moved in front of the cave entrance. "There's another kind of timeline. One where certain key points in history are set, but there's some leeway for smaller details to flow. But to protect those key moments, the world itself will make certain alterations impossible. If you go out there, the forces of temporal causation could kill you."

Fellone glared at him. "You're just trying to scare me."

"It could be what was happening when you ran into those soldiers."

The possibility alone was enough to give her pause. She stared out at the sea for a moment. "Then they would have gotten me. But they didn't."

"Because I was there to bring you back."

"By changing things by killing those men."

"Perhaps they weren't important." It was a stretch of probability and he knew it.

Fellone clearly knew it too. "And what are the other types of timeline that Kav-whatever guy talked about?"

Retyar didn't want to say, but there was no backing out of this now. "There's another possible kind where events are not fixed. Someone could go back and change things as much as he wanted, even to the point where the place he came from would be lost forever. He would be the only thing left of the old world, but that old world would still have existed, or he wouldn't be here."

Fellone stared out at the water, probably trying to sort out that last sentence.

"That's not the worst possibility, though," Retyar continued. "The timeline could be both open and closed. What happens if you go back in time and make it so you were never born, but reality needs you to be born in order to keep you from being born?"

"Uhm . . . ."

"Things can start happening that are beyond human comprehension. The laws governing cause and effect could be destroyed or reshaped in ways no one can understand or control. You could ruin the whole world, Fellone. Do you want that?"

From the look in her eye, he saw he had lost her. He could hardly blame her. This was his first time verbalizing all this out loud. It sounded nuts even to him, and he was the time traveler here.

But destroying the world's natural causal order was a real risk, no matter how crazy it sounded, and it was his responsibility to prevent such disaster.

"Is it my fault there are Leverie soldiers in Senkani's

woods?" Fellone asked suddenly. "Am I making the province fall apart by not dying?"

As before, the girl surprised him with how quick she was to draw conclusions based on ideas she'd rejected just moments prior. Like when she had suggested him a pirate, Retyar considered going along with her. Even if her fear wasn't accurate, it put the time paradox problem in terms that she could relate to. Still . . . .

"No, them being there is unrelated." He had decided he would tell her the truth. It wasn't something he could start going back on now. "According to the histories, Leverie is at the start of a civil war that's supposed to last several years. It was triggered by an attempted assassination of Crenden Redleaf and Crendess Ellaniel, who retaliated against the crenden of Creedport."

Fellone's eyes went wide. "Someone tried to kill Ella and Arzan? What happened? Are they okay?"

"I imagine they're fine right now," Retyar said. "At least, they're supposed to be alive until the Vron Empire sweeps in."

The blood drained from her face. "The empire?" she said in a small voice.

Retyar was halfway to cursing himself for the slip before remembering he'd decided to be fully honest anyway. He rested his arms on his knees and drew in a breath. "According to history, the empire arrives in 4789 and takes the country with barely a fight. Most of the ruling nobility are executed, though members of House Leverie and House Redleaf still remain provincial rulers for the next few decades until Leverie is merged into the surrounding lands as a greater territory."

"House Redleaf? Then Arzan and Ella will be okay?"

Retyar shrugged. "The only time their names specifically come up are in accounts of the civil war and when they go into battle against the Vron invasion force. Whoever wrote the encyclopedia entry on Leverie either didn't know what eventually became of them or didn't think it important."

Fellone pushed out her lips. "Well, the writer was stupid."

That earned a smile from him. He splayed his hands. "Leverie is a small country. It doesn't last long in the grand scheme of things. It barely leaves any legacy to my era. I think that the amount of information this writer provides is a great honor." He put his palms on the stones under him. "But yes, I've spent the last six years wishing there was more."

Fellone was quiet for a long while, her eyes cast over the water. Retyar gave up trying to read past that violet stare. The silence dragged on long enough for him to return to deep, if fruitless, contemplations on what he was going to do if the girl seriously set her sights on escape.

Chapter 53

The second time Charva was let in the Council command tent, the space was a different kind of beast. It still had the rugs and wall hangings, as well as the mirrored lamps, but gone was the small table with the war map. Instead, a large circular table had been assembled, and around it sat the Leverie crendens who had come to war.

"Why is she in here?" Odavan demanded loudly the moment she passed through the flap.

"Because Loftham, Athar, and I summoned her," Warth said. "As for why we summoned her, that's thanks to this tit-for-tat nonsense you started back in Creedport. So quit your whining and keep your belt on."

Loftham straightened his collar with a bony hand. "The Council is deliberating the reestablishment of the Order of Aiv Chahai. It has become clear that this war is taking longer and becoming far messier than anyone anticipated. We called Charva to the Council because she is the only woman of standing in camp and because she has been petitioning for the Order to be brought back for several days now." He smiled to her. "Take a seat please, my dear."

There was a vacant chair between Loftham and Athar, and despite the irritating wheezing and heavy breathing of the latter, she was glad to be next to people she might consider allies.

Odavan made no attempt to hide his scowl. "*We're* the ones who need to bring back the Order? In case you missed it, the Redleafs were the fiends shooting men in the back and executing the injured out there."

Charva still had a hard time believing what she'd seen at the end of the battle. She'd been as dumbfounded as the rest when the gates opened and Ellaniel had walked out in her lace-covered armor and red capelet. She had been more horrified than anyone to see her once friend mercilessly slit a helpless man's throat. *Ella, what has this war done to you?*

"Let me ask you a question, Odavan," Warth said. "The next time you capture a Senkani soldier, what can we expect your men to do to him?"

Charva saw the tightness in Odavan's jaw, could almost imagine the sound of his teeth grinding. "I would treat him as the codes require," he said stiffly.

Athar snorted, or perhaps that was just the start of a wheeze. "Doubtless."

Ylnavar cleared his throat. "I concede that we can no longer put off the Order's reinstatement. Our attempt to storm the wall has shown us that we need to spend more time on preparations, and that gives an opportunity for Aiv Chahai to be recruited from the provinces. That said, Charva will have nothing to do with it."

Mansar nodded aggressively. "She's not a neutral party. She fought on the Redleafs' behalf back at Creedport."

Loftham opened his mouth, but Charva spoke first, "You don't need a neutral party. The Aiv Chahai have never been neutral. Their one purpose is to keep their own side in check."

Odavan slammed his palm on the table. "You killed one of my ckols!"

"Your ckol was about to commit a summary execution of a daughter of the aristocracy," she shot back.

"It was a battlefield!"

"Ellaniel was on the ground and defeated. It's almost as if your ckols had explicit instructions that she not make it of that field alive. You certainly would have benefited from her death, wouldn't you, Odavan?"

Odavan sputtered and lifted his hands, aghast. He flicked his eyes at Athar. "I will not have these baseless accusations impinging upon my honor."

"What kind of orders did you give them, then?" Charva demanded.

"I sent them to intercept the cavalry unit slaughtering my

troops!"

"So your men overstepped themselves. Guess what," Charva locked eyes not only with Odavan, but also with the other crendens in turn, ending with Ylnavar, "I already am an Aiv Chahai, and I was acting in my capacity on that battlefield."

Ylnavar rapped that wood block of his on the table. "Admirable try, Charva, but we all know you are only deciding this retroactively."

"I take her claim as valid," Loftham said. "She is trying to stop unnecessary violence. Her heart is in the right place, Ylnavar."

Mansar shook his head. "You're going to let her take on titles at her own whim?"

"The Order does not answer to the Council and does not receive its authority from any man," Charva said. "I don't think you people here at all understand what the Aiv Chahai are."

"A gaggle of women with too much time on their hands!" Odavan said.

She tapped her finger on the table in irritation. "The Order is named after a woman of the First Era. It is a tradition dating back to before the scattering of humanity across the seas. In that time, there was a city—"

"Oh, for the love of—we're going into stories now," Odavan muttered.

"Let the lass speak!" Loftham said.

"It's a waste of—"

"Odavan, shut your mouth!" Warth roared.

The entire tent went quiet at the outburst. Even Charva was taken aback, but she snatched advantage of her opening. "In the First Era, during humanity's First War, there was a city that marched against its rival in the Great Competition. The name of that city has been lost to time, buried beneath an act of infamy that few people can now imagine. This was a world before the codes, when mankind was discovering the cruelties it was truly capable of.

"In the course of the war, this city went forward and found their enemy arrayed in an open field, ready to receive them. The battle was bloody, so hard-fought that it lasted the entire day and ended only when the defenders were killed down to the last soldier. The winners celebrated their victory, and, drunk on their success, marched into their enemy's streets. With no one strong enough to oppose them, they slaughtered the remaining men, pillaged the city's wealth, and raped every woman they found. Only once they were content did they return back home.

"When they reached their city, their women received the soldiers with a grand celebration. There was feasting and music and dancing in the streets. It lasted until one of the wives, a woman named Chahai, discovered what it was her husband had done. Furious that he had broken his vow to her, she fought with him, resulting in him falling out a window to his death.

"The city elders were quick to take hold of Chahai when they saw the body in the street. Singing and dancing ended as she was put under judgment for murder. The aiv, which was the title they gave to widows, was found guilty, but not before she revealed to all gathered what crimes their men had committed. Though she was executed, it was the city that was doomed. Now aware of what had transpired, the rest of the women also declared themselves aiv, saying that the men who had broken their vows were dead to them. They separated themselves from their husbands, promising never again to share their beds. For the remainder of their lives, they held to their word, and theirs was the city's last generation.

"Their conviction gave rise to a legacy not passed through ties of blood. The other women of Originate saw what had happened and decided they would not allow things to come to the same end for them. Many of them determined to travel with their men to war, calling themselves Aiv Chahai and watching to keep their husbands faithful. In the millennia since, the Order has continued its existence throughout the six continents, reinstated wherever there is conflict."

"And the war codes require that the Watchers have access to the army," Loftham put in. "Some of you might not like it, but the Order is by its very nature independent of the Council's authority. I stand by the position that Charva was fully within her rights to intervene in the Battle of Creedport."

"A Council that does not recognize the Aiv Chahai will be seen as illegitimate, not only by the people, but also by its neighbors," Warth said. "Leverie has been at peace for so long that we may have forgotten about the Order, but I'm certain many others beyond our borders have not."

"And they will pass . . . judgment on us," Athar wheezed.

Charva saw that she had an effect on the remainder of the Council. Odavan sulked silently while Ylnavar stared hard at the far end of the tent. Mansar brushed his beard in thought.

"The Council will vote on the matter of reinstituting the Order of Aiv Chahai," Ylnavar said at last.

"That's not something for the Council to vote—" Charva started.

"It is, and we will," he cut her off. "Those in favor of the Order?" The Speaker raised his hand.

Everyone else voted in favor, though it took some effort on Odavan's part to raise his arm. Charva did her best not to look smug.

"Those in favor of recognizing Natsha Leverie as Order head?"

She froze.

"Natsha is a well-respected woman of good standing," Ylnavar continued. "As both a member of the House and a widely regarded master of a trade, she would provide the Order with a positive reputation more likely to encourage honorable volunteers. Do any have other suggestions?"

Charva stood. "The Council cannot decide—"

The Speaker rapped his block. "Sit down!"

Loftham put a hand on her sleeve. "You've had your say, my dear. I believe you have the country's best interests at heart. Have a little faith that we do as well."

She clenched her fists and forced herself back down.

Warth raised his hand. "I favor Natsha. I would trust her to be an honest commander of the Aiv Chahai."

Odavan quickly added his vote, and Charva was sure it was only to oppose her. The others followed with their agreement.

"It is settled," Ylnavar said. "Natsha Leverie is recognized as leader of the renewed Order of Aiv Chahai."

Ersch was waiting anxiously for her when she stepped out of the Council tent.

"My liege, how did it go?" he asked, handing her back her sword.

Charva gave him a reserved grin and held up a letter with Ylnavar's seal stamped across the front. "The Council recognizes the Order. I'm to deliver this to my new superior in Highcity. Natsha's to be head of the Aiv Chahai."

Ersch snorted. "They recognized someone else after all. I was positive you'd wrangle them all into accepting you as head."

She smiled. Nice that someone had faith in her.

The crendens started making their way out of the tent behind her and joining up with their guards. Charva moved the two of them further away from prying ears. "Remember the point. This was an opportunity for us to gather clues." She said it as much as a reminder to herself as for him.

"And now they're sending you away from all your suspects."

He was right, and she wondered if it was paranoia to consider it to be on purpose. "Any word from our agents?"

Ersch glanced around even though they had already found a fairly private area. "Something, but not much. Some of the mercenaries came back to Creedport the night of the attack. It was late at night and the storm heavy, so the gate guard remembered them straight away when asked."

"They can't have stayed in the city for long."

"We have a witness who might have seen them leaving. A fisherman setting out before dawn saw a boat slipping around the eastern wall."

"In through the front to make it clear they're here to take payment from my father, then disappear from sight so they can return to their real master." Charva mulled it over. "Did the agents search the coast for this boat?"

"Still in progress."

Charva tapped her forehead. "Well, if I'm being sent away

from the Council, at least I'll have the opportunity to investigate elsewhere. What do you say to a trip to Woodwise after Highcity?"

"I say that's a great place to be poking around."

A group of soldiers came their way, prompting the two to move along through the camp. Charva couldn't help but notice the men carrying bundles of shovels towards the front. Somewhere in the distance, she also heard woodcutters' axes busily at work.

"They've started sapping," Ersch said, noticing her attention. "I expect it'll be more effective than their catapults, but it will take a while."

Charva set her jaw and continued on. She wouldn't be sorry to be leaving this madness behind for a bit.

She knew the camp well enough by now to find the open pens serving as the army's stables. Their horses were recently fed and groomed, and the caretakers were quick to have them in harness. As they tightened the last of the straps, a trio of scouts came riding in.

"To rot with those dirty Senkani," one of them said, reining in his horse and dropping to his feet in a cloud of dust. "Grasnakar didn't deserve to go out like that."

Another of the scouts spit as he handed off his reins. "We talkin' about the same Grasnakar? Sure, he was fun enough around the tavern back home, but the power went all to his head soon as they named him sergeant."

"Still. Ambush in the dead of night with slingstones?"

Charva cocked an eyebrow. "Slingstones?"

The last soldier to have spoken did a double take at her and straightened. "Aye. Least, that's as far as we can figure, your grace."

"You can't pierce armor like that with a sling," the other scout said. "Chain, maybe, but not gambeson, and not blazin' plate!"

"Well, weren't arrows. Or crossbow bolts. Or spears or pikes."

"And what else is there?"

"What did these wounds look like?" Charva asked.

"Like someone spiked 'em, or hit 'em with a slingstone. Each of 'em was hit once, either in the chest or the head."

"Went straight through their armor!"

"Warpick?" she suggested.

"A what?"

"They're an anti-armor weapon," Charva said. "It's like a warhammer, but with a spike at the head."

"They long enough to go in one side of a person and come out the other, armor and all?"

Charva thought back to the ones she'd seen in Falcone. She shook her head.

"Couldn't be a hand weapon anyway," the first soldier said. "Not the way the bodies were arranged. Got picked off while they were still charging."

"Anything else unusual?" Charva asked.

The first two men shook their heads, but she caught the third shifting uneasily. Charva set her eyes on him.

"It's just a bauble." The man fidgeted as both of the others stared at him. "Look, it's just a piece of brass. Wanted a war souvenir." He relented under their withering gazes and produced a small polished cylinder from his pouch. "Probably fell off someone's coat or something."

Charva had a hard time imagining how the object would attach to any piece of clothing. She plucked it from his palm, admiring its perfect shape. One end of it was open, revealing the hollow cavity within, while the other was molded in a solid end that protruded a thin rim. On the flat surface she thought she could see tiny etchings. She shifted it in the light and brought it close to her eye. Yes, there was something written around outside a circle inset in the cap's center. *.309 T4 L VsN 159.* The letters and numbers were incredibly precise. Whoever had made it was a master craftsman.

"This was near the bodies?"

"Yes, your grace."

Very curious. She fished through her pouch and pulled out a silver coin. "Thank you, soldier. I'll be taking this."

The man accepted the coin with a look of pleasant shock. Likely he'd resigned himself to an unconditional loss. Charva swung up into the saddle and spurred her horse out of camp.

"Was that worth a silver coin?" Ersch asked as he followed beside her.

Charva looked at the bauble under the flashes of sunlight

they rode through before slipping it in her pocket. "Never mind that. Let's make it quick to Highcity."

Chapter 54

Maltan never would have imagined that being a prisoner could make him feel like a thief.

Following his little chat with General Nevygar, the Vron had placed him under house arrest inside the Breakpeak palace. Sentries stood watch at his door and windows, but otherwise his life was now the pinnacle of luxury. From the plush furniture and ornate rugs to the blown glass lamps and intricate tapestries, every inch of his surroundings gushed money and excess. And his keepers apparently had orders to bring him whatever he asked for. It was the greatest irony that he should receive more honor in enemy hands than in the lap of his own people.

He was almost tempted to take it as his due, but he knew himself better than that. He didn't deserve any of this. The blood of a child was on his hands, and such a crime would always outweigh any accomplishment he might achieve. Aside from that, these things were not the Vron's to give. The palace belonged to the rightful rulers of Breakpeak, and to accept anything here as his would make him complicit in the empire's theft.

And so, he asked for nothing more than some paper and a pen, and for the days he was left to his own devices, he spent his time working at theorems and equations. He had a stack of pages twelve inches thick when a knock finally came from the hallway.

"The general requests your presence," the soldier said,

holding open the door.

Maltan put down his quill and gave a nervous smile. "And here I was beginning to think he'd forgotten about me."

The soldier offered no response as he led him out of the palace building and back to the patio where he and Nevygar had had their first meeting. The glass table was absent, and the general waited with his eyes cast over the city, his silver cape rippling gently in the breeze.

"Sir." The soldier saluted and left when Nevygar waved a dismissive hand.

Maltan stepped up to the low wall near the general. At least he wasn't afraid of heights.

"It's quite the city, isn't it?" Nevygar asked "I have been many places, seen my fair share of the world. Many of the towns and villages and plains and forests roll into one in my mind, but for every generic sight, there is a city, a mountain, a glade, a river that has its own distinct character. It is why I never grow tired of travel."

"A man can travel without conquering every city he sees."

Nevygar finally turned to him and smiled. "Come with me, Honorable Maltan."

The general started walking, and Maltan followed beside him as directed. They came to the palace gates, picking up a set of bodyguards before continuing out to the city's main avenue.

"I apologize for leaving you without company these few days," Nevygar said. "Things are always busy right after a city's capitulation." The streets they walked were fairly empty. Traffic between the ornate aristocratic houses consisted mostly of imperial soldiers on patrol. Nevygar noticed Maltan looking around at the shuttered windows.

"It's common we purge the local aristocracy," Nevygar said. "Don't worry, most are not harmed, simply relocated. People find it easier to integrate into the empire when their old authority is not present to confuse their loyalties."

"Where do you send them?" Maltan asked.

"Far enough away that there's no one around who cares about them. The members of the House we found here are on their journey to a territory well within the empire. They have a choice of retirement in the countryside. Their children will be given an education in our schools, and hopefully become well integrated into Vron society."

This was not what Maltan had expected. "Very generous terms for the defeated."

"I do not do this everywhere. There are some places where I feel the original crendens and crendesses administered their rule in wisdom and let them continue as vassals. Other times, they are so incompetent and corrupt that the sword is too good for them." His dispassionate tone set Maltan's hairs on end. He wondered how the crendens of Leverie would stack up in Nevygar's mind.

"What does the empire have planned for Breakpeak?"

The walkway now was steep enough that the hem of the general's cape trailed along the ground. They were leaving the noble quarter and true to Nevygar's words the city here was more alive. The man held out his arm. "Look around and tell me what you see."

Maltan obliged and cast his eyes over the metropolis. Things were actually the most normal he'd seen since coming to this city, with people fully back to their normal routines. There were washerwomen, children running errands, artisans and craftsmen working out front their shops. They all regarded the general and his bodyguards with masked hostility.

"I see a stone slope shaped by hundreds of years of habitation," Maltan said. "I see buildings with foundations carved into the very stone and streets smoothed by endless footsteps. I see people whose families have lived here for generations upon generations."

Nevygar nodded. "You see a city well established in its ways. The people here are accustomed to living on this towering piece of rock. They're content with the familiar, but it holds them back from their potential. Tell me, Maltan, can you think of a way to make this city better?"

"I admit, it would be a lot easier if one didn't have to walk a mile uphill to get to the palace."

The general stopped and planted his hands on his hips. "My thoughts exactly." He gestured over the city stretched out below them. "With our outside perspective, that answer is obvious. How many of them even think of the problem after living with it their entire lives?"

"What would you have them do? Level the city?"

"You're a tinkerer. Think creatively."

Maltan rubbed his beard. "A lifting mechanism."

Nevygar slapped his hand on Maltan's shoulder, an intense look in his eyes. "Think of it. People and goods able to traverse the city without effort. As it stands, elderly are stuck at home or by the gates because they lack strength for the climb. Women and children break their backs every morning carrying pots of water to their kitchens. Commerce is restricted to the lowest levels. The people here have adjusted to these realities because they have to if they want to live inside the walls, not because they like to."

"And what do *you* get from building a lift?"

Maltan had difficulty deciding if Nevygar's smiles were charismatic or egotistic. "I get credit. I know that outside the empire I am known only as a man of destruction, but inside I have a legacy. I endeavor to leave cities in better shape than I found them. Think of it as a hobby of mine."

Maltan shook his head. "Self-justification for your murders."

"Yes, it is a justification. And is that bad? Every man follows a path that he believes is right. Even the most abhorrent criminal will give you reasons for what he does. In the end, who determines which perspective is the correct one?"

"Common decency determines it be the one that brings others no harm."

"No harm," Nevygar repeated, bemusement in his voice. "In what category do you place those who stand by while his neighbor dies?"

"An age-old logical trap," Maltan said. "You're going to follow up by asking if it is right to end one life to save another. Then you're going to ask if it can be right to take a few lives to better the many."

The general chuckled. "A trail of reason you're obviously familiar with."

"And a trail that's wrong. Killing innocents is never justified, no matter what benefit may come of it. Intentionally doing so makes the beneficiaries no better than bandits."

"Then we are all bandits, Honorable Maltan. In some way or another, everyone has benefited from the deaths of others. There is no nation in this world that has not waged war, no nation that has not carved out its borders by way of bloodshed."

"I shall not dispute it. That does not mean it is just to continue their evils."

The general shrugged, his armor clinking with the motion. "Justice is ever a matter of perspective. Doesn't the administration of justice involve violence and death?"

"Justice is balanced retribution."

"I wonder if that's a notion that your own countrymen believe in."

The wry manner in which the general said the words raised a shrill warning in Maltan's head. "What do you mean by that?" he asked carefully.

"Interesting stories have been finding their way west," Nevygar said lightly. "Apparently, your very own Crenden Thrake took enough issue with some fellow of House Redleaf and tried having him killed. The Redleafs have been going on a rampage, already killing hundreds in retaliation."

"What?!" Maltan demanded, forgetting himself in shock.

"The Aristocracy of Leverie is embroiled in civil war. Your noble ideals do ring somewhat hollow, all things considered."

Maltan's mind pieced it together in an instant. That was what the purge and Maltan's exile would have been setting up. With him and Charva's supporters out of the way, there would be no one around to rein in Thrake's grudges and ambitions. Except that House Redleaf would never take a blow sitting down.

"The fool," he growled, and he heard in his own voice a degree of anger he'd never directed at another person before.

He turned to the general. "I don't suppose you'd be willing to let me return home."

Nevygar puffed through his nostrils. "And let you truly waste yourself? Your people have made it clear they don't want you there, tinkerer. Wash your hands of them."

It took a moment to draw himself back to the discussion. "And ally myself with someone even worse?" He shook his head. "If my country is truly tearing itself apart, I don't see how that has any bearing on my stance here."

"Really? I see it as very relevant. That is the very land in which you've focused your teachings of justice. Look what it's wrought them."

"In spite of me, not because of me." Charva rose to mind. He desperately hoped the girl was safe. He hoped just as much she hadn't been driven to participate in the madness.

"The world will ever contrive to spite you," Nevygar said. "Your sense of justice runs counter to how reality works. The web of human society is too complex and too contingent upon context and perspective to be boiled down to your simplistic moral imperative."

"Let's say I agree. Perhaps I have been wrong in my moral stance. You are still the empire threatening everyone I know and care about. Why should I help *you*?"

Nevygar grinned. "You and I are alike. We are born into our obsessions. For years, you have tried to suppress yourself, but inside you will never change. Just as I will always yearn to conquer, you will always yearn to invent. All I need to do is break the lock that holds. At some point, Honorable Maltan, you will see just how silly you're being and rejoin humanity." He waved his hand around him. "And the world will be a better place for it."

Maltan stared at him, not bothering to continue the argument. The general shook his head with a patient smile and gestured back up the slope. "Well, in the meantime, we can at least have lunch."

Chapter 55

Charva swung off her horse and planted her feet on Highcity's paving stones. The last time she had stood here in front of Natsha Leverie's shop had been her first meeting with Ellaniel. It felt like both yesterday and an eternity ago.

"I was expecting something a little fancier," Ersch commented.

The elegant doorway and sign with Natsha's name were the only things distinguishing the building from its plain-faced neighbors. Regardless, Charva knew, as did every fashionable woman in the aristocracy, that this was the place to come for the best needlework in the country. She tied her horse to a post that didn't quite look meant for the purpose and stepped inside.

She hadn't actually entered that time several years ago. She was sure she wasn't the only one who'd ever been taken off guard by the unexpected size of the shop, stretching far deeper than the narrow front suggested. Shelves brimmed with cloth of every imaginable color, embroidered in every possible pattern. Natsha's assistants were visible in the far back under shafts of sun pouring in from overhead skylights. The woman herself stood examining an orange dress with yellow feather patterns wrapped around the sleeves.

"Natsha," Charva said, drawing her letter as she walked up, "I have a message for you from the Council."

Natsha turned and looked her up and down with narrowed eyes. "Swords remain outside the shop. Such vulgar tools disrupt my artist's senses."

Charva smiled. "Get used to it. You've been appointed as

head of the Order of Aiv Chahai."

The letter hung in the air as Charva held it between them. The bewilderment on Natsha's face almost made the trip worth it alone. The woman slowly folded the dress and set it aside before taking the letter and breaking the Council seal.

"Those fools," Natsha said after a quick read. "They expect me to lead some form of military organization?"

"The Aiv Chahai aren't fighters," Charva said. "They merely watch to ensure the soldiers don't break the war codes."

Natsha tossed the letter away, the paper fluttering onto a stack of lace. "Oh, is that all? And what about the shop? Do you know how many personal orders I have to fill this month?"

"We're at war. It's the Council's command." In Charva's opinion, being so flippant about the state of the country made her a terrible choice to head the Watchers. As far as Ylnavar was concerned, that probably made Natsha perfect.

Natsha sighed long and loud. "I'm going to make Ylnavar pay for this. Already bad enough that all the male work is off trudging through the woods. If the shop goes in the red this month, I'm taking it out of the House coffers."

Charva shrugged and plucked up the letter of appointment. "I've delivered the Council's message. Do you have orders for me, Head Watcher?"

"That you get out of my sight," Natsha growled.

"I can help with recruiting."

"Fine, just go!"

Compared to the terrors she'd recently been faced with on the battlefield, followed by the hanging threat of execution for treason, the high-society anger Natsha radiated towards her almost brought a smirk to Charva's face. She turned on her heel and left the shop, shutting the door just as the older woman smashed a hanging rack on the floor.

"That didn't sound too good," Ersch said.

Charva shrugged. "An aristocrat whose world is embroidering handkerchiefs was just told she has to oversee a war. What did you expect?"

"What's our next step?"

She slipped out the letter Natsha had so carelessly

discarded. The seal was cracked clean in two, but if she pressed it together the insignia looked perfectly intact. She smiled. "It's time for us to snoop."

A few moments later, they stood before the Highcity palace. Though sitting in the shadow of the huge Council dome, it was still a sight to see, what with the meticulous scrollwork adorning its white stone walls. After Glasscastle, it was likely the second most expensive palace in Leverie.

Charva stepped up to the entry guards. "You, there."

The men stood straight to attention. "Your grace."

She held up the letter, seal out. "Charva Leverie, agent of the Aiv Chahai under Natsha Leverie. I'm conducting an investigation on behalf of the Council. I'm searching for any information regarding a mercenary with two scars crossing his face, or any of his fellows. Do you recall seeing them?"

The men glanced at each other, and Charva wondered if she had gone overboard in her bluff. Ersch shifted beside her, his ckol insignia catching sun.

"Don't recall someone with that description, your grace," one of the guards said. "Is there a specific time you think this scarred fellow was around here?"

"Anytime in the last few weeks. Day or night."

"Then I certainly haven't seen him."

"Nor I, your grace," the other guard said.

Charva nodded. "I will see myself to the barracks to interview more of the guard. Carry on."

She stepped into the palace, and the moment the doors shut behind them she turned to Ersch and handed him the seal. "If I remember right, the barracks are in the south wing. I'll meet you back outside the gate."

"Where are you heading?"

"A curmudgeonly old man's study."

Ersch raised an eyebrow. "If you're not at the gate in an hour, I'm coming looking for you."

Charva gave him her most charming smile then swiveled on her heel and set off. "Naturally."

With Ylnavar out on the Senkani siege, the palace would be less busy than normal, but voices still leaked out into the corridors. Only a few paces in, a maid came out of the rooms. Charva's pulse quickened, but she gave herself a purposeful air and the servant woman only offered a curious look before moving on.

Flame and embers, what am I doing? Trespassing in the Speaker's palace had to carry some severe penalties, and considering her current standing with the Council . . . .

"Another conscription pass is out of the question!"

She jumped through an open doorway an instant before two lower nobles entered the hall. Servants were one thing. She wasn't sure she could bluff her way past these fellows.

"The crenden insists they need more troops for a south crossing."

"There's no one else to spare! The plantations are running on skeleton shifts as it is!"

"Plantation workers aren't the only ones we can call on."

"They're the most indebted to the House. The average folk don't like what happened at Creedport. It was a massacre!"

"You want to deny our crenden his soldiers because the commoners are grumbling?"

The arguing voices faded off, letting Charva slip back out into the empty hallway. She discretely peeked into a few more rooms until finding the one she wanted. Ylnavar's study was similar to her father's but with more shelves and a musty smell. She was tempted to crack open a window even if it risked drawing attention.

There had been plenty of time during the trip here for her to imagine what kind of clues she should look for, but in the end she had no idea. Just keep an eye out for anything that seemed suspicious. Going up to what looked like the ledger shelves, she slipped out a monstrous binding with 4780 inked along the spine and opened it to the current month. As she'd hoped and dreaded, the pages recorded transactions from a few coppers to sales and purchases in the hundreds of golds.

"I guess it's too much to ask that he wrote 'assassination contract' in red?" she muttered sliding her finger down the scribbles and blotches. Getting through the month took some time. Nothing stood out to her as particularly strange.

Next were the correspondences. She swept her eyes around the room searching for where Ylnavar kept his letters. The shelves were all books and bindings, so probably the drawers behind the desk.

Right on the mark. She found mountains of pages all jumbled up inside, many of them sitting atop broken seals and empty envelopes. There wouldn't be enough time to look through every one even if she had all day. She focused on the names. Correspondences with other crendens, trade talks with Whitesail, Ranisa, and the Federation, a few personal notes from his nephews on the plantations—

Footsteps in the hall brought Charva's heart up into her throat. She slid the drawer closed with a too-loud clatter and ducked behind the desk. Shoes squeaked steadily over the stone floor, passing the study and then receding down the other way. "You're Charva Leverie. Keep your nerves."

Six continents, I'm talking to myself.

She took a steadying breath and got back to business.

At least half an hour later, she still had found nothing. She clicked a second drawer closed in frustration, then noticed another built into the desk. One last place she would try. She grabbed the handle. It wouldn't budge. She spotted a small lock installed in the corner.

Well, if he's hiding anything incriminating . . . .

She couldn't go bashing it open. She contemplated giving lock picking a go, but remembered her abysmal attempts at the storage room locks when she was twelve. *Not going to bother putting myself through that torture again.*

But maybe the key was around. Would Ylnavar really carry it with him all the way to Senkani? A circuit of the room bore fruit. The key was under a small candle stand in the far corner. Charva felt quite proud of herself as she turned the lock and exposed a new stack of documents. Her smile dimmed as she found most of them were simply more personal correspondences.

"Guess he's clean after all," she muttered.

She was just about to close the drawer when one letter drew her eye. It was signed in her father's name, the day after the harvest festival attacks. She started to read the first sentence when a door slammed in the hall nearby, followed by the approach of squeaky footsteps. Her hand automatically stuffed the letter in her pocket as she snapped the drawer shut with the other. *Too loud!*

The footsteps stopped in front of the study and the doorknob turned.

Embers!

Charva ducked behind the desk. The door opened and the footsteps transitioned from polished stone to rich carpet. She didn't dare peek the corner to see who it was. The person shuffled across to the ledgers and slid something off the shelf. She heard the man sneeze and mutter something to himself, followed by some scribbling. It felt like an eternity before he finally strode back out, but the ordeal wasn't over.

"Drance, ring the maid. There's a dreadful amount of dust in the crenden's study."

The words spurred Charva out of her cover. The door still hung open, but the clerk was on his way down the hall. She dashed to the candle stand and practically threw the key back in its place. Should she wait for the clerk to leave the hall, or .
. . .

A service bell rang in another room. She didn't waste another instant getting out the door. The clerk was a dozen paces away, his back to her. She moved carefully, keeping her boots from making more than a whisper. She made it three steps before the maid—the same one she'd passed earlier—rounded a corner ahead of her. The woman gave her another curious look.

Charva forced a smile and circled around to the main entrance. She nodded to the guards on the way out and met up with Ersch at the gate. Only then did a chill breeze make her realize her back and sleeves were damp with sweat.

"Find anything?" Ersch asked.

Charva let out a breath she'd been holding. "Far as I could see, it looks like Ylnavar's clean. How about you?"

Ersch shook his head. "No one's seen anything of this scarred mercenary or his friends."

She led them off the palace grounds and didn't look back. "Okay, then. On to Woodwise."

Chapter 56

Arzan walked across the market square cobblestones, his cape trailing behind him as he inspected a new line of forty volunteers.

But not the kind I wish we needed.

The volunteers weren't for the shield wall nor the archers, but the Aiv Chahai. The women standing in front of him were of a broader range than his men, stretching from those in their teens all the way to one with so many wrinkles it would make a willow tree jealous. Also unlike his soldiers, he wasn't quite sure what qualities he should be looking for, or even if it was his place to look for them at all. Once again, he felt the gaping hole of Filgneir's absence. He would have known the ins and outs of the Watcher codes.

Arzan sighed and halted before the center of the line. "I thank you women for answering Captain Vighkon's call. It's become clear with the extended fighting that we need to reinstate the Order of Aiv Chahai. The Council forces have declared they will be enlisting their Watchers, and according to the codes we must do the same. The Order you are joining has had an important role in the dignity of humanity since the First Era, one that—"

Armor clinked as Ellaniel appeared at his side. Her presence created a storm of emotions in him, not least of which was anger. He'd explicitly told her she was to stay at the palace.

"One that ensures that in fighting monsters," he continued, "we do not become monsters ourselves. Be aware that this is a dangerous task. Do not expect to be protected more than any soldier. You will be exposed to arrows, to catapults, and if things get bad, even spears and swords. For your own defense, you will be given armor and weapons, and will be shown how to use them."

One woman in her late thirties wearing merchant clothing raised her hand. "Who's going to be in charge?"

"I—"

"Are we serving under Crendess Ellaniel?" one of the younger ones asked excitedly.

A freckled woman in a white wool dress grabbed the teen by the shoulder. "The Watchers aren't fighters."

"But the crendess fights!"

"Her grace is a military commander," the freckled woman said. "Only a woman can be a Watcher, but not all women *are* Watchers." Arzan noted how careful she was not to look at Ellaniel as she spoke.

A stocky girl stepped out of line. "I want to serve in battle! I'll be the crendess' sword and shield and show these Leverie swine what we're made of!"

Arzan groaned inwardly. Things were going the exact opposite of what he wanted. *Senkani women can be* too *spirited.*

Ellaniel shifted, her hand resting on the pommel of her sword. She opened her mouth, but Arzan took her by the arm and pulled her away from the volunteers, far enough that they wouldn't hear their conversation. "I'm not recruiting soldiers here, Ella, and I gave you instructions you were not to come to the square."

She glared at him. "You're letting the Council win."

"I'm not having this discussion with you right now."

"Oh, so now you aren't speaking to your own wife?"

"Ella—"

"You're losing sight of our goal!"

He pounded his breastplate. "I'm defending Senkani's honor!"

She threw out her hand and scoffed. "By agreeing to Ylnavar's demands right after our first victory? By tying our hands behind our backs with these codes that they themselves spat on until they were of benefit to them?"

"It's not Ylnavar's fault I'm reinstating the Watchers," he said.

"Oh, well it certainly seems like—"

"It's yours."

She crossed her arms and he could see her jaw muscles knotting.

"You were out of control in that battle. What you did was cold-blooded murder. We are seeking justice, Ella, not vengeance."

"How was that not justice?" she demanded, her voice like a chill breeze that brought threat of a storm. "Like for like. Those who killed our captured will die when in our hands."

"Those found guilty in a proper trial," he said.

She struck her palms against him, shoving him back. "They're all guilty! Every one of them that takes up the sword! Every one that defiles my father's memory by standing against me!"

Arzan grabbed her firmly by the wrists. It hurt him to see this. It hurt him to see the hatred burning in her golden eyes. Not righteous anger. Hatred. He let go of her arms and held her instead in an embrace.

"The man who murdered your father deserves to die. For striking our city, Thrake, Woodwise, and the Council need to be held to account. I will see this done," he raised his hand to her cheek and turned her face to look in her eyes, "but not on account of my personal grudge. I do this because it is my duty. I am crenden of Senkani, and it is my responsibility to carry out just retribution according to what the crime deserves. Nothing less and nothing more."

He saw his words had an effect on her. There was a struggle in her, a pinch of her lips and tightening of her eyes. She spent a moment before meeting his gaze. "You are my crenden and my husband. I will do my best to submit to your judgment."

He pressed his mouth into a thin line. That wasn't how he wanted her to take this, but it would do. He held her tight, even if her armor put a limit on how much she'd feel it. "I love you, Ella. This is because I want to keep you whole."

She hesitated before putting her arm around him. "Your sense of honor is why I love you."

Vighkon coughed after allowing them a moment. "The volunteers are still here, my liege."

Arzan nodded. "All right, let's finish this business."

The women volunteers had gotten to chattering with each other in Arzan and Ellaniel's absence, but quieted the moment they approached.

Ellaniel took a breath. "We are accepting Watchers only. It is appreciated that some of you wish to fight, but unless the walls themselves are breached, that remains the men's role."

The stout girl who'd been eager to join Ellaniel's guard jumped forward desperately. "Your grace! That's not—"

"War is not a game!" Arzan said. *Even if I've been guilty of calling it that in the past.* "It is not waged for fun nor for glory! We fight because it's necessary, and thus far it's not necessary that we join a girl into the ranks of our soldiers. You should hope also that we never get to that point."

The girl glowered at the ground and turned away. "It's not fair the crendess gets to fight."

"You are dismissed!" He didn't care anymore whether he had that authority or not as he looked over the rest of the women. "Anyone else who is in this for the sword, leave."

After a bit of shifting, some did, including the girl. Of those who remained, Arzan pointed to the woman in the white wool dress. "For now, you are appointed head of the Order. You shall have the responsibility of deciding where to place your Aiv Chahai and will report to me any transgressions by our troops. Speak to Captain Vighkon about obtaining your equipment and receiving basic combat training."

The woman nodded. "Yes, my liege!"

Arzan gave the women one more look and turned to leave. Ellaniel followed with him, her armor clinking. "Thank you for turning down the ones who wanted to fight for you," he said.

"Well, I want ckols, not milk maids," she answered. "We're waging war to kill the enemy, and I'm not handicapping myself any more than the codes require."

Arzan's cheek twitched. So the blood lust was still there. He was going to have to stay vigilant with her. With her and with himself. Despite his speech, he'd had moments during the battle where anger had taken control.

Do not become the monster you fight.

That danger motivated him, as much as their goal of justice, to find Senkani victory.

Chapter 57

"Picturesque," Ersch commented as he and Charva trotted their horses past the Woodwise gates.

"I suppose," Charva said.

Woodwise always struck her as a strange place. The people who built it couldn't decide whether it was a city or a plantation, and instead created some bizarre halfway point between both. The buildings, mostly wood, but with a few stone walls thrown in the mix, never touched. The avenues were so uncomfortably wide that even with the typical urban bustle they felt desolate. And of course, there were the rows and rows of trees that shaded everything and left a constant layer of leaves over the cobbles.

"I wish the city founders had been more sensible. It takes forever to get anywhere."

Ersch shrugged. "I like it."

Charva shook her head. "To each his own, I suppose."

"How are we planning on getting in the palace this time?"

Not with the Council seal, unfortunately. They had returned it and the letter it was attached to as discretely as possible to Natsha's shop before leaving Highcity.

"We'll think of something. But that's not our first stop."

She remembered Ellaniel telling her Odavan's family estate was in the northeast part of the city. They found it after asking directions only once. The building blended into its surroundings, being of the same wood panel style of its neighbors and no larger than the merchant homes along the rest of the avenue. They took their horses around to the stable at the side and handed the mounts off to a young servant.

"You never lived in one of the lesser estates, did you?" Ersch said as they crossed the short gravel path to the front step.

"Mhm." That was one side effect of having both a father and a grandfather who were crendens. Charva had faint memories of the time before Thrake was appointed, but even then she'd lived in the palace with her grandparents.

Ersch did the honors of rapping the knocker. Within a short span, a maid unlocked the door and eyed them questioningly. "We've no visitors on appointment today."

"Council business having to do with the war," Charva said. "Is Demrow in?"

"I'm afraid that—"

"Bitella, for the last time, tell Jirgvon it's not my worry! I pay the overseers to deal with his problems and they're the ones to take care of it!"

The maid rolled her eyes, caught herself, and motioned for them to wait as she went back in. It wasn't long before the same voice shouted, "Well, why's the Council bothering me? Odavan's crenden, have him fuss over politics!"

"It's the Council, Demrow!" a woman shouted back. "Quit grumbling for one moment and see them in!"

"I'm doing that, you shrew! Did I say I'm not letting them in?"

The maid returned with a neutral mask of a face. "The master will see you. Please follow me, your grace."

Charva returned Ersch's arched brow expression with her own as they entered the small mansion. Their boots clomped loudly across the bare wood floor until they came to a cozy room with several plush armchairs around a fine table. At least, she thought it was a fine table. Details were hard to see under a thick layer of jumbled paper. Hunched over it all, his thick, meaty hand and silver pen poised over a fresh sheet, was Demrow Leverie himself. The man was just as Charva remembered him from House gatherings. He was thick all around, being as good a human impersonation of a barrel as could well be possible. It was hard for her to reconcile his flattish face with the fact that he was Odavan's father. After all, Odavan was, well, a lot more pleasant to look at.

"Don't just stand there wasting my time," Demrow said

with a growl. "What does the Council want?"

Charva drew in a breath to speak, but the man broke her off with a slap against the table. "Ah, I recognize you! You're the squirt that slipped an oiled eel down my trousers that time in Thartay!"

She felt her cheeks grow suddenly hot. She cleared her throat. "That was many years ago."

"So what? I don't buy that horse urine about people changing with time. A man or woman's character's the same whether child or shriveled prune, or anything in between."

"Demrow, if you don't stop insulting everyone like that, I'm really going to throw all these pages in the fire."

Charva startled at the tall woman in a dolphin embroidered dress who stepped into the room behind her.

"What was I just saying, Vilra? You can't change the way a dog acts."

Charva frowned. "Actually, it's normal to train—"

"And I wasn't insulting the girl, just stating facts."

Vilra sighed. "Please excuse my husband, dear. He's merely upset that he's stuck on a part of his book. Take a seat and I'll have the tea and pastries brought about."

"There's no room for that on the table," Demrow said. "Let's just hear what this is about and have done with it."

Charva finally took one of the chairs and sank into its cushions while Ersch posted himself casually by the door. "I am here in my capacity as an Aiv Chahai. I'm conducting an investigation regarding a group of mercenaries that may have been here some weeks ago."

"Mercenaries? Why come to me about that?"

"I was thinking your son might have hired them as guards." An idea occurred to her. "The Council has been looking for them in hopes of attaining some experienced sword arms for the war."

Demrow rifled through a stack of pages. "Then go on looking. We've never had use for the professional soldier sort. What need do we have for more than a smidge of muscle and a stick here in Woodwise? Hashan was out of his mind when he listened to that fool Redleaf and started raising an army. An army! What would we even use it for? That's the idiocy of martial forces, trying to control things through brute strength.

Security and wealth come from land and labor and steady cart schedules."

Charva had trouble following his fast ramblings. "So, neither you nor Odavan hired any sellswords this past year?"

"You deaf? That's what I'm saying. Do you have any other questions or can I get some peace and quiet?"

Vilra found that moment to step back into the room, the maid in tow with refreshments. "The noisiest thing in this house is you, Demrow. Her grace is staying until we've been passable hosts."

Truthfully, Charva would have preferred to be on her way now, but she'd feel bad ruining Vilra's efforts.

Demrow grumbled to himself as his wife cleared a spot on the table for the tray of tea and sweetbread. When the maid started filling the cups, he positively glared daggers. "I'd better not find a single spilled drop!"

Vilra sat beside her husband. "Maybe one of these days you'll actually keep the table in order."

Charva accepted her tea, conscious that her sword was starting to get quite uncomfortable pressed against her side. Cushions were nice, but she didn't like seats this enclosed. "What is it you're writing?"

She expected her interest would lighten his mood, and she was rewarded when his scowl weakened ever so slightly. "Contemporary history! I'll make sure the world remembers Leverie as more than just 'that place that sells silks'."

"Stop using such lofty words," Vilra said. "It's an autobiography."

Charva fought a sudden urge to throw her tea across the pages. She drew in a breath, hoping the aroma would instill her with calm.

"That's what histories are," Demrow said. "A man needs to be proud of his own story. Everyone else is all obsessed with carts and ships and how much of what's inside of them. Yes, it's all good for the country. I own plantations just like everyone else in the House. But when they're all dead and dust, the name people know will be Demrow Leverie."

"That doesn't seem the most fair," Charva said. She took a small sip, trying not to burn her tongue.

"What's not fair about it? I'm the one putting in an effort.

Besides, I'm the perfect representative of the House. When people look back and ask who the Leverie were, let the example be a true full blood who loves his lineage. I ask you, do you think it would be fair if our House were remembered for the likes of Hashan?"

Vilra tsked. "Don't speak ill of the dead."

"I'll speak ill of anyone I like, and Hashan deserves it. Fraternizing with the Redleafs, marrying his daughter off to them. Look where mixed blood got us!"

Charva inhaled some more tea aroma. "I don't think that's the problem."

"You think that bloodlust is from the Leverie side? The Redleafs were always too fond of sharpened steel, and you only need to look in that Ellaniel's eyes to see her strong Originate heritage. All these stories from the front prove how much of her people's savageness is in her."

Before she knew it, she was on her feet. She clicked the teacup down on the tray, liquid sloshing over the lip. She would love to call him the greasy son of a weasel that he was, but she managed to catch herself and force a polite smile. "I'm afraid I must be leaving after all. Thank you for the tea, Vilra."

Vilra gave her husband an angry look and nodded to Charva in resignation. "At least take some of the sweets for the road?"

Waiting for a cloth or paper would mean more time in Demrow's proximity, and she didn't trust herself against that kind of provocation. She wondered whether it would be her tongue or her fist that she first lost control of.

"I think the sooner I continue with my mission the better."

She and Ersch left the room so fast only the maid had time to follow. The woman rushed ahead and opened the door for them. As Charva stepped over the threshold, the maid leaned in close. "Was that true about the eel?"

Charva sighed. "He was the same loudmouthed buffoon back then. Alas, I'm no longer a child or I'd stick another down his trousers."

The maid gave her an approving smile. "If you aren't really in a hurry, I'll give you a whole basket of pastries."

"It's true I don't have much time to waste. However . . . ."

She weighed the wisdom of revealing too much about her intentions, but decided it was safe enough. "I'm heading to the palace, and I'd prefer to have a look about without my presence being too . . . conspicuous."

"Oh, I wouldn't worry about that, your grace. Things are busy enough down there these days that, well, you'll see when you get there."

Charva and Ersch exchanged a look on their way back to the stable.

"What do you think she meant by that?" Ersch asked.

She shrugged. The stable boy saw them coming and had their horses for them in good order.

"I thought you were about to punch our esteemed host at the end there. How would *that* scene have been portrayed in that book of his?"

The thought of Demrow's account of her possibly being the only one future generations would hear stopped her dead with one foot in the stirrup. "Flame and embers, I'm starting a journal when this is over."

When they reached the palace grounds, they found out immediately what the maid had been talking about.

"I don't think the fields outside Creedport looked this bad," Ersch said.

Laborers were at work everywhere around building. Ellaniel had described to her the beauty of her father's gardens, but Charva would never see it. Whatever plants were left lay dead on their sides in forlorn heaps, their roots clawing air rather than soil. Barrows filled with dirt rolled off the premises. Carts of stone slabs rolled in. Already half the ground was paved with polished granite. Upon the flattened, sterile surfaces, sculptors were at work chipping away at life-sized representations of men and women in aristocratic garb.

"Not what I was expecting to see." Charva led the way through the open gate, her presence drawing no attention from the well-dressed artisans. One of the stoneworkers she passed had a portrait of Odavan set up on an easel and referenced it with every hammer of his chisel.

"Didn't realize his narcissism was quite on that level."

The doors of the palace were just as easy to breach as the gate. No guards were in sight as more laborers roamed the halls with planks of wood and buckets of tools. Sawing strokes assailed her ears from every direction, and the ensuing sand dust set her sneezing. Room after room had been gutted of furniture and was practically in the process of being rebuilt from the ground up. Not only was it effortless getting in here, it was also pointless. It would have been anyway. This used to be the home of the victim, not the planning place of the perpetrator.

"Shall we leave?" Ersch asked.

Even if there was no reason not to, Charva felt she should at least make a complete round while they were here. They ascended to the second floor, passing more rooms under complete renovation. In the midst of it all, there was one set apart from the others. It was empty of furnishings and decoration, but the floor and walls were still intact. Significantly, bouquets of flowers lay piled in the center.

Charva entered. "This must be the place where it happened."

"All the evidence is gone," Ersch said.

"Truly." She strode the length of the outer wall, noting the ease with which someone could enter the windows. As she contemplated the murder, she thought of how close Ellaniel had been with her father. So much different from Charva's relationship with Thrake. She felt an inappropriate spike of jealousy that she pushed down. Her own father was still alive. What's more, he was willing to make amends. Ellaniel deserved sympathy, not envy.

She noticed Ersch inspecting the flowers. "Something interesting over there?"

He pointed down and Charva joined him to find a note tucked in amongst the petals.

"Dear Uncle, I thank you. You did not deserve this end."

She didn't know how much she should read into the words. He thanked him for what? For backing Odavan as heir? For dying early? How sincere was the second sentence?

Whatever the case, they weren't getting answers here.

"Well, this was a waste of time," she said.

"Where to next?"

Very good question. For now, she settled on returning to their horses.

Chapter 58

Maltan walked through Breakpeak's lower marketplace, trying not to get jostled too badly by the rivers of people all around. Trade was booming with the opening flood of imperial goods in the past few days. He had little idea what might have been sold here before the war, but now everywhere he looked there was more variety than he'd ever seen. In the span of several strides, he passed jewelry, fine tools, perfumes, scented candles, decorative trinkets, and numerous things he couldn't identify. People thronged to these foreign goods, their curiosity overcoming whatever fears of the empire still lingered. They turned out in even greater droves when they saw the amazingly cheap prices.

He looked upon the goods with mixed feelings. It was true that such prosperity was a wonder. On the other hand, he couldn't help but see the broader view. The empire created all this abundance through blood and suffering.

The soldier who'd been posted as his guard and escort leaned over a small box of stone dice. "I've been wanting to replace that set I've lost! Hey, stop here, tinkerer."

Maltan obliged, eyeing the box absently.

"You easterners are such boring gamblers," the soldier went on as he inspected some of the pieces and tested their weight. Maltan tried to remember the man's name, then wondered if he'd even heard it. "The only dice I can find out here are six-sided."

"I'm not a gambler," Maltan said. "How many sides do

imperial ones have?"

The soldier held up a die carved out of some blue-green stone. "Twelve. Least that's what I go for. Some fellows like the twenty faces."

Maltan couldn't help factoring what numbered dice would allow for a balanced form. "I never really thought about it, but you could go fairly high if you use triangular faces."

"Saw one with sixty once. Now *that* was a monster. Pity the poor craftsman who had to make the thing. Rolled well, though." The soldier paid for his new collection and slipped the pieces in his pocket.

Chainmail clinked on plate as a hand clamped down on the guard's shoulder. "And what do we have here?"

A sense of déjà vu washed over Maltan as he saw the Aiv Chahai at the soldier's back. "My escort is not causing me problems this time, I assure you." As much as he disliked the Vron as a nation, he didn't feel like getting this soldier in trouble that wasn't due.

The Watcher flicked her eyes across Maltan's face in bewilderment.

"Oh, he's my charge," the soldier said. "The general has me entertaining him."

Recognition lit her sharp features. "Ah, he's that tinkerer! Well, don't lose him."

The man leaned in and gave her a quick kiss. "My watch ends after I return him to the palace, which shouldn't be much longer. I'll see you by the mural at the market entrance."

She grabbed him by the shoulder as he started to turn away. "Don't think you're escaping that easily."

Maltan saw the soldier's sheepish smile. "It's just for the occasional game with the unit."

"You say that now, but I know it'll only be a week before I'm the one paying for all our food. Again."

"That only happened once. Wait . . . are you the one who took my old dice?"

"Why do you think I became a Watcher? It was to keep you out of trouble." She wagged her finger. "You can wager ten silvers a month. No more. I'll see you after you return the tinkerer." With a smile, the woman weaved her way back into the crowd.

"A lovely wife you have," Maltan said.

The soldier nodded and grinned. "Any woman who joins the Watchers for you is worth her weight in gold."

"Well, I wouldn't want to be the cause of leaving her waiting." Maltan led the way through the rest of the stalls until they came to the main avenue.

"You really didn't want to buy anything?" the soldier said. "The general's given you a decent allowance, after all."

An allowance of stolen coin, he thought. "Seeing is enough." They started up the incline. The market being so near the gate, the way to the palace posed a daunting climb. He tried to put Nevygar's request out of his mind, but it wasn't easy. With every step, and then every bead of sweat, the mechanics of a practical lifting mechanism knocked on his thoughts.

At least his escort's banter helped serve as a distraction. "She's right, obviously. Gambling's stupid. Why throw my money on the table when there's less than half odds I'll even make as much back? But then, life itself's a gamble, isn't it? Whether you're a success or failure at life, there's as much chance involved as effort. Whether you live or die on the battlefield, you can't ever be totally sure you'll come out on top. Who knows where the arrow will fall, or what day you'll be in the first rank against a good shield wall? When I get through a bad day with naught a scratch on me, it just feels like a day I should try my luck with the stones, you know?"

The words left Maltan wondering about his own luck in life. How much chance had been involved in his getting noticed and patronized by the old crenden and crendess of Creedport? His being born in Leverie was certainly something completely out of his control. How much also was he really to blame for the death of that child? The guilt he harbored, that he'd heaped upon himself for years, resisted the notion of his innocence. If he hadn't created that machine, the boy would have never been caught in it. Yet Nevygar's words chipped at his reasoning. No matter what path one took in life, no matter how hard one tried to work for the good of all, there would always be accidents and tragedies.

Along the climb, they came upon a woman even older than he, struggling with heavy breaths and a sack of grain hung over her shoulder. Maltan halted. "Do you need some help?"

"If you'd be so kind," the woman gasped. Whether from exhaustion or plain apathy, she didn't react at all to the presence of a Vron soldier beside him. Maltan reached for the sack, but his escort beat him to it.

"Don't burden yourself, tinkerer, I have it."

They gave her a few moment's rest until she no longer struggled for air. "Thank you so very much," she said once she was ready to continue the ascent. "My son used to help me with such things until he married and set up a farm in the southern valley. I encouraged him to go, but that was when my legs were still strong."

"Sorry to hear about that, auntie," the soldier said. "Don't be afraid to ask anyone in uniform for help if you need it. We're here to serve the subjects of the empire, after all."

The old woman talked more of her family as they made their way to her home. Maltan wondered at how attentively the soldier listened, even speaking every once in a while of his own parents he had left behind. Most interesting was that the man wasn't an ethnic Vron. He hailed from Trevenar Province, formerly of the Bravan Aristocracy.

"Bravan was a terrible place back in the time of my grandparents. The crendens were as corrupt as they come, stealing from people without a care. When the empire came in, they completely wiped the Houses and installed their own governors. Suddenly everyone was guaranteed the same rights under imperial law. My family rose from berry pickers to respectable merchants because the Vron gave them a fair go." The soldier grinned. "Lucky roll for us. Only fair to give other people a turn though, right?"

They reached the old woman's door. It was a lived-in little home, nestled amongst a row of similar houses and distinguished only by a planter of lavender on the porch. The soldier carried the sack to her kitchen and bid her good day.

"Not much further to the palace," the soldier said. "Just up through the noble quarter and we're there."

"So you believe conquest is a good way of making the world better," Maltan said.

The soldier looked at him as if he'd just declared he had

the ability to walk to the moon. "How else is everyone supposed to have their rights guaranteed by the empire?"

"There must be options that do not involve the spilling of blood."

The soldier knocked his helmet. "Ha! Just try getting a corrupt, stuck-up noble to treat commoners fair! There's aristocrats who'd die before they gave a lowborn man a smidgen of respect."

Maltan thought of Thrake and his impossible hardheadedness. He could agree there. "It isn't just the nobility the empire hurts. What of all the common men on the battlefield? They would be people like you, would they not? They aren't motivated by the need to keep others down, but to protect their countries and their families."

"Sometimes progress hurts," the soldier said. "That's just the way the world is. Yeah, some folks died back home in Bravan, but in the end, we were better off for it. Things ain't perfect, tinkerer. Lot of times, we just have to do the best we can with the numbers the dice give us."

Maltan stroked his beard, reflecting heavily on the words the rest of the way up to the palace.

Chapter 59

Arzan abandoned his horse and ducked low as he followed the scout through the screen of trees. He held his scabbard tight and avoided shifting his armor as much as possible. The ckols at his flanks moved with stealth, chainmail held tight. Aiding them further was the thick early morning fog that enveloped them as they left the trees and entered the cultivated field beyond. Arzan couldn't see a thing beyond ten paces, and could barely even hear the flow of the river that he knew was nearby.

A waist high wall of stone materialized ahead. Huddled in front of it were dozens of men with knives, spades, and pitchforks. A handful had hunting bows. Arzan settled in amongst them without a word.

A younger fellow did a double take at his arrival and opened his mouth in awe, but Arzan put a finger to his lips. "*No sound*," he mouthed. Vighkon slipped in beside them. He followed the order for silence as strictly as anyone, but the sense of disagreement on his face was clear as day. Arzan knew a crenden shouldn't be here. It was stupid tactically and strategically. Fortunately, he had no one above him who could actually order him to stay in the city.

After what happened during the previous battle, there was no one he could trust to do things properly.

In the silence, several noises drifted in undisturbed from past the wall. Water lapping against wood. Low voices. Creaking timbers and shuffling feet.

Boards slushing into dirt.

Arzan slipped his sword free and poised to leap over the wall. Around him, ckols and farmers gripped their weapons and awaited his lead.

Splashes. Boots squishing in mud. More scraping of wood. He tried to get a sense of how many rafts had landed. Six? Eight?

He drew in a breath and vaulted over the stones. Confident the men were right behind him, he raced towards the water's edge. Low crops and berry bushes materialized out of the fog. A shed wafted into view. With another several quick strides, the first of the Leverie soldiers solidified before him.

The nearest soldier uttered a startled cry and stumbled backwards, his foot catching on the edge of the beached raft he'd stepped from. Arzan ignored him, instead thrusting his longsword into the unguarded neck of the next man in line. He didn't give the man time to register his own death before ripping the blade free and slashing at a second target. After that it was all chaos. His ckols and the farmhands joined the fray, crashing into the beachhead landing in a flurry of iron and ringing steel.

"We're ambushed! Retreat! Retreat!"

Arrows lashed out at the few who tried to get back on the rafts. The points buried themselves in their gambeson coats, doing no damage but spurring them faster in their escape. On the river, more rafts loaded with enemy soldiers floated into sight.

Arzan didn't have time to check up and down the beach. He parried a sword strike at his head, his blade singing from the impact. His counterattack missed the Leverie's face and skated across his helmet. Cursing, he blocked and deflected a few frustratingly nimble attacks. Another opening appeared, but the man dodged to the side of Arzan's thrust. Fed up, Arzan kicked him back, granting himself a chance to flip his sword and grab it by the blade. The Leverie recovered and swung. This time, Arzan swatted the slash aside with his armguard and came in with a murderstroke, slamming the crossguard square in the side of his enemy's helmet. The man grunted and staggered, his eyes losing focus. Arzan stepped in and pulled the armor off the fellow's head. He flipped his sword back around to wield it by the hilt. The poor bloke was still struggling to recover from his daze as Arzan swept his head from his shoulders with a two-handed blow.

Amidst Arzan's momentary reprieve, a farmer shoved a Leverie soldier to the shallows nearby. The man rammed his pitchfork hard into the soldier's chest, audibly cracking ribs even if the chainmail and padding kept the iron from breaking flesh. A few more blows put him out of the fight for good.

A crossbow bolt skated off Arzan's shoulder plate. He looked at the approaching rafts, getting a good estimate of the scores of Leverie rowing through the fog before Vighkon blocked his view with his shield.

"I've given up trying to keep you off the front line, but don't just stand there with bolts raining down on you!" the captain said. Arzan noted his ckol's right sleeve was slashed in several places, revealing the mail beneath.

"How long until our reinforcements?"

"If you'd have bothered to wait just a little longer, the messenger would have arrived and told us."

"We couldn't afford to give them a beachhead."

A farmer screamed and fell as a sword cut through his thin tunic. Arzan raised his guard and rejoined the fray with Vighkon at his side. Together, they finished off a set of Leverie hounding on an isolated pair of Senkani. They had no time to celebrate their victory as another raft reached the shore and ten men in chain and plate jumped into the fight.

Arzan really wished his ckols had time to form a wall. The fresh enemy troops were on them in an instant. He fought back-to-back with Vighkon, blades coming in from every angle, scraping his armor in search of the gaps. Desperate flurries of steel rent the air. Arzan's blade arced blood as he blocked and parried. Red droplets sprayed and splattered his face with each impact against his sword. At last, some of his ckols forced their way in to take off the pressure, shouting the name of Senkani.

They pressed the attack. Arzan took the openings he could. A slash at an exposed wrist here. A leg thrust there. Few of the Leverie bore shields, and the Senkani made sure they paid dearly for it. The enemy fell back before them, and Arzan and his men chased after. They didn't even notice the next raft until another group charged and split the Senkani forces back into a melee. Vighkon made a valiant effort to keep himself between Arzan and the momentum of the enemy, wooden thuds sounding with every blow he took with his shield. A Leverie ckol in Blueturf colors bashed his own shield into Vighkon's, knocking him off balance and letting a second man duck in and grapple him from the side. When Arzan moved to help, another Blueturf ckol with a shield stepped in the way.

Arzan kicked, desperate to aid the captain. His opponent's shield held firm, his reward instead coming in the form of a flanged mace aimed at his head. He just barely caught the shaft with his sword, the force of the impact rendering his arms numb. The Leverie ckol pressed the advantage, shoving the shield in Arzan's face.

"The Redleaf is here! Let's take him down!"

Where are those reinforcements! Arzan realized too late the cost of his earlier aggression. He should have backed off and regrouped before this wave arrived. He danced backward, dodging a mace swing and buying himself some distance.

Fortunately, everyone was either busy or hadn't heard the ckol's shout. The Blueturf man looked about, irritation plain on his face. He twirled his mace and readied to continue the fight. "Looks like I have you to myself, crenden."

Arzan knew he had little hope of getting out of this unscathed. The ckol was just as well armored as he was, not counting the shield. His sword would be next to useless. On the flip side, the mace posed a very serious threat.

The ckol moved in, shield up, mace hidden behind. Arzan kept his guard high, knowing a blow to the head would be the end of him. The mace came down. He received the shaft with his sword and felt the ckol try to hook his weapon. Before his opponent could yank the blade from his hands, Arzan stepped forward in the direction of the pull. He disengaged the blade and grabbed the shield's edge as he kicked at the ckol's shins. The ckol growled, but didn't stumble. The mace came around for a glancing blow off Arzan's shoulder plate. Arzan put his weight into the shield, trying to push it lower and also use it for his own protection against the mace. He struck blindly around the edge with the pommel of his sword, hoping to catch the ckol's elbow, but found nothing.

The mace connected hard with his back. His vision blurred with the pain. He was certain a rib had cracked even through his cuirass. The next he knew, he was fending off a follow-up strike. He didn't remember letting go of the shield. He blocked another blow, pain jolting through his back from the force. The mace crashed into his arm without him seeing it coming. He twisted away in a pathetic dodge that nonetheless caused the next strike to glance of his breastplate. His foot caught in an irrigation ditch and he fell just out of reach of a swing at his head. His breath went out of him in an agonized whoosh as he hit the ground on his back. Consciousness reeling, he struggled to focus on the enemy ckol standing over him. The man dropped his knee on Arzan's chest, pinning him down for good and shoving his back further into the ground. Pinpricks of light danced across his vision as he gasped for air.

"Guess the war's over now," the ckol said.

An arrow snapped against the ckol's helmet just shy of his face. The man flinched to the side, taking the pressure off his chest. Arzan filled his lungs, ignoring the burning pain. He pushed himself up and punched. His steel gauntlet connected with the man's jaw and he felt bone break. The ckol reeled back, mouth spewing blood. Arzan scrambled forward to attack again. His enemy issued a wild swing with the mace that landed on the side of Arzan's leg, making him stagger, but not stop. Arzan grabbed him by the throat and shoved him to the ground, his fingers clawing into his windpipe. The ckol released his shield to fend him off with his bare hand. Arzan's hold slipped, but he went with it, dropping his elbow into the ckol's neck. The ckol's eyes bulged. Blood spat out of his broken mouth into Arzan's face. Arzan rolled away, letting the fellow grasp at his crushed throat for the last moments of his life.

Breathing hard and fighting against pain, he broadened his attention and saw that the battle was winding down. Bodies, too many in Senkani red, lay in the mud. As consolation, thrice as many dead wore the myriad of Council colors. Two lone rafts rowed frantically back towards the eastern shore, harried by a pair of hunters with bows.

Vighkon threw his battered shield to the ground and limped hurriedly to Arzan's side. "The crenden's hurt!" The captain said nothing else, but his eyes when he dropped down and took hold of his shoulder communicated plenty. Vighkon blamed himself for letting the enemy separate them.

"I'm pretty sure I'll survive," Arzan said. He opted not to try proving it by moving. His whole left side felt, well, like someone had been wailing on him with a mace. He didn't even want to look to see how badly dented his armor was.

Shouts announced the arrival of the Senkani infantry. Arzan slipped off his helmet with his right hand and craned his neck to see ranks of soldiers materialize out of the fog.

The company commander came with the surgeon, finding Arzan just as he had managed to sit himself upright on an overturned barrel. "I'm sorry we couldn't arrive in time to help. We discovered a second landing force while making quick march. Caught us both by surprise, but we formed a wall and pushed them back across the water. Won't be making another attempt with what they got."

Arzan nodded, then winced as the surgeon started unbuckling his armor. "How many did we lose?"

"Haven't counted," Vighkon said, "but it looks like about half of our ckols seriously injured or killed. I think only a few of the farmers made it out. The second and third waves hit us hard."

"Two deaths and five major injuries in the infantry," the company commander said.

"What were the numbers that tried to cross?" Arzan asked.

"Hard to say with all the fog. At least a hundred."

"In all the gray, perhaps they'll fear we have more men waiting here than they've seen. If—ah!"

The surgeon lifted the chain and padding and probed at Arzan's back. "Got you good here, my liege."

"I could have told you that if you'd asked." He cringed at the glare the surgeon gave him. "Sorry. How bad is it?"

"You're not coughing up blood, so there's that. The ribs are fractured at the very least, but it could have been far worse. Where else were you hit?"

Arzan pointed to his arm and leg before turning his attention back to the commander. "Double our scouts along the shore. We should also have a unit on patrol—perhaps one to two hundred strong."

"It will be done."

Arzan nodded before gritting his teeth at his physical hurt and the sight of a limp Senkani body being carried away from the battlefield. *Bloody shyles, I hate this war.*

Chapter 60

"But it's a question of ethics," Retyar said. "That kind of approach to education brings up all kinds of moral problems."

Waylar shrugged as he leaned in on his elbows, his pen perched on his upper lip. Random jumbles of notes sat spread upon the library table between them, all in Waylar's near unintelligible script. "It's already standard practice here in the University. You remember what they drilled into us with the first-year classes? 'The greatest thing you will take away from your higher education is not memorized facts, but the scholar's mindset'. The foundational principle behind this whole place is that people need to be shown the correct way to think."

"You mean shown how to properly conduct research and verify information."

"That—" Waylar took his pen in hand and used it to point at Retyar— "exactly illustrates my point. They have you thinking that there's one way to evaluate knowledge. You can't even conceive that it is only one of several, or even many valid methods of analyzing the world."

"I think there's a very good case to be made that the one they teach is the right one," Retyar said. "It's the logical system that lets us develop technology. You think any of this stuff that Laski's studying would even exist without the principle of logical inquiry?"

Laski shifted her glasses at the table's far end, but didn't look up from her textbook on wave mechanics. "Don't drag me into your philosophical craziness."

"Technology has always existed," Waylar said. "Humans will always adapt their environment to suit them. Do you think every civilization through history adhered to the logical system? Yet there's no people who haven't created things."

Retyar shook his head. "Logic is innate to human nature. Even if the concept isn't formalized in a society's philosophy, it will still manifest through people's actions."

"And then what's the point of instilling the principle of logical inquiry in students through education?"

"Well, even if everyone has some sense of logic, it takes training for it to be fully refined."

"But is that what's really happening?" Waylar asked. "Would you say that all of your classes have had intuitive logic? Don't tell me you agree with how Professor Drayus shot down your paper on technological nonobsolescence."

That was putting the iron poker in the wound. "Of course not, but he's just one person in the entirety of the modern educational establishment."

"He's symptomatic of modern education. University is meant to maintain the mental box that some pompous aristocrats set up centuries ago."

"And so you want to tear down the University system," Retyar said. "On a feeling that there should be other ways to think. What do you imagine could happen if you're wrong?"

"I'm not."

"Well, that's not an arrogant way of putting it."

A small pile of books landed on the corner of the table by Waylar's arm. "Found them all, finally!" Thesha stood straight, dusting her hands on her skirt.

Retyar craned his neck to look back at the shelves Thesha had disappeared into as soon as they all arrived at the library. "What took so long? That was, what, forty-five minutes?"

"Some idiot put two of them in the Volcana section instead of Fractora." She placed her hands on her hips and beamed with achievement as Waylar picked up one of the books and scanned the table of contents.

"You think you can prove your theory about the Sandspring empress?" Retyar asked.

"I'm sure of it," Thesha said. "I just need strong evidence

that Parshvahaven was being accurate with his Oasis Tribes oral transcriptions."

"That might be a bit of a trick," Waylar said. "Parsh doesn't have the best reputation thanks to his history on the War of the Seven Lillies."

"Why? What did he write there?" Retyar scratched his chin, trying to remember.

Thesha sighed. "He wrote the Four Petals had an army five hundred thousand strong."

"The problem is, none of our illustrious professors believes the Four Petals could have had a population base to support something like that," Waylar said. He ducked away from Thesha's glare. "Hey, don't get angry at me. I'm on your side. It'd be awesome if an army like that really existed."

"Anyway, Parshvahaven's rep isn't the biggest obstacle," Thesha said. "What really makes this paper hard is that everyone just *knows* that the Oasis Tribes are the bad guys in the story and that the Tiger Daughter is the tragic victim. If what Parshvahaven recorded is true, then it's actually the empress who's the villain."

"And publishers of children's books everywhere will drown in each other's tears," Laski muttered. "I wonder how long it will be before people start figuring out us Ytanians aren't the bad guys."

"You can't be scared of rewriting history if you know the textbooks are wrong," Thesha continued, ignoring her. "The Tiger Empress doesn't deserve all the romanticizing she gets."

"I thought you liked things traditional," Retyar said. "When did you start wanting to knock down heroes?"

Thesha shrugged. "I need something to pass for a thesis." She looked at her watch and snatched the book from Waylar's hands. "Should get going."

"Your folks are still in town?" Retyar tried to hide his disappointment.

"See you guys." She disappeared down the steps without a backwards glance.

"Been doing that a lot lately," Laski noted.

"Well, it's not every month her family comes to visit," Retyar said.

Waylar clapped his hands. "So, anyway, I can prove it to you that our modern logical system isn't completely sound."

Retyar grimaced. "We're not done with this topic?"

"Computers. They're supposed to be the ultimate logical system. Program them with a formula, give them data, and they'll give you a perfect answer according to the rules we set. Give them the same inputs and they'll give the same outputs every time."

"Yes, obviously."

"Except they don't."

Retyar only stared at him, brow raised.

"They *don't*," Waylar repeated emphatically. "Have a computer run the same calculation enough times and eventually you'll get an anomaly. How many times have you had a program crash on you when you were doing the same thing you did five minutes ago?"

"You . . . ." Retyar was momentarily at a loss for words. "Seriously? There's a million mundane explanations for that. Conflicting codes from parallel processing, memory overload, electrons jumping a flawed logic gate."

"That's how we reason it out, but can you actually ever prove those causes? The most experienced computer tech will always have those cases where he just scratches his head and shrugs after going through every possible issue. He has to give up, because the computer's right and we're wrong."

Retyar reached across the table and put a hand on his friend's shoulder. "Waylar, stick with stocks and economic history."

Waylar raised his arms. "Laski, you get what I'm saying, don't you?"

"I said leave me out of your craziness."

"One of these days, the world will see a paradigm shift and history will remember you in the same light as people who revered the absolute power of kings." A buzzing in his pocket mercifully stopped him before he could go any further. He slipped out his wireless phone—one of the modern ones that flipped open with a little text display underneath—and looked at what was written on the screen. He snapped it closed and pointed at Retyar and Laski. "You're lucky you have time yet to amend your ignorant ways."

Retyar waved him off. "Yes, yes, we peasants shall meditate and reflect upon the profound words of Waylar the Benevolent. Hurry up and cash in your investments before the market dips. I assume that's what your text was about again."

Waylar grinned as he gathered up his notes and shoved them in his satchel. "I'm not sharing any of it with Retyar the Sarcastic."

In a moment, it was just Retyar and Laski sitting alone at the table. He looked over the banister for a second, watching the students on the main floor hunched over their isolated projects, then turned to his own books.

"You still haven't asked Thesha out yet."

Retyar glanced up at Laski. She practically exuded forbearance as she turned a page in her textbook.

"Never seems to be the right time," Retyar said.

Laski closed her book with a thump. "Then make the right time. Six continents, Ret, you're never going to say anything to her at this rate."

"With all the advice you're giving me, I imagine you've got plenty of experience with human courtship practices."

She averted her eyes and blushed the moment his gaze made contact. "It's common sense, isn't it?"

Retyar sighed and slumped his shoulders. "All right, fine. You're right, it's taking a long time. Right now just doesn't seem best, though. We're all working hard on our research, and whatever free time she's got left over she's spending with her folks."

"Doesn't that make it convenient?"

"How so?"

"Well, if you ask her out and she says yes, her parents are right here for introductions."

Retyar stared at her.

"You know, to make it more . . . ." Laski trailed off and pursed her lips. "Raze it, that's not how Govunari do relationships?"

"Meeting the parents generally isn't the first step, no. Is that how it is with Ytanians?"

"Kinda, it is. If you're serious, at least."

He thought about it for a little. "I suppose that doesn't sound too bad. At least, if the girl's parents aren't psycho."

"Or the guy's."

"Fair point." His eyes wandered to the cover of Laski's textbook. "I thought you already finished with that level."

She quirked the corner of her mouth. "I did. I'm just going through some old stuff after this discussion I had on the weave."

"Don't tell me you got into a flame war over wave mechanics."

Laski narrowed her eyes on him. "I am *not* a twelve-year-old Ledgerweave newbie. I know how to stay civilized online."

"So, if you were twelve, wave mechanics is actually a topic you would start a flame war over."

"There was no argument! This guy was just asking a bunch of questions about waves and frequencies. Some of it got pretty basic and metaphysical, like what are waves on the most fundamental level? At first I thought he was some basement theorist who fancies himself a misunderstood genius. Then he started going into high-level wave theory. The way he started getting on, I'm sure he really is somebody. Like government engineer or something."

"Why would anyone like that be asking questions on an open Ledgerweave forum?"

"I haven't got a clue," Laski said. "It's ridiculous, but I can't shake the feeling he's for real." She paused. "It did get weirder. He started making these references to some guy named Kahverengi."

"The philosopher who wrote *On the Feasibility of Time Travel*?"

Laski stiffened. "Oh." She dug her fingers into her hair and leaned on her arms over her closed book. "He *was* a razing goader! He got me!"

"Sounds like this engineer would make great friends with Waylar."

"One Waylar's enough," Laski said with a groan. "Can't these people at least stay out of the physical logics?"

"If it makes you feel any better, Kahverengi argued quite emphatically against pursuing time travel," Retyar said. "If you run into that guy again on the weave, you might point that out."

"Right, and feed the goader."

"Which do you think he is, a Waylar or a goader?"

Laski thought a moment. "A Waylar. Doesn't matter, though. Either way, I'm staying off that forum for a while." She drew a circle on the textbook cover with her finger. "How did you hear about that Kahverengi guy? Standard reading for history majors?"

"I take it you don't watch movies much."

"Engineering major."

"Who has time to get into deep philosophical debates with Ledgerweave pseudo-geniuses. Besides, you're fast enough to skip levels. Surely you can spare three hours every now and then."

"I wouldn't say 'fast'. It's that I study instead of wasting those three hours."

Retyar shrugged. "All right, I'll let you get back to studying, then." He had his own paper to work on as well. He'd jotted only a few sentences down before Waylar started the whole tangent about alternative reasoning.

Laski started to respond before clamming up and digging in her satchel for another book.

A good chunk of time went by with them getting some proper studying in. Several pages into his writing though, Retyar noticed Laski's finger fidgeting around on the same line she'd read several minutes ago. He set his pen aside. "Okay, what's still bugging you?"

She jumped in her seat. "Nothing."

"If you insis—"

"Fine! Why is it that Kahverengi would—" She pressed her lips together when she realized he'd dropped the question.

Retyar quirked an eyebrow.

Laski drew in a slow, calming breath and let it back out. "Why would this Kahverengi have written some whole thing about the possibility of time travel only to say not to try? That seems kind of counterintuitive."

"Not really. It's like a criminal psychologist analyzing all the different ways people break the law, but still saying you shouldn't break the law. You can be fascinated by something without condoning it."

"I guess."

"That describes historians pretty well, actually. If you think about it, most of us get disturbingly fixated on wars and tyrants. Those are the exciting parts of the story, but what does that say about us?"

He noticed Laski seeming to bore into him with her lime green eyes. "What?"

"Insight into these sorts of things comes so easily to you."

Retyar laughed. "I don't know if I'd call it insight. More like musings."

"They're musings I wouldn't be able to come up with."

"And I wouldn't be able to understand half the stuff you do about mechanical theory."

"You could if you studied it," Laski said. "Honestly, it's only because I study nonstop that I've gotten as far as I have. It's not like I have a special mind for any of it."

He was surprised at the sudden self-deprecation. "You put the time in. That's a skill of its own."

"I only put the time in because I've got something to prove. I'm just motivated by wanting to show Ytanians can be smart too. I don't have the driving passion that you and Thesha and Waylar have for your field."

"But you do have a passion," Retyar said. "You wanting to prove the worth of your people is probably a more worthy goal than what I have."

Laski shifted her glasses and rested her chin in her hand. The lamplight reflected prominently in her eyes. "A great job I'm doing of it if I get made a fool by some random clown on the weave."

Retyar leaned in. "Laski, that sort of thing happens to everyone. Don't get embarrassed about it, and especially don't let it get you down."

She huffed. "Easier to say than do."

He shook his head. "Even if you weren't smart, and believe me you *are* smart, the thing you really have going for you is your persistence. Maybe you're right that it's not particularly easy for you to understand the stuff you're studying, but you push yourself day after day to be where you are. Most people don't have it in them to keep at this sort of thing."

"Well, that's an impressive skill to have," Laski said,

rolling her eyes.

"It's the best skill to have," he said seriously. "In my book, you've already proved Ytanians are as good as the rest of us."

She blinked and pressed her lips tight for a few moments before having to rub her eyes under her glasses. She gave him an awkward smile. "I see I'm not the only gullible one, then."

Retyar chuckled. "Right. So, are you still aiming to beat your elders to graduation?"

Laski turned back to her textbook, still grinning. "Won't be hard if you keep flunking your thesis papers."

Chapter 61

Sunlight glinted in Retyar's eye as he twisted the steel arrowhead around in his fingers. He blinked away the afterimage, and the memory of the night when it got lodged in his vest, left behind as the shaft broke off and bounced away. The little triangle wasn't too much different from the item, flat white and sharp, that he held in his other hand. A tooth the shyle had left in his vest the night he'd saved Fellone from the river mouth.

He hoped there wasn't anything more coming to kill him on her account.

Putting the two little blades in his pocket, he picked a stack of dried fish off the rocks and turned back to the cave. Inside, the girl sat hunched over the tablet, fully engrossed in its contents. She'd taken him up on his offer and been glued to the device every waking moment. Couldn't blame her. He leaned over and looked at the corner of the screen.

"Battery's running low. Time to power down and let the solar cells charge."

Fellone pressed her lips tight in annoyance, but turned off the device and handed it over.

Retyar held up the dried fish. "Hungry?"

The waves crashing outside would have drowned out the sound, but he knew her stomach had to have a fierce rumble going. That was another thing chewing at his conscience. A kid her age needed plenty to eat, and he still had trouble breaking out of his minimalist gathering habits. If he had finally stopped wrestling so much with his paranoia every time he caught a fish for himself, that anxiety was now back with a vengeance as he tried catching for two.

Fellone grabbed one of the stiff slabs of fish meat and stuffed it whole into her mouth.

"Good thing I picked out the bones," Retyar said.

She ate the next piece more slowly. "When can we have some real meat?"

"Squirrels aren't as easy to catch. Or as safe. They're more closely linked with humans, more likely to affect the timeline with their absence."

"I still think you're wrong," she said.

He crossed his arms and leaned against the cave wall.

"I think you're meant to be here. You're supposed to save Leverie from the civil war or the Vron. You're supposed to —"

"Meant to come here by who?" Retyar broke her off.

"I don't know. It doesn't matter."

He took a pebble and tossed it at the wall. "History's meant to play out the way it's recorded in that encyclopedia. Do you see me written in there?"

"You don't see me either."

"Because you weren't important enough to be remembered in the histories."

"Not this history, maybe," Fellone said. "This one was written by the Vron."

"How do you know that?"

"Because the Vron won. Ella told me history is written by the victors."

"Right. So obviously there wasn't any time traveler who stopped them."

"Unless your history only exists to show you what happens if you don't do anything."

Retyar sighed. "We've been over this. My world only comes into being if the Vron conquer Leverie. If I stop the Vron, I won't exist in the future. If that happens, I can't end up here to help Leverie."

"Then it doesn't hurt to try."

"Unless, I don't know, my trying something destroys space time."

"But you've already changed things, Rety."

This kid's going to argue this point until the world ends. Hopefully not literally. *Did she just call me Rety?*

"No. No more talk of this. It's the end of this kind of conversation."

"But—"

"No trying to change history if you want to read anything on the tablet. That's the condition."

"You're a coward," she muttered.

Retyar nodded. "Yeah. I'm scared. I could destroy everything. That's something you need to take to heart." He walked out of the cave, teeth clenched in frustration—at her and himself. He set up the tablet's solar charger, telling himself as he did that the girl's words weren't going to damage his resolve. He had decided a long time ago the best course of action. He was sticking to it.

But what if I'm wrong?

If changing things wasn't as dangerous to reality as he thought, then what did it say of him that he was sitting on knowledge that could save lives?

Even then, altering history means ending far more lives. The billions of people in my time will never even exist.

He was in a no-win situation. He'd been in one for six years.

A rustling in the brush snapped him out of his internal monologue. The memory of Leverie soldiers flashed through his mind. His pistol was in hand in an instant.

Branches parted and a wild boar strutted into the clearing. The creature turned milky eyes on him, likely not even seeing the human it had stumbled upon.

Retyar sighed. "Get out of here, old fellow. You've no idea how much I miss bacon."

The boar bumbled its way back into the brush. Retyar holstered his gun, only then noticing Fellone peeking out of the cave.

"No pork, then?"

He tugged his shirt to cover over the pistol. "Nope."

She picked at some specks of dirt caking the granite cave wall. "That little thing's a gun, right? Like that rifle you always have on your back."

"I'm going out to gather some more vegetables. Don't touch the tablet until it's at full charge." He strode away from the cave, intent on retreating into his own thoughts, as pointless as they always were.

Chapter 62

Ellaniel rushed up just as the western gate finally swung open, allowing the red-clad Senkani soldiers to file into the city. It had taken just hours for the force to march out and meet the enemy's attempted river crossing. It took a day and a half for them to return. Most of the soldiers were in fine shape, but plenty moved along with a limp, leaning against their fellows, here and there wrapped up in bandages splotched with blood. Their shields bore the marks of fierce fighting, none more so than the crenden's ckols.

"Arzan? Where's Arzan?" she demanded, taking hold of a ckol's arm.

"Right behind us, your grace. The captain's with him."

Ellaniel caught sight of the stretcher. Whatever anger still lingered in her towards her husband melted when she saw the splints at his arm and leg, the red staining the neck of his tunic. Vighkon muttered something to him with a forced smile as she approached. Arzan laughed before cutting himself short with a pained grunt.

"Arzan. How . . . " She choked, but forced herself to finish the question. "How bad is it?"

The surgeon carrying the foot of the stretcher opened his mouth, but Arzan spoke over him, "Not as terrible as it looks. Broken arm, fractured leg, a few bad ribs. The blood's from someone in a lot worse shape than me."

Ellaniel reached out, hoping to touch him, but fearful of causing hurt. "I . . . ."

Arzan dropped his bravado and used his good hand to pull her close. Her hair brushed the side of his face, their foreheads nearly touching as he looked into her eyes. "For the pain in your face alone, I'm sorry I was so reckless."

"I thought that's what makes a Redleaf," she said wanly. She lowered her head against his and let herself feel comfort in his presence.

She heard Vighkon order the crenden set aside. In moments, Arzan's stretcher was down atop a layer of blankets while Ellaniel sat beside him on the cobblestones. The ckols set up a perimeter guard a little distance away, giving them privacy.

"They made three crossing attempts," Arzan said. "I ran into a ckol with a mace on the first one. Had to leave it to the sub-commander for the other two. They didn't have the cover of fog for those. Hard-fought."

"What about now? Can you command the wall?"

He went silent, his expression dark.

"Arzan?"

"I must."

She touched his chest lightly on what looked to be his uninjured side. "You can't even use crutches with your arm hurt."

His jaw muscles tightened as he closed his eyes.

"Arzan, I made a mistake," she lied. She knew it was what he wanted to hear and she knew that she should have been sincere. Despite understanding she'd overstepped the line, she couldn't be sorry about killing any of Odavan's men. "When the Council learns of your injury, the force of their whole army is going to fall on us. When that happens, do you think Senkani will deserve a crippled commander?"

"When that happens, I don't want you standing in the face of that wave." He looked at her and brushed his fingers through her hair. "It was my mistake to have you there in the first place. My fault to have you on the field in Creedport. My own shortcomings have exposed you to too much."

Ellaniel held his hand, keeping it entangled in her hair. "This is a war. We've all been hurt. It's only going to get harder before it's all over, but we need to press forward regardless to find the end. You can't command. No one else is suitable. You have to decide what's best for this city."

"It's still a decision, isn't it?" Turmoil washed over his features. She imagined him going through the names of potential commanders in his head. There were the other Redleafs, but to a one their skills were those of merchants and vinemasters, with no inclination towards war strategy. Their officers were trained at lower-level tactics, not how to control broader actions. From how long Arzan's deliberation took, he wasn't pleased with the performance of the sub-commander who'd taken his place for the river defense. Ellaniel was the only one left. Her and Vighkon.

"Vighkon has better military understanding," Arzan said.

Ellaniel's disastrous cavalry maneuver at Creedport wouldn't be forgotten, nor should it be. "I've learned from my mistakes. I'll show you I have if only you give me the chance. Vighkon won't take command. You know him—he'll never leave your side."

Arzan drew in a breath and started to push himself up. "Then I will just have to—"

"It's impossible." She put her hand to his shoulder and it was too easy to hold him down. She shook in rage at whoever had reduced him to this shape, but also welcomed the opportunity it opened for her. "Accept it, Arzan, I need to be the one. I'm not ill-suited. The people respect me. They'll follow my command. I know something of strategy from what you've taught me, from what I've watched of you, and from what I've learned from experience already."

Arzan knitted his brows, his expression agonized. Ellaniel waited until at last he withdrew his hand and turned his head from her. "You have command. Protect our city."

Ellaniel released a breath. She touched her forehead to his. "It shall be done."

Two hours later, Ellaniel left the palace fully armed and armored. Dark lace draped over polished plate, her hair and crimson capelet flowing loose at her back. Her shield bore the newly painted image of a red tree against a black field. Around her, the ckols still fit to fight created a bubble of steel to escort her through the city. Women, children, and old or injured men stood straight and watched her pass. Encouragements showered her from all sides, only growing in number and fervor as she went, leaving families behind for idling soldiers. When at last she reached the wall, the shouts solidified into a single chant, roaring from the throats of a thousand men. Ellaniel hadn't at all expected this reception, but she grinned as she recognized the word that had once been thrown at her as a jibe and insult. As she climbed the gate tower to the ramparts, the stone stairway shuddered with her name.

"Goldeye."

Chapter 63

Crenden Thrake entered the study with a hopeful stride, his haggard face lightening as he found Charva waiting for him in the chair by his desk. "You've returned. How much progress have you made?"

"Not as much as I would have liked." When her father glanced at Ersch, she nudged her chin towards the door. Her ckol went to wait outside. Given how briefly she'd known him, she was a little surprised how much she trusted the man, but she didn't want to argue the point right now to let him stay. She'd fill him in later. Once the latch clicked shut, she went on, "I spoke with the Council, at least as many as were outside Senkani. I'm suspicious of several of them, though I've not enough to pin anyone with anything."

"Who in particular do you think we should focus on?" Thrake asked. He settled into another of the guest chairs. The choice distracted her. Charva couldn't remember the last time they'd sat in this room and he hadn't put his desk between them. It was such a small thing, and something she wanted to ignore, but she inexplicably had to blink back a welling of tears.

She cleared her throat, hoping her expression hadn't slipped. "I think we should keep the closest eye on Ylnavar and Odavan. The Speaker's always hated both you and Arzan. He's obsessively strict about order, and you two were always throwing things into disarray. As for Odavan, with Hashan dead he becomes crenden. Straightforward motive."

Thrake laced his fingers in thought. "I don't believe it's Ylnavar. It's not order he's obsessed with. It's rules. He's a man for procedure, and this conspiracy flies in the face of that."

"So Odavan, then. He kills Hashan, pins the blame on you, then hides behind Ylnavar's zeal."

"A fine theory, but we need proof."

Charva leaned into her armrest. "I already tried snooping around Highcity and Woodwise. Managed briefly to get into Ylnavar's books and letters."

Thrake arched his brows. "I feel I shouldn't be surprised at that."

"Of course not. Sadly, I found nothing of consequence. However," she reached into her pocket and withdrew the letter she'd taken from Ylnavar's drawer. The paper was woefully crumpled now after days of travel. "I've a question about this."

Her father took the letter and smoothed it out. "What is it?"

"A message you sent to the Speaker proclaiming your innocence. I don't know what it is, but something . . . " she trailed off as Thrake rubbed his beard and frowned.

"I didn't write this."

Charva suspected he might not remember. Her gaze involuntarily strayed to the cabinet near the window and the gouged wood no one had bothered yet to repair. "Well, there was a point right after the incident when you weren't exactly . . . ."

The crenden grimaced. "That's not what I—never mind. Better that I show you." He got up and circled his desk to thumb through some documents in the drawer. He came back with a sheet and handed both it and the letter over to her.

She started to read aloud, "'*Order to all members of the city guard, gate and harbor are to be*'—"

"Never mind the words!" he interrupted. "Look at the writing."

Charva did so, focusing on the lines. They were in Thrake's hand, but distinctly messier than she'd ever seen. Many of the letters she could only discern from the context. She compared it to the message from Ylnavar's study, which was sharp and perfect.

"The one I handed you was written when I was . . . was

having my episode," Thrake said. "Everything I penned those couple days is like that."

She gripped the letter tight. "This is a forgery."

Thrake paced the room. "But why? What is the purpose of this? Why put words of innocence in my mouth when my stance was already a given?"

"That doesn't matter." Charva found herself smiling. "If we can trace this letter, find who delivered it to Ylnavar, then we can find our culprit." She sprang to her feet. "I'm going back to Senkani. This letter was sent to Ylnavar, which means he was being tricked and isn't the one behind the plot. I can ask him directly about how he received it."

Her father caught her by the trailer of her sleeve. "There's time enough to wait." He pointed out the window, where the sun was starting to cast long shadows in the streets. "I'd rather not have you riding through the woods at night. Not with a war and assassins on the loose."

She had to admit, the prospect wasn't all that appealing when phrased like that. "At first light, then."

Thrake worked his jaw, struggling for words, or with them. "Charva, would . . . would you care to share dinner?"

The query left her flatfooted. "I suppose I could."

Her sleeve fluttered free. "I shall see you in an hour, then."

Charva nodded and went out into the hall. She barely noticed Ersch step in behind her as she made for her room.

The western sky was settling into a waning glow when Charva left the palace grounds for a stroll through the city.

"That was an interesting dinner," Ersch commented in a low tone.

She wouldn't disagree there. Most of it had consisted of silence and awkward half-sentences. She and her father couldn't connect over normal topics, but he had at least tried. In the end, Thrake did relate a few memories of her mother. He'd rarely ever spoken of her before.

"He's changed," Charva said. "I never really thought

anyone could become so different, but this whole thing, the assassins, the Council, losing Throrne . . . ." She knew she shouldn't feel warmth, not after mentioning the horrors that had brought this about.

Ersch picked up on her cheer. "I don't think I've ever been witness to a more uncomfortable family dinner and you're practically gleaming."

"He's trying to mend things."

"Did you already forget that he has Honorable Maltan in exile?"

The reminder dampened her mood. "There's messengers out. They'll bring Malty back."

Ersch drew in a patient breath. "As you say, my liege."

The two of them fell quiet. They passed by a lamp keeper stepping on a stool and sneaking his match stick past a glass cover to set a light. The oil would last the hour or so past sunset people would need to pack up shop and head home, or in her case get some fresh air before bed.

"Some alms, please, yer grace. City's not been kind to me this day."

Charva looked sidelong at the beggar sitting by the mouth of a narrow alley. She reached for her pouch and tossed the man a copper. As she tightened her purse amidst his muttered thanks, she noticed an odd shape in with the coins. She pulled out the odd brass cylinder the soldiers had found in the Senkani woods.

"Do you think Lavler's Blacksmith is open still?"

Ersch shrugged. "Depends how many orders he's got."

Not long later they were at the blacksmith's threshold, orange light casting against the walls from the blazing furnace within. The lack of metal hammering on metal made it simple enough to knock on the door frame to get an apprentice's attention and have themselves led to Lavler. The squat blacksmith was busy holding a length of steel within the flame and didn't look back as he shouted over the roar of the furnace, "Don't be bothering me, you fool! Can't you see I'm timing the heat?" He pulled the red hot metal free and plunged it in oil.

"Crenden's daughter to see you, Lavler."

The blacksmith hooked his tongs on the rack and turned.

"The aristocrat girl always prancing around with a sword?" He looked up at her, his round face ghastly in the furnace light. "I don't do weapons. Honest tools bring enough business my way."

Only moments dealing with the sweltering heat inside the workshop and Charva had to wipe a layer of sweat from her face. "I'm not commissioning anything, truly. I was just hoping for a professional opinion." She produced the piece of brass.

Lavler took the object in his thick-gloved hand and held it what she thought was dangerously close to the furnace as he looked it over. "Pretty little bauble. What about it?"

"I was wondering if you might have some idea what it is."

"Not the kind of thing I work with." He held it back out to her. "Something that small and shiny, you might try taking it to Fizram across the street. Jeweler."

"I don't think it's jewelry."

"Well, then you already know more about it than I do."

"I see. Thank you for your time."

Outside, the gentle sea breeze made its existence unpleasantly known through her sweat moistened dress.

"Told you it was just a decoration," Ersch said.

"Lavler said he didn't work on weapons."

"Not visiting the jeweler's, then?"

Charva shrugged. "We're already here." They crossed the street to a little building with large windows. A sign above the doorway, lit by a nearby street lamp, depicted a collection of fancy rings. The door was yet unbarred despite the hour, and a little bell announced their presence as they entered.

"Yes, yes?"

She always imagined jewelers as tall, bony men, and Fizram lived up precisely to her expectations. He even had the wispy gray hair combed sideways across his scalp.

"I want to know whatever you can tell me about this?" she said, giving him the piece of brass.

"Always, always happy to oblige a daughter of Leverie." He took the object over to his counter, where he had a mirrored lamp burning gently. "Let's see. Brass. Quite nicely fashioned. I wonder why it would be— Ah, letters on the end. No, letters and numbers. '.309 T4 L VsN 159'. Hmm, I wonder what that stands for. An interesting dimple there in the center."

"Do you know what the thing might be?" Charva asked.

"Not jewelry, I should think. No place to attach a string. My guess is that it's a vial, but I find it intriguing that it's so small. Whatever it held would have had to be quite potent to be worth the trouble."

"Could it have been for poison?" Ersch whispered to her.

"Could make sense, but they said all of the soldiers were killed by something like a slingstone," Charva answered. She addressed the jeweler, "Anything else you can discern?"

The man scratched his ear. "Hmm, on closer inspection, I feel that these letters on the bottom were stamped, not engraved."

"Would that mean anything?"

"Only that stamps are meant to be reused. There are likely more where this came from."

Somehow, that sent a chill running down her spine. She thanked Fizram and left.

The sun was fully set, the streets in this part of town entirely empty. Some hammering echoed out from the blacksmith's workshop, but otherwise the city was falling silent. Charva was just started on the way back to the palace when a man she recognized as one of her father's agents approached her under lamplight.

"I've been looking all over for you, your grace. One of ours just returned. We've found the scarred mercenary."

Chapter 69

The day was bright and clear when Retyar stepped onto the green of the University castle courtyard. Graduation. It was a day long in coming, and yet it still felt like so little time had passed since he'd enrolled.

A classmate he knew in passing slapped him on the shoulder as he dashed by. "Congratulations, Ret!" He disappeared into the mass of other students, repeating his commendations to everyone he recognized.

Retyar straightened his tuxedo and smiled as he wove his way through the crowd, eyes trying to scan the faces within the courtyard and atop the wall simultaneously. He thought he caught sight of his parents and brothers in the stands up above. It was quite a sight, seeing all the people gathered on the platform extensions that had been rigged there. He waved with a white-gloved hand, doubting at the same time his family would be able to pick him out of the hundreds of people around him.

"Ret. Ret!"

Laski materialized out of the crowd, silky black coattails flying behind her as she rushed up and grabbed his arm. "Come on, we've got to snatch our seats before we're stuck on opposite ends of the field!"

He let himself get dragged along through the rows of chairs. "Is Thesha here yet?"

"No, but Waylar is. He's been twitchy as a caffeinated hamster since the moment he stepped through the gate." She slowed down. "Are you really, seriously, finally going through with it?"

Retyar grinned, trying to fight off a bout of weightlessness in his gut. "I've wasted way too much time. Here we are at graduation. There's no better time to ask her than this, and if I don't I might as well just give up and admit I'm a coward."

"Yeah." Laski gave him a strange, distant look before shaking her head and taking him to the far right edge of the middle rows, where Waylar was sitting with chin in his fist and his heel tapping the grass at about two hundred times a minute.

"Calm down, buddy!" Retyar said. "Keep that up and I'll start renting you out to construction sites as a dirt compactor."

Waylar drew in a deep breath, stopping his leg jittering and forcing a smile. "Hey, Ret."

Retyar plopped down next to him. They were nice seats, he thought. Even though they were folding chairs, they were nicely molded hardwood. Worn yet sturdy, they'd probably seen generations of students off to the outside world. Somehow, in that moment, the feeling really struck home that he was graduating. He also felt that this had to be the day that he asked Thesha out.

Laski sat down in the next chair and leaned in. "So, you going to do it before or after the ceremony?" she asked in a whisper.

Retyar tugged at his collar. "Which do you think is better?"

"Before. Put it off any bit longer and I'm going to punch you."

"You know, I feel like the two of you are always leaving me out of the loop," Waylar said.

"It's just girl stuff," Laski told him. Retyar looked at her, not quite sure how aghast he should be at her choice of wording. Waylar chuckled and let it drop. He started shaking his leg again.

Retyar felt a little concerned now. "Waylar, you've got a lot of nerves for something as simple as a graduation ceremony. All we have to do is sit here and wait for our turn to pick up a little scroll."

Waylar chuckled. "Yeah, I look like a mess, don't I?" He smoothed his hair and seemed to reflect. "You know, this might be the last day the four of us hang out together. Ret, Thesha, and I are heading off to the Museum, but this could be the last time we see Laski."

It was one of those things Retyar had tried not to think too much about, and especially not right now. But seeing her face drop a little, he couldn't ignore it. "We'll still keep in touch. Anyway, Laski's off to bigger things than we are. I'm sure you've got laboratories scouting you from all over the place."

Laski shrugged. "Not quite. I'm not even twenty yet, you know. I'll probably see if I can apprentice in Haylane."

"No one intrigued by the youngest woman to graduate in your field?"

"There was this one offer. Pretty nuts. It looked like some military contractor. With a little digging, I found out they've got this facility up in the Brittle Mountains by Crystal Ebb and they seem to be hiring all sorts of people all of a sudden."

"Some sort of big breakthrough? That not something you'd be interested in?"

She shook her head. "And get sucked into top secret land? I'm making a name for Ytanians, remember?"

A bell chimed out a series of clear notes.

"Fifteen minutes till they start," someone called.

A student tried to take the empty seat next to them. Waylar instantly shooed him off. "Spot's taken."

"Thesha's taking her sweet time," Laski muttered. She squinted through her glasses up at the guest stands. "I think that's my folks!"

Retyar tried to follow her gaze. "Where?"

"In the green and pink." She raised her arm and waved.

He didn't mention just how tacky that color combination was. That was one thing about Ytanian ethnic garb he couldn't get used to. He also decided not to point out the wide berth other guests gave her family.

His mind turned away from the people and the ceremony and instead to what he was going to say to Thesha. A dozen different lines went through his head, each of which he tagged as cringingly cheesy after more than five or ten seconds of deliberation. He wished he'd given the details a little more thought before this morning, but he also knew why he hadn't.

"What if she doesn't want to take our relationship in that direction?"

Laski pressed her lips tight and shook her head. "Ret . . . ."

"What if she just wants us to be friends and colleagues? If I ask her out and she says no, I don't know if that'd be possible anymore. I don't think we could work together."

"Six continents," Laski said with a sigh. "Things already are awkward. From what I see, this hidden crush already has you at the tipping point. If you don't say anything," she crossed her arms, "I'm sure it *is* going to eat you up. Do you want to spend the rest of your life as a secret admirer?"

Retyar clasped his hands together, letting the weight of her words sink in. He nodded. "Raze it. I'm asking her. I'm just straight up asking her."

"I also want to say your fear of breaking things by asking is painfully cliché. That's the plot of every romance movie out there ever."

Retyar laughed despite himself. "Okay, that's a bit harsh. And how would you even know that? I thought you didn't watch movies."

"I can try new things, can't I?"

"If you're new to movies, how do you know what's cliché for romances?"

"Well, uh . . . That's kind of all I've been watching, I guess?"

He chuckled.

"Found you!"

Retyar turned his head to see Thesha sidling down the crowded row towards them. His breath caught at her unexpected appearance. Instead of the standard black tux, she had a navy blue dress with ribboned arms and dark green shoulder capes. Her brown hair was done up in a laurel braid and short tail, fully baring her slender neck.

"Late fifty-third century graduation dress," she explained as she came close. On reaching her chair, she spun around to show off every angle. "The University technically never excluded it from the dress code. You wouldn't believe how long it took to set the ribbons just right! They aren't actually sewn in like you'd expect."

He'd never seen her more beautiful. She filled out the clothing perfectly, as if the design had been crafted just for her, and with her radiant smile it left him speechless.

"You're such a nerd," Laski said. She flicked her eyes at Retyar and jabbed him with her elbow.

Retyar's mind jolted back into something resembling coherence. He swallowed, shoving down his doubts and fears. He started to get to his feet. "Thesh—"

A hand on his shoulder suddenly pushed him back in his seat. "Hold that thought, Ret," Waylar said. "Thesha. Step here for a sec?"

Though not normally quick to take offense, Retyar found a few choice words lined up on his tongue. He opened his mouth just as Waylar led Thesha to the open grass beside their row. "Actually, could *you* hold that thought for—"

"Just a minute, Ret," Waylar said forcefully, and that was the first inkling he had that something bad was up. His friend turned back to Thesha, who had her brow raised in expectation. A few students in other rows also looked on in curiosity. "I thought up a bunch of different ways to do this, but figured simple was best. Thesha Dinria," he got to his knee, "will you marry me?"

A gasp went through their area, with a girl or two squeeing in delight. Shock struck Retyar still as a statue. The first of his nerves to recover quirked his mouth into a disbelieving smile. What kind of absurdity . . . .

He saw Thesha's face. She was the picture of unbridled joy, her mouth a wide, gaping smile and her eyes wide in excitement.

Retyar had horribly, terribly misjudged something.

"Yes."

It felt like the castle walls came crashing down on his shoulders. Laski leaped to her feet beside him. "*What?!* Where did this come from?"

If anything showed in Retyar's expression, Waylar was too drunk with his own happiness to notice it. "I've a confession to make," he said, grinning from ear to ear. "We've actually been dating for a while now. We didn't want to say anything and make things awkward with our study groups."

Retyar pieced together how the two of them always seemed to leave early. Now that he saw it, it was so obvious.

Music began blaring out of the towering speakers. Students who had still been standing found the last of the chairs. Retyar followed with numb obedience as Laski forced him to swap seats, putting herself between him and the engaged couple. He stole only one final look to his right and the glowing aura of happiness surrounding Thesha and Waylar, then fixed his gaze straight ahead. The graduation ceremony progressed in a haze. He vaguely heard the University president giving some flowery speech on his pride in this generation and expectations of the things they would accomplish. At the end of it, an admin listed off the students of exceptional achievement. Retyar clapped mechanically when he heard Thesha's and Laski's names. Through all of it, Laski kept fidgeting and glancing to either side of her, as if she was somehow responsible for this mess.

At long last, the speaker called the students to stand and file down to the podium to receive their diplomas. Retyar walked down the grassy aisle, celebratory music mingling with cheering families. When the plodding line carried him to the front, he forced a smile and grabbed the scroll with hands that weren't his. The line carried him back away, depositing him in the open field amongst festive graduates. He kept on walking, ignoring Laski's voice calling his name.

With a spirit crushed to powder, he strode through the gate and didn't look back.

Chapter 65

Retyar stood staring at the vacant cave, his fingers in the empty space within his holster as his eyes took stock of the flat bedding for the third time. His anger faded and turned into a tired resignation.

He'd realized something was wrong about fifteen minutes ago. He was out gathering fruit about a quarter mile along the coast. Lifting his cloak as a makeshift basket, he'd noticed his pistol was missing. No doubt Fellone had stolen it before he'd woken, and now she was gone, together with the tablet.

He knew he had to set out immediately to find her, but couldn't summon the energy. Instead, he slid his back down against the wall, listening to the crashing waves and squawking seagulls. He put his face in his hands, wondering at his own stupidity. Why tell the girl his story? Why let her see the encyclopedia? It didn't make any sense, yet he'd done it anyway. His actions had gone against every line of rationality, against every principle he'd tried to stand for in this place. He knew what he'd done was wrong.

Why had he set himself up to fail in his only mission?

"I'm so tired," he whispered.

And that was it. So what if the timeline changed and his world was lost? He wasn't built to this task. By now, he couldn't even kid himself anymore that it was possible not to mess up history in some way just by existing. How much of a fool did he have to be to think he could preserve things, to keep a single pebble from falling?

He thought of the people he'd known in his own world. His parents, his brothers. He longed for the days he'd spent studying with Thesha, Laski, and Waylar. After all this time, he didn't even feel the bitter heartbreak that had chased him to that backwater security job. He just wanted the company of friends.

"But they're gone," he said, his voice reverberating in the stone-walled space. "Dead, all of them. The changes compounding over hundreds of years will wipe them from existence."

It was a fact he'd been refusing to acknowledge, but somewhere in his subconscious he'd already accepted it. The crashing waves measured out the moments as he came to terms with this reality. After a long while, he finally thumped the butt of his rifle into the ground and pushed himself to his feet. He remembered the day he'd graduated, thought of the lesson he probably should have learned from it.

Sometimes, waiting was the worst thing you could do.

He stepped out of the cave.

Charva shifted in her seat, still trying to get used to the mail shirt underneath her simple dress. The weight wasn't so much of a problem—the armor was perfectly fitted and belted well around her waist—but she just didn't like having so much *stuff* layered over her. Still, it wasn't all bad. The light padding and mail trousers under her skirt were a good buffer against the wooden bench as the wagon bounced on every flaming ditch the driver could lay his eyes on.

One of the wheels found an especially jarring hole that sent her skull banging against the ceiling frame. A high pitched-squeak escaped her mouth. Ersch had his hand on her head in an instant. "Driver, slow down! No point getting to Three Corners with speed if we have to spend a week mending when we get there."

"I'm fine, keep the pace," Charva ordered, ignoring the throbbing pain.

Ersch eyed her with concern, but she merely slouched

lower to avoid any more ceiling encounters. She stole a glance out the open back at the second wagon following behind them. From the outside, it looked like any other supply vehicle. That was the best way to get six of her father's ckols through the provinces. Like her, none of them wore any open signs of their identity. Ckols running loose through someone else's land would be frowned upon even in the best of times.

"What do you think this mercenary fellow's business is in Pundur's city?" Ersch asked, bracing himself in his seat.

Charva rubbed her fingers over the sheathed daggers hidden up her sleeves. It felt so odd not having them against her skin. "I suppose we can ask him that when we catch him."

The road smoothed out some, allowing Ersch to lean his elbows on his knees and steeple his fingers. "You think the assassins are working for Pundur?"

The thought didn't mesh with what she knew of the man, but there was no way to be sure. "Whether they are or aren't, we're doing this on our own. No contact with the Three Corners guard. The fewer people involved, the less chance our target will catch wind." Despite Ersch's concerns for their safety and comfort, she wished they could move faster. Without knowledge of why the scarred mercenary was in Three Corners, they'd no way of telling how long he'd stay put. The Creedport agent in the city would keep watch on him, but a lot more could go wrong trying to meet up and coordinate an ambush if he took to the road.

"I feel it's strange our agent's only seen the one," Ersch went on. "The company your father hired was fifteen all told."

"You think it's a trap for us?"

He shrugged. "Best to be prepared."

Charva tapped her sword with a smile. "Certainly."

The driver shouted at the horses. "Whoa! Whoa!" The wagon slowed, then stopped. Ersch shared a glance with her before hopping out.

"What's going on?"

She felt at her daggers again to reassure herself they were there. Ersch and the driver exchanged a few short words she couldn't make out, then there was a span of silence. Charva felt the urge to peek out, but restrained herself. The fewer people had a chance to see and recognize her the better. That didn't stop her from keeping a keen ear and loosening her sword in its scabbard. No doubt the ckols in the other wagon were doing the same.

A little time passed before Ersch walked back in sight. "Traveler asking if we've seen a girl on the road."

Charva relaxed. "Have we?"

"Driver says he hasn't, so the fellow's sure she went the other direction."

"Towards Senkani? That doesn't sound good."

"Maybe she went in the woods?" He looked back around the wagon. "He's started walking again."

She thought a moment. "Ask if he'd like a ride."

The displeasure was plain on Ersch's face. "There are plenty of other wagons traveling this road, my liege. We've more important things than to be picking up strays."

"I don't like abandoning a man searching for his family. Leaves a bad taste in my mouth."

He sighed. "If you say so."

The shout stopped Retyar in his tracks. He turned around again to see the man with the sword beckoning him over.

"We've room in the wagon if you want."

Retyar mulled over his options. The offer would have panicked him any time before today, but his mission now was changed. The sword gave him pause, but he wasn't defenseless. He shifted his rifle on his shoulder, careful not to loosen the cloth wrapping.

"That's something I'll gladly accept."

He followed the man around to the back of the first wagon and clambered aboard. It was a little more spacious than it appeared from the outside, at least in depth. The ribbed ceiling supports holding up the fabric cover were a little low.

It was only once he was seated and the driver clicking the horses back into motion that he noticed the woman further in. The lighting there was somewhat dim, but she still looked incredibly attractive. Or maybe that was just a side affect of being out of female company for several years straight. No, at the very least she was a great deal pretty, with light features that were just the right mixture of smooth and athletic. She wore a plain green dress, but carried what looked like a rapier sword. Did they use rapiers here in Moshon? Something here felt off, but it was too late to decline their invitation now.

"Hello," he said. "Thank you two for letting me ride."

"The driver will keep a lookout for any children on the road," the woman said. "You can stay there at the back so you have a view of anyone we overtake."

Retyar nodded, and felt more at ease having a seat with good escape options. Under the woman's gaze, he felt conscious of his rough and dirty appearance. It was a couple weeks since he'd last washed the makeshift cloak he'd found a year ago with some flotsam. His pants were still the same ones he'd arrived in this time with, and though he'd done his best to keep them functional, there were rips and holes, not to mention plenty of stains. At least his boots were still good. Sturdy things those were. *And also very out of place*, he thought. Made of pitch black synthetics and rubber, their texture had to stand out like a sore thumb. He subtly shifted the edge of his cloak to cover his feet.

Metallic scrunching accompanied every bounce of the wagon, drawing Retyar's attention to the man's chainmail shirt. He thought the armor to have an interesting sound quality to it, and kind of wanted to touch the stuff. The University had had plenty of plate armor on display in the Castle, but all the chain sets were always kept behind glass.

He chuckled to himself. Only a few hours since giving up his old world for lost and he was somehow back in nerd scholar mode.

"Do you live around these parts?"

Retyar blinked at the woman's question, hesitated, then answered, "Along the coast. Rather out of the way."

"Is this girl your daughter?"

Technically, he could say she was some random kid he'd half kidnapped. "Just someone I was looking after. She got displaced by the war."

"Trying to get back to her family, then."

Something must have shown on his face.

"They're not alive, I take it," she said quietly.

Retyar nodded. "That's what I gather."

"Why's she running from you, then?" the man asked. Retyar noted the same look of suspicion in his eyes as from the first moment he'd hopped from the wagon. He considered it really might have been a mistake getting a ride from them. He wanted to look outside to see how fast they were moving, how great a danger he'd be in of getting trampled by the second wagon if he jumped, but restrained himself. Letting the man know he was rattled would be as bad as admitting he was some kind of criminal.

Retyar shrugged. "I think it's one of those things where she just wants to go home."

The explanation didn't look to allay the man's suspicion, but it didn't heighten it either. He nodded and didn't ask anything more.

Retyar eyed his armor and the woman's sword. "Are you joining the army?"

"We're merchants," the woman said. "Heading to Three Corners. You can't say it's smart to travel westward unarmed these days."

"That's an interesting sword."

She smiled.

"Looks like a rapier."

The woman cocked her eyebrow. "Oh, so you know a thing or two about blades." She patted the weapon's hilt. "I picked it up in Falcone."

"You've traveled far. That trip must have earned you a lot of coin."

She smiled again in a way that made him feel he'd made some unintended joke. "It was profitable." The wagon hit a rough patch of road, forcing all of them to brace themselves. "Flame it! You know, one thing that's different between us is they pave all their major highways."

Retyar thought of his Govunari and how it wasn't just the main roads that got good treatment. *If she only knew the kinds of societies that were possible.* "What was your overall impression of that land?"

The woman thought a moment. "I suppose I'd say it was a

place of greater extremes. Bigger cities. Bigger buildings. Bigger mountains. They have kings there still, and it felt like it was normal that there was always a war raging someplace. The streets were always as busy as the main thoroughfare back home, and sometimes it seemed there were as many beggars as grocers in the markets. Yet despite all the problems, there were amazing sights to see."

"You like it better here, though."

"When it comes down to it, there's never any place like where you came from."

And that had Retyar picturing what the land that would someday become Govunari would look like today. He wondered if he could feel at home there, or if it would be just as alien as the country he was in now.

"What part of the continent were you on?" he asked. "I hear the Falcon's Heart is a lot like here, but there are places like in the Feathers where the rain comes down frozen in the winter."

"Actually, I was—" she stopped, then suddenly crawled closer. He heard mail shifting with her movements as she sat down across from him and looked into his face. Her lips quirked. "You're playing with me. You're Falconian."

She saw his eyes clearly now, and at the same time he saw hers. They were a deep blue that he'd only ever seen in movies and pictures, dark in color but somehow bright in spirit.

Retyar failed to think of anything witty to say before the woman leaned back. "What in the six is a Falconian doing all the way out here in the woods, taking care of a Senkani war orphan?"

"Living?" he answered.

She narrowed her eyes at him, then laughed. "Obviously. But how did you come to be in Leverie?"

He unconsciously tugged his cloak a little tighter around him. He might try the same story he'd first used on Fellone, but he doubted it would fly with this woman. There wasn't anything else he could think of.

"No offense, but that's something I'd like to keep to myself," he said.

"I see," she said, crossing her arms.

He readied himself for the inevitable follow-up questions, but the woman instead turned her head to watch the passing woods.

"That's it?"

"Is there anything else you'll be willing to tell me?"

"Honestly, I'd prefer not to."

She bobbed her head at him with a bounce of the wagon. "A man who travels so far from his home and settles in the wilderness is a man who doesn't want to be found. There are secrets I respect. After all, it's the least I can do if I hope for someone not to delve into mine."

The statement validated an inkling that had been lurking in the back of Retyar's mind. The clues were there.

"A wagon with no cargo. A man and woman armed and armored who don't offer their names. Whoever you are, you aren't simple merchants."

The man gave the woman the sort of look that said he was irritated she'd given it away, but didn't voice his sentiment. She rolled her eyes at him. "He was already figuring it out on his own."

"Which is why we should have just passed him by."

"Look, I know what you people are up to is none of my business," Retyar said. "I've plenty of experience keeping things to myself."

The woman slapped her companion on the shoulder. "See? A man of discretion. Of course, if he'd rather not involve himself with us . . . ."

Retyar shifted his feet. "I doubt whoever I find next on the road will have much to say about Falcone." There were some things he'd be happy to talk about.

The smile returned to the woman's lips.

Chapter 66

Charva hopped down to the paving stones as the wagon drew to a stop just inside the Three Corners city gates. She pulled her scarf close about her face and lifted her light cloak carefully over her sword, thankful the morning chill masked her purpose. Ersch dropped beside her and rubbed his hands together for warmth, his eyes surveying the stream of farmers, traders, and laborers coming and going through the wall. Not far away, the second wagon deposited its own passengers—her father's ckols disguised as common labor, their shortswords stowed in large bags hanging at their sides or from their shoulders.

Another set of feet struck the ground next to her. The Falconian gazed this way and that, taking in city and people. He seemed almost overwhelmed by the numbers around him. Indeed, it was something even Charva wasn't too used to. Three Corners was one of the more densely populated cities in Leverie.

Travelers on the road had seen the girl of his riding up front on an open cart. He'd been surprised when the sightings had gone off the Senkani road and towards Three Corners. After a bit of thought, he did say there might be someone here she knew. It turned out his and Charva's destinations were the same. He had stayed on and camped with them the night, but now it was time for them to part.

"I hope you find the girl," Charva said.

The Falconian nodded and shifted the strange covered rod strapped to his back. "So do I. Thank you again for the ride."

"Let it not be said that Leverie has forgotten kindness.

Besides, you were good company."

Even Ersch had warmed to the man somewhat. At the least, he didn't cast any glares his way anymore.

An older woman separated from the throng, hesitantly looking over Charva and the wagon. "Um, Dancer?"

That was the pseudonym their agent in the city was supposed to address her by. Charva turned her full attention to the woman.

"Ensam said he would meet you at Moonsleet Courtyard by the South Corner," the woman told her. "He'll be there at mid-morning, or else an hour past noon if you're late."

Charva thanked her and turned to bid the Falconian a final farewell, only for him to already be gone. She pinched her lips into a thin line. Rude. *Well, truly to business, then.* She had Ersch relay their destination to the other ckols. They all split into twos, making their own way to the meet-up point while the wagon drivers jockeyed for a spot near the gate. If things got hot, they might well need a quick getaway.

Retyar felt a little guilty leaving the wagon people without a proper goodbye, but he had a hunch he didn't have much time to lose in finding Fellone. He waded through the crowded street, trying his best not to be overwhelmed setting foot in his first city after six years. It was unreal. There were so many people here. So many colors. So many sounds and smells. When along the shore, he'd sometimes imagined the waves were crowds of people, but this sea was so much different, with individual voices, shouts, and conversations that he merely had to focus on to hear. Aromas he'd forgotten existed triggered long-lost memories, even if they were mixed in unfamiliar combinations. Cooked meats competed with rotting refuse, steamed rice with wood smoke, unwashed bodies with perfumes. Men and women jostled him as they passed, none of them so much as looking him in the face, oblivious to the special significance of this stranger in their midst.

This is a city six hundred years in the past. This is what no history book, what no movie can truly capture. This is real.

Staring at living history right before his eyes threatened to push him to the point of tears. His feet brought him to the end of the block before he remembered his purpose. He shook his head and focused. Looking around, he searched for someone who might have been by the gate earlier in the morning. The guards were obvious candidates, but he'd rather leave them as a last resort. He instead approached a young fruit seller nearby.

"Four coppers a basket," the woman said as he approached. "If you want to complain about the prices, take it up with the Council for starting a war."

He was flattered she thought he could pay at all. He fished in his bag as if looking for money. "Did you happen to see a girl with purple-tinted hair and a crutch come into the city this morning?"

"Don't remember." The woman didn't even spend a second to think.

He turned around to find someone else. There was a shoe cleaner across the street. Retyar walked up as he busily scrubbed mud off the boots of a pudgy merchant.

"If you're tired of her walking all over you, the answer's just to stop giving in," the shoeshine said. "Buying her new dresses every week, getting her those premium meats every evening, letting her gallivant across the province with your finest carriage whenever it strikes her fancy—it'll drive you to the poor house!"

"I can't just stop it all!" the merchant said with a whine. "She'll hate me if I do that. 'What's the point of being a merchant's wife if I can't do anything with the money?'"

"Well, tell her she won't be a merchant's wife much longer if she doesn't learn some moderation."

The merchant puffed, his face a picture of anguished despair.

Retyar stepped in. "Excuse me, would you happen to have seen a girl with purple-tinted hair and a crutch enter the city sometime this morning?"

The shoe cleaner's gaze went to his boots without even visiting his eyes. "Six continents, those are a mess! I've half a mind to take my brush to these things even if you haven't the coin to pay me. It's criminal letting you sully the streets like that."

Retyar smiled reluctantly. "Thank you for the offer, but I don't have the time. About the girl . . . ?"

"Wasn't even wearing shoes, that one. So wild she'd even give my friend's wife here a run for her money."

The merchant spluttered. "Look here. Pushy is one thing, but calling her wild is something else entirely!"

"See, it's that attitude as lets her have her way with everything."

"Excuse me, but the girl," Retyar said.

The shoeshine waved his arm in a vaguely westerly direction. "Went that way, but it was near an hour ago."

"Thank you." Retyar pushed back into the crowd to follow Fellone's trail.

"Dancer is a silly name," Charva said as she and Ersch navigated Three Corners' streets. He'd been the one responsible for thinking up her cover when they'd hastily formulated their plan.

Ersch grinned. "It suits you, if you'll beg my pardon."

"When you marry and have kids, let your wife do the naming."

"That's no fun."

The South Corner wasn't hard to find. Three Corners was one of Leverie's older cities, enough so that it had a distinct Old Quarter, surrounded by the original three-sided wall. After winding through streets flanked by one and two story brick buildings, they came to an iron bar archway crowned with a crescent moon. Inside, the Moonsleet Courtyard spread a comfortable twenty paces across, its far side situated against the outside of the old wall, the rest of it bordered by a teal-painted gathering house with wooden awnings.

Her father's agent wasn't yet there. The only others present were a pair of old men playing a game of fortress in the far corner. Charva and Ersch took up a table and bench beneath one of the awnings to wait. The smell of frying eggs and fish wafted to her nose, making her wish they had time for a more decent breakfast than the stale travel cakes she'd been made to endure.

"Wonder why it's called Moonsleet," Ersch said.

Charva shrugged. "Enchanting, wherever it came from."

A man entered the courtyard, dressed in unassuming workman's clothes. He spotted them immediately and approached with a casual swagger. "Dancer, nice to see you here early."

Charva straightened. "Ensam, I came as quickly as I could after hearing of your business offer. Are you ready to show us the property? Our partners should be with us any moment."

"I passed them on the way in," Ensam said. "I'll take you right there."

They left the courtyard and wound through the populated main streets, the ckols trailing a good distance behind. Although she was sure Ensam would give them a heads-up when they were close to their mark, Charva couldn't help keeping an eye on the crowds for the face of the hardened mercenary she'd seen those weeks ago in Creedport. She felt at her daggers and sword, lifted the scarf a little higher over her face, then chided herself. *Rein in your nerves, Charva.*

Ensam's path took them through the walls into the Old Quarter. Many of the buildings looked newer, with clean paint and smooth exteriors, but others were absolutely ancient. Sagging walls with crooked windows. Doors darkened from years of service, sitting in frames of splintering wood. Stone thresholds worn down the center in inch-deep depressions. Despite it all, those buildings were filled with as much life as any of their neighbors, if not more.

"Ever been to Three Corners before?" Ensam asked.

Charva shook her head. "First time."

"Not a bad place. Might look a tad rundown in spots, but the people are good, and Crenden Pundur's rule is easy."

"How long have you been assigned here?"

"Not so much assigned as recruited," he said quietly. "My home's on the east side. Your father pays good coin for me to keep him abreast of the local markets. At least, that's what this used to be all about."

"I'm sorry to involve you in something so dangerous."

"Don't be. This is the most meaning my job's ever given me. Just make sure you catch the eels who started this war." He suddenly put his hand out, stopping them in their tracks. A teenage boy waved from the next corner up ahead. "Here we are. The fellow should be just around this bend."

"That boy's the one you have on the mercenary's tail?" Ersch demanded, voicing Charva's own concerns.

"The lad's smart and quick on his feet," Ensam said defensively.

Ersch shook his head, muttering. Charva put a hand on his shoulder. "We're taking things from here anyway. Ensam, your report said the mercenary's alone?"

"Been watching him three days now. Hasn't talked to anyone who looks like a warrior."

They came up on the corner, where the youth stood peeking at the street beyond. He glanced at them as they arrived. "Hey, Dancer." His forced casual tone betrayed the kick he was getting from his role. "Been real quiet this morning. The scarred man's just lounging about watching the palace."

Charva looked around them at the moderately busy street, conscious of how painfully obvious the youth's clandestine activities were to every passerby. *Well, he's not been spotted yet.* She stood behind him and peeked out herself.

Retyar asked around some more and had an easier time getting pointed after Fellone. With how fast she got around, her leg must be healing better than he'd given credit.

A few minutes after leaving the marketplace, the directions had him lost in a maze of painted brick walls. He wished he'd gotten a good look of the place from outside, preferably at an elevation. He had little idea of how big the city even was.

Eventually, he came upon a wall far older than the buildings leading up to it. He knew it immediately for what it was. In Govunari, any city with a history had an old wall that marked the early city limits. The moment he laid eyes on it, he also realized he'd been going about this the wrong way. He'd been so overwhelmed after getting off the wagon he'd forgotten Fellone's objective. She had to be heading to the palace, where she'd find Crenden Pundur, a friend of the Redleafs. Logically, the palace would be here in the old quarter.

Retyar stepped through the open gate into a neighborhood layered with age. Oddly enough, it was here that he got his biggest dose of nostalgia. The old quarters of cities back home had always been old, and this felt like walking right into one of them. There were no power lines or antennas or traffic signs, but those were minor absences he could ignore. If he forgot everything that had brought him here, he could let himself believe this was simply a district of Crystal Ebb left behind in the push to modernity. If he left these old walls, he could be back in his own time. Maybe, just maybe, all this nonsense could be over, fading away like some strange dream.

He stopped himself before the delusions could take further hold. If he let himself get dragged down that path, he'd end up as bad a wreck as in his first year. No, he had to focus on finding Fellone.

A courier gave him directions to the palace and he made it within sight of the gates. He hoped he wasn't too late. His search earned him a glimpse of two familiar faces. The man and woman from the wagon were standing at a corner, eyeing a nearby warehouse. He chuckled to himself at meeting them again so soon, but he didn't have time to say hi. If Fellone was already at the palace—

A mountain of tension drained out of him as he spotted her. The girl was at the same corner as the wagon people, hobbling past them toward the palace gate down the road. Six continents, he'd made it in time!

But he wasn't out of the woods yet. How was he going to confront her? She'd certainly make a scene. There were plenty of people around, including the palace guards. Not only that, but Fellone also had his pistol. Would she pull that on him? He didn't think the girl had it in her to do something like that, but then why did she take it in the first place?

Well, I'll just have to try. He stepped forward.

The mercenary was easy to spot. He was seated on a warehouse's front step, elbows on his knees, eyes focused away from them down the street. Like the boy said, the avenue had a good view of the palace. Specifically, the front gate two blocks down. She squinted at the man, trying to determine if it was the same person she remembered. The profile looked the same, but she couldn't be completely sure from this distance.

"What's the plan?" Ersch asked.

"First, have the other ckols do a careful sweep of the area just to be sure he's really alone. Once they're done, they'll cover the other angles. I don't think we should do the capture here. Too many people around, too close to the palace. We'll wait till he moves, keep a circle around him, and strike when the opportunity arises."

Ersch nodded and started signaling the ckols. Charva continued watching the mercenary. She felt sure now that this was him. The way he carried himself, the thick cloak that would easily conceal an armor breastplate, and his fixation on the palace all added up. Once they captured him, they'd finally start getting some answers.

She was so intent on their target that she didn't notice the girl with the crutch hobbling along the street until she was right in front of the warehouse. Charva frowned and leaned forward. Hadn't the Falconian been looking for a girl with a crutch? *Of all the places!*

No time to dwell on coincidences. She wished she were under circumstances where she could try reuniting the two of them, but she didn't have the luxury of getting sidetracked. They'd just let her pass on.

Except that wasn't what happened. The girl hobbled near the mercenary, then did a double take and stopped. The mercenary turned his head to the raggedy child and froze. The two of them stared at each other just long enough for Charva to realize something very bad had just happened.

"Embers! We need to move!"

Retyar quickened his strides, intent on catching Fellone before she got to the end of the block. His sudden haste brought him colliding with a man in a dark cloak. Retyar caught his balance and muttered an apology. The man hurried on with nothing more than an annoyed grunt. It looked like he started pulling something from inside his cloak, but Retyar turned back to Fellone.

In the course of his little incident, the girl had come to a halt in front of the warehouse. She was staring down at a man sitting on its steps. The man jumped to his feet with a shout, "You!"

The mercenary shouted at the girl and everything happened at once.

The girl pulled something from the bag at her side and pointed it at him.

Charva jumped out of cover and reached into the folds of her cloak for her sword. "Now!"

The Falconian appeared out of nowhere, dashing like mad with that stick of his in hand.

Ensam fell, clutching a crossbow bolt lodged in his chest.

And a naked blade swung right at Charva's face.

Chapter 67

Retyar didn't know at first why he reached for his rifle. An instinct, perhaps. The next moment, the man at the warehouse steps had a sword in hand. The man slapped Fellone's gun aside and raised her by the front of her dress. Retyar couldn't see his face, but he could make out the fear and anger and hatred in Fellone's as she swatted with her crutch. "Murderer!" she screamed.

The man raised his blade. "I don't know how you survived, girl, but you're not—"

Retyar swung his rifle with all the momentum of his charge. The man saw it coming. He threw Fellone to the cobbles and twisted his blade to block. Retyar's rifle stock clashed with the sword, braced with an armored forearm to stop it in the air inches from the man's scarred face. He kicked Retyar in the gut, sending him sprawling on his back. Adrenaline drowning out the pain, Retyar rolled away from a slash and bounced to his feet.

The man didn't let off. Retyar barely caught another slash with his rifle, the fabric cover flying free as the blade scraped down the barrel. A follow-up thrust cut through the outer part of his cloak, sending him dodging sideways. His hand fumbled for the charging handle on his rifle and he cursed at his unpreparedness. He was going to die here. If only he'd gone in ready to shoot!

The scarred man sent another swing at Retyar's neck, and he knew the moment he saw it coming that he'd be too late to block. Mid-attack, a wooden crutch clobbered the man in the back of the head, throwing his aim so the blade only sheared a few whiskers off Retyar's beard. Retyar took his chance and cracked the butt of his rifle into his opponent's face. The man's head snapped back, blood spurting from a broken nose as he fell hard to the cobblestones.

Retyar stood gasping over his fallen enemy. He looked at Fellone, who loomed nearby, her tiny shaking hands holding tight to her crutch. The girl glared at him defiantly. "Well?"

The clash of steel drew his attention up the road. For some reason, the wagon people had gotten into a fight of their own. One man lay in the street, blood pooling from a crossbow bolt to the chest. Shouts rose from the opposite direction. The palace guards saw something was up.

Retyar grabbed Fellone and lifted her off her feet, then ran down a side street as fast as his legs would carry him.

Steel screeched on steel as the attacker's sword slid down Ersch's blade, the edge slicing the air right in front of Charva's eye. She jerked her head back and pulled her rapier from its scabbard even as the cloaked mercenary dodged away from the point of Ersch's weapon.

Ersch shouted something at her as he pressed into his counterassault, but Charva couldn't hear the words. *One inch and I'd be dead.* All she could see was the blade that had almost hacked into her skull. *Just one inch.*

Something tugged at the hem of her skirt. She broke out of her paralysis and looked down at Ensam. His chest shuddered with frantic, uneven breaths as his tunic, pinned to his body by the crossbow bolt, soaked through with his blood. Crossbow bolt . . . . Where was the crossbowman?

She raised her eyes. If he was already set for another shot

—

The crossbow was only one of her worries. More cloaked men were assaulting the rest of her ckols, two of whom were already down. A quick count told her she was outnumbered. Ersch only had one opponent at the moment, but two more raced out of an alleyway in their direction.

Flame and embers, this had been a bad idea.

But she was already here. She tried to will her sword hand to stop shaking. It didn't work. She tugged free from Ensam's grip anyway, cut her skirt down the center, and lunged into the fray.

The reinforcements got within striking range. She parried the blade of the first to make a thrust for Ersch's exposed back. His sword flailed aside, but something else rammed her hard between the ribs. Against her natural instinct to back off, she shifted her momentum into the threat. A second mercenary's eyes went wide at seeing his sword fail to run her through. She slashed her dagger at his face, felt the sickening scrape of the blade's edge against his skull as it sliced his forehead.

The mercenary jumped back, but Charva was open to the first one. His sword lashed out, cutting across her chest. It did nothing more than expose the mail shirt beneath, and before he could do anything else, Ersch's opponent suddenly tumbled into him. Her ckol had the man in some sort of arm lock that let him twist the mercenary about with ease. Charva would have laughed if these people weren't still trying to kill her.

"Get this guy off me!" the mercenary cried as Ersch maneuvered him around as a shield. The first backup fellow glanced between the ckol and Charva, wary of making another move. The other one kept his distance also, his hand pressed to his forehead trying to staunch the blood flowing into his eyes.

Shouts arose from up the street. The city guard were almost on the scene. "S-s-stop where you are and . . . and lay down your arms!"

The mercenary who'd slashed her grabbed his injured friend by the arm and ran. Ersch's captive struggled helplessly. "Hey!"

Charva assessed the current situation. The guard were only several building lengths away. She certainly wasn't chasing after the fleeing mercenaries. The rest of the ambushers were breaking off like the first, leaving a handful of her father's ckols still standing. The scarred mercenary was nowhere to be seen, and neither were the crippled girl and the Falconian. Ensam looked like he was still alive, if gravely injured. The boy knelt weeping at his side.

She smacked their captive on the head with the hilt of her sword, knocking him cold. She pointed to the ckols. "Have them carry him to the wagons!"

Ersch shoved the body into one of the other ckols' hands. The man set off immediately. Charva faced Pundur's men. "I'm starting to suspect we didn't plan this thing out too well."

The city guard were on them, or rather had come to a halt a few paces away. They had swords in hand, but in their wide-eyed, nervous regard of the bloody scene they were a far cry from the hardened foes she had just fought.

She could buy the others some time.

"You," Charva pointed to the youngest looking of the lot with her sword. He jumped the moment she spoke. "The man here's been hit by a crossbow. He needs a surgeon."

A senior guard wiggled his foot into proper sword stance. "Now wait here. Who—"

"Aiv Chahai." She wiped her dagger on her skirt and slipped it back up her sleeve. "I'm on a special assignment from the Council." She turned back to the younger guard. "What are you waiting for?" she barked. "Can't you see this man's bleeding to death?"

The man saluted and ran off. Any fear the older guard had now disintegrated. "You don't have authority over my men!" he said, his face red. "And who's that fleeing behind you? Who're they carrying? They need to return this instant! The lot of you are to be taken in for questioning!"

"That would be impeding Council business." Charva paced, trying to discourage anyone from flanking around her, but also conscious that there was still a crossbowman out there somewhere. She prodded the spot where she'd been struck in the ribs and winced. That was going to hurt for a while.

"My master's the crenden, not the Council," the guard said. "Take it up with him." His men started to fan out.

Charva sighed. Time to be stupid again.

She leaped forward and swung wildly with her sword.

The guardsmen rooted themselves and raised their weapons to block. Instead of letting her blade connect, she slipped straight though them and dashed up the street. Ersch used his fancy grapples to tangle up two of the guards, and then was right on her heels.

"Stop 'em!"

I need to quit putting myself in these—ow! Charva's foot kicked something hard that went spinning across the stones in front of her. "Flame and embers!" She ignored the throbbing pain in her toe and sprinted down an alleyway, rebounding with her shoulder off a brick wall and only speeding up from there. Bursting into another populated street, she almost hit a woman walking by. Ceramic crashed on stone as the woman dropped her jug of milk and screamed. Charva really wanted to sheath her sword, but she dared not slow down. *I hope no one decides to play hero by confronting the armed madwoman.*

For instance, someone like the new trio of guardsmen hurrying up the street in front of her. With one look, they stopped and drew their swords. Charva locked her feet, setting her boots scraping as she slid to a halt. Ersch clamped his hand around her wrist and pulled her into another alleyway.

Rotting refuse squished underfoot and shouts followed behind. Charva struggled to keep her balance as she flew over ground slick with putrid-smelling waste. Once or twice, she almost slashed Ersch by flailing about. At least she heard the guardsmen having the same trouble chasing them.

They swung around a corner. The new alley split into several branches, and she revisited her memory of the nearby streets to figure how many were likely dead ends. Most all probably, so she just picked one at random. Her eyes latched onto a set of low-hanging clotheslines. Maybe they could climb? *No, won't work.*

Another desperate thought occurred to her. She leaped and snatched some clothing off a line as they went past, then pulled Ersch into an alley branch the moment their pursuers came in sight. She felt relief at seeing the path opened into another street. They hurtled into the open, but Charva reeled Ersch to a halt. She tore off her scarf, draped the stolen cloth over her shoulders, and dropped her sword behind a barrel. Ersch saw what she was doing, but didn't have a disguise on hand. Instead, he simply dropped by a nearby threshold and curled up on his side like a drunk with a hangover.

Charva started walking back the way they'd come. She barely took two steps before the guardsmen spilled out of the alley. They hesitated, looking both ways along the street, then latched on to another alley close enough for their quarry to have disappeared into.

"There! Into that one!"

She put her hand to the wall and leaned over to catch her breath the moment they were gone. She heard Ersch laugh.

"That actually worked!" he said, standing and dusting himself. "What would you have done if the alley were a dead end?"

Charva shrugged. "Tried the other oldest trick in the book? Two lovers on a furtive meeting? A little disappointing we didn't go that route. Would have been my first kiss."

Ersch coughed, his face turning red, and he quickly reached behind the barrel to retrieve her sword. "Back to the wagons, then?"

It caught up to her what she'd just said. *Why does my tongue do this to me?* She accepted her weapon back and slid it in its sheath, turning away as she did to hide her burning cheeks. "Truly, let's."

City folk gave Retyar odd looks as he zipped past, but these quickly turned to suspicious glares as screams echoed from the scene of the fight. He turned into an alley and forced himself to slow as he twisted through several corners. Fellone remained conspicuously silent until he came to a halt in a narrow space between a pair of two-story buildings and set her down, a hand firmly on her shoulder to keep her from running. Or, well, limping.

"You should have killed him," the girl said. Anger still burned in her violet eyes.

"Because killing someone in broad daylight in the middle

of a populated city is such a great idea." Retyar shook his head at the craziness he'd gotten into. Again. "What in the six were you doing pulling a *gun* on someone? Do you—wait. The pistol. Did you get it back?"

Fellone crossed her arms. "You picked me up before I had a chance."

Retyar fell back against the alley wall and put his hand over his eyes. "Raze it. That . . . . Raze it! The city watch will already be all over that place."

"You should have killed him," Fellone repeated. "He was with the people who murdered everyone."

He glanced back the way they'd come. "What? Really?" He shook his head and rammed the butt of this rifle into the ground. "That doesn't matter. You recklessly interfered with the timeline. What were you thinking? I thought you understood what was at stake."

"Avlan has blue eyes."

The statement was so out of nowhere that Retyar could only stare.

"The encyclopedia talks about Avlan the Goldeye, who visits the Vron capitol in 4795 bearing tribute to the imperial Senate. It doesn't say where he's from, only that he amused the Vron with his golden eyes. Well, Avlan is Ellaniel's son, and her eyes are gold, but his eyes are blue like Arzan's."

Retyar blinked, his mind starting to catch up. "That—"

"Things are already changed from your history, but none of the scary stuff you explained has happened. You're still here. The world's still here. But things are changed."

The girl's eyes were alight with purpose. Her tone challenged him to argue with her.

Instead, Retyar laughed. He couldn't help it. A ten-year-old had done what he couldn't in half a decade. She'd gone and falsified a time paradox. Or maybe confirmed one. Either way, she had the gumption to act.

"So then, what? You're trying to get to Crenden Pundur and have him take you back to Senkani?"

The question seemed to throw her off balance. She'd certainly expected him to dispute her evidence, not challenge her objective. In an instant, her expression went back to its belligerent resolve. "I'm going to stop the empire."

Retyar sighed and chuckled. He should have guessed she'd dream big. He shook his head at the absurdity of everything, then grabbed her by the arm and started leading the way to a main avenue.

Fellone started to struggle. "Where are you taking me?"

He looked at her. "We're off to see the crenden of Three Corners."

Charva and Ersch escaped the city without pursuit. A good distance out, one of her ckols waved them off the main road. They turned into a copse of wood far from any farmhouse, where they found the rest of their surviving party. Their captive was conscious, face down with a ckol's boot on his head and a cloth stuffed in his mouth. Another ckol bound the man's hands and feet. The mercenary's cloak was off, his steel breastplate lying in the dust nearby, next to a sword and knife.

The ckol with his heel on the prisoner looked up at their approach, his eyes registering her and searching behind her. "What of the others?"

"We saw no signs of being followed," Charva said.

"What about Hlarce and Bearns?"

The ckol who'd waited for them on the road came up from behind. "Just them and the driver."

Charva realized they were talking about the ckols they'd lost in the city. "If they live, we have to hope the city guard will care for them."

"This rat's son better be worth it. They even got Rebarus in the leg. Didn't notice till we were out of the the city. He's bleeding hard." The ckol finished binding up their prisoner with a harsh tug. The rope tightening put a literal sound of tension in the air.

"This will be." Charva knelt next to the captive. "Sit him up."

The ckols roughly lifted him into position. The mercenary flicked his eyes at them as they took up position at his sides, their hands on his shoulders.

Charva focused on irises that were on the verge between dark blue and violet. Moshon, but that didn't say much. She sniffed, picking up the sent of ale.

"Splashed a drink on him," one of the men explained. "Pretended we were bringing him home from a night at the tavern."

She nodded and stood, her jaw tight. She'd never interrogated someone. What was she willing to do to make him talk? Did she have it in her to get brutal? She thought of all the blood being shed on the mercenaries' account. This man was a murderer. It was the aristocracy's place to punish such crime, wasn't it? *I've killed. I can do other things if the need arises.*

But she was also an Aiv Chahai.

She remembered seeing Ellaniel kill the wounded soldier outside Senkani and felt sick. No, the codes had to be upheld. Bluffs or sweet talk it was.

She bent back down and pulled out the man's gag. "Right, then. You're not the exact person we came here for, but you'll do. Let's have a chat."

The mercenary pressed his lips tight. She tried to gauge his age and figured something between thirties to mid-forties. She wondered how many situations like this he had been in over the course of his career.

"I'll cut straight to the main question. I know you're part of the group that assassinated Crenden Hashan and attacked the Redleafs. Who do you work for?"

"Crenden Thrake," he said, expression flat.

Charva drew one of her daggers and rested the blade beside his neck. "Oh, please. You know who I am. That spiel won't get you anywhere."

"It's the truth. That's what you wanted, right?"

Charva leaned closer, twisting the dagger's point to prick the skin. She put all the threat and venom she could into her voice, "Who hired you to start a war?"

Blood trickled down to the mercenary's tunic. He didn't flinch. "You're in over your head, lass."

"I'm in a position to kill you right here," Charva said. "You'd have it coming." She withdrew the blade. "But I know you're only a mercenary. What you do, you do for coin. I'm willing to let you go, trade your life for information. Surely your contract isn't worth dying over."

The mercenary smirked. "You don't have it in you to kill a man in cold blood."

"Cold blood? Is that what you call executing a murderer?" She shrugged. "Look, what your company is being paid, I'll triple it. It'll all go to you. No splitting it with your mates."

The mercenary's smirk stayed in place. He didn't speak.

"Loyalty to your fellows? I'll promise I won't go after them, only your employer. You'll get rich, you and your friends'll get the chance to leave the aristocracy."

Still he didn't speak.

"What more do you want, mercenary?"

"You can't afford my price," the man said.

"At least name it. My House has deep pockets." She slid her dagger across his tunic, slashing the fabric. "Don't tell me you prefer us to get the information from you the hard way? I'm warning you, the deal's only going to get worse from here."

The smile of his stayed on his face even after a crossbow bolt cracked through the back of his skull. Charva fell on her butt as his head lolled forward and his body went limp. Ersch and another ckol jumped to put themselves between her and the source of the attack. The other two ran to catch the crossbowman. She saw it was already too late. The cloaked figure at the woods' edge was mounting his horse and spurring it away. He reached a full gallop before any of the ckols even got close to his hiding spot.

Charva recovered from her shock, which gave way to frustrated rage. With a scream, she snatched up the mercenary's sword and hacked it into a tree. The culprit behind the war had been in her grasp!

"Unhitch and saddle the horses," she ordered. "We're riding after him. We'll search the whole countryside if we have to."

"It'll be right into another ambush," one of the ckols said. "We'd be completely crushed this time."

She bit her lip, repressing the urge to shout at him. He was right. They'd barely survived their last encounter. It was foolhardy to try again when the enemy knew they were coming. This lead was a dead end for them.

"Senkani, then," she said. "We'll ask Ylnavar about the letter." Funny that it actually felt safer riding into a war.

The ckol nodded, but with a bitter scowl. He'd given wise advice, but it didn't make him happy. He glanced towards where their injured companion he'd mentioned earlier lay by the base of a willow. "One of us should stay with Rebarus."

"You'll all stay," Charva said. "See if you can do anything for the ones we left in the city. Get everyone to Creedport and report to my father."

The ckols saluted.

Charva and Ersch went to their wagon and climbed aboard. "We'll double back towards the city and then take a round-about path to Senkani," she told the driver. "See anything suspicious on the road and turn us around immediately."

"Yes, your grace."

"Don't like this feeling we're running with our tails between our legs," Ersch said.

Charva held tight to her seat and kept watch behind them for any sign of chase as the driver clicked the horses into motion. "It doesn't make sense. They're a mercenary company. They shouldn't be so devoted to their job that they'd be this tight-lipped and willing to kill their own."

"What do you think he meant? How big is this conspiracy? Maybe there really is more than one crenden involved."

"I don't like the idea of that." Either way, she had to keep forging on. This plot was already killing hundreds and destroying the country, and with the mercenaries operating in Three Corners, she got the sense they weren't yet through creating trouble.

Ersch sat back and grunted. He pulled his bag around and pulled something out, tossing it atop his discarded cloak.

"What's that?" Charva asked.

"That thing you kicked your foot into when we started running from the guard. I think it belonged to the girl the scarred man grabbed."

She'd completely forgotten about that. She leaned over and picked it up. It was a sort of metal contraption the likes of which she'd never seen before. "You look at it yourself?"

Ersch shook his head. "First time taking it out of my bag."

The only vaguely recognizable part of the object was the thing that looked a little like a crossbow trigger. "You think it's a weapon?"

"Makes sense. She didn't look at all happy with that friend of ours."

Charva held it so that her finger rested inside the trigger hoop. Her hand fit comfortably in the grip. "It's got a lot of complicated shapes." She pointed it at the road behind them and pulled the trigger. The mechanism gave, but nothing happened, not even a click.

"Probably just the mount for a crossbow," Ersch said. "You see the hole in front? Maybe the bow frame locks in there?"

Charva peered in the hole. "She clearly meant to use it as it is, though."

"She was also a kid under duress," he pointed out.

With a shrug, she tossed it back onto the cloak. "Really expensive crossbow, if that's what it's for."

Ersch scratched his chin. "Maybe she stole it from the mercenaries. That crossbowman they have is an amazing shot. Must have a quality weapon or set of weapons."

"Be something interesting to see when we finally get them." She tapped her foot, already impatient to reach Senkani.

Chapter 68

The Council's attack came at dawn.

It wasn't obvious. The troops didn't marshal in sight of the wall. There was no rallying battle cry. Instead, it started underground, with picks and shovels, the final stage in a weeks-long process. Ellaniel only knew it was happening when a messenger ran up the steps to meet her on the battlement.

"Your grace, we hear them at the foundations."

She held her ear to the merlon and heard the sound herself: metal hammering on stone. She turned, her armor clinking, and looked out at the eastern fields. In the time since the siege's start, the ground had become overrun with weeds, the greenery masking bodies that none but the carrion birds had bothered to attend. The Senkani knew, had known since the start, that the Council had six tunnels leading down the slope towards the walls. They tracked the progress by listening and by watching for sagging soil and stunted plants. Ellaniel had taken Arzan's advice about it to heart. Let the Council fully commit. Let them waste their time and their treasury, only to crush their efforts at the last moment.

In the literal sense of the word.

"It's time. Destroy them," she ordered.

The command relayed itself along the wall and the men sprang into action. Wood and sinew groaned and locks clicked as soldiers put tension to the ballistae. The wall rumbled underfoot as others dragged and scraped heavy stones into position. Ellaniel drew in a deep breath, waiting for the result of all their preparations. The men lifted the stones up atop the defenses. They balanced the blocks on the battlements, let them teeter a long moment, then sent them toppling. She leaned out just as the nearest one thudded hard into the ground, buckling the soil and sinking deep.

The ballistae launched their heavy bolts with a snap. The missiles slammed into the ground with powerful thumps, precisely aimed for the sapping tunnels. They pounded the fields as fast as the crews could load the artillery, until Ellaniel saw the dirt shift and crumple.

The soldiers atop the wall cheered, and she smiled in grim satisfaction. One more victory for Senkani.

Someone issued a cry of alarm. "Look to the enemy camp!"

Ellaniel turned and saw the Leverie forces flooding out from behind the front line of tents. Thousands of their soldiers poured down the slope with shields and ladders.

"Archers to position!" she shouted. "Swords and pikes ready on the ramparts!"

The clamor of arms and armor filled her ears as men hastened to obey. The ballistae clicked on their mounts as their crews adjusted aim.

"Loose arrows when in range!"

She watched with calm anticipation the enemy force trampling across the overgrown fields. The Leverie had broken against their walls before. They would do so again.

Arzan watched the enemy army charging in the distance while he himself sat safe on the balcony outside his study. He heard the faint sounds of battle, the murmur of battle cries. This far away, Avlan easily drowned out the noise playing with his building blocks on the floor.

"She'll be fine," Vigkhon said from behind Arzan's chair. "The walls are impregnable to the likes of the Council."

All it takes is a well placed arrow. A moment of inattention. He remembered her limp body in the bloody fields of Creedport. "You're right," he said, willing the words to be true. "She'll be fine." Speaking it didn't help him take his eyes off the walls.

"When's Momma coming home?" Avlan asked, looking up from his blocks.

Arzan combed his hand through his son's hair. How backwards this was. It should be the husband going to war while the wife stayed and cared for the children. It shamed him that it had come to this. No matter Ellaniel's arguments, it felt like he'd failed. "Shouldn't be long, Avlan. The Leverie will run away today and she'll be back with us for dinner."

"It's been a long time since she's seen me."

"Only a few days," Arzan said with a smile. "Not even more than a week."

"How many days are in a week?" Avlan asked with a frown.

"Seven."

Avlan counted on his hands. He went through all ten fingers and the Arzan's face dropped. He turned to Vigkhon. "Bring Kalla here."

His cousin arrived within moments. "Yes, my liege?"

He beckoned her close to whisper in her ear, "Kalla, how much time did Ella spend with Avlan while I was gone?"

The corners of her mouth tightened and she gripped her skirt. "Not much."

"What do you mean by 'not much'?"

Kalla avoided his eyes, looking instead at Avlan, and darting away even from him. "Not at all."

The answer left him completely confounded. "Why?"

"I think you should ask her yourself."

Arzan blinked and then shut his eyes. He wished now more than ever that he was there on the wall beside her.

The wall rumbled and a terrific crack snapped the air. Ellaniel swung away from the chaos of repelling the ladders.

A section south of the gate crumbled before her eyes, eaten up in a massive cloud of dust.

"The wall is breached! The wall is breached!"

She caught a runner who'd missed sighting her in all the action. "How did that happen?"

"We misjudged one of the tunnels, your grace. The men were going to drop more stones, but the assault disrupted them."

Six continents, this wasn't supposed to happen.

"Send all reserves to the breach!"

"Yes, your grace." The runner disappeared past the mass of soldiers defending the battlements.

The breach didn't afford the section in front of Ellaniel any relief. The Leverie saw success and redoubled their push. Arrows peppered the wall, forcing the defending archers to cover. Soldiers climbed with better tactics than the first assault, sending alternating men with shields and spears. The Senkani could only hold them off so long before a few of the enemy finally found purchase on the wall. Ellaniel coordinated a company of reinforcements to the areas in most need, but it was too little too late. The Leverie just kept coming, gaining their footholds and inching them ever wider.

"Archers, off the wall and to the rooftops," she ordered. "Everyone else, fall back to defending the towers." She almost gave the command to sabotage the artillery, but remembered their mounts wouldn't let them point into the city.

She looked eastward at the ocean of enemy soldiers massing at the ladders and felt dread seep into her. She realized now how much she'd relied on Leverie cowardice. She saw a line open up in the enemy forces. A covered contraption rolled downhill, aimed straight for the gate. Battering ram.

"Ballistae, target the—" cut herself off. The artillery crews were already in retreat. "I need men with me!"

Screams and shouts drowned out her voice. She assembled her force herself, grabbing soldiers on her way to the nearest tower. They descended with her and rushed to the gate. They arrived with the ram already pounding away, each blow coming with a crack and a tortured groan. Though a dozen soldiers braced the doors, it was only a matter of time before the wood itself splintered apart.

Ellaniel arrayed the men in a shield wall just out of range of the gate's swing. That would give enough space for the Leverie to expose themselves to the archers still up top.

With a snap, the right door came off its hinges and fell atop a set of Senkani. The rest of the men retreated behind the shield wall. A massive cry rose from outside and then the enemy stormed through the gap, scrambling over the mangled beams and crushing those trapped beneath even further. Senkani archers pelted them from above, downing a small handful who then got trampled underfoot by those behind. The very front of the charge faltered as they saw the shield wall, but the men still pouring through forced their advance straight into Senkani steel. The double row of defenders buckled several feet against the crush of men pressing their shields and swords. Ellaniel lent her weight to their back, little though it was.

The left door crashed inward, widening the flow of soldiers. Reinforcements came to bolster the shield wall, just in time to save the line from collapse under the new onslaught. Ellaniel got lost in a storm of thrusting blades and ear-piercing screams. "Hold!" she shouted. "Hold!"

She didn't know how long it went on. When a ckol reached in and pulled her out of the battle, they were at least a hundred feet from the gate. "Your grace, this shield wall won't last much longer. You need to organize the next line of defense."

She looked at the men still in the struggle. They gave way by inches in the span it took to blink. "We need to help them."

"We need to give them a place to fall back."

Ellaniel relented. She chased the ckol up the street, glancing over her shoulder to try and get a sense of the overall battle. Not much could be seen for all the buildings. Not far from the fighting, she found a mass of soldiers running around in confusion. She picked out a reserve sergeant. "Tell me what's happening."

"Much of the wall is lost, your grace. Last I saw, four of the towers were holding, but the rest have fallen and the Leverie are entering everywhere into the city."

"Our remaining towers are getting isolated," another soldier said angrily. "They need relief."

"The towers can hold." Ellaniel removed her helmet long enough to wipe the sweat from her face. "Their role now will be to harass the enemy's rear. How are our archers?"

"On the rooftops, as ordered," the sergeant told her. "It won't be long before their quivers run dry, though, even with the boys running resupply."

"I ordered the reserves to the breach. What became of them?"

Someone else stepped forward. "I just came from that fight. They're still holding the breach, and the streets around it besides."

Ellaniel nodded. She considered having them stay to disrupt the Leverie advance, but unlike the towers those men would be quickly overrun once surrounded. "Tell them they're to withdraw. They're to form up at, um, the Thorshia Wagonhouse crossroads. I want them to barricade every street in that area." She looked to the rest of the men around her. "All of you, we're setting up another shield wall here. Keep the ranks loose enough for men to pass through, but ready to close on my order."

The first shield wall had already crept to within twenty paces. She wondered at how they'd been able to hold the Leverie this long without breaking. She couldn't see past their line of backs, but she heard the massive force they fought, the screams and cries of a thousand men out for blood.

The moment the new formation was ready, she rushed up behind the soldiers still engaged. The noise of battle forced her to scream at the top of her lungs to be heard. "Senkani, fall back! Break and run!" Even with the order, it took her ckols pulling at the men's shoulders to get the message through. The formation broke, some few seeing what was happening, most others only sensing that the wall was disintegrating around them. The last didn't realize anything before the now unopposed Leverie washed past and over them. Ellaniel ran in the center of the retreat, blocking out any guilt for the men she'd just opened to the enemy. She felt the rabid Leverie a mere breath behind her. The instant she swept through the new defensive line, she gave the order to close. Shields snapped in place just in time, halting the enemy with a fresh wall of wood and steel.

The men from the first line staggered to safety, most dropping their equipment and falling to the ground in exhaustion. Ellaniel counted twenty in their number. One near her bowed down and started openly crying, someone's name repeatedly on his lips. Blood covered them all, and their shields were battered almost to pieces. She felt the urge to comfort them, but there was no time. "On your feet! The new wall can't hold them here for long. Get somewhere you won't trip them up."

Movement on the rooftops caught her eye. Several Senkani archers retreated westward, their quivers empty. One paused, looking down at the next street over. He turned to the shield wall and cupped his hands to his mouth. "They're flanking!"

Ellaniel clenched her fists. "How many?"

The archer didn't hear her over the din of battle and continued moving. She summoned her ckols around her. "We need to meet them before they have our backs."

"Your grace, if they're anything like the surge here—"

"Then all is lost anyway." She made for the intersection behind the battle line and rounded the block. Perhaps it would only be a dozen or so. When she came within sight of the enemy, her heart sank. It wasn't as bad as the main avenue, but there were easily a hundred Leverie.

"We can't hold against this many," one of the ckols said. "Street's too wide for the eight of us to form a wall."

Ellaniel drew her sword and steeled her resolve. "Then we don't defend."

"Your grace—"

"You heard me. Raise your sword, ckol."

The approaching Leverie were of lower quality troops, with gambeson and mixed city colors. Only a few of them had shields. She told herself she and her ckols could take them.

The Leverie saw them advancing and slowed, then to her bewilderment came to a complete halt. Those in back shouted out, "Why'd you stop?"

"The Goldeye is here."

The Leverie held their weapons uncertainly, their stances tense. Ellaniel nearly gaped in astonishment. They were afraid.

She smiled. She scared them! Something in that revelation exhilarated her. Sudden confidence spurred her to point her sword at them. "Men of Leverie!" she cried, and she saw some of them flinch at her address. "How despicable you are to break down your neighbor's walls, to tread her streets with swords drawn! How deplorable you are to heed the commands of murderers and betrayers! Have you the decency left in your souls to be men and not animals, to walk away from this evil? Or will I cut you down here, feed these streets with your blood?"

Many of the men glanced uneasily at each other.

"She's just a woman!" someone shouted. "There are only seven ckols with her. Are you more terrified of them or of our crenden's wrath?"

The words prodded a few forward. They banged their swords against their shields. "Come on, you wimps."

Ellaniel dropped the point of her sword to face the ground behind her and advanced in an easy walk. It was the sort of thing her fight instructor had done to her on the first week of training. It had unnerved her then. It did the same thing to the men in front of her now. Those who had stepped up stopped. The rest shuffled backwards. *Six continents, what sort of stories have they started telling about me?*

Whatever they were, she liked it. "I see none of you value your lives."

One of the soldiers roared and charged, raising his sword high like a boy on his first day of training. The ckol left of her lunged in, thrusting his blade through the soldier's padded armor straight into his chest. The rest of the ckols charged as one. They cut down the first row of terrified Leverie with practiced efficiency. The enemy started to break under the sudden onslaught, and Ellaniel gave them the last push. She pounced into the fray, swinging her sword through an opening in a soldier's feeble guard and slicing open his neck. The man dropped his weapon and grabbed at his gushing artery, horror in his dark blue eyes. She kicked him in the chest, knocking him to the ground, and screamed her rage. The mass of

Leverie ran.

Ellaniel watched them flee. She stepped on her fallen opponent, placing the sole of her boot atop his chest as his life drained from his veins. With a laugh, she flicked the blood off her sword. *Let me be your nightmare, oh men without honor.*

Ellaniel put her reputation to use. Senkani held desperately throughout the day, but wherever the Leverie posed the greatest threat, the crendess rushed to the vanguard. Each time the enemy saw her, men slowed in fear, and the effect only built with every encounter. The defenders' morale soared with her presence, and their chanting voices cowed the Leverie even when she wasn't in direct line of sight. She hardly even had to fight, but simply energize the soldiers around her into ferocious assault.

Funny how much sway the mere image of a person could hold.

Even with Ellaniel's new-found power, she couldn't be everywhere. The enemy's sheer numbers inevitably pushed them back. By late afternoon, just after repelling another force of a half hundred trying to round one of their flanks, Ellaniel received news of the former reserves getting forced from their position.

She shook her head in frustration. "We're losing the eastern half of the city. Have everyone fall back to the river. We'll hold the bridges." Those were the last good chokepoints they had. Not only that, if the fighting crossed the river, they would have the women and children to consider. No more empty buildings if they gave ground on the western side. As she calculated her plans, she noticed a plume of dark smoke to the southeast. "What's—"

"Arrows incoming!"

Two ckols raised their shields to cover her just as the missiles landed, bouncing off armor and cobblestones.

Ellaniel pushed the shields out of the way so she could see the enemy archers. They had taken a page out of the

Senkani tactics and sent men up to the rooftops on either side of the street. Meanwhile, a new shield wall advanced down the middle.

"Keep shields raised as we fall back to Central Bridge," she ordered. She pointed to her ckols. "All of you, hide in the buildings. Wait for the archers to cross the rooftops as they chase us, and then slaughter them."

The ckols nodded and set themselves to the task. Ellaniel kept her own shield up as she kept pace with the retreating formation. Several more volleys of arrows rained ineffectively upon them until the archers decided to move up. She peeked around the edge of her shield enough to see the men jumping and climbing from rooftop to rooftop. It wouldn't be long before they came upon the ckols lying in wait.

The columns of smoke from earlier distracted her from the action. She thought they were starting to look bigger. *Six continents—the city's on fire!*

The archers fell into the ckols' trap. Her men jumped atop the thatch and cut a dozen down in an instant. One of the remaining Leverie slipped and tumbled over the edge with a scream, landing headfirst in front of his compatriots' shields. The soldiers paused long enough to dispatch reinforcements into the buildings. The ckols finished off the rest of the archers and withdrew before the Leverie from below could engage.

Ellaniel's eyes flicked repeatedly towards the sky. The smoke grew as she watched. She assessed the angle of the rising plumes, trying to judge the wind's strength and direction. Which way was the fire spreading?

The Senkani line retreated as fast as the Leverie advanced. The ckols came back down to her and she demanded a report.

"At least six hundred in this group, your grace. I saw other units navigating the streets nearby, but we'll reach the bridge before they can converge on us."

"And that fire to the southeast?"

The ckol's face was grim. "Whole area around the wagon house is aflame. Must have happened when they flushed out the men holding there."

As he spoke, the first smell of smoke reached Ellaniel's nose. "Which way does the wind blow?"

"Northerly."

There was hope for Senkani. Costly hope, but hope nonetheless.

"Send word to the city folk. Wet the rooftops along the western bank and hold the bridges at all cost."

The ckol caught on to her intent. "It will be done!"

The smoke thickened as they reached the river and the sun approached the horizon. The Senkani shield wall blocked the western end of the bridge ten ranks deep, bolstered by other soldiers who had fallen back before them as well as youths who'd yet been kept from the action. Up and down the retaining wall, women worked the bucket chains to drench the rooftops.

The Leverie pursuing them halted at the bridge's far side and eyed the defenses. A few archers tested them with arrows to no effect. A pair started to aim at the bucket women, but someone grabbed the men from behind. Ellaniel wasn't sure, but she thought she saw long hair flowing out from under the person's helmet. What—

The Aiv Chahai. That's right, the Council had recruited Watchers.

Good thing ours haven't been interfering with anything.

Her thoughts got drowned in a banging of weapons on shields. The Leverie readied to charge. She glanced up at the smoke. *We need to buy ourselves more time.*

Ellaniel pushed through the shield wall. As before, the sight of her gave the enemy pause. She held up her sword. "What's the matter? Is there no man among you who thinks he can best me?"

She braced her shield just in time to catch an arrow. Its iron head lodged in the wood, the point poking through to stare her in the face. More bows snapped, showering her with arrows. Several thudded into her shield, sending shocks up her arm. One glanced off her leg armor. A shaft shattered against her shoulder plate.

The Senkani archers returned a volley. She heard them hit wood and steel, but they also scored a couple screams.

"Your grace, fall back!"

She lowered her shield just enough to see a trio of Leverie break and charge her. "Hold the line!" she shouted behind her. One of her attackers caught an arrow in the neck and tumbled to the ground in a crash of steel plate. The other two struck as one, assaulting her on either side. She blocked the left with her shield, dodged the blade on the right.

"Save her!"

"Hold!" she howled.

She danced to the side, refusing to be easily surrounded. An arrow swooshed past her head. She blocked a strike, parried another, saw an opening and slashed one man's sword hand. He dropped his weapon with a hiss. Before the other could react to the new dynamic, she rammed him with her shield. That put the second man off balance, but the injured one was now behind her. She jumped back and slammed her pommel in his face. The one in front recovered and charged, but she rebounded and sent a quick thrust through his neck. Blood sprayed as she pulled her sword free and arced it behind her, flicking more blood through the air.

The remaining man retrieved his sword while holding a hand to his broken nose. He just barely got into stance before an arrow lodged in his back, piercing through chain and cloth. Another arrow came from the other side of the bridge, hitting Ellaniel in the chest and shattering against her armor, wood shrapnel bursting from the impact. More missiles flew past as the Senkani and Leverie archers traded shots.

"Your grace!"

Ellaniel relented and retreated. The Senkani opened for her and accepted her back with a deafening cheer.

Her display had the desired effect on the Leverie. Their shield wall remained rooted in place on the eastern end of the bridge. The Senkani took to jeering, but Ellaniel didn't have the energy left to stop them. Thankfully, the enemy stayed put, not brave enough to answer with anything more than arrows and a few counter insults.

The sun dipped below the treeline. Shadow embraced the city and crept up the ever thickening, ever spreading pillar of smoke. As the day's light dimmed, the inferno's glow grew increasingly impressive. Orange flames licked the rooftops of buildings mere blocks away. Smoke stopped being just a smell and now made it harder to breathe. The Leverie finally realized their predicament. Their shouts tapered off, some men coughing and most looking over their shoulders at the coming fire.

We did it. Elated, Ellaniel stepped atop the retaining wall. "This is where it ends, men of Leverie. I'll laugh at your graves after you burn."

The Leverie looked like they had trouble comprehending their fate, but their disbelief turned quickly into terror. They charged, but as a mob rather than an army. They crashed against the Senkani shield wall, hacking wildly, kicking, trying to shove their way through. The Senkani didn't budge, except to strike back with sword and spear tips.

The wind picked up, covering the bridge with smoke and ash while the flames leaped from building to building. The fire reached the river with frightening swiftness. Ellaniel held her capelet to her mouth, her eyes watering. Those Leverie at the far end of the bridge gave up trying to push their way through and started jumping into the water. Senkani archers, freshly restocked with arrows, rained death upon them. Any men with armor thick enough to protect them succumbed to the weight and sank beneath the surface. Soon, Ellaniel had difficulty telling if the red in the water was more from reflected firelight or blood. The roar of the flames mingled with the screams of those trying to escape.

Into the mix of burning wood and thatch came the smell of burnt hair and flesh. She fought the urge to gag at the scent, settling instead with coughing at the smoke. The Leverie gave one final push. They met with no better success than before, and got cut down to the last man. After that, the only battle left for Senkani to fight was against the sparks of flame flying across the river.

Chapter 69

Arzan picked his way through a scene that was one of any ruler's worst nightmares. Senkani had won the siege, but at what cost? Vighkon lent the injured crenden his aid, letting him step gingerly through Senkani's blackened streets. Rain pattered gently around him, the lingering end of the storm that had helped douse the fire shortly after midnight. Rivulets of soot-blackened rainwater flowed between the cobblestones. Steam rose from smoldering wrecks to either side. The many houses with stone walls now looked dead and empty, their roofs gone, their doors gaping, windows shattered. Anything made of wood was now a pile of charred beams.

He said nothing as Vighkon helped him around a corner, sidestepping a pile of stones from a collapsed wall. In this new street, they found the bodies. Scores of Leverie littered the ground. A few were fully burnt, their charred black flesh contrasting with steel mail washed clean of soot by the rains. Others were more whole, with reddened and blistered skin, or else completely untouched, looking like they'd simply lain down to sleep and never awake. It had been the smoke that killed all these, no doubt.

They reached the bridge, where the bodies of those who had tried breaking through the shield wall lay piled up at the western end. A few Senkani were starting the task of clearing a lane. Arzan looked over the side at the muddy current.

"Water's higher than normal, even accounting for the rains."

"Bodies clogging the north grate, my liege," one of the men said. "A few lads are working on it."

Arzan nodded, feeling sick.

He found Ellaniel standing silently nearby. Her helmet was off, her hair plastered to her head and shoulder plates. Dark circles hung under her eyes from a sleepless night, same as Arzan.

"This was where we decided I should know how to fight," she said as Vighkon helped him come beside her.

"What?"

She pointed to the bridge and to the building next to them. They were outside the theater house. "This was where the mob attacked me after we married. It was over there you saved me from getting thrown in the water."

Arzan remembered that incident with embarrassment. That hadn't been a good way to introduce her to his people.

"Now those city folk who hated me see me as their leader," she went on. "I'm one of them, and they proudly follow me." There wasn't irony in her voice. Only reflective contemplation. "Do you think I'm deserving of it?"

He wanted to reach out and hold her, but with only one good arm he couldn't do that and keep himself steady against the captain.

Ellaniel pressed herself to him instead. He tolerated the harsh edges of her armor as she put her head to his shoulder. Even with all the plate, he felt her tension flow out of her. He wished again that he had been there to command instead. The fire and the battle had been terrible enough to behold from a distance. It had to have been horrendous up close. That sort of thing was supposed to be his burden to bear, not hers.

"Does anyone know how the fire started?" he asked.

"Haven't even begun to question anybody," she mumbled. "Don't think I can start until after some sleep."

"Let's get back to the palace, get dry."

"Mmh."

Vighkon cleared his throat. "Will I be carrying the both of you, then?"

Ellaniel chuckled and backed off. "I can still walk, I hope."

They started on their way home, leaving the destruction of

war behind them. Rain plunked on Ellaniel's and Vighkon's armor. He wanted to bring up the issue of her avoiding Avlan, but that could wait. For now, there were more pressing matters. Rest, for one thing, but something else even before that.

"This is a victory, but it's not the end of the war."

Ellaniel had a dangerous look in her eyes. "It's the beginning of the end. The Council's army is broken. Our scouts say their soldiers are fleeing to their home cities. I've already issued the order for our able-bodied men to ready for march tomorrow."

Arzan felt conflicting emotions. He knew this was the time to push back, but he didn't like that Ellaniel had given the order without even consulting him. He certainly didn't like that she would still be leading the army into the next battle. But what was there he could do about it?

"The end of the war's in reach," he said quietly. "Stretch out and take it."

Chapter 70

Charva rode through Highcity's gate in a foul mood, wet and dirty. Her plan to speak with Ylnavar had been set back by the Council's defeat. Even though they tried riding to Senkani through the night, the sudden rainstorm delayed them until after sunrise. By the time they arrived, they found the Council's camp empty and half the city burnt to the ground. Seeing the devastation drove Charva to tears, but she moved on without delay. She might even have caught up with Ylnavar on the road had their wagon not gotten bogged down in the mud. When they broke an axle, she decided to give up on the struggle and saddled the two horses.

Within Highcity's walls, the streets were a bustle of frantic activity. Commoners everywhere were boarding up windows and doorways and carrying away belongings. Arguments punctuated all the clatter, some between husbands and wives, others between commoners and guards. People raced back and forth across the road, as or else blocked the path with carts and possessions, slowing Charva's horse enough that she might as well have dismounted and walked to the palace. With the shifty glances that some gave her, she could be sure her horse wouldn't stay there waiting for her if she did so.

They plowed on through, reaching one of the main crossroads just as an official stepped up onto a crate. "Hear the crenden's words!"

A few of the folks nearest him stopped and listened. Most others merely slowed their activities or ignored the man altogether. Still, it gave Charva and Ersch an opportunity to move a little faster.

"All able bodied men are to report to the walls for rearmament and organization! The crenden grants amnesty to all those who fled the siege of Senkani so long as these men report for the defense of Highcity!"

An egg shot through the air and cracked against the official's face. "To blazes with that!" a man shouted. "No more of us are dying for the sake of these nobles' squabbles."

"The crenden sent my brother to burn in Senkani and it's still not enough for him?" a woman screamed.

"I suppose he'll want more of our daughters as well!

The official fumed as he swiped the egg off. "This is your crenden you insult! By penalty of imprisonment, you are bound to heed his decree!"

Charva prodded her horse to increase speed. This wasn't the sort of scene she wanted to—

A glass bottle slammed the official in the chest, throwing him off balance and toppling him to the ground. He scrambled back to his feet. "Arrest that man!"

She lost all control of her horse as the street erupted in violence. She couldn't even tell if it was the handful of guardsmen or the instant mob that threw the first punches. The air filled with furious shouts and flying debris.

"Order! Order!"

"Out with the guard! Out with Ylnavar!"

Charva yelped as her horse spooked and reared, throwing her off into a family trying to escape the fray. It was all tangled limbs jostling until Ersch found her arm and bulled a path for them through the crowd.

"Our timing could have been better," Ersch said.

Charva dodged a fruit that ricocheted off someone's head. "Flame and embers, who's even fighting who?"

They ran from the mayhem, but not before she saw swords coming out of sheaths, both guardsman and commoner.

"We need to reach Ylnavar immediately."

They came to the palace to find the same guards on duty from her last visit. The men had their hands on their scabbards as they watched the street beyond the courtyard, not giving any heed to the stream of officials hurrying in and out through the open doors. They did note Charva and Ersch as they approached.

"You two!" one of the guards said.

Charva nodded. "Need to see the crenden."

The guard stepped in the way and held up a shaky hand. "W-we're onta your subterfuge. Crenden says no one on the Council authorized an Aiv Chahai to snoop around the palace."

"Yes, I lied to you. Mind letting us through so we can save the country?"

"Not on your life, trickster."

The other guard nudged his friend. "Uh, hey. I think it's starting . . . ."

They all looked towards the city. Commoners were marching up the street, at least a hundred strong or more. No few were geared up in mail and gambeson and holding sword or spear.

The guards abandoned her and ran across the courtyard. "Shut the gate!"

Charva didn't delay. She skipped up the steps into the palace, hurrying past a gaggle of frightened accountants and heading for Ylnavar's study. Guards ignored her and Ersch as they dashed out of the building, armor clattering. One ckol remained outside Ylnavar's door, his stone-faced demeanor in sharp contrast to everyone else. He held up his hand as they drew near. "Wait here, your grace." He knocked at the door without turning. "My liege, Aiv Chahai Charva here to see you."

There was a hard bang inside the room. "Of course it's her! Why not add every annoyance on top of it all!"

"Let's dispense with the unpleasantries, Ylnavar," Charva called. "I have a lead on Hashan's killers."

Angry voices grew audible from outside. The mob was getting larger and closer.

The door swung open. Ylnavar was an uncharacteristic, disheveled mess, his white hair in disarray, his fine clothes wrinkled and mud splattered. "Knowing you, you'll keep pestering me until I hear your ridiculous story. You've a short moment, girl."

Charva stepped inside, pulling the forged letter from her

bag and holding it between them. "How did this come to you?"

He snatched the letter from her hand. "This?" He glanced at his desk. "How did—the guards said—you came in here and spied on me? You petty thief!"

"Yes and yes. Punish me later. For now, I need to know who gave you this forgery."

The voices in the city steadily grew in volume. Charva could start making out words, and they were not favorable to the crenden.

Ylnavar scowled and shook his head, though at the mob or at her she couldn't tell. Likely both. "'Forgery'? So now you seek to convince me of your father's innocence by saying his claim of innocence is fake. Your reasoning boggles the imagination. Out of here with you."

Charva jumped as a rock sailed through the window, spraying glass all across the carpet. Ylnavar whirled and thrust his head into the hall. "Why are these ingrates not already dealt with? The city guard are to put the imbeciles down!"

An official came running up the passage and stopped before the crenden, huffing from the exertion. "The guard are overwhelmed. The entire populous is up in arms against you, my liege!"

"What?!"

"Th-they're rebelling against the call to re-mobilize. Our men issuing the decree have all been lynched."

"Are they insane? The Redleafs are readying their army as we speak. They're probably already on the road."

"And that army is coming for House Leverie," Charva said. "Why should they die again for your skin?"

Ylnavar thrust a bony finger into his chest. "I am their rightful leader! The men marching to our city are criminals and fiends!"

Another stone flew through one of the remaining windows. More missiles pelted the building's exterior. The shouting became impossible to ignore.

"It's your fault they're after us!"

"You killed my sons!"

"Murderer! You sent my daughter to her death!"

"Take responsibility for this, crenden!"

Ylnavar finally listened to them with her. His open rage sank into threatening stillness. Slowly, he went to his desk and sat.

"Highcity is no longer yours, Ylnavar," Charva said.

The crenden gripped his seat's armrests. "Fools. *Fools!*"

Charva stepped up to his desk and placed her palms atop it. "Who delivered the letter from my father?"

Ylnavar shook his head and glared at the broken windows, at the stones and refuse assaulting his carpets. For a moment, she thought he might not have heard her. "A regular messenger," he said. "Who else?"

"Where can I find him? What's his name?"

He barked a disdainful laugh. "You think I would remember which one? Even if I did, there'd be no finding him in all this."

Charva clenched her jaw. Another dead end. She felt Ersch's hand on her shoulder. "My liege, we need to leave."

She nodded and turned.

"You can try Roth," Ylnavar said, stopping her in her steps. "He was the first to receive a letter from Thrake, in time to bring it to the Council's attention in Woodwise. In fact, you should be able to try anyone. It seems copies of that letter went out to every crenden."

The new lead renewed Charva's hope. "Thank you, Speaker." She left the study and was several paces gone when Ylnavar called out to her again.

"You're chasing shadows, girl. Your father's to blame for all of this."

A loud crash punctuated his words.

"They're in the palace!"

Charva and Ersch ran amidst a current of terrified clerks and weeping servants heading for the rear exits. She heard the mob rampaging through the halls, smashing glass and furniture, and shouting for the crenden's head.

Palace staff clogged the back doors as they all tried getting out at once, locking the two of them inside as the mob's shouts grew closer. Ersch drew his sword. "Make way for her grace!"

His efforts only resulted in more screams and desperate

fighting to get out. A score of city folk with weapons rounded the corner behind them. "Grab them! Let none of Ylnavar's minions escape!"

Charva bared her blade and pressed her back to the servants pushing at the exit. The mob didn't break its momentum, but smashed into her. She slashed at the arm of a man who snatched at her wrist, causing him to howl in pain. Something jabbed her in the abdomen, caught by her hidden chain mail shirt. The mass of bodies behind her gave way. She stumbled out into the open air, caught her balance, and ran.

A servant already had a ladder against the estate wall and was starting up. Others shoved to be next. Charva shot a glance over her shoulder and saw Ersch kick a commoner back into the palace and slam the door shut. A guard heaved a planter on its side to jam it closed. She slowed to let Ersch catch up with her. He waved her on. "Go!"

Even as he shouted, more of the mob rounded the corner of the palace. "There! They're getting away!"

Must every day now involve me running for my life?

Charva sheathed her sword and poised herself before dashing for the wall. The servants continued quarreling with the ladder as she jumped and kicked up the brick surface. She caught the top with her fingers, but hung in place. She struggled to hold on, much less pull herself up. After an embarrassing couple of moments, her feet found someone's shoulder and she pushed on over. She landed and rolled, then looked to see Ersch climb after her, managing the whole thing much more impressively than her. He dropped to his feet, buckling to one knee with a grunt. At the ladder, a maid screamed as someone grabbed her by the skirt and pulled her out of sight. Charva shut the sound out of her mind as she held Ersch's arm and fled with him away from the palace grounds.

More city folk circled the Council dome, waving swords at the guards and throwing stones at the windows. The two gave them a wide berth and made for the north gate. Along their course, they passed the body of an official tied to a lantern post and stabbed through the chest. Charva shook her head at the scene without stopping.

The gate proved easy to pass. The guards were gone and apparently no one had thought to block nobles from escaping the city. She breathed easy once they were on the switchback heading down the wooded slope.

"That was not how I expected our day to turn out," Ersch said.

Charva felt at the hole in the front of her dress. This was two times now her armor had saved her life.

"What now?" he asked.

She stomped down the path. "We keep following our lead."

Chapter 71

The door creaked open, interrupting Retyar and Fellone's game of fortress just as he was about to make the finishing move.

"The crenden has returned," the servant said. "Please follow me."

Fellone jumped to her feet, grabbing up her crutch. She still used the same one Retyar had found for her in the woods, despite him trying to talk her into accepting something better from the palace staff. She'd adamantly refused, and he wondered if it was her rebelling against their diagnosis that she'd always walk with a limp.

The two of them trailed behind the servant, twisting through a small maze of stone corridors until they entered the palace's audience hall. The room was vastly smaller than the equivalents he'd seen in movies back home, with space for about twenty-five people to stand comfortably. Then again, the large, heavily muscled man pacing through shafts of sunlight streaming down from the high windows was a crenden, not a king. *But most monarchs in history were hardly as rich as that anyway. This could very well be more representative of most realities. That chair of his is pretty elaborately carved and looks on the level of things I've seen in the National Museum. I wonder—*

Crenden Pundur's jaw dropped the moment he saw Fellone. He rushed over and gripped his massive hands around her tiny shoulders. "Fellone! The men spoke the truth!

You live!"

"Rety here saved me. The people who attacked the mansion threw me in a river, but he found me and took care of me."

Pundur looked at Retyar in all seriousness. "Rety, is it?"

"Retyar Venon," he said.

"You belong to a House?"

"No, your grace. Second names are simply common where I'm from."

"I see. Well, you will be generously rewarded, I assure you. Fell, I'm sure you know that Senkani is in a war, but I will send word immediately to Arzan and Ellaniel."

"That's something that can't be done," Retyar said.

The crenden frowned at him. "Excuse me?"

Fellone nodded. "Listen to him, Pundur." She shared a glance with Retyar. The two of them had talked this over. "We can't let any more people know I'm alive."

Pundur stepped back, his eyes narrowed. "What is it you need to tell me?"

"A great deal," Retyar said. "Crenden Pundur, there are certain things which you are going to have a hard time believing. But first, close the door."

It took only a second of consideration before Pundur nodded to his ckols. Once the room was shut, he sat down and bid the two of them take the audience chairs. "This is about the conspiracy, isn't it? You think those vile murderers will come to finish the job if they discover dear Fell's still alive. Do you know something about them? Who they work for?"

Retyar took his seat, propping his rifle against his armrest. "It's actually a matter unrelated, though there's certainly the possibility the killers might still threaten Fellone's life."

"The empire's going to invade Leverie," Fellone blurted.

Pundur stroked his beard. "Yes, that's obvious. That's why I've been staying out of this stupid civil war. I can't waste Three Corner's army killing our own kin when the Vron are creeping up on our borders."

"It's going to happen in four years," Retyar said.

The crenden's eyes widened. "You have information on their plans?"

Retyar smiled inside. He'd dreamed of this sort of

moment countless times over the last few years. And the moment terrified him. The power of knowledge, the magnitude of change he could bring about—the weight of this responsibility was crushing. With the reality in front of him, he wanted nothing more than to slink back to his cave. But he'd made his decision, and it was too late to turn back now. "I come from the future," he said. "I know when the Vron are going to invade because I have a history text from hundreds of years ahead of your time."

The room was silent. One of the ckols snorted a laugh before stifling himself. Pundur's mouth gaped, then went tight; his face transitioned between bewilderment, anger, and pity. He turned to Fellone. "My dear, I promise you that I'm doing everything in my power to prepare for the empire's inevitable arrival. This man will receive his due with full gratitude. If he's willing, I'll even have one of my healers see to his—"

Retyar reached into his satchel and pulled out the tablet, switching it on and flipping the screen for the crenden to see. "Can a madman make a thing like this, your grace?"

Pundur blinked at the fanciful startup animation dancing across the tablet's glowing surface. "What . . . What manner of contraption is this?"

"This, your grace, is a portable library. It contains the equivalent of thousands of books, including a comprehensive history of the world up until the year 5414. That is the year I come from."

The crenden reached out his hand, but stopped himself short, closing his fingers. "Don't think you can trick me into believing your nonsense with a simple trinket like that. I've seen enough con artists and stage plays in my time. So you have a little dancing drawing and glowing glass. Waste any more of my time and intelligence and you'll find your welcome in my palace cut drastically short." His voice was threatening, but despite it, Retyar could see doubt and fear in his eyes.

"I will give you proof," Retyar said. "Do you have traders coming in from out of the country? Preferably ones who travel fast and far?"

"Any crenden does," Pundur said. "Stupid question."

"Which ones are due?"

Pundur shook his head. "I warned you not to waste my—"

"Where are they coming from?"

"This is your last—"

"Pundur, give him a chance!" Fellone said.

"Ckols, escort—"

"King M'caveer of Anturian passed away two weeks ago from a lightning strike while traveling the road to Cinderglade," Retyar said. "He was succeeded by his second son M'shavar. Three days ago, a naval fleet commanded by Admiral Sada of the Karadees Pact delayed his assault on the Brasarans after sighting a leviathan in the South Windseed Atolls. Yesterday, wildfires burned through Asaruma, destroying the Grand Fresco painted by La Aw Un. Tomorrow, Princess Fujrih of the Eighty Hills will be celebrating her twentieth birthday, and her mother will surprise her with a gift of three dwarf elephants and a set of Miluran bronze bells. In six days, a riot will break out in the city of Bander, wherein the famous marble statue of King Valouris will be toppled and broken into four parts. Eight days from now—should I keep going?"

The crenden and his guards were all still.

Pundur flexed his hands and tightened his jaw, but didn't give another order to his men. "Halmar," he said. "I have a trader coming in tomorrow from Halmar."

Retyar let out a tight breath. He had him. He saw the wonder in the crenden's eyes, the only sign of victory in the man's otherwise carefully impassive face. Wonder and a renewed tinge of fear.

Yeah, I'd be terrified too in his shoes.

"Halmar." Retyar didn't need to reference the tablet to know that it was a country on the far eastern coast of Moshon. Their major exports were peanuts and dye. Thanks to his extensive reading these past few years, he also knew:

"If he's taking the Windings River, I'm guessing he's been traveling about two weeks," he said. "Likely, he was there to hear about the opening of Crendess Jracka's Art Hall."

"Halmar's not a challenge," one of the guards spoke up. "Two-week-old news could already have reached here by coastal ship."

"But if he's going up the Windings, he'd also be traveling through the Aristocracy of Vesalar," Retyar replied. "When he arrives, ask him if they've caught the Indigo Killer. As it turns out, he's actually a she—one of Crenden Malrian's daughters who was jealous of palace staff prettier than her. Your man will be missing the trial, though, which is today. Her House is going to find her not guilty, but the Council will overrule and hang her tomorrow morning."

Crenden Pundur sat down in his chair, his hand tugging his beard and mustache. Fellone leaned in on her crutch. "You believe him now, right?"

Pundur narrowed his eyes. "Escort him to the second floor guest rooms. He's to be held under strict house arrest. No visitors, no outside contact of any kind."

"Pundur!" Fellone said.

Retyar put a hand on her shoulder. "It's all right, Fell."

"But—"

The guards came to Retyar's sides and he followed their escort. There wasn't any reason for him not to. He'd just won.

And this world isn't going to be the same.

Chapter 12

Highcity had been conquered well before Ellaniel entered its streets. She rode her horse with head held high as the local denizens knelt on either side of the Senkani column. At every street corner they passed, dead guardsmen hung tied to lampposts and statues, pools of dried blood caking the stones below them.

"The flies are a nuisance," she said. "I want the bodies removed by sundown."

One of her company leaders nodded. "I'll see to it immediately, your grace."

She swept the bowed heads all around her and smiled at the easy capitulation. Yes, the tides were turning.

Their parade terminated at Ylnavar's palace, in the shadow of the neighboring Council dome. Both buildings were a mess of shattered windows and soiled walls, with debris strewn all about the grounds. The only people in sight were a group of youngsters drawing on the stonework with chalk. The youths stopped and gawked as the Senkani formed up and Ellaniel guided her horse to the front steps.

"Children, where is Crenden Ylnavar?"

One of the youths pointed inside the palace. "His study, your grace."

A carriage arrived behind her. Ellaniel dismounted as a ckol opened the vehicle's door and helped Arzan out of the compartment. As their soldiers filed into the palace, Arzan looked around at the ruined grounds, Vighkon giving him support.

"Not how I imagined this playing out," he said.

One of their men returned from inside. "All clear, my liege."

"Did you find the crenden?" Ellaniel asked.

The soldier's face was tight. "I believe so."

Ellaniel and Arzan shared a glance before following the soldier. Shattered glass and ceramic crunched underfoot as they strode through empty hallways. Doorways hung ajar on either side, no few smashed and hanging at odd angles. In some places, blood smeared the floors and walls. Ellaniel reflected that the old her would have been horrified by the scene, but she'd been front and center to far worse these past weeks.

The door to Ylnavar's study was completely thrown from its hinges. Ellaniel nodded to the Senkani soldiers flanking the passage and entered. The room here was a worse mess than the halls. Books and ledgers lay strewn about the entire floor, a sea of paper surrounding shattered furniture. Ylnavar sat at the base of his desk. The man was unmistakably dead, beaten to a purple mess, head set at an unnatural tilt. A swarm of flies jumped into the air as she approached to make sure of his identity. The smell hadn't built as strong as it could, thanks to the destroyed windows, but she still gagged as she leaned in.

It's him.

She stepped back, acid rising in her throat. This scene brought her mixed feelings. The man was dead, finally, yet she hadn't been here to see his life drain from his eyes. To kill him herself.

"Take the body and bury it in the House plot," Arzan said quietly.

Ellaniel gaped at him. "Are you forgetting what he's done? It's thanks to Ylnavar that we have this war on our hands. Thrake would already be brought to justice by now if it weren't for him."

"And he has paid the price. What more will you have done?"

"I would love to set the body out for the wolves. I'll settle for burning it."

Arzan shook his head. "You're letting your hatred get the better of you. Think about what that will accomplish, Ella."

She laughed. "Justice?"

"Vengeance. Justice has already found him. The penalty for his crimes has been served, and what's left is to treat him with the respect still due."

"He killed hundreds of our people. Thousands of his. What respect does he deserve?"

"That of Speaker of the Council. Crenden of his city. Head of his House. The respect that comes from being a person, no matter how twisted or misguided he may have been."

Ellaniel glared at him, the suggestion that Ylnavar's titles were worth a single thing triggering her to anger. "Those who have a hand in defending the people who killed my father and attacked our son—none of them will get any mercy from me, Arzan."

He didn't answer with any counterpoint. No anger, no agreement. Only a profound look of worry.

"He doesn't deserve an honorable burial," she repeated.

"Everyone deserves one," Arzan said.

Ellaniel fingered her scabbard. "You're the crenden. Do what you want." She turned and left the room.

Arzan stayed behind, wrestling with his own mixture of feelings. He was satisfied that one of their chief enemies was dead, but he couldn't shake an overwhelming sense of sadness and pity. Somehow, looking down Ylnavar's mangled old body, he had trouble feeling hatred. Frustration, yes. Anger, yes. But when he tried to summon hatred, all that rose was sorrow. He left Vighkon's aid and held himself up by the back of a mangled chair as he watched the soldiers wrap the body in a cloth and carry it out.

"Permission to speak, my liege," Vighkon said.

Arzan nodded.

The captain eyed the body on its way out the door. "I think her grace is correct. He shouldn't be afforded respect."

"So you don't think his punishment is already enough?"

"The Speaker is dead. Anything we do to his body now won't affect him in the slightest. What effect it has is on those now living. It will be the last the people see of him, and it will be a message on how his actions should be remembered."

"What, then?"

Vighkon thought a moment. "His people burned because of him."

Arzan weighed his suggestion. "Burning a man's body is the worst insult to his legacy."

"The people need to see clearly their villains."

Arzan sighed and turned to one of his ckols. "See it done. Have them bring wood in front of the palace gate." Perhaps Ellaniel would view this as a concession to her. That could patch things up or encourage her attitude, but he decided not to let either considerations taint Vighkon's advice.

As the ckol went out, another man came in. "My liege, if you're done with the Speaker, there's something else you may wish to see."

He didn't like the grimness in the soldier's face. He liked it even less when they exited the back of the palace to greet a pile of rotting corpses. Men and women, all dressed in servants' clothing. Crows busied themselves picking at their flesh.

"These . . . Ylnavar is one thing, but these at least deserved a trial," Arzan said. "Set to finding their kin. They'll be buried where their families will." He left before the sight could disgust him further.

When they rounded the palace, Ellaniel stood waiting for him. She waved to a soldier, who brought forth a prisoner.

"The Highcity folk handed her over," Ellaniel said.

Natsha Leverie retained a noble bearing even with her hands tied behind her. She regarded the savaged palace with a stone cold expression, which didn't change when she set her eyes on the Redleafs. "Are you happy with the mess you've caused?"

"Why her?" Arzan asked.

The woman spat. "Probably because I'm the only Leverie

left in the city." She looked at Ellaniel. "Do you feel nothing? Your cousins here were slaughtered. The House's Highcity branch is gone."

"And why did they leave you alive?" Ellaniel demanded.

She laughed bitterly. "Why indeed. I thought it was their women being made Aiv Chahai they were angriest about." Her voice quieted. "My girls talked them down, even drew their swords for me."

Ellaniel frowned. "'Your girls'? Why would they—"

"She's head of the Watchers," Arzan deduced.

"By some silly notion of Ylnavar's," Natsha said. "I must thank him. It saved my life. But this ancient nonsense that women will somehow keep the world at all sane by joining the army is ridiculous. Take dear Ellaniel here."

Ellaniel narrowed her eyes and stepped closer, her armor clinking. "What about me?"

Natsha smiled disdainfully. "Nothing."

"Ella," Arzan said before she could rise to the bait.

She restrained herself and backed off. "What are we going to do with her?"

"We have three options. Keep her imprisoned—" Natsha closed her eyes, "—release her—" Ellaniel's face soured, "—or . . . " he paused, not quite sure he wanted to say it. "Or we make her crendess of Highcity."

Both women stared at him. When they recovered their speech, they started at once.

"What are you—"

"You can't be serious!"

"She is the last Leverie in Highcity," Arzan said, "thus the only legitimate candidate to rule. The post could be hers, on one condition."

"Assuming I were inclined to accept," Natsha said slowly, "what is it you want?"

"That Highcity be a vassal to Senkani for the duration of the war."

Ellaniel grabbed him by the arm and pulled him aside. He winced in pain at his injuries, nodded to Vighkon and followed with her.

"We don't need her!" she hissed. "Let's just appoint our own governor."

"And then after the war, what? Are we going to hold onto Highcity indefinitely? I've no interest in ruling anything beyond Senkani."

"Appoint a Leverie at the war's end, or establish a new House," Ellaniel argued. "Natsha worked for Ylnavar."

"Did she? You know her personality, Ella. More likely than not, she did her best to make Ylnavar's life miserable for taking her away from her shop."

"Yes, I know her—stuck up enough to match the Speaker. We don't need to deal with someone like her!"

"Actually, we do." He had Vighkon take him back.

"I can guess what your wife's opinion is on this matter," Natsha said. "I'm sure I agree with her, at least on the end point. You know my stance on barbarism. I know what you will demand of Highcity—more soldiers. I will have nothing to do with that."

Arzan's leg throbbed, and he seated himself on the step of his carriage. "That's why I want you on our side, Natsha."

She and Ellaniel both frowned.

"Do you study history?" he asked. "All too often, war puts in power those who have a hard time setting down the sword after the fight is won. I want someone in Highcity looking for excuses to withhold the troops, not reasons to push them into the field."

"That's ridiculous!" Ellaniel said. "You can spout those ideals in peacetime, but we can't have half our soldiers refusing to move forward when victory is in sight."

"Do you think numbers alone are what win wars? If that were so, Senkani would already have lost. We beat the enemy back because every man in our army believes in this fight. I'll tell you now, regardless of whether Natsha accepts being crendess, we will receive the same number of soldiers from Highcity, because not a single man will be required to join us."

Natsha shifted her feet. "What do you mean?"

"Volunteers only," Arzan said. "If I appoint a Senkani man as crenden of Highcity, I'll give him no authority to compel service in the army. But if you are crendess, neither will you have power to stop anyone from joining me."

"Not much point in taking the throne, then."

"I still don't like it regardless," Ellaniel said.

"This isn't your decision, Ella."

"Arzan—"

"That's the end of it."

His wife clenched her fists and pressed her lips to a thin line. Faster than anyone could react, she grabbed Natsha by the collar and shoved her against the carriage.

"Ella!"

Vighkon stepped forward, but Arzan put a hand out to stop him. Ellaniel and Natsha locked gazes for a long moment before Ellaniel pushed her once more and stormed away.

Natsha tried to maintain her stiff bearing, but Arzan saw her trembling.

"That woman had a sword at her side the first time she stepped into my shop. She was a brilliant artist with needle and thread, but I couldn't stand to have her carrying an instrument of war onto my premises. I see which side of her bore fruit. Tell me, Crenden Arzan, how much of that beautiful artist is left?"

Arzan said nothing. He didn't want to admit in front of her that the question already tortured him.

"I had heard that you were a man who knew of strategy, but you look little more than a fool to me. You wish me to be crendess? Very well. Natsha Leverie will cede Highcity as a vassal to Senkani. Outside the terms of this agreement, be assured that I will fight you tooth and nail."

Arzan didn't go so far as to smile, but he did nod. "In time, I hope to prove I've acted in wisdom." He waved for Vighkon to aid him. "If not, you will have Ellaniel to contend with."

They searched the palace grounds and found Ellaniel sulking in the main hall. She glared at Arzan as he approached.

"What is this?" she demanded. "Everything you've done today has been to countermand me."

"Well, perhaps you should stop attempting to challenge my every decision," Arzan said.

The anger in his wife's eyes was enough to set kindling afire. "All you've been doing today is to benefit our enemies. I thought we were on the same side."

"*Justice* is what we seek. That means we will fight the Leverie, but it also means there must be a point where we stop."

"We stop when every murderer and every accomplice is dead, Arzan!"

"Then prepare to pile up the bodies to the moon, Ella, because to fulfill that goal will mean this war will never end."

"Well, I'll at least settle for the heads of every member of the Council who sided with Thrake." She shoved her finger into his chest. "Nothing less."

Arzan pressed his lips together. "What *justice* demands, Ella." He turned back for the door, the scent of smoke wafting in from the pyre being lit outside.

Chapter 73

Charva tossed the weird crossbow grip restlessly from hand to hand as the wagon rolled past the cotton fields of Glasscastle province. "Driver, how much farther?"

"Once we come into sight of the walls, it'll be a quarter hour to the gate."

Ersch slid his whetstone over his blade one last time before sighting the edge. "In other words, the same answer you got a half mile ago. And a half mile before that."

She stopped juggling the metal contraption. "I'm the noble here. I'm supposed to have the privilege of bugging you without getting any mouth."

Ersch slid his sword into its scabbard with a grin. "As you say, my liege."

She glanced over him. "What do you think of our current course?"

Ersch grew serious. "I'm concerned about Creedport. The Senkani are sure to be at our gates soon."

"All the more reason for us to make haste to Glasscastle," she said. "When we finally get solid evidence of the conspiracy, we can take it to Arzan and Ellaniel and stop their attack." *If only we could get it faster.* Thinking about the delay set her fingers fiddling with the contraption. She watched the cotton fields outside, rows upon rows stretching on towards the distant wood line. Workers labored throughout the fields, maintaining a sense of normalcy in this corner of the country. She wondered what Roth's reason was for staying out of the war.

Her thumb found a small switch on the contraption's side.

She looked down and inspected it, flicking it a few more times. Out of curiosity, she tried the trigger. Unlike before, it didn't give at all.

Hmm.

What else might she be missing? She studied the contours more closely. There was a spot at the top that looked like it was meant to move, a sort of latch or something. She wondered if—

The top gave under her tinkering, sliding backwards and opening the latch slightly. She slid it further, pushing against a tension trying to keep it closed. The latch rotated all the way open and the sliding piece came to the end of its track with a click. Intrigued, she tried turning the contraption to look inside the latch, but her grip slipped and everything snapped back into place.

"Finding something interesting?" Ersch asked.

"Maybe. Let me just . . . ." She started sliding the thing open again when the wagon hit a bump. Her hand rammed it all the way open and something popped out and hit her nose. "Embers!"

She rubbed her face and searched around the wagon. It took some moments for her to find the little metal cylinder rolling back and forth along the floorboards. When she did, her breath caught.

"My liege?"

Charva fished in her pocket and pulled out the tiny vial the soldiers had found outside Senkani. She held it beside the new item. No mistaking it.

"That looks like the same sort of vial," Ersch said, leaning in. "A bit shorter and fatter, though."

"But still full!" Excitement washed over her. The brass vial was topped with a rounded copper cap. It was stoppered tight, and try as she might she couldn't get the thing open. Her eagerness turned to frustration as her hands grew sweatier and made it harder and harder to even find purchase. She gave it to Ersch to try, but he had no better luck.

"Why would a little vial like that even be inside a crossbow grip?" Ersch asked.

"Good question." Charva frowned and then started sliding the latch open again to try to put the vial back in. To her surprise, she saw a second vial already snugly in place.

She had a sudden, silly idea. She pointed it at the road behind them and tried pressing the trigger. It didn't move.

Oh, yeah, the switch.

She flicked it with her forefinger and tried again.

With a deafening bang, the contraption leaped out of her hand, clipping her ear as it sailed past her head. The whole wagon lurched as the horses panicked. The driver brought the animals quickly under control and shouted back, "What was that?"

Charva's heart raced. "That scared me." She looked around the wagon. "Where'd it go?"

Ersch picked it off the floor by his foot. "What did you do?"

"I'm going to figure that out," she said, taking it. "This thing's a lot more than—ow!" She snatched up her hand after burning it in something caught in the folds of her skirt. She looked down and saw one of the small brass vials, absent its cap. "What in the six?"

The pieces clicked in her mind. "Driver, halt the wagon."

They hadn't even come to a full stop when Charva hopped out into the dust cloud of their wake. The mysterious vials. The loud bang. The soldiers with pierced breastplates after strange cracks in the night . . . .

A few cotton laborers some distance out looked up from their work as she marched along the roadside, her eyes roaming for a suitable target. She found a signpost about a dozen paces ahead. That would do.

Ersch hurried up behind her. "My liege, what are you—?"

"Tell the driver to keep hold on the horses." She gripped the top of the contraption and slid it back just far enough to confirm it had another vial in place, then pointed it at the sign. She drew in a breath and pulled the trigger.

She expected the noise and the force this time and didn't flinch. She saw the burst of flame spew out the front, saw another empty vial fly out of the side. Saw the bottom of the sign instantaneously erupt into splinters.

The horses spooked again and the driver yelled something unintelligible.

Arm still outstretched, Charva couldn't help but gape. She

ran to the signpost to inspect the damage. The wood had been at least an inch thick, but whatever had hit it had gone straight through, taking a good chunk off the bottom along the way. Try as she might, she couldn't find the projectile anywhere behind it.

"What is that thing?" Ersch asked.

"I . . . I don't . . . " She held the contraption in front of her. "It's not part of a crossbow. This is the whole thing. How in the world does it . . . ? A weapon like this . . . ." She opened the latch to find yet another vial ready to go. "It even loads itself! How many of these vials are in here?"

The sheer magnitude of the power she held in her hand left her speechless. She had to suppress a grin, as well as the urge to test it one more time.

Wherever this thing had come from, she wasn't giving it back.

Charva forced herself to keep focused as she entered the city of Glasscastle. There would be time enough to take the vial contraption apart and figure out how the incredible thing worked after she saved her House.

"Straight to the palace?" Ersch asked.

She nodded. "Hopefully it won't be a long chat." The last time she and Roth had spoken, things hadn't exactly been civil. Not that Ersch would know anything about that.

As with any city, Glasscastle had its own character to it. The place had grown up from small beginnings back before the forest had been cleared for cotton, and even now wood served as the preferred material of choice. With its maze of two- and even three-story buildings, it was closer in appearance to Three Corners than to Woodwise, but the streets were wider than Pundur's city and paved in brick.

That was as much attention as Charva gave to the details as they made for the province's namesake. The Glasscastle palace wasn't truly a castle by any stretch of the imagination. The only form of security to speak of was a wrought iron fence around its perimeter, used in lieu of a customary wall in order to show off the building inside. And to be fair, the exhibit it contained was an architectural feat. Three stories high, its east and west faces were set with finely polished windows showcasing the ornate riches of the crenden's residence for all to admire. She had never seen it, but the Glasscastle Leverie boasted that the silhouette the palace made at dawn and dusk was a beauty to behold, the very arrangement of furniture and guards coming together as a work of art against the rising sun.

"What are the chances Crenden Roth is the one we're looking for?" Ersch whispered.

Charva tried to imagine the womanizer conspiring anything beyond getting a pretty girl into bed. "I wouldn't give his intelligence that much credit."

"That's harsh."

Perhaps the attempted arranged wedding colored her judgment a tad. "Doesn't hurt to be careful, I suppose."

The gate sentries saw them coming and sent a runner to the palace. With hardly a delay, a servant ushered them in through the glass double doors and into the labyrinth of wall-to-ceiling windows.

"Is this your first time seeing the Glass Palace, your grace?" the servant asked. "Most are curious how our artisans create such large and clear panes. I like to point out the incredible engineering that went into crafting a three-story building with hardly any load-bearing walls. Before you leave, perhaps you might enjoy a tour of—"

"Some other time."

"Of course. Here is the parlor. Make yourselves comfortable."

Charva settled into a plush armchair, Ersch taking his place behind her.

"Not sure I'd ever feel too at ease in such a place," Ersch said.

Charva felt the same. The building offered no sense of privacy. She could see into every room on this floor, her view obstructed only by furniture and strategically arranged brick pillars.

Ersch rubbed the stubble on his chin. "I wonder where he goes when he's got a woman—"

"Not something I want to know," Charva interrupted.

"Yeah, best not to dwell on that."

The glass walls gave them the benefit of seeing Roth approach long before he reached the parlor. He came down from a far staircase, the sight of him wavy and warped through all the panes. He had a pretty redhead on his arm whom he dismissed before heading their way. It felt a bit awkward watching him wind his way closer. She realized just how much she took for granted the clean, sudden introductions afforded by proper walls.

Roth finally entered the room, chaperoned by a pair of guards, and nodded with a hesitant smile. "I was not expecting a visit from the esteemed daughter of Creedport." He smoothed his oiled hair. "What brings you here, Charva?"

She crossed her leg over her knee. "I'll get straight to the point. There was a letter you received from my father after the murders. Ylnavar says you presented it to the Council in Woodwise. How did you receive that letter?"

"Yes, straight to the point." Roth fingered his neck in the same spot that had once felt Charva's dagger. "A bit odd of you to ask after a letter your own father sent."

"Who delivered it to you?"

The crenden raised an eyebrow. "I've no idea why you'd care to know that, but far be it from me to offend Charva Leverie. It was one of my regular messengers. Markavar, I believe. I remember because it was unusual to hear anything from Thrake since, well . . . ." He hid his mouth and coughed.

"Markavar's House employed? Where can I look for him?"

Roth waved his hand. "The post house is outside the gate to the right."

Charva stood. "Well, I'm as eager to be out of your company as you are to be out of mine. Thank you for being so efficiently accommodating."

"A pleasure, Charva." The false smile on his face said otherwise.

She wasted no time leaving the room and the palace.

"I gather there's some bad history between you two?" Ersch said.

"Not that much. He just tried to marry me once."

"Oh." From his expression, her answer only raised more questions. "His help came far easier than the other crendens so far."

Charva smiled. "Well, I give him credit. He understands better than the others that it's simpler to just step aside where I'm concerned."

The post house was shorter than the buildings around it, its double doors open for ease of access. They entered and came before a long counter manned by a middle-aged clerk with long sideburns.

"I'm looking for a messenger named Markavar," Charva said.

The clerk pulled out a sheet and glanced it over. "Let's see. I think I remember him heading off to—"

A man rushed in from the street and leaned over the counter to whisper to the clerk. Confusion and surprise flashed across the clerk's face before the messenger backed off and left the way he'd come.

Charva raised an eyebrow. "What was that about?"

The clerk cleared his throat and looked down at his record sheet. "You were asking after Markavar? I expect he'll be back sometime tomorrow. If you wish to wait for him, I can recommend a lovely inn just down at the corner."

She eyed the sweat on the man's hands and the tension in his shoulders. An alarm bell gonged in her head. With the warning signs came the sense of victory. Her quarry had finally given himself away.

"Thank you for the suggestion," she said, trying not to sound excited. "Will you send word as soon as he's arrived?"

"Certainly, your grace."

With a nod, she went out into the street, and immediately grabbed Ersch by the arm. "We've got him."

Ersch looked back at the post house. "Did I miss something?"

"That messenger who came in told the clerk to lie about Markavar. It's a ploy to get us to stay here."

He frowned. "And we're doing what they want?" Ersch said. "If they're trying to keep us here, it could very well be a trap."

"Truly."

Ersch leaned in close. "We don't have enough manpower to fight back," he whispered.

"What are we going to do, then?" Charva demanded. "We don't have time to gather more people from Creedport."

"We know Roth is up to something. We can back off, tell the Redleafs to focus on Glasscastle."

"'Arzan, we think Roth was behind the killings because his messenger clerk told us the deliveryman would show up tomorrow.' If that convinces him, then I'm the First Emperor."

"And what do we accomplish by falling for an ambush?"

"The ambush itself will be the evidence. We don't even need to catch any of them, just know that they came for us when we started poking around here. As soon as we see them, we run."

"Last time we tangled with the mercenaries, we almost died, and we had more than just the two of us," Ersch said.

Charva exposed the vial weapon in her bag. "But we didn't have this."

His expression made it clear what he thought of her confidence.

"Come now," she said. "We're the good guys. We always come out on top in the stories." *And this is the last chance we have of saving Creedport. There's no time to return with reinforcements before Senkani lays siege.*

"Surely there's another way."

"Can you name it?"

"Go back to the palace and confront Roth directly."

"Where he's surrounded by all his ckols. That's better than my plan how?"

"We'd at least have a chance of grabbing him and forcing them to let us go."

Charva smirked. "I need to be careful. My foolhardy abandon is rubbing off on you."

"It has a better chance of success than us waiting for them to get us!"

"Well, we can't run away," she said, balling her fists on her hips.

Ersch looked up and down the street and took a deep breath. "My liege, I will willingly die at your command. I just want to make sure that you make it through in one piece."

She forced a smile. "Naturally."

Without her expecting it, Ersch put a hand on her shoulder. "I mean it, Charva."

The use of her name caught her off guard. Her mouth opened, but she blanked on any words to say. It didn't help that when she looked in his eyes there was something more than a bodyguard's concern in there. Something more, possibly, than a friend.

She cleared her throat and composed herself before grabbing his hand and lifting it off her. "We will do what we need to do. If you are my ckol, you will follow my orders." She turned around, not sure she liked this inside glimpse she'd seen of him. Not sure she didn't like it. Whatever the case, she couldn't get tangled up in distractions. Not now. This right here was her chance to be her city's hero. She felt at her daggers and rubbed the hilt of her sword as she walked towards the inn. Time for round two.

That wasn't to say Charva was completely stupid. Staying overnight at the inn would be suicide if they were right and this was a trap. After sending out a letter to her father, they rented a room on the second floor, then sneaked out a window just after sunset and found a recessed hiding spot between some unevenly spaced storefronts where they could watch the door. After the glimpse of something Charva had seen in Ersch's eyes, every stretch of silence felt awkward.

A lamplighter went by in the deepening gloom, raising his match rod to the street lanterns, but there was fairly little traffic in their corner of town. Charva reached into her bag and absently flicked the vial weapon's trigger lock back and forth. Her mind wandered to the question of where the contraption had come from. Where had the girl acquired it? She was nearly certain the child was the same one the Falconian had been looking for. The more she thought about it, the more inclined she was to think the wrapped thing he had at his back was another vial weapon. Specifically, the one that used the longer vials. Meaning he'd killed the Woodwise sentries. Who was he, and whose side was he on?

Charva heard a rustling in Ersch's direction, as if he was about to say something, but he kept his silence. She drew in a long breath and drew the vial weapon. In the dark, she followed its lines with her fingers, hardly able to see the edges in the gloom. Long moments went by. Hours. Foot traffic dwindled until it died altogether.

"We should start a watch rotation," Ersch suggested eventually.

They did. The whole night passed without incident, Charva having a hard time sleeping even when her turn came to rest. Dawn arrived and the city awoke to find her still fidgeting with the vial weapon, her eyes sour.

"Perhaps we made a mistake?" Ersch said.

Was it twisted of her to be disappointed? She watched a wagon roll on up the road, heavily laden with bales of cotton, then stole a glance at the Glasscastle palace's shining top peeking up over the nearer rooftops. Did her dislike of Roth make her too quick to jump at any signs of guilt?

A handful of men flowed out of the inn, patrons who looked a lot better rested than Charva felt. Someone in a messenger's garb jogged over from the direction of the post house and entered the building. Charva sent Ersch to greet him.

He hurried across the street and into the inn, coming back out with the messenger behind him. Charva strode up. "I thought I might have time for a morning errand, but I see Markavar must be back?"

The messenger, a young man about her age, nodded. "Not an hour yet since he checked into the post house, your grace."

"I'll see him immediately."

The messenger set out to lead them. Charva followed, wondering if the delay had really been for Roth to concoct a story and school whoever it was they were to meet. She felt an idiot, realizing now how much more sense that would make than murdering her in the night. This wasn't Three Corners. Everyone here knew who she was. It would be a battle of deduction and wit after all.

She thought that right up until the messenger led them

around a turn that wasn't at all in the direction of the post house. Unlike the path before, this one stood conspicuously empty. No laborers, no women heading to market, no wagons. No guards.

Charva and Ersch drew their swords without preamble as the messenger dashed for an alley. Men in dark cloaks emerged from every corner, completely surrounding them. Charva and Ersch pressed back-to-back, blades raised.

"I'll admit," she said, "I was starting to doubt you'd really show."

One of the mercenaries stepped forward, a dark sack clutched in his hand. He pulled back his hood, revealing the scars crisscrossing his face. "Wanted to gather everyone up. Everyone in my crew's been itching for a rematch after what happened to Wetim."

"Oh, is that the man you put a crossbow bolt through?"

"Yeah, and we're going to have you pay for his sacrifice."

"Lovely." Charva forced her cool. The exits were covered, but only by two or three men each. She and Ersch would punch through one of the escapes and flee like mad. Or . . . .

She counted the total number of mercenaries. Eight. How many vials did the strange contraption hold? Perhaps she could find out.

She pulled the weapon from her bag and whipped it to aim at the scarred man.

"My liege, what are you—" Ersch started.

She pressed the trigger without hesitation. A loud bang clapped off the buildings around them as flame spurted out the tube and the weapon kicked in her hand. The mercenaries jumped back, none more than the one she'd shot. The man looked down at his chestplate and fingered the small hole over his shoulder. "What in the . . . ."

Yes! Charva smirked with glorious satisfaction. "You're all so very dead."

"Take her down!"

"Just try it!" She took aim at the next mercenary and pressed the trigger. He flinched, but nothing happened. Embers! Only three shots? No. She turned the weapon in her hand and saw a spent vial lodged in the latch. She fiddled with the contraption only for something to fall out the bottom.

The mercenaries charged. Fighting panic, Charva shoved the broken weapon into her bag and swapped her sword to her main hand. She blocked a heavy blow, the force pushing her against Ersch's back and making her arm numb. In the corner of her eye, she saw the other mercenaries closing in.

"Okay, we run!"

Ersch grunted behind her. Off to the side, one of the mercenaries lowered his crossbow. *Six continents, he's been shot!* She parried another strike, then felt a hand on her arm. She tried breaking free, only to get a fist to her gut. As she doubled over in pain, someone pulled a cloth over her head and pinned her to the ground. Cold hands pried her fingers off her sword. She heard Ersch shout her name, before a crack to her skull ended her fight.

Chapter 79

Charva awoke to the taste of dust and mildew, a cloth gag stuffed in her mouth and a sack tight over her throbbing head. The sack didn't come off when they threw her into a cart, nor when they dragged her into a building with wooden floors. It stayed on when they shoved her, stumbling, down a flight of rough stairs, hands clamped tight over wrists already bound with ropes. She struggled as they hit the bottom, but the mercenaries only clamped down harder and her kicks hit nothing except air. Someone backhanded her across the face, stunning her.

"Feisty, isn't she? Search her."

Next she knew, she felt them tugging at her dress and ripping the fabric. Her daggers clattered to the stone floor. She tried screaming past her gag as they took off her mail and padding, then groped through her underclothes.

"Nothing else."

They tossed her, freshly bound, near naked, and shivering into the corner of the cellar. She heard the flat of a blade tap against stone nearby.

"You don't want to move, lass."

She tried to control her racing heart and fight down the terror that made her shake as much as the cold. Her mind attempted frantically to concoct some way out of this, but she was blind, exposed, and unarmed. And Ersch. *Embers, they shot him!* She didn't hear him, but that didn't mean he was dead. He had to have survived. He had to have gotten away. He'd come for her. Somehow. He wasn't dead. He couldn't be.

Stupid. I should have listened to him. I'm so stupid.

A door creaked open and a set of footsteps descended into the room over squeaky planks. The steps came towards her, and the glow of a lamp brightened the hood in front of her eyes.

"Charva Leverie," Roth's smooth voice was steeped in disappointment. Or was it regret? He snapped his fingers and the mercenaries held her arms and ripped off the hood. She looked up at her captor as he held an oil lamp to her face. His violet eyes only momentarily flitted across her bare skin before they locked on her gaze. "You just had to do this to yourself."

Anger breached through her fear and she kicked him in the shin. The crenden didn't even wince at the barefooted attack. One of the mercenaries struck her in the thigh with his armored boot. She choked and bit down on her gag as tears ran down her face.

Roth stepped back and paced the cellar, shadows creeping back and forth with each step. "What am I going to do with you? You just had to go snooping around the aristocracy trying to ruin the plan. You had to come around here asking about that letter."

"I told you that forgery was an idiot move," the scarred mercenary said. He'd gotten his chest armor and shirt off for one of the other men to treat his shoulder wound. "Bloody six, where did this weapon come from?"

"Straight through plate!" someone said. "We giving that thing to Kash?"

A click. "I think she only had the one shot."

"We'll talk about her toys later," Roth said. "The important thing right now is her."

"If you want to focus on your fumble with the letter, I'm all ears," the scarred mercenary said.

"The forgery was a necessary element! Criticize me all you want, but you weren't there at the Woodwise meeting. Redleaf was about to convince the Council to put Thrake on trial. I needed to get Ylnavar to oppose him and push Senkani into rebellion."

"And that letter brought her here."

"No plan can ever be completely watertight. Thrake's

bout of madness is testament to that." The crenden stopped in front of her and smirked. "It seems she's dying to say something. Loose her mouth. No one will hear her screams down here."

One of the mercenaries obliged and removed the gag. Charva spat, trying to expel the cloth's foul taste. The mercenary slapped her. "Manners or blood."

Roth touched his shoulder. "No need for that. A little spit never hurt anyone." He crouched and dabbed his finger in her saliva as he licked his lips. A shiver of revulsion coursed through Charva's body. She swallowed the blood of her broken cheek.

"You're scum, Roth," she said, "but I never expected you to do something like this to your country. What's your goal? What do you even gain from this war?"

He set his lamp on the floor and crossed his arms atop his knees. The light from below made him positively ghastly. "I'm doing this *for* the country."

"You're destroying it!"

"Destroying part of it to save the rest. Leverie is doomed, Charva. Only a few see it, and they think they can stave it off with sticks and straw. I'm the one guaranteeing that the House has a future."

"What are you even talking about?"

He leaned close, causing her to jerk back and hit her head against the wall. Roth smiled. "You know, if you hadn't so rudely threatened to remove a certain favored part of my anatomy, I might have been inclined to tell you. We could have been working together." He waved his hand and the mercenary shoved the gag back in her mouth. "You'll take your questions with you to the grave. But not before you serve a useful part in the plan." He turned to the scarred man. "Captain, you've been trying to figure out how to push Three Corners into the conflict?"

The mercenary nodded. "You have an idea?"

Roth slid his eyes over Charva. "I think maybe an unfortunate death could be just the thing we need. A daughter of the aristocracy, found murdered in the streets of Pundur's city, and carrying documents implicating certain members of his personal council in Thrake's conspiracy to assassinate

Crenden Hashan." He bent over her. "A beautiful plan, don't you think? Pundur will face two choices. Either he denounces his officials and joins the war against Leverie corruption, or else the Redleafs declare him their mortal enemy."

If Charva's mouth were still free, she would have bit the monster's throat. Instead, she struggled uselessly against the mercenaries' hold, getting her ankles pinned for good measure.

Roth shook his head. "I'm sure you think yourself a hero. So do the Redleafs. So did your father. Every man, every woman, they're heroes of their own stories. But what is it you've accomplished? You didn't save Maltan. You didn't save your brother. Your friends from Senkani are marching to your city's destruction and their own. Your ckols are all dead, save that favored dog of yours, but he's bleeding and will be finished before noon. Your very life is only going to forward my objective. Reflect on that as you draw in your last breaths."

The crenden straightened and regarded her from a distance. Charva glared at him. She wouldn't let his words dig at her. She wouldn't give in to the terror writhing in her chest.

He turned and started back up the stairs. "I hate that you found me out," he said, wood squeaking underfoot. "I really do."

Chapter 75

Arzan grimaced as Vighkon helped him through the tent flap into the open air. His injuries still sent jolts of pain through him with every other movement. It was his curse that as much as he wanted to just lie down and recuperate, he needed far more to be where the fate of his people was to be decided. Even if he made a fool of himself hobbling around on one leg, his arm hooked around his chief bodyguard, that was more tolerable than sitting at home waiting to hear of victory or defeat. If most of his men would be happy enough with Ellaniel leading the army in the final assault on Creedport, that changed nothing. Rather, it made him all the more apprehensive.

The war camp bustled with activity as Arzan slowly and deliberately made his rounds, checking in on his sergeants and logistics officers. He glanced frequently at the forested hill hiding Highcity's walls to the south. Their supplies from Senkani were mostly in, and they waited only on one thing from their new vassal before going on the march. Around noon, it finally arrived.

"Highcity's volunteers are entering the camp," a messenger reported.

Arzan nodded and sent him on his way, then made for the space they'd set as a marshaling ground. By the time he and Vighkon arrived, the Highcity folk were already there, lined up and receiving weapons. A good number of them had gambeson and mail, but still the majority wore simple clothing. They would be men who'd avoided conscription for

Ylnavar's army.

Off to the side, Ellaniel dismounted from her horse, having escorted the force of well near three hundred.

"And what's with that face?" Arzan asked as he drew near.

His wife patted her horse, then came and helped the captain sit Arzan down on a stool. "We could have raised more by conscription."

He smiled at her stubbornness, trying not to get distracted by the oddly appealing scent of her sweat. "Are five hundred volunteers not enough for you?"

She folded her arms, her armor clinking with the motion. "All right, I'm impressed. In fact, it still doesn't make sense to me why we ended up with so many. We were killing each other a week ago!"

"And their rebellion against Ylnavar and the House shows what they thought of that, doesn't it? These volunteers believe in our cause."

"I'm not sure that's the primary reason they beat the Speaker to death."

Arzan tugged at his cape's clasp. "I guarantee you they will be far more valuable than any force we might have raised through coercion."

She raised her brows at him.

He pointed to the new soldiers. "Look at them. What do you see?"

Ellaniel stared at the men being handed spears and shields. "Whatever it is I say, I'm sure you'll point out something else."

"Is there any taunting or jeering? Does it seem like any Senkani and Highcity are going to try gutting each other tonight?"

As if to drive home his case, a group of Senkani burst out laughing at a volunteer's joke.

"No," Ellaniel conceded.

"These men will augment our army in a way conscripts never could. They *chose* to help us, and that means a lot, both to them and to us."

Ellaniel brushed a lock of hair from her face. "*I* still don't trust them," she muttered.

"Well, that's fine so long as you don't show it. And you're not going to show it. That's your crenden's order."

She was quiet for a moment, a look of disagreement on her face. With a sigh, she lowered her arms. "May we discuss something in private?"

Arzan saw a nearby supply tent that seemed empty of people. He motioned to Vighkon, but Ellaniel was faster, stooping low and putting his arm around her shoulder. "Well, captain, I suppose you can finally have a little break from carrying this invalid everywhere."

The shadow of a smile crossed Vighkon's lips. "Can't compete with a beautiful woman for your favor, my liege."

That elicited a chuckle from her.

"I must declare how much I miss holding you without all this steel in the way," Arzan said. "You don't need to be in full armor all the time, you know."

The mirth slipped from her face. The two of them entered the tent alone and Ellaniel helped him down onto a crate before pulling the flap closed.

"So, you really don't like having to accept the Highcity volunteers as equals in our army."

"I don't like it, but I'll concede to your wishes," she said. "I want to speak about something else."

He held a hand to his aching ribs. "Oh?"

"What are our plans after we take Creedport and bring Thrake to justice?"

"What do you mean?"

Ellaniel flexed her fingers, the motion audible with her gauntlets. "You know what I'm talking about."

He did. It just wasn't something he felt ready to discuss.

"Odavan doesn't deserve my father's city," she said.

"I agree, he doesn't," Arzan said.

"There's a but in there, and I know what it is."

He pressed his lips tight.

"We're going to go over it, Arzan."

"I don't think the war should be extended lightly," Arzan said. "Don't lose sight of the fact that more of our people die with every battle. If the remaining provinces sue for peace, we should allow things to proceed to trial."

"I can't let him stay in power!"

"And where will things stop? Are we going to crush every crenden that followed Ylnavar?"

"Why not? They *attacked us*, Arzan. They burned our city. You talk of trials, but who would be the judges? Members of House Leverie! They'll hand down feather light sentences, if that. Are you going to accept this?"

The question gave him pause. Several weeks ago, he would have unhesitatingly answered no. Something had changed. Seeing the brutality this war had awakened, things didn't feel so black and white as they used to.

Ellaniel gaped at his silence. "You would." Disbelief and betrayal showed in her golden eyes. "You were the one who declared this war! You were the one who raised our army and promised my father's killer would pay for his crimes, that those who got in our way and aided that murderer would be given the same fate! How can you have a change of heart now, right when we're starting to win?"

"How much are we going to destroy, Ella? How long will this war go on for?"

"As much and as long as it has to!"

Arzan's hand tightened around the pommel of his sword. "Do you want Avlan to grow up knowing only war?"

Ellaniel hammered a crate with her fist. "This is for his sake! Unless the House of Leverie is ground to submission, they will always threaten us, always threaten our son!"

"So it's for his sake that you abandoned being his mother?" he all but shouted.

It was Ellaniel's turn to stand speechless, her mouth hanging open.

"Yes, I heard from Kalla how you no longer even show your face before our son. I was on the balcony with him after my injury only to learn he hadn't seen you for weeks!"

"That's not fair to—"

"It's not fair to him, Ella! You're the one who's lost sight of things. You've become so war-hungry you're forgetting what it's like to live."

Ellaniel unbuckled her gauntlet, removing the steel glove and slapping him in the face. "You have no idea what you're talking about!" Despite the pain on Arzan's cheek, his wife was the one with tears glistening in her eyes. She turned around.

"Ella . . . ."

"Let's just . . . finish with Thrake. We agree on that, don't we?" Ellaniel slipped the armor back over her hand and composed herself before throwing the flap aside and leaving. Arzan winced as he probed the inside of his cheek with his tongue. *Six continents, she can hit.*

Vighkon entered a moment later. "Her grace was not looking happy."

Arzan shook his head. "We're at war. We're not supposed to be happy." He accepted the captain's aid to stand. "Now, let's see about getting this army moving. We've a battle to fight."

Chapter 76

The last glow of sunlight peeking between the rundown shack's boards finally faded into darkness. Memories of Charva's childhood flitted through her thoughts, trying to keep her mind off her approaching murder. She tugged weakly at the ropes binding her to the room's center post, tried again to bite down and grind through the cloth that stole all moisture from her mouth. All her struggles to escape had been pointless. The mercenaries were all far stronger than she, and professionals. They left no opportunity for her when loading her onto the wagon to Three Corners. They'd kept unfailing watch during the whole trip, allowing her no privacy even to relieve herself. Not trusting to her gag, one of them had kept a tight hold on her throat and jaw to keep her silent as they passed in through Three Corners' gates. Every opportunity she thought she might have to do something they stifled before she could act.

Her hope in Ersch coming to her rescue sputtered and died as soon as they took her from Glasscastle. She didn't know if Roth had been speaking true about his injury, but wounded or not, he wouldn't be able to save her if he didn't know where she was.

Wood scraped across the floorboards in the next room over. Another mercenary coming to join the one keeping sentry at her door. They muttered greetings to each other, then started speaking, low and gruff.

" . . . Roth really the best . . . ."

"Captain says it'll work."

" . . . trust that all of it . . . . these idiot nobles."

The other one laughed and spoke a little louder. "They don't even know the first thing about war. Their Council gave all their commoners swords instead of spears. Works for Senkani 'cause of their crenden's readying program, but these other greenhorns?"

"Senkani's sweeping the floor with them for a reason."

"Not for much longer. We need to balance this fight. Creedport can't fall just yet."

"Three Corners'll help with that."

"Not enough. The captain's going to pick one of us to be a tactical adviser to the Leverie, you can be sure of that."

"Wouldn't be too bad having my own command. These Redleafs seem like worthy foes."

Something startled Charva by scampering around in the room's shadowed corners. She hit her shoulder against the post, making enough noise for the mercenaries to pause their discussion and push the door open a crack. Seeing she was still in place, they shut it back up.

"Too bad she's not on our side. Got Vavre pretty good. Gonna be one nasty scar to add to the rest."

"What's this thing she used on the captain?"

She perked her ears at hearing a metallic click. *They have the vial contraption with them.*

"Right through his armor. If she'd hit a little lower . . . ."

"How you figure it works?"

More clicking. "Not a clue."

"She's right here. We could get it out of her."

"Cap says we're not to rough her up more than we have to."

"There's that piece that fell out, remember? We probably won't figure it out on our own without catching her ckol."

A hard snap. "Loud as a ballista, this was."

"Not something I'd like to use, that's for sure. What's wrong with a proper crossbow?"

There was a brief silence. "Sorry, didn't mean to remind you of Wetim."

"Forget it. How much longer?"

"We need the streets empty. Wait till the lamps are wavering."

The conversation lapsed, leaving Charva to both silence

and sinking darkness. A breeze brushed through the dilapidated walls, giving her a chill. The thin dress they'd provided her following her brief encounter with Roth left a lot to be desired.

She tried once more at her bonds, but it was no use. Hot tears burned at her eyes with the certainty this would be her last night.

As the evening dragged on, she went back to the question of what Roth and the mercenaries were up to. It seemed clear it wasn't just a war they wanted. For some reason, they were working to keep it going, and to involve as many of the provinces as possible. Did they truly mean it that their plan required Creedport to remain standing? She felt she should get some solace from that, but there was none. She didn't want this to be her end.

The hour finally arrived when the mercenaries opened the door, spilling lamplight into her little prison. She squinted her eyes and tensed.

"Sorry, you don't get any final words, yer grace. Nothing personal any of this."

One of the men pinned her already tied ankles as she tried kicking with all she had. The other clamped down on her wrists with one hand while undoing the knot binding her to the post with the other. She pulled with every desperate ounce of strength, but even with her two arms against his one, he held tight.

"You've her legs?"

In answer, the mercenary pulled her calves up to his shoulder as the other heaved her upper half onto his. She squirmed as they hauled her out of the building into the night air. The street lamps flickered and sputtered, hardly competing with the moon's blue glow. The city stood silent around them, so much that she had hope her gagged screams might actually be heard. Perhaps someone was still awake in the houses they passed. A mother nursing a baby, an insomniac, anyone.

Her captors showed no fear of the same. They strode as if their job was no more urgent than delivering sacks of rice to the local storehouse. No home showed any sign of stirring. Windows remained shuttered, doors remained barred, every crack dark.

"This spot's good."

The mercenaries placed her on her back on the cold stones and one of them pinned her with a knee across her middle. She yanked at her ropes to no effect. The other man produced a sheet of folded paper and planted it in a pocket of her dress. "Things are going to get interesting in the city over the next few days." He drew a dagger from his side.

Charva wanted to scream, to threaten, to plead. The mercenary's blade glistened in the moonlight as he held the point to her chest. "I'll at least make it quick. You deserve that much, eh?"

She drew in a breath and struggled with every fiber in her body, fueled by every drop of terror and desire to live. She knew with certainty it wasn't enough. Flame and embers, she was going to die.

A burst of footsteps scratching across the cobblestones stole the mercenary's attention. He dodged to the side, raising the dagger in defense. Charva heard steel on steel, felt the pressure on her stomach lift. She watched with wide, unbelieving eyes as three figures battled in the dark, blades singing and sparks flying. Someone was saving her!

Her rescuer swung a hard blow that knocked the weapon from one of the mercenaries' hands and sent it clattering beside her. She rolled and grabbed it.

"Just kill him already!"

"You try it! Where's your—" the mercenary suddenly did a flip and landed on his back.

Charva cut furiously through the ropes at her wrists. Her hands came free, a little wet from slicing her own arm in her haste. She set to liberating her feet as her savior grappled with the second mercenary. She was sure it was Ersch. Only he fought like that. She cut through the last thread and jumped to help. Two steps out, the fallen mercenary tripped her back down. She landed on her shoulder, but held the dagger tight and kicked her adversary in the face. Hoping she'd stunned him, she twisted around and raised her blade for a finishing strike. The mercenary wasn't quite senseless. As her arm was raised, he punched her in the side. Charva bit down on her gag against the pain and thrust the dagger with all her might into his ear. His body jerked, then went slack.

Nearby, Ersch had his opponent in a solid chokehold. The mercenary tried with no luck to tear the ckol's arm off his neck. He resorted to flailing at Ersch's face, clawing at his eyes. Charva went up and kicked him in the groin. She followed up with a crack to the head with her dagger's hilt.

"Sorry I was late," Ersch said as he lowered the unconscious mercenary to the ground.

Charva undid her gag. The cloth didn't come easy from her mouth, having bonded to her tongue after sucking out all moisture. "How . . . how did you find me?" She had no success keeping her voice from shaking.

"I found that messenger who led us into the trap. Made him list all the places he'd run messages to these people. Found a group of them and overheard them scheming something for Pundur. Figured they took you to Three Corners."

Charva's eyes filled with tears and she hugged him tight. "Thank you."

He hesitated before putting his hands on her shoulders. "Where to now, my liege?"

"Anywhere but here."

"I think maybe we should take this one with us. Go straight to the Redleafs."

That made sense, but all she wanted right now was to be away. Her moment of helplessness repeated in her mind, the image of a dagger poised over her heart making her shudder.

I'll get over it. I have to get over it. Ersch is right. We need to get to Arzan and Ella.

"I . . . " she took a single step and swooned. She blinked, wondering why the moonlight seemed to be fading and why it was suddenly so hard to keep her eyes open.

Ersch sensed something was wrong. "My liege?"

Charva felt at the throbbing in her side. Her hand came away bloody. *Flame and embers. That wasn't a punch.*

The last thing she heard before blanking out was Ersch calling her name.

Chapter 77

The knock came seven days after Crenden Pundur's order to place Retyar under house arrest. He knew from the strength of the rap that it was a ckol rather than the palace servants, and he had his tablet under his arm and his rifle slung as the Leverie warrior opened the door.

"The crenden asks for your presence."

Retyar followed the ckol through the hall to a doorway where Fellone was impatiently thumping her crutch. The girl looked up, excited and worried. "Rety! Are you—"

"No communication!" the ckol said.

"But—!"

"It's fine, Fell," Retyar said. "We'll talk after the audience."

She pursed her lips and held her tongue with an angry frown.

The ckol opened the door, leading him into a study with carpeted flooring and two windows overlooking the palace courtyard. Crenden Pundur sat at the far end from the door, his desk bearing a map of the continent so large the edges hung over the sides. Retyar nodded respectfully. "Your grace."

Pundur pointed a meaty finger to a chair at the desk's side. "Sit."

He obliged, setting the tablet in his lap and his rifle against the armrest.

"My man came in from Vesalar on schedule. He did hear

about the Indigo Killer. Everything matched. Over the week, I've also gathered further news and reports from across the continent. My people have kept you under careful watch, making sure you have had no contact with anyone. They did not to speak to you or provide you with any information whatsoever. You've had nothing except your supposed glass library, and now you are going to answer my questions."

Retyar nodded. "Fire away."

The crenden paused. *Right, that wouldn't be an idiom they use here.*

"First will be Ranisa," Pundur said. "What can you tell me about events there in the last week?"

"Crendess Allamur stepped down four days ago," he said immediately. "The House appointed her son Kilv to take her place. That storm earlier also flooded the Muram's banks worse than usual, causing damage to Talma Province and ruining their vegetable crops. Other than that, things should be pretty bland for a few months."

"Whitesail."

"They finished mobilizing another army to throw at the Vron in Heartsong. This one is under the leadership of Ysmar, and is mostly light infantry, with a small number of archers and cavalry in the mix. He'll be crossing the border later this afternoon. The Whitesail Council is sending Leverie a letter urging an end to the civil war and a commitment of soldiers to fight against the empire."

Pundur sighed heavily. "If so, it'll fall on deaf ears." He eyed Retyar. "As for Leverie . . . ."

"Not only is the Council scattered and in chaos, but Crenden Ylnavar of Highcity is dead, having been beaten to death by his own people. The Redleafs have declared Highcity a vassal of Senkani, installing Natsha Leverie as crendess before continuing their campaign against the House."

Pundur ran his fingers through his beard. "And what developments in the Federation?"

"Nothing in the histories about their aid against the Vron, unfortunately," Retyar said. "Right now, they're too busy squabbling over the cost of flax. Their Council just approved a quota system allotting a maximum allowable harvest for each province."

"I have a trader come in from Marloo. What happened there last month?"

"Um, where is that?"

The crenden put his finger down on the map. "East Volcana."

Retyar drew a blank. "I'll have to look it up. Give me just a minute."

Pundur shot up from his seat and rounded the desk. "I want to watch you do this."

"You're welcome to, your grace, so long as you don't touch."

The man loomed over Retyar's shoulder as he typed in "Marloo" and the current year. The tablet took a moment to reference the index before giving a list of encyclopedia entries. Retyar sifted through the article previews, searching for anything linked to last month. "Oh, wow, the Splendor Fleet is sailing right now?" he muttered. "Can't believe I missed noticing that."

"Incredible," Pundur whispered. "There," he pointed. "Show me that."

Retyar obliged, opening an entry on a ceremonial succession duel. The words popped onto the screen. "Between Prince Ra'ha Zelum and Quel'Al the Anointed. It ended—"

"In a draw." Pundur went back around the desk and crashed down in his seat, his eyes never leaving the tablet. "Amazing. You passed all my tests, but I still can't believe it. You're from the future? Ridiculous."

"I absolutely agree, your grace."

"So, why are you here?" the crenden asked, waving his hand towards the window and his city. "Why would someone travel hundreds of years through time simply to walk into the palace of a small, inconsequential province in a tiny little country like Leverie?"

Retyar grasped his rifle and wobbled it around on its stock. "I'm here by accident. I was trying to stop someone from altering history and ended up stranded with no way back."

"And people where you're from can just go gallivanting

through time?"

Retyar shrugged. "As far as I know, the two of us are the first. Some scientists—I guess you'd call them tinkerers here—they figured out the method. They kept it secret and were doing their best to prevent anyone from ever using it. I have no idea how it actually worked—I was just tasked with guarding the device, and that didn't turn out too well."

"And now you're actively trying to change things."

His hand tightened around the barrel of his gun. "It's too late to turn back. Fellone's the one who confirmed it. I've already started to alter events just by existing in this time. The Pebble Effect."

Pundur rubbed his fingers together. "You're saying something doesn't match your library?"

"Something small, but it's all the evidence needed to confirm the timeline's been altered. Avlan, the son of Crenden Redleaf—his eyes are gold in my history, but here they're blue."

The crenden frowned. "How would that even—"

"It's a ripple effect resulting from small changes in environment and timing. The slightest of alterations can lead to different genetic combinations at conception. It's very likely that a large portion of Leverie's newborns from the point of my arrival are alternate versions of the people who lived in my history."

"They're different people? But that would mean—"

"My world is gone. Irreversibly." Retyar tapped the edge of his tablet, locking his emotions away as he said the words. "And my knowledge of the future is becoming obsolete. It's possible I've only got one shot at putting it to good use."

Pundur rubbed his armrest, his brows knit. "That only makes the question stronger. Why spend this single opportunity on us?"

Yes, why indeed. With the information in the encyclopedia, he could make himself rich, could weasel his way into power in some major kingdom, maybe even establish his own empire. But he'd hardly even considered those paths.

"Fellone asked me to help save her home," he said. "That's good enough for me."

Pundur stared, his lips parted. At length, he put a hand to his mouth to stifle a laugh. "And the fate of the country rests with a child. Far be it from me to waste little Fell's efforts! Very well! Let's hear what you have in mind for us."

An hour later, the crenden stroked his beard as Retyar finished laying out his plan and backed off from the map.

"Simple in principle," Pundur said. "Massive and precise in the undertaking."

"Assuming history follows its same course, we have four years to prepare," Retyar said.

"Considering this 'Pebble Effect', however, there's a good chance a lot of things will start changing. These materials— gathering them alone will create significant waves in the markets."

"Which is why we need to make wise use of our time. Spread out our orders. Purchase from multiple regions in relatively small quantities."

"It's going to be expensive."

"Winning a war often is."

Pundur leaned back in his chair and stared out the window. "I so very much want you to be a charlatan. Not just the money—I can't believe this civil war is set to last another four years. I would think the Redleafs have practically won already."

"They're still outnumbered," Retyar said. "Woodwise has an army equally trained and equipped, and they're going to hire a mercenary tactician equal to Crenden Arzan's abilities."

"And where are they even finding this mercenary? One of the lot hired by Thrake, I wonder?"

"Don't get involved, don't take sides. According to the histories, Three Corners stays neutral through the entirety of the war. We need to preserve this chain of events to have the maximum control when the time comes to make a difference."

Pundur crossed his arms. "And this is the only way? Not that I'm complaining, mind you. I simply wonder if there are other advantages you could give us. What wonders do you have aside from your library of light?"

"I didn't come through the Rift with a whole lot."

"What of that stick you carry? What's hidden under those wrappings?"

Retyar tightened his fingers around the rifle. "I'll be forthright with you, Crenden Pundur. There are other methods I could employ to win you this war. The problem is, they involve giving you weapons that would drastically change the world. I don't want to stop the Vron Empire only to see the rise of the Leverie Empire."

"Leverie's not so aggressive as to do something like that!"

"Perhaps you're right. But knowledge is hard to contain once it gets out. When people learn of my world's weapons, would you be happy with them falling into the hands of Ranisa? Whitesail? The Federation?"

"I suppose that would depend upon the weapon," Pundur said.

"I assure you, we're talking about the kind that would give you pause."

One of the ckols, who had thus far been standing quietly by the door, slammed his fist into the wall. "My liege, this is ridiculous! If he has some unbelievably deadly tool, we should be relying on its power, not this delicate plan he's concocted for us!"

"Ckol Wystro—"

"I will have my say if it means being stripped of my title!" the ckol said. He speared his finger at Retyar. "How do we know his trap will work the way he says? We could simply be luring the Silver Tide to Three Corners so their legions can overrun our city. If I'm to stake the lives of our people, our families on this man, I want it to be in a form that we can see for our own eyes!"

Pundur rubbed his fingers and eyed Retyar's rifle. *Raze it, this isn't good.*

"I'm afraid I agree with Wystro," the crenden said. "I want to see what your weapon is before I make up my mind."

"I steadfastly decline," Retyar answered. "It's my way or nothing."

"I feel I understand your dilemma, but as crenden, I'm

responsible for the lives of my province. As much as I wish not to antagonize someone who has shown us this much favor, I still need to choose the path that offers Three Corners the greatest chance of success."

Ckol Wystro and the other guard beside him placed their hands on their swords. A bead of sweat rolled down the side of Retyar's face, but he wasn't going to back down. "Make a move to steal my equipment and you will be sealing Leverie's fate. You won't get a thing from me, and if you try, I *will* kill you."

The room was silent, each man weighing the options. If even one of the Leverie made the wrong choice, Retyar would have no recourse but to defend himself. Unlike with the run-in with the mercenaries, this time he did have his rifle loaded and the trigger at easy access.

"Back down, Wystro," Pundur said. "That's an order."

"My liege—"

"Back down!"

The ckol's jaw muscles knotted and he stepped back. Retyar let out a quiet sigh of relief.

"That's my decision, Retyar Venon," the crenden said. "You have position of head captain with every authority needed to carry out your plan to stop the Vron."

Retyar nodded, now feeling a whole new weight on his shoulders. *Here I am. This is what I've decided to do with my power.*

"First order of business," Retyar said, "no one is to know who I really am. I'm simply your head advisor or accountant —whatever you can reasonably call me. You've hired my services because training your army has put a strain on finances. That should explain why you're suddenly making some odd trade deals."

"I'll establish that as your cover," Pundur agreed. "Can't exactly tell anyone the real truth anyway without looking like a madman."

"Next, everything is going to be compartmentalized. Aside from the people in this room, no one will have the full picture of what we're doing. If we proceed correctly, no one will even suspect our actions have a military application."

"Interesting use of the word 'compartmentalized', but

sounds good."

"Trust me," Retyar said. "We do this right, we can win."

Pundur looked down at the map, at the tiny blob that was the Aristocracy of Leverie. To the west, the markers delineating the massive boundaries of the Vron Empire. "Honestly, you're the only shot we've got."

Chapter 78

The electric fence hummed with menace as Retyar strode along the compound perimeter. A few days into his job at Obsidian Aerodynamics and he was finally getting less intimidated by the facility's level of security. To really get used to it, though—that was going to take a lot longer.

A shoulder nudged him closer to the fence. "You ready to touch it yet, rookie?" Khyle asked, the signature dumb grin of his stamped across his face.

Retyar glared. "I trust it works, Khyle."

"Come on, it's not that bad. Like touching a doorknob after dragging your feet across the carpet. Just a hundred times stronger."

"If it's not that bad, why even bother electrifying it?"

"'Cause them engineers are stupid, right?"

Retyar shook his head, eyeing the eight foot fence topped with razor wire. "How many times have *you* touched it, then?"

Khyle laughed. "Poked the links my first day. Threw me straight on my rear, it did!"

Wonder how many brain cells that fried.

The two of them reached their guard tower and Khyle knocked on the support beams. "Shift change."

The previous watch climbed on down, the first man looking ready to hit the sack. "Mornin', boys, and good night."

Khyle slapped him on the back. "Night shift's not good

for your health, Dryce."

"Since you're so interested in my well being, how about you volunteer for graveyard next rotation?"

"You know I'm spooked by the dark."

Retyar secured his rifle and climbed the ladder. Old wood squeaked and groaned every inch of the way, a contrast to the fresh, high-tech fence that separated him from the grid of concrete buildings inside the compound. Up top, he squared up to the railing and popped the lens covers from his binoculars, setting his eyes on the morning forest.

Khyle reached the observation platform and immediately took the single chair in the corner. "You gotta learn to build camaraderie, Doc Venon."

"That what you call ticking everyone off?"

"See, like that!"

"I'm the quiet, brooding type. I figure that's a better personality for someone who's got to stare at nothing every day. Anyway, don't call me doc."

"Turning people into sticks-in-the mud is a university specialty, I see."

Retyar didn't respond, but peered through his binoculars at a boring piece of shrubbery. Khyle muttered something to himself and chuckled as he pulled out a set of earphones.

The next few minutes passed in dull silence, making Retyar rethink his attitude. He'd taken this job so he could run away from his mistake, but silence and nothing to focus on forced his mind to loop back to the one thing he wanted to forget.

You should have taken Laski's advice so much earlier. It's your fault, Retyar Venon. You're a coward and you lost your chance with Thesha.

He turned his eyes on the distant city line of Crystal Ebb, its modern towers rising high over the forest treetops. He counted the buildings, tried to figure how many stories he could tally.

You should have seen it coming. She obviously liked Waylar from the first day they met. You should have taken the initiative then.

He wished he could prod Khyle back into his annoying banter, but his pride held him back. He shook his head at himself. This had been so stupid.

Someone knocked at the tower's base. "How's the view, fellas?"

Khyle shot to his feet and tore the buds from his ears. "View's great, sir! Deer and squirrels all over the place. Really brings out the nature-lovin' woodsman in me."

Sub Captain Mrylt climbed on up the squeaky ladder to join them. "Great place, isn't it?" he said, hands on his hips as he took in the broad stretch of nature. "I like walking the trails in my time off—the public ones, of course. Dumb idea to go hiking inside the buffer zone."

Retyar was still trying to remember everyone, but Mrylt was pretty easy. He was a grizzled veteran type who'd most definitely seen action in the military. "Doing the rounds, sir?"

"That I am." Mrylt took the chair and sat. "Mind if I do? Ah, it's tough getting older."

Retyar reassessed the man's age. Maybe it was the outdoor sun, but he seemed more wrinkled now than when he'd seen him last night. More gray streaked along the sides too, which was strange. He remembered noting his hair was only slightly peppered.

Mrylt sighed and stood. "Well, better get to it. Been getting reports about you, Khyle."

Khyle swallowed visibly. "The good kind, sir?"

"The bad kind. Slacking on the job, namely." The sub captain held out his hand. "Here, lemme see your pistol."

The gun was in Mrylt's palm in a snap. "I keep it oiled and everything, sir."

Mrylt popped out the magazine and inspected the slide. "Your knife."

"Keep that oiled too, sir," Khyle said, shoving the grip into the sub captain's hand.

"It's stainless, genius," Retyar muttered.

Mrylt nodded. "At least this seems in order." He checked his watch.

"Other slackers to inspect?" Retyar asked. Something felt off about the sub-captain's visit.

"Nah, I've only got you two."

A shot went off inside the compound. Mrylt moved in a flash, slashing Khyle's throat with his own knife. Retyar jumped back in horror, hitting the low wall of the guard platform and nearly toppling over the side. Mrylt aimed his pistol at Retyar, and he dodged a split second before the sub-captain fired. The first shot went wide, but the second and third punched him hard in the shoulder and side. Mrylt had no chance for a fourth as Retyar bull-rushed him and knocked him cursing over the wall.

More gunshots rang out, but they were in the distance, somewhere inside the compound. Retyar dropped to his knees, breathing hard. He felt at his body, found the two lumps of lead lodged in his vest. He let out a long, ragged breath, shocked at what had just happened.

Khyle. Retyar saw Khyle's throat gurgling blood as he grasped weakly at the legs of the chair. There was nothing Retyar could do for him, and he felt like retching at the drawn-out, torturous death.

"What in the six is going on?" He pulled out his radio. "This is tower three. We've been attacked by . . . by an inside agent. We have a man down. Repeat: We have a man down."

A low hiss was the only response. That and the gunfire within the compound.

"Raze it." He tried to see the fighting, but couldn't spot a thing. Turning his binoculars on the other towers, he couldn't find the other guards either. "Raze it."

He unstrapped his rifle and chambered a round with a shaky hand. Should he hold position? Whatever was happening, it seemed to be an inside job. And they needed his help more in there than out here.

Do I really want to run into a gunfight? It was a stupid, spur-of-the-moment decision that had brought him here in the first place. This wasn't the military, so no court martial if he just walked out into the forest.

Doesn't matter. You signed on to this job. You took on this responsibility.

Retyar restrapped his rifle, took a deep breath, and climbed down the ladder.

On the ground, he found Mrylt's broken body. The man was sprawled on his back, pistol and bloody knife to either side of him. Retyar bit his lip and crept closer. He was still alive.

"Can't believe I messed that up," Mrylt said with a groan. "Can't even feel my legs."

Retyar pointed his rifle at him and kicked the pistol out of reach. "What's going on here? You trying to steal some prototype tech? You work for the Milscray or something?"

Mrylt croaked a laugh. "You've no idea, Venon. We're here to keep Govunari safe."

"Yeah, that's obvious," he said dryly. "I guess when the defense forces arrive we'll all find out. Don't think you're getting away with this."

Retyar turned around to a punch to the face. When he regained his senses, he was on his back, a gun pressed to his head. "Don't worry, Mr. Venon." He recognized the man as a guard from the front gate. "We're ready for them."

The traitor pulled the trigger.

Part III:
Wave

Chapter 79

The mallet came down with a solid whack, wedging the block of wood in position for another engineer to hammer in the nails. The clash of tools was the sound of half a year of hard work come to its conclusion, and Maltan felt a swell of satisfaction looking up at the manifestation of his designs. Rising from the outer cliffs of Breakpeak, the bank of four massive windmills would be a new signature landmark for the towering city. *It's incredible how fast the imperials were able to construct all of these.* And perhaps just as incredible how quickly his own resolve not to do this had worn down. *In the end, it seems I can't not do this.*

He'd never worked with anyone like the men Nevygar had assigned him. No common laborers, these were both knowledgeable in the physical sciences and disciplined to a fault. That was, it turned out, what it meant to be a Vron legionary.

A distinct, authoritative set of footfalls approached along the stone street. "You're going to miss the opening ceremony, chief engineer," Nevygar said, coming up beside him. The peak's perpetual wind sent ripples through the general's silver cape as he looked up at the massive white sails straining against their locking mechanisms.

"I'm not so interested," Maltan said. "I leave publicity events to the politicians."

"Are you telling me you will miss the first complete operation of your grand invention? Come, tinkerer! You must be the one to give the signal."

"The signal can be given from here. This is where the main lever is, in fact."

The general grabbed him by the shoulder and sighed. "You are coming with me. That's an order."

Maltan reluctantly accompanied the Vron commander down the main avenue and towards the main plaza. The path ran parallel to the two ramps that would serve as the track for the new lift. In the center of each ramp, three grooves were cut right into the stone. Sturdy chains ran through each groove, which would connect to the drive mechanism powered by the windmills. The lift platforms would grab these chains by means of a manually operated set of claws and be pulled up and down the city. It would have been easier to set the mechanism in motion and ride it down, but he supposed it would be more proper after all to share the opening moment with the people of the city.

"How does it feel?" Nevygar asked. "Before now, you've never had the liberty of utilizing these kinds of resources."

"Liberating for me, perhaps," Maltan said, rubbing his fingers through his beard. "That's not the word I would use for the people these materials come from."

"And why not?"

"Theft and coercion are how this project is funded."

"Taxes and tribute," Negygar corrected.

"Euphemisms."

"No, they are one side of the social contract. The empire brings the people order, universal laws, roads, and public goods. It raises the human condition, expands the horizons of the common man. These things cost money, and it is the obligation of the people benefiting to pay for the service."

"A contract is accepted by two willing parties," Maltan said. "You may try to justify your robbery, but the fact remains the empire forces people into this deal at the point of a sword."

"In a generation's time, no one will think anything of it. I tell you now, the core provinces would rather die than go back to the old ways."

"You're obligated to say as such."

The general fingered the scar running down his face.

"Tinkerer, the people of the empire enjoy the highest level of prosperity the continent has ever known. Trade flourishes, and with it, the commons have found unprecedented wealth. Every year, the empire's splendor is enhanced with improved roads, better housing, clean water." He hooked his thumb in his sword belt and gazed down at the city. "Six years ago, there was a blight in the Aristocracy of Duranth. Four-fifths of their crops went bad. Tens of thousands starved. Many thousands more succumbed to rot sickness when they tried eating the spoiled harvest. Their Council begged the empire to come to their rescue, and we did. We imported so much grain that the roads were packed ox's nose to cart's end for miles at a stretch. Our legionaries renewed their fields and established better systems of irrigation. Today, thanks to the empire's efforts, Duranth is well on its way to becoming a chief exported of food goods."

Nevygar stretched out his hand in a sweeping gesture beyond the walls. "This is a story played out time and again. Vron's might allows us to aid the people of Moshon. That is our greatest goal."

Maltan stroked his beard, his thoughts on the general's claims. He doubted he had told the full story, but it was likely true the empire had done some measure of good for the continent. After all, here they were, building something not for military use, but the benefit of the people.

Leaving the former noble quarter, they entered the commons. Many of the city folk were still tending to business at home, though plenty were heading down to the main market, chatting animatedly until they spotted the general and his entourage of guards. At length, Nevygar and Maltan reached the lower city.

The main market was filled near to capacity, commoners standing about from one end of the clearing to the other. Men and women of all ages were in attendance, no few of them with young children hoisted on their shoulders for a better view. *Has my work really drawn this much attention?*

In Leverie, even Maltan's greatest achievements had ever only attracted crowds of a hundred or so for their unveilings. Here were well over a thousand, all waiting to see his mystery machine in action. He didn't know quite what to think, or what was meant by the tightening in his chest.

"My bet's on it being some sort of flour mill," one of the commoners said to a Vron soldier lounging against a nearby building. In the months since the city's surrender, the people had grown surprisingly friendly with the imperials.

"Flour mill?" the soldier answered. "How's this supposed to be a flour mill?"

"Well, what else do you use windmills for that would be any use in the city?"

"I could think of half a dozen—oh, general, sir!"

Nevygar returned the soldier's salute. "Good morning, private. Good to see everyone getting along. Help clear a path, would you?"

"Yes, sir!"

The soldier joined the front of Nevygar's guard to cut an avenue through the crowd. The general and Maltan made their way amidst the sea of people to reach a railed wooden platform at the base of the ramp. Nevygar stepped aboard and held out a hand inviting Maltan to follow. "Stand with me, tinkerer."

Maltan climbed onto the platform and turned to face the multitude of curious onlookers. The buzz of conversation rose in strength. Many of the children held up high pointed his way and called for people to look. He'd never been particularly afflicted by stage fright, but this many eyes focused on him put him in a cold sweat. What was he doing up here?

Nevygar put a hand on his shoulder and held his other out to the crowd. "People of Breakpeak! Less than a year ago, this beautiful city entered under the authority of the great Vron Empire. Before your surrender, you heard tales designed to instill fear in your hearts, to make you believe that my glorious country was here to enslave, plunder, and kill. You have seen in these months that nothing could be further from the truth! We are here not as tyrants, but as helpers, with a mission to make the continent of Moshon strong as it has never been before. The empire uplifts through the order of law and the power of engineering. Today, Breakpeak takes but its first step on the path of progress."

The general turned to Maltan. "The honor is yours."

Maltan looked out at the crowd, at the faces marked here with excitement, there with skepticism. He wondered at his role in the empire's politicking, at what benefit this could have for the darker side of empire. But he had come this far, and no matter how he looked at it this would only be good for the people of this city. He swept his gaze over the crowd, rubbed his fingers, and finally opened his mouth.

"Engage the lift!"

A soldier blew a set of clear notes on his trumpet, which Maltan heard relayed up the city slope. In the far distance, the windmills' sails unlocked and began to turn. A moment later, the chains began to rattle in their channels. Maltan felt a grin spread on his face and placed his hand on the platform's control lever. *And now, it works or it doesn't.*

With little effort, he pulled the lever, closing the claws beneath the platform and catching the chain. The platform jolted into motion, lifting them up the slope atop smooth rollers. The crowd let out gasps and shouts. Looking down, he saw amazement in a thousand faces. He understood in that moment that he hadn't just created a machine. He had just shown this city an entirely new world. Under Thrake's thumb, Maltan had been led to believe his inventions were a hindrance to society. Here, seeing the awe and excitement in the people of Breakpeak, he understood that this could be the beginning of a new era. This could be the start of an age of engineering. Memories arose of years toiling alone in his tower, dreaming of a day when the knowledge he had could bring humanity to something greater than it was. A world where the only limit of one's accomplishments was imagination itself.

The lift rose, carrying Maltan to the fulfillment of that dream. He turned to the general. "What's next?"

Chapter 80

Branches whipped against Ellaniel's breastplate and helmet, plunking and scraping as she galloped her horse with reckless speed through the mulberry grove. Her prey was just visible in front of her, crashing through the foliage as fast as his horse would carry him. *He's not getting away. Not this time.*

The rider ahead made a sharp turn, escaping from her sight. She steered her horse through the same spot, shooting into a hundred-foot clearing filled with carnage. Swords and shields clashed on all sides as her unit fought against the Woodwise ambush. Instead of a proper battle line, the fight was broken into clumps of ten to twenty per formation.

Her adversary, now clearly identified by the mint green lieutenant cords dangling from his shoulders, veered between two groups of Woodwise spearmen. "The Goldeye is on me!"

The spearmen closed ranks behind him and raised their weapons. Ellaniel screamed in fury and jumped her horse through the formation, swinging at the nearest enemy as she flew past. She felt her sword slash across mail, but getting through the line was good enough. As soon as she was on the other side, she heard a shout and crash behind her. Looking back, she saw one of her ckols rolling on the ground, his horse writhing on its side.

She returned her focus forward. The lieutenant had

stopped fleeing and was now joined by an escort of four cavalrymen and half a dozen crossbowmen. "Shoot her!"

"Defend the crendess!"

A volley of arrows cut into the Woodwise ranks, sent at them by a nearby unit of Senkani archers, but it was too late to stop the crossbowmen from loosing. Her horse took a bolt to the shoulder and fell, sending her tumbling in the dirt. It took a moment after coming to a stop to regain her senses. When she did, she saw the Woodwise were dismounted and two of their crossbowmen were grasping at arrow shafts embedded in their bodies. The lieutenant, uninjured, pushed himself unsteadily to his feet.

Ellaniel gritted her teeth and stood, glad to note her sword and shield were both still in hand. The Woodwise officer saw her coming and raised his sword.

A trumpet blared somewhere in the distance, drawing his attention to the north. He glanced at Ellaniel, then at his soldiers. "Break and withdraw!"

"You won't escape!" Ellaniel shouted. She charged as the officer ran and disappeared into the rows of mulberry trees. The men who'd defended him stayed to challenge her, but the remainder of her ckols tore in, their horses trampling them into the dust. Ellaniel followed after the lieutenant without pause.

Her quarry's path was easy to trace. The young trees were planted close together here, and a running man couldn't help snapping shoots and branches with every step. She kept her shield up, parting the foliage ahead of her. Her sword remained ready to strike at any moment, its keen edge slicing effortlessly through every leaf it touched.

Getting further away from the chaos of the battle, she could hear the lieutenant's armor and heavy breathing not far up ahead. She picked up her pace.

He moved faster as well, sensing the hunter near at hand. Branches cracked with greater urgency, but then suddenly stopped, giving way to the sound of boots on gravel.

Ellaniel burst out of the grove five paces behind the lieutenant as he raced towards a long plantation building. The man rammed his shoulder into a doorway, crashing it open and disappearing inside. She didn't spare a moment to think as she went in after him.

A blade lashed out the instant she entered the shadowy entryway, landing on her outstretched shield. The lieutenant cursed and stumbled his way further into the room. Ellaniel followed more by sound than sight. After the bright midday light outside, all her maladjusted eyes could make out were vague outlines of broad shelving, broken up by narrow aisles the length of the room.

She chased the lieutenant's silhouette down one of the center paths. He grabbed a shelf and tried tipping it to block her. It didn't budge, and the attempt instead let her close the gap and ram him with her shield. The man crashed into the shelf on the opposite side with a grunt. The wood cracked under his weight, dropping him even further and pouring the shelf's contents right on top of him.

Ellaniel stood over her prey, her eyes finally starting to adjust. She smirked as she saw the silkworms layered all over him. "Having fun there, lieutenant? Don't worry, they don't bite—"

The lieutenant kicked her square in the middle. She smashed through one of the shelves, landing in the next aisle over, covered in splinters, chopped mulberry leaves, and silkworms. As she scrambled to her feet, another pair of men burst in, wrestling over a sword. Shouts and clashing steel carried from outside. Over at the far end of the room, someone kicked open another door. "Lieutenant, this way!"

Ellaniel charged after him as he ran, jumping into the second room just as the lieutenant reached the exit. She feared she was going to lose him, but right then the door blew inwards and caught the officer in the face. Arzan rushed in, thrusting his longsword through a Woodwise soldier's neck. He blocked another soldier's swing with his arm plate and kicked back, sending his opponent into a wall of cocoon frames. Ellaniel finished that one off with a quick thrust through his throat.

"This," Arzan said, pulling his sword from the first soldier and placing his foot on the lieutenant's chest, "is the end of the road for you."

After finishing up the rest of the skirmish and ensuring the Leverie forces were no immediate threat, Arzan turned his attention to their captive inside the temporary command tent. Blood dripped down the lieutenant's face from a broken nose as he sat tied to his chair. The man was far more intent on watching the red liquid drop to the dirt than in looking up at the crenden and crendess.

"Good job chasing him down, Ella. How did you even separate him from his unit in the first place?"

Ellaniel set her helmet atop the strategy table and shook out her hair without a word. Arzan sighed softly to himself and leaned over the seated prisoner. "If you haven't guessed, we've some questions for you. Eight months ago, we thought it was going to be a simple march from Highcity to Creedport. When Woodwise showed up, it wasn't entirely unexpected, but we thought we'd be able to fight you and push on." He tapped his fingers on his sword's pommel. "We didn't expect Odavan to suddenly develop these new hit-and-run tactics. Nor for him to restructure his army so drastically, creating sophisticated signals and tiers of authority. Neither did we anticipate he'd so smoothly coordinate with the other crendens in some sort of rotating guard duty around Creedport."

The lieutenant sat quiet, still not looking up.

Arzan inched closer. "How did Odavan suddenly turn into a tactical genius?"

"I shan't divulge a thing to traitors to the Council," the prisoner said, his words stuffy from the broken nose.

Steel clicked and scraped as Ellaniel clenched her fists. "Traitors? That's rich coming from a man who's fighting the daughter of his crenden."

"Odavan is the rightful crenden of Woodwise."

"He's a scoundrel and an opportunist who sided with my father's murderers!"

"My liege was properly voted in," the lieutenant said stubbornly. "He had Hashan's blessing."

"The blessing to march an army on his daughter?"

The man swallowed. Arzan narrowed his eyes. "You know something's wrong with all this."

"I will be true to my loyalties. You are enemies to the Council and to Woodwise."

"Really?" Ellaniel said. "You really want to insist on me being your enemy?"

"Odavan is the proper—"

Ellaniel grabbed him by the hair and drew her sword before pulling his face close to hers and digging the tip of her blade into his neck. "Odavan is a traitor, a villain, and a fool," she hissed. "Where is he getting his new tactics?"

The lieutenant gulped, a drop of blood trickling down his neck. Arzan took a step forward. "Ella—"

"Back off, Arzan," she growled. She put more pressure on the blade. "What's changed?"

"Pavris!" the lieutenant gasped. "Captain Pavris! He's a mercenary who showed up just after you took Highcity. Offered Crenden Odavan his services in leading the army."

Arzan fiddled with his cape clasp, wondering how reliable this information was. "And this Pavris, where did he come from?"

"No one knows. Even the crenden's too reluctant to look a gift horse in the mouth and ask."

"And it's only him?"

"Haven't seen or heard of anyone else."

"What does he look like?" Ellaniel demanded.

The lieutenant started to shake his head, stopped short when the motion drew more blood. "Rough. Scary. Got two big scars crossing his face."

Arzan shot Ellaniel a narrow look. "Do these scars run here and here?" he asked the lieutenant, tracing a path with his finger.

He frowned. "Yes, exactly."

Arzan rubbed the hilt of his sword, remembering the night that had started all this, the man who'd tried to kill him and Ellaniel. He turned to the guards at the entrance. "See the lieutenant out. Put him with the rest of the captives."

The guards nodded and picked up the prisoner. As they exited through the flap, Arzan caught a glimpse of a Highcity Aiv Chahai join the escort. Ellaniel saw her too, and displayed her usual distaste for the women. Arzan pressed his lips tight, not going to argue with her again over the necessity of keeping to the codes. The codes she had just been dancing on the edge of breaking.

But it had gotten them significant intelligence.

"This captain of Odavan's army is one of Thrake's agents who attacked us that night," he said.

She placed her hands on her hips, her expression fierce. "And now earning double coin from Thrake and Odavan to lead Woodwise's army."

Arzan adjusted his cape clasp and thought. "Maybe—"

Ellaniel slapped her helmet off the table, sending it clattering in the dirt. "They know! They all flaming know! It's not just Thrake behind all this—it's the entirety of House Leverie!"

"That's not something we can certainly—"

"Odavan's hired the very mercenary who tried to assassinate us, Arzan!"

He grit his teeth and bent over the strategy table, his eyes trying to focus through the anger to look at the map objectively. Multiple armies protecting the prize, together outnumbering Senkani several times over, and each steadily growing in proficiency as the war raged on.

"Do you have a suggestion?" he asked.

Ellaniel jabbed her finger down on the map. "Woodwise. Thrake can wait and rot in Creedport while we pay my cousin a visit."

Arzan chuckled grimly. "At this rate, we'll end up taking every city in Leverie before hitting Creedport."

"If that's what it takes for justice to be served."

As much as he wished the war could be ended with one last assault, this last half year had demonstrated the futility of that approach. Thrake's defenders had to be dealt with before any new advance on the city could be possible.

"All right, then. To Woodwise we go."

Chapter 81

Another basket's worth of freshly harvested potatoes tumbled into the pile, and Charva bit her tongue in annoyance.

"Lot more where these came from," the farmhand said before stepping out from under the tarp and heading back into the field.

"Why do we even have to scrub these?" Charva muttered, dipping a large spud in the water bucket in front of her and swiping it with her rag.

The woman next to her snatched the vegetable and went at it with her own cloth. "How many times do I have to tell you? Harder! I want spotless golden nuggets." She held the cleaned potato up for Charva's scrutiny.

I'm calling you Gold Spud from now on, Charva thought, but she didn't voice the retort. She owed these people.

Despite her grumbling, the farm work helped. It was better than the weeks and months she'd spent in bed, healing both from the stab wound itself and from the delirium of blood poisoning. It was an incredible thing that Ersch had managed to get her treated and stowed away across the Whitesail border without the assassins following their trail.

Another farmhand stepped under the tarp. Charva tossed a cleaned potato into the next basket and shifted a little to the side to make more space for the pile to grow.

"I hope it's not too much of a problem to borrow Dancer for a moment?"

Charva looked up. It was Ersch there, bare-chested, skin shiny with sweat. Gold Spud sighed irritably. "This isn't a charity we're running here. This produce needs to be ready for market tomorrow, and that ain't happening if I let the two of you prance around playing love games."

"She's right," Charva said, scrubbing down another potato. "Is it something that can wait till evening?"

"Tenark is sending me on an errand into town. I'll be gone until the day after next."

Her chest seized up at the news. *I'll be alone for two days.* She was barely getting used to having Ersch out of hearing range.

No sooner did the fear surface than the anger followed. *I'm Charva Leverie. I'm a flaming adventurer. I don't get scared being alone at night.* But she remembered the fight in the dark. Remembered the day of helplessness and approaching death. The knife cutting into her—

I hate this! I hate this, I hate this, I hate this! Why do I have to keep thinking about that?

"I'll just be a minute." Without bothering for permission, she stood and crossed the potato field. They passed a half dozen men harvesting spuds from the loose soil before reaching the bean trellises by the road. The trellises didn't reach anywhere near head height, so it wasn't as if they were hidden, but it still gave them the greatest sense of privacy short of walking several minutes to the workers' house.

"What is it you need to talk about?" Charva asked. She thought she did a good job of keeping her voice steady. *Please, please, don't leave me on my own.*

Ersch shifted his feet and hooked his thumbs in his belt. "How well has your wound healed?"

Charva automatically touched her hand to her side. "I don't think there's any more chance of it reopening."

"I suggest it's time we crossed the border, went back to Leverie."

Her heart thudded and she felt the chill that attacked her whenever the plan came up. Memories of being bound and at the full mercy of Roth's mercenaries came unbidden to her mind's eye. She bit her lip and shook her head. "Not yet."

Ersch closed his eyes, let out a deep breath. When he opened them again, he focused straight at her face. "When?"

"When I'm ready."

"When, my liege?"

She thought of being bound and gagged, of having her own blood on her hands. "We don't have to go back." *Did you just say that? Charva, are you giving in to fear?*

Ersch stared at her, his expression impassive, for what felt an eternity. She knew his valuation of her had just dropped with her words. In truth, her own assessment of herself did the same. But she'd said it. This was an option, right?

"We don't have to return," she repeated, telling herself she was just considering possibilities. "Whitesail's much the same as Leverie. We can live here. Or if not, we can go south to the Federation."

"My liege, Creedport needs us."

"We're only two people who barely escaped getting murdered."

"And we know about Roth."

"We've sent letters."

"Last we've heard, Leverie is still at war. Our messages clearly haven't gotten through."

"And you think we will?" Charva was shaking. She couldn't help it. "You think the two of us can get to my father or get to Arzan and Ella if Roth's mercenaries are able to catch even our letters?"

"You'll abandon our home, then?"

She held to the trellises and hung her head. "The mercenaries said Creedport couldn't fall. Roth claimed he was saving the country somehow."

"You'll take the word of those scoundrels who tried to kill you?"

"We can't go back."

"It's our duty to—"

"We return and we die, Ersch!" Charva saw that he wouldn't understand. He hadn't been on the brink like she had, hadn't helplessly watched as his life ended, drained away. "Look, we don't need to be tied to Creedport or to Leverie. We can travel the world, find a new start somewhere else! We can sail the seas. No ties. No obligations."

Ersch shook his head. "But—"

"We wouldn't be separated by class. It wouldn't be inappropriate for us to . . . ."

The statement gave him pause. She saw the yearning in his eyes, the feelings he'd left unspoken all these months. He looked away quickly, perhaps so she wouldn't see, perhaps out of a war he fought with himself. "I thought all you ever wanted was to be crendess of Creedport."

Charva pressed her lips together and looked out across the road. A group of horsemen were coming from the west, but she didn't focus on them. "Some things in life we have to give up on."

Ersch lowered his eyes. "This isn't like you. Steadfast determination was what made Charva Leverie special." His tone of voice made it clear—she'd let him down.

"I—"

"I have that errand to run in the city," he said. "I hope when I get back some of the old Charva will be here." He turned away and started for the workers' house.

Charva watched him go, cursing the hand life had dealt her, but also seeing how pathetic her curses were. She'd been born with better cards than most. It was her own fault if this was where they'd landed her.

I'll get over this. I'll figure out how to fight through it.

She returned to her post.

"Lovers' spat?" Gold Spud asked at seeing her.

Charva didn't answer, only grabbed a fresh potato and set to scrubbing. Again and again, her mind tortured her with the question of what Ersch would do if she didn't get over her fear of going back. She imagined him abandoning her and getting himself killed. Again the vision of a blade in the dark made her breath catch and her hands shake.

She hated herself. Hated how fragile she had turned out to be after the bravado she had put out all her life.

A whistle cut through her thoughts. She looked up to see dread in Gold Spud's face before she hid it behind her usual harsh facade.

"What is it?" Charva asked, searching the fields with unease.

"Nothing us women need to be concerned with. Keep washing."

Her eyes caught hold of the group of horsemen at the edge of their fields. Male laborers from all around were gathering about them. Charva jumped to her feet, drawing a curse from Gold Spud. She approached the growing crowd just as one of the horsemen raised the banner of Whitesail.

"By order of the Council, one in four are called to the defense of our brothers in Heartsong. We ask first for volunteers to the army."

One man Charva knew to be two years short of twenty immediately stepped forward. "I will fight for the honor of our crenden!"

"Glory will be yours," the horseman said. "Any others?"

No one else moved.

"Very well. The rest shall be selected by lots."

Charva looked about at the thirty or so farm hands. She found Ersch's gaze from across the gathering. He gave her a reassuring nod. *It's one in four odds. Don't panic.*

The lots went quickly. When the last throw was called and Ersch wasn't selected, Charva breathed easy. She weaved through the crowd, stepping past a woman wailing as she hugged her unlucky fiancé. Before she could reach Ersch, however, someone spoke up, "I wish to have someone take my place!"

The lead horseman grimaced. "Unless someone elects to replace you, the selection is final."

The man who'd spoken pressed his fingers to his chest. "I have worked hard for my country all my life. I will not be sent off to die ahead of a deserter!" He pointed at Ersch. "If anyone's sent to the front, it should be him!"

Charva stopped dead in her tracks. *No.*

"Is this accusation true?" the horseman asked. The rest of the crenden's men abandoned a conversation amongst themselves and nudged their beasts forward.

A few mutterings passed between the farmhands. "I saw him the first day he arrived," one man offered. "He had blood on him and was carrying a sword."

No. Charva pushed her way in front of the horsemen. "He's not a deserter!"

"What's his explanation, then? In half a year, you and your boyfriend've never said what brought you here." Charva looked back and saw that Gold Spud had left her job behind as well.

The nearest workers backed away as the horsemen slipped their swords from their scabbards. "The accused is to stand before us."

"He's not a deserter!" Charva repeated. *Only I am.* Flame and embers, she shouldn't have waited so long to leave. "He's never been in the Whitesail army!"

"Silence, woman," the head horseman said. "I'll hear the story from his mouth."

The dismissal set her blushing in anger. *I'm a crenden's daughter.* But that didn't matter. Not here, in a foreign country where she hid her name. She was nothing here. Even her weapons were gone.

Ersch advanced with solid steps through the lane the laborers opened for him. "She speaks the truth. I have never served in the army."

The horseman shifted in his saddle as his mount dug restlessly at the soil. "And the account of you carrying a sword?"

Ersch looked at her. Charva swallowed and nodded.

"I'm from Leverie," Ersch said. "We were caught in the violence there and fled across the border hoping for safe harbor."

The horseman regarded him for a long moment before speaking. "Your story makes the more sense. We're far closer to the Leverie border than to Heartsong. If you were fleeing the western front, you would not cross the entire country of Whitesail with blood still on you."

Charva let out a breath.

"Step in with the other conscripts."

She choked. "What?"

The horseman turned so that his blade arm faced her. "He didn't desert from the Whitesail army, so I have no authority to execute him. I do have authority to enlist anyone I deem fit."

"But—"

"You Leverie disgust me. Whitesail sheds its blood to defend the aristocracies from the empire, and instead of sending us aid, you people fight amongst yourselves. It's high time at least one of yours did his part holding back the Silver Tide."

"You can't—"

The horseman pointed his blade at her. "Know your place! Another word and I will consider it obstruction of the crenden's business."

Ersch jumped in front of her. "Don't touch her! I'm going with you."

"Ersch . . . ."

He turned and whispered in her ear. "I'll escape as soon as I can. There's a crossroads with a covered well on the way to Three Corners. We'll meet there."

"They'll be watching you."

He smiled. "You think I can't handle a few Whitesail lackeys?"

"Enough goodbyes," the horseman said. "Fall in order."

Ersch squeezed her shoulder. He drew away from her ear, but lingered with his face a finger's breadth from hers. The moment lasted but a heartbeat before he turned to join the conscripts.

Charva felt empty as he walked off. Despite his plan, she felt certain she would never see him again. He was the last thing she had. She'd lost her city, her friends, her country, her identity, and her courage. She was going to lose him too.

"I volunteer as an Aiv Chahai!"

Ersch swung around. "Charva, no."

The horseman looked down at her, eyes narrowed. "Your loyalty to your man is admirable, but the ranks are already swelled with enough Watchers."

"An Aiv Chahai cannot be denied access to the war," Charva said. "I will go with him."

Another voice called out from behind her, "I will be an Aiv Chahai as well." It was the woman who had been crying over her fiancé's conscription.

The horseman grunted and shrugged. "So be it."

Ersch hissed as she stepped beside him. "What are you doing?"

"We escape together or not at all."

After a moment, his scowl turned to a grin. "Glad to see the old you is coming back."

It wasn't, but she didn't correct him. All she knew now was that without him at her side, she might as well be dead.

She just had to fight the fear that they'd both end up dead anyway.

Chapter 82

Maltan took in the city of Alsabriem with avid fascination. A proud sign just inside the outer gate proclaimed it The Crossroads of Heartsong, and it more than lived up to the title. Wide avenues converged from every cardinal direction, each named after the city with which it connected.

"The economic heart of the country," Nevygar said as he rode horseback beside Maltan's wagon. "Where people tread, so too flow goods and money."

"How did you capture this city?" Maltan didn't see anything more than mild fear and disdain in the faces they passed. The fields outside had been well tended and the walls intact.

"The crenden surrendered to us three weeks ago, after we obtained a majority of Alsabriem's neighbors. He is merchant-minded, after all, and he knows that his city is nothing without partners in trade. Even if the Council's armies managed to hold us off, Alsabriem would go bankrupt without access to the northern provinces."

"The city sold itself out for money, then."

"Yes, and why not? Money is a city's lifeblood. Without it, the city withers and dies. Would you subject the people here to poverty and want for the sake allegiances they were arbitrarily born to?"

"Is fealty to the empire any less arbitrary?" Maltan asked.

"No, honorable tinkerer, it is based upon strength." The general pointed to cartloads of stone and gravel towed by columns of imperial engineers. Maltan had seen many of these already on the trip from Breakpeak, paving the previously dirt highway with tireless efficiency. "The empire has the unparalleled power to protect and destroy, to build up and tear down. There is nothing arbitrary about it."

Maltan tapped his finger against the wagon's side. "And for the sake of argument, if someone else were to come with greater power than the Vron, would you consider it right for your territories to leave you? Would you let them go without reprisal, taking it simply as a matter of course?"

"If there were ever a power strong enough to challenge the Vron in such a way, well, then I must wonder if we would even be capable of reprisal. Either way, the point is moot. No one in Moshon has the strength to resist the empire." He pointed ahead of them before Maltan could respond. "But that will be a discussion for later. Here is our destination."

The wagon driver came to a halt at the edge of a broad trench that cut the length of the city. It took a moment before Maltan recognized what it was he saw. "A canal bed."

"Generations ago, Alsabriem not only connected every city in Heartsong, but also served as a terminus to the Gilgashay Tributary system to the west. War and bitter relations with the tributary aristocracies saw a decline in traffic, and eventually the Heartsong Council deemed the canal too expensive to maintain."

"And after so many years, this is what is left," Maltan finished. He stepped down from the wagon and assessed the dry canal bed. Wild grasses and brambles covered most of the ground, obscuring what little bits of the stone retaining wall weren't already buried in dirt. Here and there, the poorer elements of society had staked out their own little portions, erecting humble tarps and lean-tos. *There should be someplace decent we can relocate them*, he thought. *Probably inconvenient living there anyway.*

"And this must be the engineer of Breakpeak we've heard of!"

Maltan turned to find a small group of men in rich silks and cottons. Nevygar nodded to them. "Representatives of the local merchant guild. They have been quite eager to work together with us on this project."

"Much to be gained from re-linking the waterways," one of the merchants said, propping one foot up atop the canal wall. "The Gilgashay rivalries are ancient history, and since we've both been taken in by the empire, we're all the same people now, aren't we? Time for trade to flourish."

"Besides, this canal has been a blight on the city as long as anyone can remember," another of them said. "All it does is get stupid people drowned every time the rains come."

Maltan stroked his beard. "I imagine it should be fairly easy. Simply dredge up all the silt. Hardly something you need me for."

"To make it as before, yes," Nevygar said. "But I have an eye to widen it from the original, as well as extend the system to every one of the coastal cities. Our surveyors note some interesting elevation issues to overcome."

"Well, that changes everything," Maltan said, smiling. "Let me see your maps."

Later that afternoon, Maltan walked the canal's edge, his mind stuffed with plans and ideas. This project was far bigger than anything he had done back home, bigger even than his work in Breakpeak. It wasn't just the scale, but also the challenge. Nevygar had not been lying about the terrain. The number of locks needed would be staggering if they couldn't devise a new way of connecting the canal to the eastern coast cities. He couldn't wait to go scout out the land for himself so he could start crafting solutions.

A call for help shook him from his thoughts. He looked ahead, but saw only an imperial Aiv Chahai sitting by the canal, leisurely eating some fruit. He figured he had mistaken the sound until he heard it again, coming most definitely from a nearby alleyway. He cast a glance at the Watcher, confused that she hadn't reacted, and then hurried to the source of the call. Within the alleyway, he found a trio of soldiers holding a commoner by the arms, one of them touching a sword to the man's neck. The blade might have even been drawing blood, but it was hard to tell from all the bruising and blood already covering the man's skin.

"What's going on here?" Maltan demanded.

"Attempted sabotage," one of the soldiers said. "Nothing to concern yourself over, tinkerer."

"I didn't do anything!" the captive cried.

One of the soldiers punched him in the face.

Maltan felt queasy at the scene. "Even if he's guilty, torture is against the codes. Bring him to your captain and be done with it."

"There's too many of these rats for that. We've the general's approval."

"This man—" Maltan started.

"Was caught red-handed messing with the paving carts. I've a friend who had his leg crushed from a stunt like that."

Maltan shut his mouth. He saw the anger in the soldiers' faces. He didn't think he had the words to stop this. As sick as it made him to turn his back, he had nothing else but to leave the alley and seek out the Aiv Chahai.

"You! You're supposed to be watching against things like this."

The woman took a bite from her fruit and wiped some of the juice from her mouth onto her silver sleeve. "I'm here 'cause I promised my cousin's wife I'd keep him off the local harlots," she said, her cheek bulging. "I couldn't care less what happens to some lowlife saboteur trying to get us killed."

"It's your job to enforce the codes!"

"Lay off, old man. They're not going to kill him."

"What's your name? I'm reporting you to your superior."

She swallowed and smirked. "I don't have to tell you a thing. Get back to the engineering corps where you belong."

A scream came from the alleyway, making Maltan's jaw clench. What was there he could he do?

Knowing all too well it would take too long to be of any help, he started back in the direction of military command. He hurried past a scattering of city folk drawn to the commotion, but kept back by the Aiv Chahai's presense. For a brief moment he considered enlisting their help, but cast that aside. It would be worse to incite a riot. This city had avoided widespread bloodshed. He wouldn't be the one to bring that down on them.

I need to have Nevygar order a stop to this kind of nonsense.

He retraced his steps until he reached the set of merchant houses on the edge of the noble quarter commandeered for imperial use. The former occupants had all been die-hard Heartsong loyalists who fled the city after the crenden's surrender. Now, silver banners hung from the eaves of every building and imperial soldiers guarded every corner.

The men posted at the general's mansion nodded at the sight of him and let him through into the antechamber. Nevygar was just within, inspecting a stack of documents held out for him by an aide. He looked up. "Your walks aren't usually so short."

"I'm not usually interrupted mid-thought by groups of hooligans posing as Vron soldiers!"

The general's face went deadly. "Did some of my men not recognize you? They are all under strict orders not to—"

"I'm fine. A poor man in an alley by the canal is not. I found three soldiers beating him into an unrecognizable bloody pulp. That and an Aiv Chahai who refused to lift a finger over the crime. She didn't even care the man hadn't a fair trial over his supposed sabotage."

"Ah." Nevygar looked back down at the papers and spoke to the aide, "Make sure the crenden has a chance to see these arrangements by day's end. I want his seal on them when I set out in the morning."

"Yes, sir."

The aide left and Nevygar stepped beside Maltan, placing a hand on his shoulder. "Not the most pleasant thing to stumble upon. Perhaps some tea would be good to settle your nerves."

"My nerves will be fine on their own! See that a surgeon is sent out to help that man! And the soldiers responsible should be reprimanded immediately!"

Nevygar smiled and led him into the lounge. "It would be in bad form to discipline men carrying out my wishes."

The words set Maltan's blood cold. He stopped in his tracks. "You . . . you're saying you've *ordered* that people in this city be beaten to within an inch of their lives?"

With a sigh, Nevygar let him go and stood in front of a silk tapestry. It was a wonderful piece of art depicting some old part of the city. "Perhaps you have forgotten that this is a war."

"A war, maybe, but that was hardly a battle. The man had a right to a trial and protection against torture."

"Oh, but it is a battle, tinkerer. Not all military engagements are shield wall on shield wall. A saboteur is as much an enemy as a charging man with a sword. Considering that wars are won or lost on the basis of sound logistics, the former is possibly even more dangerous than the latter."

Maltan threw his arm. "Then arrest them! You don't need to resort to this barbarism."

Nevygar clasped his hands behind his back and shifted his eyes to regard him. "Have you thought through the repercussions of that approach?"

The question made him laugh. "Excuse me?"

"Let's say we do arrest every saboteur," the general said. "Do you realize how many there are in this city alone? In the first week after the surrender, we had dozens of instances of tampering, not to mention all those who came up with every fabricated excuse not to aid us in our needs. Do we arrest them all? Put every one of them on trial?"

"If that's what it—"

"And what does a trial even mean? It will be our word against theirs. A fair trial is only ever legitimate when it has an impartial judge. Do you expect to find one here?"

"But—"

"And once we find them guilty, what then? Do you think Alsabriem will love us when we put the saboteurs to death? Do you think that will quell rebellion, or simply set the families of the dead in eternal enmity with us?"

"The codes, general," Maltan said.

Nevygar lifted his chin. "I respect the intent of the codes, but at the end of the day they are a human construct. One cannot blindly follow their precepts, yet ignore their purpose. I tell you, when all is said and done, my way will be better for everyone."

Maltan clenched his teeth, but finally sat. Even if he didn't like it, Nevygar's argument made sense. He closed his eyes and saw again the man in the alley. Beaten, but left alive.

"No great good comes without toil and hardship," Nevygar said. "Remember that we work towards goals that not everyone sees. For everyone's sake, we must press on even when some stand in opposition."

Maltan breathed deeply and touched his nose to his laced fingers. His mind agreed with Nevygar, but he still felt ill at the violence.

The general strode behind him and placed a hand upon either shoulder. "Just like Breakpeak, Alsabriem will be a better place."

Maltan nodded. He would believe. "I must get back to work." He stood and left the lounge, trying his best to put the afternoon's events out of mind.

Chapter 85

Charva pulled the thin blanket tighter against the dreary weather, her eyes focused on the wagon floor where the toes of her boots touched against Ersch's. Days of constant travel had her tired and sore, but she hardly noticed. She only waited. Waited a chance for her and Ersch to escape.

"You think we're in Heartsong yet?" one of the conscripts asked.

"You not been paying attention?" someone else said. "All the signboards today've been pointing to Needlegrate."

"That in Heartsong?"

"It sure ain't part of Whitesail!"

Charva raised her gaze to the scattered woods around them. It could have passed for a section of the Leverie countryside. The province of Three Corners, maybe. Nature didn't care so much about human borders when crafting its terrain. Up ahead of them, about a dozen other wagons full of Whitesail conscripts rolled along the dirt road, while a matching number rattled on behind them. She and Ersch had been here in the center of the train the whole trip, making it impossible to sneak away.

"Can't wait to send the silvers packing back to their Senate." Charva recognized the voice of the teen from her farm.

War's different from what you're imagining, kid, she thought. She'd never seen the imperial army in person, but they had to be just as professional as Senkani. What chance would a young man fresh off the potato field have against them?

Ersch shifted across from her. He leaned forward and whispered, "We're getting close to the war, I'd wager. It needs to be tonight at the latest."

She nodded. "There's been no opening, though."

"Then we'll have to make one." He abruptly grabbed her hand and reached into the satchel he'd brought with him. "I didn't get around to telling you after you recovered. I managed to take this off that mercenary in Three Corners." With a discreet glance to ensure no one was looking their way, he pressed the vial weapon into her palm.

Charva's breath stopped as the steel touched her skin, flooding her memories with the day of her capture.

"I don't trust the thing, but it was easier to keep hidden than our swords. Thankfully, I saved the box with the vials, so you should be able to shoot with it."

She didn't want to take it. The thing was a reminder of her naive stupidity. She had no choice, though. One of the conscripts started to turn his head and she slipped the weapon into the folds of her skirt.

"Tonight," Ersch mouthed.

Charva started to nod, but the wagon came to a sudden halt. The occupants all looked ahead to the rest of the motionless wagons.

"What's going on?" one of the conscripts asked.

A mounted soldier came riding down the line. "On the ground! Everyone line up! Left side, left side!"

Murmurs rose as the conscripts started disembarking. Charva glanced at Ersch. Perhaps an opportunity to escape was finally here.

She gripped the vial weapon tight as she jumped down into the damp, sticky soil. She lost her balance as the mud sucked at her boots, but Ersch caught and steadied her.

Well, maybe this isn't the easiest place to try and run.

As further discouragement, a group of horsemen came trotting along. She noted their crossbows, cocked and loaded.

"March!"

The line started moving, and Charva couldn't help wondering if this was how slaves had felt in the old days.

"Where are we going?" someone asked in a low voice. She recognized it as the other woman who'd volunteered as

Aiv Chahai.

"Just stay with me," her boyfriend said.

Several clear trumpet notes sounded somewhere in the distance, sending a shiver down Charva's spine.

"Hurry it up!" the first horseman called.

They left the wagons behind and rounded a bend, coming into sight of several companies of soldiers with white uniforms and shields. A few were lined up in the first signs of formation, but most were busy securing armor and checking weapons.

Not good.

An officer sized up the newcomers and set them in a square fifteen across and six deep. Being from the middle wagon, Charva and Ersch ended up in the center of the formation. From there, most of her view was blocked, except for slim cracks between the ranks. She tried to keep her breathing steady and glean what she could of their surroundings. They were formed up just to the south of the Whitesail army. A little to the east, she saw the tops of tents. On the west was a long stretch of muddy ground that terminated in a stream. The grassy bank on the far side rose up a few feet before turning into a screen of trees.

Which way do we run? We can't get caught up in a battle.

Another series of trumpet notes told her it was already too late for that.

Charva squeezed the vial weapon. *We were supposed to have time!* Could she and Ersch try shooting their way past the horsemen? No. There couldn't be too many more vials, and the noise the weapon made would attract whatever cavalry were left.

The soldiers finished lining up. "Granite and Slate Companies, move out!"

"Where are our weapons and armor?" someone ahead of her asked. "They need to give us those, right?"

"We're not fighting. We just got here."

"You sure about that? That's not a very big army."

"Quiet in the ranks!"

A pair of officers came into Charva's thin line of sight. One of them pointed to the conscripts and then the stream. The other started arguing, but low enough that the words didn't carry.

Hooves pounded the ground. "They're at the second grove!"

One of the officers won the dispute. He broke away from the other and approached the conscripts. "All of you, thank you for coming here for the sake of your country. You were to be given basic training before your first engagement, but we've unfortunately come under assault by a detachment of imperial soldiers. Don't worry, you will not be put into battle. The enemy only needs to see that we hold the numerical advantage." He turned. "Sergeant, give them the shields and spears we have left on hand."

The fiancé from the farm shoved aside the men in the row in front of him. "Wait, take the women out of the formation!"

The officer looked between the ranks at the young man before glancing at his girlfriend and Charva, and at the small number of other women from other farms. "They stay in."

Ersch put his hand on Charva's shoulder. "Aiv Chahai are not fighters!"

"Like I said, your unit will not participate in the battle, and every head is important. No more useless babble. Anyone who steps out of line from here out will get a bolt through the chest. Do I make myself clear?"

Ersch flicked his eyes at her, his jaw muscles tight. Charva tried to keep her breathing even and slow her heart. She searched about the bit of clearing she could see. *Where are the Aiv Chahai already attached to the army? Don't they have anything to say about this?*

The logistics officers finished handing out their weapons, which were sufficient only for the first two rows. The shields were barely enough to cover the front. Charva and Ersch got nothing.

"Move out!"

Charva grabbed onto Ersch's arm as the formation started forward. The untrained mass lost most of its cohesion, turning into more of a blob than a square. The sucking mud didn't help matters. It got a little easier when they reached the wood planks set down as a stream crossing, but then her footing went from sticky to slippery. She kept her skirt above her knees to keep it from dragging in the current. While she held onto Ersch for balance, someone else grabbed her for the same as they tread through the cold, murky water.

Another series of trumpet notes split the air, closer than before. For certain it came from beyond the screen of trees along the far bank, now the near bank. The men around her had mixed levels of enthusiasm. A few looked ready to chance their luck with the mounted crossbowmen at their flanks. Others kept eager eyes forward.

"Should've given me one of them spears," someone grumbled behind her. "What kind of rotten setup is this?"

"Just stay with me," the fiancé said to his girl. "Whatever happens, don't let go."

They reached the grassy bank and scrambled up to the treeline.

"Shields front! Shields front!"

The conscripts stamped their way through the bushes and low branches until abruptly coming out into a broad meadow of knee-high grass.

"Form up!"

"Six continents, we're close," one of the shield bearers said.

Charva couldn't see a thing ahead of the unit, but a trumpet call sounded disconcertingly near. She heard shouts and marching feet to the right of the formation. "Ersch, can you make anything out?"

He pushed himself up on his toes and swiveled his head about. "The officer was right. We've got the silvers outnumbered, but not by much."

Whitesail's going to lose this battle. But maybe that was to their advantage. "Be ready for the rout," she whispered.

He nodded.

Another string of trumpet notes, faster paced than before. A shout. Someone started banging wood on wood. In seconds, the air filled a rhythmic clash of hundreds of spears and shields. Charva's hairs stood on end at the raw aggression projected in the noise. Two of the men ahead of her shared a look and began stomping their feet in unison. It spread through the rest of the formation, and soon the very ground was shaking under her, sending tremors up her legs. It was exhilarating and terrifying all at once.

The Vron answered with a trumpet blast louder than all the others, so sudden that the Whitesail lines went still. The trumpet blared again, and was followed by a vicious roar that made more than one man flinch. On its heels was another war cry, lower in volume, but just as ferocious. And it grew closer.

In the direction of the main Whitesail army, she just barely heard someone shriek, "Brace!"

Wood crashed once more on wood, but this time it was joined by singing steel and bloody screams.

"What's going on?" Charva demanded.

"The imperials are—" Ersch started.

"The silvers have their backs turned to us!" someone up front shouted. "We can charge and take 'em!"

"No, we're told to stand here. We can't go charging with only thirty spears."

"One man can turn a battle. You know the songs."

"You can't leave the rest of us alone!" someone called from Charva's row.

"Our side's starting to break! We need to charge now or we lose!"

Charva cast a wild and pointless look around her. "Ersch, why isn't an officer taking charge?"

"I . . . I think he's gone."

"Our side's fleeing!"

"We need to charge!"

"Six continents, they're coming for us!"

All argument died. The formation collapsed in the span of a heartbeat. The front line broke first, pushing and screaming their way back. For the first time, the scene ahead opened up to her, letting her see the perfect wall of silver shields rushing in. In the next instant, the wave of bodies carried her away. It was all she could do to keep her feet and not get trampled in the stampede to escape. She couldn't even tell where Ersch was.

The ground disappeared beneath her as they hit the bank. *When did we pass the trees?* She hit the back of the man in front of her, sending his face into the back of the one in front of him. Her feet didn't even find purchase before someone shoved her to the side. Her left foot finally touched down only for her to get pushed again. She slipped face first into the frigid stream.

Get up! Get up!

Water rushed past her ears. A kick landed in her side even as she scrambled with one hand along the wood crossing planks. Her head broke the surface to screams and the sound of steel cracking through bone.

Move!

She stood. Someone tried shouldering his way past her, but she latched onto his arm to help her gain momentum. She got three steps before the man shook her off. "Stop dragging —" he looked back and his eyes went wide.

Charva ducked instinctively and heard a blade whoosh past her ear and land in flesh. The man dropped, his body tripping her into the water. She landed this time on her hip, facing the enemy. The imperial loomed over her, cold blue eyes regarding her from within his polished helmet. At his side, blood dripped off the tip of his sword into the brown current.

Charva sat paralyzed. The memory of the last time she'd been stabbed froze her limbs in place. The imperial drew back his sword.

A woman's scream jarred her enough to dodge the thrust. She twisted to the side, letting the blade pass an inch from her chest. The motion brought her off the edge of the crossing plank. Her body slipped into the muddy stream bed, her head falling below the water. She fought with the sludge, trying to get as far away from the soldier as she could. When finally she pushed up, spluttering for air, she was sure she should have gotten out of his reach. Her heart stopped once she opened her eyes. He was still right there.

To blazes with this stream.

The soldier dropped to his knee and raised his sword. The man was just like the mercenary in Three Corners. Emotionless. No sign of regret nor remorse. For him, her death would just be another day on the job.

With a familiar roar, Ersch tackled the imperial. The two of them splashed into the water right next to her, the soldier's shield nearly clipping her in the face as it sailed free. Charva tried to get some distance, but the muck stubbornly held her close. The two men thrashed at each other, half blind. Ersch managed to grab the soldier's sword hand, but without free use of his legs couldn't utilize his throws. They struggled over the blade, a contest of brute strength.

Charva wanted to help, but she could barely move. She tightened her fists and realized she was grasping something in her right hand. She looked down. *Flame and embers!* By some insane luck, she had held on to the vial weapon through all the chaos.

She pulled back the top and let it snap back into place. Just as she raised it at the imperial, the two men twisted around. She lowered the weapon, horrified that she could have shot Ersch.

"Turn him this—"

Ersch broke the sword free from the imperial's grip. He swung the sword around, aiming at the soldier's neck. The soldier threw up his arm in defense and the blade caught in his wrist. The man screamed, but it was a sound of fury more than pain. Almost faster than Charva's eye could follow, the imperial bared a dagger with his remaining hand and plunged it into Ersch's chest.

"No!" she screamed. She lifted the vial weapon and pulled the trigger. The contraption jumped in her hand with a bang and a flash of flame at its mouth. A ping sounded off the imperial's helmet. At first, she was sure whatever the thing shot had deflected, but the soldier collapsed into the water, blood turning the current red around his head.

Charva tore her wide eyes off the dead imperial. She strained against the muck to grab Ersch just as he slowly started to fall. "Ersch?"

He was looking at the dagger, his hand wrapped weakly about the hilt.

"Ersch?"

He leaned heavily into her, unable to support his own weight. He swallowed, then opened his mouth. "I . . . . "

His light faded from his eyes.

The world around Charva ceased to exist. She held Ersch in her shaky arms, not believing this was real. He couldn't be dead. They were supposed to escape together. He was supposed to be her loyal companion. She was supposed to repay him for everything he'd done for her.

He wasn't supposed to leave her.
Alone.

Some time later, an officer in white rode across the planks and stopped next to her. She had the vague sense she had missed a battle, but didn't care. The officer's shout came as if through a haze, "Commendations all around for drawing the imperials in and breaking their formation. Everyone still fit to fight is now a regular. Welcome to the war."

Chapter 89

"Jarsoon, get over here and secure that rigging!"

With a groan and dramatic spread of his arms, Jarsoon turned from the *Merryway*'s starboard rail and thumped over to work the ropes. "This smell is killing me, cap," he said through the wet cloth tied to his face. It seemed to do nothing against the retched stench of rotten eggs that rose from the ship's hold.

Captain Braussi scratched at the thick hair on his arms and turned the wheel, adjusting the *Merryway*'s course to stay center of the Windings River. "A job's a job."

"You don't have to take every job that comes our way—especially when it involves blistering Volcana merchants who don't know how to do a proper barrel seal!"

"Suck it up or you can swim to shore!"

Jarsoon rolled his eyes. "You're running a skeleton crew as it is, cap. Four men for a six-man sloop? I'd like to see you make the rest of the trip to port after chucking me overboard." He finished resecuring the line and glanced up at the mainsail. Decent breeze. Enough to nudge them faster than the current, but not enough to clear out the smell of their cargo. "Black blistering sulfur," he muttered. "Why can't the dye merchants find something less foul to make colors out of?"

The complaints were still swirling around his head when he heard something thunk against the side of the hull. Looking around, he saw Amkar and Shalms, the two other sailors, leaning over the rail by the bow. "Hey, we bump something?" he called.

Shalms shrugged. "Someone just dropped an oar ahead of us."

Next to him, Amkar grinned and picked at his scruffy blond beard. "Hey, you know the joke about the Ranisa oarsman?"

Shalms started trudging back to work. "No, Amkar, and no one wants to hear it."

"Aw, come on. It involves a cat and pretty maidens and everything." Amkar started telling it, but Jarsoon wasn't listening. He instead had his eyes on the river, his mind on rumors that had been going around at the last port in Whitesail.

"Hey, captain, you think there might have been something to those claims of pirates?" he asked.

"No pirates on the Windings," the captain answered. "Who ever heard of brigands in the central aristocracies?"

True. But it was unusual times, what with the empire coming in from the west and the Leverie provinces in civil war. Sure, they were still in Three Corners waters, but . . . .

He narrowed his eyes. Who were those three people along the north shore?

"Hey, cap," he said as the strangers hopped into a raft and pushed off towards the *Merryway*.

"They . . . they coming for us?" the captain said.

Jarsoon felt a sudden chill. "They have swords!"

The captain cursed and spun the helm. "We have the wind with us. We'll outrun them just fine."

The men in the raft waved their arms and shouted something, but Jarsoon didn't bother trying to listen. He ran to the crew quarters and grabbed his shortsword, as well as Shalms' long butcher knife. The captain always laughed when Jarsoon suggested they get boarding spears. Well, who would be laughing now?

Captain Braussi, apparently. Jarsoon heard the man's booming cackle as he went back out on deck.

"See, what did I tell you?" he said, pointing at the raft now falling in their wake. "Set off too late to intercept with something so slow. We'll be around that next bend in no time and never see another sight of 'em."

"Still shouting taunts at us, cap," Amkar said, leaning out over the stern.

Jarsoon handed Shalms his knife and joined Amkar in the back. Yep, the pirates were shouting. He mockingly put his hand to his ear. "You saying something, you lowlifes?"

"Drop anchor!" they called.

He shook his head with an incredulous grin. The brazen nerves of some people.

"Um, fellas?" Shalms spoke up.

The tone of his voice set Jarsoon's hairs on end. He turned slowly. Out ahead of them, another ship, a schooner, was coming in sight around the bend. It was anchored against the current, but with plenty of men up on deck. Men armed with swords, spears, and crossbows.

The captain spun the wheel, turning them hard to port. That would swing them the long way around the bend and wide around the pirates, but Jarsoon immediately saw it was the worst thing they could do.

"Cap, we have to cut past them!" he called, racing up to the helm. "Don't go wide!"

"We ain't going anywhere near those killers!"

The pirates pulled anchor and dropped the sails.

Bloody shyles. Too late.

"Shalms, Amkar! Ready to defend!"

"We'll be fast enough!" Braussi said. "We have the momentum!"

Jarsoon's eyes stayed locked on the pirate ship, which was getting underway with frightening efficiency. They had their sails spread and catching wind. With the *Merryway* taking the outside of the turn . . . .

"Adjust those sails, you bafoons!" the captain shouted. "We need to catch as much wind as—"

Jarsoon leaped down to the maindeck. It was no use trying to slow his racing heart as he stood straight, his hand tight on the grip of his sword. Across the water, the pirates were gathering speed. There was no hope of outrunning them.

"This is going to get messy," Jarsoon said, taking stock of their opponents. Four pirates with spears, two with swords, and four with crossbows. The *Merryway* began finishing the turn and the pirates closed in.

Captain Braussi straightened their course and slammed his fist on the helm. "Well, this is it, boys."

"Shalms, get ready over there," Jarsoon said. "Amkar, stay behind cover until I can get you one of their weapons. As soon as they—"

Braussi stormed up and slapped him across the face. "What in the six are you trying, boy? Put that sword down! We're surrendering!"

"Cap—"

Something wooshed past and thunked into the far railing. Jarsoon felt something warm trickle down his arm and looked down to see a slash in his sleeve and flowing blood. Lifting his gaze, he saw one of the crossbowmen respanning his weapon. The other three had their aim on Jarsoon and Shalms.

Shalms dropped his knife and raised his hands.

"Let it go, son," Braussi said, hand tight on Jarsoon's shoulder. "None of this is worth dying over."

Jarsoon always thought he'd have the courage to fight in this kind of thing, but now even his knees were shaking. Ashamed, he let the sword fall to the deck.

The pirates came alongside the *Merryway* and secured the boarding planks. The two men with swords crossed over first, followed by the spearmen, while the crossbowmen remained on their ship.

One of the swordsmen pinched his nose. "What in the six continents is that smell?"

"Our cargo's sulfur," Captain Braussi said.

Two of the spearmen went to the barrels lashed to the middle deck and pried one open, revealing the yellow powder.

"Search below deck for the moneybox," the swordsman said.

Jarsoon knew they wouldn't find much. The *Merryway*'s last trade had been settled on credit, and aside from living and operating expenses, the captain's money was all deposited in the Leverie public bank. That reinforced just how stupid it was for Jarsoon to have tried fighting. There wasn't even anything aboard for the pirates to steal.

They made plenty of ruckus searching the cabins. He heard them smashing open drawers and upending furniture. While they were at it, one of their men took the helm to keep the *Merryway* steady with the other ship.

It took some time before the pirates came back top. One of them threw Braussi's moneybox to the lead swordsman. "All we found, boss."

The pirate leader flicked the lip up and set his jaw at the contents. He glared at the captain. "Where do you hide the rest of it?"

Braussi grit his teeth. "That's all we've got with us."

The pirate glared at him a moment, then snapped his fingers and pointed to Shalms. One of the spearmen backed Shalms against the mast and touched the tip of his weapon to his belly. "You want to try me, mud slurper?" the leader said. "Tell me where the rest of the money is or you'll be seeing your crew's entrails decorating the deck."

Jarsoon's feet rooted themselves in place as he felt the blood rush from his head. Captain Braussi went utterly pale as well.

"I'm telling you, that's all there is!" Braussi said. "My suppliers know I'm good on credit!"

The pirate leader rested the flat of his blade on his shoulder and sighed. "Muddy waste of time." He flipped the sword and slashed it across the captain's throat.

"Cap!" Jarsoon screamed. He started forward, but a strike to his head toppled him to the deck. His vision swam, refocusing just as Braussi fell nearby. The older man's hands clutched at his neck, useless against the flow of blood gushing around his fingers. His frantic eyes found Jarsoon. His mouth opened, but issued more blood instead of words.

No. No, drown it, no!

"Kisl, what in blazes was that for?"

"What, you care about our marks now? You didn't object when we threatened this knucklehead here."

"That was a bluff! The local crendens have ignored us so far because they've got a war to fight, but if we start killing people we'll have their soldiers to deal with."

Jarsoon found the strength to crawl towards Captain Braussi. *I should have fought!*

A pirate stomped the deck beside Jarsoon, and the tip of his spear touched his cheek. "Don't you start messing around, you little—"

Jarsoon grabbed the shaft of the spear and focused his weight into it. The blade thrust down and lodged into the deck. The pirate cursed, but he couldn't draw back the weapon as Jarsoon lifted his shoulder up into the villain's stomach. Fear and agony and rage surged in his veins as he roared and pushed the pirate up, throwing him at least six feet.

The other pirates turned. Jarsoon knew he was as good as dead now, but he was going to go down fighting. He ran and scooped up his sword just in time to use it to block a slash from one of the scoundrels. Another of the pirates thrust a spear, missing Jarsoon by a hair as he desperately twisted to the side.

"Surround him!"

Jarsoon put his back to the railing, three pirates forming a half-circle in front of him. He flailed his sword to keep them at bay, but knew this was the end. The criminals closed in, spear points primed to thrust. Jarsoon growled through grit teeth, bracing for the pain of a blade in his gut.

A crack split the air and something flew into a pirate's chest. Jarsoon blinked at the crossbow bolt lodged in the man's body, as shocked as he was. He tried to turn to see where the shot had come from and saw a man jump between the ships and land on the *Merryway*. Clad in chainmail and armed with a longsword, the man charged straight for the pirates.

Jarsoon gaped in shock as the newcomer tore through the pirates with expert precision. The first spearman thrust and got the shaft of his weapon slapped aside, leaving him open for a slash across the throat. The man kicked the chocking pirate into one of his fellows and engaged the third pirate surrounding Jarsoon. The pirate parried a single slash with his sword, but failed to defend against the following cuts to his arms and a stab to the chest. The second pirate disentangled himself from the dying man clutching at him and charged. Jarsoon wasn't even sure how the swordsman killed him— only that it took a mere flick of the wrist and the pirate was down with blood seeping onto the deck.

The rest of the surviving pirates knew what was what. They tossed their weapons and jumped into the river.

Jarsoon's savior watched to make sure the pirates were swimming away before wiping off his blade and sliding it back in its sheath. He checked on Captain Braussi's motionless body and shook his head, then moved on to assess Jarsoon, Amkar, and Shalms. The other two were white as a sheet, but otherwise unharmed. Finally, the man turned towards the pirate ship. "Might want to get over here, unless you plan on piloting that thing all by yourself."

A fellow ran and jumped the gap between ships just as the two vessels pulled enough apart for the planks to fall. He landed hard, a covered sword or rod of some sort nearly slipping from his shoulder, but kept his feet. The newcomer ambled over on unsteady land legs. "Sorry I only got the one shot off. Crossbows take ages to reload!"

"That was better than enough. Honestly, I'm impressed you hit him, Retyar."

The man named Retyar shrugged. "Different from what I'm used to, but not too different. And you've seen me at the practice range! I can clearly hit a target!"

"Better than you can swing a sword, I'll grant you that."

Jarsoon tore his eyes away from the captain's body. The two of them had traded plenty of jabs over the years, but Braussi had become something near to a second father to him. He'd give the captain a full and proper send-off and a personal account to his family. But for now . . . .

"Well, I think I had better ask who you are so I can give proper thanks for saving our lives."

The warrior pulled a patch from his pocket. "Ckol Mazeari in service to Crenden Pundur."

Retyar knelt down by one of the dead pirates. "Retyar. Also in service to the crenden. We arranged a purchase of a large cargo of sulfur, but on our way to the trade heard of pirates harassing ships on the Windings River. We saw you heading into their trap and tried to flag you down. I'm sorry we weren't successful."

Jarsoon clenched his fists. *It's my fault.*

Retyar touched his shoulder. "Who's in command of the

ship?"

Breathing deep, Jarsoon pointed to Braussi.

The crenden's man sighed sorrowfully. "I'm sorry. Second in command?"

Amkar and Shalms were both older, but Jarsoon was more commonly the one left in charge in the cap's absence. "That's me."

"Permission to inspect the cargo?"

"It's just sulfur."

Retyar nodded. "That's exactly what we're buying." He went down below deck, emerging only after some time. "All intact. We will stay aboard until reaching port. The crenden will pay the full contract price, as well as for all your losses and injuries."

"It's our own fault for being so foolhardy."

For the first time, Jarsoon noticed the green of Retyar's eyes. Odd. "You don't know how important this shipment is for the aristocracy. We're the ones who should have safeguarded the transport better. Accept the payment and take good care of your ship and crew, captain."

It took a moment for Jarsoon to realize the title of address. Amkar put his palm on Jarsoon's back. "We'll get to port and then sort all this out, eh? For now, we can finish this trade in the captain's memory."

Jarsoon breathed in deep. "Yeah. Yeah, we'll do that."

Chapter 85

Arzan snapped his horse's reins taut between his hands as he sat and surveyed the enemy formation. It was a sight he had been waiting to see for months. Rows and rows of troops in Woodwise blue stood at the far end of the fallow fields, perhaps two thousand men strong. Behind and around them, nothing but open ground and low boundary markers. Their banners ruffled in the breeze and the early afternoon sun shone off their helmets and swords, while up above a murder of crows circled and awaited a feast.

"I don't like this," he said.

"We can take them," Ellaniel answered beside him. Her horse pawed at the loose soil, just as eager as its master. "We're evenly matched in number."

He didn't look behind at the Senkani and Highcity soldiers at his back. They had just finished forming a line, having marched here to the field of combat eager for blood. They certainly matched Woodwise man to man, but with a heavier proportion of archers, as well as a clear advantage in artillery in the form of five ballista crews.

"It doesn't feel right for them to meet us straight on. Up until now, they've insisted on hounding us in surprise ambushes. They've done everything to avoid a pitched battle."

"There's no longer a choice," Ellaniel said. "The terrain doesn't favor that tactic here. Not enough to keep us from the city."

Arzan wasn't convinced. There were more open areas this

side of the province, but it was still called Woodwise for a reason. Senkani would have to pass through several more forested areas before coming to the city, so why did the enemy commander mass here?

A scout came galloping to the front. "My liege, we've not found any sign of reinforcements lying in wait. It's clear for at least three miles in all directions."

The report did more to unnerve him than set him at ease. *What about the other crendens? Where are they?*

Ellaniel seemed to read his mind. "If the Council is trying to take this chance to strike at our own cities, they'll find the garrisons more than a match."

Out across the fields, the enemy remained in place, unmoving. No shouts even from their commanders. Arzan eyed them a moment more, a sense of foreboding tugging at him as he fingered the clasp of his cape. He gritted his teeth before he raised his arm. "Center infantry, set the wall one hundred shields across, ten deep. Remaining infantry, split into six squares. One square stand at each flank. The rest stay in reserve. I want the archers formed behind the left square and artillery in front of the right."

His unit commanders went to carry out the orders. In the distance, the Woodwise shuffled their own formation. They didn't try to copy the Senkani, but rather formed a sort of stagger pattern, similar to merlons set flat on the ground.

"This commander thinks he's Harth the Unbreakable," he muttered.

"What?" Ellaniel asked.

Arzan pointed. "That's the style used in Originate during the era of the Stone Legions."

"What's it for?"

"Unit rotation and breaking the other side's line." He shook his head. "Only works if your men have trained extensively in it. Otherwise, they're liable to break once the forward squares start getting surrounded."

Ellaniel smiled as she eyed the enemy. "Let's rout them, then."

Arzan frowned. This felt more and more wrong. From the level of strategy he'd seen of Odavan's captain so far, he couldn't believe the man would use this formation without knowing its shortcomings. *What am I overlooking?*

"My liege, the men are in position."

He drew in a breath and shook his head. "Advance until the archers and artillery are within distance."

The army moved forward, creeping closer until they were in range for volleys.

Well, whatever they're plotting, they have to close with us first. "Archers, commence attack. Artillery, maintain a steady assault on the right flank, but reserve five bolts per crew."

The men set to carrying out his orders. Wood groaned and creaked as engineers put tension to the ballistae. At the opposite end of the army, archers stuck their arrows in the dirt, ready to snatch up in rapid shot. Across the field, the enemy still stood in place, though he could see men fidgeting about.

"Archers, notch!"

Arzan let his sergeants shout the commands as he silently sat and watched. The Woodwise lines raised their shields high as a mass of Senkani arrows launched skyward. Just as the missiles reached their peak, the first ballista bolt sprang forward. The artillery tore a hole in the enemy formation an instant before the arrows landed. Hundreds of wooden thunks told him most of the volley had been ineffective, but a handful of screams carried to his ears, not all of them from the right flank.

A second volley was set to flight, together with another ballista bolt. Arzan braced himself, ready to call his men to defend against an enemy charge or counterattack, but to his vexation nothing came. A third volley landed, then a fourth and fifth, and still the Woodwise stood their ground and took it.

The close knit of Ellaniel's eyebrows told him she was as confused about this as he was. "Why are they letting us dwindle their numbers?" she asked quietly.

Arzan hailed a scout newly come in. "Anything to report?"

"No, my liege. No sightings of anything at all."

"Maybe the mercenary captain decided he wasn't getting paid enough," Vighkon suggested.

Ellaniel hissed. "I hope not. He needs to be here for me to

twist my blade in his gut."

The morning wore on until the last of the arrows and most of the bolts were spent. The Senkani archers stepped back and the Woodwise lowered shields bristling with feathered shafts. The right flank was all but obliterated, a few clumps of haggard soldiers standing surrounded by red soaked soil and over a hundred mangled bodies.

"Shields, make ready."

Arzan took in a long, steadying breath. *All right, no more second guessing. Keep alert, but do not hesitate.* "Infantry forward. Artillery, launch four barrages as the men close. Hold the fifth bolt at the ready."

The ballista crews obeyed and pounded the Woodwise lines as the Senkani and Highcity soldiers marched in, shields tight. Splinters and blood exploded into the air with every hit. The screams of the dying grew louder as Arzan inched his horse along behind his men. The army came within the last hundred feet of the enemy.

"Shields, halt. Form up."

He gave them a handful of moments to straighten out.

"Ballistae, launch!"

The artillery loosed the last of their bolts, smashing into the Woodwise formation. Before any of the bodies hit the ground, Arzan shouted, "Infantry, charge!"

With a roar, the Senkani and Highcity men raced at the enemy. The Woodwise braced against the tide.

Their shield arms will be tired from fending off the arrows. We shouldn't have trouble—

A whistle cut him off mid-thought. The Woodwise split their ranks just as the attackers were nearly on them. Arzan's throat tightened and his eyes went wide in horror. The enemy's solid formation had been hiding two dozen ballistae of their own.

"No—"

The artillery loosed as one, ripping into the charging force at point-blank range. Splintering wood, snapping bone, and bloodcurdling cries of anguish sounded all along the line. Those not hit directly by the barrage stumbled to a halt mere feet from the enemy shields.

The voice of a Woodwise commander bellowed into the

air, "Attack!"

Arzan spent a wasted heartbeat with his mouth agape as the enemy closed and engaged the shattered Senkani wall. He quickly shook himself out of it. "Reserves, bolster the line! Don't let the wall break!"

The Woodwise had abandoned their previous staggered formation, and were instead molding to the fractured Senkani line, pressing hard into the holes created by the ballistae. With the reserve units pushing directly in to fend off collapse, Arzan had nothing left to maneuver. It was a straight-on test of strength. He looked over the thousands of soldiers and locked on to the enemy commander mounted at the rear of his army. From this distance, he had no way of telling if he was the hired assassin he'd faced so long ago now in his city's square.

He looked back at the battle. Was there something he could do? Could he and his ckols strike the flanks? Would the enemy commander's guard attempt to intercept them? His hands tightened on his reins.

"Ella, can you tell how many men their commander has around him?"

She stood in her stirrups and shielded her eyes against the sun. "I count sixteen cavalry."

"Our ckols are twelve." There used to be twice as many between them, but the war had taken its toll.

"My liege, I advise you not—" Vighkon started.

"We're doing it," Ellaniel interrupted. Her golden eyes burned.

Arzan drew his mace. "We ride." He urged his horse into motion, Ellaniel right beside him. He no longer tried to dissuade her from the fights. In the back of his mind, he wondered if there was some truth to what people said about her Originate blood. As much as he wanted to keep her out of harm's way, perhaps she was born to this.

He galloped for the right flank. The Senkani at least had local superiority here, thanks to the beating dished out by the artillery. His men were pushing hard, and if Arzan hit with the cavalry it could be enough to put some to rout.

"They're coming for us," Ellaniel called.

Behind the raging battle, the Woodwise cavalry raced to

intercept. The commander was with them, but at the rear of the pack. *Murder in the dark. Ambushes in the woods. This man is a coward.* The thought made him want to beat him down even more. How dare someone like him take and destroy so much?

Arzan held his mace in his left hand and pointed it out at the Woodwise commander. The man's head was turned his way, and Arzan felt certain he saw the promise.

They came to the edge of the battle and he steered his horse around to aim at the enemy flank. The Woodwise cavalry accepted the bait, forming a wedge and hurrying to cut him off. The Senkani ckols built their own wedge behind him as he turned to meet them head to head. Arzan flourished his mace in his mainhand and grabbed his shield, shouting in fury as the two forces met. He was the first to strike, smashing the opposing point man in the face. The enemy's helmet twisted around with the blow, hiding the gore, his own mace slipping free from his mistimed swing. Arzan ducked an attack from the next rider, then deflected a sword on the left with his shield. He hit another cavalryman with a glancing blow to the shoulder plate. The commander was the last behind him. Arzan didn't have his mace ready as he sped past, but he saw the man's face.

Yes, it was him. He couldn't forget those cold, ruined features. This was the man who had set the spark to begin this all. Yet as he slowed to a trot and turned around, goosebumps covered his skin. The mercenary captain hadn't attacked him. He'd watched Arzan ride past and smiled.

Arzan checked the damage. He had lost three riders to the enemy's four. Seven horses cantered away from the fight without direction, a couple of them dragging their lifeless masters through the dirt, one foot caught in the stirrup.

Ellaniel rode her horse in circles, not stopping. The black lace covering her right arm plate hung loose, the fabric slashed. "It's him!" she said. "He's the one from the festival!"

Arzan watched the enemy horsemen form back up. Their commander shielded himself once more with his men.

"We take him down this time," Arzan called. "On me!"

He charge the moment they were ready. His mace held high, he grit his teeth against his horse's gait. The formations closed. He swung at the new vanguard. The shaft of his weapon connected with the enemy's and slid up, catching on the flanged head. The mace tore from Arzan's grip. He grabbed at his sword, raising his shield to fend off an attack from the next horseman. The rider after that went down with a startled shout as Arzan slashed at the man's mount across the neck in the same motion as his draw. He made sure to have his sword ready this time for the commander, holding it point out to bury in the mercenary's throat.

The commander saw him coming and parried. Blade scraped across blade, trailing sparks until they sheered free into open air. Arzan grunted in frustration, turning his horse to circle around for another clash.

The Woodwise cavalry didn't match his desire. They galloped back towards the center of the battle line, their horses kicking up clods of dark soil in their wake.

"Don't let him escape!" Ellaniel shouted from right behind him.

"We'll be right behind their entire army if we follow!" Vighkon said. "It's suicide!"

A piercing whistle cut through the clash of war. Before his eyes, the Woodwise line drew back. For a brief moment, Arzan thought they were sounding the retreat, but then he saw the ballistae reloaded and exposed. They shot their bolts in a second barrage, ripping into the Senkani who tried going after the Woodwise soldiers. His gut twisted.

We're losing.

He reined in his horse, letting Ellaniel shoot ahead of him. She slowed and turned around. "What—"

"We're going back."

She pointed her sword after the commander. "We can still win if we kill him!"

It was too late for that. The mercenary officer was skirting close to the infantry, many of whom now saw the Senkani horsemen.

Ellaniel finally stopped. She let loose a cry of wordless rage and turned her horse back the way they'd come.

The two armies met again as they rode around the flank. Arzan kept his eyes on the line, noting spots where their side was beginning to crumble. This was the first time in the entire war his men were actually *running*. He bit down on his pride.

"Retreat! Break off the fight!"

He rode across the length of the battle, repeating the order. There were groups that followed the command immediately, turning on their heels and fleeing the fight. Far too many were either too engaged or too stubborn and stood their ground against increasingly messy odds. Arzan was helpless as the enemy overwhelmed their suddenly exposed flanks. He couldn't help but feel he'd just killed them.

Two long calls of the whistle rose through the shouts and screams. Arzan's jaw tightened as he expected the Woodwise to charge on the heels of the fleeing Senkani. Instead, the enemy drew back, even pulling their ballistae along with them. The surviving Senkani holdouts hesitantly peered over their shields and watched the enemy go. As they stood there in confusion, a line of lightly armored Aiv Chahai filtered through the Woodwise soldiers and stopped several paces from the dead and injured strewn across the field.

Arzan blinked, not believing what he was seeing. "*Now* they respect the codes?"

"What are they doing?" Ellaniel asked.

"Allowing us to collect the wounded." He shook his head, unable to reconcile this with the rest of the war. Not able to forget the image of the Woodwise commander smiling at him during the fight. What kind of treachery was this?

But he couldn't ignore the offer. His men had watched their friends and family slaughtered outside Creedport the last time they had left their wounded behind. He surveyed his soldiers. Battered units stood in formation, eyes on him.

"Save those you can," Arzan said.

The men returned to the field, shields raised in caution until they came to the injured. The Woodwise army remained true to the codes and didn't cross the Watchers' line.

"Do they actually remember the meaning of honor?" Vighkon asked.

Arzan looked at the Woodwise troops. Maybe they did. When he spotted the mercenary commander, the idea faded. The way the man sat on his horse, it didn't speak of respect. No, he was only smug. He had the stronger army, and he was rubbing it in.

Arzan dug his heel into his horse's side, turning away from the field. He would make this man regret his false mercy.

Chapter 86

"Column, halt!"

Dust swirled as Charva stopped in her tracks amidst the thick mass of Whitesail soldiers. She took off her helmet and wiped sweat and grime from her face, not caring that it marred her uniform's white sleeve. The sergeants hated when the troops did that, but what were they going to do to her? It wasn't like she had anything left to lose. She let some of the heat dissipate from her head before putting the helmet back on with a lazy swoop.

The officers kept the column in place for some time, leading the soldiers around her to whisper guesses as to the reason for the delay. Being at the edge of the formation, Charva had a clear view of the empty fields of rolling grasslands to her left. The vast landscape stretched far to a series of low mountains in the distance. A few lone trees stood thin and straight across the scene, breaking up the monotony, but overall it felt like a fitting reflection of Charva's heart. Even given many months' time in grueling drills and training to separate her from Ersch's death, she was still empty, her spirit numb.

"Column, shift right!"

She followed the drill and sidestepped with the rest of the formation, leaving the left half of the road free. The midday heat continued to wear on her, but she bore it without complaint. No, she welcomed the suffering. She deserved every ounce of it and more. The memory of Ersch's last moment went again and again through her mind. It had been all her fault.

Murmurs started filtering in from the front of the formation.

"The scouts found imperials."

The soldiers next to her tightened their grips on their shields and spears. Along the road, a second column started marching past, kicking up a fresh storm of dust. She ignored them, letting her eyes wander the white coat of the soldier in front of her. She fixated on the details of the stitching and the weave without really thinking anything of either.

A streak of motion counter to the march's flow caught her attention an instant before a hand latched onto her arm, pinching her even though the layers of fabric and mail.

"You!"

Charva had a spark of recognition. It was the man from her farm who'd been followed by his fiancée. She hadn't seen either of them since . . . . *Mud and bloody water. Ersch's sightless eyes.*

The man shook her hard. "You're the one who put it in her head to volunteer! As if this army even has any Watchers! It's your fault she died in that dirty stream!"

His eyes held the same hollowness she felt in her own soul.

"A dog's death to you!" He shouted. "Let the Vron take your eyes and split your throat!"

The soldier behind her grabbed him. "Get off her, you maniac!"

The man only squeezed tighter and pulled her from the column. "It's your fault!" He raised his fist. She did nothing to protect herself. *If he's ready to kill me, that's justice, isn't it?*

"Hey!"

Someone pulled her to the side, ramming her helmet into a shield and stunning her. Shouts and dust and scuffling overwhelmed her senses until a command split through the chaos, "All right, quit it! Order in the ranks!" An officer came trotting between the columns, sword in hand. "What's the cause of this disruption?"

A soldier pointed to Charva and the man who'd grabbed her. The two of them were the only ones now standing apart from the formation. "Them. The fellow started yelling at—"

"I don't need the details," the officer interrupted. "There's no excuse for breaking discipline as we're about to start a battle. Sergeant, have these two placed at the front of the company."

The unit commander was just stepping onto the scene. "Sir, the man's not part of my—"

"I've no time to argue. Put them in the front."

"Understood, sir."

The fiancé glared at her in silent hatred as a pair of soldiers escorted them to their new position. Charva didn't say a word, didn't argue. The escorts selected the men from the front rank to be replaced. The soldiers they pointed out wasted no time moving back, their relief plain. Their escorts shoved Charva and the fiancé side by side into the opened spot.

"Welcome to death's door," the soldier next to her muttered.

The man from her farm laughed bitterly. "We die together, then."

Off in the distance, a trumpet blared a string of notes. Despite her best efforts, the memory of Ersch's death flooded back to her. She felt the chill of the water, the slime of the stream bed. She felt the weight of Ersch's body in her arms.

"Granite company, move out!"

"It wasn't supposed to be like this," the man said quietly. "We would have been married by now. She was a wonderful woman. Always knew how to pick me up when I was feeling down. Always knew how to find the good in things."

"Limestone company, move out!"

"Love shouldn't lead you to death." The man's shoulders shook as he sobbed soundlessly. He leaned into his spear as if the weight of the world was crushing against his back.

"Basalt company, move out!"

The unit ahead of them began marching, clearing the road and stomping through the knee high grasses.

It is my fault, Charva thought. *Everything.*

"Clay company, move out!"

Weeks of drills made her keep pace with the rest of the unit without her conscious effort. Her feet left the packed dirt road and crushed blades of green grass to sink into spongy soil. The formation followed the sergeant's lead to stand behind Limestone and Basalt, affording Charva a view of the Vron army creeping over the crest of a far hill. Hundreds and hundreds of polished helmets shone in the sun in perfect rows, topping solid walls of silver shields. She watched their approach with an unshakable sense of inevitability.

"I should have left with him earlier," she whispered. "I shouldn't have volunteered. I should have let him try to escape on his own." Her fingers tightened on her spear. "I shouldn't have been there. I shouldn't have forced him to come back." The imperial soldiers became blobs in her vision. "I should have helped him, should have shot sooner." A tear rolled hot down her cheek, its trail quickly turning cold. "He shouldn't have saved me."

Silence reigned in the ranks as the imperials closed in on them, the rhythm of their boots a countdown of the seconds before the battle.

The officer who'd ordered her placed at the front was now just up ahead, conversing with another man on horseback. "They're spread wide. We need to match them or they'll envelop the flanks."

The other nodded without enthusiasm. "I hate putting Clay in front, but so be it. Basalt, face right! March! Clay, move up!"

In moments, Charva was flush with the rest of the army's first rank. There stood nothing left between her and the Vron except open grassland. She took a breath. *This is the end, then.* There was a peace in that. This was payment for failing everyone who mattered to her. It was only fair.

The Vron came to a halt seventy paces from the Whitesail lines. They were an impressive sight, their painted silver shields impeccably straight. Their commander rode lengthwise before them, shouting a stirring speech for his men. The Whitesail officer did the same for his own army, booming his own encouragements or entreaties or challenges. Charva didn't listen to the words. Whatever they were, they weren't meant for her.

The commanders both finished up and rode to the rear of their respective forces. A string of trumpet notes started the Vron forward. A whistle prodded the Whitesails. Charva's legs carried her onward. Step by step, she drew closer to the silver shields and the steel blades hidden behind them. The soldiers around her leveled their spears.

She closed her eyes. *I'm sorry I failed.*

A voice came in her ear, low and defeated, "I was wrong. You don't deserve this."

Her eyes snapped open. The fiancé was staring at her, the self loathing she felt mirrored clearly in his face. "Wha—"

The Vron trumpet blared and the air filled with an ear-splitting battle cry. The imperials charged.

"Brace! Brace! Brace!"

The Whitesail spears proved useless at keeping the Vron at a distance. The imperials shoved them aside with their shields and smashed into the line as one. An imperial soldier rammed Charva full force, throwing her off her feet and into the man behind her. Sharpened steel flashed around her shield, slashing through the shoulder of her uniform and baring her chainmail shirt. The soldier at her rear struck back, thrusting his spear over her head and catching metal on the other side of the imperial's shield.

"You don't deserve this."

Both sides crushed her between their shields, men screaming in fury and pain in every direction. She tried to maneuver her spear, but it was impossible in the tight press all around. Blood splattered her uniform, turning white to red. She didn't fight, but let the battle rage around her.

All I need to do is put my face out above my shield. That's all it'll take and I'll be dead.

"Whitesail!"

The strength behind her surged, pushing the line forward. The sword beyond her shield lashed out and loosed a spray of blood. A lifeless arm fell and rested on her shoulder. She felt her stomach churn and she forced down her vomit.

"Glory to the empire!"

It felt like she would be ground between the two shield walls. Her boots scraped along the ground. The line moved with her hopelessly pinned between each side. She struggled even to breathe.

And then the pressure stopped. As if by mutual consent, the armies drew away. Charva fell to the ground, a body right on top of her. She thrashed to get the weight off, and as the dead man slipped and thumped to the ground she saw the long pile of corpses marking the battle line. Having been kept upright by the press of the shield walls, they would have created a buffer keeping those still alive from reaching with their weapons.

She turned aside and retched. Gasping for air, she tried to keep her head from reeling. She succeeded in focusing her vision on the body next to her. It was the man from her farm. His neck was pierced, blood wetting his throat and face, his uniform soiled from blood, dirt, and the former contents of Charva's stomach. His eyes stared sightlessly at her, accusingly.

No, not accusingly. His last words had been a statement that he didn't blame her.

Her vision blurred with tears. She dug her fingers into the trampled and blood-soaked turf and bowed her head. He didn't blame her. He absolutely should have, but he didn't.

The Vron trumpet blared and weapons drummed on wood like the beating heart of a massive monster.

She reached over and closed the man's eyes. Whatever he had decided, she still couldn't forgive herself. But she knew Ersch wouldn't want her to die here. Grabbing her shield and spear, she steeled herself and pushed back to her feet. Voices roared and weapons waved, and Charva went to rejoin the ranks.

Chapter 87

The hamlet was fairly large, with near a hundred squat houses of stone and wood lining the dirt road. Ellaniel knew the people here would be familiar with Arzan, considering his regular rounds of the province. She wondered about their existing impression of her as she guided her horse to the elder's house in the community's center. Every head turned her way when she passed, respect in the eyes of the adults, curiosity and awe in the children's. Most of those eyes turned to both hope and dread as they noticed the carts rolling along behind her.

The elder stood waiting for them outside his humble abode. He looked every bit his part, from the closely trimmed white beard to the lovingly embroidered coat of red and sea green silk that had to be as old as his status. "Welcome, my crendess. What brings you to this part of Senkani?"

Ellaniel dismounted and removed her helmet. Heat rose off her head, a welcome relief that would last until the hot sun started roasting her bare skin instead of baking it through the steel. "I come to return a number of men home who served valiantly on the field of battle," she said, waving her arm to the carts.

The elder hurried past her with long strides. The soldiers manning the carts undid the panels so he wouldn't have to climb up to see the wounded. He grabbed the hands of two men sitting at the edge, bandages wrapped across their bodies. "Ring the bell!"

A little child ran up to a crude bronze bell on a post next to the elder's house and pulled the rope with a vigorous tug. The sound that issued from it was more a clatter than a ring, but it was loud enough to serve its purpose. As people trickled in from the fields, the elder went to the other carts one after the other, his eyes scanning the injured. After checking the last, he came back to Ellaniel. "Your grace, I have a son by the name of Narkam. Is he still with the army?"

The question took her unprepared. Seeing the look in the elder's face, she cursed herself for not thinking to seek out that information before coming here.

One of the wounded soldiers hobbled over on his crutch. "Nathum, I'm sorry. Narkam was among the fallen in the fields of Woodwise. I witnessed him struck down by the first volley of artillery."

It was like an ember fading to black as the life went from the elder's eyes. He shrank down, his silk coat suddenly seeming too big for his frame.

"He was a brave soldier," the man went on. "He was as much an inspiration to us as you always were. In the south of Creedport—"

Nathum put up a hand. "I apologize, Fitheur. I will hear of his service later. For now, I wish to be alone."

Ellaniel grabbed him firmly before he could leave. "I hate to ask more of you, elder, but I have further reason being here. Would you please lend me your authority?"

"You are crendess. You have power to do what you wish." The old man slipped away into the shadows of his home.

The elder's grief threatened to crack the stone with which Ellaniel had encased her heart, but she grit her teeth and willed herself not to forget her mission.

She turned back to the growing crowd and waited, her hand resting on her pommel. She let families find their loved ones and help them from the carts. It was a relief that most of these men's injuries were of the sort that would heal. Some of those Arzan was bringing home had lost limbs, or worse.

After a fair amount of time, she ordered a ckol to ring the meeting bell. The clattering drew the people before her, most with thankful faces.

She climbed onto her horse to be in view of all. "Men of Senkani, as you know, the war still goes on. We suffered heavy losses in the battle with Woodwise, and the army needs to be replenished. I ask for volunteers to replace those I bring back to you."

A young man was the first to jump forward, but an older woman grabbed his arm and pulled him back. "But mother —"

"Your brothers already joined the army, and one of them's come back nearly dead! We can't afford to have you gone. Who will tend the field?"

"Let him go," an old man called. "It's for the greater good of Senkani."

"There's no greater good if we all starve to death," another woman said. She cast a quick look to Ellaniel. "Begging yer pardon, yer grace, but our community's already spared all the fighters it can. We're barely managing to feed ourselves this season, much less send our part to the army."

Ellaniel tightened her jaw. "I am exceedingly grateful for all that you have provided thus far. Unfortunately, we need more. We don't have enough strength to break Woodwise and capture Creedport. If we replenish the army now, however, we can strike the Leverie while they are still weakened. We will be able to end this war within the month."

"And we thought the war would be finished in a week when this all started," someone said.

A man stepped in and thrust a finger at the one who'd spoken. "The Leverie must be crushed! So what if it's turned out not to be easy? They burned half our city to the ground, not to mention all the farms they razed during the siege!"

"Are *you* going to volunteer, then?"

The man thumped his chest. "I will!"

"But the crops," the earlier woman said.

"We will make do," Ellaniel called out. "We all do what we must in this war. I realize things will be hard, but do not think I am a stranger to difficulties. I have fought on the battlefield. I have been beaten down. Yet I always refused to give up or stand down, and I know that the people of Senkani are made of even sterner stuff than I am. I have faith that you will find a way to keep our province fed, but also make our army strong."

"The spirit of Senkani never submits!" a man said.

The woman let show a look of exasperation, but didn't argue further.

Satisfied, Ellaniel drew her sword and raised it to the sky. "Who else will join me?"

Several more men stepped forward. A few looked barely halfway through their teens, but she didn't turn them away. *Numbers matter, even if we put them in the back.*

A woman advanced right behind one of those younger ones. "I'll follow my brother as a Watcher."

Ellaniel fought back a scowl. "We don't need Watchers."

"You're an Aiv Chahai, are you not, your grace? You keep watch over your husband."

"I have no interest in handicapping our side," Ellaniel said. "I fight. I don't go about stopping our men from doing what's needed to make sure our enemies die and we live."

The young woman shrank down and spoke more quietly, "But your grace, aren't the Aiv Chahai required by the codes of war?"

Why does everyone care so much about these codes? She considered rejecting the woman outright, but knew she'd hear no end of it from Arzan. "Fine."

The woman pursed her lips and quickly stepped beside her brother and put a hand on his shoulder. Ellaniel shook her head. "Any others?"

A few more men and women deliberated with their families before joining the ranks. In the end, Ellaniel left with half as many as were brought back wounded. It was still better than nothing, but she could only hope the rest of the province was being more cooperative.

If we lose another battle, Arzan and I won't have the luxury of asking, she thought, snapping her reins and setting her horse forward. *We'll win this war, whatever it takes to motivate them.*

Chapter 88

Felkem trudged down the dirt road in obstinate determination. He was hungry. His feet hurt. The hot sun made it so his shirt was soaked through with sweat. That didn't matter. Nothing was going to make him turn back from his promise.

Well, the thought of Ma's and Pa's furious faces might do that. Felkem sweated even harder as soon as he imagined them figuring out that he'd sneaked away from Uncle Meselk's farm. He shook his head to clear the vision and firm his resolve. No, he would keep moving. His honor demanded it. And it didn't matter if he was only ten—honor was honor. Even Pa said as much.

Felkem hit a rock on the path, smashing up his big toe even through his shoe. He hopped and sucked in a full lungful of air, but fought off the tears. Honor. He kept walking.

There weren't a whole lot of people on the road. Ma had mentioned that the path ahead was closed off. Something to do with the same reason the crenden had bought their farm, forcing them to move in with Uncle Meselk. He thought that was weird. Wasn't this the main road from Three Corners to Senkani? Even with the war, lots of common folk had to cross between the provinces. The fields of crops on either side of him often went to feed hamlets on both sides of the provincial border. It wasn't as if you could just stop people from crossing over.

At least, that's what he thought until he saw the wall.

Felkem couldn't believe it. Going right through what used

to be Old Man Carnhaln's carrot field was a wall of giant logs stood up in a row. It wasn't through the whole field quite yet. There were scores of people still working on it, carting more logs over, digging pits, tying ropes. Felkem wasn't sure, but it looked like they were trying to cross off the whole farmland from one treeline to the other. And that would leave his family's farm on the opposite side.

He balled his fists. This was an unexpected obstacle, but he couldn't let that turn him back. Whatever the crenden was doing, Felkem still had a mission to accomplish. He was getting past this wall.

He still had to pause. There were a lot of those strangers working on the project. He was pretty sure any one of them would stop him if they knew he was trying to get to his family's farm. The crenden's order had been very specific about them staying away.

Felkem left the road and crouch-walked through Lim's rice field. The crop was still maturing and only about three feet high, but that was enough. He made his way to the next field over, which had a barley crop. After that, he was sort of close to one of the gaps in the wall, but would have to cross open rows of cabbage. He waited and watched the workers until they were all walking away to fetch a new log. Heart pounding, he raced up to and through the gap, jumping over the pit where they were going to set the wood.

As soon as he landed on the other side, his breath caught. "What . . . But . . . Where's the farm?"

Out north of the wall, everything had been turned upside down. *Actually* upside down. Houses and shacks and barns were gone. Property stones were gone. Crops were gone. And far off in the distance, around where Felkem's family's farm was supposed to be, was a big hole in the ground. Scores and scores of workers were shoveling more dirt, and dozens of carts were sitting around nearby with endless barrels.

Felkem just stared, dumbfounded. How was he ever going to find what he was looking for? How was he going to fulfill his promise?

A hand came down on Felkem's shoulder. His heart jumped into his throat. Eyes wide, he tilted his head back to look into the face of a man towering over him. "Uh . . . Um . .

. . ”

"You're not supposed to be out here," the man said. He was dressed more like a merchant than a worker, and his eyes were colored strangely green. "Where are your parents?"

"Um . . . ." The idea of lying and saying he was the son of one of the laborers popped into his head, but he shoved that down. Lying was against honor, even if it made it harder to fulfill another honor. "I'm here by myself. Ma and Pa don't know I came here."

The man pressed his lips tight for a moment. "Well, going against the crenden's orders is a serious offense. Are you going to tell me why you ran off from your parents to sneak into this field?"

Felkem broke from the man's grasp and turned around, steeling himself. "I need to find Gurar's box of game stones!"

The green-eyed man quirked his mouth and sighed. "Kid, violating the crenden's orders to get a toy is—"

"They're not my stones!" Felkem said, placing his fists on his hips. "They're Gurar's. I promised I would keep them for him since his pa doesn't like him playing games. He says it only distracts him from his work on the farm, even though that's not true. Game stones is all Gurar's really good at, but he's really good. He even has a match tomorrow with the local stone king, and I know he'll win the crown, but he can't play because I wasn't able to bring him his box because I had to keep it hidden outside the house because Gurar's pa got my pa to say he wouldn't let me encourage him and—"

"Okay, okay—take a breath!" the man said.

Felkem felt his cheeks flushing and tears threatening to roll from his eyes. He fought to harden himself up again, terrified that he might actually start crying. "Pa says it's important to keep promises," he forced out. "You keep your promises to keep your honor, and honor's the thing that makes the world work."

The man regarded Felkem a moment. Lips pressed tight, he turned to look out over the fields that were no longer Felkem's home. "Well, little guy, I guess that counts as a reason."

"Then—"

"But there's no way we're letting you get any closer to the

work."

Felkem felt his heart sink. "That's not—"

"Your father's right about honor," the man said. "My honor binds me to protecting the work that's going on over there. I can't let a kid go rummaging all over the place."

"I'll be extra careful!" Felkem said. "I won't get in anyone's way!"

"You're going to sift through all those mountains of dirt? And then still have time to get home before your friend's game?" The man shook his head before sitting down on a log. He tapped the spot next to him. "Take a seat."

Felkem hesitated.

"Look, if you're going to run, good luck trying to find those stones while I'm chasing you."

With reluctance, Felkem sat on the log. The crenden's man nodded and reached down to pluck a green stalk of grass, which he twirled in his fingers.

"Honor's definitely important," the man said. "Did your father teach you that there's two types of honor?"

Felkem frowned. "No." He was really suspicious of the words the man was using. Last time someone had talked like this, it had been Jragin the carpenter's son trying to twist things around to make it so he hadn't *actually* been "stealing" from the tanner.

The man stopped twirling the stalk and balanced it by the center on his finger. "Well, there are. There's the honor of reputation and there's the honor of justice. Can you guess what the difference is?"

"Um . . . ."

"Someone who acts honorably according to justice puts principle above himself. He has a steadfast standard of right and wrong. When he sees oppression, he confronts it. When he sees a lie, he exposes it. When he sees the weak, he supports them. He will do these things even if he finds that he himself was in the wrong. If he spoke an untruth, he will admit it. If he committed a crime, he will submit to punishment."

Felkem felt uncomfortable with where this was going.

The man pinched the grass stalk and with his other hand stripped the green seeds off the end. "A lot of people, however, mix this up with the honor of reputation. Having an honorable reputation is definitely good. Society will trust you, love you. Everyone wants it—even the lowest of criminals. But while living by the honor of justice will often get you an honorable reputation, the truth is it can be a pretty hard path. It's so much easier to just pretend."

He held up the now seedless stalk. "The man pursuing the honor of justice may attain a reputation of honor, but many more choose to fake honor. They will puff out their chests and come to blows with whoever challenges their reputation. They will wear expensive clothes and give themselves impressive sounding titles. They will make promises they have no way of keeping."

Felkem shot to his feet. "It's not my fault! You're the one who made it so I can't keep my promise! I didn't know we were going to move and our land was going to be dug up!"

"We never know the future, kid." The man paused. "Well, not—anyway, the power we have often isn't as reliant on our own abilities as we think it is. Promises are based on the assumption that things tomorrow will be like things today. Or even worse, that things will be better than they are today."

"But it's still your fault!"

The man leaned forward. "Look, what's the point of your promise?"

"I . . . ." Felkem had to focus his thoughts. "Gurar needs a set of game stones for his match."

"Right. You made a promise to keep his set for him. You can't keep your promise. If you want to be honorable, you have to take responsibility for that. Do you know what that means?"

"Um . . . ."

The man stood up. "There's some laborers taking a break outside the work area. Come with me."

Felkem followed cautiously as the man led the way along the wooden wall. When they reached the road, they found a number of workers sitting in groups of three or four in the dirt. Felkem saw that some of them were playing board games. The nearest was a couple of men competing at fortress while their friends watched on. Somewhere else, they were betting at cups and marbles. A third group . . . .

A set of game stones!

The crenden's man went up to the group with the game stones. "How's it going?"

The laborers stopped mid-clash. "Chief! I thought you were checking on the barrels!"

"Got sidetracked. Hey, this kid here's in a bit of a bind. How much would you be willing to sell that set for?"

"These things? I nabbed 'em dirt cheap since the colors don't match too well. If you want it, I'm fine with three coppers."

The crenden's man turned to Felkem. "Well? Willing to take that deal?"

"I . . . ." Felkem eyed the set. Honestly, it wasn't a very good set. Nothing like Gurar's old ones. But his friend didn't need the stones to be pretty for him to win. He just needed stones. "But I don't have three coppers on me."

"Can you get three coppers?" the crenden's man asked.

Felkem nodded. It would be most of his savings, but he had that.

"All right." The crenden's man reached into his money pouch and gave the worker his coins. "Kid, next time you or one of your family goes into the city, give your coppers to one of the guards and tell him they're for Chief Retyar. And let him know if your friend won his match."

Felkem felt the onset of tears again, but this time for a whole different reason. He fought them back as he nodded.

The laborers finished up their game, settling the bet they'd made on the outcome, and the one dropped his stones in their box and handed them over. Felkem took them gratefully with both hands. "Thank you."

The crenden's man patted him on the shoulder. "Be careful with your promises, kid, and good with your honor. Be a man that Three Corners will never want to lose."

"I will be. And I'll get you your coppers." Felkem felt far more timid knowing that this wasn't just any follower of the crenden, but some kind of chief. But he respected honor, and that made him good in Felkem's book. He bowed his head in gratitude. "Gurar will be sure to win!" His objective had been achieved in an unexpected manner, but he started on his way back home.

Chapter 89

Charva thumbed the last of the vials into the spring box and slapped it into the slot in the weapon's grip, locking it in place with a satisfying click. She pulled the slide, loading the first vial, and let it snap back forward. Five vials. Five shots.

A lot of good that would do her against an army of two thousand.

The new Whitesail captain shouted orders as Charva tucked the vial weapon under her belt. She couldn't see him, nor the endless rolling plains around her, past the rows of soldiers. "Granite and Slate, tighten your ranks! I won't have so much as a grasshopper slip between you! Hold your spears proper! You think you scare anyone with those limp wrists?"

Charva had made a decision after the last battle. She could torture herself over her failures and guilt when she was out of this and there weren't people counting on her. Until then, she would fight.

Her odds for survival were better this time around as she was a few ranks deep in the formation. The officer didn't see her as she pushed her spear off from against her shoulder and caught the shaft in her hand. She spared a glance at the female soldier next to her. Dill, she thought her name was? Now that she was forcing herself to pay attention, she knew just why the unit was called Clay. All the other companies were named after stones, but hers was weaker than the weakest rock. Almost half women, it was where the Whitesail aristocrats had decided to shove any girl foolish enough to try volunteering for the Aiv Chahai. She didn't know whether it was outright contempt for the codes or just disdain at having noncombatants on the field, but there weren't truly any Watchers in this army.

The officer's voice continued shouting at the forward companies, "I said closer! Do you *want* those Vron swords slitting you open?"

"They're already tight as clams," the soldier ahead of her muttered. He was just tall enough to be able to see the field.

"What are the imperials doing?" Charva asked.

The soldier glanced back at her over his shoulder. "Hey, you're the one the old captain put in the front rank that time. Surprised you're still alive."

"Doing better than he did. Broke his back falling from his horse, was it? Are the imperials still holding position?"

He nodded. "They've got a solid line. I think our commander's scared of advancing on them."

"That's why he's blowing out all that hot air."

"Trying to stall for time."

Charva chose to view it as a blessing. "Maybe we won't have to fight today."

"Forward line, prepare to move out!"

The solder glared at her for jinxing them.

Charva twisted the butt of her spear into the springy soil and didn't respond. *I'm not shaking*, she thought. Nightmares still haunted her dreams. Flashes of memory from Ersch's death and from Three Corners still harassed her days. Since the time she had found her resolve, however, she had been able to push through.

A hand tapped her on the shoulder, barely felt through her chain and padding. She turned to look at the woman next to her.

"Um, you've been in battle before, right? What do I do to, um, not die?"

Charva tapped her spear to her shield. "You always stay behind this."

"Always stay behind the shield," Dill repeated, her voice quavering. "All right."

"Forward line, advance!"

I need to do more than just survive. Charva felt again at the vial weapon, then tightened her grip around her spear. Ersch had wanted her to live as the person she used to be. *I need a sword.*

"Reserve lines, advance!"

Clay company started forward. Scrunching chain and knocking wood filled her ears as the unit marched. Most of the soldiers were still inexperienced, though, and the formation lost some of its cohesion, letting her catch glimpses of the field ahead. She saw the backs of hundreds more Whitesail soldiers, helmets and speartips glistening in the sun.

"Formation, halt!"

"Clay company, straighten out, you dregs!" their sergeant ordered.

The gaps closed up, blocking out Charva's view before she had a chance to see any of the enemy. She knuckled the soldier in front of her. "Hey, how close are—"

"Arrows!"

She snapped her eyes upwards in time to see a mass of arrows hit the peak of their arc. In an instant of panic, she realized their disjointed training hadn't included anti-archer maneuvers. She also knew it wouldn't have mattered. Clay was packed too closely to be able to raise shields.

The arrows hit. Steel tips bounced off helmets and mail. She felt one smack her in the shoulder, the shaft behind it snapping and throwing splinters against her cheekguard. The soldier to her left screamed in agony as an arrow caught him in the foot. He wasn't the only one. There were screams all around from men and women hit in the legs or feet.

"Charge! Before the next volley, charge!"

The front units shouted a battle cry and raged forward. Charva bit her lip as she saw another volley of arrows launch skyward. Clay endured this shower better than the first as people crouched down or held their shields close to protect their unarmored legs. Charva received an arrow to the dome of her helmet, and another scratched a shallow groove along her shield.

"Reserves, what in the six are you doing? Quit huddling around like idiots!"

Charva grit her teeth. Next to her, the injured soldier gurgled a cry as he yanked the arrow from his foot.

"Move it, Clay!"

"Wait, I can't—"

"Move! Move! Move!"

The unit stumbled more than marched, leaving behind the soldiers too wounded to keep up. Another volley of arrows rained down. Charva sidestepped a soldier halted in her tracks, her hand grasping the shaft of an arrow planted in her throat.

"Faster, dregs!"

The soldier behind pushed to speed her up. The bottom of her shield caught on a large clump of dirt. Not expecting the snag, she stepped her foot down on the bottom of the board, leveraging the whole shield out of her hand. "Wait, my—"

The unit shoved her past, not giving her a chance to so much as bend down. She heard the boots of every soldier behind her stomping all over her lost equipment.

Embers.

The sounds of fighting dominated ahead. She still couldn't see the enemy, but they were close enough that the archers couldn't arc their shots.

She gripped her spear tightly in both hands as the company came to a halt. Steel rang and screams rent the air. On her right, Dill was shaking and crying. *Well, can't count on her . . .* She tried to measure her own breathing and keep her nerves. She tapped the soldier in front of her. "How's the battle going?"

"Can't tell."

The Vron trumpet blared. A heavy snap cut through the din, followed by more screams and howls.

"Six continents, Sandstone is breaking."

The captain's voice came from the unit's left. "Don't let the line collapse! Clay, into the breach, now!"

Flame and embers!

The unit rushed forward to close the gap, shoving aside the bloodied remnants of Sandstone as they fled annihilation. She thought she saw one man with his arm ripped clear off. *What in the world happened to them?*

Clay's sloppy shield wall slammed into the imperial line, compressing into the fight. The shield of the soldier at Charva's back pressed her into the soldier at her front. She instinctively took a handhold of the front soldier's uniform to anchor herself and tried desperately to keep a grip on her spear. People roared and jostled, and Charva could do nothing against the flow of the back-and-forth shoving match. She put as much of her weight into the press as she could, but it was hard for her to find purchase in the squishy soil.

Squishy? She started to look down, only to be interrupted when the soldier ahead of her snapped his head back and smacked his helmet against hers. She heard a gurgling noise before the imperials pushed in a wave, winning several steps. The Whitesails pushed back, but the Vron pulled away at the same moment. The soldier in front of Charva fell forward and planted his face in an imperial shield. His body sagged to the ground, his throat sliding down the shield, leaving a smear of dark red against the silver paint.

Charva's eyes went wide. She was on the front line. She saw the bloodied Vron swords poking through their shield wall. Saw the dead splayed on the ground. She felt the force of a dozen men and women at her back, pushing her towards those razor sharp blades with no shield of her own.

Well, if I'm going to die here, I'm not making it easy.

And that meant doing something crazy.

With a scream she hoped sounded more menacing than terrified, she rushed in and grabbed the top of the imperial's bloodied shield. Using the fallen body of the Whitesail soldier for a little extra height, she jumped up and kicked against the shield behind her.

The look of shock on the imperial's face was almost reward enough as she sprang over his shield, spear poised. She thrust her weapon straight through his gaping mouth, lodging the point in the bones of his neck. She braced herself for the storm of swords inevitably coming for her.

Instead, the Vron trumpet sounded. The imperials parted beneath her, dropping her to slam to the ground. The moment she hit the trampled grass, something let loose a deafening snap. She sensed something whoosh past her and heard a crash of breaking wood. She raised her head in confusion and found a ballista sitting at the end of the open lane in the imperial formation.

A ballista? Why is a ballista—

She broke off her own question as her eyes latched onto the artillery crew. More specifically, one of the crew. Even more specifically, the sword sheathed at his side. She recognized its length, the style of its basket guard. It was a rapier.

All other thoughts emptied from her mind. She was taking that sword.

She scrambled as the imperial formation started to close. Several soldiers took swings at her, but they were too startled at her choice of direction to land accurate hits. Their blades missed the gaps in her armor, slashing and stabbing uselessly against her mail. She made it all the way through just before the imperials locked the shield wall back in place, and caught the ballista crew completely by surprise.

"Hey! One of the—"

Charva kneed the engineer in the groin and grabbed the guard of his sword. The other five turned as she pulled the blade free of the scabbard and flipped it around to wield it by the grip. The man she'd stolen it from fought against the pain and swung at her. She danced out of his reach, letting his fist pass her by, then leaped in with a thrust. He dodged, but not well enough. The tip of the rapier caught him in the side of the neck, piercing deep before she cut her way out, severing the artery. He touched his injury and looked down at his bloody hand.

"You Whitesail scum. You've killed me." He slowly eased himself against the frame of the ballista, blood gushing out onto his silver uniform.

Charva whipped the blood from the sword. "Occupational hazard, no?"

The other engineers drew their swords.

She hopped around the ballista, placing it between her and three of the imperials. The remaining two attacked at once. A blade cut the air by her ear as she bent her head out of the way, but the other one hit her brutally in the ribs, felt hard even through her armor. She grit her teeth against the pain and held the second blade against her body. The imperial tried pulling the weapon free, but she kept it tight, twisting to force him between her and the first engineer.

"Blazing rat!"

She let go and shifted to parry an imperial rounding the artillery. She ducked under a follow-up blow and weaved through the ballista to slip out the other side.

"Got that right, Lerav," one of them said. "This one *is* a rat."

"Quit running and face us like a man, coward."

Charva laughed and twirled her sword. "Sorry, being a man doesn't quite appeal to me at the moment."

The imperial named Lerav shook his head in disbelief. "The sergeant got done in by a girl?"

One of the others scratched his chin. "Actually, Pvar and I had money riding on that."

"On his own girl killing him, not some Whitesail she rodent in the middle of nowhere!" He turned back to Charva. "You and me, sludge rat. One on one. I'll show you how a real swordsman fights."

She looked out at the plain, wondering if she could just high tail it. Not too far away, there were a lot of bored-seeming archers. Not the smartest thing to risk. She eyed the engineer and his colleagues.

"We can't waste time on her, Lerav. We need to load another bolt."

"To flames with the bolts! I'm getting the sergeant's sword back."

Two of the others started towards her. "You don't need a stupid duel for that."

Charva drew in a breath and tightened her hand on the hilt. Five on one, then.

Five . . . .

The two men lunged. She swapped the rapier to her left and with her mainhand grabbed the vial weapon from her belt. She moved into the swing of the one of the soldiers, catching the crossguard to her shoulder instead of the blade to her neck. His head turned to her sword, but it was the vial weapon she pressed to his chest. The contraption kicked with an ear-splitting bang as she pulled the trigger. The soldier stumbled away, a bewildered look on his face before he collapsed to the ground.

The other imperial flicked his eyes to his fallen comrade and tried for a disarm. Charva parried clumsily with her rapier, letting his blade slice the back of her right hand. Holding tight to her weapons, she lunged in. The soldier jumped back, his focus on the vial contraption. Charva aimed a slash at his head and scraped her sword point across his helmet. His attention turned back to the blade and she rushed in and put the vial weapon to his heart. The soldier started to curse as she pulled the trigger. *Bang.* She twisted his sword arm in hers, preventing any last attacks as the life drained from his body.

The three remaining engineers hung back.

"Did you see that? The she rat punched right through their chain."

"What is it, some spring hammer or something?"

Lerav bobbed his sword and sneered. "Just don't let her touch you with it."

They moved in to flank her. She waited, letting them come within about five paces before she pointed the vial weapon at the one on her right and shot. The instant after she felt the kick, she dashed at the one on the left. He thrust at her, but she dropped under it, rolling right to his feet before thrusting her own blade straight up from beneath. The point of the rapier slipped inside the hem of his chain armor to skewer him from gut to lung. He went rigid and squealed, a sound she cut short with a shot through his chin.

The last one, Lerav, roared and smashed her off her feet as she tried to pull her sword free of the body. She lost her grip on the rapier, but not the vial weapon. She landed on her back and spent her final vial, shooting him square in the chest.

He didn't stop or even flinch. She rolled aside just in time to avoid his sword as he put his full weight into a falling stab. The blade sank deep in the ground, but he instantly pulled it free and kept at her.

"Not so fast, rat!" The man kicked her in the head, knocking her helmet off even despite her chin strap. Her hair flew loose, black strands blocking her eyes. She tried to clear her vision, but only succeeded in plastering the hair in place with the blood from her hand. She saw with one eye Lerav moving in. She flailed awkwardly with the vial weapon, but he knocked it away with ease and struck her hard in the side. She gasped in pain.

"I'm going to take my time with you. Stealing the sergeant's sword, killing my crew." He kicked her in the stomach as she tried rising to her knees. Her vision spun and she nearly blacked out as she fell back to the ground clutching her belly. "I bet you think you're really something." He pushed her onto her back and pinned her with a foot on her chest. His heel dug through her armor into her sternum. She clawed at his leg to no avail. The man leaned in and rested the point of his sword on her throat. She coughed, driving the steel into her skin. Lerav leered down at her. "You lose, girl. You . . . lose . . . ."

Without further warning, the engineer collapsed to the side. Charva lay frozen, uncomprehending. After several moments, she turned her head. The imperial lay beside her, his eyes blank. His silver uniform was soaked red from the spot where she'd shot him an eternity ago. She started to laugh, only to stop short as black dots flooded her vision and throbbing pain coursed through her body. "Flame and embers, I'm a mess."

She managed to peel her hair from her eye and look down at herself. Her uniform was hardly more than ribbons. "I'm not taking this mail shirt off for as long as I live." Only after groaning out the words did she realize how ominous that sounded.

The battlefield was a lot different when she finally recovered the strength to sit up. The Whitesail army was in rout, the Vron chasing them down. All eyes were to the east. Here on the western side, she actually had a chance of getting away. She forced herself to her feet and retrieved the vial weapon and the rapier. Taking one more look at the mayhem she'd wrought, she also decided to take the scabbard from the artillery sergeant, as well as the man's water skin. Once her spoils were firmly hanging from her belt, she pointed herself north and started walking.

Chapter 90

Endless plans and figures filled Maltan's head as his carriage rolled along the smooth imperial road in through Breakpeak's gates. The canal project was coming along amazingly well. Bare months after his first survey of the rugged eastern terrain, Vron engineers were already cutting stone and laying out the groundwork for the massive embankments he'd started outlining. The sheer scale of it was far beyond what Maltan would have dreamed ever seeing completed in his lifetime just two years ago. Vron discipline, skill, and engineering promised to make it possible within a decade.

The carriage rolled to a halt at the imperial stables. A soldier swung open the door and kicked a wooden step into place for Maltan's convenience. "Welcome back to Breakpeak, chief engineer."

Maltan climbed down to the paving stones, smiling distractedly. "Do you know if the general is here yet?"

"He hasn't checked in his horse. He's usually back from the camp inspections by sundown, though."

The sun was still high, only three hours past noon. "I'll be waiting for him in the palace."

"Understood, chief."

Maltan hummed happily as he walked across the city's lower square. He was pushing seventy now, but was more invigorated than ever. He had purpose. His efforts were building Moshon a better future.

He stopped in the center of the square and looked up at his first contribution to humanity here under General Nevygar's patronage. The lift track was even more admirable to him now than when he'd completed it. The test of time was the greatest obstacle any invention ever faced, and here, half a year after the grand opening, the lift platforms faithfully maintained their steady advance up and down the city's steep slope. According to the army's reports, there hadn't been a single major issue in its operation.

"Stupid imperial nonsense."

Maltan turned to face the scrawny basket seller sitting on a blanket amongst his wares. "Pardon?"

The basket seller pointed to the lift. "It's stupid. An injustice. Do you have any idea how many houses they tore down to build that?"

Apparently, the merchant didn't recognize him. "In fact, I do. I also know that every one of the owners was compensated for the loss."

"Not like they had a choice. 'Look here, we've a few gold coins. You've got a week to pack up and leave.' Never mind that many of those houses were in the family for a hundred years."

"It was a generous sum for each of them," Maltan said. "It was fair, and for the good of the whole city."

The merchant scoffed. "The good of the city, eh? It's only good for the people living in the Uppers. And who are they? The nobles, of course. Aristocrats and the pompous silvers who run the palace."

A woman selling carved keepsake boxes in the next space over threw up her hands. "My parents use the lift all the time. It's good for folk who live in the Middles too. Most people love the new machine."

"Well, then let them pay for it. But of course the empire won't charge a toll. No, they need to levy a tax—a percentage from everyone! The lift is just a fine little justification, even if it only costs a tiny fraction of what they take from us to keep that contraption working."

"The tax isn't just for the lift," Maltan said. "It goes to pay for the roads and canal as well."

The basket seller clicked his tongue and scowled. "And

who asked for that? Breakpeak got along just fine with our old roads. This isn't for us—it's for the empire's armies and the—" he stopped abruptly, his eyes narrowing. "Wait, I do know you. You're the imperial engineer."

Before Maltan could utter a word, the basket seller spit at his feet. "Nothing more to say to collaborators."

Maltan bristled at the slight, but caught himself and swallowed down his sense of injury. "I . . . appreciate your perspective."

With a nod, he continued the rest of the way to the lift. His journey up the city, smoothly rising on the wooden platform, was more conflicted than he would have wished. *The man's just being silly. Society is improving—they just don't all see it yet. They need to get used to the change.*

At the palace platform, the imperial guards saluted him. No one interrupted him on his way to the general's quarters. A lone sergeant stood by the door, his hand resting lazily on his hilt. Maltan took up a spot nearby and waited.

After some moments, he found himself fidgeting as he thought about the discussion in the marketplace. The guard took the wrong meaning from it. "You can wait inside if you want, chief engineer. They really should put some chairs out here."

Maltan opened his mouth to refuse, but thought better of it. Sitting wouldn't be so bad. "Thank you."

The guard let him inside. Maltan strolled across the thick crimson rug to one of the guest chairs by Nevygar's desk and set himself down. *The taxes are fine,* he thought. *Moshon's traditional condemnation of them lacks nuance and flexibility. It's not like the empire is forcing it out of people who can't pay. Ah, stop being bothered by this, old Maltan. Get back to planning the canal.*

His eyes wandered the general's desk and stopped at a letter sitting at the far corner. It was half unfolded, one side bearing the broken seal of the Vron Senate. He looked away, resting his elbow on his corner of the desk and wondering what kind of trouble he could get in by reading the general's correspondences.

Of course, it can't be that important of a message, or else he wouldn't have left it sitting in the open . . . .

All the more reason why he shouldn't bother with it.

But perhaps it contained the Senate's views on the canal project. Maltan had to admit he was curious what they thought. He often wondered how aligned Nevygar's ideals were with those of the Vron homeland.

He cast a glance at the closed doorway. No sounds of footsteps from the hall.

Why not.

Quietly as he could, Maltan rose from his chair and circled the desk. He gently lifted a partial fold of the paper to reveal the whole letter.

> *General Nevygar of the Vron Empire, Commander of the Eastern Front,*
>
> *As we have discussed in previous correspondences, the Senate grows impatient with the pace of progress in the east. We appointed you to this post with the expectation that you would expand the empire's borders more effectively than your predecessor. Instead, you have told us time and again that we need to show patience, that we must wait for plans and opportunity to ripen.*
>
> *It is the opinion of the Senate that the time is far past ripe. Heartsong's armies are crushed, and their allies from the Aristocracy of Whitesail have lost their teeth biting into Vron iron. Your agents in Leveric have furthermore annihilated the military strength to Whitesail's back. There is nothing left to oppose you. Fresh legions are en route to Heartsong. You are to take these forces and execute our plans of conquest. You are ordered to hand jurisdiction of the new Imperial province of Heartsong over to Governor Evrim, who will be accompanying the legions. Let him oversee these efforts at civilization you have begun.*
>
> *For the Glory of Empire,*
> *Pescar, Senator in Service to the People of Vron*

Maltan's hands shook. He read one particular passage

over again. "Your agents in Leverie."

No. It can't be.

The guard shifted his feet outside. Heart hammering in his ears, Maltan waited for any sound of approach in the hall. Hearing none, he reached for the drawer in the side of the desk. He eased it silently open and found a disorderly pile of letters, many with the Senate seal. With unsteady hands, he smoothed them out atop the desk one after another. It wasn't long before he found what he was looking for.

> . . . *I am encouraged by the progress being made in the Aristocracy of Leverie. I feel that your decision to make use of the agents put in place by General Darmine has been the correct one. News of the setbacks experienced fighting Whitesail have served to erode, to some extent, the people's confidence in the eastern campaign. If Leverie's armies can be weakened with this civil war prior to the empire's arrival, it would set the stage for easy victory, which is sorely needed to bolster public opinion. Keep me apprised of the situation.*

Maltan stood back and put his hand over his mouth, his thoughts in disarray. *Six continents! I've been working with the architects behind the Leverie war!*

"Welcome back, general."

For a single moment Maltan froze in absolute horror. He shook himself and snapped into motion, snatching the letters and shoving them back into the drawer. He dashed around the desk, stopping at a shelf and bending near its contents just as the door swung open. Nevygar strode in, armor clinking with each step, his silver cape fluttering behind him.

"Honorable Maltan, good. We've ironed out the land agreements for the last stretch between Wyin and Garphan. It's the same area we were hoping for."

Maltan pulled a book from the shelf and kept his eyes locked on its cover. He didn't dare look up and betray the anger seething within him. "Excellent. That . . . that's excellent news."

Nevygar settled into his chair. In the corner of his vision,

Maltan saw him rest his elbows on the desk and lace his hands. The general was staring at him. "Is something troubling you?"

"Nothing," he said, far too quickly. He held up the book. "This, um, just brought back some memories."

The general cocked an eyebrow. "*On Standardized Accounting?*"

Maltan slipped the book back in place. "They were . . . old memories."

"I see. In any case, I'm sure you were waiting for me with some purpose."

"It wasn't significant. In fact," he turned for the door, "I think I should get back to drawing some schematics."

"I'm afraid I must insist that you stay, Honorable Maltan," Nevygar said, stopping him in his tracks. He heard the desk drawer being pulled open. When he slowly faced Nevygar, the general was paging through his letters, his expression impenetrable. "Sit."

Maltan obeyed. Sweat trickled down his neck as he gripped the armrests of his chair.

"I recall leaving one of these letters atop the desk here." Nevygar plucked the sheet from the pile and held it high. "Would you happen to know how it placed itself inside the drawer?"

Silence condemned Maltan as strongly as any confession.

"That I should have made such a mistake." Nevygar set the letter down and smoothed it over with his palm. "Tinkerer, what am I to do? We are working together so well, you and I."

"You have thrust my country into civil war," Maltan said. "You betrayed my trust."

"I have done nothing different than what you have always seen," Nevygar said. "I am bringing the greatness of the Vron Empire to every corner of Moshon, using the tools available to me."

"There is nothing great about destruction!"

"No, but from the ruins of destruction we build civilization. From the beating down of outdated institutions and orders, we leave space for progress. I assure you, when this is all done, Leverie will experience greater prosperity than it has ever imagined, and none of its children or grandchildren will remember or care for the way things used to be."

Maltan stood. Never before had he so dearly desired to strike another person. "I cannot believe I served you."

Nevygar sighed. "Guards, enter. Escort Chief Engineer Maltan to the guest wing. He is to be kept under house arrest."

As the soldiers flanked Maltan, the general leaned back in his chair. "You will not be held for long, tinkerer. Leverie will soon be part of the empire, and when that happens, I'm sure you will have no objection to shaping your old home into something quite grand."

Chapter 91

Charva crossed her arms and glared at the thin rock outcropping in the cliff above her. This was three times now she'd come back to this spot.

"You'd think a woman so well traveled would have a better sense of direction," she muttered to herself. She looked back the way she'd come. If she turned around now, she wondered about her chances of finding her way to the entrance of this labyrinth of brown cliffs and ravines. A trip through the lesser passes of Heartsong's northeast mountains was turning out to be a bad idea. Not that she'd had much of a choice. The eastern border was impassable with all the fighting, and the main passes to the coast were tightly controlled by the empire. She might have a chance of posing as a local, but that would mean ditching her sword and armor.

And so she was going to starve to death in some fortune forsaken mountains.

They're not even tall mountains. Such a boring place to die!

With a sigh, she resigned herself to more wandering. Maybe there were traveler markers she'd missed. She patted her satchel, checking how much she had left of the rations she'd bartered for in the foothills. "With my luck, I'll have to start figuring out how to catch rabbits."

She went a little ways before a voice called out to her, "Nice sword you have there."

Charva drew her blade and spun around, eyes searching the crevices and ledges surrounding the path.

A lanky man in mail stepped into view a few feet above

her. He had his sword sheathed and his hands raised in the air. "No harm. Just saw you coming by here several times. You lost?"

She didn't ease her stance. "Not so lost as to ask directions from a bandit."

The man parodied a look of hurt. "Hey now, that's not a nice accusation."

"Truly." She took a wary step backwards, ready to run once she had enough distance to turn around.

"Hey now, wait up! You know how to use that sword?"

She stopped again and raised an eyebrow. "Looking for a fight?"

"Maybe, though not with you, for sure."

Understanding brought an incredulous smile to her lips. "Are you trying to recruit me?"

"Told you she wouldn't want to," someone's voice echoed from beyond the first man.

"Stow it, Flegs," the lanky man said over his shoulder. "I've got a feeling about her."

"A gut feeling, or a heart feeling?"

Several other voices made suggestive noises before breaking out laughing.

"Hey now, knock it off. She's pretty, but not *that* pretty."

Charva sniffed and started walking. The man called out desperately, "Wait!" Boots scraped down rock as he slid his way to the path and ran after her.

"Ah, ah," Charva held her sword up.

The lanky man held out his hands as the tip hovered in front of his nose. "Look, you're a deserter, right? From Whitesail? I can tell from the ring pattern on your mail."

"I took the armor off a dead soldier."

The man gave her a smile that was somehow charming despite the handful of teeth missing on his left side. "'Course you did. Now see, we're all deserters too. Least, that's what our commanders would call us if we ever showed our faces again. But we're still opposing the empire. We're freedom fighters."

"Good for you."

"Yeah, but listen! There's an imperial convoy coming through here, see? Not that big, but they're carrying supplies for the canal project. We're going to raid them. Now, if you help us, we'll give you a cut, and I'll even draw you a map out of here."

Directions would be really useful. Charva weighed the deal. "How many imperials are we talking in this convoy?"

The man clapped his hands in victory. "Our source says twenty."

"And how many with you?"

"Fifteen, but hey, wait, we've got surprise and a few tricks up our sleeves."

She thought it over a little longer. *Flame and embers, why not.* She sheathed her sword. "All right."

The man elbowed empty air. "Yes!" He put his hand out. "Serath."

Charva hesitated, but shook. "Dancer."

"No offense to your parents, but that's a weird name."

She opened her mouth to throw back an insult of her own, but Serath turned on his heel and called to the rest of his gang. "She's on board, boys and girls!"

He led her up a little crevasse to where his men were gathered on a wide landing. They were a motley crew of wide-ranging age and size, and they were by no means limited to swords and spears. She saw axes, hammers, bows, crossbows, and even a polearm. Everyone was equipped with at least gambeson and mail, and three even wore various amounts of plate.

"Guys, this is Dancer," Serath said. "Dancer, this here's Plax, that's Ylf, the one with the polearm's Leal. Cath, Durkanny, and Eram are originally from the Heartsong army. The sisters are Anty and Seorie. In the back there are . . . ."

Charva's attention waned as he listed the rest of the names, but she waited until he was done until asking, "How long should it be 'till the imperials get here?"

Leal looked up at the sun. "We've probably a couple hours. The source said—"

A soft bird call echoed down to them.

"Okay, well, they made good time, I guess."

The crew scurried into position. Cath and the sisters put winches to their powerful crossbows, several others strung their bows, and Plax and Ylf rolled a large wooden barrel close to the drop. Everyone else crouched low by the edge, blades and hammers in hand.

"What's that?" Charva asked, pointing to the barrel.

"Pitch," Serath said, scarcely a second before Plax pried off the top and Ylf started striking a piece of flint to light a torch. "We use it to block the passage."

"Seems expensive."

Serath gave her his gap-toothed grin. "It was a gift from a convoy we raided a month back."

A silly idea popped into Charva's head as Ylf's torch poofed to life. "Do you have any spare swords?"

Serath raised an eyebrow. "Yeah, why?"

Charva flashed a smile of her own. "I'm feeling creative."

He showed her a bundle of swords rolled up in a brown cloth. "Straight from a Vron armory."

She took one and tested the edge on a corner of the fabric. Satisfied, she brought it to the barrel of pitch and dipped it near to the hilt.

Serath slapped Flegs on the back. "Told you I had a feeling about her!"

Before long, they started hearing the sounds of horses and carts. Charva knelt by the ledge with the rest of the crew and waited. *Feels good to have the advantage over the imperials for once.*

The convoy came into view. She counted five carts, with four soldiers and one driver to each. They were all packed high with uniform crates. The vehicles rolled steadily closer, their occupants oblivious to the men and women poised above.

When the first cart came near to the barrel of pitch, one of the soldiers riding it perked up. "Do you smell something?"

The hidden archers and crossbowmen rose and launched the opening volley. Several imperials went down, thrashing at the arrows and bolts lodged in their necks.

"Ambush!"

Plax kicked the barrel of pitch over the side. It smashed against the hard ground with a crack, splashing black goo across the passage floor. Ylf threw the torch after it, but not before Charva touched her pitch-covered sword to the fire. Flames raced up her blade, and she gripped it tight as she leaped down beside the first cart.

An imperial hopped off the cart to greet her as she recovered from the drop. He banged his sword against his shield. "Come at me, brigand!"

"Gladly." She charged in, acrid smoke billowing around her. The imperial raised his shield against her attack, but Charva hit the top of the board and slid the flat towards her. Burning pitch slopped down onto the soldier's hand, earning a cry and a backwards dance as he dropped the shield. She chased after him, flicking her sword to splatter globlets of fire at his face. He flailed with his blade, trying to fend off the unconventional attack. "You little—"

She thrust in, slipping past his confused guard to impale him through the throat. The sword cut clean through to the bone, making a brief sizzling sound on the way through. The imperial's mouth went wide, but no voice issued forth.

She let go of the now blisteringly hot hilt and drew her rapier in time to parry a strike from a second imperial come in from the side. Singing steel competed with whinnying horses and screaming men. Charva dodged and deflected one attack after another until Durkanny came to her aid to smash the imperial in the back of the head with his warhammer.

"Thanks," Charva said, the soldier splayed motionless at her feet.

Durkanny nodded curtly and moved on, rejoining the fight elsewhere. Charva let the rest of the crew finish off the skirmish as she got a little further away from the blazing pitch for some clear air. It was only a matter of moments before the battle was over and Serath came striding along the captured carts, a handful of prisoners getting thrown to the ground behind him.

"Hey now, did you all see that?" he called. "I take back what I said. Your parents named you aptly indeed!"

"Did we lose anyone?" Charva asked, slipping her rapier back into its sheath.

Serath displayed his gap-toothed smile. "Nope. Today was a good day. A few nicks here and there, but nothing a few stitches won't fix."

Charva nodded and picked up one of the fallen imperial's swords. She climbed into the nearest cart and wedged the blade under the lid of a crate. Serath came and lent his strength, and the planks came apart with a tortured squeak.

"Well," she said, tossing the bent sword aside and scooping her hand into the crate's contents, "not the most impressive thing people have lost their lives over." She held up a handful of iron nails.

"A little disappointing, I admit," Serath said. "Still, it puts a dent in the imperial war machine."

"I suppose you could use them to build a barricade in the pass or something."

Serath laughed, but also rubbed his chin. "Not a bad idea. I like the way you think, Dancer."

"Flattered. Now, if you don't mind, I'll go grab myself a coin purse while you draw me a map to the coast."

He put a hand on her arm before she could get down. "I just want to say it—you're welcome in our crew. We could sorely use someone with your skill and wit."

She had to admit, the offer was a bit tempting. This escapade was just what she'd imagined adventure being like when she was a kid. More than that, she actually kind of liked this group.

She tipped her head. "I appreciate the invitation, but I have an obligation to take care of."

Serath let her go with a look of disappointment. "Well, it would be rude to insist."

Dust puffed up around her as she landed in the dirt and walked to the imperial she'd buried her flaming sword into. She had relieved him of his purse and was counting the coins when Flegs escorted a terrified captive driver up by the cart.

"I'm Heartsong, not imperial! Please, please don't kill me!"

"Hold your horses, man. No one said anything about taking your life. We just want to know what's going on with the canal project. What's the progress? What areas have the weakest army presence?"

Charva poured the coins back into the pouch. *Should be enough to book me passage to Leverie.*

"The project's a little upset. The schedules are all off on account of Chief Engineer Maltan being put under house arrest. There's a new project head, and he's changing a lot of the building priorities."

Charva pulled the purse straps too tight around her belt and whirled on the driver. "Chief Engineer Maltan?"

The driver shied away at her intensity. "Y-yes. The one General Nevygar took a liking to."

She found her mouth gaping. "Nevygar? What—how?" She shook her head. "Never mind that. Where is he now?"

The driver shared a glance with Flegs, who looked intrigued at Charva's interest. "Breakpeak. He's being held in the city palace."

Serath walked up with a sheet of paper. "All right, I've got you a map to the nearest coast city. It'll take about—"

Charva snatched the map from his hands and slapped it against the side of the cart. "Give me directions to Breakpeak."

Chapter 2

Woodwise's western gate tore from its hinges with a sharp snap and thudded heavily to the ground. Arzan raised his sword and shouted over clashing steel and battered wood, "Forward!"

Ellaniel stuck close to him as they pushed with the mass of Senkani troops past the ram and into the city. She couldn't see anything beyond their ckols and a few ranks of their own soldiers, but the howls and screams of men injured and dying told her the fighting still raged nearby. Senkani had taken the advantage in this battle, pushing straight to the gate and dividing Odavan's army in two outside the wall. The bold move must have taken Woodwise by surprise. Their mercenary commander, cunning as he was, probably expected Arzan to be rattled and cautious after Senkani's previous defeat.

We are not intimidated, Ellaniel thought, her grip tight on her sword as she marched victoriously into the city.

Setting foot inside Woodwise set loose a storm of emotions. The familiar main avenue was little changed from how she remembered, yet at the same time looked so different. It felt like a window into her childhood, a part of her distanced by her marriage to Arzan, by her father's murder, and by her searing hatred for the House. It was like confronting a part of her that was, but which she could never be again.

"Forty men to the ramparts on either side," Arzan ordered. "Take out those archers. Five companies will escort us to the palace. The rest are to hold the gate."

Their soldiers flowed through the broken entryway and formed squares. Ellaniel shook herself from her introspection and marched to the head of the lead formation. Arzan stood at her side, but nodded to her. They'd agreed it was her place to command from here.

Ellaniel pointed her sword into the city. "To the palace."

They advanced through empty streets layered with fallen leaves. The sounds of battle faded behind them until they were almost impossible to hear above the footsteps of hundreds of soldiers. No one challenged the Senkani marching through the broad central avenue. She approached every intersection with caution, setting soldiers to plug the crossroads with shield walls while the rest of the force passed through. It was all eerily quiet.

They found the palace gates with blood already spilled ahead of them. Fifteen or so men lay dead in the street, half in Woodwise blue, the others in commoner clothing. The gate itself hung ajar, its corner propped against a fallen guard. She shared a glance with Arzan, then commanded the soldiers to fan out and surround the palace.

"Much like what happened in Highcity," Arzan said.

"He had better not be dead already." She stepped through the gate. And froze.

The grounds were completely changed from when her father had been alive. Gone was the beautiful garden, the trees and flowers and brick pathways bordered with grasses. Gone were the benches where she'd spent countless hours practicing her embroidery while enjoying fruit picked fresh off the branch. Gone were the little clearings where she had watched her mother practice her sword stances. Instead, the beautiful living artwork her father had spent a lifetime crafting and cultivating was replaced with a drab surface of dead marble. Where once there had been carefully pruned trees, there now stood lifeless statues with arrogant eyes.

Ellaniel tightened her fists and shook with anger. *"Odavan."*

She stormed up the front steps and threw the doors wide before her ckols had a chance to clear the way ahead of her.

"*Odavan!*"

The interior of the palace had been remodeled as well. Silly paintings lined yellow walls with turquoise moldings. Thick runners covered up the floors. Even the layout seemed changed, with doors spaced at unfamiliar intervals.

Her home. Her father's home. It had been desecrated.

Someone appeared in the passageway ahead of her as she took her first rage-fueled step into the building. He was dressed in commoner clothing, but her ckols quickly stood between him and their crendess, swords raised. The commoner stopped and knelt just out of sword range. "My liege. This way—we have the crenden in his study."

Armor clinked as Arzan stood next to her. "Who are you?"

"Your grace, I was among the men Crenden Hashan selected for shield wall training. When Odavan took power and ordered the army to march against Senkani, I refused and was sent home. Seeing that Crendess Ellaniel was retaking the city, I and my fellows stopped Odavan before he could flee."

Ellaniel drew in a breath to compose herself. *There are those who stayed loyal to my father.* After all the fighting and betrayal, she had given up on such a possibility. "Take . . . take me to him."

The man stood and led them eagerly to Odavan's study. Two ckols went in and confirmed it was safe before Ellaniel and Arzan entered. They found four more men without uniform flanking Odavan's chair, two of them with firm hands on the Woodwise crenden's shoulders.

Her cousin looked on the verge of sickness even before he saw her. As soon as his eyes latched onto her face, he squirmed. "No! Let me go!"

Ellaniel took four steps and stabbed her sword down into Odavan's desk. He cried out and pressed himself further into his chair. "C-Cousin, wait!"

"You want me to wait? Did you wait before taking my father's seat and uprooting everything he built?"

"I was the designated heir," he squealed. "I did nothing

wrong."

She reached across the desk and grabbed Odavan by the collar before yanking him to within an inch of the still wobbling blade. "You marched an army to the defense of my father's killer and attacked me!"

"It was by Ylnavar's command! It was the Council!"

"The Council was wrong!" She threw him back in his seat, where he cowered with tears streaming down his face. "All that time you spent goading and insulting me when we were little. All those times you mocked me for my eyes and gloated that you were to be the next crenden. But this is what you are—a sniveling, opportunistic coward." She grabbed the hilt of her sword and yanked it free. "Vigkhon, bring him."

Arzan pointed to another of the ckols. "Send message to the battle that Odavan is ours."

They took Odavan out in front of the palace, where the troops cheered at their victory. Ellaniel had the captain place their captive on his knees. "Those men here, Odavan, you've killed their brothers. You've burned their homes and trampled their fields."

Odavan clawed his fingers around her greaves. "Cousin, please! We're family!"

Ellaniel crouched down. "Then, as family, tell me one thing. Where is the mercenary captain you hired to head your army?"

"H-Him? He abandoned us two days ago. Left behind the second half of his pay."

Arzan sighed. "Of course. Always one step out of our grasp."

"It doesn't matter," Ellaniel said. "No doubt he's running off to his true master. We'll find him in Creedport."

"Y-Yes!" Odavan said. "Thrake's the true villain! Cousin, he's betrayed us both!"

"Oh, by failing to kill me for you?"

"Cousin—"

"Stop calling me that," she said putting her face up to his. "What's wrong with calling me by the name you always used for me?"

Odavan's mouth opened and closed like a beached fish. "I-I . . . ."

"Go on. Aren't I the barbarian woman with blood too uncivilized for House Leverie? What did you always call me?"

"Ellaniel, please—"

"Well, maybe you were right. I am the Goldeye, here to be what you said I was."

She stood and looked to Arzan and tightened her fingers on the hilt of her sword. "Do you object?"

Arzan stared at Odavan. "Do what will give you closure, Ella."

Odavan put his arms around her leg. "No!" he wailed.

Vigkhon tore apart his grip and held him back.

"For all your gloating, I never wanted to rule Woodwise, cousin," Ellaniel said. "It's because of you that I need to."

She swung her sword and chopped through flesh and bone. Odavan's head sheared from his body, landing face first on the marble flagstones. A deafening cheer rose from the soldiers at her back, and she raised her bloody sword, its red coat glistening in the daylight. Even though it was impossible for her to be heard, she shouted, "Justice is done!"

It took some time for the celebratory shouts to die down, but when they did she found her father's old soldiers kneeling by the palace steps.

"Hail Ellaniel Leverie Redleaf, Crendess of Woodwise!"

Chapter 93

Charva placed her hands on her hips and gazed up at the lift line ascending through the center of Breakpeak. The scale. The elegance. The beauty of the enormous windmills gracing the top of the sloped city. She smiled. *It's magnificent.*

She tapped a passing commoner on the arm. "Maltan built that?"

"Uh, yes?"

She nodded and grinned wider. *Magnificent.*

Following a few more moments of glee, she shook herself and started for the bottom boarding station. Seeing the pair of imperials guarding the lift, she did her best to straighten her silver uniform. It was the smallest one she'd managed to get from the convoy guards in the mountains, but even so it was too large around the shoulders. The soldiers ahead didn't seem too attentive, so she hoped they wouldn't notice the ill fit, nor the rough Watchers patch the sisters had sewn together for her.

She stood in line and waited for the next lift to come rumbling to the plank. An operator on board pulled a lever and stopped the contraption, letting half a dozen passengers off before calling, "Ready to board."

City folk started filing in, but one of the guards perked up and looked straight at Charva. "Hey, Watcher."

Charva tensed.

"What are you doing standing in line? Everyone, move aside. Vron first."

She let out a sigh of relief and walked past onto the lift. She greeted the operator and leaned into the railing as everyone else stepped on. The operator reengaged the lift, snapping them into motion.

Charva beamed as she rose upwards, tiled rooftops slipping by on either side. Her thoughts went back to the days she'd spent in Maltan's tower, watching his little contraptions shift and whirl. *You finally did it, Malty.*

The lift reached the second boarding station. The operator let three off, trading them for an Aiv Chahai. Charva made certain to keep to the far end with her back turned. Nonetheless, she felt the woman's gaze as the lift carried on. At the next stop, she tilted her head. Her eyes connected with the imperial woman's.

Great.

Charva stepped off the lift, but heard shifting mail as the Watcher followed after her. "Excuse me, private."

Pretending not to hear, Charva continued up the street.

"Private!"

With no other choice, she stopped and faced the imperial. "Yes," she flicked her eyes over the woman's rank insignia, "sergeant?"

The Aiv Chahai crossed her arms. "It's a minimum ten years hard labor for impersonating an agent of the empire."

Charva blinked and feigned innocence. "What?"

The sergeant poked Charva's shoulder patch. "What kind of pathetic imitation is this? My eight-year-old daughter can sew a better insignia."

"I'm sorry, sergeant," Charva said. "I just came from the front. My uniform got ruined in the fighting and I had to put this together from salvage on the trail." She soured her face. "I, um. My hands weren't too steady after washing the blood out of it."

The Watcher looked her over again, unsure. Her eyes narrowed deeper. "Then let's make a trip to requisitions."

Charva worked up a few tears, trying to make it seem like she'd been holding them back. "Thank you, sergeant! This is my first time in the city and the directions they gave at the gate didn't help any!"

The sergeant's face softened a little. "All right. I admit I had a hard time when I first joined up."

Oh, that worked!

"What army were you attached to, anyway?" the sergeant asked, moving to guide her.

Embers. "Uh . . . ." She grabbed the sergeant by the side of the head and slammed her skull into the nearest wall. The woman fell to the ground in a heap. Charva ducked down and checked for a pulse, feeling extraordinarily guilty. Thankfully, the sergeant was alive. She hooked her arms under the imperial's armpits just as a pair of city folk turned the corner.

"Sarge, how many times do I have to tell you to watch your step in this flaming city?"

The locals hurried on their way, allowing Charva to drag the Aiv Chahai into an alley and set about giving herself a promotion. The sergeant's uniform turned out to be a better fit around the shoulders, but decidedly loose at the chest. *Well, I can run and jump. So there.*

She used her previous uniform to tie the woman up. "Sorry for giving you trust issues."

Eager to leave the scene of the crime, she went back to the lift station. Wearing a proper Watcher uniform helped her feel like she belonged, which in turn helped a lot with her acting. As the next platform reached the boarding plank, she folded her hands behind her and lifted her nose, adopting the haughty imperial overlord look that would prompt people to steer clear and not ask questions.

The lift brought her all the way to the top of the city without further incident. The station was right by the palace, and Charva strolled in through the gated courtyard and front door as if it were her own home in Creedport. None of the guards gave her a second glance, but she was mindful to provide other Aiv Chahai a wide berth as she traversed the polished hallways. It took little time for her to understand the size of the building and respect the maze of passages. Before the servants and guards had a chance to notice how lost she was, she drew in a deep breath and approached a young Watcher doodling by a window. "Private."

The woman startled, squeezing her sketch pad to her bosom and snapping a salute. "Yes, sergeant!"

Charva suppressed a snicker. "Where is Chief Engineer Maltan being held?"

"North wing. Follow this passage until the pot with the

yellow flowers, then turn left. It'll be the fourth door on the right."

"Thank you."

She followed the private's directions until spotting the door flanked by two guards. She loitered around the corner and tried to formulate a plan.

Mere moments into her plotting, a voice roared behind her, "Why in the six do you have that?"

Charva stiffened as a soldier crossed her way. No, an officer. The man had a lieutenant's insignia.

"Excuse me?" She tried to ignore her racing heart.

The lieutenant pointed to her sword. "I'd recognize that hilt anywhere. That's Sergeant Givain's rapier."

Charva swallowed, her mind racing. *Don't panic.* Despite everything, she smirked. "Not since I won it from him."

The imperial stopped in front of her and leered down from his impressive height. "Nonsense! Givain is the best duelist in the Forty-Ninth."

She glanced down at the weapon. Oh.

"How did you really get his sword, mouse?"

Charva kept the quirk in her lips. "He *was* the best in the Forty-Ninth before I came along."

"Liar. There's no way he would have lost to a woman. You stole it, or cheated it from him."

"Truly. I bet it's not actually Givain's prowess you're defending. You just don't want to admit I'm better than *you*."

The officer reddened. "That's enough. Courtyard. Now."

Charva's mind finally caught up to what she was doing. "You-you mean right now?" She checked again his height and the two handed sword at his hip. *I. Am. Stupid.*

"This instant!" the lieutenant all but roared, his hand on his pommel.

Another officer rushed up from a side passage. "Lieutenant, they're waiting for you in the—" he stopped dead in his tracks as the lieutenant turned, his face contorted in suppressed rage. "Whoa, did someone kill your cat?"

"Ten minutes, Rakthan! I need to teach this Watcher a lesson!"

"The governor's already been waiting. Now, Helear."

The lieutenant seethed. "Fine!" He pointed at Charva.

"Courtyard. Half an hour."

She watched him storm off with the other officer and breathed a sigh of relief. *I'll be sure to be long gone by then.*

Off down the hall, the guards to Matan's door were both staring at her.

Well, nothing for it.

She strode up. "I'm here to see the chief engineer."

The guards glanced at each other. One shifted his belt. "You really beat Givain?"

"Yep," she passed on putting any bravado into the statement. No point inviting any more duels.

The two men whistled and opened the door for her. "Go right ahead, Watcher."

Charva suppressed her surprise. That was . . . easier than she anticipated.

She stepped into the room, the guards clicking the door closed behind her. Her heart raced in her chest as she surveyed the chambers. The place was a mess. Papers and books lay strewn about, furniture upended. Maltan's tower had been cluttered, but never disorderly. Fearing for his safety, she hurried to the next room. The moment she reached the threshold, her breath stopped.

There he was.

Maltan sat hunched in his chair over an empty desk. As in the first chamber, papers lay scattered across the floor. He was dressed more finely than any time she could remember, but at the same time he looked so much more frail and old.

She choked up, her legs getting wobbly. As she put a hand out to steady herself, her fingers shifted a plate of untouched food on the stand beside her. The dish clacked.

"Just leave it all there," Maltan said in a defeated voice.

Charva swallowed. "Malty."

Maltan slowly raised his head, then turned to face her. "Charva?"

She ran and embraced him, tears running down her face. "Malty, I missed you!"

He hugged her back. "What-what are you doing here?"

A laugh escaped her lips. "It's a long story. I got chased out of Leverie by Roth's men, then got conscripted into the Whitesail army. After I escaped, I heard about you being chief engineer for General Nevygar. Malty, what in the six happened?"

Maltan's face darkened. "I've made a grave mistake. I helped the enemies of Leverie."

"What, you mean by building that lift? That's really amazing—"

He slammed his fist down on the desk. "The Vron are the ones responsible for the Leverie civil war!"

Charva blinked and frowned. "What? No. Roth's the one responsible. He admitted it straight to my face."

His mouth opened in surprise. "Roth?" He shook his head. "He must be a puppet. He's working for the empire to pit the provinces against each other and wear down our armies so they can be easily defeated by the Vron legions. General Nevygar has already left with a fresh army from the homeland, and it's my fault. I helped him solidify their rule here in Heartsong."

Charva stepped back. She felt her hands shaking. "The empire is marching on Leverie?"

A knock sounded at the main entryway. "Things all right in there, Watcher?"

"Um, y-yes," Charva stammered. She turned to look around at the rest of the room. "How are we going to escape from here?"

"You came in here without a plan? Not that I can call myself shocked."

Charva tapped her forehead. "Oh, to blazes with it." She took Maltan's hand and led him to the front door. "Open up."

The door creaked inward. The guards saw her escorting Maltan. "What's this?"

"What's this?" Charva snorted and hauled Maltan forward by the front of his shirt. "Do you know he hasn't been eating his meals? Who's in charge here? Do you want him starving himself to death?"

"That, um—"

"I'm taking him to the kitchens. I'll force something down his throat if I have to!"

Maltan picked up on the ruse. "You can't force anything out of me, and you can't force anything into me! I'll not serve the machinations of the empire any longer!"

She pulled him out into the hall. "Enough of that, old fool."

The guards looked at a loss as they followed Charva away from the chambers.

Out of the room. Now what?

"Kitchens are down that way," Maltan whispered.

She followed his directions as she tried to figure out their next move. *Well, if he hasn't been eating, maybe stopping at the kitchens actually isn't a bad idea.*

"Trying to get away, are you?" A hand clamped around the back of her neck and towed her off course. It was Lieutenant Helear.

Embers!

"We're settling this now, and that sword is mine."

"I'm busy, lieutenant."

"Too bad."

"Don't worry, Watcher, we've got him."

For a very brief moment, she thought the guards meant they were going to get her free. Instead, they took hold of Maltan.

"We'll be cheering for you on the sidelines, sergeant."

"Um, that's not—" Charva started.

Another soldier started jogging through the palace. "Helear's dueling a Watcher!"

"Ha! Poor girl doesn't stand a chance."

"Wait, is this the woman with Givain's sword?"

Great. She'd come in trying to be sneaky and ended up being the talk of the palace.

By the time the lieutenant dragged her to the courtyard, they already had an audience of more than twenty soldiers and Aiv Chahai. *Because when making a covert getaway, you want the whole palace guard detail watching you. Good going, Charva.*

At least she could see the city out through the eastern arches, for all the good that did her.

"Twenty silvers on Helear!"

"I'm putting twenty-five on the Sister," a Watcher called. Right next to her, the private with the sketch pad was excitedly framing the scene with thumb and forefinger.

"Keep up your delusions that a woman will someday

defeat one of the dueling kings," a soldier said with a smirk.

"She's got Givain's sword. That means she already beat one of the kings."

"Rule set of fours and six," Lieutenant Helear said, pulling off his uniform and baring the chain shirt underneath. He tossed the cloth aside and drew his sword.

Embers. We're using real edges? What's fours and six? Charva flexed her arms, feeling sweat roll down her face. She cast her eyes about, trying to spot any way out of this. She caught Maltan's gaze. He balled his fists, his guards holding his arms at either side, and looked ready to cause a scene. Charva shook her head. She wasn't going to have him act as a distraction. They'd both get out of here, or neither of them would. She was tired of leaving people behind.

The only way out was to win the duel. Charva drew her sword and settled into her stance. She could do this. It sounded like the imperial Aiv Chahai didn't have a great dueling record, but how many of them had fought on the field like she had?

Helear gripped his sword in both hands. "Don't mind me cutting that uniform up, Watcher?"

"What makes you think you'll be able to touch me?" She didn't want anyone to see she was wearing a Whitesail chain pattern underneath the imperial cloth.

"I'll act as ref," a soldier said, stepping between them.

"I'll be merciful and not give you *too* many bruises, woman," the lieutenant said.

Charva merely flourished her sword without another word.

The self-appointed referee chopped his hand through the air and stepped away. Lieutenant Helear immediately charged in with a lateral cut. Charva danced back, letting the blade miss her by half an inch. He continued pressing forward, crisscrossing his attacks as she kept just out of reach.

"Hey, stop running away!" someone called. "Give us a good fight!"

The lieutenant stepped in faster than she could back off, forcing her to parry. His sword hit hers hard, numbing her hand and sending the sound of clanging metal clapping off the walls.

"Don't listen to the boys! Let him tire himself out!"

She narrowly deflected several more blows, each coming closer to scoring a hit. Forget tiring *him* out—it was all she could do to keep hold of her sword as his pounding wore at her arm.

"Where's all that spunk now, Watcher?" Helear demanded.

Charva's back hit against the edge of the courtyard. The lieutenant struck hard. She managed to block, but the force pushed the blunt edge of her sword into her chest. He pressed into the bind, pinning her against the base of the arch. With his offhand, he clamped her blade to the wall as well to keep her from attacking. Their audience hollered.

"This is the part where you beg me to let you forfeit," he said between clenched teeth.

Since when was that her style? She buckled her legs and slipped downwards. She let her sword stay high, but twisted and grabbed his back with her free hand, simultaneously tangling her leg behind his knee. It wasn't the best leverage, but she managed to pull him just enough that his chest touched the back edge of his weapon.

"Point!" the referee called.

"What?!" Helear shouted.

"Edge contact," the soldier said. "One point to the Watcher."

The Aiv Chahai cheered.

"Come on, that's cheap!" a soldier shouted.

The referee raised his hand. "Reset!"

Charva and the imperial returned to the center of the courtyard. The lieutenant didn't hide his fury, but glared daggers at her. "That won't work twice."

"Don't worry, I've got plenty more tricks," she answered. *In a real fight, that move would have been pointless.* She did her best to keep her arm from shaking with exhaustion.

The ref dropped his hand. Helear charged in with a feint, dodging to the side as Charva thrust at his chest. She bent back to escape a slash, heard the blade swish past her face. The next attack forced her to parry, putting more strain on her arm. Teeth grit, she braced her left forearm against the back of her sword to better absorb the blows. It meant less reach if she tried attacking, but at this point she was stuck on the defensive anyway.

Helear didn't even seem like he wanted to get around her guard and score a point. He wailed away at her sword, determined to break down her endurance. Charva backed away to lessen the pressure, but angled her movement into a circle so she wouldn't be pinned to the wall again.

"What's the matter? Too tired to hit back?" Helear's downward swing hit her guard so hard she stumbled. "Come on!"

Charva's blade was too tied up to strike. Hoping she wasn't breaking the rules, she kicked her heel into the lieutenant's shin. He grunted and eased his assault ever so slightly. It was just enough that she managed to dodge his next swing. She kicked him in the leg again, harder, and flicked her blade, forcing him off balance as he bent to avoid losing a point. She tried to take advantage of his bad stance and whipped the tip of her sword at his chest, but he recovered too quickly, catching her blade with his. The rapier bounced aside, singing in her hand.

Helear shouted and swung his sword into her side. The blade caught her just below the ribs, the force jarring her through the chain and padding.

"Point!"

She staggered away from the blow, the male soldiers taking their turn to cheer. *Embers, he's tough.*

"Half point to the Watcher from unarmed contact."

The lieutenant spit and cursed. Charva raised her eyebrows as she got her feet back under her. *Well, I guess this rule set isn't so bad.* She was still starting to feel she was going to lose this. These imperial duelists weren't called kings for nothing. *Does that matter, though? Do I really have to win to get out of here?*

They returned to the center of the courtyard and took their stances. Helear didn't bother saying anything as the referee raised his hand.

"Alarm! Alarm! Impostor in the city!"

Everyone turned to the Aiv Chahai running in through the palace gates.

"Someone took a Watcher's uniform in the Lowers!"

Well . . . embers.

Charva did the only sensible thing she could think of—she took advantage of the distraction and rammed Lieutenant Helear in the temple with her guard. She swiveled around even as he collapsed to the ground and saw Maltan break away from his escorts. The two soldiers, and most everyone else for that matter, still had their eyes on the messenger. They swiveled their heads and started after Maltan, not yet registering Charva as a threat as she dashed in and swept their legs out from under them. For the briefest moment, as they sprawled on the stones, she contemplated running them through, but stayed her hand and simply grabbed Maltan by the arm. "Run!"

As she turned back around, she saw that people were starting to realize what she was doing. Someone pointed. "It's her!"

Charva and Maltan dashed through the eastern arches and onto the path to the gates, but stopped short as the sentries ahead drew their blades. She glanced over her shoulder. The soldiers and even half the Watchers were closing in fast, swords in hand.

"You can jump, right, Malty?"

She didn't give him a chance to respond before sheathing her sword and pushing him towards the outer fence. The iron bars were a good seven or six feet high, but they were set into the steep slope, making it "only" a four-foot hurdle if they placed it right.

"Now!"

They both jumped and caught the tops of the bars. For a wonder, Charva managed to get her foot purchase and twist her body up and over. She perched just long enough to help pull Maltan after her, puffing and shaking. The two of them dropped to the ground and tumbled several yards downhill until hitting a solid wood wall with a pair of heavy thumps.

Charva immediately braced herself against the wall and pushed herself up, ignoring her many new bruises and scrapes.

"Catch them!"

Soldiers were climbing the fence after them as well as racing out the gates. Rumbling drew her attention further downhill, and she realized the low wall they were up against was along the guide track for Maltan's lift. One of the lifts had just departed the platform and was beginning its descent off to their left. The operator was its lone occupant, and he had his face turned towards the palace with narrowed eyes.

"Malty, hurry!" She urged him onto the track without the faintest shadow of a plan. The first of their pursuers dropped from the fence, but lost his footing the same as the fugitives. He rolled into the wall with a curse and a grunt as Charva started an awkward descent down the track, the lift chain slipping along by her feet.

The operator searched around in desperation as she approached, but found no help nearby. "Catch her!" someone shouted. "In the name of the empire, grab her!"

Charva drew her sword and leaped onto the platform. The operator backed into the far rail before braving up and rushing at her, fists raised. In some other circumstance, she might have admired his courage, but right now she didn't have time to waste. She pierced him clear through the heart, then kicked the body off the blade and spun to deflect a cut from a soldier who landed on the lift. Maltan punched the imperial in the jaw, clacking the man's teeth, but it did nothing more than draw his ire. The soldier elbowed Maltan in the face, sending him crashing into the control lever.

Charva was in mid-strike as the platform disengaged from the chain and plunged. She caught a glimpse of a second soldier trying for the rail and grabbing air before all her focus went to frantically holding on as the lift careened downwards. Screams sounded from below. The lift crashed into the next platform and her grasp tore free from the beam, sending her flying into the front railing. The wood hammered her in the waist, forcing the wind out of her with a *humph* and flipping her into the lift they'd just hit.

She groaned and tried finding the floor with sluggish limbs. Her waist throbbed in agony. She thought she heard voices, small and distant. She blinked hard, slowly clearing her vision.

"Surround the lift! Stop that Aiv Chahai!"

Get up, Charva, she told herself. The world righted. Charva pushed up to her knees with a cough and she spit after tasting blood. Her sword was teetering on the lift's edge between the rails and right next to a merchant holding to his head in a daze. She grabbed it and stood, ignoring the shrieking pain in her side.

Maltan was next to her, still trying to regain his bearings. Aside from a red gash across his forehead, he looked fine. The lift they were on was still moving, though the uphill side was caved in from the impact. The body of the operator she'd killed seemed to still be up above. The second lift's operator lay badly injured at her feet. Besides him and the merchant, there was one other passenger getting his legs under him. Off to right and left, soldiers were tearing through the streets and hopping across rooftops to catch up.

"I really should have put more safety mechanisms into the system," Maltan muttered as he dabbed his sleeve into the cut on his face.

She put her sword in its sheath. "Everybody hold on. I've got a very bad idea."

Maltan saw her put her hand on the control lever. "No, that really is a very bad—"

Charva pulled the lever, disengaging the chain claws. The lift lurched and careened down the slope, slipping out of reach of the pursuing soldiers. It also sped right for the next lift in line. That lift's passengers had just enough time to jump out and onto the boarding platform before thousands of pounds of wood came slamming in. Charva barely hung on as the impact shuddered through her.

"W-well, that wasn't so—" she started.

Something cracked. The wood groaned and shuddered under her.

Maltan drew in a deep breath and closed his eyes. "Keep holding on."

The lower lift's brakes gave out with a pair of snaps. Her hands went white and numb as she clenched the rail and her stomach floated up into her throat. Their mass of three platforms smashed into the next lift down, snapping it loose and absorbing it into the rolling disaster. They hit the next and the next. The city streaked by in a blur of tan and brown.

Flame and embers, this was stupid!

With a bang the clump of lifts reached the bottom of the

track, smashing through the boarding platform and skidding through the lower square. Fruit and vegetables splatted against the rail as they tore through vendors. A tarp whipped overhead, part of a corner post whacking the wood inches from her head. Just as she was expecting the next impact to kill her, the lifts lurched to a halt in a spray of glass beads.

She lay still, her hands remaining tight on the rail as dust settled on her skin. She heard screams all around her, drowning out the sound of her own frantic breaths.

Six continents. How many people did that just kill?

"Move, move! Make way for the guard!"

Charva forced herself up and looked about for Maltan. He was already sitting, staring out at the mangled marketplace around them and shaking his head with tears in his eyes. She grabbed him by the arm, beads raining off her sleeve. "Come on, Malty!"

He didn't argue as they dropped to the ground and stumbled through the wreckage. To her relief, she didn't actually see any bodies. Perhaps enough people had spotted the lifts coming for everyone to get out of the way. Or almost everyone. A little further out, people limped along with cuts and bruises, some of them helped by imperial soldiers. A squad of guards rushed on past towards the lifts. "Check for the passengers!"

The chaos was enough that the two of them were able to make it to the stables without problem. They weren't even challenged, the stable hands having run to the square to help. Charva picked out a pair of horses already saddled and ready to travel.

"Where are we going from here?" Maltan asked, his back conspicuously turned to the ruined square.

"Isn't it obvious? Now we go home."

Chapter 91

Arzan rode his horse past the last trees into the open fields south of Creedport. Finally, at long last, they were at the end of the road. *He* was at the end of the road. The war would end today.

The joint Senkani, Highcity, and Woodwise army marched behind and around him, their steps ranging from practiced precision to amateurish shambling. Regardless of each man's proficiency, he could sense in them, could see in their eyes that they were as determined as he to see this day through. One last battle. One last push. Then everyone could finally go home.

The fields were empty of people, unharvested vegetables standing alone in orderly rows that would soon be trampled into the ground. Thrake's banners flew above the walls, over the tops of hundreds of heads wearing polished helmets. They were the only defenders in sight. After the capture of Woodwise, the rest of the Leverie crendens had slunk away to their own provinces, leaving Creedport to its own devices.

Ellaniel rode her horse alongside his, her golden eyes aflame. She already had her sword in hand. "Today," she said, "Thrake dies."

Arzan nodded and tightened his helmet strap. "Today."

"Report from the coast scouts!" a messenger called. "Ship approaching the harbor!"

Ellaniel clashed her sword against her shield. "We can't let Thrake escape out to sea! All companies, begin the assault!"

Charva jumped from the ship to the pier, not waiting for the dockworkers to shove the gangplank into place. She would have had to make the leap anyway, since the throngs of people clogging the docks stampeded aboard the instant the ramp was down.

"I knew I shouldn't have docked here," the captain shouted.

Charva ignored him and caught Maltan's eye as he pressed up against the handrail. "I'll find you at the tower, Malty."

"Don't wait for me," Maltan said. "Go!"

She nodded and shoved her way along the dock to solid ground. After getting past the mass of clamoring people desperately trying to get to the ship, she found empty streets and boarded windows. Creedport was braced for war.

She ran, making for the main avenue. Tears of joy at being back home threatened at her eyes, but she held them back with the knowledge that everything was on the verge of crashing down. She needed to find her father.

It didn't take long for her to hear that the battle had already begun. Siege weapons cracked over the steady roar of angry voices—faint, but impressive in how far they carried.

The palace loomed to her side. Two lone guards stood at the gate, their eyes nervously turned to the south. Charva caught hold of a lamp pole, halting herself right in their faces. "Where's the crenden?"

The nearer guard jumped and dropped his spear, while the other swiveled around and leveled his weapon at her. "Who —"

"My father," she snapped. "Where is he?"

The eyes of the guard pointing his spear at her widened in recognition. "Your grace? You're back! How—never mind! Crenden Thrake is at the south gate, organizing the defense."

Charva nodded sharply and ran. The streets remained empty up until two blocks from the wall, where ranks of men gripping axes and makeshift spears stood anxiously behind wood barricades. She hurried past them, conspicuous in her shining mail. Nearer to the gate, she found proper soldiers in Creedport green, most of whom were braced against the door as a ram battered savagely at the center. She tried to tune out the shouting and crashing as she swept her eyes across the scene, trying to find her father.

"Arrows!"

Feathered shafts pelted the wall and bits of the street beyond. Charva kept her arms above her head to fend off any lucky hit. A not-so-fortunate soldier screamed and fell off the ramparts after an arrow caught him in the neck.

"The ladders are closing! Don't let them reach the wall!" She recognized her father's voice shouting the order. He was up on the rampart, halfway between the gatehouse and the first tower to the west. She rushed up the gatehouse stairwell, the stones shaking under her feet as the battering ram pounded away. She reached the top just as a row of Creedport archers loosed a volley out at the mass of soldiers marching on the city.

Supply runners jostled through with baskets of arrows as Charva pushed her way along. One of the carved merlon lizards exploded into a spray of stone chips on getting hit dead center by a ballista bolt. An archer stepped back in a daze, his hand pressed to his bloody face.

"Stop, soldier, this area is—" the ckol who had put up his hand to halt her narrowed his eyes, then gasped in surprise. "Your grace!" He turned on his heel and dashed away. "The crenden's daughter is back! Her Grace Charva is back!"

"Volley incoming!"

Arrows rained down on the wall, lodging into gambeson or clattering on stone.

"Return volley! Loose!"

The archers released a flurry of arrows down on the enemy. As they collectively bent to grab more ammunition, Charva caught sight of her father standing in the midst of his ckols. She felt emotions well up in her chest. Not as strong as when she'd been reunited with Maltan, but there nonetheless.

The crenden pointed out at the Redleaf army. "The ladders are at the wall! Swords in position! Defend the—"

The ckol who'd seen Charva finally reached him and

waved excitedly in her direction. Thrake turned and saw her. His jaw dropped. He shoved an archer out of the way as she took the last few steps to reach him, then grabbed her in a crushing embrace. She heard his voice croak in her ear, just barely audible to her over the chaos around them. "My daughter! I though you were dead."

Charva found herself hugging him back, not quite able to make words. It was insane. A war raged around them, but all her mind could do was try to remember any time during her childhood that her father had shown love for her so.

An arrow skidded off Thrake's plate armor, ending the moment. He pushed her back to arm's length, fear in his eyes. "You shouldn't have returned now of all times. The city is going to fall. You can't be here when the Redleafs breach the gates."

"Father, I discovered who is behind the assassins. It's the Vron! The empire is marching an army on Leverie this very moment!"

Wood thumped on stone as the siege ladders hit the wall. A sergeant raised his ax. "Swords! Defend the city!"

"We have to stop the fighting," Charva said. "We have to unify the aristocracy against the coming invasion."

Her father's eyes had turned distant. "The Vron . . . . I was the one who spoke most loudly against preparing Leverie against the empire. I fought Arzan on the matter in the Council."

"The Vron saw that as an opening to pit us against each other, wear us down for an easy victory."

"It's my fault," Thrake said.

"Destroy the ladders! Don't let them up!"

Steel rang against steel. The Senkani were at the battlements. Below, the ram continued booming against the gate.

Resolve crystallized within Thrake's blue eyes. "I need to give myself up. Surrender."

Charva shook her head and held his arm tight. "They could kill you immediately. You won't have a chance to explain what's happening."

"Then you will speak after I'm dead. We need to stop the fighting and preserve as much of our forces as we can."

"But—"

"It's the only way, Charva."

She saw it for the truth. Still, she couldn't let him go. However much of a fool he'd been, however much he'd attempted to smother her over the years, he was still her father. And now, here, he was finally a better man. The man she had always wanted him to be.

"There must—"

"A well reasoned plan." The voice came from right beside them. Charva turned, but only caught a glimpse of a soldier twisting away from her and slipping into the frenzy of bodies. Thrake tipped sideways and looked down at a dagger hilt protruding from just below his chestplate. Charva stood frozen in horror as dark blood soaked his tunic.

The Senkani forces flooded the ramparts.

"Everyone on those walls or at the gate!" Arzan shouted. "We're holding nothing back!"

He'd already sent the archers to cover the east and west gates, with the command to shoot anyone trying to flee. Scouts reported that the ship in port had taken on its passengers, but was having trouble with departure. They might just make it to the harbor in time. If not, he hoped Thrake was not on board, but found he wasn't too worried. Even if he escaped, Arzan decided this would be enough. He was tired of this fighting. Whether Thrake lost his life or his city, it would be a justice Arzan could be content with.

With a crack, the south gate gave to the battering ram and swung in, panels splintered. The soldiers whooped in victory. Arzan took a breath and tightened his grip on his sword. Beside him, Ellaniel's armor clinked.

"The city is open! Charge!"

Charva drew her blade in time to parry a strike from a Senkani soldier. She fended off two more attacks before he got drawn off by the soldier beside her. The battlements were getting fast overrun, Creedport defenders falling left and right. Several of her father's ckols barely managed to pull him from the fray, the rest rallying around her. Grief clawed at her heart, but unlike the times before that it had swallowed her soul, she successfully focused herself on the immediacy of the fight. *He'll live. He'll live . . . .*

A man in Woodwise blue cut down a soldier and engaged the ckol guarding her left flank. More of the enemy poured up onto the wall, swelling the press of attack. There simply weren't enough defenders to hold them off.

"Fall back to the towers!" Charva shouted. "Get to the barricades!"

The ramparts were so clogged with bodies—standing or fallen—that she had little hope of following her own order. In both directions, allies were shoulder to shoulder, enemies practically nose to nose. It was like her time in the shield wall, except without even the semblance of formation. And there was no ground for the defenders to give. As she watched, the force of the attackers started pushing Creedport soldiers over the edge and screaming to their deaths on the street below.

"Death to the murderers!"

The press of attackers broke through her father's ckols' protective boundary. The ckol in front of her wasn't so much stabbed as impaled on a relentless mass of sharpened steel. His body became a cushion between her and a half dozen swords as the mass shoved her right up against the edge of the wall. She teetered, snapping her gaze down at the ground already littered with broken men. Of to the side, a few defenders tried jumping to the nearest rooftops with varying success.

The enemy pushed her further, bringing her heels out over empty space. She grabbed at the ckol's body, but it started to slip loose from the blades. In desperation, she followed the other soldiers' lead and jumped, twisting around and putting everything into the leap. She didn't even have time to pick a target. She saw the tiled rooftop an instant before she hit, her shoulder colliding painfully on the baked clay. She tumbled helplessly along the steep slope. Her hands scrambled for purchase, catching hold of the edge tiles right in time as her body rolled out into empty air. The joints of her arms screamed at her as she stopped her forward momentum and brought herself swinging back towards the building's outer wall. Just as she braced to hit, the tiles came loose, dropping her. She crashed through a cloth awning and landed, quite luckily, in a big, open crate of yarn.

She let herself lie there a few moments to catch her breath. "Bless the weavers in this city."

The continued sounds of fighting urged her to get on her feet. She pulled herself out of the crate, noticing as she did the bloody print she left on the wood. Looked like her left hand had been scratched up rather bad, opening up her wounds from Heartsong. On the plus side, her sword was lying on the cobbles nearby. She scooped it up and started down the narrow street at a slight limp, grateful that she wasn't worse off than that after jumping off a city wall.

She wound her way through the twisting alleys, not quite sure where she was trying to go. *Arzan and Ella. I need to find them.*

That would mean going back towards the fighting, and if she did that, would she even be able to parlay? No one would bother pausing the fight for a sole woman screaming in all the chaos.

As she moved past intersections, she caught glimpses of Senkani soldiers hunting down fleeing defenders. Shouts and screams carried from every direction, echoing off the stone walls. Where would Arzan and Ellaniel go in person?

The same place as before.

Charva followed familiar paths, snaking through the tight city streets until she reached the palace. About thirty or so soldiers and city guardsmen were rallied in front of the gate. It was obvious they had no one in charge, the way they gathered about in formless clumps. One of the men recognized her as she stepped into the open.

"Your grace? You've returned?" then quickly, "Is the crenden with you? We need orders."

Her hand throbbed, and she felt crusted blood on her skin

crack as she balled her fist. "Form a line against the south."

The men rushed to comply, locking shields in as good a wall as they could manage in the broad avenue. "We'll defend you with our lives, your grace."

"Just hold until I give the word." There really wasn't much this group could do for her except buy time. Not against the Senkani, not against . . . . She cast her eyes about the street, watching for any sign of the imperial assassins. Were they finally going to kill her too? If they had their crossbowman here, then . . . . *Well, then that's that. I'm dead.* She was tired of death coming at her from every direction.

The sound of soldiers marching reached her ears. Her fingernails bit into her palm. She willed her hand to relax.

"Here they come!" a guardsman shouted. "Stand firm!"

She watched through the gaps in the single layer shield wall as the Senkani soldiers approached in solid formation. Not all the red on their shields was paint.

Are the Redleafs with them? Please be with them.

What she was doing looked more and more like another idiot idea in a long string of her idiot ideas. She was going to die here. But then, it was only natural that her recklessness would catch up to her some day.

She had to do what she could if it meant a chance of saving her home.

"Men of Senkani," Charva called. She nudged two guards out of her way and stood just in front of the defensive line. "I would speak with the Redleafs."

The Senkani soldiers hesitated just as they were winding up to charge.

"We're done talking," a man with a sergeant's patch said. "Surrender or die. Justice has come to Creedport."

"I will speak with your crenden," Charva repeated.

"She's trying to buy time," a soldier said. "Thrake must be on his way to the ship!"

Charva shook her head in frustration. "You're all imbeciles."

"Out of our way, woman! You'll get no mercy if you try helping Crenden Thrake."

"So be it," she muttered, and readied her sword.

"The wall is ours!"

Exuberant soldiers raised their weapons and cheered as the remaining Creedport defenders fled down the street, the Senkani vanguard hard on their heels. Thrake's men didn't even bother rallying behind the wooden barricades, but simply ran for dear life. Arzan stepped over a set of bodies in green and surveyed the carnage they'd wrought in the quick battle. "Any sign of Thrake?"

His men glanced at each other in question, all of them returning blank looks or shaking heads. Arzan fiddled with his cape clasp. *I'd hoped for the kind of unexpected honor he'd had in the first battle. Looks like we should have followed the old plan and secured the docks first.*

Ellaniel strode ahead of him. "Hurry. We need to capture that ship."

"Two hundred men follow the wall east and west," Arzan ordered. "Leave twenty at each gate and have the rest continue to the port. A hundred hold this gate. Everyone else with us."

His men eagerly stepped into formation in front and behind. In moments, they were marching into the city up the main avenue. Arzan felt the weight of victory with each step. No one opposed their advance, and he even saw spears and shields abandoned in the street. Off in the distance, he could make out the mast of the ship at port. Looked like they were still having trouble with the launch.

As they made their way northward, a messenger came running up. "My liege, a line of Thrake's men are making a stand outside the palace."

Arzan nodded. "Make sure our soldiers hurry and lock down the port. I will secure the palace first, but the defense there may still be a ruse." To the troops, "Double time!"

The palace, when they arrived, was a mess. From the row of half a dozen bodies in the street, he discerned the Creedport soldiers had formed a line across the main avenue before falling back to the gate. There, ten defenders were trying to fend off thirty Senkani shieldsmen. They were making a valiant show of it, but the attackers were already starting to scale the fence on either side to surround the enemy.

"This will be over quick," Ellaniel said. "Send another company over the fence and they'll have no choice except—"

She cut off as a figure darted away from the gate and sprang at the first Senkani to slip onto the palace grounds. Light glinted off narrow steel before it pierced through the attacker's throat. The soldier flailed his sword uselessly about as the woman who'd struck him danced back out of reach and rushed for the next incursion. She was already thrusting her rapier at a second soldier as the first tottered and fell.

"Hold the assault!" Arzan ordered. "Everyone climbing, off those fences!"

"My liege," the forward sergeant started, "we've almost —"

"I said back off!"

The sergeant recoiled and hastily conveyed the order. Arzan stepped toward the fence even as his men pulled away from the fight. "We'll crush 'em at your order, my liege," a soldier muttered as he passed.

Arzan patted his shoulder. "You've crushed them quite well already."

Without his own soldiers in the way, it was clear the Creedport men were much the worse for wear, many of them barely standing. But that was hardly his concern. His eyes were on the woman walking to meet him from the other side of the fence. He stopped just far enough from the bars to be out of range of her sword.

He nodded. "Charva."

Despite the fluidity she'd displayed moments earlier, Thrake's daughter looked like she was on the verge of collapse. Instead of her usual falconian dress, she sported a mail shirt with numerous spots of missing and bent rings. Her left hand was badly bloodied, her sword shook, and it seemed to pain her just standing straight. She gave him an exhausted smile, the type one saw on someone who'd finally reached the end of a long, harrowing journey. It disappeared after she took a deep breath and schooled her face.

"Arzan, we need to talk."

Ellaniel settled in beside him. "There's nothing to talk about, Charva, except for you to tell us where Thrake is."

Armor clicked and feet shuffled as the soldiers on both sides watched, ready to reengage.

"The Vron Empire is marching on Leverie," Charva said, her eyes level on Arzan's. "This civil war was their plot to divide us. They're on their way here right now."

"I am tired, Charva," Ellaniel told her. Arzan heard the leather squeak as she tightened her hand on her sword's grip. "I am tired of everyone getting in my way. I am tired of all the lies and the justifications. You have one chance to—"

"No, *you* listen to *me*!" Charva snapped. "You have no idea what I have been through! Do you know where I've been while you were riding about destroying our country? I have bled honoring my promise to get your father's killer. And it's not Thrake—it's Roth of Glasscastle, who's been working as a Vron agent to pave the way for an imperial invasion."

Ellaniel responded with a disgusted chuckle. "That's it? That's the story you've decided to spin?" She narrowed her eyes. "Where. Is. Your. Father?"

Arzan sighed. Ellaniel should know brute force was never going to work on her. "Charva, it's no use wasting our time. Our men are already taking the docks, and others are guarding the gates. Delaying us only results in more deaths."

"Flame and embers, you two!" Charva flicked her sword, whipping blood from the blade. "Look, we surrender. Just stop trying to kill everyone long enough for me to show I'm telling the truth."

"I've no patience left for this," Ellaniel said.

"I will bring you to him. Just promise—*promise*—that you'll *listen*."

"We see him first, and then we talk," Arzan said.

Charva gripped the fence and rested her head on the bars. "All right." The relief in her voice was so strong, it was almost enough to convince Arzan of her sincerity all on its own. She quickly stood back and turned for the gate. "This wa—"

"My liege!" A messenger came running up from the direction from the docks. "My liege, there's something you need to hear!"

"It will wait," Arzan said. "Her grace is taking us to Thrake."

"Senkani is in danger!" the messenger blurted. "A sailor —he says he witnessed a Vron armada unloading along the Senkani coast!"

Charva dropped to her knees. "Too late."

The messengers' words were so utterly horrible that Arzan's mind refused to decipher their meaning. He stared dumbly at the soldier for several moments. "What?"

Ellaniel rushed up and grabbed at the fence. "What do you mean too late? What's going on?"

"I'll bring you to my father," Charva said. She pulled herself back to her feet, the relief he'd seen now all but gone. "And then we'll plan out our counterattack."

Chapter 95

As much as Charva had tried to convince herself otherwise, she knew what it was she'd find on reaching her father. The scene was as terrible as she expected. They were in the back room of a tavern not far from the wall, a single shaft of sunlight spilling through the window to fall on the blood-soaked body of Creedport's crenden as he lay dying on a dirty, straw-stuffed mattress. A small group of ckols and surgeons stood at the edges, solemn witness to the inevitable. The smell of death hung in the air—the scent of bile, human waste, sweat, and blood. She knelt down by Thrake's side, taking his hand in hers. She didn't know which of them was shaking more.

"Father, Arzan and Ellaniel are here."

"Is the fighting stopped?" Thrake asked. His voice was strained as he fought against the agony of his wound. She tried not to look at the bandages that glistened dark red.

"Yes," she said, "but the empire is already here. There was report from sea that the legions were seen landing in Senkani. A rider also arrived a moment ago bearing word that the city is under siege."

Armor clinked as Arzan drew near. Ellaniel stayed where she was, silent and unmoving. Thrake's ckols watched closely, hands on the pommels of their swords. "Even if we quick marched from here immediately, we'll be too late," Arzan said. "Senkani can't defend the walls against that kind of professional army—not with the numbers we left behind."

"We're both fools," her father wheezed. His grip tightened on her hand and his teeth clenched for a long moment before he finally found a chance to snatch a sharp intake of air. He spoke his words in a rush, desperate to get them out. "Here at the end of my life, I see how petty . . . our squabbles."

"Thrake, I have one question," Arzan said. "Were you the one who sent the assassins against us? Did you kill Hashan?"

"I had nothing to do with the order."

Arzan stood still, his face inscrutable. After a long stretch, he knelt down and bowed his head. "I offer my sincerest of apologies. By my word, if we were not under invasion, I would offer you my life in payment this very instant."

"The one thing no one could ever criticize you over was your honesty," Thrake said. He choked back another wave of pain. His fingers squeezed Charva's knuckles like a vise. Armor clinked, and she glanced just in time to see the end of Ellaniel's capelet trailing behind her out the room.

"I wonder if your mother would have forgiven me for the role my idiocy played in all this," Thrake said.

"I'm sure she would," Charva said without even thinking. "I remember that much of her, at least."

"Throrne was the one who took after her." His gaze was distant and tears rolled down the corners of his eyes. "I wanted so much for him to rule."

"I don't blame you for that any more, father." She tried to blink back the tears blurring her vision.

"I promised I would nominate you, Charva. Now you and I are the only ones of the House left in the city." He raised his arm with a jerk. "I demand you all to witness. I declare Charva Leverie crendess of Creedport."

The ckols in the room put their hands to their hearts, and Arzan stood in acknowledgment. "Hail Charva Leverie, crendess of Creedport!" the ckols boomed.

For all she'd wanted this moment to come, she felt nothing as it played out. She squeezed her eyes shut, trying to staunch the tears that flowed even as she thought she was going numb.

"Is there really no way to save you?" she asked quietly.

"There's only so much anyone can do about the wound the crenden received," one of the surgeons said. "It may take hours yet, however."

Her father spasmed in pain. "I can't stand . . . another quarter hour of this." He grit his teeth and groaned. "One . . . one of you. My last command. Put an end to it."

Chara's lips quivered as she looked to the ckols. It was like watching a dream. The men nodded grimly. They played a quick set of coin tosses and the loser stepped forward and drew his blade. She felt Arzan pull her gently away. The scene seemed surreal as the ckol cut the shaft of sunlight with his sword, poising it over Thrake's heart.

"Are you ready, my liege?"

"Can anyone ever be ready? Just do it."

Charva shuddered as the ckol thrust his sword through the crenden's chest. Thrake gasped one last time before his body slowly went slack and sight went from his eyes. She stared, feeling empty in her soul.

"There will be time for you to grieve," Arzan said, "but right now, mourning is a luxury not afforded us. Let's go, Charva."

His words pulled her back from the brink, and only then did she realize how close she was to the haze of despair that had hit her after Throrne's and Ersch's deaths. She shot to her feet and turned for the exit, desperately trying to focus her mind on the action they had before them.

It was Arzan who lingered in the doorway. "I came to this city seeking to kill him. I leave wishing I could have saved him."

Ellaniel escaped the room of Thrake's deathbed to vomit in the tavern's main hall. She clung desperately to the corner of the bar, her legs draining of strength. The armor she'd grown so accustomed to wearing now felt like stone pulling her to the floor. Her lungs betrayed her, denying air no matter how much she gasped for breath.

What have I done?

She saw the faces of those she'd killed, felt their blood splashing her own face and hands. Odavan's head lay disembodied on the marble flagstones, eyes wide in terror.

"You've the blood of Originate, Goldeye. You don't belong in the aristocracies. You're a brute." Odavan's words, spoken long before she'd proven him right.

She was on hands and knees, not remembering having fallen. She heaved at knowing herself for a murderer.

It's not my fault. I was tricked.

It was a quiet voice in her mind protesting against her guilt. The greater part of her knew it didn't matter to the people whose blood she'd spilled, the families who'd lost sons, brothers, fathers, and husbands. If anything, it made it worse. They'd died at her hand over *nothing*.

You're a monster, Ellaniel.

A monster.

She reached for her blade with a trembling hand. She didn't deserve to live.

The door to the back room swung open. She heard people hurrying for the street. Arzan's distinct stride went several paces before pausing. His hand touched her shoulder plate and she looked up into his face. She could see the same kind of haunting in his eyes that afflicted her own soul, but his hid behind a strong resolve.

"Later, Ella. Right now, we need to save Avlan."

Her throat choked up at the thought of her son in imperial hands. She wanted more than anything to hold him close, but she recoiled at the thought of tainting him with her touch. "Go without me."

Arzan frowned and closed his face to hers. "Ella, what have we fought for all this time? Wasn't it our son? Are you giving up now that we know who our true enemies are?"

Her eyes slid to the floor. "I'm—I'm not worthy! I can't face Avlan as a murderer. He doesn't deserve a mother like me."

He brushed his hand across her cheek. The metal plates of his gauntlet clicked right below her ear, but his fingers were warm where they touched her skin. He held her firm, forcing her to meet his eyes. "We're what he has."

Hot tears rolled down her cheeks. A sob fought in her chest, but she latched her hands on Arzan's armor and held tight. He was right. It didn't matter what she was. She was going to get to her son even if it killed her, and woe to anyone who got in her way.

She sucked in a breath, steeling her body, and Arzan helped her to stand. "Let's go."

"Messenger!" A soldier in Woodwise blue came bursting in from the street. "Vron messenger requesting to speak with Crenden Arzan!"

The rider in imperial silver was standing at attention beside his horse as Arzan arrived with a retinue of a dozen ckols and double that in soldiers. Despite the armed welcome, and the tens of soldiers already circled around the imperial, the messenger showed no signs of intimidation. His eyes skimmed Arzan up and down. "Crenden Redleaf? I bear a message from General Nevygar, commander of the eastern campaign."

Arzan crossed his arms, trying not to let show how disoriented he felt. He had put on a solid front for Charva and Ellaniel, but he was still trying to wrap his head around Thrake's innocence and the invasion. He'd thought he would at least have a day to let this new reality set in before first meeting the new enemy.

"And what," he put authority into his tone, "does this general of yours have to say to me?"

"The general wishes to parlay," the messenger said. "If you arrive in Senkani by mid-morning tomorrow, he is willing to grant you an audience and discuss terms."

Mid-morning. He looked up at the waning sun.

"And if I arrive later?"

"He will assume you declined his offer. This is, however, your first and last chance for negotiation."

Enough time to get there on horseback, if he rode through part of the night. Impossible to make it with the army. "And I'm supposed to trust he won't simply kill me?"

"There's no guarantee at all, your grace," the messenger said. "You only have his word that he wishes to speak, and speak only." The imperial smiled and nodded before stepping into the stirrup and mounting his horse. "My own advice? The mouse should listen to the lion's offer before biting the beast's paw." He kicked the horse into motion, riding it between ranks of sour-faced Senkani and disappearing towards the gate.

Arzan bit his lip and fidgeted with the clasp of his cape. Beside him, Vighkon let out a displeased grunt.

"Get me my horse," Arzan said. "I'm off to meet a lion."

Chapter 96

An hour past sunrise, Arzan and his ckols rode through the eastern gate of his city. When he'd left, he was its ruler. He returned a beggar.

The walls were undamaged, as were the new constructions that had been put up since the fire of the Council siege. The fields outside had been clean as well. One wouldn't be able to tell Senkani had fallen, except for the army of men in silver uniforms lining the main avenue. The imperial soldiers stood at silent attention on either side as the horses clomped along the cobbles. The occupiers were each spaced four feet apart, equipped with shields and armed with alternating sword and spear. They stretched the entire length of the street all the way to the palace.

They're showing me they have plenty of men to spare even while keeping the rest of the city secure. They were here only as the first step in conquering the aristocracy.

Arzan found the palace gate wide open and a clear path to the courtyard. He dismounted, noting the crossbowmen stationed on the surrounding rooftops. His anger built as he stepped through the gate and found the Vron settling into his home.

And his blood went cold when he saw Avlan standing beside a crouching man with a feathered helmet. The imperial was saying something Arzan couldn't quite make out. Arzan rushed up fast enough that the Vron guards readied their weapons.

"Get away from my son!"

Avlan saw him and tried to run forward, but a soldier held him firmly by the shoulder. The feathered officer stood and faced Arzan, his silver cape rustling. "Crenden Redleaf. I suggest you put that away before something unfortunate happens."

Arzan looked down at the sword that had somehow found its own way into his hand, then at the crossbows aimed at him from above.

"Don't hurt my papa!" Avlan shouted, struggling against his captor.

"No one needs to be hurt today, so long as your father agrees to be civil," General Nevygar said. "After all, he is only here to talk."

Arzan wanted nothing more than to cut the imperials to pieces, crossbow bolts bouncing off his armor, but he knew he'd be overwhelmed by the men on the ground before he got within ten feet of his son. Jaw clenched tight, he snapped his sword back into its scabbard. He heard his ckols sheath their weapons as well behind him.

Nevygar smiled. "Civil." He flicked his finger and the soldier pulled Avlan to the palace entry, where he was taken into Kalla's arms. Her eyes met with Arzan's and she nodded. He doubted there was anything she could do about the half dozen more guards surrounding her, but he knew she would follow her husband's lead into death if anyone tried harming her charge.

"Now then, to business," Nevygar said. He removed his helmet and held it against his side before starting along the length of the palace, beckoning Arzan to join him. "Let us discuss this as one man of authority to another."

Arzan bit down his still simmering anger and approached to walk beside the general. "What are your terms?"

"First of all, for you to put in the effort to stop thinking me a tyrant."

"That's a bit difficult when you march into my city with an army and hold my son hostage."

"The empire uses the means it must in order to bring progress to Moshon," Nevygar said. "We seek to create a unified continent, prospering under one law and one economy, with universal rights for all."

"If servitude to your empire is so desirable, why do you spread it with the sword?"

The general halted his steps, brushing his fingers along the stonework of the palace. "I assure you, crenden, that in a year's time, you will be asking that very question with an entirely different attitude."

In a year's time, we'll have you scrambling for your ships as we tear you to bloody scraps, Arzan thought. "Enough silly platitudes. What is it you actually want from me?"

Nevygar brought his hand away from the wall. "I want you to continue what you're good at. I want to give you your city, and a good chunk of Leverie thrown into the bargain. How would you like to rule as vassal governor over the Imperial Province of Senkani? I will give you power over Creedport, Highcity, Three Corners. Considering your wife is crendess of Woodwise, I think it fair to add her domain to the list."

Arzan coughed a laugh. "Oh, you think to bribe me over? General, I have spent the last few years fighting a war for freedom against exploitative powers. I am not going to end it by kneeling to a new overlord, and I am not going to be the one who imposes my will on others."

"Isn't that what you've been doing?" Nevygar asked. "Imposing your will, I mean. You have amassed your own little coalition of cities through sword and spear, crushing your enemies beneath you and demanding their fealty."

"Only so far as they opposed the administration of justice!" Arzan said, but as he spoke it he knew it was exactly the wrong thing for him to argue. There had been no justice in what he had done.

"You did it to preserve your House," Nevygar said. He clasped his hands behind his back and paced. "The Leverie had been hounding you for generations, encroaching on your land, your markets, your power."

"It was not about power."

"No, of course it wasn't! It was about survival. The House of Leverie aimed to devour you whole." The general stopped and lifted his chin. "You and us, we share similar motives. The Vron did not start as conquerors." He continued his pacing, his steps slow and methodical. "We were attacked by our neighbors for enacting a new form of government. The aristocratic councils were afraid of our Senate, a ruling body controlled not by the nobility, but by popular democratic vote. They sent army after army, tore our cities to the ground. By sheer will and a little bit of cunning, we fought them back to their borders, and then to make sure they would never wage war on us again, we pressed on into their homes."

Nevygar fingered the scar on the side of his face. "That was the Vron's first conquest. We succeeded in our goal. Under our control, those aristocracies never again rose up against us, and we even integrated them into the democracy. But do you know what happened then?"

Arzan wasn't interested in this history lesson, but the general went on without prompting.

"When the dust settled, we found that our borders were three times larger, and we suddenly had four times the enemies. By winning one war, we ended up fighting another. And then another. Each time we were victorious, our reputation became all the more terrifying."

A subtle wind ruffled Nevygar's cape. He looked out at the rooftops of the city, poking up above the palace wall.

"I'm to believe the evils of the Vron Empire are simply a misunderstanding?" Arzan asked. If his city weren't occupied by their legions, he'd feel bemused.

"Wouldn't you call it a misunderstanding if someone declared your war against the Leverie evil?"

Arzan clenched his fists. "It was."

The general paused.

"I let my rage get the better of me and ignored the laws I agreed to uphold. I destroyed the very system that would have shown me the truth and brought me actual justice. In my mistake, I killed hundreds, thousands of innocent men. What I did was evil. I admit that in full."

A moment passed in silence, Nevygar's eyes narrowed on him. At length, he smiled. It was a small smile, just the faintest upturn of the corners of his mouth. "It is one ruler in a hundred who will admit such a thing, even to himself." He fingered the pommel of his sword. "I see that there will be no games with you. Very well. I will give it to you straight. I know you and Senkani. You have been a thorn in House

Leverie's side, and you are all but guaranteed to be a thorn to the empire. That gives me two options. First, I can win you over fully and completely, obtaining your absolute obedience through persuasion, threat, or guile. Or second," he stepped in close so that he need only whisper his words, "I can destroy you utterly. I will have my legions break in every door and slaughter every man, woman, and child within these walls, starting with your boy."

It took every ounce of self-control Arzan had not to free his sword and stab it through the general's face. "You have the gall to call yourself anything other than the embodiment of evil?"

"I do what must be done for the greater good."

"If the greater good needs villains to champion its cause, then I'm not interested in what it's selling."

Nevygar sighed. "A pity." He stepped back and raised his hand. "Kill the boy."

Arzan roared, drawing his blade and slashing in one movement. The general caught it deftly with his own. A trio of crossbow bolts hammered Arzan's armor, but he shrugged off the attacks as he reached out for Nevygar's throat. Someone caught him by the elbow as his fingers were inches from the general's neck, and something slammed into the side of his head. The next he knew, he was on the ground, his ears ringing. Or was that the singing of steel on steel?

Half a dozen men were on top of him, pinning him down. His face pressed into the cold cobblestones, he could just make out his ckols fighting desperately as they were overwhelmed by hordes of soldiers in silver uniforms. Arzan shouted in rage, trying with all his strength to push off his captors until Vighkon, the last of his ckols to remain standing, was forced to the ground with his arms twisted behind him.

Once the fight was ended, Nevygar crouched down in front of him, his silver cape pooling on the stones. "You understand now that you are powerless, Crenden Redleaf. I give you one last opportunity. Declare fealty to the empire, or watch the death of your city."

Tears blurred silver, steel, and stone into one in Arzan's vision as his fury burned away into despair.

It was halfway between noon and dusk when Arzan and his ckols met the army coming up from Creedport. They had pushed their horses hard for the first mile or so after leaving Senkani, but had long since slowed to a trudging walk. The air had taken a chill, the sun hiding behind a thick curtain of dark gray clouds.

Ellaniel and Charva rode to the front of the column within moments.

"What of Avlan?" Ellaniel asked quickly. The reins were pulled taut between her hands.

He closed his eyes and bit his lip, ashamed at the news he brought.

"Arzan, what happened?" Charva demanded.

The army was at a halt, every head within sight turned to him. Arzan couldn't stay here. Not in front of all the men. He dismounted and marched off the road, waving for the two women to follow.

Leaves and twigs crunched underfoot as they stepped through the brush, walking until they were out of view and out of hearing of the army. They came to a halt, but Arzan still had trouble facing them.

"I can tell the news is bad," Charva said, "but you need to give it to us sooner rather than later."

"Senkani shall officially side with the empire."

Charva tapped her forehead and bit her lip. "The city's already been won over? It's only been a day. How can—"

"Not the city," Arzan said. He put everything he had into keeping his voice steady. "Senkani. Me." He pointed back towards the road. "The army."

Ellaniel wrung her hands. "What have they done with Avlan?"

"Avlan and the whole city are hostage. The Vron will kill all of them if we don't follow General Nevygar's commands."

His wife leaned back against a tree and buried her face in her hand. "No."

"I . . . " Charva fiddled with the fancy guard of her sword. "They can't be that ruthless. Even the Vron wouldn't—"

"He's serious." Arzan slammed his fist into a nearby trunk. "And even if I can't be sure it's not a bluff, can I ask my men to take action that would see their families dead?"

Charva stood quiet. She looked about, her gaze shifting between him and Ellaniel. "You said you have to follow Nevygar's commands. So, what are they?"

Arzan broke bark between his fingers. "He wants Senkani to march south and engage with Three Corners."

"You and Pundur are the only ones left in Leverie with any army worth speaking of. Throw you two at each other and all his legions have to do is sweep through the country and knock."

"We're giving them Leverie," Ellaniel whispered.

"No, I will not surrender to this!" Charva said. "I am not giving up this country without a fight!"

Arzan turned on her. "What's the point in fighting if everyone you're protecting is dead?"

Charva took a step back, but from there held her ground. "If we give in, the deaths won't stop with Senkani."

"Your family isn't on the line here."

"No, they're already dead!" He saw the hurt in her eyes, and the flame of anger.

Arzan flexed his fingers, anguish and confusion roiling within him. What was the right thing to do?

He drew his blade with a roar. Charva pulled her own sword free with wide eyes, but Arzan embedded his weapon in the trunk of a tree. He released the hilt, letting it wobble freely in the air, and stormed past her.

"Arzan?"

He barely heard the two scramble after him. His thoughts were a mess at the impossible choice. *How? How can I do one or the other?*

"This is the last time I'll say it, the road is closed. You'll have to turn around or else move to the side until the army's passed."

A carriage was stopped at the head of the army. A sergeant stood beside it, helmet tilted back as he spoke up to the driver. Arzan ignored them and grabbed the reins of his horse, but didn't mount. A light drizzle started falling around him. *What am I supposed to do?*

Charva's voice approached from behind, "Arzan, we're not done talking."

He tightened his grip on the leather straps in his hand. "I don't see how things can be solved with words."

Wood creaked as the carriage door opened. Charva grabbed him by the arm and leaned close. "We have to find another option."

How he wanted to. He had spent the entire ride out from the city trying to think of one. "There's nothing we can do."

"Oh, I think there's something."

Ellaniel gasped. Arzan looked to see her covering her mouth, her wide eyes fixated beyond him. He turned and instantly dropped the reins.

"It . . . it can't be!" he breathed.

A girl leaned on a crutch beside the carriage. She tucked a lock of purple-tinted hair behind her ear and beamed a wide smile.

"I've been dying to see you again," Fellone said. "There's someone in Three Corners you need to meet."

Chapter 97

Retyar steepled his fingers together and leaned forward in his chair, listening to the soft patter of rain against the command tent's fabric. His heart pounded in his chest, and he took to slowly rubbing his hands together in quiet anxiety.

"If you don't calm down, you'll make *me* nervous," Crenden Pundur said from just in front of him, hunching over the strategy table in the center space. Warm light from the oil lamps played across the large man's armored form, creating a striking contrast to the cold view visible out through the slit beyond him.

"The rain could ruin everything."

"We've had rains before, and you assured me it wouldn't be a problem."

Retyar drew in a calming breath. He forced his hands apart, placing one on the covered rifle propped against his chair. "You're right. *I'm* right. It won't be an issue." *It'll work*, he assured himself again silently.

The tent flap lifted up and a ckol poked in his head, water dripping from his helmet's nasal guard. "They're here, my liege."

Pundur slowly lifted his shoulders and crossed his arms. He glanced at Retyar with a mirthless grin. "This is it, then."

Retyar bit his lip and nodded. "Yes, this is it."

"Show them in."

The tent flap opened wide, allowing a train of figures to file on inside. Armor clinked and jingled, and Retyar studied the people before him with fascination. Their boots and lower leggings were caked with mud, their hair and fabric soaked through from the rain, but none of it detracted from the awe he felt. Regardless of the relatively small role they played, these were men and women who shaped the history of the world he knew.

The man in the lead would be Crenden Arzan Redleaf. He was heavily outfitted in plate, almost as well as a Falconian knight. He bore no heraldry, unless one counted the brilliant red cape, but he exuded the bearing of a ruler. He had handsome features, though his stubbly beard testified to someone used to shaving who now hadn't the time. His dark blue eyes had an intensity that made Retyar nervous about drawing their attention.

The woman beside the crenden had to be his wife, Ellaniel. Fellone said she was nicknamed Goldeye, but even so he was struck by how vibrant her irises were. He knew of a few celebrities from his time that would be envious of that color. He really liked the aesthetic of her armor, with the black lace draped over her arms and legs and the capelet colored red to match her husband.

Charva Leverie was next, and he was pleased to have guessed right—it was the woman who'd given him a ride to Three Corners. She wore chain, rather than plate like the other two, visible beneath a green tunic. A rapier with an exquisitely shaped ivy basket guard hung at her hip.

Behind Charva was an old man with gray hair and a wispy beard. His clothing was far more pedestrian than the others, and he didn't seem to carry a weapon. Retyar wasn't sure if he was supposed to know him, or if he was just an aide to one of the others.

Fellone took up the rear, hobbling in on her crutch before pulling the flap closed. "Here we are!" she said cheerily.

Arzan wasted no time in walking up opposite to the table from Pundur. "Fellone hasn't told us anything other than that you protected her and have a way of defeating the Vron."

Ellaniel held the girl close. "I still can't believe you're alive."

"You can all take a seat it you like," Pundur said, pointing out the chairs to either side.

"Truly grateful for that," Charva said as she pulled her charcoal hair through thumb and forefinger, wringing it of water. She plopped down without bothering to draw the furniture closer to the table. "Flame and embers, I've got so many bruises from the past few days I can't even distinguish one ache from another."

"You don't look it," the old man said, pushing another chair toward the strategy map and frowning at the parchment as he sat.

Charva tapped her side. "Trust me. Beneath all this, I'm more blue and purple than white."

"We don't have time to be getting comfortable!" Arzan snapped. "Pundur, the Vron want me to kill you! They have my city as hostage, and—"

Pundur drew himself to his full height. "Arzan, sit down!"

Crenden Redleaf shut his mouth, and Retyar saw his jaw muscles go tight. At length, the man stomped over to grab a chair and pull it to the table. After dropping down in a cacophony of clashing steel, he went on in a quieter voice, "I'm taking a great risk even speaking with you. The imperials will know I'm here. I'll do my best to convince them I'm trying to make you surrender, and it'll be the truth if I don't think your plan is good enough." He made a fist in front of him. "Nevygar's bringing Avlan with his army. If he has reason to believe . . . ."

Pundur nodded. "We figured that was the sort of bind you were in. Now, since you're on the empire's leash, I can't exactly give you all of the details. You only have my assurance that we've got something up our sleeve that can destroy their entire army."

"That's too vague to go on," Arzan said. "I've seen their legions. They can match both our forces put together. Besides that, they've got experience and a legendary general."

"Well, I can't give you specifics, but I can give you something to go on." Pundur turned his head and nodded to Retyar. "I want you to meet—"

Charva shot to her feet and thrust her finger. "You!"

Retyar couldn't help but smile at the excitement on her face. "Took long enough."

"You're totally different without the beard and vagabond

clothing," Charva said. "Though, I should have figured it out sooner after seeing Fellone."

The old man raised an eyebrow. "You know this fellow?"

She grinned, reaching into the bag at her side. She pulled out something black and angular and slammed it on the table. "It take it this is yours?"

Retyar drew in a deep breath and let it out in a sigh. "So, you're the one who snatched it."

Charva pointed to his covered rifle. "That there. It's something like this, isn't it? It uses the same sort of vials, but bigger."

It took a moment for him to figure out was she talking about. "Vials . . . . Oh, cartridges!" He chuckled. *Never thought of them like that.* "I'm sorry, but that's something of a secret." He eyed her. "You've used it?"

She slipped out the magazine and showed it was empty. "Saved my life in Heartsong, actually."

Retyar squinted. "Heartsong?"

"Yeah, I was conscripted into the Whitesail army and, well, it's a long story."

He clapped his hands. "I knew it! You're the Dancing Flame!"

She frowned. "The what now?"

"Hmm," he scratched his chin, muttering, "but according to the legend you never left the imperial province of Whitesail."

"Well, the empire's here in Leverie two years ahead of schedule," Pundur said. "Obviously, things have changed."

"I think," the old man said, "that there is a very interesting story behind this friend of yours. However, if it takes this long even to get his name, I believe there are more productive topics to focus on with the Senkani and imperial armies converging on us."

"I was going to give you his name before I was rudely interrupted," Pundur said, crossing his arms.

Charva winced and sat down again. "Sorry, you're right. More important things right now."

Pundur cleared his throat. "This is Retyar Venon from the Kingdom of Govunari in Falcone. He came to Leverie for reasons that will stay his own, but I have come to trust him a great deal. He's in fact the one who saved little Fellone's life from the Vron assassins and explained to me their plot."

"So you knew about the truth of all this," Ellaniel said quietly. She had taken a chair off to the side, Fellone sitting next to her. "Why didn't you tell us? Why didn't you try to stop us?"

Pundur lowered his head and pressed his palms together. "I did, didn't I? Back when you first mustered the army, wasn't I there telling you to be reasonable?"

"You didn't say anything about the empire!"

"I didn't know that part back then."

"But you did later, and then kept silent!"

"I—"

"I kept him from revealing the empire's involvement," Retyar said. "For our trap to work, we needed the imperials to follow through with their plan." If the Redleafs were going to pin the blame on anyone, let it be on him. *It's best that Pundur stay on good terms with them, and . . . . Raze it, Crenden Arzan's eyes are scary.*

He felt a sweat break out as the Senkani crenden assessed him, weighing. It wasn't that he was overtly hostile. More that he seemed a confident judge, and someone you simply didn't want to disappoint.

"You deemed it an acceptable trade-off to allow thousands to die in an unnecessary civil war?" Arzan asked.

Retyar pressed his lips tight. There was no way for Arzan to know about the price Retyar was paying, of how big his decision had been. He was changing the flow of history, and it was only at this very point that he could feel confident of where he was directing it.

Even so, it's still true I let all those people die.

It's also true that what I'm doing will kill even more. Wipe out an entire world of people before they can even exist. And that's if this even works. Most of the pieces are in the places we expected, but with it two years ahead of schedule, who knows what else is going different.

But it was too late to go back, and neither could he explain what it was he was sacrificing.

Pundur spoke up for him anyway. "This man has lost more than you know, Arzan. He's giving up a lot to help us."

Arzan regarded him a long moment further before turning his gaze on Pundur. "You trust him, and I trust you. Right now, all that matters is the answer to one question. How confident are you that you will truly destroy the Vron?"

"I know better than anyone that nothing is ever a hundred percent," Retyar said, "but we need it to happen, and I will make sure it does."

Charva tapped the pistol with her finger. "If he's got anything else like this ready, I'll vouch for him."

"It's that impressive?" the old man asked. "You didn't mention anything about that contraption to me.

"I was kind of preoccupied, Malty. I'm sure you'd love to play with it, though."

Retyar reached out and grabbed the pistol. "Nope."

Charva huffed. "I am not going to stop bugging you for that back," she muttered.

"What exactly does it do?" Arzan asked.

"Shoots stuff," Charva said. "Able to punch straight through chain. I took out an artillery crew with it. You Falconians are a nasty bunch."

Retyar ground his teeth at the unnecessary information she was spreading around. Pundur was rubbing his chin, and he could practically see the wheels turning in his head as he tried piecing things together. How many years until the people in this room figured out the principles behind firearms?

A matter for later.

"Are you ready to go with our plan?" Retyar asked.

Arzan looked to Charva. "If she and Pundur both are convinced you can really beat them."

"It's not just a matter of defeating the Vron," Ellaniel said. "We have to beat them fast enough that Nevygar doesn't have time to harm Avlan."

"Or," Charva put in, "we could try a little something just before they spring the trap."

The old man—Malty, was he called?—brushed his fingers through his beard. "You're suggesting someone goes in and rescues the boy?"

"I'm in," Ellaniel said immediately.

"Is that even possible?" Pundur asked. "He'll be in the

center of the army."

"Not likely," Arzan said. He was looking down at the map on the table. "They wouldn't have a hostage in the middle of the formation. That would simply be ridiculous. No, they'll put him back in the reserves before the battle starts."

"Even then, there'll be a lot of soldiers between us and Avlan," Pundur said.

Charva smiled coyly. "That I think I can manage."

Retyar dropped a hand to his armrest. "Wait, are you telling me you're going in there yourself?"

"She's become something of an expert at infiltration," Malty said.

She nodded. "Thank you."

"The getting out part could use some work, however."

"Hey, we're both in one piece!"

Arzan regarded her solemnly. "You are honestly willing to go through with this?"

Charva leaned forward. "I'm the best qualified, aren't I? As a Leverie, if this is what it takes to get you on our side, I'll do it. Besides, Avlan's my nephew too."

"Five times removed," Pundur said.

"Who's counting?" Charva turned to Retyar, her blue eyes shrewd. "I do have a condition." She pointed to the pistol. "Malty's right. Chances are, I'll have to fight my way out, and it'll be very useful if I had that thing. With a fresh set of vials, of course."

He shook his head before she got halfway through. "No."

Pundur sighed. "Retyar, I know how stubborn you are on this weapon of yours, but she's putting herself in a great deal of danger here for our sakes."

"We've been through this, Pundur. It's non-negotiable."

"It gives me the best chance of getting Avlan out alive," Charva said.

Ellaniel stood. "If you're refusing to help us save Avlan, Senkani is not following along with your plan."

All eyes were on him. Retyar bit his lip, wishing again, as he occasionally did, that he'd never left his cave. Was he going to have to make a world-altering choice every step of the way? He couldn't see another option. He grudgingly placed the pistol back on the table, then rummaged in his bag for his two extra magazines. "This is the last ammunition I have for it. Twenty shots. If you have to use it, make it count, because I'm not making any more."

Charva reached out with a grin, but Retyar held the magazines back. "And if you're in, this is what you're all going to do . . . ."

Chapter 98

Arzan clung to newfound hope as the joint Senkani, Highcity, Woodwise, and Creedport army came within sight of Pundur's forces. It was early morning on the day after their council. Arzan's side had ridden back just before dusk, their roles clearly defined. They still hadn't been told what exactly Pundur and Retyar's trap was, but he was ready to bet everything on their plot. There was a way of fighting back against the empire, and he was sure he wouldn't be able to live with himself if he didn't take it.

A horse splashed through a puddle to his left, its rider shielding his eyes against the eastern sun. He was one of the Vron liaisons Nevygar had assigned him. *More realistically, my handler*, he thought. "I don't imagine the general wants me to charge in immediately," he said aloud.

The imperial smirked. "No rush, your grace. You can wait for the imperial army to arrive before you begin the assault. They're only about an hour behind, and I'm sure the general would like to observe your enthusiasm first-hand."

Bloody shyles, are all silvers this smug?

He restrained himself from antagonizing the man. Waiting on the legion's arrival was what he wanted. He set about assessing the terrain and planning how to deploy the army. Pundur's men were set up on a broad palisade about three hundred paces away. The fortification was set up in a natural choke point, or at least as near as one could find in the area leading up to Three Corners. It spanned a clearing in the woods about a third of a mile across, broken in the center by a steep mound of stone. The eastern side was on flatter ground than the west, and was the portion that received the road through a narrow gate. It also had the larger visible presence of soldiers.

Arzan called in his lieutenants. "I want the five most experienced companies forming the front of the assault. They're to cover the battering rams as they make for the gate."

The officers glanced at the imperial liaison, clearly unhappy at their assignment. "Are our boys simply soaking up arrows, or are we sending our archers out to trade feathers?"

"Our munitions are still low after the siege of Creedport," Arzan said. "I don't want to risk the archers when we only have a handful of volleys anyway." It was a good enough excuse to minimize the number of men out there.

"How about that section of the palisade to the west? Looks to be sagging from the rains."

"Too hilly for the rams. We'll just focus on the eastern side." *And that bait isn't meant for us.*

"Too bad Crenden Pundur was unwilling to accept your terms of surrender," the imperial commented. "He could have made this a lot less painful for the both of you."

Arzan remained silent as he stared at the palisade.

"By the way, where's your wife and the Crendess Charva? I don't believe I've seen them since they rode back with you."

He nodded to the rear, where the logistics personnel were already pitching tents. "Over there possibly. I don't think either of them has the stomach for this fight."

The imperial shrugged. "Understandable." He reached out and patted his horse's neck. "You will see that this is worth it, your grace. It may not seem so now, but Leverie will be a better place before long."

Arzan puffed his nose, but didn't argue. *You don't realize how right you are.*

Retyar had seen Pundur's army mustered on a couple of

occasions already, but he still found it impressive. Three thousand men stood up on the palisade or in reserve behind it, with an additional six hundred light cavalry at the ready by the gate. It was one thing to read about armies in history books. It was another entirely to actually witness that many men armed and armored. As he walked through mud trampled through with grass, he noted that he hadn't ever even seen that many horses total in his life until now.

"Retyar, you fool of a Falconian, stop mucking about and get up here!"

He followed the voice to see Pundur waving at him from atop the palisade left of the gate. He shifted his rifle and jogged to the nearest ladder. On reaching the top, he found the old man Malty had already joined the crenden and was sweeping the north with a telescope. Fellone was beside them both, peering over the battlements on tiptoes.

"That's an army that's seen years of hard fighting," Pundur said, pointing his chin out beyond the wall.

The sight garnered Retyar's respect. The Redleaf/Leverie army was already there, several companies fanning out in preparation for attack. The front lines were composed mostly of soldiers in Senkani red, but with two blocks on the side colored in Woodwise blue. Behind them, soldiers from Creedport and Highcity milled about in less cohesion. The sheer number of armed men facing them down set his hairs on end, even if he knew the Redleafs were going to do their best to pull their punches.

"How many soldiers is that?" Retyar asked quietly.

"I think Arzan managed to scrape together a little over four thousand, including from Charva and Natsha," Pundur said.

"We're a little outnumbered, then," Retyar said, "but we've got the defender's advantage."

"Half a defender's advantage," Pundur said.

Malty lowered his telescope. "An interesting strategy. I wonder if the Vron will take the bait."

Retyar eyed Pundur, wondering how much of the plan he had shared. "I just told him where we're trying to draw the silvers," Pundur said defensively. "Don't worry, he's to be trusted. Even if he wasn't, it's not like he'll have a chance to go sneaking off to the imperials."

"I've been their 'guest' longer than is comfortable. Right now, my biggest regret is that I've little to offer you in way of aid."

"So, Malty, what exactly are you?" Retyar asked.

Pundur barked a laugh while a small smile tugged at the corners of the old man's lips. "Charva's the only one who ever calls Honorable Maltan that name," Pundur said as he slapped Retyar on the back.

Maltan rolled the telescope between his palms. "I was a tinkerer patronized by Charva's grandparents, before Thrake became crenden. I haven't done much for Leverie since then, but I think we can all be certain that my new crendess will have a great deal of work for me once this is all over." He looked back northward at the Redleaf army, his expression clearly adding, *if we survive.*

Retyar pursed his lips. A man of the sciences. Great. His hope not to accelerate technological advancement just got more and more strained. He sighed. "Mind if I see that telescope?"

The old man held it out. "Be gentle. It would take months to acquire a replacement."

He peered through the glass, bringing the Senkani forces into focus. It had good magnification, possibly even better than his binoculars, though of course without the benefit of serving both eyes. He whimsically contemplated the possibility of clamping it to his rifle, but cast aside the thought. He planned never to use the weapon, and even if he did, there wasn't enough spare ammunition to properly zero the scope.

He started to give it back. "Good quality. I—"

"Save that sentence," Pundur said, snatching the telescope straight from his hands and training it on the road beyond the Redleaf forces. "The imperials have arrived."

Nevygar began matching landmarks to the map in his head the moment the Leverie came into view. His imperial legion marched in precise step beside his horse, a sound as familiar and comforting to him as his own heartbeat, despite being muddled by the moist ground. *I've been gone too long from this. Playing politician and nation builder has its place, but this is where I belong.*

Crenden Arzan had his forces already arrayed and ready for the assault. Nevygar noted that he was facing off against the strongest part of the Three Corners palisade. From the look of it, he aimed to batter down the wall rather than use ladders, and for that he needed the flatland on the eastern side of the clearing.

Nevygar called his senior captain. "Begin setting up camp. Make it look like we'll be sitting back to watch, but put two companies to work preparing ladders."

The Redleaf might think him cruel, but in reality he was merely practical. He wanted to win this with the fewest number of Vron casualties.

A runner came up from the rear of the column. "General, Crenden Roth has arrived and wishes to speak with you."

Nevygar grunted in distaste. "He's supposed to be in Glasscastle preparing eastern Leverie for the transition."

"Shall I turn him away, sir?"

"No. Settle him in the camp. I'll deal with him later."

"Very good."

He watched the runner go, then on a whim turned his horse back towards the center of the column. His lungs filled with air made humid from the million puddles burning away under the sun's heat. Row upon row of soldiers saluted him in his passing until he reached the Redleaf boy riding in front of a young private. Not far distant, his short nursemaid glared daggers as she followed along on foot, her hands bound and leashed to another soldier.

"How has the journey been for the brave little lad?"

"Been having a swell time, general," the mounted soldier answered. "Never seen the likes of our legion on the march."

The boy glowered at Nevygar. "He's lying. The crenden and crendess of Senkani will beat you like they beat the Council."

Nevygar forced a smile. The bliss of youth. "The camp's being set. Find a place for him and keep him safe."

"Absolutely, sir."

He let the soldier go and stayed in place a moment longer, his eyes on his troops. At last, he kicked his horse into motion. He had an army to command and a battle to win.

"The soldiers never stop coming," Ellaniel murmured to herself. From her hiding place just within the woods northwest of the clearing, she could see the imperial army spreading across the fields. And spreading. And spreading.

"That's more than I've even seen before," Charva said from beside her. She was changed out of her green outfit, instead wearing the silver uniform of a Vron Aiv Chahai, accented by a few slashes in the fabric. "I sure hope that Retyar fellow truly knows what he's doing."

Ellaniel shifted her chain shirt under her blue Watcher uniform. She wasn't used to armor without plate. It felt too exposed. Worse, she didn't even have her shield. But this was what the plan called for. If it meant saving Avlan, she'd go out in a shift if she had to.

"Charva," she said quietly, "why do you go through all this?"

The other woman leaned to the side and picked at her sword's basket guard. "Because someone needs to."

"But what is there even here for you? Your family hated you, your friends turned on you. Why not just leave, go on some adventure, make a name for yourself somewhere else?"

Charva tapped the metal with her fingernail. "I almost did. Ersch . . . he told me that would be abandoning what made me special to him."

Ellaniel hadn't asked what had happened to the man. From the flash of pain in her eyes, she knew enough not to now.

"Maybe I'm a fool, but Leverie is still my home," Charva said with a shrug.

Ellaniel lowered her gaze to stare at the sodden leaves and twigs at her knees. *She's lost almost everyone, yet she hasn't been eaten up by revenge. I'm nothing compared to her.*

In the clearing, soldiers were beginning to raise tents. She strained in the scant hope of spotting Avlan in their midst. "How much longer will we wait?"

Charva reached for her belt and drew the weapon she'd gotten from the Falconian. She fiddled with the sliding part on top before lining up the sights with the camp. "A little longer. We don't want to be too early and increase the risk of tipping our hand."

Ellaniel fidgeted, her fingers folding around the hilt of her sword. "We can't leave Avlan with them a moment longer than we have to."

"Nevygar has every reason to keep his hostages safe until we try something." Charva put the weapon away and rummaged in her bag, pulling out a metal canister Retyar had given her in addition to the vial weapon. She examined the string leading from the top.

Ellaniel drew in a breath. "Perhaps we should switch the roles. Now that I'm paying closer attention, I think I'm a better fit for that uniform. It's really noticeable how much the chest sags."

Charva shoved the canister back in the bag, her face going red. "Ella, brag about your bust one more time and I really will consider leaving you here on your own."

"Wha—" her mind caught up to the unintended insult and she snickered. "That wasn't what I—"

Charva stopped her with a finger in the air. Past the palisade, a thin line of white smoke had begun snaking its way skyward.

"That's the signal, isn't it?" Ellaniel asked. She had to fight the urge not to spring to her feet and dash for the camp.

Steel whispered gently on leather as Charva drew her blade. "Let's do this."

Chapter 99

"Aim for the shields! The shields!"

Hundreds of bowstrings twanged, throwing arrows that thunked into solid wood. The Senkani and Woodwise soldiers stormed the ground outside the palisade with feathered shafts bristling from their shields. They made it the last few feet and then split their formation to let the battering rams roll into place. The wall shuddered violently under Retyar's feet as the siege weapons went to work. He did his best not to lose his balance while he passed behind the archers, his eyes on the distant, massive silver ranks of the Vron legion hanging back from the battle. He had thought the Leverie forces impressive. A wall of twenty thousand men was something else.

When are you going to advance, Nevygar?

"Brace that gate, soldiers! Give it everything you've got!"

Retyar came up beside Pundur. The crenden wasn't even looking at the surging mass of red and blue at the palisade's base as he shouted commands at his men. "More reinforcements to the weakened wall! If that thing falls before I say it can fall—"

A scream amongst the Senkani ranks drew a wince from the large man. "I said aim for the shields!"

"It has to be somewhat believable," Retyar said. He looked down, bracing himself against the shake of the rams at work, and was grateful that the attackers weren't using ladders.

"Sir expert in all things General Nevygar," Pundur said,

"how long until that fool tries for the flank?"

"Basic hammer and anvil. Before he moves to hit us from the back, he needs to be confident we're locked up with Arzan's forces."

"In other words, the Senkani need to actually break through and engage," Maltan said. Retyar hadn't even noticed him behind Pundur's hulking form. He had his telescope back and was peering through it at the Vron army, his mouth tight. "I think I see them gathering wood. They're definitely up to something."

Retyar looked around. "Where's Fellone?"

Maltan pointed left along the palisade. "She said she had better get started now if she hopes to, in her words, 'get there in time for the good stuff.'"

"I don't want this dragging out," Pundur said, cringing as more men screamed below and the rams continued smashing into the timbers under their feet. "Let's just draw them in right now."

"Not yet." Retyar nodded at the little signal fire he'd had lit a little ways behind the defenses. "We need to give the crendesses time to get Avlan."

Charva trudged through spongy soil and thigh-high grasses on her way towards the Vron camp, Ellaniel held tight at her side. By now, the imperials already had a virtual town set up, with dozens of tents raised and pegged and more on the way. On the north side of the clearing, screened behind the tents and the bulk of the army, soldiers set axes to trees, chopping off branches and setting them out to make ladders.

"Flame and embers," she muttered. "With how fast they're doing this, they could storm the wall in half an hour."

"We need to finish this fast, then," Ellaniel said.

They got close enough to the camp that someone took notice. A lone Aiv Chahai walking around one of the tents stopped and lowered a spear. "What's this?"

Ellaniel took the cue and started struggling. Charva twisted her arm and kicked her leg, forcing her to the ground and putting a knee to her back. "Woodwise scout spying out our positions," Charva called. "Help me with her!"

The imperial Watcher rushed over to assist. "Hold on, I'll get her left side."

Charva let go as soon as the woman was close and sprang up to grapple her with an arm around the throat. She clamped her hand over the imperial's mouth before she could call out. Ellaniel scrambled to her feet and drew her sword to the Watcher's face. "Struggle and you're dead."

They guided the Watcher around the nearest tent, making sure they were in the clear before pushing her inside. They left her gagged and tied behind a stack of supplies, absent her uniform.

"I think I'm getting good at this," Charva said.

Ellaniel fingered the corporal's knot on the shoulder of her new outfit. "I think this is Parim cotton with yellow Glemear dye. It must cost a fortune to clothe this army."

Charva glanced at the sergeant's décor on her own uniform. "I don't think mine's as rich as yours."

"Your loss." She surveyed the men and women moving about further within the camp. "Where do we search first?"

"Let's just start looking anywhere for now," Charva said with a shrug.

"I thought you were an expert on this."

"It's about improvisation. Rigid thinking is what gets you caught."

They skirted the outer parts of the camp, getting a feel for soldier concentrations. Most of the Vron were in the formation staring down the palisade. Those with the tents were too busy at the task of organizing supplies to give the two any attention.

"There," Ellaniel nudged Charva and pointed her chin towards a tent guarded by two soldiers.

"Let's hope that's it."

"It has to be. How do we get inside?"

Charva weighed their options. "Wait here. I'll check it out."

"Not without me!" Ellaniel grabbed her wrist.

"Yeah, there's a *ton* of imperial Aiv Chahai with Originate blood. They won't be suspicious at all of the only woman in the whole country with golden eyes."

"That's—"

"Make way!"

The two barely escaped to the side as a group of soldiers hurried through carrying a completed ladder. Once they were gone, Charva saw that Ellaniel had her face turned away, her hand holding some of her hair by her eyes.

"You have a point," Ellaniel said grudgingly.

"I'll make it quick."

Charva straightened her back and strode up to the guarded tent. *All right, gotta come up with a story. The chef ordered me to find a box of seasoning that got misplaced during unloading. It must be in one of the tents, but we're not sure which.* She reached the tent and opened her mouth, but the soldiers nodded before she could speak. "Watcher."

She swallowed her first sentence and nodded back, more than a little disappointed as she moved the flap aside without the slightest challenge. *That was no fun.*

Her annoyance disappeared immediately as her eyes adjusted to the inside of the tent. Avlan was right there in the center, sitting on the bare grass, a private standing over him. There was one other soldier guarding Kalla off to the side, as well as two Aiv Chahai leaning against a stack of supply crates at the back. The imperials gave her a cursory glance before turning back to Avlan with an air of long-suffering patience.

"And when he beats you here, he's going to chase you all the way back to your Senate and tear the whole thing down!" Avlan said.

The young private next to him tugged sharply at the collar of his uniform. "Kid, quit it! I've already told you, there's hundreds of thousands of Vron soldiers between here and the homeland, and a hundred thousand more in the capitol. Your dad doesn't have a chick's chance in a cat's cage of scaring us."

"He'll beat them all!"

"Oh, I'm sure!"

"Stop arguing with him, you knucklehead!" the other soldier said. "He's just a boy."

"I'm not just a boy! I'm the son of the bravest crenden in

Leverie!"

Charva realized how long she had spent simply standing in awe at the scene. She held in a giggle and walked across the tent as the little debate dragged on. Kalla lifted a withering glare away from the ground and passed her gaze over her. Her eyes narrowed, then opened wide in surprise, then narrowed again in suspicion all in the span of three heartbeats. Charva raised a finger to her lips and winked. She hoped Ellaniel's friend would realize her presence here wasn't as an enemy.

At the back of the tent, the Aiv Chahai were doing their best to ignore the childish arguing up front. "I haven't seen Travasha since we left Heartsong. Did she get placed in a different unit?"

"Pregnant. She was dropped from the campaign right before we got on the boats."

"Again! That settles it. She's doing it on purpose!"

Charva passed her hand over the crates the women were leaned against. "Not here, not here," she muttered. "On to the next tent."

She went back out without incident. Ellaniel was where she'd left her, but somehow had found a helmet. With her gaze down, the rim helped shadow her eyes. "Is he there?"

Charva nodded. "Now we get in position and wait."

"Your men could be a bit more enthusiastic. At this rate, it will take all day to break that gate in."

Arzan ground his teeth and didn't respond to the imperial liaison. He shifted his gaze towards the imperial line before snapping it back away. He hoped the Silver hadn't noticed.

"The longer they drag this out, the more men you'll lose, crenden." The liaison tossed his reins from hand to hand. "Of course, that's your call to make."

A pair of men carried a stretcher away from the palisade. The wounded soldier screamed in pain at the arrow lodged in his leg. The number of casualties so far had been minimal compared to the other battles they'd fought, but . . . . Arzan clenched his jaw. *To be losing men for a ruse . . . .*

He hoped he had bought enough time. "Send in another company," he ordered. "Smash that gate!"

Ella, you better be ready.

"General, the Redleaf is sending in more men."

Nevygar already saw it, but nodded to the officer anyway. He trotted his horse in front of the army, silver shields flush in a line, soldiers unwavering.

"Companies one through four, hold position. Companies five through twelve, prepare ladders."

He turned to look at the land leading up to the western section of the palisade. The hills were enough to hinder siege engines, but his infantry could cross the space in moments. They would be over the defenses well before Crenden Pundur's forces could redeploy.

"Almost too easy," he muttered.

"It's not as if Three Corners has any experienced strategists," one of his officers said. "Besides, not much they can do outnumbered as they are."

As much as Nevygar hated sending his men into a bloodbath, he still missed the challenge of a good opponent.

The roar of distant voices announced the event he had been waiting for. The eastern palisade was breached. Nevygar drew his sword and raised it above his head. "Trumpets, sound the advance!"

The sound of sharp notes pierced the air.

"Nevygar's advancing," Charva hissed. "Move!"

Ellaniel gripped her sword tight and kept pace with her as they maneuvered around tent pegs to get behind the one holding Avlan. She willed Charva to move faster, watching as she slipped a dagger from her sleeve and slit an opening.

"Count to thirty," Charva whispered.

Ellaniel nodded and crawled quietly inside, marking the time in her head. She came in right behind a stack of piled supply boxes. Just on the other side, she heard two women chattering, but couldn't be bothered picking out the words.

Eleven, twelve . . .

One of the soldiers at the front of the tent spoke up, "Hey, sergeant, back already?"

Sixteen, seventeen . . .

"I think the spices might be in this one after all," Charva answered. "I shouldn't be long."

At the edge of hearing, Ellaniel made out the quiet slap of a blade hitting flesh, followed by the crash of an armored body hitting the ground.

"Wha—"

His words turned into gurgling.

Someone inside the tent drew a sword. "Leshure? Report!"

Thirty!

Ellaniel rounded the crates, blade poised. The two soldiers and two Watchers were all focused on the front of the tent. She hacked down one of the Aiv Chahai with a clean strike to the neck. The second one turned, her eyes going wide. The imperial woman managed to deflect Ellaniel's lunge with her arm, the blade slicing cloth and hissing across mail. She tried going for her sword, but Ellaniel palmed her in the face, dazing her. The next moment, Ellaniel's blade was slitting the woman's throat.

"Behind you!" Kalla shouted.

Ellaniel spun to find one of the soldiers charging her. She whipped up her sword to parry. The man slammed her with his shoulder instead, throwing her into the stacked crates. The boxes tumbled, depositing her in a mess of awkward limbs. The soldier raised his sword for a downward thrust, but stopped as a dagger rammed its way into the side of his neck. He reached for the blade in a panic, but Charva yanked it out before his hand touched and kicked him to the ground.

"S-Stop! N-No one move!"

The last remaining soldier backed against the side of the tent, Avlan held tight in front of him. He had his sword against her son's throat.

Ellaniel pushed herself to her feet.

"Don't move!" the soldier said. His arm shook as his eyes flicked to his fallen comrades.

"Let. Him. Go," Ellaniel growled.

"S-Stay back!"

Kalla dashed up from the side and grabbed the soldier's sword arm. He turned to her with wide eyes. Ellaniel crossed the space before he could even look back and thrust her sword down just behind his collarbone. The steel cut to his heart and his body went limp. She let him drop, sword still lodged in his flesh.

She stood there, breathing heavy, her hands shaking now that the fight was over.

"Mama?" Avlan's voice cracked. Tears ran unchecked down his cheeks and his lip quivered.

Ellaniel started to raise her arms to take him in an embrace, but stopped. Her hands were coated in blood. "A-Avlan." Was that terror in his face? *No, I can't bear him to see me like—*

Her son put his arms around her and hugged tight, pressing his face and his tears into her uniform. Ellaniel choked up, her vision blurring as she hugged him back. She put her mouth to the top of his head. "I'm here."

Charva hit her on the shoulder. "Ella, we have to go!"

Ellaniel sniffled and gently pushed Avlan away. "Come on, we'll get you out of the camp." She held him with one hand as she wiped her eyes and picked up one of the soldiers' swords.

"What's all that crying, Avlan?" Kalla asked. She'd already fetched a weapon herself. "A moment ago you were talking down two imperial soldiers!"

"I'm not crying!" Avlan said.

"I'm still amazed how intensely he was goading them," Charva said. "He didn't even notice me scouting the tent."

"I did too notice you Aunt Charcoal! I knew I couldn't give you away!"

Charva chuckled and took up position beside the exit. Kalla took the other side. "You know how to use that?" Charva asked, nodding to the sword in Kalla's hands.

"I took a few lessons."

"Okay, well, we're going to make a break for the woods to the north. We'll probably pick up some pursuers. I'll try to get them to focus on me. You three just get to the forest, and then turn east until you reach the Leverie army."

"That sounds a lot like you don't intend on coming with us," Ellaniel said.

"We're getting Avlan out of here," Charva said. "No time to argue on the methods."

A voice came from behind the tent, "Hey, did someone cut this?"

"Embers." Charva threw the flap open. "Come on!"

The sounds of battle faded to a low roar that undercut the pounding of Retyar's boots on the wood ramparts. He'd just passed the rocky rise that marked the center of the palisade. Glancing north, he saw the line of silver shields growing closer. The enemy was moving fast, their formation dipping and rising with the contours of the land.

"They'll be at the wall fast!" Pundur shouted behind him.

Retyar nodded, more to himself than to the crenden. In his head, he calculated the distances, the speeds. *Nevygar left a few companies behind, but that's not unexpected. This will still work.*

He caught sight of Fellone's purple hair ahead. The girl had found a few blocks of wood to stand on, letting her peer out over the battlement. Beside her, guarded by twenty soldiers, was the thick length of rope that everything depended on. It ran out over the defenses, one end disappearing into the grasses on the north side, the other secured to a pair of horses on the south.

"Retyar, I have to admit I'm getting nervous," Pundur said. "That's a *lot* of soldiers."

From the look of it, the Three Corners forces were feeling the same way. Retyar noticed them fidgeting as they stared at the enemy.

"You're really lucky you aren't up here," one of them

called down to the horsemen. "They've enough troops to fill Third Point Square ten times over."

Retyar stopped beside Fellone.

"You going to pull it yet?" the girl asked.

He eyed the Vron camp. "Everything needs to be in place."

Charva stepped over the bodies of the two guards laying dead in the grass, only the slightest bit hidden to any passersby. Ellaniel held Avlan close and followed her out. *Yeah, three blood-covered women and a boy aren't suspicious at all.*

"Fast walk, don't run," Charva said quietly as they started northward.

She saw several soldiers moving about beyond the tents to either side of them. All were too busy with whatever tasks they were at to afford the trespassers any attention.

"I think someone's noticed the bodies," Kalla said. "Soldiers are running."

"Okay, a little faster," Charva said.

"Alarm! They've taken the hostages!"

Charva grabbed Ellaniel's arm. "Keep the pace. Don't run."

Ellaniel glanced over her shoulder. "They're going to—"

A group of men rounded a tent. "He promised me the whole country! I'm not going to stand for—" Crenden Roth stopped short a foot from Charva's face. "Oh, blaz—"

Charva surprised even herself with how fast she stabbed her dagger through his gut. She had the satisfaction of seeing his eyes bulge before Ellaniel shoved her aside and rammed her own sword through his chest. "For my father, traitor."

Roth's body fell, slipping free from Ellaniel's blade to land in a lifeless heap. His entourage stumbled back in horror. "M-Murder!"

"There they are!"

Charva drew her rapier and faced the approaching soldiers. "Okay, *now* it's time for you three to run."

The shrill notes signaling a camp intrusion brought Nevygar's head around. As he looked, a plume of yellow smoke rose up over the tents.

"So the Redleafs cannot be tamed." He turned to his lead captain. "The assault is to continue. You have command. Sound for the companies that remained behind to advance on the Senkani army."

"Where are you going, sir?"

Nevygar maneuvered his horse around towards the east. "I'll be taking command of the harder battle." He urged his horse into a gallop. Only once the wind was blowing in his ears did he realize his teeth were bared in a grin.

The Vron trumpets sounded as the enemy army drew closer and closer. Retyar watched the troops carefully, but didn't see any change in their advance.

"That was a signal for the reserve force to move on Crenden Arzan," Maltan said. He puffed in exhaustion, having just caught up with Retyar and Pundur, and dabbed sweat with his sleeve.

"You know their codes?" Pundur asked.

Maltan nodded. "I had plenty of time to learn while hearing their drills in Heartsong."

"We're good, then," Retyar said. He was still anxious at seeing Charva's signal inside the camp. The yellow smoke grenade meant they had Avlan, but were fighting their way out.

"It's about time to spring the trap, isn't it?" Pundur said. He pressed his palms against each other and bit his lip. The imperial troops were getting close enough that Retyar thought he could see individual faces.

Retyar inhaled slowly. "Yeah, it's about time." He put his

hands on the makeshift earmuffs he had hanging around his neck. They were simple cotton pads strapped on the ends of a strip of spring steel. Not the most comfortable, but they would work. He turned to the horsemen below and raised his arm.

"Reform the line!" Arzan shouted. "The imperials see what's happening! Reform the line!"

"You're making a big mistake," the Vron liaison said. He was unhorsed, flanked by two Senkani with swords drawn.

"You should really stop speaking," Arzan said. "With every word, I get closer to snapping your neck. Shields ready!"

"Go!" Retyar cut the air with his arm, sending the two riders galloping away from the palisade. The coiled slack in the rope quickly unraveled behind them and whipped taut. The line streamed by beside him, pulling at the hundred yards of flint strikers now under the imperial army's feet.

"You may want to cover your ears." *And hope that the rains didn't—*

The hills exploded.

Chapter 100

Over ten thousand Vron soldiers disappeared into a string of massive orange flashes. Grass flattened in a wave of power that raced out in all directions. Arzan had only an instant to try to comprehend what he was seeing before the sound hit him like a physical thing. The next he knew, he was on his back in the mud, his horse tearing away in a panic. He pushed back to his feet and stared in awe at the ball of white smoke rolling skyward. Everyone around him had come to a shocked halt and gaped in amazement. Fifty paces out, the Vron reserve force floundered and turned to the sight, many covering their ears.

"What in the six was that?" a sergeant asked in awe.

Something plinked against Arzan's shoulder plate. More plinks sounded from throughout the army and Arzan realized it was raining pebbles and soil. Something heavier bounced off the top of a shield—a Vron helmet.

"Shields up!" Arzan shouted. *We're almost half a mile away!*

More came down. Stones, weapons, bits of armor. The downpour lasted several moments. Once it subsided, there could be no doubt.

The imperial legion was destroyed.

Arzan smiled. He pushed his way to the front of the army and pointed his sword towards the stricken imperials that had come to fight him instead of storming the palisade.

"Charge!"

Charva shot a silver through the forehead. The vial weapon projectile ripped through the man's skull and pinged the back of his helmet and he dropped flat on his face. She followed with a warding slash with the rapier in her left hand as another soldier tried to come in from her flank. "You mind giving up? You see that massive plume of smoke? That means you've lost."

The soldier pressed on, bashing her sword aside. "I'll surrender when my general tells me to!"

Charva tripped on a tent peg and landed hard on her back. *More bruises to the collection*, she thought miserably. She shot the soldier through the chest, piercing chain, flesh, and bone as he tried coming at her. The look of confusion on his face when his legs gave out under him was starting to get familiar.

She regained her feet only for three more imperials to round into sight. She aimed the vial weapon and shot, hitting one of them in the gut. He doubled over in pain, but the other two charged with a shared battle cry. The one on the right took a vial to the chest without slowing. She pulled the trigger again to an empty click. She turned the weapon over and saw the top was open and the box was empty. *Embers!* She juggled her weapons, swapping her sword to her mainhand in time to deflect a blow.

"We're taking you down, Leverie. No one breaks into a Vron war camp and gets away with it." The right soldier arrived first and tried battering down her guard, but she weaved her sword out of the way, letting his face open to a bash from her hilt. He staggered back with his hand cradling a broken nose. The other soldier came in at her. Charva guarded high.

It was a mistake. The imperial stabbed low, taking her in the thigh. She screamed in pain, feeling the blade nick bone. He pulled it back out to parry her thrust, then ducked as she chucked the empty vial weapon. She deflected a high strike, but intentionally left her right side open. The soldier went for the opportunity, not noticing the dagger she drew in her offhand until it was already in his neck.

She readied herself for the first soldier even before the second hit the ground. He didn't come. He was already down, blood blossoming on the chest of his uniform where she'd shot him earlier.

"Die sooner, will you?" she muttered.

She took a step, only to be blinded by white hot pain. She looked down at her injured thigh. "I . . . I don't think that's artery blood," she said hopefully. It was a lot of red regardless.

Trumpets sang in the distance. She forced herself to move and pick up the vial pistol where it lay at the base of a tent. *Whatever I can do to give Ella and Avlan time to escape.*

She slipped out the empty vial box and slapped in her second and last replacement. More soldiers found her. She leveled her aim and pulled the trigger.

The Vron shield wall solidified into a solid mass right before the Senkani and Leverie charged in. Wood crashed on wood, steel hissed on steel. Enraged voices roared in challenge.

Arzan pressed into the thick of the fight. He hacked away at a Vron shield with a borrowed ax, gouging out gaps in the wood to reveal the frenzied face of the soldier behind it. The next few moments were a mad exchange of stabs and slashes, of shoving and screaming. The shield walls ground against each other, crushing men into solid rows of sharpened steel on either side. Arzan didn't have a shield of his own, but his heavy armor was enough, fending off every attack as he hacked at wood and mail and bone.

Break! We have the advantage! Break!

The Vron didn't. On the periphery of his senses, he heard their signal trumpets blaring. He didn't know what they communicated, but whatever it was, the imperials weren't budging an inch except for what they lost in lives.

He bellowed in fury, slamming his ax head into the

helmet of an enemy soldier. Even though the man went limp, the press kept his body upright. Arzan felt himself pushed back by the unrelenting force of a hundred men. "Don't give them ground!" he shouted. The moment he did, he realized it was already too late. He was the furthest forward, his shieldsmen no longer guarding his flanks. He felt a hand grab the back of his armor and pull him away as four Vron tried attacking him at once. He got out of reach of their blades. They didn't follow, giving the Leverie space to reform the line at ten paces.

"I don't know why I even try keeping you alive, my liege," Vighkon said, his hand firmly on Arzan's cuirass. "Barring you from the front line is like holding a squirrel off its nuts."

Arzan labored to catch his breath. His armor felt oddly tight. Looking down, he saw why—the plate was so dented the chest piece was practically concave.

The Vron trumpets continued blaring their signal notes. The imperial formation seemed to melt and then instantly reform, the men in front pulling back and getting replaced by fresh troops from the rear.

"This isn't like any army we've faced," Vighkon whispered.

"No, it's not." Arzan filled his lungs. "Lock shields!"

The trumpets gave one more command and the silver wall surged in.

Retyar listened to the Vron signals and watched the imperials reengage the Leverie line. He passed his hand through his hair and tried to keep his head. This wasn't how it was supposed to go. "We decimated their main force. They should be surrendering right now."

"Someone's keeping them together," Maltan said. "Those signals are giving precise orders to hold the Senkani at the front while one company circles around to intercept the Three Corners forces coming from the palisade."

Fellone slapped her crutch against the battlements. "I told

you, I saw someone riding away before you set off the powder."

"It was Nevygar after all," Pundur said. "He realized Arzan was crossing him and left to take charge of the eastern force."

"He has fewer than six thousand men remaining," Maltan said, his telescope pressed to his eye. "We still have the numerical advantage."

Retyar watched the imperial legion morph and maneuver before it started getting obscured by the colossal cloud of smoke drifting in from the minefield. *Numbers alone don't mean a thing against professionals.* "Where's our cavalry? Why aren't they riding out?"

"The explosion spooked the horses all to the moon," Pundur said. "Didn't you notice the ones that raced through here screaming?"

The curtain of smoke completely covered the battle. It did nothing to block the distant roar of voices and the intermittent trumpet calls. He paced, frustrated and, he admitted to himself, more than a little scared. *I messed up. We're going to lose this.*

And the Vron were going to go home with a new weapon in their arsenal.

He balled his fists and turned back toward the shrouded battle. Pundur and Maltan were consulting with each other, going over plans that Retyar knew wouldn't work. Not with Nevygar in command. Retyar breathed in and pulled his body up over the battlement.

Pundur stopped. "You fool! What are you doing?"

"Fixing things," Retyar said. He hung from his fingers, looked down at the ground below, and dropped.

Chapter 101

Retyar buckled his knees as he made contact and rolled sideways into the dirt. Mud squelched between his fingers as he straightened out. Pundur shouted something at him from above as he wiped his hands on his pants. Ignoring the crenden, he checked on the sword at his waist and the chain shirt he wore over his Obsidian ballistic vest. Last, he took the rifle from his shoulder.

"So, I'm doing it after all." He loosed one end of the cloth wrap and unwound the covering. Blackened steel and polymer frame peeked out at him as he piled the fabric at his feet. Once fully exposed, he swept the charging handle, cycling the action with a heavy metallic click to load a round into the chamber. His hand fit snugly around the grip as he readied his finger above the trigger.

The field was eerily peaceful as Retyar took his first strides forward. All that stood between him and the thick haze of smoke was a pleasant carpet of green grass swaying in a light breeze. The sun was at a nice angle, comfortably warm. The ground was spongy beneath his boots.

Within twenty steps, the scent of burned sulfur filled his nose and the sun dimmed around him. He found the smell bringing up memories of King's Day, when millions of people would set off fireworks all through the night. He'd wondered as a kid if the booms pounding the air were what real war sounded like.

He stepped on a piece of plate metal hidden in the grass.

He soon found bodies, mangled and torn to shreds. Grass eventually gave way to cratered dirt. He didn't hear any screams or groans. The legion had been precisely on top of the mines, with the blast strong enough to kill with concussion alone anyone who managed to miss the flames. The trap probably hadn't even needed the shrapnel stones set atop the buried powder kegs. More smoke still rose up from fissures in the ground, together with wisps of steam.

It was a long trudge before he left the grisly scene behind. Drawn toward the distant roar of battle cries, the clashing of steel, he roamed the smoke with his grip tight on his weapon. Trumpets continued signaling commands. There was enough ground to cover that he had time to think. He thought of his old world and the people he used to know. If by some chance, they would somehow still have come to exist, he'd destroyed that possibility today. *I killed ten thousand people.* He still had trouble wrapping his head around it. Never mind the effect such a thing would have on the timeline, would he be able to sleep with this carnage he'd wrought?

The smoke lightened as he drew nearer to the battle. He saw the backs of the Vron lines. They were fighting hard, all focus on the enemy, except for those carrying the wounded to the rear. Retyar cast his eyes about, looking for mounted officers. He saw a few in either direction, but far enough that the smoke still obscured their uniforms.

The trumpet sounded from the right. That must be where the general was. He started that way just as a company came quick marching from the left. "Move out of the way! Get—"

"He's not one of ours! Right wing, take him down!"

Raze it. Retyar lifted his rifle and sighted on the soldier in the center of the formation. The report of his shot was almost deafening even with his makeshift earmuffs. The bullet took the soldier between the eyes, pinging the backside of his helmet, hitting the soldier behind him, and then glancing off the armor of a third to catch someone in the neck.

"What the bloody shyle? Shields!"

"Good luck with that," Retyar said. He aimed and fired, ripping through wood and steel to drop two more soldiers with a single shot.

"Charge him!"

Retyar showed no mercy. He emptied the magazine, dropping soldiers two, three, four at a time. They didn't even make it within thirty feet of him before their formation disintegrated, half of it from soldiers stumbling over the dead and wounded, half from others turning and running, screaming in terror.

"I am Retyar Venon!" He shouted, dropping the spent magazine into his hand and swapping it for another as he advanced on his foes. "The Vron Empire has reached the fields of Leverie, but it will go no further!"

More soldiers fled, leaving only one who raised his sword in challenge. "For the glory of—"

Retyar shot him in the face. The imperial's body crumpled like a sack of grain.

"Where I'm from, there's no glory left in war," Retyar muttered. He turned around. "Now, where's my prey?"

"Rotate fresh troops to Third Company's left! A group of ckols is trying for a flank on Fifth Company—get spearmen in position to intercept!"

The signal officer trumpeted Nevygar's orders, setting silver-clad soldiers into motion. Nevygar kept his eye on the enemy battle line. They were weakening in several spots, but not quite yet to the point of a break or rout. Crenden Redleaf had regained his head since the initial charge and was giving orders from behind his forces, his red cape waving as he rode to and fro. The man was a competent commander with a mind for the intricacies of strategy. He knew the strengths and weaknesses of his men, how much they could take, where to put them, when to pull them out.

"General," a captain spoke up. "This will be a close battle, but even if we win, what's the point? We haven't enough forces left to take the aristocracy." He glanced at where the main part of the legion had met its astounding doom.

"You don't see?" Nevygar said. "When we capture Three Corners, we will have the means to rewrite the rules of engagement. The power that Crenden Pundur's engineers have developed—the ability to wipe out a force of ten thousand men in the blink of an eye . . . . Do you not understand what the empire could do with such a power?"

"I . . . . Yes, general."

"Speaking of which," another of his officers said, "does anyone know what those cracking sounds were earlier?"

"Enemy reinforcements!"

The palisade gate was reopened, letting through a column of Three Corners cavalry. At least a hundred had already made it out. Nevygar hadn't seen them earlier because of the smoke.

"We'll need more men on the right flank," he said. "Where's First Company? They should have been here by now."

An officer pointed. "I think that's their runner."

When Nevygar looked, he saw the man moving as if wolves were on his heels. He came straight to the general, his eyes wild, and dropped immediately to his knees. "General! First Company is destroyed! The enemy has set a monster upon us!"

"Soldier, that is not how a warrior composes himself!" Nevygar barked.

The captain squinted and shielded his eyes. "Who's that?"

The runner shot to his feet in dismay. "He's coming!"

The hairs on Nevygar's neck stood on end. He set aside his displeasure with the runner and looked up at the man approaching along the back of the imperial line. He walked steadily, confidently, purposefully. In his hands was a weapon of a type Nevygar didn't recognize. In that moment, he realized he'd made a miscalculation. The Leverie had more than one trick up their sleeves.

"We need to stop him." Nevygar thrust his finger at the lone enemy and bellowed, "Anyone who's not engaged, take him down!"

Retyar was sure now the man with the feathered helmet

was the famous Vron general he'd spent years reading about. The man pointed straight at him, and a dozen guards and officers on horseback charged with swords drawn. It didn't feel like Retyar was facing down a legend as he calmly put the stock of his rifle to his shoulder. Nevygar and all his soldiers were just men. Men protected by nothing better than the tin cans he used to shoot out in the woods as a kid. He put the general in his sights and pulled the trigger.

The rifle's report alone spooked the horses out of control. It was all the riders could do to keep from getting thrown. They didn't see their commander slip from his mount and splat in the muddy ground.

A man with a lieutenant's shoulder cord was the first to wrestle his horse back to order. He pointed the beast at Retyar and galloped forward in determination. Retyar put a bullet straight through his chest.

This time, the others saw the man fall back from his saddle. Retyar didn't wait for their reaction before lighting them up. In seconds, all that was left were bodies and a few men writhing and gasping on the ground. He walked between them to the signal man. The officer was shaking atop his horse, knuckles white as he gripped his trumpet. "You." Retyar raised his rifle. "Sound the surrender."

Chapter 102

Arzan saw Ellaniel approach with a retinue of soldiers, Avlan held tight at her side. He went to them as fast as he could, impeded by a painful limp from an unlucky spear that found its way between his leg plates. He barely noticed the injury as he took his wife and son into a tight embrace.

"Papa, your armor hurts!"

Arzan let go and tried to laugh, but choked instead. "You're both okay."

Ellaniel passed her fingers across his tortured chestplate. "Are you?"

"Nothing serious."

She nodded and turned on her heel. "We have to go back for Charva. She stayed behind to hold off pursuit."

Arzan grit his teeth. "That idiot! Vighkon, horses!"

In moments, he and Ellaniel were mounted, together with all that remained of their ckols. They rode past the columns and columns of surrendered Vron soldiers, separated from their mounds of swords and shields by a line of united Leverie troops.

"Was the general killed in that . . . whatever it was?" Ellaniel asked.

"That Retyar took care of him," Arzan said. "We would have lost."

They passed into open ground and rode hard for the imperial camp, Arzan gritting his teeth against the sharp throbbing in his leg. Pundur's cavalry had already secured the area, rounding up several hundred soldiers and Aiv Chahai and lining them just outside the perimeter.

"Any sign of Crendess Charva?" Arzan asked one of the horsemen.

"We only just finished bringing in the captives, your grace. I did see evidence of a fight over that way, however."

Ellaniel was already heading into the camp. Arzan followed after her.

They found over a dozen bodies strewn about one of the major lanes. Ellaniel half jumped, half stumbled off her horse and ran between them, eyes searching. "I don't see—"

"There!" Vighkon shouted. He dismounted and rushed to a tent whose side was sagged in. As Arzan rode up to it, he saw Charva enveloped in the fabric. Her skin was pale, even for her, while her silver uniform was soaked red. She wasn't moving. Arzan dropped to the ground as Ellaniel knelt by Charva's side.

"No, no," Ellaniel breathed.

Charva's eyes cracked open and rolled at seeing them. "Took you long enough," she mumbled weakly.

"She's alive!" Arzan said. "A surgeon, quickly!" He bent his good knee. "Hang in there, Charva."

She closed her lids, but raised an eyebrow. "What, not even a little bit of awe at how many of them I got?"

Ellaniel dug her fingers in Charva's hair and leaned close, smiling. "You cheated."

"Come on, I deserve at least a little praise."

Arzan put a hand gently on her shoulder. "You did admirably. Thank you."

Charva quirked the corner of her mouth. "There. That's more like it."

Retyar leaned on his rifle and gazed at the thousands of Vron prisoners and the many bodies set in rows beneath white sheets. He still didn't know what to think of his actions. Had he done the right thing?

Was that the most important question?

How was what he had done even possible? There was no

denying now that the timeline was changed in a major way. Defeating a Vron legion—defeating General Nevygar himself —that would definitely alter world history, with effects rippling across the six continents. And yet the encyclopedia remained the same, still recounting events as Retyar had been taught in school. Just as strange, Retyar was still here. He still existed, even though the changes in the timeline should have prevented him from ever being born.

Is it somehow possible my world still exists?

He'd likely never know. If no one had come for him yet, they likely never would.

With a heavy sigh, he slung his rifle and strolled across the trampled grasses, no particular destination in mind. Soldiers stopped and nodded as he passed. In their eyes he saw respect, awe, gratitude, fear. Definitely not the sort of looks he'd ever expected to garner in life.

"You fool of a Falconian! There you are!"

Crenden Pundur dropped a meaty hand on Retyar's shoulder and squeezed. "You saved our country, friend. You've provided a service we can't repay."

Retyar opened his mouth, but found he didn't have a response. Time would tell whether he'd brought these people a blessing or a curse. With the natural timeline disrupted, with technologies from hundreds of years in the future unleashed, who could tell what tomorrow would bring?

Pundur narrowed his eyes. "What is it? Is this not the end of the Vron after all?"

"No, it's not that. According to the histories, the Ikashan Rebellions are about to start out west in a few weeks. The empire's hands are going to be too full to mount another expedition here in the east for a long time. Not with their star general and an entire legion defeated."

The crenden gave him a knowing look. "You're thinking of home, then."

Retyar shrugged.

"You're absolutely welcome to live in Three Corners. You'll be in the lap of luxury, spared nothing you desire. You are the hero of Leverie!" Pundur's cheek twitched. "I promise I won't even ask for any of your marvels."

Retyar allowed himself a smile. "Thanks. I expect I'll

take you up on that."

Pundur slapped him on the back. "You'd better!" He turned his head at hearing someone call for his attention. "Until later, then, my friend."

He watched the crenden leave. He felt a bit better as he continued on his aimless wandering. His feet took him away from the soldiers and up to the rocky mound at the palisade's center. Without really thinking, he sat down and pulled out the tablet. He stuck in the battery, lighting up the scratched and dirty screen. He stared at the icons for a few moments, then up at the battlefield.

There's going to be stories about this, aren't there? About me.

They would be accounts through the eyes of people without a clue of what had truly happened. They wouldn't know who he was or how he knew the things he knew. It would have to be that way.

But maybe in a few hundred years' time, someone would once again create computers and be able to understand him.

He opened up his text program and began to write.

Epilogue

Captain Thadale stood beside the helm of the imperial patrol ship *Serpentgale* and watched the vast sea. The waters were calm today, the winds brisk, snapping the sails and his silver uniform. Perfect conditions for the search.

"It's a strange mission, captain, if you don't mind me saying," the helmsman said.

"What's strange about it?" Thadale asked. "We get reports of ships threatening the trade lanes all the time." He glanced down at the Vron marines lounging about on deck. Most were relaxed, only a few busying themselves with oiling their equipment or sewing up tears in their uniforms. Thadale let their leisurely attitude slide. He knew from experience that theses men were ones to be counted on when it came to a fight.

"They're odd tales though, sir," the helmsman went on. "Never heard of a ship made of steel and no sails."

"Exaggerated. How would something like that even float?"

The helmsman rubbed the wheel's spokes. "Then there's folks who say it isn't a ship at all, but an island of metal risen up in the middle of the sea. The most bizarre things ever to reach my ears."

Thadale thought he heard something thud. He held up a hand and stepped up to the starboard rail. He frowned at the waters, seeing a length of plank wash by. "Debris in the water! Watch for survivors!"

Sailors and marines rushed to the sides, grabbing hooks and rope. "Eyes peeled, men!"

The helmsman looked more nervous when Thadale

returned to him. "Debris? We're in open sea. No rocks to smash against. You think it could be a leviathan?"

A wild thought occurred to Thadale. If one could make a ship out of steel, ramming might actually be a viable tactic. A chill went down his spine. How would anyone guard against that kind of attack? What nation would even dream up such a thing?

A shout came down from the crow's nest, "Ship ahoy! Quarter forward from starboard!"

Thadale snatched the telescope from his belt and scanned the waters, dreading to find the steel monstrosity. "Where? Where's the—?" A vessel materialized into view. He sighed in relief. "It's a shore boat! Ready ladder!" So someone had survived from the wreck. For sure they would have answers to put to rest his crazy speculations. "Helmsman, turn towards their boat."

Water sprayed against the prow as the *Serpentgale* adjusted course. The boat of survivors drew nearer, and able to see easily with the naked eye.

"Is it just me, or are they coming on way too fast?" The helmsman asked.

Thadale knit his brow. The man was right. They were closing as if the shore boat was being driven by a full wind. *What in the twelve seas?* "Draw sails!"

The crew pulled the sails closed. The *Serpentgale* slowed, dragging along without wind. The shore ship continued on with speed, getting closer and closer. Thadale noted now the oddity of its shape. The hull was bulbous and ridiculously thick, and painted a glossy black. The men aboard were just as strange, clad entirely in black armor with a lacquered shine. Not just chest and greaves, but completely head to toe in the style of Falconian knights. "This is wrong," he whispered. He leaned over the banister. "General quarters! All hands on deck!"

He heard the first mate strike the bell and the stomping of boots on timber as men emerged from below. Sixty marines lined up behind the rails with sword and shield at the ready, another sixty taking position behind them with bows and crossbows.

The shore ship came nearer, and Thadale became aware of

a bizarre buzzing noise. The vessel passed parallel with his ship, water churning just behind it. His sailors and marines gawked at the strangers as they went by. *How is that thing moving?* Thadale wondered. Even as he asked himself the question, the black vessel turned, incomprehensibly coming around and matching the imperials' course. The occupants reached out and took hold of the rope ladder hanging over the *Serpentgale*'s side.

Thadale swallowed and stepped down to the main deck, hand involuntarily on the pommel of his sword. Four of the black armored men climbed up over the rail and silently surveyed the hundreds of Vron surrounding them. He eyed them for weapons. They possessed no blades he could see, but held strange metal contraptions in their hands. The two sides stared for some moments before Thadale cleared his throat. "Who are you?"

The armored man at the lead turned his head. Thadale felt another chill shake his spine. Where were their eye slits? Their helmets were perfectly enclosed, their smooth face plates lacking any hint of holes.

"This is a Vron ship?" The voice was eerily clear despite the helmet.

"This is a vessel in service to the Senate and the people of Vron," Thadale answered. "We are investigating reports of merchants getting harassed in these waters. Are you . . . " He fought off a shudder. "Are you the ones responsible?" *Stay rational, Thadale. They are only four men, no matter how strangely equipped.*

The leader of the armored group regarded him with his unsettling blank gaze. "Ship's log."

"Excuse me?"

"Give me your ship's log."

Thadale would have normally laughed at such a request. Right now, every fiber of his being told him he shouldn't dare.

"Are you the ones harassing our merchants?" he repeated.

The stranger didn't answer.

Thadale swallowed and forced himself to regain his sense of authority. "If you refuse to explain your presence here, I must presume your guilt." He raised his hand. "Arrest them."

Faster than he could blink, the strangers raised their metal contraptions and filled the air with a stream of ear-splitting cracks. Thadale dove to the deck, his hands pressed to his head to block the sound. He smelled smoke and blood. When he looked up, he saw his men strewn across the ship, most of them dead or writhing in agony. His body locked up in fear.

The lead stranger waved to one of his fellows. "Get the log."

The subordinate stepped past Thadale with an unhurried stride. On his way, he dropped a long metal box that clattered on the deck. He pulled another one from a full belt at his waist and slapped it into his weapon.

One of the remaining men in black armor leaned towards the leader. "We using the plastics?"

The leader tilted his gaze, as if listening to something. After some moments, he shook his head. "Captain wants to make sure the Anchor's fire control is properly calibrated."

"That should be fun."

They waited until their man was back with the leather-bound log from the first mate's cabin. The four climbed over the side and back to their boat.

Thadale finally raised himself up on trembling arms, his breath ragged. He heard the buzzing below and staggered to the rail in time to see the assailants sail off without sails. He struggled to comprehend what had just happened.

This needs to be reported to the Senate.

He turned to take stock of his crew. They'd tend to the wounded and then immediately—

The planks suddenly heaved beneath his feet, fire blasting all around him. He landed hard in the water. His arms flailed until he caught hold of a large beam that had a moment ago been part of the *Serpentgale*'s mast. All around him, the sea was littered with splintered wood and torn fabric. Blood colored the water red around men pierced through with the ship's broken fragments. Thadale felt a sharp pain in his own side and saw that he was bleeding out into the water himself.

The black boat returned, floating through the wreckage. The men in black armor saw Thadale and steered close.

"W-Who are you?" Thadale asked.

The last thing he saw was the quick flash of flame after

one of them raised his weapon to Thadale's face.

To be continued in
Kahverengi's Dilemma,
Book II:
Instance War

Appendix I

The Six Continents and their associated eye colors:

- Originate
  - Brown and gold
- Falcone
  - Green and gray
- Volcana
  - Orange and red
- Moshon
  - Blue and violet
- Evena
  - Violet and orange
- Fractora
  - Full color spread

Note: exceptions and variations will exist, including particularly rare eye colors within certain communities.

Appendix II
The Aristocracies and their Governance

The Moshon aristocracies practice a form of government unique from the rest of Dunya. After overthrowing their monarchies early in the continent's history, the merchant class took on the mantle of power. Rather than adopting the notion of absolute right of kings, however, they opted for a more mercantile approach. The ruling merchant families took on House names, with members of their Houses being appointed as heads of city-provinces. Known as crendens/crendesses, these individuals serve to maintain order in their territories and operate as master of the local House branch. They are responsible for resolving disputes, maintaining roads and bridges, and leading the army in times of war. Notably, these services are financed through the House's own coffers, with no taxes levied from the public. The House must be adequately profitable in order to run the province. To this end, the general public are often eager to support the House's commercial enterprises for the sake of ensuring prosperity and order for the whole community. For the most part, this means plentiful labor and competitive supply contracts for the House. House monopolies in their given trades are not criticized, but rather celebrated. Competition in the House trades is more likely to take place at the national or international level, between crendens and countries. Important here is the institution of the Councils. These governmental bodies are made up of each nation's ruling creandens and crendesses. They are focused on national and international matters, most commonly on the issue of trade. It is through the avenue of Councils that multiple provinces will coordinate focus of production, contentious resource distribution, and united strategies for dealing with foreign entities. The Council also serves as a judicial body in the event of a crenden or crendess committing serious crimes. In the event that armed conflict is necessary, the Council has the power to declare war and arrange general strategy.

Appendix III
Major Characters

No House affiliation:

Retyar Venon
-Security guard and history graduate from fifty-fifth century Govunari.

Gricall
-Beloved advocate for workers' rights in Senkani province.

Fellone
-Gricall's only daughter.

Captain Vighkon
-Head of Arzan's ckols.

Ckol Magar
-Ellaniel's head ckol.

Captain Ulman
-Head of the Creedport city guard.

Ersch
-Nephew of Captain Ulman.

Maltan
-Tinkerer living in Creedport's tower.

General Nevygar
-Celebrated and feared commander in the Vron legions.

Thesha Dinria
-Fellow student in Retyar's college history program.

Laski
-Ytanian engineering student and Retyar's friend.

Waylar Unavin
-Economics major and Retyar's friend.

Grigon Ashkyn
-Rogue scientist formerly employed by Obsidian Aerotech.

Kahverengi
-A classical time travel philosopher.

House of Redleaf:

Arzan Redleaf
-Ruling crenden of Senkani.

Kalla Redleaf
-Arzan's cousin.

House of Leverie (Creedport Branch):

Thrake Leverie
-Ruling crenden of Creedport and enemy of Arzan.

Charva Leverie
-Thrake's daughter.

Throrne Leverie
-Thrake's son and younger brother of Charva.

House of Leverie (Highcity Branch):

Ylnavar Leverie
-Ruling crenden of Highcity and Speaker of the Council.

Natsha Leverie
-The best embroiderer in the country.

House of Leverie (Woodwise Branch):

Hashan Leverie
-Ruling crenden of Woodwise.

Ellaniel Leverie
-Hashan's daughter.

Odavan Leverie
-Ellaniel's cousin.

House of Leverie (Three Corners Branch):

Pundur Leverie
-Ruling crenden of Three Corners.

House of Leverie (Other Cities Branch):

Mansar Leverie
-Ruling crenden of Blueturf.

Roth Leverie
-Ruling crenden of Glasscastle.

Athar Leverie
-Ruling crenden of Harean.

Loftham Leverie
-Ruling crenden of Bluhall

House of Goldquarry:

Warth Goldquarry
-Ruling crenden of Quarry Hill.

Acknowledgments

The publication of this book is the product of a long journey. Many years ago now, there was a guest speaker who came to my school to give us kids an inspirational talk about the fun of storytelling. I sadly can't remember the name of this guy, but he was the one who sparked in me the desire to write. Going off his prompts, I was crafting the beginning of my first novel that very afternoon. It wasn't the novel you are holding in your hands now (for which you should be very thankful), but it put me on the first step of a road that is now twenty years long and still going, so long as the Lord wills.

Through these years were many people who deserve recognition for giving me the ability to reach this point. First, my parents, who have not only provided me with incredible support and encouragement, but also gave me a foundational footing of literary inclination, the value of pursuit of understanding, and a moral anchor. Without them, my feet would never have had ground to walk on.

Second, I want to thank the rest of the family for their support. Grandma Zenny, I know you really wanted me to use my real name, but you will have to settle with me mentioning yours. As for you aunties and uncles and brothers, you know who you are.

Next is a very big thank you to the Burbank writers group. You provided me with invaluable feedback and suggestions. Without you, I would not have a story of this quality (such as it is), and might even still be floundering about trying to finish the thing. In particular, I want to give a special shout-out to Adrienne, Julie, Jim, and Nancy. Your loyalty to the group and incredible insights are very much appreciated. I'm sorry that two of you have not been able to keep on through the upheaval of the pandemic.

Special recognition goes to Owl in the Brush, who did an incredible job with the cover art and chapter headers. I recommend checking out his other work at owlinthebrush.com.

In terms of resources I've used for doing research, I've read and watched a lot of material. The community of the sword on YouTube, however, have been especially helpful. There are a few channels that I think deserve special recognition: Shadiversity, Skallagrim, Metatron, Scholagladiatora, Lindybeige, and Tod's Workshop. These are not only very educational, but also quite entertaining.

Next, I want to thank my beta reader Chris, as well as my alpha readers Gail, Stacy, and Cindy. I may or may not have addressed your concerns to your satisfaction, but your thoughts were very welcome.

I thank the members of the Interrobangs writers group for additional feedback on the first few chapters. You caught some things that would have dragged down the narrative significantly.

Thank you to the BookBaby team for proofreading and providing me with an avenue to get this book out to the world.

To anyone I neglected, I'm sorry to have left you out. Hit me up so I can include you in book 2.

Above all, praise and glory to God, in whom is all wisdom, love, power, and understanding. Without Him, there is nothing possible. With Him, nothing is impossible.

A note from the author

"For a righteous person falls seven times and rises again,
But the wicked stumble in time of disaster."
Proverbs 24:16

What makes a hero?

In the era I am writing this, there is something of a crisis going on in the realm of entertainment media (and society at large). A lot of people are noticing that the characters and stories being churned out by Hollywood and many major publishers seem flat and uninteresting. This is despite obvious attempts at checking endless boxes on the list labeled "diversity". It is also despite writers supposedly freeing themselves from chains of arbitrary traditions and moral codes. Why is it that these people who claim unprecedented artistic freedom have so much difficulty making compelling narratives?

Part of the issue, in my opinion, is that the prominent writers of our day are not writing heroes. They are writing gods.

A hero is someone who overcomes adversity. The greater the adversity, the greater the heroism of the person who overcomes. Who do we cheer for more? The man who climbs a thirty-foot hill or the man who climbs Mt. Everest? The one who climbs the mountain, of course. Human beings are driven to root for those who face the greater hardship.

But what if we were to shake things up a bit? What if the man climbing the hill was a man with broken legs and a mind haunted by demons showing him visions of despair whenever he looked up to the crest? And what if the man climbing Mt. Everest were a Kryptonian with the ability to fly? Suddenly things become reversed. The obstacle of the hill seems insurmountable and the obstacle of the mountain is a joke. Hardships are relative to the capabilities of the person facing them.

A further element of heroism is that of purpose. What is

there to lose if the person fails? Money? Pride? Life? In the example of our two men, what if the Kryptonian flying up the mountain simply wants to see a nice sunset, while the broken man going up the hill needs to rescue his kidnapped daughter from a group of necromancers in need of a human sacrifice? In this case, the mountain man will only lose a moment of peaceful satisfaction, but he can catch another one tomorrow. The man going up the hill will have lost the life of his child. The degree to which the person facing adversity cares about the outcome in turn influences us in who we want to watch and support.

Another aspect of this purpose is whether it is for the benefit of the self or the benefit of another. We respect those who do good for others. We disdain those who only care about their own pleasure. Because of this, we admire the man trying to save his daughter. At most, we empathize a little with the Kryptonian wanting to see some sights.

Connected is what the man who would be a hero is willing to sacrifice to achieve his objective. The only thing the Kryptonian needs to sacrifice is a little of his time. The man on the hill may need to give up some of his sanity to face the demons, as well as push himself up onto his broken legs at the risk of them never being able to heal. And he will do it again and again if he needs to. The amount that the person struggling is willing to pay in order to succeed is another big factor in who we think is worthy of reward.

With all that we have built up, the greater hero is obviously the man climbing the hill. The problem with many of today's writers is that they would rather use the man climbing the mountain. It is not their intention to write heroes. They are writing gods.

A hero is someone we can emulate. He or she is a role model for overcoming adversity. Gods, by contrast, are beings of power. They may show some human characteristics, but those serve only as flavors to help you choose which to pray to for favor. A modern writer will put a protagonist in a wheelchair, but instead of showing the hardships of being without legs, will have that character do everything a whole person can do without any effort. Nay, they can actually do those things better. They will put a woman in a misogynistic society and have her victorious in arm-wrestling every man. They will have children be wiser than all the adults. Very typically, these characters will be given token adversities, overcome every time as a matter of course. These aren't heroes. These characters are patron gods. They are the gods of people in wheelchairs, of women, of children, of ethnic minorities, or various letters of the LGBTQ+ acronym.

The great irony, of course, is that these man-made gods fall flat against the God with a capital G. The God of the Bible is a shining example of a true hero. Here we have the inverse of these patron gods. The Lord is one of ultimate power, but He surrenders His immortality to be a mortal man. He suffers through the trials and temptations of humanity, through hunger, through weariness, through mockery, and pain. He sweats blood knowing the final hurdle He has to face, and yet He willingly gives Himself up to humiliation, torture, and execution as a falsely accused heinous criminal by the humans He created. Why? Not for Himself. He did it because that was what was needed to overcome an insurmountable obstacle—the penalty that was facing the people He loves. He is not some mere patron god who will justify your identity in some superficial marker. He is a God who dives into icy waters and feels the bite of the cold to rescue those who are drowning. Cling to Him, and He will joyfully embrace you with hands scarred with the price of your purchase out of the slavery of sin and your impending penalty.

That is a hero.

Who is Jesus?

There's a question that many people throw out, sometimes as a challenge, sometimes in genuine honesty: If God is loving, good, and all powerful, how is it that He allows evil and suffering?

This is a question that has stumped many who believe in God. It's used as a "gotcha" by plenty of atheists. However, this is because we have a tendency to not fully appreciate what it means for God to be both loving and good. God doesn't just do good. He *is* good. He is the Source of good, the Standard of good, and Perfect in His goodness. Contrast that with us. However we may delude ourselves, we are not good. All of us fall short of God's glory. We are liars, thieves, blasphemers, boasters, coveters, adulterers, and murderers, in deed and in heart. We are tainted. But God is holy, righteous, and good, without fault nor blemish. He is so holy that no one who is less than perfect in goodness can approach Him without being destroyed.

And therein lies a big problem. You see, God is also the Source of life. He is the one who created us and gave us breath. He is the one who sustains the universe and sustains us. What do you think happens when you become disconnected from that Source of life? You get what we see in the world around us. You get decay. You get sickness. You get death. And that is only right. If you reject God's standards of good, why should He extend to you His life? On the contrary, if He is righteous and good, then it is His place to condemn you to death. And that is exactly what humanity faces. God is all powerful, yes. And that means the whole world is subject to destruction, down to every single person who falls short of His perfect standards.

But the story doesn't end there. God has another trait, and that is love. While God has the right to judge us, He does not *want* to condemn us, because He loves us. We have separated ourselves from God in our sins, but God has offered us a way to become reconciled to Him. He is perfectly good and holy

—infinitely so. And what happens when you take the finite sins of a man or woman and wash them with infinite holiness? As it happens, this if what God did.

Two thousand years ago, God entered into His creation in the form of a man. The name by which we call this Man in English is Jesus. This comes from the Greek pronunciation Yaysoos, which itself came from the pronunciation of the name in Hebrew and Aramaic of Yeshua. In the original language, it literally means "God saves". After living a perfect life without sin, He surrendered Himself to be nailed to a cross and die. Before Jesus breathed His last breath, He said, "It is finished." What did He finish?

A mission started from the day the first man Adam fell from goodness. In that day, God condemned Adam and Eve for their disobedience and banished them from paradise, but at that same time promised that they would have a descendant who would crush the head of the serpent who deceived them. He also dressed Adam and Eve in animal skins to cover their nakedness. This may seem a small detail, but together with the promise of this descendant, it was an important foreshadowing in the story. From the same moment God condemned man to die, He set the foundation for him to be saved. When God appeared to Abraham generations later, He made a promise of One to come who would be a blessing to the nations. After bringing Israel out of Egypt by the hand of Moses, God established Israel as a priestly nation. Important in their tasks was the sacrificing of animals and the sprinkling of their blood to stave off God's judgment of sins.

That's a strange thing, isn't it? How would killing an animal save you from God's justice? The Israelites sinned day after day, but somehow sacrificing an animal and sprinkling its blood on people and on the ground drove away God's wrath? It doesn't seem to make sense. I mean think about it. You're before a judge for a serious offense. What you've done is so bad that the only adequate payment is your life. And so you bring out an animal, kill it, and give its blood to the judge?

It's strange because it wasn't about the animal. It was another piece of foreshadowing. It was a ritual pointing to something God was going to do.

That something was the death of Jesus on the cross.

An animal life is not equal to a human life. But let's say a person comes to the judge you are facing and says, "Take my life in place of his." In that case, we have something of equal value.

Now replace a mere person with God. The life of God, the very Source of all life itself, is by its very nature of greater value than all other life combined. That substitutionary payment covers the sins of the entire world.

"I have come that they may have life, and that they may have it more abundantly." (John 10:10)

Infinite life and holiness to cover our finite sins. After all, God knows that those of us who have fallen short of His goodness cannot make up for it in any way. No amount of good deeds or endless prayers can bridge the gap. Something defective does not become redeemed by fulfilling its intended purpose only some of the time. You cannot buy your way to Him with money or riches that He gave you in the first place. You cannot purge yourself to holiness through penance when your rightful punishment is the loss of the thing you are trying to obtain.

And so He gave us a gift. A free one. Anyone, no matter what sins you have committed, can receive this gift and be born anew. You will have all of your faults covered before God and finally be able to approach Him. As evidence of this, Jesus rose bodily from the dead after He had been crucified. He conquered death, and this power He extends to all who accept His gift and believe in Him. But only if you believe in Him. This is the balance of perfect justice and perfect mercy: the condemned's choice of whether to repent and recognize the Judge. And yes, when the time comes, God in His infinite power and goodness will wipe away all suffering and evil. All of it, including the evil that is within all of us. When this is done, only those who have accepted His life and His blood and cling to His gift by believing in Him will remain standing, because no one is good except God.

"If you declare with your mouth, 'Jesus is Lord,' and believe in your heart that God raised him from the dead, you will be saved."

Romans 10:9

About the Author

Born twice in Los Angeles, California, Zeph now resides in Riverside County. A fan of old school Star Wars and the Lord of the Rings, he also enjoys the Total War, Battlefield, Elders Scrolls, Soulcalibur, and Soulsborne franchises. His all-time favorite anime is Fullmetal Alchemist: Brotherhood.

www.zephyraxiom.net